THE DICKENS DIGEST

The DICKENS

Four Great Dickens Masterpieces

DAVID COPPERFIELD · PICKWICK PAPERS

CONDENSED BY MARY LOUISE ASWELL

WHITTLESEY HOUSE · McGRAW-HILL BOOK

DIGEST

Condensed for the Modern Reader

OLIVER TWIST · MARTIN CHUZZLEWIT

ILLUSTRATED BY DONALD McKAY

COMPANY, INC. · NEW YORK AND LONDON

PUBLISHED BY WHITTLESEY HOUSE
A division of the McGraw-Hill Book Company, Inc.

Printed in the United States of America by H. Wolff, New York City

Editor's Note

"IN EVERYBODY," Chesterton says, "there is a thing that loves babies, that fears death, that likes sunlight; that thing enjoys Dickens." In everybody, that is, who reads him. But there is a growing majority of people who "always wanted to read Dickens, but never got around to it," or who loved him as a child but know that if they read him again, particularly if they read him aloud, they would be bound to skip. This book is for them.

What the *Dickens Digest* offers is not a skeleton of the novels chosen, but the essential narrative in the words of its creator, freed of the prolixity that annoys modern readers. I have been a Dickens lover for too long a time to be willing for anybody to miss the pleasure and privilege of reading him. My purpose has been to reproduce faithfully scenes, dialogues, descriptions that acquaint the reader with the essential Dickens, omitting nothing that contributes to the rapid progress of the stories and the characters. My first concern, as the choice of titles shows, is to give the reader Dickens's most famous, most familiar characters.

To bring these four gigantic books within the compass of a single volume it was necessary to eliminate, first of all, padding. It was also desirable. All four of these books were written as serials or in monthly numbers. Their plot complications, their repetitions, their digressions, their "rant and cant" were by-products, not only of the nineteenth-century taste for a leisurely style, but of the pressure under which Dickens wrote, hastily, almost without plan, entirely without opportunity for careful revision and correction. The padding, then, came out first. Next, some of the social satire was dispensed with, satire that in tone and intention means little to the reader today. Finally, the technique of compression learned through long experience in book condensing eliminated the circumlocution that accounts for much of Dickens's verbosity. And the four novels were brought down to the length of one.

Indirect Language

It will be obvious to many that, however seriously I have felt my responsibility to those who are reading Dickens here for the first time, my judgment of the significance of the material chosen is not infallible. Other tastes, other selections. I can only say that readers who have come to the pages of the *Dickens Digest* as if today were the first day of their genesis have reacted as did those readers a hundred years ago who awaited impatiently each fresh appearance of the immortal characters.

David Copperfield. "Of all my books, I like this the best," Dickens wrote in his Preface. Perhaps most of us do, not because we read our own story in David's, as his biographer did, but because we meet here people who enrich immeasurably our emotional lives: the Micawbers, the Peggottys, the villains! Uneasily aware of the shade of Dickens over my shoulder as I cut his text, I was almost persuaded of a lightening of the atmosphere when, having read the scenes between Mr. Murdstone and David and his mother at least ten times, I found my tears falling like rain as I finally typed the version you read here. And if I have held firmly to the main threads of the narrative, no one, I think, can complain of that.

Oliver Twist. "The key of the great characters of Dickens is that they are all great fools," Chesterton said. Only Mr. Bumble, then, in this tale, belongs in that supreme category. But the novel represents, as Chesterton also said, the talent for horror that is next to Dickens's talent for humor; and it is one of the best of his social tracts. As for Oliver himself, and Fagin, Bill Sikes, and the Artful Dodger—they will not die as long as young readers are encouraged to meet them. Those of us who read *Oliver Twist* in our childhood will never forget some of the scenes that are reproduced here almost verbatim. It is my belief that the memories of those who read the novel in this version will be as richly stored.

Martin Chuzzlewit. This novel, alone among those included in the *Dickens Digest*, is not a contemporary favorite. The other three, along with the Christmas stories, *A Tale of Two Cities*, and *Great Expectations* (all comparatively short), are most in demand at libraries and bookstores. But I believe that the elements I have minimized in the condensed version (the complexity of the plot's ramifications, the monotony of the satiric repetitions, the satire which has become dated or was overdrawn to begin with) are the very elements which have impaired the popularity of this diffuse, exuberant, in part brilliant book. If my efforts help restore to living English speech Mrs. Gamp, Mrs. Prig, Mrs. Harris, and that synonym for hypocrisy, Mr. Pecksniff (you will find them all in Webster's dictionary!), then this experiment has been worth while.

The Pickwick Papers. Here the problem of condensation was something quite different. The "plot" is almost entirely a series of episodes. Which to choose, since our space, like Mr. Weller's vision, is limited, was the burden of many sleepless nights. First to come out were the interpolated tales which most *Pickwick* devotees admit they skip. After that it was a matter of selection, but I think that I have been able to include most of the scenes that flash upon that inward eye of *Pickwick* fanciers.

My problem, like that of Donald McKay, who illustrates the *Dickens Digest,* has been to bridge the gap between the taste of the nineteenth century and the taste of today. Our combined hope is that we have selected those elements in Dickens which are for all time; and that the sunlight surrounding Mr. Pickwick and Sam Weller, Mr. Micawber, Sairey Gamp, will shine unobscured upon the memory of their creator.

M. L. A.

Contents

DAVID COPPERFIELD

WHETHER I shall turn out to be the hero of my own life or whether that station will be held by anybody else, these pages must show. To begin at the beginning, I record that I was born (as I have been informed and believe) toward the small hours on a Friday night, at Blunderstone, in Suffolk. I was a posthumous child. My father's eyes closed upon the light of this world six months before mine opened. There is something strange to me, even now, in the reflection that he never saw me; and something stranger yet in the shadowy remembrance of my childish compassion for his white gravestone lying alone in the churchyard.

He had once been the favorite of an aunt who was the principal magnate of our family. But Miss Trotwood, or Miss Betsey, as my poor mother called her, when she sufficiently overcame her dread of this formidable personage to mention her at all, was mortally affronted by his marriage, on the ground that my mother, whom she had never seen, was "a wax doll."

On the afternoon of what I may be excused for calling that eventful Friday, however, my mother was sitting before the fire, very timid and sad, when, lifting her eyes to the window, she saw a strange lady coming up the garden and had a sure foreboding that it was Miss Betsey. She opened the door.

"Mrs. David Copperfield, I *think*," said Miss Betsey.

"Yes," said my mother, faintly.

"Miss Trotwood," said the visitor. "You have heard of her, I dare say?"

My mother answered she had had that pleasure.

"Now you see her," said Miss Betsey.

When they were both seated, my mother, after vainly trying to restrain herself, began to cry. "Why, bless my heart!" exclaimed Miss Betsey. "You are a very Baby!"

My mother was unusually youthful in appearance; she hung her head, as if it were her fault, and said, sobbing, that indeed she was but a childish widow and would be but a childish mother if she lived.

"Oh, tut, tut, tut!" said Miss Betsey. "When do you expect—?"

"I am all in a tremble," faltered my mother. "I shall die, I am sure!"

"No, no, no," said Miss Betsey. "Have some tea. What do you call your servant?"

"Peggotty," said my mother.

"Peggotty!" repeated Miss Betsey, with some indignation. "Do you mean to say that any human being has gone into a Christian church and got herself named Peggotty?"

"It's her surname," said my mother, faintly. "Her Christian name is the same as mine."

"Here, Peggotty!" cried Miss Betsey, opening the parlor door. "Tea. Your mistress is a little unwell. Don't dawdle." Having issued this mandate, she sat down as before, with her feet on the fender and the skirt of her dress tucked up.

"Now, child," said she, "from the moment of the birth of this girl—"

"Perhaps boy," my mother took the liberty of putting in.

"I have a presentiment that it must be a girl," returned Miss Betsey. "Don't contradict. From the moment of this girl's birth, child, I intend to be her friend and godmother, and I beg you'll call her Betsey Trotwood Copperfield." There was an interval of silence, broken by her occasionally ejaculating "Ha!"

"You were an orphan, weren't you, and a governess?" she went on presently. "What did David do for you?"

My mother answered with some difficulty, being increasingly indisposed. "Mr. Copperfield," she said, "was so considerate and good as to leave me a hundred and five pounds a year."

"He might have done worse," said my aunt. The word was appropriate to the moment. My mother was so much worse that a messenger was dispatched for the doctor, who was considerably astonished, when he arrived, to find an unknown lady of portentous appearance sitting before the fire, with her bonnet tied over her left arm, stopping her ears with jewelers' cotton.

Mr. Chillip was the meekest of his sex, the mildest of little men. He sidled in and out of a room, to take up the less space, and carried his head on one side in modest propitiation. Making my aunt a little bow, he said, in allusion to the jewelers' cotton, as he touched his left ear,

"Some local irritation, ma'am?"

"What!" replied my aunt, pulling the cotton out of one ear like a cork.

"Some local irritation, ma'am?"

"Nonsense!" replied my aunt and corked herself up again.

Mr. Chillip could do nothing but retreat upstairs. At half-past twelve, his duty done, he came down again. He sidled into the parlor and said to my aunt, "Well, ma'am, I am happy to congratulate you."

"What upon?" said my aunt, sharply.

Mr. Chillip was so flustered that he made her a little bow and gave her a little smile, to mollify her.

"Mercy on the man, what's he doing?" cried my aunt impatiently.

"Be calm, my dear ma'am," said Mr. Chillip, in his softest accents. "There is no longer any occasion for uneasiness. All is now over, ma'am, and well over."

"How is she?" said my aunt, folding her arms.

"Quite as comfortable," returned Mr. Chillip, "as we can expect a young mother to be."

"And *she*. How is *she*?" said my aunt, sharply.

Mr. Chillip laid his head a little more on one side and looked at my aunt like an amiable bird.

"The baby," said my aunt. "How is she?"

"Ma'am," said Mr. Chillip, "I apprehended you had known. It's a boy."

My aunt said never a word but took her bonnet by the strings, in the manner of a sling, aimed a blow at Mr. Chillip's head with it, put it on bent, walked out, and never came back.

The first objects that assume a distinct presence before me as I look back into the blank of my infancy are my mother, with her pretty hair and youthful shape, and Peggotty, with no shape at all and cheeks and arms so hard and red that I wondered the birds didn't peck her in preference to apples. I believe I can remember going unsteadily from one to the other, and I have an impression of the touch of Peggotty's forefinger as she used to hold it out to me and of its being roughened by needlework, like a nutmeg grater.

What else do I remember? Let me see. There comes out of the cloud, our house. Here is a long passage—what an enormous perspective I make of it!—leading from Peggotty's kitchen to the front door. A dark storeroom opens out of it, and that is a place to be run past at night. Then there is the parlor in which we sit of an evening, my mother and I and Peggotty—for Peggotty is quite our companion, when her work is done, and brings the little bit of wax candle she keeps for her thread, and her workbox with a view of St. Paul's Cathedral on the top, into the parlor when we are alone. Now we are playing in the winter twilight, dancing about the room. When my mother is out of breath and rests herself, I watch her winding her bright curls round her fingers and straightening her waist, and nobody knows better than I do that she likes to be so pretty.

Peggotty and I were sitting by the fire one night, alone. I had been reading to her about crocodiles and was dead sleepy; but, having leave, as a high treat, to sit up until my mother came home from a neighbor's, I would rather have died than have gone to bed. I propped my eyelids open and looked perseveringly at Peggotty, whom I thought lovely. I knew that if I lost sight of her, for a moment, I was gone.

"Peggotty," said I suddenly, "were you ever married?"

"Lord, Master Davy," replied Peggotty. "What's put marriage in your head?" She answered with such a start that it quite awoke me.

"If you marry a person and the person dies, you may marry another person, mayn't you, Peggotty?"

"You *may*," said Peggotty, "if you choose, my dear."

"You ain't cross, I suppose, Peggotty, are you?" said I; she had been so short with me. I was quite mistaken: opening her arms wide, she gave me such a squeeze that two of the buttons on the back of her gown flew off. "Now let me hear some more about the crorkindills," she said.

We had exhausted the crocodiles when the garden bell rang. And there was my mother, looking unusually pretty, and with her a gentleman with beautiful black hair and whiskers, who had walked home from church with us last Sunday.

As my mother stooped down to kiss me, the gentleman said I was more highly privileged than a monarch—or something like that. And somehow I didn't like him or his deep voice, and I was jealous that his hand touched my mother's in touching me. I put it away.

"Oh, Davy!" remonstrated my mother.

"Dear boy!" said the gentleman. "I cannot wonder at his devotion. Come, let us shake hands!"

My right hand was in my mother's, so I gave him the other.

"Why, that is the wrong hand, Davy!" laughed the gentleman.

My mother drew my right hand forward, but I was resolved not to give it him, and he went away. At this minute I see him turn round in the garden and give us a last look with his ill-omened black eyes.

Peggotty had not said a word, and I fell asleep in the parlor. But I half awoke to find her and my mother both in tears. "Not such a one as this, Mr. Copperfield wouldn't have liked," said Peggotty. "That I say, and that I swear."

"Good Heavens!" cried my mother. "Was ever poor girl so ill-used by her servants as I am! How can you dare—you know I don't mean how can you dare, Peggotty, but how can you have the heart—to make me so uncomfortable, when you know that I haven't, out of this place, a single friend to turn to?"

"The more's the reason," returned Peggotty, "for saying that it won't do. No! No price could make it do. No!"

"And my dear boy," cried my mother. "Is it to be hinted that I am wanting in affection for my precious treasure!"

"Nobody went and hinted no such a thing," said Peggotty.

"You did, Peggotty!" returned my mother. "You know you did!" At this we all fell a crying and went to bed greatly dejected.

Whether it was the following Sunday when I saw the gentleman again, I cannot recall. But there he was, and gradually I became used to seeing him, though with the same instinctive jealousy. Peggotty began to be less with us of an evening. My mother deferred to her more than usual and we were all three excellent friends, but we were different from what we used to be.

One day Mr. Murdstone—I knew him by that name now—came by on horseback and proposed to take me with him to Lowestoft. We went to a hotel there where we met two gentlemen. "And who's this shaver?" said one of them, taking hold of me.

"That's Davy," returned Mr. Murdstone. "Davy Copperfield."

"What! Bewitching Mrs. Copperfield's incumbrance?" cried the gentleman.

"Quinion," said Mr. Murdstone, "take care, if you please. Somebody's sharp."

"Who is?" asked the gentleman, laughing. I looked up, curious to know.

"Only Brooks of Sheffield," said Mr. Murdstone. I was quite relieved; at first I really thought it was I. But there seemed to be something very comical in the reputation of Mr. Brooks of Sheffield, for the gentlemen laughed heartily. Then the one called Quinion said, "And what is the opinion of Brooks of Sheffield in reference to the projected business?"

"Why, I don't know that Brooks understands much about it at present," replied Mr. Murdstone, "but he is not generally favorable, I believe." At which they laughed the more.

It was probably about two months later when Peggotty said to me coaxingly, "Master Davy, how should you like to go along with me and spend a fortnight at my brother's at Yarmouth?"

"Is your brother an agreeable man, Peggotty?" I inquired, provisionally.

"Oh, what an agreeable man he is!" cried Peggotty, holding up her hands. "Then there's the sea; and the boats and ships; and the beach; and Am—" (Peggotty meant her nephew Ham).

So our visit was arranged. It touches me nearly now, although I tell it lightly, to recollect how eager I was to leave my happy home. I am glad to recollect that, when the carrier's cart was at the gate, a grateful fondness for the old place made me cry and that my mother cried too. I am glad to recollect that, when the carrier began to move, my mother called to him to stop, that she might kiss me once more. I am glad to dwell upon the earnestness and love with which she lifted up her face to mine.

As we left her, Mr. Murdstone came up to her and seemed to expostulate with her for being so moved. I wondered what business it was of his.

2

"HERE'S my Am!" screamed Peggotty when we arrived at Yarmouth. He was waiting for us at the public house, a huge, strong fellow with a simpering boy's face that gave him quite a sheepish look, and, carrying me on his back, he walked past boat-builders' yards, riggers' lofts, smiths' forges, and a great litter of such places until we came out upon a dull flat waste, when he said, "Yon's our house, Mas'r Davy!"

I looked in all directions, but no house could *I* make out. There was a black barge not far off, high and dry on the ground, with an iron funnel sticking out for a chimney and smoking very cosily, but nothing else in the way of a habitation that was visible to *me*. "That's not it?" said I. "That ship-looking thing?"

"That's it, Mas'r Davy," returned Ham.

If it had been Aladdin's palace, I could not have been more charmed with the romantic idea of living in it. There was a delightful door cut in the side, and there were windows in it; but the wonderful charm of it was that it was a real boat, which had been upon the water hundreds of times and which had never been intended to be lived in, on dry land.

We were welcomed by a very civil woman in a white apron, and by a most beautiful little girl, who wouldn't let me kiss her but ran away and hid. By and by a hairy man with a very good-natured face came home, who was presented to me as Mr. Peggotty, the master of the house.

"Glad to see you, sir," said Mr. Peggotty. "You'll find us rough, sir, but you'll find us ready."

After tea, when the door was shut and all was made snug (the nights being cold and misty now), it seemed to me the most delicious retreat that the imagination of man could conceive. Little Em'ly had overcome her shyness and sat by my side on a locker which fitted into the chimney corner. Peggotty at her needlework was as much at home with St. Paul's and the bit of wax candle as if they had never known another roof. Mr. Peggotty was smoking his pipe. I felt it was a time for conversation and confidence.

"Mr. Peggotty!" says I.

"Sir," says he.

"Did you give your son the name of Ham because you lived in a sort of ark?"

Mr. Peggotty seemed to think it a deep idea but answered, "No, sir. His father giv it him."

"I thought you were his father!"

"My brother Joe was *his* father!" said Mr. Peggotty.

"Dead, Mr. Peggotty?" I hinted, after a respectful pause.

"Drowndead," said Mr. Peggotty.

I was very much surprised by this and began to wonder whether I was mistaken about his relationship to anybody else there. "Little Em'ly," I said, glancing at her. "She is your daughter, isn't she, Mr. Peggotty?"

"No, sir. My brother-in-law, Tom, was *her* father."

I couldn't help it. "Dead, Mr. Peggotty?" I hinted, after another respectful silence.

"Drowndead," said Mr. Peggotty.

I felt the difficulty of resuming the subject but must get to the bottom of it somehow. So I said, "Haven't you *any* children, Mr. Peggotty?"

"No, master," he answered, with a short laugh. "I'm a bacheldore."

"A bachelor!" I said, astonished. "Why, who's that, Mr. Peggotty?" pointing to the person in the apron.

"That's Missis Gummidge," said Mr. Peggotty. But at this point my Peggotty motioned me not to ask any more questions, and informed me later, in the privacy of my cabin, that Mrs. Gummidge was the widow of my host's partner in a boat, who had died very poor. Mr. Peggotty was but a poor man himself, said Peggotty, but as good as gold and as true as steel.

Almost as soon as it was morning, I was out on the beach with little Em'ly, gathering shells. "You're quite a sailor, I suppose?" I said gallantly.

"No," replied Em'ly, shaking her head, "I'm afraid of the sea. It is cruel to our men. They are fishermen, you see."

"Your uncle Dan must be very good, I should think?" said I.

"Good?" said Em'ly. "If I was ever to be a lady, I'd give him a sky-blue coat with diamond buttons, a cocked hat, a large gold watch, and a box of money."

"You would like to be a lady?" I said.

Em'ly laughed and nodded, "Yes." Then she ran along a jagged timber which overhung the deep water at some height, with a look that I have never forgotten, directed far out to sea.

The light, bold, fluttering little figure turned and came back safe to me, in spite of my fears. But there has been a time since when I have wondered whether, if the life before her could have been revealed to me then and if her preservation could have depended on a motion of my hand, I ought to have held it up to save her. But that is premature.

Of course I was in love with little Em'ly. The days sported by us as if Time had not grown up himself yet but were a child, too, and always at play. I told Em'ly I adored her and that unless she adored me too I should be reduced to the necessity of killing myself with a sword. She said she did, and I have no doubt she did.

I soon found out that Mrs. Gummidge, however, did not always make herself so agreeable as she might have been expected to. Hers was rather a fretful disposition, and she whimpered more sometimes than was comfortable. "I am a lone lorn creetur," were her words one forenoon when the fire smoked, "and everythink goes contrairy with me."

"Oh, it'll soon leave off," said Peggotty, "and besides, you know, it's not more disagreeable to you than to us."

"I feel it more," said Mrs. Gummidge.

It was a very cold day. Mrs. Gummidge's peculiar corner of the fireside seemed to me to be the warmest and snuggest in the place, as her chair was certainly the easiest, but it didn't suit her that day at all. She was constantly complaining of a visitation in her back which she called "the creeps."

"It is certainly very cold," said Peggotty. "Everybody must feel it so."

"I feel it more than other people," said Mrs. Gummidge.

Accordingly, when Mr. Peggotty came home that night from The Willing Mind, a public house to which he went occasionally, this unfortunate Mrs. Gummidge was in a very wretched condition. "What's amiss, old Mawther?" Mr. Peggotty said.

"Nothing," returned Mrs. Gummidge. "I'm sorry I should drive you to The Willing Mind, Dan'l."

"Drive! I don't want no driving," said Mr. Peggotty. "Don't ye believe it."

"Yes, yes," cried Mrs. Gummidge. "I know that I am a lone lorn creetur and not only that everythink goes contrairy with me but that I go contrairy with everybody. It ain't a fair return. If thinks must go contrairy with me, let me go contrairy in my parish. Dan'l, I'd better go into the House and die and be a riddance!"

Mrs. Gummidge retired with these words, and Mr. Peggotty, who had not exhibited a trace of any feeling but the profoundest sympathy, said in a whisper, "Poor thing! She's been thinking of the old 'un!" And whenever Mrs. Gummidge was overcome in a similar manner, he always said the same thing, and always with the tenderest commiseration.

At last the day came for going home. All the time I had been on my visit I had thought little about home, but the nearer we drew to it the more excited I was to get there and to run into my mother's arms. Peggotty, however, instead of sharing in these transports, tried to check them (though very kindly) and looked confused and out of sorts. When we arrived and I looked in vain for my mother, she took me into the kitchen. "Peggotty!" I cried. "Not dead, too? Oh, she's not dead, Peggotty?"

Peggotty cried out, "No!—I should have told you before now," she said, "but I couldn't azackly bring my mind to it. Master Davy, you have got a Pa. A new one." She gave a gasp, as if she were swallowing something hard, and took me to the parlor, where she left me.

On one side of the fire sat my mother; on the other, Mr. Murdstone. My mother arose hurriedly, but timidly I thought. "Now, Clara, my dear," said Mr. Murdstone. "Recollect! Control yourself, always control yourself! Davy boy, how do you do?"

I gave him my hand. After a moment of suspense, I went and kissed my mother; she kissed me, patted me gently on the shoulder, and sat down again to her work. As soon as I could creep away, I crept upstairs. My old dear bedroom was changed, and I was to lie a long way off from my mother.

I was awakened from the miserable sleep into which I had fallen by my mother and Peggotty, but I thrust my mother from me with my hand. "This is your doing, Peggotty, you cruel thing!" she said. "Davy, you naughty boy! Peggotty, you savage creature!" And she turned from one to the other in her pettish, willful manner. "When one has the most right to expect the world to be as agreeable as possible—!"

I felt the touch of another hand. It was Mr. Murdstone's.

"What's this?" he said. "Clara, my love, have you forgotten? Firmness, my dear!" He drew her to him. I knew as well, when I saw my mother's head lean down upon his shoulder, that he could mold her pliant nature into any form he chose, as I know, now, that he did it. "Go you below, my love. David and I will come down together."

When we were left alone, Mr. Murdstone looked steadily into my eyes. "David," he said, "if I have an obstinate horse or dog to deal with, what do you think I do?"

"I don't know."

"I beat him. I make him wince and smart. I say to myself, 'I'll conquer that fellow'; and if it were to cost him all the blood he had, I should do it. As for you, we shall soon improve our youthful humors."

God help me, I might have been improved for my whole life by a kind word at that season. A word of encouragement and explanation, of welcome home or reassurance that it *was* home, might have made me respect instead of hate him. I thought my mother was sorry to see me standing in the parlor presently so scared and strange and that when I stole to a chair she followed me with her eyes more sorrowfully still—missing, perhaps, some freedom in my childish tread—but the word was not spoken, and the time for it was gone.

When Mr. Murdstone stepped outside that evening to greet his elder sister, who was coming to stay with them, my mother hurriedly and secretly took me in her embrace as she had been used to do and whispered me to love my new father and be obedient to him. Then Miss Murdstone arrived, and a gloomy-looking lady she was, greatly resembling her brother. She brought with her two uncompromising hard black boxes, with her initials on the lids in hard brass nails. When she paid the coachman, she took her money out of a hard steel purse, and she kept the purse in a very jail of a bag which hung upon her arm by a heavy chain and shut up like a bite. When she looked at me, she said, "Is that your boy, sister-in-law?"

My mother acknowledged me.

"Generally speaking," said Miss Murdstone, "I don't like boys. How do you do, boy?"

She began to "help" my mother the next morning and was in and out of the store closet all day, making havoc in the old arrangements. Almost the first thing I observed in Miss Murdstone was her being constantly haunted by a suspicion that the servants had a man secreted somewhere on the premises. Under the influence of this delusion she dived into the coal cellar at the most untimely hours and scarcely ever opened the door of a dark cupboard without clapping it to again, in the belief that she had got him.

"If you'll be so good as to give me your keys, my dear, I'll attend to everything in future," she announced to my mother, who did not, however, suffer her authority to pass from her without a shadow of protest. One night when Miss Murdstone had been developing certain household plans to her brother, my mother suddenly began to cry. "I don't ask much," she said through her tears, "I am not unreasonable. I only want to be consulted sometimes. I am very much obliged to anybody who assists me, and I should be quite broken-hearted if anybody was to go—" (for Miss Murdstone made a jail delivery of her pocket handkerchief and threatened instant departure). But the next morning my mother earnestly and humbly entreated Miss Murdstone's pardon and never afterward gave an opinion on any matter, without first ascertaining hers.

There had been some talk of my going to boarding school, but in the meantime I learned lessons at home. Shall I ever forget those lessons! They were presided over nominally by my mother, but really by Mr. Murdstone and his sister, who found them a favorable occasion for giving my mother lessons in that *firmness* which was another name for tyranny. I believe I was kept at home for that purpose.

Let me bring one morning back again. I take a last drowning look at the page as I hand the first book to my mother and start off at a racing pace while I have got it fresh. I trip over a word. Mr. Murdstone looks up. I trip over another word. Miss Murdstone looks up. I redden, tumble over half a dozen words, and stop. My mother says softly, "Oh, Davy, Davy!"

"Now, Clara," says Mr. Murdstone, "be firm with the boy. Don't say, 'Oh, Davy, Davy.' That's childish. He knows his lesson, or he does not know it."

"He does *not* know it," Miss Murdstone interposes awfully. My mother glances submissively at them, shuts the book, and lays it by as an arrear to be worked out when my other tasks are done.

There is a pile of these arrears very soon, and it swells like a rolling snowball. The bigger it gets, the more stupid *I* get. When my mother (thinking nobody is observing her) tries to give me the cue by the motion of her lips, Mr. Murdstone comes out of his chair, takes the book, boxes my ears with it, and turns me out of the room. I had been apt enough to learn when my mother and I were alone together, but after six months of this treatment I was almost stupefied.

One morning when I went into the parlor with my books, I found my mother looking anxious, Miss Murdstone looking firm, and Mr. Murdstone binding something round the bottom of a cane, which he poised and switched in the air as I came in. "Now, David," he said, "you must be more careful today than usual."

This was a good freshener to my presence of mind. I began badly and went on worse. Book after book was added to the heap of failures. My mother at last burst out crying, and Mr. Murdstone rose, taking up the cane. "David, you and I will go upstairs," he said.

When we got there, he suddenly twisted my head under his arm. "Mr. Murdstone! Sir!" I cried to him. "Pray don't beat me! I have tried to learn, sir, but I can't learn while you and Miss Murdstone are by. I can't indeed!"

"Can't you, indeed, David?" he said. He cut me heavily, and in the same instant I caught his hand in my teeth and bit it through. It sets my teeth on edge to think of it.

He beat me then as if he would have beaten me to death. Above all the noise we made, I heard them running up the stairs and crying out—my mother and Peggotty. Then he was gone; and the door was locked outside; and I was lying, fevered and hot, and torn, and sore, and raging in my puny way, upon the floor.

How well I recollect, when I became quiet, what an unnatural stillness seemed to reign through the whole house! How well I remember, when my smart and passion began to cool, how wicked I began to feel!

My imprisonment lasted five days. If I could have seen my mother alone, I should have gone down on my knees to her and besought her forgiveness; but I saw no one except Miss Murdstone, who brought me my meals without a word. On the last night I was awakened by hearing my name spoken in a whisper, and putting my own lips to the keyhole I whispered back, "Is that you, Peggotty?"

"Yes, my own precious Davy," she replied. "Be as soft as a mouse, or the Cat'll hear us."

"How's Mamma, dear Peggotty? Is she very angry with me?"

I could hear Peggotty crying softly on her side of the keyhole, as I was doing on mine, before she answered. "No. Not very."

"What is going to be done with me, Peggotty dear? Do you know?"

"School. Near London. Tomorrow," was Peggotty's answer. Then she fitted her mouth close to the keyhole and delivered these words through it, shooting in each broken little sentence in a convulsive burst of its own.

"Davy, dear. If I ain't been azackly as intimate with you. Lately, as I used to be. It ain't because I don't love you. Just as well and more, my pretty poppet. It's because I thought it better for you. And for someone else besides. What I want to say, is. That you must never forget me. For I'll never forget you. And I'll take as much care of your mamma, Davy. As ever I took of you. And I won't leave her. The day may come when she'll be glad to lay her poor head. On her stupid, cross, old Peggotty's arm again. And I'll—I'll—" Peggotty fell to kissing the keyhole, as she couldn't kiss me—I patted it with my hand, as if it had been her honest face —and so, with tears, we parted.

3

THE cart might have gone about half a mile the next morning, after I had said good-by to my mother, and my pocket handkerchief was quite wet through, when the carrier stopped short, and to my amazement Peggotty burst from a hedge and climbed into the cart. She took me in both her arms, squeezed me to her stays, crammed some bags of cakes into my pockets, put a purse into my hand, and without a word (and without, to my belief, a solitary button on her gown) got down from the cart and ran away.

The purse had three bright shillings in it, which Peggotty had evidently polished up with whitening. But its most precious contents were two half crowns folded in a bit of paper, on which was written in my mother's hand "For Davy. With my love." As for the cakes—I offered one to the carrier (whose name was Mr. Barkis), and he ate it at one gulp, exactly like an elephant.

"Did *she* make 'em, now?" said Mr. Barkis, always leaning forward, in a slouching way, with an arm on each knee.

"Peggotty, do you mean, sir?"

"Ah!" said Mr. Barkis. "Her."

"Yes. She makes all our pastry and does all our cooking."

"Do she though?" said Mr. Barkis. He made up his mouth as if to whistle, but he didn't whistle. By and by he said, "No sweethearts, I b'lieve? No person walks with her?"

"Oh, no. She never had a sweetheart."

"Didn't she, though?" said Mr. Barkis. Again he made up his mouth to whistle, and again he didn't. "So she makes," he said, after a long interval of reflection, "all the apple parsties, and does all the cooking, do she?"

I replied that such was the fact.

"Well," said Mr. Barkis. "P'raps you might be writin' to her?"

"I shall certainly write to her," I rejoined.

"Ah!" he said, slowly turning his eyes toward me. "Well! If you was writin' to her, p'raps you'd recollect to say that Barkis was willin'?"

"That Barkis was willing," I repeated, innocently. "Is that all?"

"Ye-es," he said, considering. "Ye-es. Barkis is willin'."

When I had taken this commission on myself, Mr. Barkis relapsed into perfect silence; and I, quite worn out, slept soundly until we got to the inn at Yarmouth, where I was to have my dinner before taking the coach for London. In the coffee room, which, to my confusion, I had to myself, the waiter brought me some chops and vegetables and poured out my ale. "My eye!" he said. "It seems a good deal, don't it?"

"It does seem a good deal," I answered, quite delighted to find him so pleasant.

"There was a gentleman here yesterday," he said, "a stout gentleman, by the name of Topsawyer—perhaps you know him?"

"No," I said, "I don't think—"

"He came in here," said the waiter, "ordered a glass of this ale—*would* order it—I told him not—drank it, and fell dead. It oughtn't to be drawn; that's the fact."

I was very much shocked to hear of this melancholy accident and said I thought I had better have some water.

"Why, you see," said the waiter, "our people don't like things being ordered and left. It offends 'em. But *I'll* drink it, if you like. I don't think it'll hurt me, if I throw my head back and take it off quick. Shall I?" And he obliged me.

"What have we got there?" he said, putting a fork into my dish. "Not chops? Lord bless my soul! Why a chop's the very thing to take off the bad effects of that beer! Ain't it lucky?" So he took a chop in one hand and a potato in the other, and afterward took another chop and another potato, and after that another chop and another potato. And when he brought me a pudding, he raced me to see who should get most.

With the simple confidence of a child, I had no serious mistrust of him, though it was a little disconcerting to find, when I was being helped up behind the coach, that I was supposed to have eaten all the dinner without any assistance. "Take care of that child, George, or he'll burst!" one of the servants called to the guard. The story of my supposed appetite getting wind among the passengers, they were merry upon it likewise and asked me whether I was contracted for at school or went upon the regular terms, with other pleasant questions. But the worst of it was that I knew I should be ashamed to eat anything more and that, after a rather light dinner, I should remain hungry all night, which is what happened.

We got to London about eight the next morning, to find nobody there to meet me. While I waited in the booking office, a procession of most tremendous considerations marched through my mind. Supposing Mr. Murdstone had devised this plan to get rid of me? If I started off at once to walk back home, could I ever find my way? If I offered myself to go for a soldier, I was such a little fellow, they probably wouldn't take me. I was in the height of apprehension when a gaunt, sallow young man entered and whispered to the clerk, who pushed me over to him. "You're the new boy?" he said.

I supposed I was.

"I'm one of the masters at Salem House," he said, and told me that we should go by stage coach to Blackheath. I took heart to tell him that I had had nothing to eat all night, and after considering he said that he wanted to call on an old person who lived near by and that I could get breakfast there. We walked until we came to some almshouses and went into the room of one of these poor old women.

On seeing the Master enter the old woman said something that I thought sounded like "My Charlie!" but, on seeing me come in too, she made a confused sort of half curtsey; I was too sleepy to pay much attention. Mr. Mell soon took me away, and we reached our destination at last.

All about Salem House was perfectly quiet, for it was holiday time; the Master explained to me that I had been sent early as a punishment for my misdoing. Even the proprietor, Mr. Creakle, was at the seashore. And the schoolroom seemed the most desolate place I had ever seen. There could not have been more ink splashed about it if it had been roofless from its construction and the skies had rained, snowed, hailed, and blown ink through the varying seasons. Suddenly I came upon a pasteboard placard, which bore these words, "Take care of him. He bites."

I got upon a desk immediately, apprehensive of at least a great dog underneath. But I could see nothing of him. "I beg your pardon, sir," says I to Mr. Mell, "isn't it a dog that's to be taken care of, sir? That bites?"

"No, Copperfield," says he, gravely, "that's a boy. My instructions are to put this placard on your back. I am sorry to make such a beginning with you, but I must do it." With that he tied it on my shoulders.

What I suffered from that placard nobody can imagine. The playground where I was ordered to walk was open to all the back of the house; and I knew that everybody who came there read that I was to be taken care of, for I bit. I recollect that I positively began to have a fear of myself, as a kind of wild boy who did bite. Though I was lonely, listening at night to the doleful performance of Mr. Mell on his flute, I dreaded the time when the school bell should ring the boys back to work.

I had led this life about a month, doing long tasks with Mr. Mell every day, when I was summoned to appear before Mr. Creakle, a stout gentleman who sat with a tumbler and bottle beside him. Mr. Creakle's face was fiery, and his eyes were small, and deep in his head. But the circumstance about him which impressed me most was that he had no voice but spoke in a whisper and that the exertion this cost him, or the consciousness of talking in that feeble way, made his angry face all the angrier.

"I have the happiness of knowing your stepfather," whispered Mr. Creakle, taking me by the ear, "and a worthy man he is, and a man of strong character. He knows me, and I know him. Do *you* know me? Hey?", pinching my ear with ferocious playfulness.

"Not yet, sir," said I, flinching with the pain.

"I'll tell you what I am," whispered Mr. Creakle. "I'm a Tartar. Now you have begun to know me, my young friend, you may go."

It was a happy circumstance for me that the first boy who returned was Tommy Traddles. He enjoyed my placard so much, that he saved me from the embarrassment of either disclosure or concealment. But I was not considered as being formally received into the school until J. Steerforth arrived. Before this boy, who was reputed to be a great scholar and was very good-looking, I was carried as before a magistrate. He inquired into the particulars of my punishment and was pleased to express his opinion that it was "a jolly shame," for which I became bound to him ever afterward.

Having appropriated my money for a royal spread at which he did me the favor of presiding, he told me that night all kinds of things about the school. I heard that Mr. Creakle had not preferred his claim to being a Tartar without reason, though he knew nothing himself but the art of slashing; that Steerforth, the only parlor boarder, was the one boy on whom he never ventured to lay a hand; that Mr. Sharp and Mr. Mell, the two Masters, were wretchedly paid—that Mr. Mell hadn't a sixpence to bless himself with and that there was no doubt his mother was as poor as Job. Then Steerforth bade me good night. "I'll take care of you, young Copperfield," he said.

"You're very kind," I gratefully returned.

"You haven't got a sister, have you?" he said, yawning.

"No," I answered.

"That's a pity," said Steerforth. "If you had one, I should think she would be a pretty, timid, little, bright-eyed sort of girl. I should have liked to know her."

I thought of him very much after I went to bed and raised myself, I recollect, to look at him where he lay in the moonlight, with his head reclining easily on his arm. He was a person of great power in my eyes; that was the reason of my mind running on him. No veiled future dimly glanced upon him in the moonbeams. There was no shadowy picture of his footsteps, in the garden that I dreamed of walking in all night.

School began in earnest next day. A profound impression was made upon me, I remember, by the roar of voices in the school-room suddenly becoming hushed as death when Mr. Creakle entered after breakfast.

"Now, boys, this is a new half," he said. "Come fresh up to the lessons, I advise you, for I come fresh up to the punishment." He then came to where I sat and told me that, if I were famous for biting, he was famous for biting, too. He showed me the cane and asked me what I thought of *that* for a tooth? Was it a sharp tooth, hey? Was it a double tooth, hey? Did it bite, hey? Did it bite? At every question he gave me a fleshy cut with it that made me writhe; so I was very soon made free of Salem House.

Not that these were special marks of distinction, which only I received. On the contrary, a large majority of the boys (especially the smaller ones) were visited with similar instances of Mr. Creakle's notice. I should think there never can have been a man who enjoyed his profession more. He had a delight in cutting at the boys, which was like the satisfaction of a craving appetite, cutting a joke before he beat his victim. And we laughed at it—miserable little dogs, we laughed, with our visages as white as ashes and our hearts sinking into our boots.

Poor Traddles! In a tight sky-blue suit that made his arms and legs like German sausages, he was the merriest and most miserable of all the boys. He was always being caned, and was always going to write to his uncle about it, and never did. After laying his head on the desk for a while, he would cheer up somehow, begin to laugh again, and draw skeletons all over his slate. He was very honorable and held it a solemn duty in the boys to stand by one another. Once, when Steerforth laughed in church, the Beadle thought it was Traddles and took him out. He never said who was the real offender, though he smarted for it next day. But he had his reward. Steerforth said there was nothing of the sneak in Traddles, and we all felt that to be the highest praise. For my part, I could have gone through a good deal (though I was less brave than Traddles, and nothing like so old) to have won such a recompense.

In a school carried on by sheer cruelty, whether it is presided over by a dunce or not, there is not likely to be much learned. I believe our boys were as ignorant a set as any in existence; they were too much troubled and knocked about to learn. But Mr. Mell's liking for me made me an exception to the general body, insomuch that I did steadily pick up some crumbs of knowledge.

It always gave me pain, therefore, to observe that Steerforth treated Mr. Mell with systematic disparagement and seldom lost an occasion of wounding his feelings. It troubled me the more because I had told Steerforth, from whom I could no more keep a secret than I could keep a cake or any tangible possession, about the old woman Mr. Mell had taken me to see; and I was always afraid that Steerforth would let it out and twit him with it.

One day when Mr. Mell was keeping school by himself, he bent his aching head over the book on his desk amidst an uproar that might have made the Speaker of the House of Commons giddy. Boys whirled about him, grinning, making faces, mimicking him, mimicking his poverty, his boots, his mother, everything belonging to him that they should have had consideration for.

"Silence!" he cried, suddenly rising and striking his desk with the book. "It's impossible to bear this. It's maddening. How can you do it, boys?"

I was standing beside him, and I saw the boys all stop, some surprised, some half afraid, some sorry perhaps. Steerforth looked at Mr. Mell with his mouth shut up as if he were whistling.

"Silence, Mr. Steerforth!" said Mr. Mell.

"Silence yourself," said Steerforth, turning red. "Whom are you talking to? Mind your business."

There was a titter, and some applause; but Mr. Mell was so white, that silence immediately succeeded; and one boy who had darted out behind him to imitate his mother changed his mind.

"If you think, Steerforth," said Mr. Mell, "that I am not acquainted with the power you can establish over any mind here"— he laid his hand, without considering what he did (as I supposed) upon my head—"or that I have not observed you urging your juniors on to every sort of outrage against me, you are mistaken. And when you make use of your position of favoritism here to insult a gentleman—"

"A what? Where is he?" said Steerforth.

Here somebody cried out, "Shame, J. Steerforth! Too bad!" It was Traddles.

"—To insult one who is not fortunate in life, sir," said Mr. Mell, with his lip trembling very much, "you commit a mean and base action."

"When you take the liberty of calling me mean or base," returned Steerforth, "you are an impudent beggar. You are always a beggar, you know; but when you do that, you are an impudent beggar."

I am not clear whether he was going to strike Mr. Mell or Mr. Mell was going to strike him, but I saw a rigidity come upon the whole school, as if they had been turned to stone, and I found Mr. Creakle in our midst. "Mr. Mell," he said, "you have not forgotten yourself, I hope?"

"No, sir, no," returned the Master, "I—I have remembered myself, sir. I—I could wish you had remembered me a little sooner, Mr. Creakle."

Mr. Creakle turned to Steerforth and said, "Now, sir, what *is* this?"

Steerforth evaded the question for a little while, looking in scorn and anger on his opponent and remaining silent. I could not help thinking what a noble fellow he was in appearance and how homely Mr. Mell looked opposed to him.

"He said I was mean and base, and then I called him a beggar," Steerforth said at length. "If I had been cool, perhaps I shouldn't have. But I did, and I am ready to take the consequences."

Without considering whether there were any consequences to be taken, I felt quite in a glow at this gallant speech. It made an impression on the boys, too.

"I am surprised, Steerforth—although your candor does you honor," said Mr. Creakle, "that you should attach such an epithet to any person employed and paid in Salem House, sir."

"If he isn't a beggar himself, his near relation's one," said Steerforth. He glanced at me, and Mr. Mell's hand gently patted me upon the shoulder. I looked up with a flush on my face and remorse in my heart, but his eyes were fixed on Steerforth. He continued to pat me kindly on the shoulder.

"Since you expect me, Mr. Creakle, to justify myself," said Steerforth, "what I have to say is that his mother lives on charity in an almshouse."

Mr. Creakle turned to his assistant, with a severe frown and labored politeness. "Have the goodness to set this gentleman right before the assembled school," he said.

"He is right, sir, without correction," returned Mr. Mell.

"Be so good then as declare publicly, will you," said Mr. Creakle, "whether it ever came to my knowledge until this moment?"

"I believe not directly, though I apprehend you never supposed my worldly circumstances to be very good," replied the assistant.

"I apprehend, if you come to that," said Mr. Creakle, "that you've been in a wrong position altogether and mistook this for a charity school. Mr. Mell, we'll part, if you please. The sooner the better."

"I take my leave of you, Mr. Creakle, and all of you," said Mr. Mell, glancing round the room. "James Steerforth, the best wish I can leave you is that you may come to be ashamed of what you have done today. At present I would prefer to see you anything rather than a friend to anyone in whom I feel an interest."

Once more he laid his hand on my shoulder; then, taking his flute and a few books from his desk he went out of the school. Mr. Creakle then made a speech in which he thanked Steerforth for asserting the respectability of Salem House, while we gave three cheers—I did not quite know what for. For myself, I felt so much self-reproach that nothing would have enabled me to keep back my tears but the fear that Steerforth might think it unfriendly. He was very angry with Traddles, who thought Mr. Mell ill-used. "Who has ill-used him, you girl?" said Steerforth. "Do you suppose I am not going to write home and take care that he gets some money?" But, in the dark that night, Mr. Mell's old flute seemed to sound mournfully in my ears, and I was quite wretched.

One other event in this half year made an impression on me— an unexpected visit from Mr. Peggotty and Ham. "Cheer up, Mas'r Davy 'bor!" said Ham, when I cried with pleasure at seeing them. "Why, how you've growed!"

"Do you know how Mamma is?" I said. "And my dear, dear Peggotty?"

"Oncommon," said Mr. Peggotty.

"And little Em'ly, and Mrs. Gummidge?"

"Oncommon," said Mr. Peggotty.

I said, with a consciousness of reddening, that I supposed little Em'ly was altered too. "She's getting to be a woman, that's wot she's getting to be," said Mr. Peggotty. "Ask *him*." He meant Ham, who beamed with delight and assent. I dare say they would have said much more about her, if they had not been abashed by the coming in of Steerforth.

I am not sure whether it was in the pride of having such a friend as Steerforth or in the desire to explain to him how I came to have such a friend as Mr. Peggotty that I called to him, "Don't go. These are two Yarmouth boatmen—very kind, good people—who are relations of my nurse and have come to see me."

"Ay, ay?" said Steerforth, returning. "I am glad to see them. How are you both?"

There was an ease in his manner—a gay and light manner, but not swaggering—which I still believe to have borne a kind of enchantment. He carried a spell with him to which it was a natural weakness to yield and which not many persons could withstand. I could see how pleased they were with him and how they seemed to open their hearts to him in a moment.

The rest of the half year is a jumble in my recollection of the daily strife and struggle of our lives. I well remember, though, how the distant idea of the holidays began to come toward us and to grow and grow. How from counting months, we came to weeks, and then to days; and how I began to be afraid that I should not be sent for—and then learned from Steerforth that I *had* been and was certainly to go home.

4

Mr. Barkis the carrier received me on my way home exactly as if not five minutes had elapsed since we were last together. "You look very well, Mr. Barkis," I said, thinking he would like to know it. Mr. Barkis rubbed his cheek with his cuff, and then looked at his cuff as if he expected to find some of the bloom upon it, but made no other acknowledgment.

"I gave your message, Mr. Barkis," I said; "I wrote to Peggotty."

"Ah!" said Mr. Barkis. He seemed gruff and answered dryly.

"Wasn't it right, Mr. Barkis?" I asked, after a little hesitation.

"Why, no," said Mr. Barkis. "Nothing came of it. No answer."

"There was an answer expected, Mr. Barkis?" said I. This was a new light.

"When a man says he's willin'," said Mr. Barkis, turning his glance slowly on me, "it's as much as to say that man's a waiting for a answer."

"Have you told her so, Mr. Barkis?"

"N-no," growled Mr. Barkis, reflecting about it. "I ain't got no call to go and tell her so. I never said six words to her myself. *I* ain't a goin' to tell her so."

"Would you like me to do it, Mr. Barkis?" said I, doubtfully.

"You might tell her, if you would," said Mr. Barkis, "that Barkis was a waitin' for a answer. Says you—what name is it?"

"Peggotty."

"Chrisen name? Or nat'ral name?" said Mr. Barkis.

"Oh, her Christian name is Clara."

"Is it though!" said Mr. Barkis, pondering. "Well!" he resumed at length. "Says you, 'Peggotty! Barkis is a waitin' for a answer.' Says she, 'Answer to what?' 'Barkis is willin',' says you." After that, he slouched over his horse in his usual manner; but half an hour later he wrote inside the tilt of the cart "Clara Peggotty"— apparently as a private memorandum.

Ah, what a strange feeling it was to find that every object I looked at reminded me of my happy old home, which was like a dream I could never dream again! I walked along the garden path when we arrived there, fearing at every step to see Mr. Murdstone or his sister, but no face appeared, and I went in. God knows how infantine the memory may have been that was awakened within me by the sound of my mother's voice. She was singing in a low tone, sitting by the fire in the old parlor, suckling an infant whose tiny hand she held against her neck.

I spoke to her, and she started and called me her own boy! and kneeled down upon the ground and kissed me, and laid my head down on her bosom near the little creature that was nestling there, and put its hand up to my lips.

I wish I had died. I wish I had died then, with that feeling in my heart! I should have been more fit for Heaven than I ever have been since.

"He is your brother," said my mother, fondling me. "Davy, my pretty boy! My poor child!" Then Peggotty came running in and went mad about us both.

It seemed that I had not been expected so soon and that Mr. and Miss Murdstone had gone out. It was as if the old days were come back. We three dined together by the fireside, where I told Peggotty about Mr. Barkis. Before I had finished, she began to laugh and throw her apron over her face.

"What are you doing, you stupid creature?" said my mother, laughing.

"Oh, drat the man!" cried Peggotty. "He wants to marry me. I wouldn't have him if he was made of gold."

"Then, why don't you tell him so, you ridiculous thing?" said my mother.

"Tell him so," retorted Peggotty, looking out of her apron. "He has never said a word to me about it. He knows better. I should slap his face."

I remarked that my mother became more serious and thoughtful. I had seen at first that she was changed, too delicate. Now her manner became anxious and fluttered. At last she said, laying her hand affectionately on the hand of her old servant, "Peggotty dear, you are not going to be married? Don't leave me. It will not be for long, perhaps. What should I ever do without you!"

"Me leave you, my precious!" cried Peggotty. "I think I see myself. It isn't that there ain't some Cats that would be well enough pleased if I did, but they shan't be pleased. They shall be aggravated."

We sat round the fire and talked delightfully. I took the little baby in my arms when it was awake and nursed it lovingly. When it was asleep again, I crept close to my mother's side, according to my old custom, broken now a long time, and sat with my little red cheek on her shoulder. We were very happy; and that evening, as the last of its race and destined evermore to close that volume of my life, will never pass out of my memory.

"Ah, dear me!" sighed Miss Murdstone when she saw me the next morning. "How long are the holidays?"

"A month, ma'am."

"Counting from when?"

"From today, ma'am."

"Oh!" said Miss Murdstone. "Then here's *one* day off." She kept a calendar of the holidays in this way and every morning checked a day off. In short, I was not a favorite with Miss Murdstone. In short, I was not a favorite with anybody, not even with myself; for those who did like me could not show it, and those who did not showed it so plainly that I had a sensitive consciousness of always appearing boorish and dull. What irksome constraint I underwent, too, sitting in the parlor hours upon hours, as I was ordered to do, afraid to move an arm or a leg. What meals I had in silence and embarrassment, always feeling that there were a plate and chair too many, and those mine; an appetite too many, and that mine; a somebody too many, and that I!

Thus the holidays lagged away, until the morning came when Miss Murdstone said, "Here's the last day off!" I kissed my mother and my baby brother and was very sorry then, but not sorry to go away, for the gulf between us was there, every day. And it is not so much the embrace she gave me that lives in my mind, though it was as fervent as could be, as what followed.

I was in the carrier's cart when I heard her calling to me. She stood at the garden gate alone, holding her baby up in her arms for me to see. It was cold still weather; and not a hair of her head nor a fold of her dress was stirred, as she looked intently at me.

So I lost her. So I saw her afterward, in my sleep at school—a silent presence near my bed, looking at me with the same intent face, holding up her baby in her arms.

I pass over all that happened at school, until my birthday. How well I recollect the kind of day it was! I see the dim perspective of the schoolroom, with a sputtering candle here and there to light up the foggy morning, and the boys' breath wreathing and smoking in the raw cold air as they blow upon their fingers and tap their feet upon the floor. Mr. Sharp said,

"David Copperfield is to go into the parlor."

I expected a hamper from Peggotty and brightened at the order, getting out of my seat with alacrity.

"Don't hurry, David," said Mr. Sharp. "There's time enough, my boy."

I might have been surprised by the feeling tone in which he spoke if I had given it a thought. I hurried away to the parlor; and there was Mrs. Creakle with an open letter in her hand.

"David Copperfield," said Mrs. Creakle, sitting beside me on a sofa. "I have something to tell you, my child. You are too young to know how the world changes every day, and how the people in it pass away. But we all have to learn it, David, some of us when we are young."

I looked at her earnestly.

"When you came away from home at the end of the vacation," said Mrs. Creakle, after a pause, "were they all well?" After another pause, "Was your mamma well?"

I trembled without distinctly knowing why and still looked at her earnestly.

"Because," said she, "I grieve to tell you that I hear this morning that your mamma is very ill. Very dangerously ill," she added.

I knew all now.

"She is dead."

There was no need to tell me so. I had already broken out into a desolate cry, and felt an orphan in the wide world.

When I could cry no more, I began to think; and then the oppression on my breast was heaviest. And yet my thoughts were idle, not intent on the calamity that weighed upon me, but idly loitering near it. I stood upon a chair when I was left alone and looked into the glass to see how red my eyes were, and how sorrowful my face. I considered, after some hours were gone, if my tears were really hard to flow now, as they seemed to be. I felt that a dignity attached to me and that I was important in my affliction.

If ever child were stricken with sincere grief, I was. But I remember that this importance was a kind of satisfaction to me. When I saw the boys glancing at me as I walked in the playground, I looked more melancholy and walked slower. When they spoke to me, I felt it rather good in myself not to be proud to any of them and to take exactly the same notice of them as before.

I left Salem House upon the following afternoon. I little thought then that I left it, never to return. At Yarmouth I looked out for Mr. Barkis; but, instead of him, a fat, short-winded, merry-looking little old man in black, came puffing up and said, "Will you come with me, Master Copperfield?"

I put my hand in his, and we walked away to a shop on which was written "Omer, Draper, Tailor, Haberdasher, Funeral Furnisher, Etc." It was a close and stifling little shop, full of a breathless smell of warm black crape. Three young women, at work on a quantity of black material, appeared to be very industrious and comfortable. Stitch, stitch, stitch. At the same time there came from a workshop across the yard a regular sound of hammering that kept a kind of tune, *Rat*-tat-tat, *rat*-tat-tat, *rat*-tat-tat, without any variation.

"I have been acquainted with you," said Mr. Omer, after my dimensions had been taken, "all your life. I may say before it. I knew your father before you. He was five foot nine and a half, and he lays in five and twen-ty foot of ground."

Rat-tat-tat, *rat*-tat-tat, *rat*-tat-tat, across the yard. Presently the tune left off, and a good-looking young fellow came in. "Well, Joram!" said Mr. Omer. "How do *you* get on?"

"All right," said Joram. "Done, sir."

"My dear," said Mr. Omer to me, "would you like to see your—"

"No, father," the girl called Minnie interposed. I can't say how I knew it was my dear, dear mother's coffin that they went to look at.

I don't think I have ever experienced so strange a feeling as that of being in the chaise presently with Mr. Omer and his daughter and Joram, remembering how they had been employed, and seeing them enjoy the ride. I was not angry with them; I was scared by the young people's love making and hilarity, as if I were cast away among creatures with whom I had no community of nature. When we reached home, I dropped out of the chaise behind, that I might not be in their company before those solemn windows. I was in Peggotty's arms before I got to the door, and she took me into the house. Her grief burst out when she first saw me; but she controlled it soon, and spoke in whispers, and walked softly, as if the dead could be disturbed.

Mr. Murdstone took no heed of me when I went into the parlor, but sat weeping silently. He would open a book and look at it as if he were reading, but without turning a leaf, and then walk to and fro in the room. I used to sit with folded hands watching him and counting his footsteps, hour after hour. He seemed to be the only restless thing, except the clocks, in the whole motionless house.

If the funeral had been yesterday, I could not recollect it better. We stand around the grave. The day seems different to me from every other day, and the light not the same color—of a sadder color. Now there is a solemn hush, and I hear the voice of the clergyman, saying, "I am the Resurrection and the Life." Then I hear sobs; and, standing apart among the lookers-on, I see that good and faithful servant, whom of all the people upon earth I love the best and unto whom my childish heart is certain that the Lord will one day say, "Well done. . . . "

I knew that Peggotty would come to me in my room afterward. She sat down on my bed; and holding my hand and sometimes smoothing it with hers, as she might have comforted my little brother, she told me all that had happened.

"She was never well," said Peggotty, "for a long time. I think she got to be more timid, and more frightened-like, of late, and that a hard word was like a blow to her. But she was always the same to me. She never changed to her foolish Peggotty, didn't my sweet girl." Here Peggotty stopped, and softly beat upon my hand a little while.

"The last time that I saw her like her own old self, was the night when you came home, my dear. The day you went away, she said to me, 'I never shall see my pretty darling again.' She tried to hold up after that and many a time, when they told her she was thoughtless and light-hearted, made believe to be so; but it was all a bygone then. She often talked to them two downstairs—for she loved them; she couldn't bear not to love anyone who was about her— but when they went away from her bedside, she always turned to me, as if there was rest where Peggotty was, and never fell asleep in any other way.

"On the last night, in the evening, she kissed me and said, 'If my baby should die too, Peggotty, please let them lay him in my arms, and bury us together.' (It was done; for the poor lamb lived but a day beyond her.) 'Let my dearest boy go with us to our resting place,' she said, 'and tell him that his mother, when she lay here, blessed him not once, but a thousand times.'"

Another silence followed this, and another gentle beating on my hand.

"Daybreak had come, and the sun was rising, when she said to me, how kind and considerate Mr. Copperfield had always been to her, and how he told her, when she doubted herself, that a loving heart was better than wisdom. 'Peggotty, my dear,' she said then, 'put me nearer to you,' for she was very weak. 'Lay your good arm underneath my neck,' she said, 'and turn me to you, for your face is going far off, and I want it to be near.' I put it as she asked; and oh! Davy, the time had come when my first parting words to you were true—when she was glad to lay her poor head on her stupid cross old Peggotty's arm—and she died like a child that had gone to sleep!"

5

THE first act of business Miss Murdstone performed when the day of solemnity was over was to give Peggotty a month's warning. As to me or my future, not a word was said, or a step taken. Happy they would have been, I dare say, if they could have dismissed me at a month's warning too. I mustered courage once to ask when I was going back to school; Miss Murdstone answered dryly, "Not at all." At first I was in dread of Mr. Murdstone's taking my education in hand again, but I soon began to think that such fears were groundless and that all I had to anticipate was neglect.

"Davy," said Peggotty one evening, "I have tried all ways I could think of to get a suitable service here in Blunderstone; but there's no such a thing, my love."

"And what do you mean to do, Peggotty," says I, wistfully. "Do you mean to go and seek your fortune?"

"I expect I shall be forced to go to Yarmouth," replied Peggotty. "But as long as you are here, my pet, I shall come over every week to see you."

I felt a great weight taken off my mind by this promise; and even this was not all. For Peggotty went on to say that she was going to her brother's first for a visit and that I was to go along with her.

When Peggoty's month was out, Mr. Barkis came for us. Peggotty was naturally low in spirits; she had been walking in the churchyard very early. And so long as she remained in that condition, Mr. Barkis gave no sign of life whatever. But when she began to look about her, he nodded his head and grinned several times. "Peggotty is quite comfortable now, Mr. Barkis," I remarked, for his satisfaction.

"Is she, though?" said Mr. Barkis. After reflecting about it, with a sagacious air, he eyed her and said, "*Are* you pretty comfortable?"

Peggotty laughed and answered in the affirmative.

"But really and truly, you know. Are you?" growled Mr. Barkis, sliding nearer to her on the seat and nudging her with his elbow. "Are you? Really and truly, pretty comfortable? Eh?" At each of these inquiries[Mr. Barkis shuffled nearer to her and gave her another nudge, so that at last we were all crowded together in the corner of the cart and I was so squeezed that I could hardly bear it.]

Peggotty calling attention to my sufferings, Mr. Barkis gave me a little more room and got away by degrees. But he seemed to think he had hit upon a wonderful expedient for expressing himself in a neat, agreeable, and pointed manner, without the inconvenience of inventing conversation. By and by he made another descent upon us with the same inquiry and the same result, and then another. At length I got up whenever I saw him coming and stood on the floor.

As we were leaving him at Yarmouth, Mr. Barkis said to me confidentially, "It was all right. You know who was willin'. It was Barkis. It's all right."

In his attempts to be particularly lucid, Mr. Barkis was so extremely mysterious that I might have stood looking in his face for an hour, getting as much information out of it as out of a clock that had stopped, but for Peggotty's calling me away. I told her he had said it was all right.

"Like his impudence," said Peggotty, "but I don't mind that! Davy dear, what should you think if I was to think of being married?"

"To Mr. Barkis, Peggotty?" I said, after considering. "I should think it would be a very good thing. You would always have the horse and cart to bring you over to see me and could come for nothing and be sure of coming."

"The sense of the dear!" cried Peggotty. "What I have been thinking of, this month back! Barkis is a good plain creatur', and if I tried to do my duty by him, I think it would be my fault if I wasn't—if I wasn't pretty comfortable," said Peggotty, laughing heartily.

Mr. Peggotty's cottage, when we came to it, looked just the same, except that it may, perhaps, have shrunk a little in my eyes. But there was no little Em'ly to be seen, so I asked Mr. Peggotty where she was.

"She's at school, sir," said Mr. Peggotty. "We all on us feel the loss of her, bless you!"

Mrs. Gummidge moaned.

"Cheer up, Mawther!" cried Mr. Peggotty.

"I feel it more than anybody else," said Mrs. Gummidge. "I'm a lone lorn creetur, and she used to be almost the only thing that didn't go contrairy with me."

Mr. Peggotty said in a low voice, which he shaded with his hand, "The old'un!"

Little Em'ly, when she came home from school, was even prettier and gayer than I remembered, though she seemed to delight in teasing me, which was a change I wondered at very much. But she had such a pleasant manner of being both sly and shy at once that she captivated me more than ever; I recollect putting a short clause into my prayers, petitioning that I might grow up to marry her.

"And how's your friend, sir?" said Mr. Peggotty to me.

"Steerforth?" said I. "He was very well indeed when I came away."

"There's a friend!" said Mr. Peggotty. "If it ain't a treat to look at him!"

"He is very handsome, is he not?" said I, my heart warming with this praise.

"And I do suppose now," said Mr. Peggotty, "that in the way of book larning he'd take the wind out of almost anything."

"Yes," said I, delighted. "He knows everything, he is so clever."

"There's a friend!" murmured Mr. Peggotty, with a grave toss of the head.

"He is such a speaker," I pursued, "that he can win anybody over; and I don't know what you'd say if you were to hear him sing, Mr. Peggotty."

Mr. Peggotty gave his head another toss, as much as to say, "I have no doubt of it."

"Then, he's such a generous, fine, noble fellow," said I, quite carried away by my favorite theme, "that it's hardly possible to give him as much praise as he deserves." I was running on, very fast indeed, when my eyes rested on little Em'ly, listening with the deepest attention, her breath held, her blue eyes sparkling, and the color mantling in her cheeks. "Em'ly is like me," said Peggotty, "and would like to see him."

On the very first evening after our arrival, Mr. Barkis appeared in an exceedingly vacant and awkward condition and with a bundle of oranges tied up in a handkerchief. As he made no allusion to this property, he was supposed to have left it behind by accident; until Ham, running after him to restore it, came back with the information that it was for Peggotty. After that he appeared every evening at exactly the same hour, and always with a little bundle which he left behind the door. These offerings of affection were of a most various and eccentric description. Among them I remember a double set of pigs' trotters, a huge pin cushion, half a bushel of apples, a pair of jet earrings, some Spanish onions, a box of dominoes, a canary bird and cage, and a leg of pickled pork.

At length it was given out that Peggotty and Mr. Barkis were going to make a day's holiday together and that little Em'ly and I were to accompany them. When we were all in a bustle outside the door, I found that Mr. Peggotty was prepared with an old shoe, which was to be thrown after us for luck. "Come, old gal!" he cried to Mrs. Gummidge. "Take and heave it."

"No, Dan'l," returned Mrs. Gummidge, whimpering and shaking her head. "If I felt less, I could do more. Thinks don't go contrairy with you, nor you with them; you had better do it yourself."

So away we went; and the first thing we did was to stop at a church, where Mr. Barkis tied the horse to some rails and went in with Peggotty. When they came out, he turned to me and said with a wink, "What name was it as I wrote up in the cart?"

"Clara Peggotty," I answered.

"What name would it be as I should write up now?"

"Clara Peggotty again?" I suggested.

"Clara Peggotty *Barkis!*" he returned, and burst into a roar of laughter.

In a word, they were married. Peggotty could not hug me enough in token of her unimpaired affection; but she soon became herself again and said she was very glad it was over.

Next day I took leave of Mr. Peggotty, and Ham, and Mrs. Gummidge, and little Em'ly, and passed the night at Peggotty's in a little room in the roof which was to be always mine, Peggotty said. Then I went home with herself and Mr. Barkis in the cart. They left me at the gate, not easily or lightly; and it was strange to see the cart go on, taking Peggotty away and leaving me alone at the house in which there was no face to look on mine with love or liking any more.

And now I fell into a state of neglect which I cannot look back on without compassion. What would I have given to have been sent to the hardest school that ever was kept—to have been taught something, anyhow, anywhere! No such hope dawned upon me. Mr. Murdstone could not bear me; and in putting me from him he tried, as I believe, to put away the notion that I had any claim upon him—and succeeded.

Faithful to her promise, Peggotty came to see me every week, and never empty-handed; but many and bitter were the disappointments I had, in being refused permission to visit her. Some few times, however, I was allowed to go, and then I found that Mr. Barkis was something of a miser, or, as Peggotty dutifully expressed it, "a little near," and kept a heap of money in a box under his bed, which he pretended was only full of coats and trousers. From this coffer the smallest installments could only be tempted out by artifice, so that Peggotty had to prepare a very Gunpowder Plot for every Saturday's expenses.

At last, one day, I had been out loitering somewhere in the listless manner that my way of life engendered, when I came upon Mr. Murdstone walking with a gentleman who cried, on seeing me, "What! Brooks of Sheffield!" And his laugh coming to my remembrance, I knew him to be Mr. Quinion, whom I had once gone over to Lowestoft with Mr. Murdstone to see.

"How do you get on, and where are you being educated, Brooks?" said Mr. Quinion. I did not know what to reply and glanced dubiously at Mr. Murdstone.

"He is at home at present," said the latter. "He is not being educated anywhere. I don't know what to do with him. He is a difficult subject." When I left them, I saw them looking after me and felt that they were speaking of me.

In the presence of Mr. Quinion and of his sister, Mr. Murdstone spoke to me later that day. "David," he said, "to the young this is a world for action, not for moping in."

"As you do," added his sister.

"Jane Murdstone, leave it to me, if you please. I suppose you know, David, that I am not rich. Education is costly; and even if it were not, I am of opinion that it would not be advantageous to you to be kept at a school. What is before you is a fight with the world; and the sooner you begin it, the better."

It occurred to me that I had already begun it, in my poor way.

"You have heard me mention the counting house of Murdstone and Grinby, in the wine trade," Mr. Murdstone went on. "Mr. Quinion manages that business. He suggests that it gives employment to some other boys and that he sees no reason why it shouldn't give employment to you."

"He having," Mr. Quinion observed in a low voice, "no other prospect, Murdstone." Mr. Murdstone, with an impatient gesture, resumed.

"The terms are that you will earn enough to provide for your eating and drinking and pocket money. Your lodging (which I have arranged for) will be paid by me, as will your washing and clothes. So you are now going to London, David, to begin the world on your own account."

"In short, you are provided for," observed his sister, "and will please to do your duty."

Though I quite understood that the purpose of this announcement was to get rid of me, I have no distinct remembrance whether it pleased or frightened me. Behold me on the morrow, in a much worn little white hat, with a black crape round it for my mother, and with my little worldly all before me in a small trunk, sitting in the post chaise that was carrying Mr. Quinion to the London coach. See, how our house and church are lessening in the distance; how the spire points upward from my old playground no more, and the sky is empty!

6

So I became, at ten years old, a little laboring hind in the service of Murdstone and Grinby. Their warehouse was at the water side, in Blackfriars. Its decaying floors and staircase, the squeaking and scuffling of the old gray rats down in the cellars, and the dirt and rottenness of the place are all before me now just as they were in the evil hour when I went among them for the first time, with my trembling hand in Mr. Quinion's.

There were three or four of us boys who were employed to rinse and wash bottles, paste on labels, fit corks, or pack the finished bottles in casks. My principal associate was a boy called, because of his complexion, Mealy Potatoes; and no words can express the secret agony of my soul as I compared this companionship with that of Steerforth, Traddles, and those of my happier childhood, and felt my hopes of growing up to be a learned and distinguished man crushed in my bosom. But I kept my own counsel, and I did my work. I am solemnly convinced that I never for one hour was reconciled to it; but I bore it and, even to Peggotty, partly for the love of her and partly for shame, never in any letter revealed the truth.

The clock was at half-past twelve my first day and there was general preparation for going to dinner when Mr. Quinion beckoned me to the counting house. There I found a stoutish, middle-aged person, in a brown surtout and black tights and shoes, with no more hair on his head (which was a large one, and very shining) than there is upon an egg, and with a very extensive face, which he turned full upon me. His clothes were shabby, but he had an imposing shirt collar on. He carried a jaunty sort of a stick, with a large pair of rusty tassels to it, and a quizzing glass hung outside his coat—for ornament, I afterward found, as he very seldom looked through it and couldn't see anything when he did.

"This," said Mr. Quinion, in allusion to myself, "is he."

"This," said the stranger, with a certain condescending roll in his voice and a certain indescribable air of doing something genteel, "is Master Copperfield. I have received a letter from Mr. Murdstone in which he mentions that he would desire me to receive into an apartment in my house which is at present unoccupied—and is, in short, to be let as a—in short," said the stranger, in a burst of confidence, "as a bedroom—the young beginner whom I have now the pleasure to—" and the stranger waved his hand and settled his chin in his shirt collar.

"This is Mr. Micawber," said Mr. Quinion to me.

"Under the impression that your peregrinations in this metropolis have not as yet been extensive and that you might have some difficulty in penetrating the arcana of the Modern Babylon—in short," said Mr. Micawber, in another burst of confidence, "that you might lose yourself—I shall be happy to call this evening and install you in the knowledge of the nearest way. At what hour shall I—"

"At about eight," said Mr. Quinion.

"At about eight," said Mr. Micawber. "I beg to wish you good day. I will intrude no longer." So he put on his hat and went out with his cane under his arm, very upright, and humming a tune.

Arrived at his house that night, he presented me to Mrs. Micawber, a thin and faded lady, who was sitting in the parlor (the first floor was altogether unfurnished, and the blinds were kept down to delude the neighbors), with a baby at her breast. This baby was one of twins; and I may remark here that one of them was always taking refreshment. There were two other children, Master Micawber, aged about four, and Miss Micawber, aged about three. These, with a dark young woman named Clickett, who was servant to the family and informed me that she was "a Orfling" and came from St. Luke's workhouse, completed the establishment.

"I never thought," said Mrs. Micawber, "before I was married, when I lived with papa and mamma, that I should ever find it necessary to take a lodger. But Mr. Micawber being in difficulties, all considerations of private feeling must give way." Mr. Micawber, I understood, was a sort of town traveler for a number of miscellaneous houses. "If Mr. Micawber's creditors *will not* give him time," went on Mrs. Micawber, "they must take the consequences. Blood cannot be obtained from a stone, neither can anything on account be obtained at present (not to mention law expenses) from Mr. Micawber."

Whether my precocious self-dependence confused Mrs.

Micawber about my age or whether she would have talked to the very twins if there had been nobody else to communicate with, this was the strain in which she always talked to me, though, like her husband, she was very elastic. I have known her to be thrown into fainting fits by the king's taxes at three o'clock, and to eat lamb chops breaded and drink warm ale (paid for with two teaspoons that I had taken to the pawnbroker's) at four, telling me stories about her papa and mamma.

With this family I passed my leisure time. My breakfast of a penny loaf and a pennyworth of milk I provided myself, as well as another loaf and a modicum of cheese for my supper, which made a hole in the six or seven shillings I was paid a week; and I was so young and childish and so little qualified—how could I be other-wise?—to undertake the whole charge of my own existence that often, in going to Murdstone and Grinby's of a morning, I could not resist the stale pastry put out for sale at half price and spent in that the money I should have kept for my dinner.

I know I do not exaggerate the scantiness of my resources or the difficulties of my life. I know that I worked from morning until night, with common men and boys, a shabby child. I know that I lounged about the streets, insufficiently and unsatisfactorily fed.

I know that, but for the mercy of God, I might easily have been, for any care that was taken of me, a little vagabond.

Mr. Micawber's difficulties were an addition to the distressed state of my mind, though I have known him come home to supper with a flood of tears, and a declaration that nothing was now left but a jail, and go to bed making a calculation of the expense of putting bow windows to the house, "in case anything turned up," which was his favorite expression. But at last his difficulties came to a crisis, and he was arrested early one morning and carried over to the King's Bench Prison in the Borough.

On the first Sunday after he was taken there, I went to see him. He was waiting for me within the gate, and we went up to his room and cried very much. He solemnly conjured me, I remember, to take warning by his fate; after which he borrowed a shilling of me for porter, gave me a written order on Mrs. Micawber for the amount, and cheered up. We sat before a little fire until another debtor came in with a loin of mutton which was our joint-stock repast, when I was sent up to "Captain Hopkins" in the room overhead, with Mr. Micawber's compliments, and would Captain Hopkins lend me a knife and fork. There was something gypsy-like and agreeable in the dinner, and I used often to go back to the prison and walk up and down the parade with Mr. Micawber.

I don't know how the household furniture came to be sold for the family benefit; but when it went Mrs. Micawber moved into the prison, and a little room was hired for me outside the walls. In due time, however, Mrs. Micawber informed me that "her family" had decided that Mr. Micawber should apply for his release under the Insolvent Debtors' Act; and when he was finally discharged, I went to rejoice with Mrs. Micawber while Mr. Micawber celebrated with his fellow prisoners. "On such an occasion I will give you, Master Copperfield," said Mrs. Micawber, "in a little more flip," for we had been having some already, "the memory of my papa and mamma."

"Are they dead, ma'am?" I inquired, after drinking the toast.

"My mamma departed this life," said Mrs. Micawber, "before Mr. Micawber's difficulties commenced, or at least before they became pressing. My papa lived to bail Mr. Micawber several times and then expired, regretted by a numerous circle." She dropped a pious tear upon the twin who happened to be in hand.

"May I ask, ma'am," said I, "what you and Mr. Micawber intend to do now?"

"My family," said Mrs. Micawber, who always said those two words with an air, though I never could discover who came under the denomination, "my family are of opinion that Mr. Micawber should quit London and exert his talents in the country. Mr. Micawber is a man of great talent, Master Copperfield. The influence of my family being local, they wish Mr. Micawber to go down to Plymouth. They think it indispensable that he should be upon the spot."

"That he may be ready?" I suggested.

"Exactly," returned Mrs. Micawber. "In case of anything turning up."

"And do you go too, ma'am?"

The events of the day, in combination with the twins, if not with the flip, had made Mrs. Micawber hysterical, and she shed tears as she replied, "I never will desert Mr. Micawber. Mr. Micawber may have concealed his difficulties from me in the first instance, but his sanguine temper may have led him to expect that he would overcome them. The pearl necklace and bracelets which I inherited from mamma have been disposed of for less than half their value; and the set of coral, which was the gift of papa, has been actually thrown away for nothing. But I never will desert Mr. Micawber. No!" cried Mrs. Micawber, more affected than before, "I never will do it! It's of no use asking me!"

Mrs. Micawber having now raised her voice into a perfect scream, I was so frightened that I ran for Mr. Micawber. "Emma, my angel!" he cried, running into the room; "what is the matter?"

"I never will desert you, Micawber!" she exclaimed.

"My life!" said Mr. Micawber, taking her in his arms. "I am perfectly aware of it."

"He is the parent of my children! He is the husband of my affections," cried Mrs. Micawber, struggling; "and I ne-ver-will-desert Mr. Micawber!"

I had grown so accustomed to the Micawbers and had been so intimate with them in their distresses and was so utterly friendless without them that the prospect of being turned adrift was unendurable.

"My dear young friend," said Mr. Micawber on our last evening together, "I am older than you; a man of some experience in life, and—and, in short, in difficulties. At present, and until something turns up (which I am, I may say, hourly expecting), I have nothing to bestow but advice. Still my advice is so far worth taking that—in short, that I have never taken it myself, and am the—" here Mr. Micawber, who had been beaming and smiling, checked himself and frowned—"the miserable wretch you behold."

"My dear Micawber!" urged his wife.

"I say," returned Mr. Micawber, quite forgetting himself and smiling again, "the miserable wretch you behold. My advice is, never do tomorrow what you can do today. Procrastination is the thief of time. Collar him!"

"My poor papa's maxim," Mrs. Micawber observed.

"My other piece of advice, Copperfield," said Mr. Micawber, "is this: Annual income twenty pounds, annual expenditure nineteen, nineteen six, result happiness. Annual income twenty pounds, annual expenditure twenty pounds, ought and six, result misery. The blossom is blighted, the leaf is withered, the God of day goes down upon the dreary scene, and—and, in short, you are forever floored. As I am!"

To make his example the more impressive, Mr. Micawber drank a glass of punch with an air of great enjoyment and whistled "The College Hornpipe."

Next morning I met the whole family at the coach office and saw them, with a desolate heart, take their places.

"Master Copperfield," said Mrs. Micawber, "God bless you! You have never been a lodger. You have been a friend." I think, as she sat at the back of the coach and I stood in the road looking wistfully up at them, a mist cleared from her eyes, and she saw what a little creature I really was, because she beckoned me to climb up, with quite a new and motherly expression on her face, and gave me just such a kiss as she might have given to her own boy. Then the Orfling, who had been disbanded, said goodbye; and I went back to begin my weary day at Murdstone and Grinby's.

But with no intention of passing many more weary days there. No. I had resolved to run away. To go to Dover, to the only relation I had in the world, and tell my story to my aunt, Miss Betsey. But being a very honest little creature, I considered myself bound to remain at Murdstone and Grinby's until Saturday, as I had been paid a week's wages in advance.

On the Saturday night, then, I bade a last good night to Mealy Potatoes and ran away. As I went toward my lodging, I looked for someone to help me carry my box to the coach office; I had a half guinea for traveling expenses which Peggotty had sent me. There was a long-legged young man with a very little empty donkey cart whose eye I caught. He had a defiant manner about him that I did not much like, but a bargain was made and he rattled off, so fast that I was quite out of breath with running and calling after him to stop while I put the address on my box.

Being much flushed and excited, I tumbled my half guinea out of my pocket in pulling the card out. "Wot!" said the young man, seizing it with a frightful grin. "This is a pollis case, is it? You're a going to bolt, are you? Come to the pollis, you young warmin, come to the pollis!" And, jumping into the cart, he rattled away harder than ever.

I ran after him as fast as I could, but not daring to call out I had to leave him at last to go where he would with my box and money and, panting and crying but never stopping, faced about for Greenwich, though I had but threepence in my pocket; taking very little more out of the world, toward the retreat of my aunt, than I had brought into it on the night when my arrival gave her so much umbrage.

7

I⊤ was by this time dark, a summer night, fortunately, and fine weather. Never shall I forget the lonely sensation of first lying down without a roof over my head. But sleep came upon me as it came on many other outcasts against whom house doors were locked and house dogs barked that night. Next morning I struck into the long dusty track which was the Dover Road.

I got, that Sunday, through three and twenty miles, though not very easily. I see myself, as evening closes in, eating bread that I had bought for supper and once more lying down beneath the sky. Feeling next morning that I could go but a very little way if I were to reserve my strength, and having no money left, I resolved to make the sale of my jacket my principal business. Accordingly, I began a tour of inspection of the various slop shops in Chatham.

At last I found one that I thought looked promising. But I was not relieved when an ugly old man, with a stubbly gray beard and starting eyes, rushed out of a dirty den behind it and seized me by the hair of my head. "Oh, what do you want?" he grinned in a fierce, monotonous whine that began low, like the wind, and mounted high and fell again. "Oh, my eyes and limbs, what do you want? Oh, my lungs and liver, what do you want? Oh, goroo, goroo!"

"I wanted to know," I said, trembling, "if you would buy a jacket."

"Oh, how much for the jacket?" cried the old man, after examining it. "Oh—goroo—how much for the jacket?"

"Half a crown," I answered, recovering myself.

"Oh, my lungs and liver," cried the old man, "no! Oh, my eyes, no! Oh, my limbs, no! Eighteenpence. Goroo!"

"Well," said I, glad to have closed the bargain, "I'll take eighteenpence."

"Oh, my liver!" cried the old man, throwing the jacket on a shelf. "Get out of my shop! Oh, my eyes and limbs—goroo—don't ask for money; make it an exchange."

I never was so frightened in my life, before or since; but I told him humbly that I wanted money, that nothing else would do, but that I would wait for it, as he desired, outside. So I went outside and sat down in the shade. And I sat there so many hours that the shade became sunlight and the sunlight became shade again, and still I sat there waiting for the money.

He made many attempts to induce me to consent to an exchange, at one time coming out with a fishing rod, at another with a fiddle, at another with a cocked hat. But I resisted all these overtures and sat there in desperation, each time asking him for my money or my jacket. At last he began to pay me in halfpence at a time and was full two hours getting by easy stages to a shilling.

"Oh, my eyes and limbs!" he then cried, peeping hideously out of the shop, after a long pause, "will you go for twopence more?"

"I can't," I said; "I shall be starved."

"Oh, my lungs and liver, will you go for threepence? Oh, go-

roo!" (it is really impossible to express how he twisted this ejacula-
tion out of himself) "will you go for fourpence?"

I was so faint and weary that I closed with this offer; and at
an expense of threepence I soon refreshed myself completely, so
that I limped seven miles upon my road, sleeping then under a
haystack.

It was not until the sixth day of my flight that I set foot in
Dover. My money was all gone; I had nothing left to dispose of;
I was hungry, thirsty, and worn out; worst of all, because my first
inquiries for my aunt proved futile, I seemed as distant from my
end as if I had remained in London. At length a fly driver knew
Miss Trotwood's name.

"Old lady?" said he. "Pretty stiff in the back? Comes down
upon you sharp?"

My heart sank as I acknowledged the undoubted accuracy of
this description.

"Why, then," said he, "if you go up there," pointing toward the
heights, "and keep on till you come to some houses facing the sea,
I think you'll hear of her."

I was directed at last to a very neat little cottage with cheerful
bow windows, where a muslin curtain partly undrawn in the
middle, a large round green screen or fan fastened onto the window
sill, a small table, and a great chair suggested that my aunt might
be seated there in awful state.

My shoes were by this time in a woeful condition. My shirt
and trousers, stained with heat, dew, grass, and Kentish soil—and
torn besides—might have frightened the birds from my aunt's
garden. My hair had known no comb or brush since I left London.
From head to foot I was powdered almost as white with chalk and
dust as if I had come out of a lime kiln. In this plight I waited to
make my first impression on my formidable aunt.

The unbroken stillness of the parlor window leading me to
infer that she was not there, I lifted my eyes to the window above
it, where I saw a florid, pleasant-looking gentleman with a gray
head, who shut one of his prominent bright eyes in a grotesque
manner, nodded his head at me several times, shook it as often,
laughed, and went away.

I was so discomposed by this unexpected behavior that I was
on the point of slinking off when there came out of the house a

tall lady with a handkerchief tied over her cap and a dress rather scantily made, as if she desired to be as little encumbered as possible, carrying a great knife. I knew her immediately to be Miss Betsey, for she came stalking out of the house exactly as my poor mother had so often described her stalking up our garden.

"Go away!" said Miss Betsey, making a distant chop in the air with her knife. "Go along! No boys here!"

I watched her stoop to dig up some little root. Then, without a scrap of courage, but with a great deal of desperation, I went softly in and touched her.

"If you please, ma'am," I began. "If you please, aunt."

"*Eh?*" exclaimed Miss Betsey, in a tone of amazement. She sat down flat in the garden path.

"If you please, aunt, I am David Copperfield, of Blunderstone, in Suffolk—where you came, on the night when I was born, and saw my dear mamma. I have been very unhappy since she died. I have been slighted and taught nothing and put to work not fit for me. It made me run away to you. I was robbed at first setting out and have walked all the way and have not slept in a bed." Here my self-support gave way all at once; and, with a movement of my hands intended to show my ragged state, I broke into a passion of crying, which had been pent up within me all week.

My aunt got up in a great hurry, collared me, and took me into the parlor, where her first proceeding was to unlock a tall press, bring out several bottles, and pour some of the contents of each into my mouth. I think they must have been taken out at random, for I am sure I tasted aniseed water, anchovy sauce, and salad dressing. After a time she rang the bell. "Janet," she said to the servant. "Go upstairs, give my compliments to Mr. Dick, and say I wish to speak to him." Then she walked up and down the room, until the gentleman who had squinted at me from the upper window came in laughing.

"Mr. Dick," said my aunt, "don't be a fool, because nobody can be more discreet than you can, when you choose. You have heard me mention David Copperfield. Now don't pretend not to have a memory, because you and I know better."

"David Copperfield?" said Mr. Dick, who did not appear to me to remember much about it. "*David* Copperfield? Oh, yes, to be sure. David, certainly."

"Well," said my aunt, "this is his boy, his son. And he has done a pretty piece of business. He has run away. Ah! His sister Betsey Trotwood never would have run away." My aunt shook her head firmly. "The question I put to you," she went on, "is, What shall I do with him?"

"Oh, do with him?" said Mr. Dick feebly, scratching his head. "Why, if I was you I should—" The contemplation of me seemed to inspire him, and he added, briskly, "I should wash him!"

"Janet," said my aunt, turning round with a quiet triumph, which I did not then understand, "Mr. Dick sets us all right. Heat the bath!"

Janet, I may mention here, was one of a series of protégées whom my aunt had taken into her service expressly to educate in a renouncement of mankind and who had generally completed their abjuration by marrying the baker. Janet had gone away to get the bath ready, when my aunt, to my great alarm, became in a moment rigid with indignation, and cried out, "Janet! Donkeys!"

Upon which, Janet came running up the stairs as if the house were in flames, darted out on a little piece of green in front, and warned off two saddle donkeys, lady-ridden, that had presumed to set hoof upon it, while my aunt, rushing out of the house, seized the bridle of a third animal laden with a bestriding child, turned him, led him forth from those sacred precincts, and boxed the ears of the unlucky urchin in attendance.

To this hour I don't know whether my aunt had any lawful right of way over that patch of green; but she had settled it in her own mind that she had, and it was all the same to her. The one great outrage of her life, demanding to be constantly avenged, was the passage of a donkey over that immaculate spot. Jugs of water were kept in secret places ready to be discharged; sticks were laid in ambush; sallies were made at all hours; and incessant war prevailed.

After I had been bathed, dressed in some clothes belonging to Mr. Dick, and fed a roast fowl and a pudding, I began to be deeply anxious to know what my aunt was going to do with me; but invasions of donkeys kept interrupting my story, which she elicited from me by a series of questions. At dusk, however, she said to Mr. Dick, "What would you do with this child?"

"Do with David's son?" said Mr. Dick. "Yes. Do with—I should put him to bed."

"Janet!" cried my aunt, with the same complacent triumph I had remarked before. "Mr. Dick sets us all right. If the bed is ready, we'll take him up to it."

The room was a pleasant one, overlooking the sea, on which the moon was shining brilliantly. I remember the sensation of gratitude and rest which the sight of the white-curtained bed inspired. I remember how I thought of all the solitary places under the sky where I had slept, and how I prayed that I might never be houseless any more, and never might forget the houseless.

On going down in the morning I was more than ever anxious to know my aunt's intentions toward me, and I felt sure that I had been the subject of her reflections. After looking at me for a long time she said, "I have written to your stepfather. I have sent him a letter that I'll trouble him to attend to."

"Shall I—be—given up to him?" I faltered.

"I don't know," said my aunt. "We shall see."

My spirits sank under these words, but presently my aunt said, "I wish you'd give my compliments to Mr. Dick, and I'll be glad to know how he gets on with his Memorial."

He seemed to be getting on very well indeed, driving at it with a long pen, his head almost laid upon the paper. "Ha!" he said, when he observed me. "I shouldn't wish it to be mentioned, but it's a"—here he beckoned to me and put his lips close to my ear—"it's a mad world. Mad as Bedlam, boy!" and Mr. Dick laughed heartily. Without presuming to give my opinion on this question, I delivered my message.

"Well," said Mr. Dick, "my compliments to her, and I—I believe I have made a start. Do you recollect the date," looking earnestly at me and taking up his pen to note it down, "when King Charles the First had his head cut off?"

I said I believed it happened in the year 1649.

"Well," returned Mr. Dick, scratching his ear with his pen and looking dubiously at me. "So the books say; but I don't see how that can be. Because, if it was so long ago, how could the people about him have made the mistake of putting some of the trouble out of *his* head, after it was taken off, into *mine?*"

I was very much surprised by the inquiry but could give no

information on this point and was going away when he directed my attention to a large paper kite which was covered with manuscript, very closely and laboriously written, but so plainly that as I looked along the lines I thought I saw some allusion to King Charles the First's head again, in one or two places.

"There's plenty of string," said Mr. Dick; "and when it flies high, it takes the facts a long way. That's my manner of diffusing 'em."

"Well, child," said my aunt, when I went downstairs, "what do you think of Mr. Dick?"

I had some shadowy idea of endeavoring to evade the question, but my aunt was not to be put off. "Come!" she said. "Your sister Betsey Trotwood would have told me directly. Be as like your sister as you can, and speak out!"

"Is he—I ask because I don't know, aunt—is Mr. Dick at all out of his mind, then?" I stammered.

"Not a morsel," said my aunt. "I have a selfish pleasure in saying he has been *called* mad, or I should not have had the benefit of his society and advice for these last ten years—ever since your sister Betsey Trotwood disappointed me. And nice people they were, who had the audacity to call him mad. Mr. Dick is a sort of distant connection of mine. If it hadn't been for me, his own brother would have shut him up for life. That's all.

"He had a favorite sister," went on my aunt, "but she did what they all do—took a husband. And *he* did what they all do—made her wretched. It had such an effect upon the mind of Mr. Dick that, combined with his fear of his brother, it threw him into a fever. Did he say anything to you about King Charles the First, child?"

"Yes, aunt."

"Ah!" said my aunt, rubbing her nose as if she were a little vexed. "That's his allegorical way of expressing the disturbance and agitation of his illness. It's not a business-like way of speaking. I am aware of that; and that's why I insist that there shan't be a word about it in his Memorial."

"Is it a Memorial about his own history that he is writing, aunt?"

"Yes, child," said my aunt. "He is memorializing the Lord Chancellor, or the Lord Somebody or other, about his affairs;

it keeps him employed." I found out afterward that Mr. Dick had been for upwards of ten years endeavoring to keep King Charles the First out of the Memorial; but he had been constantly getting into it and was there now.

The anxiety I underwent before and after Mr. Murdstone wrote that he was coming to see my aunt was extreme. Then, on the day he was to arrive, my aunt gave a sudden alarm of donkeys, and to my consternation I beheld Miss Murdstone ride deliberately over the sacred green. "Go along with you!" cried my aunt, shaking her fist at the window. "You have no business there. Oh! you bold-faced thing!

"I don't care who it is!" she went on, when I informed her. "I won't be trespassed upon. Go away! Janet, lead him off!" and I saw a sort of hurried battlepiece, in which the donkey stood resisting everybody, while Janet tried to pull him round, Mr. Murdstone tried to lead him on, Miss Murdstone struck with a parasol, and several boys, who had come to see the engagement, shouted vigorously, pursued by my aunt. She took no notice of the Murdstones until, the contest over, they were announced by Janet. "Oh!" she said then, "I was not aware at first to whom I had the pleasure of objecting. But I don't allow anybody to ride over that turf. I make no exceptions. I don't allow anybody to do it."

"Your regulation is rather awkward to strangers," said Miss Murdstone.

"Is it?" said my aunt. "Janet, my compliments to Mr. Dick, and beg him to come down." When he had been introduced, she inclined her head to Mr. Murdstone, who began.

"Miss Trotwood. This unhappy boy who has run away from his friends and his occupation has been the occasion of much domestic trouble and uneasiness. He has a sullen, rebellious spirit, a violent temper, and an untoward, intractable disposition. Both my sister and I have endeavored to correct his vices, but ineffectually."

"I beg to observe," said Miss Murdstone, "that, of all the boys in the world, I believe this is the worst boy."

"Strong!" said my aunt, shortly.

"I have my own opinion," resumed Mr. Murdstone, whose face darkened more and more, the more he and my aunt observed each other, which they did very narrowly, "as to the best mode of bringing him up. I am here to take him back unconditionally, to dispose of him as I think proper, and to deal with him as I think right. Is he ready to go? If he is not—my doors are shut against him henceforth, and yours, I take it for granted, are open to him."

"And what does the boy say?" said my aunt. "Are you ready to go, David?"

I answered no and entreated her not to let me go. I said that neither Mr. nor Miss Murdstone had ever liked me or had ever been kind to me. That they had made my mamma unhappy about me. I said that I had been more miserable than anybody could believe; and I begged my aunt to befriend me, for my father's sake.

"Mr. Dick," said my aunt, "what shall I do with this child?"

Mr. Dick considered, hesitated, brightened, and rejoined, "Have him measured for a suit of clothes directly."

"Mr. Dick," said my aunt triumphantly, "your common sense is invaluable." Having pulled me toward her, she said to Mr. Murdstone, "I'll take my chance with the boy. If he's all you say he is, at least I can do as much for him as you. But I don't believe a word of it."

"Miss Trotwood," said Mr. Murdstone, "if you were a gentleman—"

"Bah! Stuff and nonsense!" said my aunt. "Don't talk to me!"

"How exquisitely polite!" exclaimed Miss Murdstone. "Overpowering, really!"

"Do you think I don't know," said my aunt, turning a deaf ear to the sister, "what kind of life you must have led that poor, misdirected baby, his mother? You were a tyrant, and you broke her heart, which is a disagreeable remembrance and makes the sight of the boy through whom you tormented her odious now. Ay, ay! you needn't wince! Good day, sir, and good-by! Good day to you, too, ma'am," she said, turning suddenly upon his sister. "Let me see you ride a donkey over *my* green again and, as sure as you have a head upon your shoulders, I'll knock your bonnet off and tread upon it!"

No attempt at defiance being made by the Murdstones, her face gradually relaxed and became so pleasant that I was emboldened to kiss and thank her. "Well, *that's* settled," said my aunt. "I have been thinking, Mr. Dick, that I might call him Trotwood." Thus I began my new life in a new name, and with everything new about me.

8

Mr. Dick and I soon became the best of friends, nor did I go backward in the favor of his staunch friend, my aunt. In the course of a few weeks she shortened my adopted name of Trotwood into Trot, and even encouraged me to hope that I might take equal rank in her affections with my sister Betsey Trotwood.

Shortly thereafter she drove me to Canterbury to look up a school, stopping first at a very old house bulging out over the road, where I saw a cadaverous face appear at a small window on the ground floor (in a little round tower that formed one side of the house) and quickly disappear. The low arched door then opened, and the face came out. It belonged to a red-haired person—a youth of fifteen, as I take it now, but looking much older—whose hair was cropped as close as the closest stubble, who had hardly any eyebrows and no eyelashes and eyes of a red brown, so unsheltered that I remember wondering how he went to sleep. He was high shouldered and bony, dressed in decent black, with a white wisp of a neckcloth buttoned up to the throat, and had a long, lank, skeleton hand with which he rubbed his chin.

"Is Mr. Wickfield at home, Uriah Heep?" said my aunt.

"Mr. Wickfield's at home, ma'am," said Uriah Heep, "if you'll please to walk in."

Mr. Wickfield I found to be a lawyer, steward of the estates of a rich gentleman of the county, and also my aunt's adviser. He had an agreeable face, though there was a certain richness in his complexion which I had been accustomed, under Peggotty's tuition, to connect with port wine; and I fancied it was in his voice, too, and referred his growing corpulency to the same cause. My aunt had come to consult him about a school for me. But she soon found that at the best one I couldn't board, and the boarding houses Mr. Wickfield showed her proved unsuitable.

"I'll tell you what you can do, Miss Trotwood," Mr. Wickfield said at length. "Leave your nephew here, for the present. He's a quiet fellow. He won't disturb me at all. The house is roomy. Leave him here."

My aunt evidently liked the offer, though she was delicate of accepting it. So did I. "Then come and see my little housekeeper," said Mr. Wickfield.

We accordingly went up a wonderful old staircase, with a balustrade so broad that we might have gone up that, almost, and into a shady old drawing room, lighted by some three or four quaint diamond-paned windows, which had old oak seats in them that seemed to have come of the same trees as the shining oak floor and the great beams in the ceiling.

Mr. Wickfield tapped at a door in a corner of the paneled wall, and a girl of about my own age came quickly out and kissed him. Although her face was quite bright and happy, there was a tranquillity about it and about her—a quiet, good, calm spirit—that I have never forgotten; that I never shall forget.

This was his little housekeeper, his daughter Agnes, Mr. Wickfield said. When I heard how he said it and saw how he held her hand, I knew what he meant when he told my aunt that he had but one motive in life.

"Trot," said my aunt, as she bade me good-by, "be a credit to yourself, to me, and Mr. Dick, and Heaven be with you! Never," said my aunt, "be mean in anything; never be false; never be cruel. Avoid those three vices, Trot, and I can always be hopeful of you."

I was greatly overcome but promised as well as I could that I would not abuse her kindness. Then, after she had gone, I sat for a while opposite the desk where Uriah Heep was working. It had a brass frame on the top to hang paper upon, and I thought, the writing he was making a copy of being between us, that he could not see me; but it made me uncomfortable to observe that, every now and then, his sleepless eyes would come below the writing, like two red suns, and stealthily stare at me for a whole minute at a time, during which his pen went, or pretended to go, as cleverly as ever. Whenever I looked toward those two red suns, I was sure to find them either just rising or just setting.

Feeling friendly toward everybody, however, after I had mustered up my spirits again, I went in and spoke to him and, at parting, gave him my hand. But oh, what a clammy hand his was! as ghostly to the touch as to the sight! I rubbed mine afterward, to warm it *and to rub his off.*

Next morning I entered on school life again and was introduced to my new master, Dr. Strong, who, in turn, introduced me to the boys. One Adams, who was the head boy, then presented me to the masters, in a gentlemanly way that would have put me at my ease if anything could.

It seemed to me so long, however, since I had been among such boys; I was so conscious of having passed through scenes of which they could have no knowledge and of having acquired experiences foreign to my age, appearance, and condition as one of them, that I half believed it was an imposture to come there as an ordinary little schoolboy. My mind ran upon what they would think if they knew of my familiar acquaintance with the King's Bench Prison? Suppose some of them had seen me coming through Canterbury, wayworn and ragged, and should find me out?

But there was such an influence in Mr. Wickfield's old house that when I knocked at it after school I began to feel my uneasiness softening away. When we had dined, Agnes set glasses and decanters in a corner of the drawing room and played the piano to us while Mr. Wickfield sat down to drink, and drank a good deal.

In good time she made tea; and afterward, when I brought down my books, showed me what she knew of them (which was no slight matter, though she said it was) and what was the best way to learn and understand them. I see her, with her modest, orderly, placid manner, and I hear her beautiful calm voice, as I write these words. The influence for all good, which she came to exercise over me at a later time, begins already. I love little Em'ly, and I don't love Agnes—not in that way—but I feel that there are goodness, peace, and truth wherever Agnes is.

When she had gone to bed, I went downstairs; and, seeing a light in the little round office and feeling myself attracted toward Uriah Heep, who had a sort of fascination for me, I went in. I found Uriah reading a great fat book, with such demonstrative attention that his lank forefinger followed up every line as he read and made clammy tracks along the page (or so I believed) like a snail.

"You are working late tonight, Uriah," says I.

"Yes, Master Copperfield," says Uriah. "But not office work. I am improving my legal knowledge, Master Copperfield. I am going through Tidd's Practice. Oh, what a writer Mr. Tidd is, Master Copperfield!"

"I suppose you are quite a great lawyer?" I said.

"Me, Master Copperfield?" said Uriah. "Oh, no! I'm a very umble person."

It was no fancy of mine about his hands, I observed; for he frequently ground the palms against each other as if to squeeze them dry and warm, besides often wiping them, in a stealthy way, on his pocket handkerchief.

"I am well aware that I am the umblest person going," said Uriah Heep, modestly, "let other be where he may. My mother is likewise a very umble person. We live in a numble abode, Master Copperfield, but have much to be thankful for. How much have I to be thankful for, in Mr. Wickfield's kind intention to give me my articles, which would otherwise not lay within the umble means of mother and self!"

"Perhaps you'll be a partner in Mr. Wickfield's business, one of these days," I said, to make myself agreeable; "and it will be Wickfield and Heep."

"Oh, no, Master Copperfield," returned Uriah, "I am much

too umble for that!—Mr. Wickfield is a most excellent man, Master Copperfield," he went on. "And I am sure you must have a great admiration for Miss Agnes."

"Everybody must have," I returned.

"Oh, thank you, Master Copperfield," said Uriah Heep, "for that remark! It is so true! Umble as I am, I know it is *so* true! Oh, thank you, Master Copperfield!" He writhed himself quite off his stool in his enthusiasm, before remarking, "I should think *you* would come into the business at last, Master Copperfield!"

I protested that I had no views of that sort and that no such scheme was entertained in my behalf by anybody; but Uriah insisted on blandly replying to all my assurances, "Oh, yes, Master Copperfield, I should think you would, indeed!" and "Oh, indeed, Master Copperfield, I should think you would, certainly!" over and over again.

I got a little the better of my uneasiness when I went to school next day, and so shook it off by degrees that in less than a fortnight I was quite at home, and happy, among my new companions. Through them I learned that Dr. Strong had married his beautiful young wife for love; for she had not a sixpence and had a world of poor relations (so our fellows said) ready to swarm the Doctor out of house and home.

Her mamma was a lady I took great delight in. Her name was Mrs. Markleham; but our boys used to call her the Old Soldier, on account of her generalship and the skill with which she marshalled great forces of relations against the Doctor. She was a little, sharp-eyed woman, who used to wear one unchangeable cap, ornamented with some artificial flowers and two artificial butterflies supposed to be hovering above them, which improved the shining hours at Dr. Strong's expense like busy bees. Each time she had carried her point she would kiss the sticks of her fan and then tap the Doctor's hand with it.

I also learned from the boys that the Doctor's cogitating manner was attributable to his being always engaged in looking out for Greek roots, which, in my ignorance, I supposed to be a botanical furor on the Doctor's part, especially as he always looked at the ground when he walked about, until I understood that they were roots of words, with a view to a new dictionary which he had in contemplation. Adams, our head boy, who had a turn for mathematics, had made a calculation of the time this dictionary would take in completing, at the Doctor's rate of going. He considered that it might be done in one thousand six hundred and forty-nine years, counting from the Doctor's last, or sixty-second, birthday.

But the Doctor himself was the idol of the whole school; and it must have been a badly composed school if he had been anything else, for he was the kindest of men. If any sort of vagabond could only get near enough to his creaking shoes to attract his attention as he walked up and down, that vagabond was made for the next two days. It was so notorious in the school that we took pains to cut these marauders off at angles and to turn them out of the courtyard before they could make the Doctor aware of their presence. His was an excellent school, as different from Mr. Creakle's as good is from evil. It was very gravely and decorously ordered, and on a sound system, with an appeal to the honor and good faith of the boys which worked wonders.

Every alternate Wednesday while I was in school Mr. Dick arrived by stage coach from Dover to pay me a visit; and those were the happiest days of Mr. Dick's life, as they were far from being the least happy of mine. He soon became known to every boy in the school and, though he never took an active part in any game but kite flying, was as deeply interested in all our sports as any one among us. After a few Wednesdays, Dr. Strong himself made some inquiries of me about him, and I told him all my aunt had told me, which interested the Doctor so much that he requested to be presented to him.

The veneration which Mr. Dick felt for the learning he had never been able to acquire he extended to the Doctor, whom he thought the most accomplished philosopher of any age. It was long before Mr. Dick ever spoke to him otherwise than bare headed; and even when he and the Doctor had struck up a friendship and would walk together by the hour, Mr. Dick would pull off his hat at intervals to show his respect for wisdom and knowledge. As I think of them going up and down before those schoolroom windows—the Doctor reading out scraps of the famous dictionary, Mr. Dick listening, enchained by interest—I think of it as one of the pleasantest things, in a quiet way, that I have ever seen. I feel as if the world might somehow be the better for it.

As if a thousand things it makes a noise about, were not one-half so good for it, or me.

One day when I met Uriah in the street, he asked me to come to his mother's for tea, if their umbleness didn't prevent me. I really had not yet been able to make up my mind whether I liked Uriah or detested him, but I felt it quite an affront to be supposed proud, and accepted. "Have you been studying much law lately?" I asked as we started off.

"Oh, Master Copperfield," he said, with an air of self-denial, "my reading is hardly to be called study. There are expressions, you see, Master Copperfield—Latin words and terms—in Mr. Tidd that are trying to a reader of my umble attainments."

"Would you like to be taught Latin?" I asked, briskly. "I will teach you with pleasure, as I learn it."

"Oh, thank you, Master Copperfield," he answered, shaking his head. "I am sure it's very kind of you to make the offer, but I am much too umble to accept it. Learning ain't for me. A person like myself had better not aspire. If he is to get on in life, he must get on umbly, Master Copperfield!"

I never saw his mouth so wide or the creases in his cheeks so deep as, writhing modestly, he led me into a low room, walked straight into from the street, where we found Mrs. Heep, who was the dead image of Uriah, only short. She received me with the utmost humility and apologized for giving her son a kiss, observing that, lowly as they were, they had their natural affections, which they hoped would give no offense to anyone. "My Uriah," said Mrs. Heep, "has looked forward to this visit, sir, a long while. He had his fears that our umbleness might stand in the way, and I joined him in them myself. Umble we are, umble we have been, umble we shall ever be," said Mrs. Heep.

I found that Mrs. Heep gradually got nearer to me and that Uriah gradually got opposite to me and that they respectfully plied me with the choicest eatables on the table, which I thought very agreeable. Presently they began to talk about aunts, and then I told them about mine, and about fathers and mothers, and then I told them about mine; and then Mrs. Heep began to talk about stepfathers, and I began to tell her about mine, but stopped, because my aunt had advised me to observe a silence on that subject. A tender young cork, however, would have had no more chance against a pair of corkscrews or a tender young tooth against a pair of dentists than I had against Uriah and Mrs. Heep. They did just what they liked with me and wormed things out of me, especially about Mr. Wickfield and Agnes, that I had no desire to tell, with a certainty I blush to think of; the more especially as, in my juvenile frankness, I took some credit to myself for being so confidential and felt that I was quite the patron of my two respectful entertainers.

I had begun, however, to be a little uncomfortable and to wish myself well out of the visit when a figure coming down the street passed the door, which was open, came back again, looked in, and exclaimed loudly, "Copperfield! Is it possible?"

It was Mr. Micawber! "My dear Copperfield," said he, "this is indeed a meeting which is calculated to impress the mind with a sense of the instability of all human—in short, it is a most extraordinary meeting. Walking along the street, reflecting upon the probability of something turning up (of which I am at present rather sanguine), I find a young but valued friend turn up. Copperfield, how do you do?"

I cannot say—I really *cannot* say—that I was glad to see Mr. Micawber there. But I was glad to see him and presented him to Uriah and Mrs. Heep. As they abased themselves before him, Mr. Micawber took a seat and waved his hand in his most courtly manner. "Any friend of Copperfield's," said he, "has a personal claim upon myself. And what are you doing, Copperfield? Still in the wine trade?"

I was excessively anxious to get Mr. Micawber away; on the Murdstone and Grinby life, at least, I had been dumb. I suggested, with a very red face, that we go and see Mrs. Micawber, who was waiting at their inn. "If you will do her that favor, Copperfield," replied Mr. Micawber, rising. "Mr. Heep! Good evening. Mrs. Heep! Your servant," and he walked out with me in his most fashionable manner, humming a tune.

"I thought you were at Plymouth, ma'am," I said to Mrs. Micawber when we met.

"I will not disguise from you, my dear Master Copperfield," said Mrs. Micawber, "that from the Plymouth branch of my family —this is between ourselves—our reception was cool. Since then,

I have consulted other branches of my family on the course which it is most expedient for Mr. Micawber to take—for I maintain that he must take some course, Master Copperfield," said Mrs. Micawber argumentatively. "It is clear that a family of six, not including a domestic, cannot live upon air."

"Certainly, ma'am," said I.

"Mr. Micawber was induced to think," pursued Mrs. Micawber, "that there might be an opening for a man of his talent in the Medway coal trade. We came and saw the Medway. I say 'we,' Master Copperfield; for I never will," said Mrs. Micawber with emotion, "I never will desert Mr. Micawber. My opinion of the coal trade on that river is that it may requite talent, but that it certainly requires capital. Talent, Mr. Micawber has; capital, Mr. Micawber has not. We saw, I think, the greater part of the Medway; and that is my individual conclusion. Being so near here, Mr. Micawber was of opinion that it would be rash not to come on and see the Cathedral. And at present we are waiting for a remittance from London, to discharge our pecuniary obligations at this hotel."

As I was looking out of window later that evening, it surprised me, and made me rather uneasy, to see Mr. Micawber and Uriah Heep walk past, arm in arm, Uriah humbly sensible of the honor that was done him and Mr. Micawber taking a bland delight in extending patronage. But when I went next day to dine with the Micawbers, I was too afraid of hurting their feeling to say that I hoped he had not been too communicative to Uriah.

We had a beautiful little dinner—quite an elegant dish of fish, the kidney end of a loin of veal roasted, fried sausage meat, a partridge, and a pudding. There was wine, and there was strong ale; and after dinner Mrs. Micawber made us a bowl of punch. As it disappeared, Mr. Micawber became more and more friendly and convivial. Mrs. Micawber's spirits becoming elevated too, we sang "Auld Lang Syne." In a word, I never saw anybody so thoroughly jovial as Mr. Micawber was, down to the very last moment of the evening. Consequently I was not prepared, at seven o'clock next morning, to receive the following communication, dated half an hour after I had left him:

"My dear young friend,

"The die is cast—all is over. Hiding the ravages of care with a sickly mask of mirth, I have not informed you that there is no hope of the remittance. Under these circumstances, alike humiliating to endure, humiliating to contemplate, and humiliating to relate, I have discharged the pecuniary liability contracted at this establishment by giving a note of hand, made payable fourteen days after date. When it becomes due, it will not be taken up. The result is destruction. The bolt is impending, and the tree must fall.

"Let the wretched man who now addresses you, my dear Copperfield, be a beacon to you through life. He writes with that intention. If he could think himself of so much use, one gleam of day might penetrate into the cheerless dungeon of his remaining existence—though his longevity is, at present (to say the least of it), extremely problematical.

"This is the last communication, my dear Copperfield, you will ever receive
   "From
     "The
       "Beggared Outcast,
       "Wilkins Micawber."

I was so shocked by the contents of this heart-rending letter that I ran off directly toward the hotel with the intention of trying to soothe Mr. Micawber with a word of comfort. But halfway there I met the London coach with Mr. and Mrs. Micawber up behind, Mr. Micawber, the very picture of tranquil enjoyment, eating walnuts out of a paper bag. As they did not see me, I thought it best, all things considered, not to see them. So, with a great weight taken off my mind, I turned back to school.

My school days! The silent gliding on of my existence—the unseen, unfelt progress of my life—from childhood up to youth! Time has stolen on unobserved, for *I* am the head boy, now! I wear a gold watch and chain, a ring upon my little finger, and a long-tailed coat; and I use a great deal of bear's grease—which, taken in conjunction with the ring, looks bad. Am I in love? I am. I worship the eldest Miss Larkins.

The eldest Miss Larkins is not a little girl. She is a tall, dark, fine figure of a woman. Perhaps the eldest Miss Larkins may be about thirty. I think continually about my age. Say I am seventeen, and say that seventeen is young for the eldest Miss Larkins, what of that? When the eldest Miss Larkins marries another, I am terribly dejected for a week or two. Agnes teased me a little, I remember, when I was taking leave of her as my school days ended. "But I shall confide in you, just the same, Agnes," I said to her, "even when I come to fall in love in earnest."

"Why, you have always been in earnest!" said Agnes, laughing.

"My wonder is that you are not in earnest yourself, Agnes," said I. "Oh, I know you are not!" for I saw a faint blush on her face. "There is no one I know of who deserves to love *you*." We had gone on in a mixture of confidential jest and earnest that had grown out of our familiar relations. But Agnes now lifted up her eyes to mine and, speaking in a different manner, said, "Trotwood, there is something I want to ask you that I would ask of no one else. Have you observed any gradual alteration in Papa?"

I had observed it and had often wondered whether she had, too. I must have shown it. "Tell me what it is," she said in a low voice.

"I think—shall I be quite plain? I think he does himself no good by the habit that has increased upon him since I first came here. He is often very nervous, or I fancy so."

"It is not fancy," said Agnes, shaking her head.

"His hand trembles, his speech is not plain, and his eyes look wild. I have remarked that at those times, and when he is least like himself, he is most certain to be wanted on some business."

"By Uriah," said Agnes.

9

I AM doubtful whether I was at heart glad or sorry when my school days drew to an end. I had been very happy at Dr. Strong's, but misty ideas of being a young man at my own disposal and of the wonderful things to be done by that magnificent animal lured me away. My aunt and I held many grave deliberations on the calling to which I should be devoted. But I had no particular liking, that I could discover, for anything.

"Trot, it has occurred to me," said my aunt one morning when I had left school, "that a little change may be useful in helping you to know your own mind. Suppose you go down into the old part of the country again and see that—that out-of-the-way woman with the savagest of names," said my aunt, rubbing her nose, for she could never thoroughly forgive Peggotty for being so called.

"What I want you to be, Trot," she continued, "is a firm fellow. A fine firm fellow, with a will of your own. With resolution," said my aunt, shaking her cap at me and clenching her hand. "That you may begin, in a small way, to act for yourself, I shall send you upon your trip, alone. I did think, once, of Mr. Dick's going with you; but, on second thought, I shall keep him to take care of me."

Mr. Dick, for a moment, looked a little disappointed; until the honor of having to take care of the most wonderful woman in the world, as he always called my aunt, restored the sunshine to his face.

So it was that I was fitted out with a handsome purse of money, and a portmanteau, and tenderly dismissed upon my expedition. At parting, my aunt said that, as her object was that I should look about me, she would recommend me to stay a few days in London. In a word, I was at liberty to do what I would.

The main object on my mind, once I got fairly on the road, was to appear as old as possible to the coachman and to speak extremely gruff. The latter point I achieved at great personal inconvenience; but I stuck to it, because I felt it a grown-up sort of thing.

"You are going through, sir?" said the coachman.

"Yes, William," I said, condescendingly (I knew him); "I am going to London. I shall go down into Suffolk afterwards."

"Is Suffolk your county, sir?" asked William. "I'm told the dumplings is uncommon fine down there."

I was not aware of it myself, but I felt it necessary to uphold the institutions of my county, so I shook my head, as much as to say, "I believe you!"

"And the Punches," said William. "There's cattle! A Suffolk Punch, when he's a good 'un, is worth his weight in gold. Did you ever breed any Suffolk Punches yourself, sir?"

"N-no," I said, "not exactly."

"Here's a gen'l'm'n behind me, I'll pound it," said William, "as has bred 'em by wholesale."

The gentleman spoken of was a gentleman with a very unpromising squint and a prominent chin, which was cocked over the coachman's shoulder. "I should think so," said the gentleman. "There ain't no sort of 'orse that I ain't bred, and no sort of dorg. 'Orses and dorgs is some men's fancy. They're wittles and drink to me—lodging, wife, and children—reading, writing, and 'rithmetic."

"That ain't a sort of man to see sitting behind a coachbox, is it, though?" said William in my ear, as he handled the reins. I construed this remark into an indication that he should have my place; so I blushingly offered to resign it.

"Well, if you don't mind, sir," said William, "I think it *would* be correct."

I have always considered this as the first fall I had in life. When I booked my place at the coach office, I had had "Box Seat" written against the entry and had given the book-keeper half a crown. I was got up in a special greatcoat and shawl, expressly to do honor to that distinguished eminence, and had felt that I was a credit to the coach. And here, in the very first stage, I was supplanted by a shabby man with a squint, who had no other merit than smelling like a livery stable!

A distrust of myself, which has often beset me in life on small occasions, was assuredly not stopped in its growth by this little incident outside the Canterbury coach. It was in vain to take refuge in gruffness of speech. I spoke from the pit of my stomach for the rest of the journey, but I felt completely extinguished and dreadfully young.

I was in the coffee room of the Golden Cross at Charing Cross that night when a handsome well-formed young man, dressed with a tasteful easy negligence which I have reason to remember very well, caught my eye; and I turned to look at him again. With a fast-beating heart I said, "Steerforth! won't you speak to me?"

He looked at me—just as he used to look, sometimes—but I saw no recognition in his face. "You don't remember me, I'm afraid," said I.

"My God!" he suddenly exclaimed. "It's little Copperfield!"

The tears came to my eyes as I grasped him by both hands. "Why, you are a very Daisy!" he laughed, and yet he was glad, too, to see how the delight I had in meeting him affected me. I asked him how he came to be there.

"Well, I am what they call an Oxford man," he returned; "that is to say, I get bored to death down there, periodically—and I am on my way now to my mother's. What are you doing here?"

Glowing with pleasure to find that he still had an interest in me, I told him how I had been adopted by an aunt and how she had sent me on an expedition. "As you are in no hurry, then," said Steerforth, "come home with me to Highgate, and stay a day or two. You will be pleased with my mother—she is a little vain and prosy about me, but you can forgive her—and she will be pleased with you. Everyone who likes me has a claim on her that is sure to be acknowledged."

Accordingly the stage coach deposited us next day at a genteel old-fashioned house overlooking London, where an elderly lady with a proud carriage and a handsome face greeted us. In the dining room was a second lady, of a slight, short figure, dark, and with a scar upon her lip. It was an old scar which had once cut through her mouth but was now barely visible except on her lip, the shape of which it had altered. I concluded in my own mind that she was about thirty years of age and that she wished to be married. Her thinness seemed to be the effect of some wasting fire within her, which found a vent in her gaunt, eager eyes.

She was introduced as Miss Dartle, and both Steerforth and his mother called her Rosa. I found that she lived there, a distant connection, and that she had been for a long time Mrs. Steerforth's companion. It appeared that she never said anything she wanted to say, outright, but hinted it and made a great deal more of it by this practice. For example, when Mrs. Steerforth observed, more in jest than in earnest, that she feared her son led but a wild life at college, Miss Dartle put in thus:

"Oh, really? You know how ignorant I am and that I only ask for information, but isn't it always so? I thought that kind of life was understood to be—eh? Isn't it, really?"

"Really what?" said Mrs. Steerforth.

"Oh! You mean it's *not!*" returned Miss Dartle. "Well, I'm very glad to hear it! Now, I know what to do. That's the advantage of asking. I shall never allow people to talk before me about wastefulness and profligacy, and so forth, in connection with that life, any more."

Mrs. Steerforth speaking to me about my intention of going down into Suffolk, I said at hazard how glad I should be if Steerforth would only go there with me. "You would be delighted to see that household," I said, describing the boat and the people in it.

"Should I?" said Steerforth. "I must see what can be done. It would be worth a journey to see that sort of people and make one of 'em."

My heart leaped with a new hope of pleasure. But it was in reference to the tone in which he had spoken of "that sort of people" that Miss Dartle now broke in again.

"Oh, but, really? Do tell me. Are they, though?" she said.

"Are they what? And are who what?" said Steerforth.

"That sort of people. Are they really animals and clods and beings of another order? I want to know *so* much."

"Why, there's a pretty wide separation between them and us," said Steerforth, with indifference. "They are not to be expected to be as sensitive as we are."

"Really!" said Miss Dartle. "Well, I don't know when I have been better pleased than to hear that. It's so consoling! It's such a delight to know that, when they suffer, they don't feel! Sometimes I have been quite uneasy for that sort of people; but now I shall just dismiss the idea of them altogether. Live and learn."

I believed that Steerforth had said what he had, in jest, or to draw Miss Dartle out; and I expected him to say as much when we were sitting alone before the fire. But he merely asked me what I thought of her.

"She is very clever, is she not?" I asked.

"Clever! She brings everything to a grindstone," said Steerforth, "and sharpens it, as she has sharpened her own face and figure these years past. She is all edge."

"What a remarkable scar that is upon her lip!" I said.

Steerforth's face fell, and he paused a moment. "Why, the fact is," he said "*I* did that. I was a young boy, and she exasperated me, and I threw a hammer at her. She has borne the mark ever since."

I could not help glancing at the scar with a painful interest when we went in to tea. It was not long before I observed that it was the most susceptible part of her face and that, when she turned pale, that mark altered first, and became a lead-colored streak, lengthening out to its full extent, like a mark in invisible ink brought to the fire. While we were talking, Steerforth more than once called me Daisy, which brought Miss Dartle out again.

"But, really, Mr. Copperfield," she asked "is it a nickname? And why does he give it you? Is it—eh?—because he thinks you young and innocent? I am so stupid in these things."

I colored in replying that I believed it was.

"Oh!" said Miss Dartle. "Now I am glad to know that! He thinks you young and innocent; and so you are his friend! Well, that's quite delightful."

He had, in fact, a dashing way of treating me like a plaything, which reminded me of our old acquaintance. I joyfully believed that I was nearer to his heart than any other friend, and my heart warmed with attachment when he decided to go with me to Yarmouth; when he sent me off alone, "to be cried over," on our arrival.

The streets looked small, of course; the streets that we have only seen as children always do. But I had forgotten nothing in them and found nothing changed until I came to Mr. Omer's shop. "Omer and Joram" it was now, but Mr. Omer was there, just the same. "Why, Lord bless my soul!" he exclaimed when I made myself known to him. "Blunderstone! Dear me, yes; the party was a lady, I think? And let me see. Barkis's the carrier's wife—Peggotty's the boatman's sister—she had something to do with your family? Well, sir, we've got a young relation of hers here, under articles to us, that has as elegant a taste in dressmaking as any duchess."

"Not little Em'ly?" said I, involuntarily.

"Em'ly's her name," said Mr. Omer, "and she's little too. But she has such a grace of her own that half the women in town are mad against her. You see, she hasn't taken kindly to any particular acquaintances, not to mention sweethearts, so an ill-natured story got about that Em'ly wanted to be a lady. Then, out of a very little, she could dress herself better than most others could out of a deal, and *that* made things unpleasant. Moreover, she was rather what might be called wayward, a little spoiled, and couldn't, at first, exactly bind herself down. But here she has been as good a girl as ever was. Worth any six."

Receiving permission to peep at her, I saw her sitting at her work, a most beautiful little creature, with much of the old capricious coyness lurking in her face but with nothing in her pretty looks, I am sure, but what was meant for goodness and for happiness and what was on a good and happy course.

The tune from the workshop across the yard that seemed as if it had never left off—alas! it was the tune that never *does* leave off—was beating, softly, all the while. I took leave of Mr. Omer, and went away to my dear old Peggotty's.

10

HERE she was in her kitchen, cooking dinner! I looked at her with a smile, but she gave me no smile in return. I had never ceased to write her, but it must have been seven years since we had met.

"Is Mr. Barkis at home, ma'am?" I said, feigning to speak roughly.

"He's at home, sir," returned Peggotty, "but he's bad abed with rheumatics."

"Don't he ever go over to Blunderstone now?" I asked. "Don't *you?*"

She looked at me more attentively, and I noticed a quick movement of her hands, as if to keep me off.

"Peggotty!" I cried to her.

She cried, "My darling boy!" and we both burst into tears and were locked in one another's arms.

Mr. Barkis, too, received me with absolute enthusiasm. He was too rheumatic to be shaken hands with, but he begged me to shake the tassel on the top of his nightcap, which I did most cordially. "I was willin' a long time, sir?" said he.

"A long time," said I.

"And I don't regret it," said Mr. Barkis. "Do you remember what you told me once, about her making all the apple parsties? It was as true," said Mr. Barkis, "as turnips is. It was as true," said Mr. Barkis, nodding his nightcap, which was his only means of emphasis, "as taxes is. And nothing's truer than them. A man as poor as I am finds that out when he's laid up. I'm a very poor man, sir!" Here his right hand came slowly and feebly from under the bedclothes and with a purposeless uncertain grasp took hold of a stick which was loosely tied to the side of the bed. After some poking about, in the course of which his face assumed a variety of distracted expressions, Mr. Barkis poked it against a box, an end of which had been visible all the time. Then his face became composed.

"Old clothes," said Mr. Barkis. "I wish it was money, sir."

"I wish it was, indeed," said I.

"But it *ain't*," said Mr. Barkis.

Steerforth had promised to follow me to Peggotty's, and his manner to me alone, when he arrived, would have won her. But his easy, spirited good humor, his handsome looks, his natural gift of adapting himself to whomsoever he pleased and making direct, when he cared to, to anybody's heart, bound her to him wholly. I sincerely believe she had a kind of adoration for him before he left the house that night. If anyone had told me, then, that all this was a brilliant game, played for the excitement of the moment, in the thoughtless love of superiority, in a mere wasteful careless course of winning what was worthless to him, and next minute thrown away, I wonder in what manner my indignation would have found a vent!

As we walked after dinner over the dark wintry sands toward the old boat, the wind sighed and moaned and the sea, Steerforth said, roared as if it were hungry for us. Then we went into the warm light room, where a picture awaited us: Mr. Peggotty, laughing with all his might, held his arms wide open; Ham held little Em'ly's hand, as if he were presenting her to Mr. Peggotty; Em'ly, blushing and shy, was stopped by our entrance from springing into Mr. Peggotty's arms; and Mrs. Gummidge, in the background, was clapping her hands like a madwoman. I was in the midst of the astonished family when Ham shouted, "Mas'r Davy! It's Mas'r Davy!"

In a moment we were all shaking hands with one another. "Why, that you two gent'lmen—gent'lmen growed," said Mr. Peggotty, "should come to this here roof on the brightest night o' my life as ever was or ever will be, Gorm the t'other one, and horroar for it—" He ruffled his hair with both hands. "This here little Em'ly, sir," he said to Steerforth, "has been, in our house, what I suppose no one but a little bright-eyed creetur *can* be. She ain't my child; I never had one; but I couldn't love her more. You understand! I couldn't do it!"

"I quite understand," said Steerforth.

"There was a certain person as had know'd our Em'ly," Mr. Peggotty went on, "when a babby, when a young gal, when a woman. Not much of a person to look at, he warn't; something o' my own build—rough—wery salt—but, on the whole, a honest sort of a chap, with his 'art in the right place."

I thought I had never seen Ham grin to anything like the extent he was grinning now.

"What does this here blessed tarpaulin go and do," said Mr. Peggotty, with his face one high noon of enjoyment, "but he loses that there 'art of his to our little Em'ly." He laid a hand upon my knee and a hand upon Steerforth's (previously wetting them both, for greater emphasis) and continued, "All of a sudden—as it might be tonight—comes little Em'ly from her work, and him with her. And this tarpaulin chap, he takes hold of her hand, and he cries out to me, joyful, 'Look here! This is to be my little wife!' And she says, 'Yes, uncle, if you please.'—If I please!" cried Mr. Peggotty, rolling his head in ecstasy. "Then Missis Gummidge, she claps her hands like a play, and you come in. Theer! the murder's out!" said Mr. Peggotty. "You come in!"

"A most engaging little beauty!" said Steerforth, as we left. "That's rather a chuckle-headed fellow for her, though, isn't he?"

He had been so hearty with them all that I felt a shock in this unexpected and cold remark. But turning quickly upon him and seeing a laugh in his eyes I said, much relieved, "Ah, Steerforth! It's well for you to joke about the poor! You may skirmish with Miss Dartle or try to hide your sympathies in jest, but I know better. And I admire and love you for it, Steerforth."

He stopped and, looking in my face, said, "Daisy, I believe you are in earnest and are good. I wish we all were!" Next moment he was gaily singing a song of Mr. Peggotty's, as we walked back to Yarmouth.

Steerforth and I stayed for more than a fortnight in that part of the country. We were very much together but occasionally went our several ways. I had no idea how he employed his time, beyond a general knowledge that he was very popular in the place and had twenty means of actively diverting himself. One dark evening I found him alone in Mr. Peggotty's house, sitting thoughtfully before the fire, so intent upon his own reflections that he gave a start when I put my hand on his shoulder. "You come upon me," he said, almost angrily, "like a reproachful ghost! David, I wish to God I had had a judicious father these last twenty years!"

"My dear Steerforth, what is the matter?"

"I wish with all my soul I had been better guided!" he exclaimed. "I wish with all my soul I could guide myself better!" His face was always full of expression, but I never saw it express such a dark kind of earnestness as when he said those words. "So much for that!" he said, making as if he tossed something light into the air, as we left the house. "You know I have bought a boat?"

"What an extraordinary fellow you are, Steerforth!" I said. "When you may never care to come near here again!"

"I don't know that," he returned. "I have taken a fancy to the place. And Mr. Peggotty will be master of the boat in my absence."

"Now I understand you!" I said, exultingly. "You have really bought it to confer a benefit on him. How can I tell you what I think of your generosity?"

"The less said, the better," he answered, turning red. "She must be newly rigged, so I shall leave Littimer behind to see it done. Did I tell you Littimer had come down?"

Littimer was his servant, a man who was in appearance a pattern of respectability; I believe there never existed in his station a more respectable-looking man. He was taciturn, soft footed, very quiet in his manner, deferential, observant, always at hand when wanted, and never near when not wanted; but his great claim to consideration was his respectability. I am particular about this man because he had made a particular effect on me and because of what took place thereafter.

"He came down this morning, with a letter from my mother," Steerforth said. As our looks met, I observed that he was now pale even to his lips, though he looked very steadily at me. "He shall see to the boat being fresh named."

"By what name?" I asked.

"The *Little Em'ly*." As he continued to look steadily at me, I could not help showing how much this pleased me, and he seemed relieved. "But see here," he said, looking before us, "where the

original little Em'ly comes! And that fellow with her, eh? Upon
my soul, he's a true knight!" When they passed on, we looked after
them fading away in the light of a young moon.

Suddenly there passed us—evidently following them—a young
woman whose approach we had not observed but whose face I
saw as she went by and thought I had a faint remembrance of.
She was lightly dressed, looked bold, and haggard, and flaunting,
and poor. "That is a black shadow to be following the girl," said
Steerforth in a strangely low voice.

At dinner that night Littimer announced to Steerforth that
Miss Mowcher wished to wait on him. "Why, what on earth does
she do here?" said Steerforth.

"It appears to be her native part of the country, sir. She in-
forms me that she makes one of her professional visits here every
year, sir."

"Do you know the Giantess in question, Daisy?" inquired
Steerforth.

I was obliged to confess that I did not.

"She is one of the seven wonders of the world," he said, laughing, but would tell me nothing about her. When she was announced, I looked at the doorway and saw nothing; when, to my
infinite astonishment, there came waddling round a sofa a pursy
dwarf, of about forty or forty-five, with a very large head and face,
a pair of roguish gray eyes, and such extremely little arms that,
to enable herself to lay a finger archly against her snub nose as she
ogled Steerforth, she was obliged to meet the finger halfway and
lay her nose against it. Her chin was so fat that it entirely swallowed up the strings of her bonnet, bow and all. Throat she had
none; waist she had none; legs she had none, worth mentioning;
for though she was more than full-sized down to where her waist
should have been and though she terminated in a pair of feet, she
was so short that she stood at a chair as at a table, resting a bag
she carried on the seat, as she broke into a torrent of words.

"What! My flower!" she pleasantly began, shaking her large
head at Steerforth. "You're there, are you? Oh, you naughty boy,
fie for shame, what do you do so far away from home? Up to
mischief, I'll be bound. Oh, you're a downy fellow, Steerforth,
and I'm another, ain't I? Ha, ha, ha! What a comfort you are to

your blessed mother, ain't you, my dear boy, over one of my shoulders, and I don't say which!"

I never beheld anything approaching to Miss Mowcher's wink, except Miss Mowcher's self-possession. She had a wonderful way, too, of pausing with her head cunningly on one side and one eye turned up like a magpie's. She now produced from her bag (plunging in her short arm to the shoulder, at every dive) a number of small bottles, sponges, combs, brushes, bits of flannel, little pairs of curling irons, and other instruments. "What a refreshing set of humbugs we are, ain't we, my sweet child?" she said, taking something else out. "Look here! Scraps of the Russian Prince's nails. They do more for me in private families of the genteel sort than all my talents. If Miss Mowcher cuts the Prince's nails, she *must* be all right. Ha! ha! ha! Well, this is not business. Come, Steerforth, let's explore the polar regions." She then asked if the table would bear. On Steerforth's replying in the affirmative, she pushed a chair against it, and begging the assistance of my hand, mounted up, pretty nimbly, to the top.

"If either of you saw my ankles," she said, when she was safely elevated, "say so, and I'll go home and destroy myself."

"*I* did not," said Steerforth.

"*I* did not," said I.

"Well then," cried Miss Mowcher, "I'll consent to live. Now, ducky, ducky, ducky, come to Mrs. Bond and be killed." Steerforth accordingly sat himself down, with his back to the table, and submitted his head to her inspection. To see Miss Mowcher standing over him, looking at his rich profusion of brown hair through a magnifying glass which she took out of her pocket, was a spectacle.

"I haven't seen a pretty woman since I've been here, Jemmy," she said, rubbing away briskly.

"We could show her one, I think," said Steerforth. "Eh, Daisy?"

"Aha?" cried the little creature, glancing sharply at my face and then peeping round at Steerforth's. "Umph?" The first exclamation sounded like a question put to both of us, and the second like a question put to Steerforth only.

"I'll leave you nothing to guess at," Steerforth said, as though in reply. "Her name is Emily, Miss Mowcher. She is at present apprenticed to Omer and Joram, haberdashers, milliners, and so forth, in this town. Do you observe? Omer and Joram. She is engaged to be married to her cousin; Christian name, Ham; surname, Peggotty; occupation, boat builder. If it were not that I might appear to disparage her intended, which I know my friend Mr. Copperfield would not like, I would add that to *me* she seems to be throwing herself away; that I am sure she might do better; and that I swear she was born to be a lady."

Miss Mowcher listened to these words, which were very slowly and distinctly spoken, with her head on one side and her eye in the air, as if she were waiting for an answer. When he ceased, she became brisk again in an instant. "Oh! And that's all about it, is it?" she exclaimed. "What's that game at forfeits? I love my love with an E, because she's enticing; I hate her with an E, because she's engaged. I took her to the sign of the exquisite and treated her with an elopement; her name is Emily, and she lives in the east? Ha! ha! ha! What a rattle I am! Mr. Copperfield, ain't I volatile?"

Looking at me with extravagant slyness and not waiting for a reply, she continued, without drawing breath, "Now, I know I'm going to break your hearts, but I am forced to leave you. You must call up all your fortitude, and try to bear it. Good-by, Mr. Copperfield! Take care of yourself, Jockey of Norfolk! How I *have* been rattling on! 'Bob swore!' as the Englishman said for 'Good night,' when he first learned French and thought it so like English. 'Bob swore,' my ducks!" With the bag, now repacked, slung over her shoulder, she waddled to the door, where she stopped to inquire if she should leave us a lock of her hair. "Ain't I volatile?" she added, as a commentary on this offer, and, with her finger on her nose, departed.

When Steerforth had had his laugh out, he told me that Miss Mowcher had quite an extensive connection and made herself useful to a variety of people in a variety of ways. Some people trifled with her as a mere oddity, he said; but she was as shrewdly and sharply observant as anyone he knew, and as long headed as she was short armed.

I was surprised, when I came to Mr. Barkis's house that night, to find that little Em'ly was there, talking to a "young woman," Ham told me, "that Em'ly knowed once and doesn't ought to know no more." When I heard these words, a light began to fall upon the figure I had seen following them, some hours ago. "Martha Endell she is," said Ham. "They sat at work together many a day, at Mr. Omer's. Tonight she creeps under Em'ly's winder, whisp'ring, 'Em'ly, Em'ly, for Christ's sake, have a woman's heart toward me. I was once like you!' Those was solemn words, Mas'r Davy, fur to hear!"

"They were indeed, Ham. What did Em'ly do?"

"Em'ly couldn't speak to her theer, for her loving uncle was come home, and he couldn't, kind-natur'd as he is, see them two together; so Em'ly tells her to meet her here, and she gives me her little purse to carry and asks me to bring her. She doen't ought to know any such, but I can't deny her."

Peggotty soon called us into the kitchen, where the three women were. The girl—the same I had seen upon the sands—was sitting on the ground, with her head and one arm lying on a chair. "Martha wants," Em'ly said, "to go to London."

"Why to London?" returned Ham.

He stood between them, looking on the prostrate girl with a mixture of compassion for her and of jealousy of her holding any companionship with her whom he loved so well which I have always remembered.

"Better there than here," said Martha, though she did not move. "No one knows me there. Everybody knows me here."

"What will she do there?" inquired Ham.

"She will try to do well," said little Em'ly. "You don't know what she has said to us. Does he, aunt?" Peggotty shook her head compassionately. Then, as Em'ly held out her hand for her purse, I saw Ham put a little canvas bag in it. "It's all yourn, Em'ly," I heard him say. "It ain't of no delight to me, except for you, my dear!"

The tears rose in Em'ly's eyes, as she put money in Martha's bosom and asked, was that enough? "More than enough," the other said and took her hand and kissed it before she went away. As the door closed, little Em'ly fell to sobbing. "Oh, Ham!" she exclaimed. "I am not so good a girl as I ought to be! Not near! Not near!"

I saw her do, that night, what I had never seen her do before. I saw her innocently kiss her chosen husband on the cheek and creep close to his bluff form as if it were her best support. When

they went away together, in the waning moonlight, and I looked after them, comparing their departure with Martha's, I saw that she held his arm with both her hands and still kept close to him.

I I

"Do you stay long here, Littimer?" said I, as he stood waiting to see the coach start that was taking Steerforth and me back to London.

"He can hardly say, just now," observed Steerforth, carelessly. "He knows what he has to do, and he'll do it." For some time after we started we held no conversation, Steerforth being unusually silent. Then I disclosed to him that my aunt had written saying she was in London and asking me if I should like to be a proctor. "What *is* a proctor, Steerforth?" said I.

"Why, he is a sort of monkish attorney," replied Steerforth. "He is, to some faded courts held in Doctors' Commons—a lazy old nook near St. Paul's Churchyard—what solicitors are to the courts of law and equity. It's a place that has an ancient monopoly in suits about people's wills and marriages and disputes among ships and boats, with very comfortable fees. On the whole, I would recommend you to take to Doctors' Commons kindly, David."

I quite made up my mind to do so and went straight to a private hotel in Lincoln's Inn Fields where my aunt had taken lodgings, it having a stone staircase and a convenient door in the roof; for my aunt was firmly persuaded that every house in London was going to be burned down every night.

If I had been round the world since we parted, we could hardly have been better pleased to meet again. When the table was cleared after supper, she put on her nightcap, which was of a smarter construction than usual ("in case of fire," my aunt said) and folded her gown back over her knees, these being her preparations for warming herself before going to bed. I then made her, according to established regulations, a glass of hot white wine and water and a slice of toast cut into long thin strips. With these accompaniments we sat down to talk.

"Well, Trot," she began, "what do you think of the proctor plan?"

"I have only one difficulty, aunt," I said. "As this seems to be a limited profession, would not my entrance into it be very expensive?"

"It will cost," returned my aunt, "to article you, just a thousand pounds."

"Now, my dear aunt," said I, "I am uneasy about that. It's a large sum of money. Are you certain that you can afford it, and that you should?"

"Trot, my child," she replied, "if I have any object in life, it is to provide for your being a good, a sensible, and a happy man. I am bent upon it—so is Dick. You have been a credit to me and a pride and a pleasure. I have no other claim upon my means; at least"—here to my surprise she hesitated and was confused—"no, I have *no* other claim—and you are my adopted child. Only be a loving child to me in my age and bear with my whims and fancies; and you will do more for an old woman whose prime of life was not so happy or conciliating as it might have been, than ever that old woman did for you."

So next morning we set out for the office of Messrs. Spenlow and Jorkins, her own proctors, in Doctors' Commons. My aunt, who had this other general opinion about London, that every man she saw was a pickpocket, gave me her purse to carry, which had ten guineas in it and some silver. Suddenly she greatly accelerated her pace, and looked frightened. I observed, at the same time, that a lowering ill-dressed man who had stared at us in passing was coming so close after us as to brush against her.

"Trot! My dear Trot!" cried my aunt, in a terrified whisper, pressing my arm.

"Don't be alarmed," said I. "There's nothing to be afraid of. Step into a shop, and I'll soon get rid of this fellow."

"No, no, child!" she returned. "Don't speak to him for the world. I entreat, I order you!"

"Good Heaven, aunt!" said I. "He is nothing but a sturdy beggar."

"You don't know what he is!" replied my aunt. "You don't know who he is! You don't know what you say! Get me a coach, my dear, and wait for me in St. Paul's Churchyard."

"Wait for you?" I repeated.

"Yes," rejoined my aunt. "I must go alone. I must go with him." She took her purse and sprang into the coach, the man following her.

While I waited, something Mr. Dick had told me about a man frightening my aunt in Dover came into my mind. I had supposed it to be a delusion of his, that she gave the man money in the moonlight. But on her giving me back her purse, when she returned, I found that all the guineas were gone. She said nothing except "My dear child, never ask me what it was, and don't refer to it," until she had regained her composure, when we went through a little low archway into Doctors' Commons.

A few dull courts and narrow ways brought us to the offices of Spenlow and Jorkins and to Mr. Spenlow, a little gentleman with the stiffest of white cravats and shirt collars, buttoned up mighty trim and tight. He was so stiff that he could hardly bend himself, being obliged, when he glanced at some papers on his desk, to move his whole body, like Punch.

"And so, Mr. Copperfield," he said, "you think of entering into our profession? I casually mentioned to Miss Trotwood the other day"—with another inclination of his body—Punch again—"that there was a vacancy here. Miss Trotwood was good enough to mention that she had a nephew for whom she was seeking to provide genteelly in life."—Punch again.

I bowed my acknowledgments and said that although it was little else than a matter of form I presumed I should have an opportunity of trying how I liked it, before I bound myself to it irrevocably.

"Oh surely! surely!" said Mr. Spenlow. "We always propose a month—an initiatory month. I should be happy, myself, to propose two months—three—an indefinite period—but I have a partner, Mr. Jorkins."

"I suppose, sir," said I, still desiring to spare my aunt, "that it is not the custom here, if an articled clerk were particularly useful, to allow him—"

Mr. Spenlow, by a great effort, just lifted his head far enough out of his cravat to shake it and answered, anticipating the word "salary," "No. I will not say what consideration I might give to that point myself. Mr. Jorkins is immovable."

I was quite dismayed by the idea of this terrible Jorkins. But I found out afterwards that he was a mild man whose place in the business was to keep himself in the background and be constantly exhibited as the most ruthless of men. If a clerk wanted his salary raised, Mr. Jorkins wouldn't listen to such a proposition. If a client were slow to settle his bill of costs, Mr. Jorkins was resolved to have it paid; and, however painful these things might be (and always were) to the feelings of Mr. Spenlow, Mr. Jorkins would have his bond. As I have grown older, I think I have had experience of some other houses doing business on the principle of Spenlow and Jorkins!

When our business was settled, my aunt showed me the advertisement of a set of chambers in the Adelphi she proposed to look at, which directed us to apply to Mrs. Crupp on the premises. It was not until we had rung three or four times that we could prevail on Mrs. Crupp to communicate with us, but at last she appeared. "For this gentleman?" said Mrs. Crupp. "And a sweet set they is for sich!"

Seeing how enraptured I was with the chambers, my aunt took them for me. Mrs. Crupp was to find linen and to cook; and Mrs. Crupp expressly intimated that she should always yearn toward me as a son; thank Heaven, she said, she had now found summun she could care for! The next day, my aunt left for Dover.

It was a wonderfully fine thing to have that castle to myself, to come and go without a word to anyone, and to ring Mrs. Crupp up, gasping, from the depths of the earth, when I wanted her—and when she was disposed to come. It was wonderfully fine; but I must say, too, that there were times when it was very dreary. As the day declined, I wanted somebody to talk to. I missed Agnes. I found a tremendous blank, in the place of that smiling repository of my confidence. Steerforth, too, had disappeared with some Oxford friends, though he had promised to come and meet my aunt. So it was particularly delightful to see him when he finally walked in, and I persuaded him to bring his friends to dine with me.

Then I acquainted Mrs. Crupp with my desperate design. Mrs. Crupp said, in the first place, of course she couldn't be expected to wait, but she knew a handy young man, who she thought could be prevailed upon to do it. Next, Mrs. Crupp said it was clear she couldn't be in two places at once (which I felt to be reasonable) and that "a young gal" stationed in the pantry, there never to desist from washing plates, would be indispensable. Now, Mrs. Crupp said, about the dinner.

It was a remarkable instance of want of forethought on the part of the ironmonger who had made Mrs. Crupp's kitchen fire-place that it was capable of cooking nothing but chops and mashed potatoes. So what Mrs. Crupp recommended was this: a pair of hot roast fowls—from the pastry cook's; a dish of stewed beef, with vegetables—from the pastry cook's; two little corner things, as a raised pie and a dish of kidneys—from the pastry cook's; a tart and (if I liked) a shape of jelly—from the pastry cook's. This, Mrs. Crupp said, would leave her at full liberty to concentrate on the potatoes and to serve up the cheese and celery as she could wish to see it done. These preparations happily completed, I bought a little dessert in Covent Garden Market and gave a rather extensive order at a wine merchant's.

Being a little embarrassed at first and feeling much too young to preside, I made Steerforth take the head of the table when dinner was announced; and he exerted himself so brilliantly that there was no pause in our festivity. I was not quite such good company during dinner as I could have wished to be, for my attention was distracted by observing that the handy young man went out of the room very often and that his shadow always presented itself, immediately afterward, on the wall of the pantry, with a bottle at its mouth. The "young gal" likewise occasioned me some uneasiness; for, being of an inquisitive disposition, she was constantly peering in at us and constantly imagining herself detected, in which belief she several times retired upon the plates (with which she had carefully paved the pantry floor) and did a great deal of destruction.

But when the cloth was cleared I abandoned myself to enjoyment, passing the wine faster and faster yet and continually starting up with a corkscrew to open more wine, long before any was needed. I proposed Steerforth's health, saying (in two words) "Steerforth, you're the guiding star of my existence." I laughed heartily at my own jokes and everybody else's. I announced that I meant to have a dinner party exactly like that, once a week, until further notice.

Somebody was smoking. We were all smoking. *I* was smoking, and trying to suppress a rising tendency to shudder. Somebody said, "Let us go to the theater!" and we went downstairs, one behind another. Near the bottom, somebody fell and rolled down. Somebody said it was Copperfield. I was angry at that false report, until, finding myself on my back, I began to think there might be something in it.

A very foggy night, with great rings round the lamps in the streets! Steerforth said, "You are all right, Copperfield?" and I told him, "Never berrer." Shortly afterward, we were very high up in a very hot theater, but the whole building looked to me as if it were learning to swim, it conducted itself in such an unaccountable manner when I tried to steady it. On somebody's motion, we resolved to go downstairs to the dress boxes, where the ladies were. Then I was being ushered into one of these boxes and found myself saying something as I sat down, and people about me crying "Silence!" to somebody, and ladies casting indignant glances at me, and—what! yes!—Agnes, sitting on the seat before me! I see her face now, better than I did then, I dare say, with its indelible look of regret and wonder. "Agnes!" I said thickly, "Lorblessmer! Agnes!"

"Hush! Pray!" she answered, I could not conceive why. I saw her shrink into her corner and put her gloved hand to her forehead. "Agnes!" I said. "I'mafraidyou'renorwell."

"Yes, yes. Do not mind me, Trotwood," she returned. "I know you will do as I ask you, if I tell you I am very earnest. Ask your friends to take you home, Trotwood, for my sake." She had so far improved me, for the time, that though I was angry with her I felt ashamed and with a short "Goori!" (which I intended for "Good night") went away. But the agony of mind, the remorse, the shame I felt, when I became conscious next day; when a ticket porter brought me a letter from Agnes!—I found, when I opened it, that it contained no reference to my condition at the theater. All it said was that she was staying at the house of her father's agent Mr. Waterbrook and that she wished to see me.

It took me such a long time to write an answer at all to my satisfaction that I don't know what the ticket porter can have thought, unless he thought I was learning to write. But at last it was done, and in due time I arrived at Mr. Waterbrook's, where I found Agnes. She looked so quiet and good that I yielded to my self-reproach and shed tears. She put her hand—its touch was like no other hand—upon my arm for a moment. "Ah, Agnes!" I said. "You are my good angel!"

She smiled rather sadly, I thought, and shook her head. "If I were, indeed, Trotwood," she returned, "I should set my heart on warning you against your bad angel."

"My dear Agnes," I began, "if you mean Steerforth—"

"I do, Trotwood," she returned.

"Then, Agnes, you wrong him very much. Is it not unjust to judge him from what you saw of me last night?"

"I do not judge him from what I saw of you," she quietly replied, "but from many things—trifles in themselves, though they do not seem so when they are put together. I judge him partly from your account of him, and your character, and the influence he has over you." There was always something in her modest voice that seemed to touch a chord within me, answering to that sound alone; and Steerforth, in spite of all my attachment to him, darkened in that tone.

Resuming her usual tone, Agnes asked me if I had seen Uriah.

"Uriah Heep?" said I. "No. Is he in London?"

"He comes to the office downstairs, every day," returned Agnes. "He was in London a week before me. I believe he is going to enter into partnership with papa."

"What? Uriah? That mean, fawning fellow, worm himself into such promotion!" I cried indignantly. "You must not allow your father to take such a mad step."

Agnes shook her head. "You remember our last conversation about papa? Uriah has made himself indispensable to papa. He is subtle and watchful. He has mastered papa's weaknesses, fostered them, and taken advantage of them, until—to say all in a word—until papa is afraid of him. Let me earnestly entreat you, Trotwood, to be friendly to Uriah. Don't repel him. Think first of papa and me!"

Agnes had no time to say more, for the door opened, and Mrs. Waterbrook, who was a large lady—or who wore a large dress: I don't exactly know which, for I don't know which was dress and which was lady—came sailing in and invited me to dinner next day; when, being plunged into a vapor bath of haunch of mutton, I divined that I was not the only guest. I was presented first, with much ceremony, to a very awful lady in a black velvet dress and a great black velvet hat, who looked like a near relation of Hamlet's—say his aunt.

I found Uriah Heep among the company, in a suit of black and in deep humility. He told me, when I shook hands with him, that he was obliged to me for my condescension, but I could have wished he had been less obliged, for he hovered about me in his gratitude all the rest of the evening and, whenever I said a word to Agnes, was sure, with his shadowless eyes and cadaverous face, to be looking gauntly on us from behind.

There were other guests—all iced for the occasion, like the wine. But there was one who attracted my attention before he came in, when I heard him announced as Mr. Traddles. He was a sober, steady-looking young man of retiring manners, with a comic head of hair and eyes that were rather wide open; it was the old unfortunate Tommy! We greeted each other with fervor but were separated at table, being billeted in two remote corners, he in the glare of a red velvet lady, I in the gloom of Hamlet's aunt. The dinner was very long, and the conversation was about the Aristocracy—and Blood. Mrs. Waterbrook repeatedly told us that, if she had a weakness, it was Blood. Hamlet's aunt had the family failing of indulging in soliloquy and held forth by herself on every topic that was introduced; as we always fell back upon Blood, she had as wide a field for abstract speculation as her nephew himself.

"Oh! There is nothing," she observed, "so satisfactory to one! There is nothing that is so much one's beau ideal of—of all that sort of thing, speaking generally. We see Blood in a nose, and we know it. We meet with it in a chin, and we say, 'There it is! That's Blood!' It is an actual matter of fact."

As these were not people with whom I believed Agnes could be very much at home, I was almost glad to hear that she was going away shortly. And it was in remembrance of her entreaty that I asked Uriah to come home to my rooms and have some coffee. "Oh, really, Master Copperfield," he rejoined—"I beg your pardon, Mr. Copperfield, but the other comes so natural—I don't like that you should put a constraint upon yourself to ask a numble person like me."

"There is no constraint," said I. "Will you come?"

"I should like to, very much," replied Uriah, with a writhe.

When I heated the coffee in an unassuming block-tin vessel in which Mrs. Crupp delighted to prepare it (chiefly, I believe, because there was a patent invention of great price moldering away in the pantry), he professed so much emotion that I could joyfully have scalded him. "Oh, really, Master Copperfield—I *should* say, Mr. Copperfield—to see you waiting upon me! But, one way and another, so many things happen to me which I never could have expected in my umble station that it seems to rain blessings on my ed. What a prophet you have shown yourself, Master—Mr. Copperfield! To think that you were the first to kindle the sparks of ambition in my umble breast! But the umblest persons may be the instruments of good. I am glad to think I have been the instrument of good to Mr. Wickfield. Oh, what a worthy man he is, Mr. Copperfield, but how imprudent he has been!"

"So Mr. Wickfield," I said, "who is worth five hundred of you —or me—" (for my life I could not help dividing that part of the sentence with an awkward jerk) "has been imprudent, has he, Mr. Heep?"

"Oh, very imprudent indeed, Master Copperfield," returned

Uriah, sighing modestly. "But I wish you'd call me Uriah, if you please. It's like old times."

"Well! Uriah," said I, bolting it out with some difficulty.

"Thank you," he returned, with fervor. "Thank you, Master Copperfield! It's like the blowing of old breezes or the ringing of old bellses to hear *you* say Uriah.—Ah! Great imprudence, Master Copperfield! If anyone else had been in my place during the last few years, by this time he would have had Mr. Wickfield (oh, what a worthy man he is, Master Copperfield) under his thumb. Un-der—his thumb," said Uriah, very slowly, as he stretched out his cruel-looking hand above my table and pressed his own thumb down upon it, until it shook and shook the room.

"You won't think the worse of my umblencss if I make a little confidence to you, Master Copperfield, will you?" he asked presently. He took out his handkerchief and began wiping the palms of his hands. "Umble as I am, the image of Miss Agnes (I don't mind trusting you with my secret, Master Copperfield) has been in my breast for years. Oh, Master Copperfield, with what a pure affection do I love the ground my Agnes walks on!"

I believe I had a delirious idea of seizing the red-hot poker out of the fire and running him through with it. But a timely observation of the sense of power there was in his face brought back to my remembrance the entreaty of Agnes. I asked him, with a better appearance of composure than I had thought possible, whether he had made his feelings known to Agnes.

"Oh, no, Master Copperfield!" he returned. "Not to anyone but you! You see, I am only just emerging from my lowly station. I rest a good deal of hope on her observing how useful I am to her father. She's so much attached to her father that I think she may come, on his account, to be kind to me."

I fathomed the depth of the rascal's whole scheme and understood why he laid it bare.

"If you'll have the goodness to keep my secret, Master Copperfield," he pursued, "and not, in general, to go against me with my Agnes, I shall take it as a particular favor."

Dear Agnes! So much too loving and too good for anyone that I could think of, was it possible that she was reserved to be the wife of such a wretch as this! I charged Mrs. Crupp to leave the windows open next morning, that my sitting room might be aired and purged of Uriah's presence.

12

On the day when I was articled, no festivity took place. Mr. Spenlow intimated, however, that when his daughter came home from finishing her education at Paris, he hoped to have the pleasure of entertaining me at his house at Norwood. I knew that he was a widower with one daughter and expressed my acknowledgment. He was as good as his word. In a week or two he invited me to drive down with him on Saturday, to stay till Monday.

"Where is Miss Dora?" he said to the servant when we arrived. "Dora!" I thought. "What a beautiful name!" We turned into a room, and I heard a voice say, "Mr. Copperfield, my daughter Dora, and my daughter's confidential friend!" All was over in a moment. I had fulfilled my destiny. I was a captive and a slave. I loved Dora Spenlow to distraction!

"*I*," observed a well-remembered voice, when I had bowed and murmured something, "have seen Mr. Copperfield before."

The speaker was not Dora. No; the confidential friend, Miss Murdstone!

I don't think I was much astonished. No capacity of astonishment was left in me. There was nothing worth mentioning in the material world but Dora. What a form she had, what a face she had, what a graceful, variable, enchanting manner! I don't remember who was there that evening, except Dora. I have not the least idea what we had for dinner, besides Dora. She had the most delightful little voice, the gayest little laugh, the most fascinating little ways. She was rather diminutive altogether. So much the more precious, I thought.

My cruel apprehension that Miss Murdstone would disparage me was happily relieved when she spoke to me alone after dinner. "David Copperfield," she said, arranging the little fetters on her wrists and round her neck, "I shall not attempt to disguise the fact that I formed an unfavorable opinion of you in your childhood. You may have your opinion of me. But it is not necessary that these opinions should come into collision here. Under existing circumstances, it is as well on all accounts that they should not." With which sentiment I heartily agreed.

All I know of the rest of the evening is that I heard the empress of my heart sing enchanted ballads in the French language—generally to the effect that whatever was the matter, we ought always to dance, ta ra la, ta ra la—accompanying herself on a glorified instrument resembling a guitar. That I retired to bed in a most maudlin state of mind and got up in a crisis of feeble infatuation, which drove me into the garden. I had not been walking long, when I turned a corner and met her. I tingle again from head to foot as my recollection turns that corner, and my pen shakes in my hand. "You—are—out early, Miss Spenlow," said I.

"It's so stupid at home," she replied. "Besides, it's the brightest time of the whole day. Don't you think so?"

I hazarded a bold flight and said (not without stammering) that it was very bright to me then, though it had been very dark to me a minute before.

"Do you mean a compliment," said Dora, "or that the weather has changed?"

I stammered worse then before, in replying that I meant no compliment, but the plain truth; though I was not aware of any change in the weather. It was in the state of my feelings, I added bashfully, to clench the explanation.

I never saw such curls—how could I, for there never were such curls!—as those she shook out to hide her blushes. Then Jip, her little dog, came running along the walk. He was mortally jealous of me and persisted in barking at me. She took him up in her arms —oh my goodness!—and caressed him. He wouldn't let me touch him, though I approached him tenderly, loving even him.

"You aren't very intimate with Miss Murdstone, are you?" said Dora. "—My pet." (The two last words were to the dog. Oh if they had only been to me!)

"No," I replied, "not at all."

"She is a tiresome creature," said Dora, pouting. "I can't think why papa chose such a vexatious thing to be my companion. Jip can protect me a great deal better than Miss Murdstone, can't you, Jip, dear?" But Miss Murdstone was looking for us and marched us into breakfast as if it were a soldier's funeral.

How many cups of tea I drank, because Dora made it, I don't know. But I perfectly remember that I sat swilling tea until my whole nervous system, if I had had any in those days, must have gone by the board. By and by we went to church. A sermon was delivered—about Dora, of course—and I am afraid that Dora is all I know of the rest of my visit.

Within the first week of my passion, I bought four sumptuous waistcoats—not for myself, *I* had no pride in them, for Dora— and laid the foundations of all the corns I have ever had. If the boots I wore at that period could only be produced and compared with the natural size of my feet, they would show what the state of my heart was, in a most affecting manner. And yet, wretched cripple as I made myself by this act of homage to Dora, I walked miles upon miles daily in the hope of seeing her, fagging through the Park long after I was quite worn out.

Mrs. Crupp must have been a woman of penetration; for even before I had had the courage to write Agnes about my attachment, she found it out. She came up to me one evening, when I was very low, to ask (she being afflicted with a curious disorder called "the spazzums," to which she was a martyr) if I could oblige her with a little tincture of cardamoms mixed with rhubarb and flavored with seven drops of the essence of cloves, which was the best remedy for her complaint, or, if I had not such a thing by me, with a little brandy, which was the next best. It was not, she remarked, so palatable to her, but it was the next best. As I had never even heard of the first remedy and always had the second in the closet, I gave Mrs. Crupp a glass, which she began to take in my presence.

"Cheer up, sir," said Mrs. Crupp. "I can't bear to see you so, Mr. Copperfull. I'm a mother myself; I know what it is, sir. There's a lady in the case."

"Mrs. Crupp?" I returned, reddening.

"When the present set were took for you by your dear aunt, Mr. Copperfull," said Mrs. Crupp, "my remark were, I had now found summun I could care for. 'Thank Ev'in!' were the expression, 'I have now found summun I can care for!' You don't eat enough, sir, nor yet drink."

"Is that what you found your supposition on, Mrs. Crupp?" said I.

"Sir," said Mrs. Crupp, "I've laundressed other young gentlemen besides yourself. A young gentleman may be overcareful of himself, or he may be undercareful. He may brush his hair too regular, or too unregular. But let him go to which extreme he may, sir, there's a young lady in both of 'em. Mr. Copperfull, I'm a mother myself, and my adwice to you is to cheer up and know your own walue."

It may have been in consequence of Mrs. Crupp's advice that it came into my head, next day, to go and look up Traddles, who had given me his address. I found him living in a place that reminded me forcibly of the days when I lived with Mr. and Mrs. Micawber. Happening to arrive at the door as it was opened to the afternoon milkman, I was reminded of them more forcibly yet.

"Now," said the milkman to the very youthful servant girl. "Has that there little bill of mine been heerd on?"

"Oh, master says he'll attend to it immediate," was the reply.

"Because," said the milkman, going on as if he had received no answer and speaking, as I judged from his tone, for the edification of somebody within the house, "because that there little bill has been running so long, I begin to believe it's run away altogether. Now, I'm not a going to stand it, you know!" said the milkman, still throwing his voice into the house and glaring down

the passage. "Are you fond of milk?" he said to the youthful servant, looking at her for the first time.

"Yes, I likes it," she replied.

"Good," said the milkman. "Then you won't have none tomorrow. D'ye hear? Not a fragment of milk you won't have tomorrow." Having deposited the usual quantity in the family jug, he went away, muttering.

Traddles was delighted to see me and welcomed me heartily to his little room. "You are reading for the bar, Mr. Waterbrook informed me?" said I.

"Why, yes," said Traddles. "It's some time since I was articled, but the payment of that hundred pounds was a great pull. A great pull!" said Traddles, with a wince, as if he had had a tooth out. "It was an unfortunate thing, but my uncle didn't like me when I grew up. He said I wasn't at all what he expected, so he married his housekeeper, and so when he died I wasn't provided for.

"Now, Copperfield," he went on, "you are so exactly what you used to be, with that agreeable face, that I shan't conceal anything.

You must know that I am engaged."—Engaged! Oh Dora!—
"She is a curate's daughter, one of ten, down in Devonshire. She
is such a dear girl! A little older than me, but the dearest girl! I
dare say ours is likely to be a rather long engagement, but our
motto is 'Wait and hope!' We always say that. 'Wait and hope,'
we always say. And she would wait, Copperfield, till she was sixty
—any age you mention—for me!

"In the meantime," said Traddles, "I get on as well as I can.
I don't make much, but I don't spend much. I board with the
people downstairs, who are very agreeable. Both Mr. and Mrs.
Micawber have seen a good deal of life."

"My dear Traddles!" I exclaimed. "Mr. and Mrs. Micawber!
Why, I am intimately acquainted with them!" I begged him to
ask his landlord to walk up, which he did. And Mr. Micawber,
not a bit changed—his tights, his stick, his shirt collar, and his
eyeglass, all the same—came into the room with a genteel and
youthful air.

"You find us, Copperfield," said Mr. Micawber, when we had
exchanged greetings, "established on what may be designated as
an unassuming scale; I am at present engaged in the sale of corn
upon commission. But you are no stranger to the fact that there
have been periods in my life when it has been requisite that I
should pause until certain expected events should turn up, when
it has been necessary to fall back before making what I may term
—a spring. You find me now, fallen back, *for* a spring; and I have
every reason to believe that a vigorous leap will shortly be the
result." He informed me privately that Mrs. Micawber was in a
state of health "which renders it not wholly improbable that an
addition may be ultimately made to those pledges of affection
which—in short, to the infantine group." Accordingly I declined
his invitation to dinner but appointed a day when they would all
come to me.

On the occasion of this domestic little party, I did not repeat
my former extensive preparations. I merely provided a pair of
soles, a small leg of mutton, and a pigeon pie. Mrs. Crupp broke
out into rebellion on my first bashful hint in reference to the cooking of the fish and joint and said, with a dignified sense of injury,
"No! No, sir! You will not ask me sich a thing, for you are better
acquainted with me than to suppose me capable of doing what I

cannot do with ampial satisfaction to my own feelings!" But, in the end, a compromise was effected; and Mrs. Crupp consented to achieve this feat, on condition that I dined from home for a fortnight afterward.

And here I may remark that what I underwent from Mrs. Crupp, in consequence of the tyranny she established over me, was dreadful. We made a compromise of everything. If I hesitated, she was taken with that wonderful disorder which was always lying in ambush in her system, ready to prey upon her vitals. One motion of her hand toward her nankeen bosom made me glad, at any sacrifice of brandy, to get rid of her. I would have done anything rather than give Mrs. Crupp offense; and she was the terror of my life.

I informed Mr. Micawber, when my guests arrived, that I relied upon him for a bowl of punch and led him to the lemons. The despondency with which he had just described to me a recent collision with a Minion of Power—in other words, said he, with a ribald Turncock attached to the waterworks (from which I inferred that his domestic water supply had been cut off)—was gone in a moment. I never saw a man so thoroughly enjoy himself amid the fragrance of lemon peel and sugar, the odor of burning rum, and the steam of boiling water as Mr. Micawber did that afternoon.

I suppose—I never ventured to inquire, but I suppose—that Mrs. Crupp, after frying the soles, was taken ill. Because we broke down at that point. The leg of mutton came up very red within and very pale without, besides having a foreign substance of a gritty nature sprinkled over it, as if it had had a fall into the ashes of that remarkable kitchen fireplace. In short, the banquet was such a failure that I should have been quite unhappy—about the failure, I mean, for I was always unhappy about Dora—if I had not been relieved by the good humor of my company and by a bright suggestion from Mr. Micawber.

"My dear friend Copperfield," said Mr. Micawber, "accidents will occur in the best regulated families. If you will allow me to remark that there are few comestibles better than a Devil and that I believe, with a little division of labor, we could accomplish a good one, this little misfortune may be repaired."

We had in my gridiron from the pantry, in a twinkling, and

immediately effected the division of labor to which Mr. Micawber had referred: Traddles cut the mutton into slices; Mr. Micawber (who could do anything of this sort to perfection) covered them with pepper, mustard, salt, and cayenne; I put them on the gridiron, turned them with a fork, and took them off, under Mr. Micawber's direction; and Mrs. Micawber heated some mushroom ketchup in a little saucepan. What with the novelty of this cooking, the excellence of it, and the bustle of it, even my appetite came back miraculously. I am ashamed to record it, but I really believe I forgot Dora for a little while. I am satisfied that Mr. and Mrs. Micawber could not have enjoyed the feast more, if they had sold a bed to provide it. Traddles laughed as heartily as he ate and worked. Indeed we all did, and I dare say there never was a greater success.

We were at the height of our enjoyment, when I was aware of a strange presence in the room, and my eyes encountered those of the staid Littimer, standing hat in hand before me. "What's the matter?" I involuntarily asked.

"I beg your pardon, sir, I was directed to come in. Is my master not here, sir?"

"No. Did he tell you you would find him here?"

"Not exactly so, sir. But I should think he might be here tomorrow, as he has not been here today."

"Is he coming up from Oxford?"

"I beg, sir," he returned respectfully, "that you will be seated and allow me to do this." With which he took the fork from my unresisting hand and bent over the gridiron, as if his whole attention were concentrated on it.

We all became in a moment the meekest of the meek before this respectable serving man. Mr. Micawber, humming a tune to show that he was quite at ease, subsided into his chair, with the handle of a hastily concealed fork sticking out of the bosom of his coat, as if he had stabbed himself. Mrs. Micawber put on a pair of brown gloves and assumed a genteel languor. When he gravely handed the mutton round, we all took some; but we merely made a show of eating it, and we all breathed more freely when he had cleared the table and was gone, though Mr. Micawber bestowed many encomiums on the absent Littimer as a most respectable fellow. "But punch, my dear Copperfield," said Mr. Micawber, tasting it, "like time and tide, waits for no man. I will drink, if you will permit me, to the days when

> *'We twa hae run about the braes*
> *And pu'd the gowans fine'*

—in a figurative point of view. I am not exactly aware," said Mr. Micawber, with the old roll in his voice, and the old indescribable air of saying something genteel, "what gowans may be, but I have no doubt that Copperfield and myself would frequently have taken a pull at them, if it had been feasible."

"As we are quite confidential here, Mr. Copperfield," said Mrs. Micawber, sipping her punch, "Mr. Traddles being a part of our domesticity, I should much like to have your opinion on Mr. Micawber's prospects. For corn," said Mrs. Micawber argumentatively, "may be gentlemanly, but it is not remunerative. Commission to the extent of two and ninepence in a fortnight cannot, however limited our ideas, be considered remunerative."

We were all greed upon that.

"Very well," said Mrs. Micawber. "Then what do I recommend? Here is Mr. Micawber with a variety of talents—*I* should say, with genius, but that may be the partiality of a wife—"

Traddles and I both murmured, "No."

"And here is Mr. Micawber without any suitable employment. Where does that responsibility rest? Clearly on society. It appears to me that what Mr. Micawber has to do is to throw down the gauntlet to society and say, in effect, 'Show me who will take that up. Let the party immediately step forward.'"

I ventured to ask Mrs. Micawber how this was to be done.

"By advertising," said Mrs. Micawber, "in all the papers. It appears to me, that what Mr. Micawber has to do is to describe himself plainly as so-and-so, with such-and-such qualifications, and to put it thus: '*Now* employ me, on remunerative terms, and address, post paid, to *W. M.*, Post Office, Camden Town.'"

"This idea of Mrs. Micawber's, my dear Copperfield," said Mr. Micawber, "is, in fact, the Leap to which I have alluded."

"Advertising is rather expensive," I remarked, dubiously.

"Exactly so!" said Mrs. Micawber, who prided herself on taking a logical view of things. "It is for that reason especially that I think Mr. Micawber ought, in justice to himself, in justice to his family, and in justice to society, to raise a certain sum of money—on a bill."

Mr. Micawber, leaning back in his chair, cast his eyes up at the ceiling; but I thought him observant of Traddles, too, and for that reason I detained Traddles as Mr. and Mrs. Micawber were departing. "Traddles," said I, "Mr. Micawber don't mean any harm, poor fellow; but if I were you, I wouldn't lend him anything."

"My dear Copperfield," returned Traddles, smiling, "I haven't got anything to lend."

"You have got a name, you know," said I.

"Oh! You call *that* something to lend?" said Traddles, with a thoughtful look. "I am very much obliged to you; but—I am afraid I have lent him that already."

"I hope there will be nothing wrong about it," said I. But on opening the letter which Mr. Micawber slipped into my hand as he left I knew that poor Traddles had been carried into the Money Market neck and heels. It was dated an hour before dinner and was couched in a sort of legal phraseology which Mr. Micawber seemed to think equivalent to winding up his affairs.

"Sir—for I dare not say my dear Copperfield,
"It is expedient that I should inform you that the undersigned is Crushed. The present communication is penned within the personal range of an individual, in a state closely bordering on intoxication, employed by a broker. That individual is in legal possession of the premises, under a distress for rent. His inventory includes, not only chattels and effects belonging to the under-signed, but also those appertaining to Mr. Thomas Traddles, whose friendly acceptance for the sum of £23 4s. 9½d. is overdue and is *not* provided for.

"After premising this much, it would be a work of supererogation to add that dust and ashes are for ever scattered

"On
"The
• "Head
"Of
"Wilkins Micawber."

Poor Traddles! I knew enough of Mr. Micawber by this time to foresee that *he* might be expected to recover the blow; but I was distressed by thoughts of Traddles and of the curate's daughter who was such a dear girl and who would wait for Traddles (ominous praise!) until she was sixty or any age that could be mentioned.

13

I was musing, half gravely and half laughing, on the character of Mr. Micawber and the old relations between us when I heard a quick step ascending the stairs. At first I thought it was Traddles coming back for something Mrs. Micawber had left behind; but as the step approached, I knew it and felt my heart beat high and the blood rush to my face, for it was Steerforth's.

I was never unmindful of Agnes, and she never left that sanctuary in my thoughts where I had placed her. But when he entered and stood before me with his hand out, the darkness that had fallen on him changed to light, and I felt ashamed of having doubted one I loved so heartily. "Why, Daisy, old boy, dumfoundered!" laughed Steerforth. "Have I detected you in another feast, you Sybarite!"

"I was so surprised at first," said I, "that I had hardly breath to greet you with, Steerforth."

"Well, the sight of me *is* good for sore eyes, as the Scotch say," replied Steerforth, "and so is the sight of you, Daisy. How are you, my bacchanal? And will you give me some supper?" While I got out the remains of the pigeon pie, he sat idly beating on a lump of coal with the poker. "I shall do it justice," he said, "for I have come from Yarmouth."

"I thought you came from Oxford?" I returned. "Littimer was here today, to inquire for you, and I understood from him that you were at Oxford; though, now I think of it, he did not say so. Have you been long at Yarmouth?"

"No," he returned. "An escapade of a week or so."

"And how are they all? Of course, little Em'ly is not married yet?"

"Not yet. Going to be, I believe—in so many weeks, or something or other. I have not seen much of 'em. By the bye"—he began feeling in his pockets—"I have a letter for you from your old nurse. Old what's-his-name's in a bad way."

"Barkis, do you mean?"

"Yes. It's all over with poor Barkis, I'm afraid." The letter was written with a plain, unaffected, homely piety that I knew to be genuine and ended with "my duty to my ever darling"—meaning myself. "It's a bad job," Steerforth said, "but the sun sets every day, and people die every minute, and we mustn't be scared by the common lot. If we failed to hold our own, because that equal foot at all men's doors was heard knocking somewhere, every object in this world would slip from us. No! Ride on! Rough shod if need be, smooth shod if that will do, but ride on! Ride on over all obstacles, and win the race!"

"And win what race?" said I.

"The race that one has started in," said he. "Ride on!"

"If your high spirits will listen to me, Steerforth," said I, "I think I will go down and see my old nurse. Wouldn't you go if you were in my place?"

His face was thoughtful, and he sat considering a little before he answered, in a low voice, "Well! Go. You can do no harm. But don't go tomorrow. Pass as much of tomorrow as you can with us at Highgate! Who knows when we may meet again, else? Come! I want you to stand between Rosa Dartle and me."

"Would you love each other too much, without me?"

"Yes, or hate," laughed Steerforth; "no matter which. Come!"

I said I would and walked with him as far as the open road. He was in great spirits; and when I looked after him going so gallantly and airily homeward, I thought of his saying, "Ride on over all obstacles, and win the race!" and wished, for the first time, that he had some worthy race to run.

We articled clerks, as germs of the patrician order of proctors, were treated with so much consideration that I was almost my own master at all times. I got leave of absence, therefore, the next day and went to Highgate, where Mrs. Steerforth was pleased to see me, and so was Rosa Dartle. But what I particularly observed was the close and attentive watch Miss Dartle kept upon me and the lurking manner in which she seemed to lie in wait for something to come out between Steerforth and me.

All day she seemed to pervade the whole house. If I talked to Steerforth, I heard her dress rustle in the gallery outside the room. When he and I engaged in exercise on the lawn, I saw her face pass from window to window, like a wandering light, until it fixed itself in one. When we all four went out walking, she closed her thin hand on my arm to keep me back, while Steerforth and his mother went on out of hearing, and then spoke to me.

"You have been a long time," she said, "without coming here. Is your profession really so engaging as to absorb your whole attention?"

I replied that I liked it well enough but that I certainly could not claim so much for it.

"Oh! then perhaps you want relief and change—excitement, and all that?" said she. "Ah! very true! But isn't it a little—eh?— for him? I don't mean you." A quick glance of her eye toward Steerforth and his mother showed me whom she meant; but beyond that I was lost. "Don't it—I don't say that it *does*, mind— don't it rather engross him? Don't it make him, perhaps, a little more remiss than usual in his visits to his blindly doting—eh?"

"It certainly is not the fact," said I, perplexed, "that I am accountable for Steerforth's having been away from home longer than usual—if he has been. I have not seen him this long while, until last night."

As she looked full at me, I saw her face grow sharper and paler and the marks of the old wound lengthen out until it cut through the disfigured lip. There was something positively awful to me in this and in the brightness of her hungry eyes, as she said, looking fixedly at me, "What is he doing? In what is that man assisting him, who never looks at me without an inscrutable falsehood in his eyes? Is it anger, is it hatred, is it pride, is it some wild fancy, is it love, *what is it*, that is leading him?" A twitching or throbbing came into the cruel mark. She put her hand upon it hurriedly and saying in a fierce, passionate way, "I swear you to secrecy about this!" said not a word more.

Mrs. Steerforth was particularly happy in her son's society that day, and Steerforth was particularly attentive to her. It was very interesting to see them together, not only on account of their mutual affection, but because of the strong personal resemblance between them. I thought it was well no serious cause of division had ever come between them, or two such natures—two such shades of the same nature—might have been harder to reconcile than the two extremest opposites in creation. The idea originated, I must confess, in a speech of Rosa Dartle's at dinner.

"Oh, but do tell me, though, somebody," she said, "because I want to know."

"Pray, pray, Rosa, do not be so mysterious," returned Mrs. Steerforth. " Don't I constantly entreat you to speak plainly, in your own natural manner?"

"Oh! then this is *not* my natural manner?" she rejoined.

"It has become a second nature," Mrs. Steerforth said. "But I remember—and so must you, I think—when your manner was not so guarded and was more trustful."

"Really? Well, that's very odd. I must study to learn frankness from—let me see—from James."

"You cannot learn frankness, Rosa," said Mrs. Steerforth quickly—for there was always some effect of sarcasm in what Rosa Dartle said—"in a better school." Then, appearing to regret having been nettled, she said kindly, "Well, my dear Rosa, what is it you want to be satisfied about?"

"Oh! it was only whether people, who are like each other in their moral constitution, are in greater danger than people not so circumstanced, supposing any serious cause of variance to arise between them, of being divided angrily and deeply?"

"I should say yes," said Steerforth.

"Should you?" she retorted. "Dear me! Thank you very much."

One other little circumstance connected with Miss Dartle I must not omit, for I had reason to remember it thereafter, when all the irremediable past was rendered plain. During the whole day Steerforth exerted himself to charm this singular creature. That he should succeed, was no surprise to me. That she should struggle against the fascinating influence of his delightful art— delightful nature I thought it then—did not surprise me either. I saw her features and her manner slowly change; I saw her try, more and more faintly, to resist the captivating power that he possessed; and finally I saw her sharp glance soften, and we all sat about the fire, talking and laughing together as if we had been children.

"She is playing her harp," Steerforth said softly, when she had left us in the dining room, "and nobody but my mother has heard her do that these three years." He said it with a curious smile, which was gone directly; and we went into the drawing room, where we found her alone.

"Don't get up," said Steerforth (which she had already done); "my dear Rosa, don't! Be kind for once, and sing us an Irish song. Let me listen as I used to do."

He did not touch her but sat himself near the harp. She stood beside it for a while, going through the motion of playing with her right hand, but not sounding it. At length she sat down, and drew it to her with one sudden action, and played and sang.

I don't know what it was, in her touch or voice, that made that song the most unearthly I have ever heard. It was as if it had never been written or set to music but sprung out of the passion within her, which found imperfect utterance in the low sounds of her voice, and crouched again when all was still. I was dumb when she leaned beside the harp again, playing it, but not sounding it, with her right hand.

A minute more, and this had roused me from my trance: Steerforth had left his seat, and gone to her, and had put his arm laughingly around her, and had said, "Come, Rosa, for the future we will love each other very much!" And she had struck him, had thrown him off with the fury of a wild cat, and had burst from the room.

When I said good night to Steerforth, I said, "I shall be gone before you wake in the morning." He was unwilling to let me go and stood, holding me out, with a hand on each of my shoulders. "Daisy, if anything should ever separate us, you must think of me at my best," he said. "Come! Let us make that bargain. Think of me at my best, if circumstances should ever part us!"

"You have no best to me, Steerforth," said I, "and no worst. You are always equally loved and cherished in my heart."

"God bless you, Daisy, and good night!" he said.

I was up with the chill dawn, and looked into his room. He was fast asleep, lying easily, with his head upon his arm. The time came in its season, when I wondered that nothing troubled his repose. But he slept—let me think of him so again—as I had often seen him sleep at school; and thus, in this silent hour, I left him.

—Never more, oh God forgive you, Steerforth! to touch that passive hand in love and friendship. Never, never more!

14

I GOT down to Yarmouth in the evening, when many of the shops were shut. But the door of Omer and Joram's was open. "I am sorry to have heard bad news of Mr. Barkis," said I to Mr. Omer. "Do you know how he is tonight?"

"The very question I should have put to you, sir," returned Mr. Omer, "but on account of delicacy. It's one of the drawbacks of our line of business. When a party's ill, we *can't* ask how the party is."

The difficulty had not occurred to me, though I had had my apprehensions, too, when I went in, of hearing the old tune.

"Bless you," said Mr. Omer, "it would be a shock that the generality of parties might not recover, to say 'Omer and Joram's compliments, and how do you find yourself this evening?' Accordingly, we're obleeged, in ascertaining how Barkis goes on, to limit ourselves to Em'ly. Minnie and Joram have just stepped down to the house now to ask her."

I inquired how little Em'ly was. "Well, sir," said Mr. Omer, "I tell you truly I shall be glad when her marriage has taken place. She's unsettled at present. Somehow she wants heart. To see her clinging to her uncle, tighter and tighter, is to see a sight. Now, you know, there's a struggle going on when that's the case."

The report his daughter and Joram brought back was that Barkis was "as bad as bad could be"; that Mr. Chillip had mournfully said that the College of Physicians, the College of Surgeons, and Apothecaries' Hall, if they were all called in together, couldn't help him. He was past both Colleges, Mr. Chillip said, and the Hall could only poison him. Hearing this, I went to the house at once, where all the family was gathered.

The coldness of little Em'ly's hand when I touched it, I can feel yet. There was a trembling upon her that I can see now. Creeping to the other side of her uncle, she bowed herself upon his breast. "It's such a loving 'art," said Mr. Peggotty, smoothing her rich hair with his great hard hand, "that it can't abear the sorrer of this. It's nat'ral in young folk, Mas'r Davy, when they're timid, like my little bird—it's nat'ral."

Peggotty took me in her arms and entreated me to come upstairs, where I found Mr. Barkis lying, mute and senseless, with his head and shoulders out of bed, half resting on the box which had cost him so much trouble. "He's a going out with the tide," said Mr. Peggotty to me. "People can't die, along the coast, except when the tide's pretty nigh out. It's ebb at half-arter three."

We remained there, watching him, a long time—hours. When he at last began to wander feebly, Mr. Peggotty whispered with much awe and reverence, "They are both a going out fast."

"Barkis, my dear!" said Peggotty.

"C. P. Barkis," he cried faintly. "No better woman anywhere."

"Look! Here's Master Davy!" said Peggotty. For he now opened his eyes.

He tried to stretch out his arm and said to me, distinctly, with a pleasant smile, "Barkis is willin'!"

And, it being low water, he went out with the tide.

After some search, Mr. Barkis's will was found in the box, at the bottom of a horse's nose bag, wherein (besides hay) was discovered an old gold watch, with chain and seals; a silver tobacco stopper, in the form of a leg; an imitation lemon, full of minute cups and saucers, which I have some idea Mr. Barkis must have purchased to present to me when I was a child and afterward found himself unable to part with; eighty-seven guineas and a half; two hundred and ten pounds; certain receipts for Bank of England stock; an old horseshoe, a bad shilling, a piece of camphor, and an oyster shell. From the circumstance of the latter having been much polished, I conclude that Mr. Barkis had some general ideas about pearls, which never resolved into anything definite.

For years and years, Mr. Barkis had carried this box on all his journeys, every day. That it might the better escape notice, he had invented a fiction that it belonged to "Mr. Blackboy" and was "to be left with Barkis till called for." He had hoarded to good purpose, leaving nearly three thousand pounds, two-thirds of it to Peggotty; the interest of one thousand pounds was bequeathed to Mr. Peggotty for life, the principal then to be divided between Peggotty, little Em'ly, and me.

I did not attend the funeral in character, if I may venture to say so. I mean I was not dressed up in a black cloak and a streamer, to frighten the birds. But I walked over to Blunderstone early in the morning and was in the churchyard when Peggotty and her brother came. We walked about the churchyard for an hour, after all was over, and pulled some young leaves from the tree above my mother's grave.

A dread falls on me here. A cloud is lowering on the distant town, toward which I retraced my solitary steps. I fear to approach it. I cannot bear to think of what did come, upon that memorable night, of what must come again, as I go on.

Mr. Peggotty's house looked very comfortable indeed that night. The fire was bright; the locker was ready for little Em'ly in her old place; in *her* old place sat Peggotty once more. Mrs. Gummidge appeared to be fretting a little, in her old corner, and consequently looked quite natural, too. "You're the first of the lot, Mas'r Davy!" said Mr. Peggotty with a happy face. He rose and put a candle in the window. "Theer we are, Missis Gummidge!" Mrs. Gummidge slightly groaned. "Lighted up accordin' to custom! It's fur our little Em'ly, sir. When I'm here at the hour she's a comin' home, I puts the light in the winder. That, you see, meets two objects. She says, says Em'ly, 'Theer's home!' she says. And likewise, says Em'ly, 'My uncle's theer!'"

"You're a baby!" said Peggotty, very fond of him for it.

"Well," returned Mr. Peggotty, "I doen't know but I am. Not to look at, but to—to consider on, you know. I'm Gormed if I doen't feel as if the littlest things of hers was her, almost. I takes 'em up and I puts 'em down, and I touches of 'em as delicate as if they was our Em'ly. There's a babby for you, in the form of a great Sea Porkypine!" said Mr. Peggotty, with a roar of laughter. "Why, at the present minute, when I see the candle sparkle up, I says to myself, 'She's a looking at it! Em'ly's a coming!' *There's* a babby for you, in the form of a Sea Porkypine! Right for all that," said Mr. Peggotty, smiting his hands together, "fur here she is."

It was only Ham, with a large sou'wester hat on, slouched over his face. "Mas'r Davy, will you come out a minute, and see what Em'ly and me has got to show you?" he said.

We went out. As I passed him I saw, to my astonishment, that he was deadly pale. He pushed me hastily into the open air and closed the door on us. "Ham! what's the matter?"

"Mas'r Davy!" Oh, for his broken heart, how dreadfully he

wept! "Mas'r Davy, my love—the pride and hope of my 'art—her that I'd have died for—she's gone!"

"Gone!"

"Em'ly's run away! Oh, think *how* she's run away, when I pray God to kill her (her that is so dear above all things) sooner than let her come to ruin and disgrace! How am I ever to break it to him, Mas'r Davy?"

I saw the door move and instinctively tried to hold the latch on the outside. It was too late. Mr. Peggotty thrust forth his face; and never could I forget the change that came upon it when he saw us, if I lived five hundred years. I remember a great wail and cry, and a paper in my hand, which Ham had given me. "Read it, sir," Mr. Peggotty said, in a low, shivering voice. "Slow, please."

In the midst of the silence of death, I read thus, from a blotted letter:

" 'When you, who loved me so much better than I ever have deserved, even when my mind was innocent, see this, I shall be far away. When I leave my dear home—my dear home—oh, my dear home!—in the morning—it will be never to come back, unless he brings me back a lady. This will be found at night, many hours after, instead of me. Oh, if you knew how my heart is torn. Oh, take comfort in thinking that I am so bad. Oh, for mercy's sake, tell uncle that I never loved him half so dear as now. Oh, don't remember how affectionate and kind you have all been to me—don't remember we were ever to be married—but try to think as if I died when I was little and was buried somewhere. Love some good girl, that will be what I was once to uncle and be true to you and worthy of you, and know no shame but me. God bless all! If he don't bring me back a lady and I don't pray for my own self, I'll pray for all. My parting love to uncle. My last tears, and my last thanks, for uncle!' "

Slowly, at last, Mr. Peggotty said, in a low voice, "Who's the man? I want to know his name." Ham glanced at me, and suddenly I felt a shock that struck me back. "There's a man suspected," said Mr. Peggotty. "Who is it?"

"Mas'r Davy!" implored Ham. "Go out a bit. You doesn't ought to hear it, sir."

I felt the shock again. I sank down in a chair; my tongue was fettered.

"I want to know his name!" I heard said, once more.

"For some time past," Ham faltered, "there's been a servant about here, at odd times. There's been a gen'l'm'n too. Both of 'em belong to one another. The servant was seen along with—our poor girl—last night. He's been in hiding about here.—Doen't stay, Mas'r Davy, doen't!"

I felt Peggotty's arm round my neck, but I could not move.

"A strange chay and hosses was outside town this morning. The servant went to it and come from it and went to it again, with Em'ly. The t'other was inside. He's the man."

"For the Lord's love," said Mr. Peggotty, falling back and putting out his hand. "Doen't tell me his name's Steerforth!"

"Mas'r Davy," exclaimed Ham, in a broken voice, "it ain't no fault of yourn—but his name is Steerforth, and he's a damned villain!"

Mr. Peggotty uttered no cry and shed no tear and moved no more, until he seemed to wake again, all at once, and pulled down his rough coat from its peg. Ham asked him whither he was going.

"I'm a going to seek my niece. I'm a going to seek my Em'ly through the wureld. I'm a going, first, to stave in that theer boat and sink it where I would have drownded *him* if I had had one thought of what was in him!"

"No, no!" cried Mrs. Gummidge, in a fit of crying. "Not as you are now, Dan'l. Seek her in a little while, my lone lorn Dan'l, but not as you are now. Sit ye down, and give me your forgiveness for having ever been a worrit to you, Dan'l—what have *my* contrairies ever been to this!—and let us speak about them times when she was first an orphan, and Ham was too, and you took us in. It'll soften your poor heart, Dan'l, and you'll bear your sorrow better; for you know the promise 'As you have done it unto one of the least of these, you have done it unto me,' and that can never fail under this roof that's been our shelter for so many, many year!"

"We have had a mort of talk, sir," said Mr. Peggotty next morning, "of what we ought and doen't ought to do. But we see our course now. My dooty here is done. I'm a going to seek my—" He stopped and went on in a firmer voice, "I'm a going to seek her. That's my dooty evermore. Ham'll hold to his present work and live along with my sister. The old boat—my wishes is, sir, as it shall look, day and night, winter and summer, as it has always looked, since she fust know'd it. Then, maybe, seein' none but Missis Gummidge here, she might take heart to creep in, trembling, and rest her weary head.

"Every night," said Mr. Peggotty, "as reg'lar as the night comes, the candle must be stood in its old place, that if ever she should see it, it may seem to say, 'Come back, my child, come back!'"

Mrs. Gummidge spoke so comfortably and softly that I hardly knew her. "All times and seasons, you know, Dan'l," she said, "I shall be allus here, and everythink will look accordin' to your wishes."

"You'll be a solitary woman, I'm afeerd!" said Mr. Peggotty.

"No, no, Dan'l," she returned, "I shan't be that. Doen't you mind me. I shall have enough to do to keep a beein' for you" (Mrs. Gummidge meant a home) "again you come back." What a change in Mrs. Gummidge in a little time! She was another woman. The work she did that day! As to deploring her misfortunes, she appeared to have entirely lost the recollection of ever having had any. I left her, when I went away that night, the prop and staff of Mr. Peggotty's affliction, and I could not meditate enough upon the lesson that I read in her.

I was sitting alone at Peggotty's that evening when I heard a knock low down upon the door. I opened it and at first looked down, to my amazement, on nothing but a great umbrella that appeared to be walking about of itself. But presently I discovered, underneath it, Miss Mowcher. When I relieved her of the umbrella (which would have been an inconvenient one for the Irish giant), she wrung her little hands in such an afflicted manner that I exclaimed, "What is the matter? Are you ill?"

"My dear young soul," returned Miss Mowcher, squeezing her hands upon her heart, "I am ill here, I am very ill. To think that I might have known it and prevented it, if I hadn't been a thoughtless fool!"

"I am surprised," I began, "to see you so distressed and serious—" when she interrupted me. "Yes, it's always so," she said. "They are all surprised to see any natural feeling in a little thing like me! Take a word of advice, even from three foot nothing. Try not to associate bodily defects with mental, except for good reason.

"If I had shown myself a sensitive dwarf to your false friend," pursued the little woman, with reproachful earnestness, "how much of his good will do you think *I* should ever have had? If I am a plaything for you giants, be gentle with me." Looking at me with a very intent expression, she said, "Do you remember what Steerforth said to me about this unfortunate girl, that time when I saw you both? I believed it was *you* who had a boyish passion for her! That wicked servant told me that 'Young Innocence' (so he called you) had set his heart upon her, but his master was resolved that no harm should come of it. They deceived me altogether, and I gave the poor girl a letter, which I fully believe was the beginning of her ever speaking to Littimer, who was left behind on purpose. I have some reason to suspect, from what I have heard, that they are gone abroad. But if ever they return, I am more likely than another, going about as I do, to find it out soon. Whatever I know, you shall know. And Littimer had better have a bloodhound at his back than little Mowcher!"

Next day Peggotty and Mr. Peggotty returned with me to London, and I took them home to tea; a proceeding, I regret to state, which did not meet with Mrs. Crupp's approval. I ought to observe, however, in explanation, that she was much offended by Peggotty's tucking up her widow's gown and setting to work to dust my bedroom. This Mrs. Crupp regarded in the light of a liberty, and a liberty, she said, was a thing she never allowed.

Mr. Peggotty purposed first seeing Mrs. Steerforth. As I felt bound to assist him in this, I went with him to that house where I had been, a few days since, so happy.

"I know, with deep regret," said Mrs. Steerforth, "what has brought you here. What do you want of me?" Mr. Peggotty gave her Emily's letter. "Please to read that, ma'am," he said. "That's my niece's hand."

She read it, sitting upright in her chair, with a stately, immovable air—untouched by its contents, as far as I could see—and returned it to him.

"'Unless he brings me back a lady,'" said Mr. Peggotty. "I come to know, ma'am, whether he will keep his wured?"

"No," she returned.

"Why not?" said Mr. Peggotty.

"It is impossible. He would disgrace himself. You cannot fail to know that she is far below him."

"Raise her up!" said Mr. Peggotty.

"She is uneducated and ignorant. Since you oblige me to speak plainly, her humble connections would render such a thing impossible, if nothing else did."

"Hark to this, ma'am," he returned, slowly and quietly. "You know what it is to love your child. So do I. You doen't know what it is to lose your child. I do. But save her from this disgrace, and she shall never be disgraced by us. Not one of us that's lived along with her and had her for their all these many year will ever look upon her pritty face again. We'll be content to trust her to her husband—to her little children, p'raps—and bide the time when all of us shall be alike in quality afore our God!"

The rugged eloquence with which he spoke was not devoid of all effect. She still preserved her proud manner, but there was a touch of softness in her voice as she answered, "I justify nothing. But it is impossible. Such a marriage would irretrievably ruin my son's career. Nothing is more certain than that it never can take place, and never will. If there is any other compensation—"

"I am looking at the likeness of a face," interrupted Mr. Peggotty, with a steady but a kindling eye, "that has looked at me, at my fireside, smiling and friendly, when it was so treacherous that I go half wild when I think of it. If the likeness of that face don't turn to burning fire, at the thought of offering money to me for my child's flight and ruin, it's as bad."

She changed now, in a moment, as she said, in an intolerant manner, "What compensation can you make *me* for opening such a pit between me and my son? What is your love to mine? What is your separation to ours? If he can stake his all upon the lightest object, I can stake my all upon a greater purpose. Let him put away his whim now, and he is welcome back. Let him not put her away now, and he shall never come near me, living or dying." She rose with an air of dignity to leave the room; but Mr. Peggotty signified that it was needless, and we departed. Before we left the house, however, Rosa Dartle intercepted me.

"You do well," she said, "indeed, to bring this fellow here!" Such a concentration of rage and scorn as darkened her face I could not have thought compressible even into that face. When the throbbing I had seen before came into her scar, she absolutely lifted up her hand and struck it.

"He is a deeply injured man, Miss Dartle," I replied. "You may not know it."

"I know that James Steerforth," she said, "has a false, corrupt heart and is a traitor. But what need I know or care about this fellow, or his common niece? They are a depraved, worthless set. I would have her whipped! If I could hunt her to her grave, I would." I have seen passion in many forms, but never such as that.

That night Mr. Peggotty set out on his travels. Rarely thereafter did I look up at the moon or stars or watch the falling rain or hear the wind but I thought of his solitary figure toiling on, poor pilgrim, and recalled his parting words.

"I'm a going to seek her, fur and wide. If any hurt should come to me, remember that the last words I left for her was 'My unchanged love is with my darling child, and I forgive her!'"

15

Taking the management of Peggotty's affairs into my own hands, with no little pride, I proved the will and came to a settlement with the Legacy Duty Office and soon got everything into an orderly train. When I took her down to our office to pay her bill, Mr. Spenlow had stepped out, the clerk told me, to get a gentleman sworn for a marriage license. And when he came back, neither Peggotty nor I had eyes for him when we saw, in company with him, Mr. Murdstone!

"Rather a good marriage this, I believe?" said Mr. Spenlow when he had gone.

I explained that I knew nothing about it.

"I understand there's money," he said. "Beauty too, I am told."

"Indeed! Is his new wife young?"

"Just of age," said Mr. Spenlow. "I should think they had been waiting for that."

"Lord deliver her!" said Peggotty. So very emphatically and unexpectedly, that we were all three discomposed.

All this time, I had gone on loving Dora harder than ever. When Mr. Spenlow told me that this day week was Dora's birthday and he would be glad if I would join a little picnic on the occasion, I went out of my senses immediately. I turn hot when I remember the cravat I bought. My boots might be placed in any collection of instruments of torture. At six in the morning of the appointed day, I was in Covent Garden Market, buying a bouquet. At ten I was on horseback (I had hired a gallant gray for the occasion), trotting down to Norwood.

I suppose that when I saw Dora in the garden and pretended not to see her, I committed a foolery which other young gentlemen might have committed. But oh! when I did drag those stony-hearted boots across the garden, what a spectacle she was, among the butterflies, in a white chip bonnet and a dress of clestial blue! There was a young lady with her—comparatively stricken in years—almost twenty, I should say. Her name was Miss Mills, and Dora called her Julia. She was the bosom friend of Dora. I learned that Miss Mills had had her trials in the course of a checkered existence, having been unhappy in a misplaced affection, and that she was understood to have retired from the world on her awful stock of experience but still to take a calm interest in the unblighted hopes and loves of youth.

It was a trying thing to find other people at the picnic spot, waiting for us. All of my own sex—especially one impostor, three or four years my elder, with a red whisker, on which he established an amount of presumption not to be endured—were my mortal foes. Red Whisker pretended he could make a salad (which I don't believe) and obtruded himself on public notice. Some of the young ladies washed the lettuces for him and sliced them under his direction. Dora was among these. I felt that fate had pitted me against this man, and one of us must fall. By and by I saw him with the majority of a lobster on his plate, eating his dinner at the feet of Dora!

I have but an indistinct idea of what happened after this. I was very merry, I know; but it was hollow merriment. I attached myself to a young creature in pink and flirted with her desperately. Then I strolled off by myself among the trees, in a raging state, where Dora and Miss Mills met me.

"Mr. Copperfield," said Miss Mills, "you are dull."

I begged her pardon. Not at all.

"And Dora," said Miss Mills, "*you* are dull."

Oh dear no! Not in the least.

"Mr. Copperfield and Dora," said Miss Mills, with an almost venerable air, "enough of this. Do not allow a trivial misunderstanding to wither the blossoms of spring, which, once put forth and blighted, cannot be renewed. I speak," said Miss Mills, "from experience of the past—the irrevocable past."

I hardly knew what I did, but I took Dora's little hand and kissed it—and she let me! All too soon we heard the others calling, "Where's Dora?" They wanted Dora to sing. Red Whisker would have got the guitar case out of the carriage, but Dora told him nobody knew where it was, but I; and *I* got it, and *I* sat by her, and *I* held her handkerchief and gloves, and *I* drank in every note of her dear voice, and she sang to *me* who loved her! That sagacious, amiable Miss Mills, too; what a kind thing *she* did! "Dora is coming to stay with me," she told me. "If you would like to call,

I am sure papa would be happy to see you!" I invoked a blessing on Miss Mills's head and stored her address in my memory.

When I awoke next morning, I was resolute to declare my passion to Dora and know my fate. Happiness or misery was now the question. Arrayed for the purpose at vast expense, I went to Miss Mills's, fraught with a declaration.

How many times I went up and down the street and round the square before I could persuade myself to go in is no matter now. Mr. Mills was not at home. I did not expect he would be. Nobody wanted *him*. Miss Mills was at home. I was shown into a room where Miss Mills and Dora were. Jip was there. Miss Mills was copying music, and Dora was painting flowers. Miss Mills was conversational for a few minutes and then left the room.

I began to think I would put it off till tomorrow.

"I hope your poor horse was not tired, when he got home last night," said Dora, lifting up her beautiful eyes. "It was a long way for him."

I began to think I would do it today.

"It was a long way for *him*," said I, "for *he* had nothing to uphold him on the journey."

"Wasn't he fed, poor thing?" asked Dora.

I began to think I would put it off till tomorrow.

"Ye-yes," I said, "he was well taken care of. I mean he had not the unutterable happiness that I had in being so near you."

Dora bent her head over her drawing and said, after a little while—I had sat in the interval, in a burning fever, and with my legs in a very rigid state—"You didn't seem to be sensible of that happiness yourself, at one time of the day."

I saw now that I was in for it, and it must be done on the spot.

"You didn't care for that happiness in the least," said Dora, "when you were sitting by Miss Kitt." Kitt, I should observe, was the name of the creature in pink. "Though certainly I don't know why you should," said Dora, "or why you should call it happiness at all. But of course you don't mean what you say. And I am sure no one doubts your being at liberty to do whatever you like. Jip, you naughty boy, come here!"

I don't know how I did it. I did it in a moment. I intercepted Jip. I had Dora in my arms. I was full of eloquence. I told her how I loved her. I told her I should die without her. I told her that I idolized and worshiped her. Jip barked madly all the time. When Dora hung her head and cried and trembled, my eloquence increased so much the more. Lovers had loved before, and lovers would love again; but no lover had ever loved, might, could, would, or should ever love, as I loved Dora. The more I raved, the more Jip barked. Each of us, in his own way, got more mad every moment.

Well, well! Dora and I were sitting on the sofa by and by, quiet enough, and Jip was lying on her lap. It was off my mind. I was in a state of perfect rapture. Dora and I were engaged. I suppose we had some notion that this was to end in marriage. But in our youthful ecstasy we were to keep our secret from Mr. Spenlow.

What an idle time it was! What an unsubstantial, happy, foolish time! Of all the times of mine that Time has in his grip, there is none that in one retrospect I can smile at half so much and think of half so tenderly.

I wrote to Agnes as soon as Dora and I were engaged, entreating her not to regard this as a thoughtless passion which could ever yield to any other. And somehow, as the remembrance of her clear, calm eyes and gentle face came stealing over me, it shed such a peaceful influence upon the hurry and agitation in which I had been living lately that it soothed me into tears. As if in love, joy, sorrow, hope, or disappointment, in all emotions, my heart turned naturally there and found its refuge and best friend.

I also hinted something to Traddles of my state, to explain why I had not seen him for some time. "Mine, perhaps you recollect," said Traddles, "lives down in Devonshire—one of ten. Consequently, I am not so much engaged as you—in that sense."

"I wonder you can bear," I returned, "to see her so seldom."

"Hah!" said Traddles thoughtfully. "It does seem a wonder. I suppose it is, Copperfield, because there's no help for it?"

"I suppose so," I replied with a smile, and not without a blush. "Is she the eldest?" I inquired.

"Oh dear, no," said Traddles. "The eldest is a Beauty. Not, of course, but that my Sophy—pretty name, Copperfield, I always think?—is beautiful too, in my eyes. But when I say the eldest is a Beauty, I mean she really is something very uncommon indeed! Then, you know, being formed for society and not being able to enjoy much of it in consequence of their limited means, she naturally gets a little irritable and exacting, sometimes. Sophy puts her in good humor!"

"Is Sophy the youngest?" I hazarded.

"Oh dear, no!" said Traddles. "The two youngest are only nine and ten. Sophy educates 'em."

"The second daughter, perhaps?" I hazarded.

"No," said Traddles. "Sarah's the second. Sarah has something the matter with her spine, poor girl. Sophy nurses her. Sophy is the fourth."

"Is the mother living?" I inquired.

"Oh yes," said Traddles, "she is alive. She is a very superior woman indeed, but the damp country is not adapted to her constitution, and—in fact, she has lost the use of her limbs. But in a merely domestic view it is not so bad as it might be, because Sophy takes her place. She is quite as much a mother *to* her mother, as she is to the other nine."

I next inquired how Mr. Micawber was. "He is quite well, Copperfield, thank you," said Traddles. "I am not living with him at present. The truth is, he has changed his name to Mortimer, in consequence of his temporary embarrassments; and he don't come out till after dark—and then in spectacles. There was an execution put into our house, for rent."

This reminds me that, in my own house, Mrs. Crupp had resigned everything appertaining to her office (the salary excepted) until Peggotty should cease to present herself. Mrs. Crupp, after holding divers conversations respecting Peggotty, in a very high pitched voice, on the staircase, addressed a letter to me, developing her views. Beginning it with that statement of universal application, that she was a mother herself, she went on to inform me that at all periods of her existence she had had a constitutional objection to spies, intruders, and informers. She named no names, she said; but spies, intruders, and informers, *especially in widders' weeds*, she had ever accustomed herself to look down upon; and she stipulated that she should not be "brought in contract" with such persons. After which, she confined herself to making pitfalls on the stairs, principally with pitchers, and endeavoring to delude Peggotty into breaking her legs. I found it rather harassing to live

in this state of siege but was too much afraid of Mrs. Crupp to see any way out of it.

What was my amazement, therefore, on coming home with Peggotty one day, to note the sudden disappearance of the pitfalls. And what was my joy to find my aunt in my sitting room, and Mr. Dick; my aunt sitting on a quantity of luggage, with her cat on her knee, like a female Robinson Crusoe, drinking tea; Mr. Dick leaning thoughtfully on a great kite, with more luggage piled about him!

We cordially embraced. "Hullo!" said my aunt to Peggotty, who quailed before her awful presence. "How are *you?*"

"You remember my aunt, Peggotty?" said I.

"For the love of goodness, child," exclaimed my aunt, "don't call the woman by that South Sea Island name! If she married and got rid of it, why don't you give her the benefit of the change? What's your name now—P?" said my aunt, as a compromise for the obnoxious appellation.

"Barkis, ma'am," said Peggotty, with a curtsy.

·"Well! That's human," said my aunt. "It sounds less as if you wanted a missionary. How d'ye do, Barkis?"

"Let me draw the sofa here, or the easy chair, aunt," said I. "Why should you be so uncomfortable?"

"Thank you, Trot," replied my aunt, "I prefer to sit upon my property." Here my aunt looked hard at Mrs. Crupp and observed, "We needn't trouble you to wait, ma'am."

"Shall I put a little more tea in the pot afore I go, ma'am?" said Mrs. Crupp. "Would you let me fetch another pat of butter? Or would you be persuaded to try a new-laid hegg? Ain't there nothing I could do for your dear aunt, Mr. Copperfull?"

"Nothing, ma'am," returned my aunt. "I shall do very well, I thank you." Mrs. Crupp, who had been incessantly smiling to express sweet temper and incessantly holding her head on one side to express a general feebleness of constitution and incessantly rubbing her hands to express a desire to be of service, gradually smiled herself, one-sided herself, and rubbed herself, out of the room.

"Dick!" said my aunt. "You know what I told you about time servers and wealth worshipers? Mrs. Crupp is one of them." I noticed how her eye lighted on me, when she thought my attention otherwise occupied, and what a curious process of hesitation appeared to be going on within her.

"Trot," she said at last, "Trot, have you got to be firm and self-reliant?"

"I think so, aunt."

"Then why, my love," said my aunt, looking earnestly at me, "why do you think I prefer to sit upon this property of mine tonight?"

I shook my head, unable to guess.

"Because," said my aunt, "it's all I have. Because I'm ruined, my dear. All I have in the world is in this room except the cottage; and that I have left Janet to let. We must meet reverses boldly and not suffer them to frighten us, my dear. We must learn to act the play out. We must live misfortune down, Trot!"

16

"TROT, my dear," said my aunt, when she saw me preparing to compound her usual night draught that evening, "not wine. Ale."

"But there is wine here, aunt. And you always have it made of wine."

"Keep that in case of sickness," said my aunt. "We mustn't use it carelessly. Ale for me. Half a pint." She drank it with quiet enjoyment, soaking her strips of toast in it. "Trot," said she, "I don't care for strange faces in general, but I rather like that Barkis of yours, do you know! She is uncommonly fond of you. Here the poor fool has been begging and praying about handing over some of her money—because she has got too much of it. A simpleton!" My aunt's tears of pleasure positively trickled down.

"Ah! Mercy upon us!" she sighed presently. "I know all about it, Trot! Barkis and myself have had quite a gossip. So you fancy yourself in love, do you?"

"Fancy, aunt!" I exclaimed, as red as I could be. "I adore her with my whole soul!"

"Dora, indeed!" returned my aunt. "And you mean to say the little thing is very fascinating, I suppose? And not silly?"

"Silly, aunt!" I seriously believe it had never once entered my head for a moment to consider whether she was or not. I resented the idea, of course, but I was in a manner struck by it, as a new one altogether.

"Well, well!" said my aunt. "I only ask. I don't depreciate her. Poor little couple! And so you think you were formed for one another and are to go through a party-supper-table kind of life, like two pretty pieces of confectionery, do you, Trot?" She asked me this so kindly and with such a gentle air, half playful and half sorrowful, that I was quite touched. "Ah, Trot! blind, blind, blind!

"Some one I know, Trot," my aunt pursued, after a pause, "though of a very pliant disposition, has an earnestness of affection in him that reminds me of poor Baby. Earnestness is what that Somebody must look for, to sustain him and improve him, Trot. Deep, downright, faithful earnestness."

"If you only knew the earnestness of Dora, aunt!" I cried.

"Oh, Trot!" she said again, "blind, blind!" and, without knowing why, I felt a vague loss or want of something, overshadowing me like a cloud.

How miserable I was when I lay down! How I thought and thought about my being poor in Mr. Spenlow's eyes! About my not being what I thought I was, when I proposed to Dora; about the chivalrous necessity of releasing Dora from her engagement, if she thought fit; about how I should contrive to live, during the long term of my articles, when I was earning nothing. I came to the conclusion that I ought to try if my articles could be canceled and the premium recovered. Accordingly I approached Mr. Spenlow the next morning.

"I am sorry to say," said I, "that I have some rather disheartening intelligence from my aunt. She has met with some large losses. In fact, she has very little left, indeed."

"You as-tound me, Copperfield!" cried Mr. Spenlow.

"Indeed, sir," said I, "her affairs are so changed that I wished to ask you whether it would be possible, at a sacrifice on our part of some portion of the premium, of course"—I put in this, on the spur of the moment, warned by the blank expression of his face—"to cancel my articles?"

"I am extremely sorry to hear this, Copperfield," said Mr. Spenlow. "It is not usual to cancel articles. At the same time—"

"You are very good, sir," I murmured, anticipating a concession.

"Not at all. Don't mention it," said Mr. Spenlow. "At the same time, I was going to say, if it had been my lot to have my hands unfettered—if I had not a partner—Mr. Jorkins—"

My hopes were dashed in a moment, but I made another effort. "Do you think, sir," said I, "if I were to mention it to Mr. Jorkins—" Mr. Spenlow shook his head. "Mr. Jorkins is very hard to move from the beaten track, Copperfield," he said. "But mention it if you will."

Evidently astonishing Mr. Jorkins very much, I went up to his room and stated my case. "You have mentioned this to Mr. Spenlow, I suppose?" said Mr. Jorkins. "He said I should object?" I was obliged to admit that he had considered it probable. "I am sorry to say, Mr. Copperfield, I can't advance your object," Mr.

Jorkins said, nervously. "If Mr. Spenlow objects—hopeless! I—I have got an appointment at the bank." With that he fairly ran away; and to the best of my knowledge it was three days before he showed himself in the Commons again.

In a state of despondency I then went home, where I found a welcome visitor—Agnes. My aunt had written her that she had fallen into adversity, and Agnes had come to London to see her, there being a mutual liking between them. She was not alone, she said. Her papa was with her—and Uriah Heep. "I do not like to leave papa alone with him," she explained.

"Does he exercise the same influence over Mr. Wickfield still, Agnes?"

Agnes shook her head. "There is such a change at home," said she, "that you would scarcely know the dear old house. They live with us now—Mr. Heep and his mother. The chief evil of that is that I cannot be as near papa as I could wish—Uriah Heep being so much between us. But if any fraud or treachery is practicing against him, I hope that simple love and truth will be stronger in the end. I hope that real love and truth will be stronger in the end than any evil or misfortune in the world."

A certain bright smile, which I never saw on any other face, died away, even while I thought how good it was; and, looking attentively at my aunt, Agnes asked how the reverse in her circumstances had come about.

"Betsey Trotwood," said my aunt, who had always kept her money matters to herself,"—I don't mean your sister, Trot, but myself—had a certain property. Betsey funded her property for some time; but, thinking she was wiser, now, than her man of business, who was not such a good man of business as he used to be—I am alluding to your father, Agnes—she took it into her head to lay it out for herself. First, she lost in the mining way, and then she lost in the diving way—fishing up treasure, or some such Tom Tiddler nonsense," explained my aunt, rubbing her nose; "and then, to set the thing entirely to rights, she lost in the banking way. And there's an end of that."

Agnes had listened at first with suspended breath. Her color still came and went, but she breathed more freely. I knew why. She had had some fear that her unhappy father might be in some way to blame for what had happened. My aunt took her hand in hers. "Now, Trot and Agnes," she said, "what's to be done?"

"I have been thinking, Trotwood," said Agnes, diffidently, "that if you had time—"

"I have a good deal of time. I am always disengaged after four or five o'clock, and I have time early in the morning," said I.

"I know you would not mind," said Agnes, "the duties of a secretary. Dr. Strong has retired and come to live in London; and he asked papa to recommend him one. He would rather have his favorite old pupil near him than anyone."

"Dear Agnes!" said I. "You are always my good angel."

Just then a knock came at the door. "I think," said Agnes, "it's papa." I opened the door, and admitted, not only Mr. Wickfield, but Uriah Heep. I had not seen Mr. Wickfield for some time. I was prepared for a great change in him; but the reversal of the two natures, in their relative positions, Uriah's of power and Mr. Wickfield's of dependence, was a sight more painful to me than I can express. If I had seen an ape taking command of a man, I should hardly have thought it a more degrading spectacle.

"Well, Wickfield!" said my aunt, and he looked up at her for the first time. "I have been telling your daughter how well I have been disposing of my money for myself, because I couldn't trust it to you. We have been taking counsel together. Agnes is worth the whole firm, in my opinion."

"If I may umbly make the remark," said Uriah Heep, with a writhe, "I fully agree with Miss Betsey Trotwood and should be only too appy if Miss Agnes was a partner."

"You're a partner yourself, you know," returned my aunt, "and that's about enough for you, I expect." He had jerked himself about, after his compliment, in such an intolerable manner that my aunt had lost all patience.

"I ask your pardon, Miss Trotwood," returned Uriah; "I'm aware you're nervous."

"Go along with you, sir!" said my aunt. "Don't presume to say so! I am nothing of the sort. If you're an eel, sir, conduct yourself like one. If you're a man, control your limbs, sir! Good God!" said my aunt, with great indignation, "I am not going to be serpentined and corkscrewed out of my senses!"

Mr. Heep was rather abashed, as most people might have

been, by this explosion and left shortly after; when Mr. Wickfield soon became more like himself, though there was a settled depression upon him which he never shook off.

And how Agnes spoke to me of Dora, listened to my praises of her, praised again, and round the little fairy figure shed some glimpses of her own pure light that made it yet more precious and more innocent to me! Oh, Agnes, sister of my boyhood, if I had known then, what I knew long afterward!

There was a beggar in the street when I went down with them, and he made me start by muttering, as if he were an echo of the morning,

"Blind! Blind! Blind!"

I began the next day with a visit to Dr. Strong. My whole manner of thinking of our late misfortune was changed. What I had to do was to show my aunt that her past goodness to me had not been thrown away. What I had to do was to take my woodman's ax in my hand and clear my own way through the forest of difficulty by cutting down the trees until I came to Dora. I got into such a transport that I felt quite sorry my coat was not a little shabby already. I wanted to be cutting at those trees.

"Now, my dear Copperfield," the Doctor said, "in reference to this proposal of yours. It's very gratifying, but don't you think you could do better? What's seventy pounds a year?"

"It doubles our income, Dr. Strong," said I.

"Dear me!" replied the Doctor. "Not that I mean to say it's rigidly limited to seventy pounds, because I have always contemplated making any young friend I might thus employ a present too."

"My dear tutor," said I, "if you will take such time as I have and can think it worth seventy pounds a year, you will do me such a service as I cannot express."

"Then be it so," said the Doctor. "And when you can do better, you will? On your word, now?" "On my word, sir!" I returned, answering in our old school manner.

I was pretty busy now, up at five in the morning, and home at nine or ten at night. But I had infinite satisfaction in being so engaged, and never walked slowly on any account, and felt enthusiastically that the more I tired myself the more I was doing to deserve Dora. I had not yet revealed myself to her in my altered character, because she was coming to see Miss Mills in a few days, and I deferred all I had to tell her until then.

Not satisfied with all these proceedings, I went to see Traddles, because I had heard that many men distinguished in various pursuits had begun life by reporting the debates in Parliament, and I wished to know how I could qualify myself for this pursuit. Traddles informed me that the mere mechanical acquisition necessary was about equal in difficulty to the mastery of six languages. But I, only feeling that here were a few tall trees to be hewn down, immediately resolved to work my way to Dora through this thicket, ax in hand. "I'll begin tomorrow," I told Traddles, whereupon he took me with him to dine with the Micawbers.

"My dear Copperfield," said Mr. Micawber when we arrived, "yourself and Mr. Traddles find us on the brink of migration. We are going to a cathedral town. In fact, to Canterbury. I have entered into arrangements, by virtue of which I stand pledged and contracted to our friend Heep, to assist and serve him in the capacity of—and to be—his confidential clerk."

I stared at Mr. Micawber, who greatly enjoyed my surprise.

"I am bound to state," he said, with an official air, "that the business habits of Mrs. Micawber have in a great measure conduced to this result. The gauntlet, to which Mrs. Micawber referred on a former occasion, being thrown down in the form of an advertisement, was taken up by my friend Heep and led to a mutual recognition. Such address and intelligence as I chance to possess," said Mr. Micawber, with the old genteel air, "will be devoted to my friend Heep's service. I have already some acquaintance with the law—as a defendant on civil process—and I shall immediately apply myself to the "Commentaries" of Mr. Justice Blackstone."

"What I particularly request Mr. Micawber to be careful of, is," said Mrs. Micawber, "that he does not, in applying himself to this subordinate branch of the law, place it out of his power to rise, ultimately, to the top of the tree. Now, for example, a judge, or even say a chancellor—" Indeed, I quite believe that Mr. Micawber saw himself, in his judicial mind's eye, on the woolsack.

"Whatever station in society I may attain," said he in a parting speech, "I shall endeavor not to disgrace, and Mrs. Micawber will be safe to adorn. Under the temporary pressure of pecuniary liabilities, I have been under the necessity of assuming a garb from which my natural instincts recoil—I allude to spectacles—and possessing myself of a cognomen to which I can establish no legitimate pretensions. All I have to say on that score is that the cloud has passed from the dreary scene, and the God of Day is once more high upon the mountain tops. On Monday next, on the arrival of the four o'clock afternoon coach at Canterbury, my foot will be on my native heath—my name, Micawber!"

17

THE time had now come for Peggotty to return home. Although Mrs. Crupp thereupon transferred her hostile attentions to my aunt, who had joined me in my chambers, and expressed her intention of bringing some of my aunt's accusations before a "British Judy"—meaning, I suppose, the bulwark of our national liberties—my aunt obtained a signal victory over her by paying her off, throwing the first pitcher she planted on the stairs out of the window, and protecting in person, up and down the staircase, a supernumerary whom she engaged from the outer world. These vigorous measures struck such terror to the breast of Mrs. Crupp that she subsided into her own kitchen under the impression that my aunt was mad. My aunt being supremely indifferent to Mrs. Crupp's opinion and rather favoring than discouraging the idea, Mrs. Crupp, of late the bold, became within a few days so faint-hearted that, rather than encounter my aunt, she would endeavor to hide her portly form behind doors—leaving visible, however, a wide margin of flannel petticoat—or would shrink into dark corners. This gave my aunt such satisfaction that she took a delight in prowling up and down, with her bonnet insanely perched on the top of her head, at times when Mrs. Crupp was likely to be in the way.

The day came when Dora was to visit Miss Mills, and I appeared promptly. But I carried desolation into the bosom of our joys by asking Dora, without the smallest preparation, if she could love a beggar?

My pretty, little, startled Dora! "How can you ask me anything so foolish?" she pouted. "Love a beggar!"

"Dora, my own dearest!" said I. "*I* am a beggar!"

"How can you be such a silly thing," replied Dora, slapping my hand, "as to sit there, telling such stories? I'll make Jip bite you!"

But I looked so serious that Dora left off shaking her curls, and first looked scared and anxious, then began to cry. That was dreadful. I fell upon my knees, imploring her not to rend my heart; but poor little Dora did nothing but exclaim Oh dear! and Oh, she was so frightened! and Where was Julia Mills! Oh, take her to Julia Mills! and go away, please! until I was beside myself.

At last, after an agony of supplication and protestation, I told her how I loved her, so dearly, and so dearly; how I felt it right to offer to release her from her engagement, because now I was poor; how I never could bear it if I lost her; how a crust well earned was sweeter than a feast inherited; and much more to the same purpose. "Is your heart mine still, dear Dora?" said I rapturously, when she clung to me.

"Oh, yes!" cried Dora. "Oh, don't be dreadful! Don't talk about being poor—"

"My dearest love," said I, "the crust well earned—"

"Oh, yes; but I don't want to hear any more about crusts!" said Dora. "And Jip must have a mutton chop every day at twelve, or he'll die!"

I was charmed with her childish, winning way. But I felt she was a little impracticable. "My own! May I mention something?" I said.

"Oh, please don't be practical!" said Dora coaxingly. "It frightens me so!"

"Sweetheart!" I returned, "there is nothing to alarm you in all this. If you will just sometimes think—not despondingly—that you are engaged to a poor man and look about now and then at your papa's housekeeping and endeavor to acquire a little habit—of accounts, for instance—"

Poor little Dora received this suggestion with something that was half a sob and half a scream.

"It would be so useful to us afterwards," I went on. "And if you would read a little—a little cook book that I would send you, it would be so excellent for both of us. For our path in life, my Dora," said I, warming with the subject, "is stony and rugged now—" but I had said enough. I had done it again. Oh, she was so frightened! Oh, take her to Julia Mills, and go away, please! So that, in short, I was quite distracted.

Well! I loved her, and I went on loving her, absorbingly, but went on, too, working pretty hard, and busily keeping red hot all the irons I now had in the fire. I did not, for example, allow my resolution with respect to the parliamentary debates to cool. I bought an approved scheme of the noble art and mystery of stenography and plunged into a sea of perplexity that brought me, in a few weeks, again to the confines of distraction. Night after night, after I came home from the Doctor's, Traddles dictated speeches to me, for practice. I really did work, as the common expression is, like a cart horse, until I used to fancy my head was turning quite gray.

One day, when I went to the Commons as usual, I found Mr. Spenlow looking extremely grave. Instead of returning my good morning with his usual affability, he coldly requested me to accompany him to a certain coffee house, where we found Miss Murdstone. "Have the goodness to show Mr. Copperfield," said Mr. Spenlow, "what you have in your reticule, Miss Murdstone."

I believe it was the old identical reticule of my childhood that shut up like a bite. Miss Murdstone opened it and produced my last letter to Dora, teeming with expressions of devoted affection. "I believe that is your writing, Mr. Copperfield?" said Mr. Spenlow. "If I am not mistaken," as Miss Murdstone brought out a parcel of letters, tied round with the dearest bit of blue ribbon, "those are also from your pen?"

I took them from her with a most desolate sensation, blushed deeply, and inclined my head.

"Miss Murdstone, be so good as to proceed!"

That gentle creature delivered herself with dry unction as follows: "I must confess to having entertained my suspicions of Miss Spenlow, in reference to David Copperfield, for some time. It appeared to me that Miss Spenlow received too many letters from her friend Miss Mills; but Miss Mills being her friend with her father's full concurrence"—a blow at Mr. Spenlow—"it was not for me to interfere. Last evening I observed the little dog worrying something. When I called Miss Spenlow's attention to it, she put her hand to her frock, gave a sudden cry, and ran to the dog. I interposed."

Oh Jip, miserable spaniel, this wretchedness, then, was your work!

"Miss Spenlow endeavored," said Miss Murdstone, "to bribe me with kisses, workboxes, and small articles of jewelry—that, of course, I pass over. At length, I obtained possession of the document. After perusing it, I taxed Miss Spenlow with having many such letters in her possession and ultimately obtained from her the packet which is now in David Copperfield's hand."

"You have heard Miss Murdstone," said Mr. Spenlow, turning to me. "Have you considered your years and my daughter's years, Mr. Copperfield? Have you considered my daughter's station in life, the projects I may contemplate for her advancement, the testamentary intentions I may have with reference to her? Have you considered anything?"

"Very little, sir, I am afraid," I answered. "But will you grant me time—any length of time? We are both so young, sir—"

"You are right," interrupted Mr. Spenlow, nodding his head, "you are both very young. It's all nonsense. Let there be an end of it. All I desire, Mr. Copperfield, is that it should be forgotten."

All! In the note I wrote Miss Mills, I bitterly quoted this sentiment. I entreated Miss Mills to see me that evening; when we resolved that she should go to Dora the first thing in the morning and find some means of assuring her of my devotion and misery. We parted, overwhelmed with grief; and I think Miss Mills enjoyed herself completely.

I was surprised, when I came within sight of our office door next morning, to see the ticket porters standing outside talking together. "This is a dreadful calamity, Mr. Copperfield," said the head clerk as I entered.

"What is?" I exclaimed. "What's the matter?"

"Don't you know? Mr. Spenlow. Dead!"

I thought it was the office reeling, and not I. "Dead?"

"He dined in town yesterday and drove down in the phaeton by himself. The phaeton went home without him. They found him a mile off. Whether he fell out in a fit or got out, feeling ill before the fit came on, no one appears to know."

I cannot describe the state of mind into which I was thrown by this intelligence. The shock of such an event happening so suddenly, and happening to one with whom I had been in any respect at variance, the appalling vacancy in the room he had occupied so lately, the insatiable relish with which our people talked about it—this is easily intelligible to anyone. What I cannot describe is how, in the innermost recesses of my heart, I had a lurking jealousy even of Death. How I felt as if its might would push me from my ground in Dora's thoughts. How I was, in a grudging way I have no words for, envious of her grief.

For six weeks I was in torment. All that time Miss Mills reported to me that my broken-hearted little Dora would say nothing, when I was mentioned, but "Oh, poor papa! Oh, dear papa!" She had gone to live in Putney with two aunts, maiden sisters of Mr. Spenlow, who were her only relations. It appeared a wonderful thing to me, but it turned out that Mr. Spenlow had left no will! What was scarcely less astonishing to me was that his affairs were in a most disordered state. By little and little it came out that, in the competition on all points of appearance and gentility then running high in the Commons, he had spent more than his professional income, which was not very large, and had reduced his private means to a very low ebb indeed. I felt as if some grim enchanter had drawn a magic circle round the innocent goddess of my heart, which nothing but the broad pinions of Time (as Miss Mills put it), capable of carrying so many people over so much, would enable me to enter!

My aunt beginning, I imagine, to be made seriously uncomfortable by my prolonged dejection, made a pretence of being anxious about the cottage, which was let, to send me to Dover. I obtained leave of absence from the Doctor with no difficulty. As to the Commons, I had no great occasion to be particular about my duties there. To say the truth, we were getting in no very good odor among the tiptop proctors and were rapidly sliding down to but a doubtful position. Mr. Jorkins, notwithstanding his reputation in the firm, was an easy-going, incapable sort of man, whose reputation out of doors was not calculated to back it up. I was turned over to him now; and when I saw him take his snuff and let the business go, I regretted my aunt's thousand pounds more than ever.

I found everything in a satisfactory state at the cottage, and walked on to Canterbury. Arrived at Mr. Wickfield's house, I found, in the little lower office, Mr. Micawber, plying his pen with great assiduity. He was extremely glad to see me, but a little confused too. I asked him whether he had reason, so far, to be satisfied with his friend Heep's treatment of him. He got up to ascertain if the door were close shut, before he replied, in a lower voice:

"My dear Copperfield. A man who labors under the pressure of pecuniary embarrassments is, with the generality of people, at a disadvantage. That disadvantage is not diminished when that pressure necessitates the drawing of stipendiary emoluments before those emoluments are strictly due and payable. All I can say is that my friend Heep has responded to appeals to which I need not more particularly refer in a manner calculated to redound equally to the honor of his head and of his heart."

"I should not have supposed him to be very free with his money, either," I observed.

"Pardon me!" said Mr. Micawber, with an air of constraint. "Allow me to offer a remark! I am here in a capacity of confidence. I am here in a position of trust. The discussion of some topics, even with Mrs. Micawber herself (so long the partner of my various vicissitudes, and a woman of a remarkable lucidity of intellect), is, I am led to consider, incompatible with the functions now devolving on me." As I left Mr. Micawber, I clearly perceived that there was something interposed between him and me since he had come into his new functions which prevented our getting at each other as we used to do and quite altered the character of our intercourse.

But what a pleasure to be the object of that sweet regard and welcome, when I found Agnes! She soon led me on to tell all that had happened since our last meeting. "What ought I to do, Agnes?" I inquired when I had finished. "What would it be right to do?"

"I think," said Agnes, "that the honorable course would be to write to Dora's aunts. Don't you think that any secret course is an unworthy one?"

"Yes. If *you* think so," said I. With a lightened heart, though with a profound sense of the weighty importance of my task, I devoted the whole afternoon to the composition of this letter, for which great purpose Agnes relinquished her desk to me. I had hoped to have no other companion in her little room. But Mrs. Heep had asked permission to bring herself and her knitting there, on pretense of its having an aspect more favorable for her rheumatics.

"I'm umbly thankful to you, sir," said Mrs. Heep in acknowledgment of my inquiries concerning her health, "but I am only pretty well. If I could see my Uriah well settled in life, I couldn't expect much more. How do you think my Ury looking, sir?"

I thought him looking as villainous as ever, and replied that I saw no change in him.

"Oh, don't you think he's changed?" said Mrs. Heep. "There I must umbly beg leave to differ from you. Don't *you* see a wasting and a wearing in him, Miss Wickfield?"

"No," said Agnes, quietly pursuing the work on which she was engaged. "You are too solicitous about him. He is very well." Mrs. Heep, with a prodigious sniff, resumed her knitting.

She never left off or left us for a moment. At dinner, too, she maintained her watch, with the same unwinking eyes. She hardly ever spoke—I question if she ever did—without making some mention of her Ury. It was evident to me that this was the duty assigned to her. Mother and son hung like two great bats over the whole house. Next day the knitting and watching began again and lasted all day.

I had not an opportunity of speaking to Agnes, for ten minutes. I could barely show her my letter. I proposed to her to walk out with me; but, Mrs. Heep complaining that she was worse, Agnes charitably remained within, to bear her company. Toward the twilight I went out by myself, musing on whether I was justified in withholding from Agnes any longer what Uriah Heep had told me in London. I had not walked far when he caught up with me. "To tell you the truth," said I, as civilly as I could, "I came out to walk alone, because I have had so much company." He looked at me sideways and said with his hardest grin, "You mean mother."

"Why, yes, I do," said I.

"Ah! But you know we're so very umble," he returned. "And,

having such a knowledge of our own umbleness, we really must take care that we're not pushed to the wall by them as isn't umble. All strategems are fair in love, sir. You see," he said, hugging himself, "you're quite a dangerous rival, Master Copperfield."

"Do you suppose," said I, constraining myself to be very temperate on account of Agnes, "that I regard Miss Wickfield otherwise than as a very dear sister? For her sake I will tell you that I am engaged to another young lady. I hope that contents you."

"Oh, Master Copperfield," Uriah said. "If you had only had the condensation to return my confidence when I poured out the fullness of my 'art, I never should have doubted you! As it is, I am sure I'll take off mother directly, and only too happy."

"Before we leave the subject, you ought to understand," said I, "that I believe Agnes Wickfield to be as far above *you* and as far removed from all *your* aspirations as that moon above us!"

"Now confess, Master Copperfield," said Uriah, "that you haven't liked me quite as I have liked you. All along you thought me too umble now, I shouldn't wonder?"

"I am not fond of professions of humility," I returned.

"There now!" said Uriah. "Didn't I know it! But how little you think of the rightful umbleness of a person in my station, Master Copperfield! Father and me was both brought up at a foundation school, and mother likewise. They taught us all a deal of umbleness—not much else that I know of. We was always to know our place and abase ourselves before our betters. And we had such a lot of betters! Father got the monitor medal by being umble. So did I. 'Be umble, Uriah,' says father to me, 'and you'll do!' And really I ain't done bad!"

It was the first time it had ever occurred to me that this detestable cant of false humility might have originated out of the Heep family. "When I was quite a young boy," said Uriah, "I got to know what umbleness did, and I took to it. I ate umble pie with an appetite. When you offered to teach me Latin, I knew better. 'People like to be above you,' says father; 'keep yourself down.' I am very umble to the present moment, Master Copperfield, but I've got a little power!"

And he said all this—I knew, as I saw his face in the moonlight—that I might understand he was resolved to recompense himself by using his power. I had never doubted his meanness, his craft and malice; but I fully comprehended now, for the first time, what a base, unrelenting, and revengeful spirit must have been engendered by this early and this long suppression.

Whether his spirits were elevated by the communication I had made to him, I don't know; but they were raised by some influence. When we three males were left alone after dinner, he induced Mr. Wickfield to drink one health after another, exulting as he held him up before me. "Come, fellow partner!" said he, at last, "*I'll* give you another one, and I umbly ask for bumpers, seeing I intend to make it the divinest of her sex."

Her father had his empty glass in his hand. I saw him set it down and shrink back in his chair.

"I'm an umble individual to give you her 'ealth," proceeded Uriah, "but I admire—adore her. Agnes Wickfield is, I am safe to say, the divinest of her sex. May I speak out, among friends? To be her father is a proud distinction, but to be her 'usband—"

Spare me from ever again hearing such a cry as that with which her father rose up from the table!

"What's the matter?" said Uriah, turning a deadly color. "You are not gone mad, after all, Mr. Wickfield, I hope? If I say I've an ambition to make your Agnes my Agnes, I have as good a right to it as another man. I have a better right to it than any other man!"

I had my arms round Mr. Wickfield, imploring him by everything that I could think of, oftenest by his love for Agnes, to calm himself a little. He was mad for the moment, tearing out his hair, beating his head, trying to force me from him. But by degrees he struggled less and began to look at me—strangely at first, then with recognition in his eyes. At length he said, "I know, Trotwood! My darling child and you—I know! But look at him!"

He pointed to Uriah, pale and glowering in a corner, evidently very much out in his calculations, and taken by surprise. "Look at my torturer," he said. "Before him I have step by step abandoned name and reputation, peace and quiet, house and home."

"I have kept your name and reputation for you, and your peace and quiet, and your house and home too," said Uriah, with a sulky, hurried, defeated air of compromise. "Don't be foolish, Mr. Wickfield. If I have gone a little beyond what you were prepared for, I can go back, I suppose? There's no harm done. Can't you see I'm as umble as I can be?"

The door opened, and Agnes, gliding in, without a vestige of color in her face, put her arm round her father's neck and steadily said, "Papa, you are not well. Come with me!" He laid his head upon her shoulder, as if he were oppressed with heavy shame, and went out with her. Her eyes met mine for but an instant; yet I saw how much she knew of what had passed.

When she came, late that night, to bid me good-by, I said, "You will never sacrifice yourself to a mistaken sense of duty, Agnes?" More agitated for a moment than I had ever seen her, she moved a step back. "Say you have no such thought, dear Agnes! Much more than sister! Think of the priceless gift of such a heart as yours, of such a love as yours!"

Oh! long, long afterward, I saw that face rise up before me, with its momentary look, not wondering, not accusing, not regretting. Oh, long, long afterward, I saw that look subside, as it did now, into the lovely smile with which she told me she had no fear for herself—I need have none for her—and parted from me by the name of "Brother," and was gone!

It was dark in the morning when I got upon the coach. As I sat thinking of her, came struggling up the coach side, through the mingled day and night, Uriah's head. "Copperfield!" said he, in a croaking whisper, "I thought you'd be glad to hear that we've made it all smooth. Why, though I'm umble, I'm useful to him, you know; and he understands his interest when he isn't in liquor!"

I obliged myself to say that I was glad he had made his apology. _

"Oh, to be sure!" said Uriah. "When a person's umble, you know, what's an apology? So easy! I say! I suppose," with a jerk, "you have sometimes plucked a pear before it was ripe, Master Copperfield? *I* did that last night; but it'll ripen yet! It only wants attending to. I can wait!"

Profuse in his farewells, he got down again as the coachman got up. For anything I know, he was eating something to keep the raw morning air out; but he made motions with his mouth as if the pear were ripe already, and he were smacking his lips over it.

18

I was walking home from the Doctor's one snowy night when I encountered, in St. Martin's Lane, a woman's face. It looked in mine, passed across the narrow lane, and disappeared. I knew it. I had seen it somewhere. But I could not remember where. On the steps of St. Martin's Church, there was the stooping figure of a man; my seeing the face, and my seeing him, were simultaneous. I stood face to face with Mr. Peggotty! Then I remembered the woman. It was Martha, to whom Em'ly had given the money that night in the kitchen. Martha Endell—side by side with whom, he would not have seen his dear niece, Ham had told me, for any treasure.

"Mas'r Davy!" Mr. Peggotty said, gripping me tight, "it do my'art good to see you, sir. Well met, well met! I had my thowts o'coming to make inquiration for you, sir, tonight, but I was afeared it was too late. I should have come early in the morning afore going away."

"Again?" said I.

"Yes, sir," he replied, patiently shaking his head, "I am away tomorrow."

When I saw him in the light of the public room to which I took him, I observed that he had every appearance of having toiled and wandered through all varieties of weather; but he looked very strong and like a man upheld by steadfastness of purpose, whom nothing could tire out. "I'll tell you, Mas'r Davy," he said, "wheer-all I've been, and what-all we've heerd. When she was a child," he said, "she used to talk to me a deal about the sea, and about them coasts wheer the sea got to be dark blue and to lay a shining and a shining in the sun. When she was—lost, I knowed in my mind, as he would take her to them countries. I knowed in my mind, as he'd have told her wonders of 'em and how she was to be a lady theer. I went across channel to France."

I saw the door move, and the snow drift in, as a hand softly interposed to keep it open.

"I went away through France," said Mr. Peggotty. "When I came to any town, I found the inn and waited about till someone turned up (someone mostly did) as knowed English. Then I told how that I was on my way to seek my niece, and they told me what manner of gentlefolks was in the house, and I waited to see any as seemed like her. When it warn't Em'ly, I went on again. By little and little, I found that the poor people knowed about me. They would set me down at their cottage doors and give me what-not for to eat and drink and show me wheer to sleep; and many a woman, Mas'r Davy, as had a daughter, I found a waiting fur me, at Our Savior's cross outside the village, fur to do me kindnesses. Some had had daughters as was dead. And God only knows how good them mothers was to me!"

It was Martha at the door. I saw her haggard, listening face distinctly.

"At last I come to the sea. It warn't hard, you may suppose, for a seafaring man like me to work his way over to Italy. I should have gone from town to town, maybe the country through, but that I got news of her being seen among them Swiss mountains yonder. I made for them mountains, Mas'r Davy, day and night. Ever so fur as I went, ever so fur the mountains seemed to shift away from me. But I come up with 'em, and I crossed 'em. Only, Mas'r Davy, it warn't to be—not yet! I was too late, and they was gone. I traveled heer, and I traveled theer, but I found no Em'ly, and I traveled home."

From some pocket in his breast he took out, with a very careful hand, a small packet containing two or three letters, which he laid upon the table. "This fust one come," he said, "afore I had been gone a week. A fifty pound bank note, put underneath the door in the night. She tried to hide her writing, but she couldn't hide it from me!

"This come to Missis Gummidge," he said, handing me another note, "two or three months ago." I read as follows:

"Of what will you feel when you see this writing and know it comes from my wicked hand! But try, try—not for my sake, but for uncle's goodness—try to let your heart soften to me, only for a little, little time! Try, pray do, to relent toward a miserable girl, and write down on a bit of paper whether he is well and what he said about me before you left off ever naming me among yourselves. Dear, if your heart is hard toward me—justly hard, I know—tell him I have wronged the most—him whose wife I was to have been—that if I was to die tomorrow (and oh if I was fit I would be so glad to die!) I would bless him and uncle with my last words and pray for his happy home with my last breath!"

Some money was enclosed in this letter also. Five pounds. It was untouched, like the previous sum, and he refolded it in the same way. "Is that another letter in your hand?" said I.

"It's money, sir," said Mr. Peggotty. "Ten pounds. But the fust was put underneath the door, and this come by the post, day afore yesterday. I'm a going to seek her at the post mark." He showed it to me. It was a town on the Upper Rhine. He had found out, at Yarmouth, some foreign dealers who had drawn him a rude map of that country. He gathered up the letters thoughtfully; put them into their little bundle; and placed it tenderly in his breast again. The face was gone from the door. I still saw the snow drifting in; but nothing else was there.

"All that troubles me, "he said, "is to think that any harm might come to me afore that money was give back. If I was to die and it was lost or stole or elseways made away with and it was never knowed by him but what I took it, I believe the t'other wureld wouldn't hold me!"

He rose, and I rose too; we grasped each other by the hand before he resumed his solitary journey through the snow.

At last, an answer to my letter came from Dora's two aunts. They presented their compliments to Mr. Copperfield and informed him that they had given his letter their best consideration, "with a view to the happiness of both parties," and that if Mr. Copperfield would do them the favor to call upon a certain day (accompanied, if he thought proper, by a confidential friend) they would be happy to hold some conversation on the subject.

To this favor, Mr. Copperfield immediately replied, with his respectful compliments, that he would have the honor of waiting on the Misses Spenlow at the time appointed, accompanied in accordance with their kind permission by his friend Mr. Thomas Traddles of the Inner Court. But, excellent fellow as I knew Traddles to be and warmly attached to him as I was, I could not help wishing, on that delicate occasion, that he had never contracted the habit of brushing his hair so very upright. It gave him a surprised look—not to say a hearth-broomy kind of expression— which, my apprehensions whispered, might be fatal to us.

I took the liberty of mentioning it to Traddles, as we were walking to Putney, and saying that if he *would* smooth it down a little—"My dear Copperfield," said Traddles, lifting off his hat and rubbing his hair all kinds of ways, "nothing would give me greater pleasure. But it won't. It's quite an old story, my unfortunate hair. My uncle's wife couldn't bear it. She said it exasperated her. It stood very much in my way, too, when I first fell in love with Sophy."

"Did she object to it?"

"*She* didn't," rejoined Traddles; "but all the sisters laugh at it. They pretend that Sophy has a lock of it in her desk and is obliged to shut it in a clasped book to keep it down."

"By the by, my dear Traddles," said I, "your experience may suggest something to me. When you became engaged, did you make a regular proposal to her family? Was there anything like— what we are going through today?"

"Why," replied Traddles, "it was rather a painful transaction, Copperfield, in my case. You see, Sophy being of so much use in the family, none of them could endure the thought of her ever being married. Indeed, they had quite settled among themselves that she never was to be married. Accordingly, when I mentioned it, with the greatest precaution, to Mrs. Crewler—"

"The mamma?" said I.

"The mamma," said Traddles,—"Reverend Horace Crewler—when I mentioned it with every possible precaution, the effect was such that she gave a scream and became insensible. I couldn't approach the subject again, for months."

"The sisters took your part, I hope, Traddles?"

"Why, I can't say they did," he returned. "The fact is, we avoid mentioning the subject; and my unsettled prospects and indifferent circumstances are a great consolation to them."

His honest face, as he looked at me with a serio-comic shake of his head, impresses me more in the remembrance than it did in the reality, for I was by this time in a state of such excessive trepidation as to be quite unable to fix my attention on anything. Ultimately I found myself backing Traddles into the fireplace of the Misses Spenlow's drawing room and bowing in great confusion to two dry elderly little ladies, dressed in black, each looking wonderfully like a preparation in chip or tan of the late Mr. Spenlow. "Pray," said one of the two little ladies, "be seated."

When I had done tumbling over Traddles and had sat upon something which was not a cat—my first seat was—I so far recovered my sight as to perceive that Mr. Spenlow had evidently been the youngest of the family; that there was a disparity between the two sisters; and that the younger appeared to be the manager of the conference, inasmuch as she had my letter in her hand.

"Mr. Copperfield!" said the sister with the letter.

I did something—bowed, I suppose—and was all attention, when the other sister struck in. "My sister Lavinia," said she, "being conversant with matters of this nature, will state what we consider most calculated to promote the happiness of both parties."

I discovered afterward that Miss Lavinia was an authority in affairs of the heart by reason of there having anciently existed a certain Mr. Pidger, who was supposed to have been enamored of her. My private opi.   's that this was entirely a gratuitous assumption and that Pidge.   s altogether innocent of any such sentiments—to which he had never given any sort of expression that I could ever hear of. Both Miss Lavinia and Miss Clarissa had a superstition, however, that he would have declared his passion if he had not been cut short in his youth (at about sixty) by overdrinking his constitution and overdoing an attempt to set it right again by swilling Bath water. They had a lurking suspicion, even, that he died of secret love.

"Our niece's position, or supposed position, is much changed by our brother Francis's death," said Miss Lavinia; "and therefore we consider our brother's opinions as regarded her position as being changed too. We have no reason to doubt, Mr. Copperfield, that you are a young gentleman possessed of good qualities and honorable character, or that you have an affection—or are fully persuaded that you have an affection—for our niece."

I replied, as I usually did whenever I had a chance, that nobody had ever loved anybody else as I loved Dora. Traddles came to my assistance with a confirmatory murmur.

Referring to my letter through her eyeglass, Miss Lavinia resumed. (They both had little bright round twinkling eyes, by the way, which were like birds' eyes. They were not unlike birds, altogether, having a sharp, brisk, sudden manner and a little short, spruce way of adjusting themselves, like canaries.) Miss Lavinia, as I have said, resumed. "You ask permission of my sister Clarissa and myself, Mr. Copperfield, to visit here as the accepted suitor of our niece." Now, although I had not received any express encouragement as yet, I fancied that I saw in the two little sisters, particularly in Miss Lavinia, an intensified enjoyment of this new and fruitful subject of domestic interest, a disposition to pet it, in which there was a good bright ray of hope. This gave me courage to protest most vehemently that I loved Dora better than I could tell or anyone believe; that all my friends knew how I loved her. And Traddles, firing up as if he were plunging into a parliamentary debate, really did come out nobly, confirming me in good round terms that evidently made a favorable impression.

"It seems to us," said Miss Lavinia, "prudent, Mr. Traddles, to bring these feelings to the test of our own observation. Therefore we are inclined to admit Mr. Copperfield's visits here. Sister Clarissa," said Miss Lavinia then, "the rest is with you."

Miss Clarissa, unfolding her arms for the first time, took my letter, on which were written some orderly looking notes, and glanced at them. "We shall be happy," said Miss Clarissa, "to see Mr. Copperfield to dinner, every Sunday, if it should suit his convenience. Our hour is three."

I bowed.

"In the course of the week," said Miss Clarissa, "we should be happy to see Mr. Copperfield to tea. Our hour is half-past six."

I bowed again.

"Miss Trotwood," said Miss Clarissa, "mentioned in Mr. Copperfield's letter, will perhaps call upon us."

I intimated that my aunt would be proud and delighted to make their acquaintance, though I must say I was not quite sure of their getting on very satisfactorily together. Miss Lavinia then arose and, begging Mr. Traddles to excuse us for a minute, requested me to follow her. I obeyed, all in a tremble, and was conducted into another room. There I found my blessed darling, stopping her ears behind the door with her dear little face against the wall, and Jip in the plate warmer with his head tied up in a towel to keep him from barking.

Oh! How beautiful she was in her black frock, and how she sobbed and cried at first and wouldn't come out from behind the door! How fond we were of one another when she did come out at last! I don't know how long I should have stayed there, oblivious of Traddles, if Miss Lavinia had not come in to take me away.

I was wonderfully relieved to find that my aunt and Dora's aunts rubbed on, all things considered, much more smoothly than I could have expected. But one thing troubled me much. It was that Dora seemed by one consent to be regarded like a pretty toy or plaything. My aunt, with whom she gradually became familiar, always called her "Little Blossom"; and the pleasure of Miss Lavinia's life was to curl her hair, make ornaments for her, and treat her like a pet child. What Miss Lavinia did, her sister did too. They all seemed to treat Dora, in her degree, much as Dora treated Jip in his.

I made up my mind to speak to Dora about this; and one day said to her that I wished she could get them to behave toward her differently. "Because you know, my darling," I remonstrated, "you are not a child."

"There!" said Dora. "Now you're going to be cross! And I am very happy."

"Well! But, my dearest life!" said I, "you might be very happy and yet be treated rationally." Dora gave me a reproachful look— the prettiest look!—and then began to sob, saying, if I didn't like her, why had I ever wanted so much to be engaged to her? And why didn't I go away now, if I couldn't bear her?

What could I do but kiss away her tears and tell her how I doted on her!

"I am sure I am very affectionate," said Dora; "you oughtn't to be cruel to me, Doady!" which was a corruption of David.

"Cruel, my precious love! As if I would—or could—be cruel to you!"

"Then don't find fault with me," said Dora, making a rosebud of her mouth; "and I'll be good."

I was charmed by her presently asking me, of her own accord, to show her how to keep accounts. I gave her a set of tablets and a pretty little pencil case, to practice housekeeping with. But the figures made her cry. They wouldn't add up, she said. So she rubbed them out and drew little nosegays and likenesses of me and Jip all over the tablets. As to the cook book I brought her—the principal use to which it was devoted was being put down in the corner for Jip to stand upon. But Dora was so pleased when she had trained him to stand upon it that I was very glad I had bought it.

And we fell back on the guitar case and the flower painting and the songs about never leaving off dancing, Ta ra la! and were as happy as the week was long. Though I occasionally awoke, as it were, wondering to find that I had fallen into the general fault and treated Dora like a plaything too—but not often.

19

I FEEL as if it were not for me to record, even though this manuscript is intended for no eyes but mine, how hard I worked at that tremendous shorthand in my sense of responsibility to Dora and her aunts. I will only add, of my perseverance and of a patient and continuous energy which then began to be matured within me, that there, on looking back, I find the source of my success. I have been very fortunate in worldly matters; many men have worked much harder and not succeeded half so well; but I never could have done what I have done without the habits of punctuality, order, diligence, and concentration which I then formed. Some happy talent and some fortunate opportunity may form the two sides of the ladder on which some men mount, but the rounds of that ladder must be made of stuff to stand wear and tear; and there is no substitute for thoroughgoing, ardent, and sincere earnestness. Never to put one hand to anything on which I could throw my whole self and never to affect depreciation of my work, whatever it was, I find, now, to have been my golden rules.

How much of the practice I have just reduced to precept I owe to Agnes, I will not repeat here. My narrative proceeds to Agnes, with a thankful love.

She came on a visit of a fortnight to the Doctor's, and I was in a flutter of pride and anxiety when I took her to see Dora. Dora was afraid of Agnes. She had told me that she knew Agnes was "too clever." But when she saw her looking at once so cheerful and so earnest, and so thoughtful and so good, she gave a faint little cry of pleased surprise and just put her affectionate arms round Agnes's neck and laid her innocent cheek against her face.

I never was so happy. I never was so pleased as when I saw those two sit down together, side by side. "I am so glad," said Dora after tea, "that you like me. I didn't think you would; and I want, more than ever, to be liked, now Julia Mills is gone." (I have omitted to mention it, but Miss Mills had sailed with her papa to India.) Agnes said she was afraid I must have given her an unpromising character, but Dora corrected that directly. "Oh no!" she said, shaking her curls at me; "it was all praise. He thinks so much of your opinion that I was quite afraid of it."

I was standing alone before the fire that night when she came stealing softly in. "Don't you think, if I had had her for a friend a long time ago, Doady," said Dora, her little right hand idly busying itself with one of the buttons of my coat, "I might have been more clever perhaps?"

"My love!" said I, "what nonsense!"

"I have forgotten," said Dora, still turning the button round and round, "what relation Agnes is to you, you dear bad boy."

"No blood relation," I replied, "but we were brought up together."

"I wonder why you ever fell in love with me?" said Dora, beginning on another button of my coat.

"Perhaps because I couldn't see you and not love you, Dora!"

"Suppose you had never seen me at all," said Dora, going to another button.

"Suppose we had never been born!" said I, gaily. I wondered what she was thinking about, as the little soft hand traveled up the row of buttons on my coat. At length her eyes were lifted up to mine, and she stood on tiptoe to give me, more thoughtfully than usual, her precious little kiss—once, twice, three times— and went out of the room.

Once again, let me pause upon a memorable period of my life. I have come legally to man's estate. I have attained the dignity of twenty-one. Let me think what I have achieved.

I have tamed that savage stenographic mystery. I make a respectable income by it. Night after night, I record predictions that never come to pass, professions that are never fulfilled, explanations that are only meant to mystify. I report the debates in Parliament for a morning newspaper. I have come out in another way. I have taken with fear and trembling to authorship. I wrote a little something, in secret, and sent it to a magazine, and it was published. Since then, I have taken heart to write a good many trifling pieces. Now, I am regularly paid for them. Altogether, I am well off.

We have moved from the Adelphi to a pleasant little cottage in Highgate. My aunt, however (who has sold the house at Dover to good advantage), is not going to remain here, but intends removing herself to a still more tiny cottage close at hand. What does this portend? My marriage? Yes!

Yes! I am going to be married to Dora! Miss Lavinia and Miss Clarissa have given their consent; and if ever canary birds were in a flutter, they are. A dressmaker, always stabbed in the breast with a needle and thread, boards and lodges in the house; and seems to me, eating, drinking, or sleeping, never to take her thimble off. They are always sending for my darling to come and try something on. Miss Clarissa and my aunt roam all over London to find out articles of furniture for Dora and me to look at. It would be better for them to buy the goods at once; for when we go to see a kitchen fender and meat screen, Dora sees a Chinese house for Jip, with little bells on the top, and prefers that.

Peggotty comes up to make herself useful and falls to work immediately to clean everything over and over again. And now it is that I begin to see her solitary brother passing through the dark streets at night and looking, as he goes, among the wandering faces. I never speak to him at such an hour. I know too well what he seeks and what he dreads.

Why does Traddles look so important when he calls upon me this afternoon in the Commons—where I still occasionally attend, for form's sake, when I have time? The realization of my boyish day dreams is at hand. I am going to take out the license. "I hope the next time you come here, my dear fellow," I say to Traddles, "it will be on the same errand for yourself. And I hope it will be soon."

"Thank you for your good wishes, my dear Copperfield," he replies. "I hope so too. She really is the dearest girl—"

"When are you to meet her at the coach?" I ask.

"At seven," says Traddles. "And really the great friendship and consideration of inviting Sophy to be a bridesmaid in conjunction with Miss Wickfield, demands my warmest thanks."

Sophy arrives in due course. She has the most agreeable of faces—not absolutely beautiful, but extraordinarily pleasant—and is one of the most genial, unaffected, frank, engaging creatures I have ever seen. I have brought Agnes from the Canterbury coach, and her cheerful and beautiful face is among us too. Still I don't believe it. We have a delightful evening and are supremely happy; but I don't believe it yet. I feel in a misty and unsettled kind of state, as if I had got up very early in the morning a week or two ago and had never been to bed since. I can't make out when yesterday was. I seem to have been carrying the license about many months. When tomorrow comes, the day of our wedding, it is all a more or less incoherent dream.

A dream of their coming into the church with Dora; of the clergyman and clerk appearing; of a few boatmen and some other people strolling in; of an ancient mariner behind me, strongly flavoring the church with rum; of the service beginning in a deep voice and our all being very attentive.

Of Miss Lavinia being the first to cry and of her doing homage (as I take it) to the memory of Pidger, in sobs; of Miss Clarissa applying a smelling bottle; of Agnes taking care of Dora; of my aunt endeavoring to represent herself as a model of sternness, with tears rolling down her face; of little Dora trembling very much and making her responses in faintest whispers.

Of my walking so proudly and lovingly down the aisle with my sweet wife upon my arm; of their whispering, as we passed, what a youthful couple we are and what a pretty little wife she is; of there being a breakfast whereof I partake, as I should do in any other dream, without the least perception of flavor, eating and drinking, as I may say, nothing but love and marriage and no more believing in the viands than in anything else.

Of the pair of hired post horses being ready and of Dora's going away to change her dress; of my wanting to carry Jip (who is to go along with us) and Dora's saying no, that she must carry him or else he'll think she doesn't like him any more; of our going arm in arm and Dora stopping and looking back and saying, "If I have ever been cross or ungrateful to anybody, don't remember it!" and bursting into tears.

Of her waving her little hand and our going away once more. Of her once more stopping and hurrying back to Agnes and giving Agnes, above all the others, her last kisses and farewells.

We drive away together, and I awake from the dream. I believe it at last. It is my dear, dear little wife beside me, whom I love so well! "Are you happy now, you foolish boy," says Dora, "and sure you don't repent?"

It was a strange condition of things, the honeymoon being over, when I found myself sitting down in my own small house with Dora, quite thrown out of employment, as I may say, in respect of the delicious old occupation of making love.

It seemed such an extraordinary thing to have Dora always there. It was so unaccountable not to be obliged to go out to see her, not to have to write to her, not to be scheming and devising opportunities of being alone with her. Sometimes of an evening, when I looked up from my writing and saw her seated opposite, I would lean back in my chair and think how queer it was that there we were, alone together as a matter of course—nobody's business any more—all the romance of our engagement put away upon a shelf—no one to please but one another—one another to please, for life.

When there was a debate and I was kept out very late, it seemed so strange to me, as I was walking home, to think that Dora was at home! It was such a wonderful thing, at first, to have her coming softly down to talk to me as I ate my supper. It was such a stupendous thing to know for certain that she put her hair in papers. It was altogether such an astonishing event to see her do it!

I doubt whether two young birds could have known less about keeping house, than I and my pretty Dora did. We had a servant, of course. She kept house for us. I have still a latent belief that she must have been Mrs. Crupp's daughter in disguise, we had such an awful time of it with Mary Anne.

Her name was Paragon. Her nature was represented to us, when we engaged her, as being feebly expressed in her name. Our treasure was warranted sober and honest. I am therefore willing to believe that she was in a fit when we found her under the boiler and that the deficient teaspoons were attributable to the dust man; but she preyed upon our minds dreadfully. We felt our inexperience and were unable to help ourselves. She was the cause of our first little quarrel. "My dearest life," I said one day to Dora, "do you think Mary Anne has any idea of time?"

"Why, Doady?" inquired Dora, looking up innocently from her drawing.

"My love, because it's five, and we were to have dined at four."

My little wife came and sat upon my knee, to coax me to be quiet, and drew a line with her pencil down the middle of my nose. "Don't you think, my dear," said I, "it would be better for you to remonstrate with Mary Anne?"

"Oh no, please! I couldn't, Doady!" said Dora. "I'm such a little goose, and she knows I am!"

I thought this sentiment so incompatible with the establishment of any system of check on Mary Anne that I frowned a little. "Oh, what ugly wrinkles in my bad boy's forehead!" said Dora and traced them with her pencil, putting it to her rosy lips to make it mark blacker and working at my forehead with a quaint little mockery of being industrious. "Don't be a naughty Blue Beard! Don't be serious!"

"My precious wife," said I, "we must be serious sometimes. Come! Give me the pencil! There! You know, my love, it is not exactly comfortable to have to go out without one's dinner. Now, is it?"

"N-n-no!" replied Dora faintly.

"My love, how you tremble!"

"Because I *know* you're going to scold me," exclaimed Dora, in a piteous voice.

"My sweet, I am only going to reason."

"Oh, but reasoning is worse than scolding!" exclaimed Dora in despair. "I didn't marry to be reasoned with. If you meant to reason with such a poor little thing as I am, you ought to have told me so, you cruel boy!"

I felt so injured by the inconsequential nature of this charge that it gave me courage to be brave. "Now, my own Dora," said I, "you are talking nonsense. You must remember that I was obliged to go out yesterday when dinner was half over and that, the day before, I was made quite unwell by being obliged to eat underdone veal in a hurry; today, I don't dine at all. I don't mean to reproach you, my dear, but this is not comfortable."

"Oh, you cruel, cruel boy, to say I am a disagreeable wife!" cried Dora.

"I am not blaming you, Dora, I am only trying to show you that you must—you really must accustom yourself to look after Mary Anne. Likewise to act a little for yourself, and me." But I had wounded Dora's soft little heart, and she was not to be comforted. I was obliged to hurry away; and I felt all night such pangs of remorse as made me miserable. When I got home, two or three hours past midnight, I found my aunt sitting up for me. "Is anything the matter, aunt?" said I, alarmed.

"Nothing, Trot," she replied. "Little Blossom has been rather out of spirits, and I have been keeping her company. That's all."

I leaned my head upon my hand and felt more sorry and downcast than I could have supposed possible so soon after the fulfillment of my brightest hopes. "Don't you think, aunt," said I, after looking at the fire for some time, "that you could counsel Dora a little, now and then?"

"Trot," returned my aunt, with some emotion, "no! Don't ask me such a thing. I look back on my life, child, and I think of some who are in their graves with whom I might have been on kinder terms. I've been a grumpy, frumpy, wayward sort of a woman; I am still and always shall be. But never do both me and Dora the injury you have hinted at!"

I comprehended at once that my aunt was right, and I comprehended the full extent of her generous feeling toward my dear wife.

"You have chosen freely, Trot, for yourself" (a cloud passed over her face for a moment) "and you have chosen a very pretty and a very affectionate creature. It will be your duty, and it will be your pleasure too, to estimate her (as you chose her) by the qualities she has and not by the qualities she may not have. But remember, my dear, your future is between you two. This is marriage, Trot; and Heaven bless you both in it, for a pair of babes in the wood!"

Dora came stealing down when I was alone and cried upon my shoulder and said I had been hard hearted and she had been naughty; and I said much the same thing in effect; and we made it up and agreed that our first little difference was to be our last and that we were never to have another if we lived a hundred years.

But everybody we had anything to do with seemed to cheat us. Our appearance in a shop was a signal for the damaged goods to be brought out immediately. As to the washerwoman pawning the clothes, I suppose that might have happened to anybody. Also the chimney on fire, the parish engine, and perjury on the part of the beadle. But I apprehend that we were personally unfortunate in engaging a servant in our long line of Incapables with a taste for cordials, who swelled our running account for porter at the public house by such inexplicable items as "quartern rum shrub (Mrs. C.)"; "half-quartern gin and cloves (Mrs. C.)"; "glass rum and peppermint (Mrs. C.)"—the parentheses always referring to Dora, who was supposed, it appeared on explanation, to have imbibed the whole of these refreshments.

One of our first feats in the housekeeping way was a little dinner to Traddles. I could not have wished for a prettier little wife at the opposite end of the table, but I certainly could have wished, when we sat down, for a little more room. Traddles was so hemmed in by Jip's pagoda, and the guitar case, and Dora's flower painting, and my writing table that I had serious doubts of the possibility of his using his knife and fork; but he protested, with his own good humor, "Oceans of room, Copperfield! I assure you, oceans!"

There was another thing I could have wished, namely, that Jip had never been encouraged to walk about the table cloth during dinner. On this occasion he seemed to think he was introduced expressly to keep Traddles at bay and barked at him with such undaunted pertinacity that he engrossed the conversation. However, as I knew how tender-hearted Dora was and how sensitive to any slight upon her favorite, I hinted no objection. "My love," said I, "what have you got in that dish?"

"Oysters, dear," said Dora timidly.

"There is nothing Traddles likes so much!" said I, delighted.

"Ye-yes, Doady," said Dora. "But I—I am afraid there is something the matter with them. They don't seem right." Diamonds twinkled in her eyes.

"Do you know, Copperfield," said Traddles, cheerfully examining the dish, "I think it is in consequence—they are capital oysters—but I *think* it is in consequence—of their never having been opened."

They never had been opened; and we had no oyster knives and couldn't have used them if we had; so we looked at the oysters and ate the mutton. At least, we ate as much of it as was done and made up with capers.

When Traddles went away, my wife planted her chair close to mine and sat down by my side. "I am very sorry," she said. "Will you try to teach me, Doady?"

"I must teach myself first, Dora," said I. "I am as bad as you, love."

"Will you call me a name I want you to call me?" inquired Dora, without moving.

"What is it?" I asked with a smile.

"It's a stupid name," she said, shaking her curls for a moment. "Child-wife."

I laughingly asked my child-wife what her fancy was in desiring to be so called.

"I don't mean, you silly fellow," she answered, "that you should use the name instead of Dora. I only mean that you should think of me that way. When you are going to be angry with me, say to yourself, 'It's only my child-wife!' When I am very disappointing, say, 'I knew, a long time ago, that she would make but a child-wife!' When you miss what I should like to be and I think can never be, say, 'Still, my foolish child-wife loves me!' For indeed I do."

I had not been serious with her, having no idea, until now, that she was serious herself. But her affectionate nature was so happy in what I now said to her with my whole heart that her face became a laughing one before her glittering eyes were dry. She was soon my child-wife indeed; sitting down on the floor outside the Chinese house, ringing all the little bells one after another, to punish Jip for his recent bad behavior.

This appeal of Dora's made a strong impression on me. I look back on the time I write of; I invoke the innocent figure that I dearly loved, to come out from the mists and shadows of the past; and I can still declare that this one little speech was constantly in my memory. I may not have used it to the best account; I was young and inexperienced; but I never turned a deaf ear to its artless pleading.

Sometimes, of an evening, when I was at home and at work— for I wrote a good deal now and was beginning in a small way to be known as a writer—I would lay down my pen and see my child-wife's blue eyes looking at me with quiet attention. "Oh, what a weary boy!" said Dora one night.

"What a weary girl!" said I. "You must go to bed another time, my love. It's far too late for you."

"No, don't send me to bed!" pleaded Dora, "pray don't do that!" To my amazement she was sobbing on my neck.

"Not well, my dear! Not happy!"

"Yes! Quite well, and very happy!" said Dora. "But say you'll let me stop and see you write. Will you mind if I say something very, very silly? Please let me hold the pens. I want to have something to do with all those many hours when you are so industrious. May I hold the pens?"

The remembrance of her pretty joy when I said "Yes" brings tears into my eyes. The next time I sat down to write, and regularly afterward, she sat beside me with a spare bundle of pens. So we went on. Dora was hardly less affectionate to my aunt than to me, and I never saw my aunt unbend more systematically to anyone. She courted Jip, though Jip never responded; never attacked the Incapables, though the temptation must have been severe; and never came in by the garden, and missed Dora from the room, but she would call out, in a voice that sounded cheerfully all over the house,

"Where's Little Blossom?"

20

I MUST have been married, if I may trust my imperfect memory for dates, about a year or so, when one evening, as I was returning from a solitary walk, thinking of the book I was then writing—for my success had steadily increased, and I was engaged upon my first work of fiction—I came past Mrs. Steerforth's house, and a voice asked me to come in.

I found Miss Dartle sitting on a seat at one end of a kind of terrace, overlooking the great city. Our meeting was not cordial. We had parted angrily on the last occasion; and there was an air of disdain about her, which she took no pains to conceal. "Pray," she said, "has this girl been found?"

"No."

"And yet she has run away! If she is not found, perhaps she never will be found. She may be dead!" The vaunting cruelty with which she met my glance, I never saw expressed in any other face. "Come here!"—as if she were calling to some unclean beast. And, with undiminished respectability, Mr. Littimer appeared, made me a bow, and took up his position behind her. The air of wicked grace, of triumph, with which she reclined upon the seat between us was worthy of a cruel princess in a legend.

"Now," said she, imperiously, and touching the old wound as it throbbed, "tell Mr. Copperfield about the flight." Mr. Littimer began:

"Mr. James and myself have been abroad with the young woman, ever since she left Yarmouth under Mr. James's protection. We have been in France, Switzerland, Italy—almost all parts. Mr. James took quite uncommonly to the young woman and was more settled for a length of time than I had known him to be since I had been in his service. The young woman is very improvable and spoke the languages, and wouldn't have been known for the same country person. I noticed that she was much admired wherever we went."

Miss Dartle put her hand upon her side. I saw him steal a glance at her and slightly smile to himself.

"Very much admired, indeed, the young woman was. What with her dress, what with the air and sun, what with being made so much of, what with this, that, and the other, her merits really attracted general notice. The young woman went on in this manner for some time, being occasionally low in her spirits, until I think she began to weary Mr. James by giving away to her low spirits and tempers of that kind and things were not so comfortable. Mr. James, he began to be restless again."

Clearing his throat behind his hand with a respectable short cough, he went on: "At last, when there had been, upon the whole, a good many words and reproaches, Mr. James, he set off one morning from the neighborhood of Naples, where we had a villa (the young woman being very partial to the sea), and left it in charge of me to break it out that, for the general happiness of all concerned, he was"—here an interruption of the short cough—"gone. But Mr. James, I must say, certainly did behave extremely honorable; for he proposed that the young woman should marry a very respectable person, who was, at least, as good as anybody the young woman could have aspired to in a regular way."

I was convinced that the scoundrel spoke of himself, and I saw my conviction reflected in Miss Dartle's face.

"This I also had it in charge to communicate. The young woman's violence when she came to, after I broke the fact of his departure, was beyond all expectations. She was quite mad and had to be held by force; or if she couldn't have got to a knife or got to the sea, she'd have beaten her head against the marble floor."

Miss Dartle, leaning back upon the seat with a light of exultation in her face, seemed almost to caress the sounds this fellow had uttered.

"But when I came to the second part of what had been entrusted to me," said Mr. Littimer, rubbing his hands uneasily, "then the young woman came out in her true colors. A more outrageous person I never did see. She had no more gratitude, no more feeling, no more reason in her than a stone. If I hadn't been upon my guard, I am convinced she would have had my blood."

"I think the better of her for it," said I, indignantly. Mr. Littimer bent his head and resumed his narrative: "It was necessary to shut her up close. Notwithstanding which, she got out in the night, forced the lattice of a window, and never has been seen or heard of, to my knowledge, since."

"She is dead, perhaps," said Miss Dartle, with a smile, as if she could have spurned the body of the ruined girl.

"She may have drowned herself, miss," returned Mr. Littimer, "it's very possible. Or she may have had assistance from the boatmen and the boatmen's wives and children. Being given to low company, she was very much in the habit of talking to them on the beach." When I indicated that I had no further questions to ask, he made a polite bow and walked away.

"He says besides," Miss Dartle observed, "that his master is coasting Spain; and, this done, is away to gratify his seafaring tastes till he is weary. Between these two proud persons, mother and son, there is a wider breach than before and little hope of its healing, for they are one at heart, and time makes each more obstinate and imperious. This is of no interest to you. But if this girl is alive, you will desire to have a pearl of such price found and taken care of. We desire that, too, that he may not by any chance be made her prey again; and that is why I, who would do her any mischief that so coarse a wretch is capable of feeling, have sent for you to hear what you have heard."

I saw, by the change in her face, that someone was advancing behind me. It was Mrs. Steerforth, who gave me her hand more coldly than of yore and with an augmentation of her former stateliness of manner, but still, I perceived—and I was touched by it— with an ineffaceable remembrance of my old love for her son. She was greatly altered. "You are married, sir, I am told?"

I answered that I had been some time married.

"And are doing well? I hear little in the quiet life I lead, but I understand you are beginning to be famous."

"I have been very fortunate," I said, "and find my name connected with some praise."

"You have no mother?"—in a softened voice.

"No."

"It is a pity," she returned. "She would have been proud of you. Good night!" As I moved away from them along the terrace, I observed how steadily they both sat gazing on the prospect and how it thickened around them. From the greater part of the broad valley interposed between them and the distant city, a mist was rising like a sea, which, mingling with the darkness, made it seem as if the gathering waters would encompass them. I have reason to remember this and think of it with awe; for before I looked upon those two again, a stormy sea had risen to their feet.

I felt it right that what had been told me should be communicated to Mr. Peggotty, and went to his lodging in London. He listened in profound silence to all I had to tell. When I had finished, he said steadfastly, "My niece Em'ly is alive, sir! I doen't know wheer it comes from or how 'tis, but *I am told* as she's alive!"

"If she should come to London," said I, "I believe there is one person more likely to discover her than any other. Do you remember—hear what I say with fortitude—do you remember Martha Endell? Do you know that she is in London?"

"I have seen her in the streets," he answered with a shiver. "I think I know wheer to look for her." I saw how carefully he adjusted the little room before we went out, put a candle ready, took out of a drawer one of Emily's dresses neatly folded with some other garments, which he placed upon a chair. There they had been waiting for her, many a night, no doubt.

We were not far from Blackfriars Bridge when he turned his head and pointed to a solitary female figure flitting along the opposite side of the street. I knew it to be the figure that we sought. We followed it for some time, to the river's brink, where it stood, lonely and still, looking at the water. I did not approach her without trembling; for this gloomy end to her determined walk, and the way in which she stood, inspired a dread within me.

"Martha!" I said as I grasped her arm. She uttered a terrified scream and struggled with me with such strength that I doubt if I could have held her alone. But a stronger hand than mine was laid upon her; and when she raised her frightened eyes and saw whose it was, she made but one more effort and dropped down between us. "Oh, the river!" she cried passionately. "Oh, the river!

"I know it's like me!" she exclaimed. "It comes from country places, where there was once no harm in it—and it creeps through dismal streets, defiled and miserable—and it goes away, like my life, to a great sea, that is always troubled—and I feel that I must go with it!"

The thought passed through my mind that in the face of my companion I might have read his niece's history. I never saw, in any painting or reality, horror and compassion so impressively blended. He shook as if he would have fallen.

A new burst of crying came upon her now, in which she once more hid her face among the stones and lay before us, a prostrate image of humiliation and ruin. Knowing that this state must pass before we could speak to her, we stood by in silence until she became more tranquil. "Are you composed enough," said I then, "to speak on the subject which so interested you—I hope Heaven may remember it!—that snowy night?"

Her sobs broke out afresh, and she murmured some inarticulate thanks for not having driven her away from the door.

"If you heerd," said Mr. Peggotty, "owt of what passed between Mas'r Davy and me, th' night when it snew so hard, you know as I have been—wheer not—fur to seek my dear niece. My dear niece," he repeated steadily. "Fur she's more dear to me now,

Martha, than ever she was dear afore. You're thankful to her, and you love her. Help us all you can to find her!"

"Will you trust me?" she asked, in a low voice of astonishment.

"Full and free!" said Mr. Peggotty.

She lifted up her eyes and solemnly declared that she would devote herself to the task fervently and faithfully. That she would never waver in it, never be diverted from it while there was any chance of hope. Mr. Peggotty suggesting to me what had already occurred to myself, I took out my purse; but I could not prevail upon her to accept any money. "I could not do what I have promised, for money," she said, "if I were starving. To give me money would be to take away your trust, to take away the only certain thing that saves me from the river." Again she repressed the tears that had begun to flow and, putting out her trembling hand and touching Mr. Peggotty as if there was some healing virtue in him, went away along the desolate road.

It was midnight when I arrived at home. I was rather surprised to see that the door of my aunt's cottage was open, and went to speak to her. It was with very great surprise that I saw a man standing in her little garden. I stopped short, for the moon was up now, and I recognized the man whom I had once encountered with my aunt in the streets of the city. Just then she came out of the house. She was agitated and told some money into his hand. I heard it chink.

"What's the use of this?" he demanded.

"I can spare no more," returned my aunt. "You know I have had losses and am poorer than I used to be. You stripped me of the greater part of all I ever had. You closed my heart against the whole world, years and years. You treated me falsely, ungratefully, and cruelly. Go, and repent of it. Don't add new injuries to the long, long list of injuries you have done me!"

"Ay!" he returned. "It's all very fine! Well! I must do the best I can, for the present, I suppose." In spite of himself, he appeared abashed by my aunt's indignant tears, and came slouching out of the garden.

"Aunt," said I, coming up hurriedly. "This man alarming you again! Let me speak to him. Who is he?"

"Child," returned my aunt, "come in, and don't speak to me

for ten minutes." At the end of that time she said calmly, "Trot, it's my husband."

"Your husband, aunt?" I sat in silent amazement.

"Betsey Trotwood don't look a likely subject for the tender passion," said my aunt, composedly, "but the time was, Trot, before you were born, when she believed in that man most entirely. He repaid her by breaking her fortune and nearly breaking her heart. So she put all that sort of sentiment in a grave and filled it up and flattened it down."

"My dear good aunt!"

"I left him," my aunt proceeded, "generously. He had been so cruel to me that I might have effected a separation on easy terms for myself; but I did not. He soon made ducks and drakes of what I gave him, sank lower and lower, became an adventurer, a gambler, and a cheat. What he is now, you see. But he was a fine-looking man when I married him," said my aunt, with an echo of her old pride and admiration; "and I believed him—I was a fool! —to be the soul of honor."

She gave my hand a squeeze and shook her head. "He is nothing to me now, Trot, less than nothing. But, sooner than have him punished for his offenses, I give him more money than I can afford, at intervals when he reappears, to go away. I was a fool when I married him; and I am so far an incurable fool on that subject that I wouldn't have even this shadow of my idle fancy hardly dealt with."

My aunt dismissed the matter with a heavy sigh and smoothed her dress. "There, my dear!" she said. "Now you know the beginning, middle, and end, and all about it. We won't mention the subject any more. This is my grumpy, frumpy story, and we'll keep it to ourselves, Trot!"

I labored hard at my book; and it came out and was very successful. I was not stunned by the praise which sounded in my ears, notwithstanding that I was keenly alive to it, and thought better of my own performance, I have little doubt, than anybody else did. But it is not my purpose, in this record, though in all other essentials it is my written memory, to pursue the history of my own fictions. They express themselves, and I leave them to themselves. When I refer to them, incidentally, it is only as a part of my progress. When my new success was achieved, I considered myself entitled to escape from the dreary debates. (I had already left the Doctor.) One joyful night, therefore, I noted down the music of the parliamentary bagpipes for the last time.

I now write of the time when I had been married, I suppose, about a year and a half. After several varieties of experiments, we had given up the housekeeping as a bad job. The house kept itself. What other course was left to take? To "form Dora's mind"? This was a common phrase of words which had a fair and promising sound, and I began immediately. When Dora was very childish, I tried to be grave—and disconcerted her, and myself too. I talked to her on the subjects which occupied my thoughts; and I read Shakespeare to her—and fatigued her to the last degree. I accustomed myself to giving her, as it were quite casually, little scraps of useful information or sound opinion—and she started from them when I let them off, as if they had been crackers. No matter how incidentally or naturally I endeavored to form my little wife's mind, she always had an instinctive perception of what I was about and became a prey to the keenest apprehension. In particular, it was clear to me, she thought Shakespeare a terrible fellow.

Formation went on very slowly, but I persevered. Finding at last, however, that although I had been all this time bristling with determination I had effected nothing, it began to occur to me that perhaps Dora's mind was already formed. Indeed, this appeared so likely that I abandoned my scheme, resolving henceforth to be satisfied with my child-wife; so I bought a pretty pair of earrings for her and a collar for Jip and went home one day to make myself agreeable. "The truth is, Dora, my life," I said, "I have been trying to be wise."

"And to make me wise too," said Dora, timidly. "Oh what a shocking boy!"

"But I shall never try any more," said I. "For I love her dearly as she is."

In fulfillment of the contract I have made with myself, to reflect my mind on this paper, I again examine it, closely, and bring its secrets to the light. What I missed in my marriage I now regarded as something that had been a dream of my youthful fancy, incapable of realization. But that it would have been better for me if my wife could have helped me more and shared the many thoughts in which I had no partner, and that this might have been, I knew.

It remained for me to adapt myself to Dora, to share with her what I could and be happy, to bear on my own shoulders what I must and be still happy. It made my second year much happier than my first and, what was better still, made Dora's life all sunshine. But as the year wore on, Dora was not strong. I had hoped that lighter hands than mine would help to mold her character and that a baby's smile upon her breast might change my child-wife to a woman. It was not to be. The spirit fluttered for a moment on the threshhold of his little prison and, unconscious of captivity, took wing.

"When I can run about again, as I used to do, aunt," said Dora, "I shall make Jip race. He is getting quite slow and lazy."

"I suspect, my dear," said my aunt, "he has a worse disorder than that. Age, Dora."

"Do you think he is old?" said Dora, astonished. "Oh, how strange it seems that Jip should be old! But you are not so old, Jip, are you, that you'll leave your mistress yet? We may keep one another company a little longer!'

My pretty Dora! We thought she would be "running about as she used to do" in a few days. But they said, "Wait a few days more," and then, "Wait a few days more"; and still she neither ran nor walked. I began to carry her downstairs every morning and upstairs every night. She would clasp me round the neck and laugh, the while, as if I did it for a wager. But sometimes, when I took her up and felt that she was lighter in my arms, a dead blank feeling came upon me, as if I were approaching to some frozen region yet unseen. I avoided a recognition of this feeling by any name until one night, when my aunt had left her with a parting cry of "Good night, Little Blossom." Then I sat down at my desk alone and cried to think, Oh what a fatal name it was, and how the blossom withered in its bloom upon the tree!

21

I RECEIVED one morning by the post, the following letter, dated Canterbury and addressed to me at Doctor's Commons, which I read with some surprise.

"My dear Sir,

"Circumstances beyond my individual control have effected a severance of that intimacy which has ever afforded me gratifying emotions. This fact, my dear sir, combined with the distinguished elevation to which your talents have raised you, deters me from presuming to aspire to the liberty of addressing the companion of my youth, by the familiar appellation of Copperfield! It is sufficient to know that the name to which I do myself the honor to refer will ever be treasured among the muniments of our house (I allude to the archives connected with our former lodgers, preserved by Mrs. Micawber), with sentiments of personal esteem amounting to affection.

"Without more directly referring to any latent ability that may possibly exist on my part, of wielding the thunder bolt or directing the devouring and avenging flame in any quarter, I may be permitted to observe that my brightest visions are for ever dispelled—that my peace is shattered and my power of enjoyment destroyed—that my heart is no longer in the right place—and that I no more walk erect before my fellow man. The canker is in the flower. The cup is bitter to the brim. The worm is at his work.

"Placed in a mental position of peculiar painfulness, beyond the assuaging reach even of Mrs. Micawber's influence, it is my intention to fly from myself for a short period and devote a respite of eight and forty hours to revisiting some metropolitan scenes of past enjoyment. Among other havens of domestic tranquillity and peace of mind, my feet will naturally tend toward the King's Bench Prison. In stating that I shall be (D.V.) on the outside of the south wall of that place of incarceration on civil process, the day after tomorrow, at seven in the evening, precisely, my object in this epistolary communication is accomplished.

"I do not feel warranted in soliciting my former friend Mr. Copperfield or my former friend Mr. Thomas Traddles of the Inner Temple to condescend to meet me and renew (so far as may be) our past relation of the olden time. I confine myself to throwing out the observation that, at the hour and place I have indicated, may be found such ruined vestiges as yet

"Remain,

"Of

"A

"Fallen Tower,

"Wilkins Micawber."

I was still reading this letter when Traddles came in with a letter from Mrs. Micawber, which ran thus:

"My best regards to Mr. Thomas Traddles, and may I beg a few moments of his leisure time?

"Though harrowing to myself to mention, the alienation of Mr. Micawber (formerly so domesticated) from his wife and family is the cause of my addressing my unhappy appeal to Mr. Traddles and soliciting his best indulgence. Mr. T. can form no adequate idea of the change in Mr. Micawber's conduct, of his wildness, of his violence. Mr. T. will not require me to depict my feelings when I inform him that I have become accustomed to hear Mr. Micawber assert that he has sold himself to the D. Mystery and secrecy have long been his principal characteristic, have long replaced unlimited confidence. The slightest provocation, even being asked if there is anything he would prefer for dinner, causes him to express a wish for a separation. Last night, on being childishly solicited for twopence, to buy 'lemon stunners' —a local sweetmeat—he presented an oyster knife at the twins! He looks with an eye of coldness even on the unoffending stranger who last became a member of our circle.

"May I now venture to confide to Mr. T. the purport of my letter? The quick eye of affection is not easily blinded when of the female sex. Mr. Micawber is going to London. Dare I fervently implore Mr. T. to see my misguided husband and to reason with him? If Mr. Copperfield should yet remember one unknown to fame, will Mr. T. take charge of the unalterable regard and similar entreaties of one who subscribes herself, in extreme distress,

"Mr. Thomas Traddles's respectful friend and suppliant,

"Emma Micawber."

"I think the two letters together, Copperfield," said Traddles when he had read mine, "mean more than Mr. and Mrs. Micawber usually mean in their correspondence—but I don't know what." Accordingly, I wrote a comforting letter to Mrs. Micawber, which we both signed; and we decided to be very punctual in keeping Mr. Micawber's appointment.

But we found Mr. Micawber already there, standing with his arms folded over against the wall, looking at the spikes at the top with a sentimental expression, as if they were the interlacing boughs of trees that had shaded him in his youth.

"Mr. Copperfield," said Mr. Micawber bitterly, after the first salutations, "when I was an inmate of this retreat I could look my fellow man in the face, and punch his head if he offended me. My fellow man and myself are no longer on those glorious terms!"

"How is our friend Heep, Mr. Micawber?" said I, after a silence.

"My dear Copperfield," returned Mr. Micawber, bursting into a state of much excitement and turning pale, "if you ask after my employer as *your* friend, I am sorry for it; if you ask after him as *my* friend, I sardonically smile at it. In whatever capacity you ask after my employer, I beg, without offense to you, to limit my reply to this—that whatever his state of health may be, his appearance is foxy, not to say diabolical."

I then mentioned that it would give me great pleasure to introduce Mr. Micawber to my aunt. "Or if confiding anything to friends will be more likely to relieve you, you shall impart it to us, Mr. Micawber," said Traddles, prudently.

"Gentlemen," returned Mr. Micawber, "do with me as you will! I am a straw upon the surface of the deep and am tossed in all directions by the elephants—I beg your pardon, I should have said the elements." He was for the most part plunged into deep gloom as we made our way to Highgate. He occasionally made an attempt to smarten himself and hum the fag end of a tune; but his relapses into profound melancholy were only made the more impressive by the mockery of a hat exceedingly on one side and a shirt collar pulled up to his eyes.

We went to my aunt's house rather than to mine, because of Dora's not being well. My aunt welcomed Mr. Micawber with gracious cordiality. And Mr. Dick was by nature so exceedingly compassionate of any one who seemed to be ill at ease and was so quick to find any such person out that he shook hands with Mr.

Micawber at least half a dozen times in five minutes. To Mr. Micawber in his trouble, this warmth on the part of a stranger was so extremely touching that he could only say, on the occasion of each successive shake, "My dear sir, you overpower me!" Which gratified Mr. Dick so much that he went at it again with greater vigor than before.

I watched Mr. Micawber so anxiously, in his vacillations between an evident disposition to reveal something and a counter disposition to reveal nothing, that I was in a perfect fever. My aunt had more useful possession of her wits, for she held him in conversation and made it necessary for him to talk. "I hope Mrs. Micawber and your family are well, sir," she said.

Mr. Micawber inclined his head. "They are as well, ma'am," he desperately observed after a pause, "as Aliens and Outcasts can ever hope to be."

"Lord bless you, sir!" exclaimed my aunt in her abrupt way. "What are you talking about?"

"The subsistence of my family, ma'am," returned Mr. Micawber, "trembles in the balance. My employer—" Here Mr. Micawber provokingly left off.

"Your employer, you know," said Mr. Dick, jogging his arm as a gentle reminder.

"My good sir," returned Mr. Micawber, "you recall me. I am obliged to you." They shook hands again. "My employer, ma'am—Mr. Heep—once did me the favor to observe to me that, if I were not in the receipt of the stipendiary emoluments appertaining to my engagement with him, I would probably be a mountebank swallowing a sword blade. For anything that I can perceive to the contrary, it is still probable that my children may be reduced to seek a livelihood by personal contortion, while Mrs. Micawber abets their unnatural feats by playing the barrel organ." He rose from his chair, pulled out his handkerchief, and burst into tears.

"Mr. Micawber," said I, "what is the matter? Pray speak out. You are among friends."

"Among friends, sir!" repeated Mr. Micawber; and all he had reserved came breaking out of him. "Good Heavens, it is principally because I *am* among friends that my state of mind is what it is. What is the matter, gentlemen? What is *not* the matter? Villainy is the matter; baseness is the matter; deception, fraud, conspiracy are the matter; and the name of the whole atrocious mass is—*Heep!*"

My aunt clapped her hands, and we all started up as if we were possessed.

"The struggle is over!" said Mr. Micawber, violently gesticulating with his handkerchief and fairly striking out from time to time with both arms, as if he were swimming under superhuman difficulties. "I will lead this life no longer. Give me back my wife, give me back my family, substitute Micawber for the petty wretch who walks about in the boots at present on my feet, and call upon me to swallow a sword tomorrow, and I'll do it. With an appetite!

"I'll put my hand in no man's hand," said Mr. Micawber, gasping, puffing, and sobbing, to that degree that he was like a man fighting with cold water, "until I have—blown to fragments —the—a—detestable—serpent—*Heep!* I'll partake of no one's hospitality, until I have—a—moved Mount Vesuvius—to eruption—on—a—the abandoned rascal—*Heep!* I—a—I'll know nobody—and—a—say nothing—and—a—live nowhere—until I have crushed—to—a—undiscoverable atoms—the transcendent and immortal hypocrite and perjurer—*Heep!*

"No, Copperfield!" he said, when I would have gone to his assistance, "no communication—a—until—Miss Wickfield—a— redress from wrongs inflicted by consummate scoundrel—*Heep!*" (I am quite convinced he could not have uttered three words but for the amazing energy with which this word inspired him when he felt it coming.) "Inviolable secret—a—from the whole world— a—no exceptions—this day week—a—at breakfast time—a— everybody present—including aunt—a—and extremely friendly gentleman—to be at the hotel at Canterbury—and—a—will expose intolerable ruffian—*Heep!* No more to say—go immediately —upon the track of devoted and doomed traitor—*Heep!*"

With this last repetition of the magic word that had kept him going at all, Mr. Micawber rushed out of the house, leaving us in a state of excitement, hope, and wonder that reduced us to a condition little better than his own.

22

By this time, some months had passed since our interview with Martha. I had never seen her since, and nothing had come of her zealous intervention. I confess that I began to despair of Emily's recovery and gradually to sink into the belief that she was dead.

I was walking alone in the garden, however, the second evening in Mr. Micawber's week of suspense, when I saw a figure dressed in a plain cloak in the road. It was bending eagerly toward me and beckoning. "Martha!" said I.

"Can you come with me?" she inquired, in an agitated whisper. "I have been to Mr. Peggotty, and he is not at home. I wrote down where he was to come and left it on his table. I have tidings for him. Can you come directly?"

My answer was to pass out of the gate immediately. We proceeded, without a word being spoken, to one of London's somber streets, where once-fair dwellings had long degenerated into poor lodgings let off in rooms. Entering at the open door of one of these, Martha beckoned me to follow her up the common staircase. Two or three times I thought I observed the skirts of a female figure going up before us. And as we turned to ascend the last flight of stairs between us and the roof, we caught a full view of this figure pausing for a moment at a door. Then it turned the handle and went in.

"What's this!" said Martha, in a whisper. "She has gone into my room. I don't know her!" *I* knew her. I had recognized her with amazement, for Miss Dartle. Martha kept one hand on my lips and raised the other in a listening attitude.

"It matters little to me her not being at home," said Rosa Dartle, haughtily, "I know nothing of her. It is you I came to see."

"Me?" replied a soft voice.

At the sound of it, a thrill went through me. For it was Emily's!

"Yes," returned Miss Dartle. "I have come to see James Steerforth's fancy; the girl who ran away with him and is the town talk of the commonest people of her native place; the bold, flaunting, practiced companion of persons like James Steerforth. I want to know what such a thing is like."

There was a rustle, as if the unhappy girl on whom she heaped these taunts ran toward the door, and the speaker swiftly interposed herself before it. When she spoke again, it was through her set teeth. "Stay there!" she said, "or I'll proclaim you to the house and the whole street!"

A frightened murmur was the only reply that reached my ears. I did not know what to do. Much as I desired to put an end to the interview, I felt that I had no right to present myself; that it was for Mr. Peggotty alone to see her and recover her. Would he never come? I thought, impatiently.

"So!" said Rosa Dartle, with a contemptuous laugh, "I see her at last! Why, he was a poor creature to be taken by that delicate mock modesty and that hanging head!"

"Oh, for Heaven's sake, spare me!" exclaimed Emily. "Whoever you are, you know my pitiable story; spare me, if you would be spared yourself!"

"If *I* would be spared!" returned the other fiercely; "what is there in common between *us?*"

"Nothing but our sex," said Emily, with a burst of tears. "Dear, dear lady, think what I have suffered, and how I am fallen! Oh, Martha, come back! Oh, home, home! You know, perhaps, what his power with a weak, vain girl might be. I don't defend myself, but I know well, and he knows well, that he used all his power to deceive me and that I believed him, trusted him, and loved him!"

Rosa Dartle sprang up from her seat, recoiled, and in recoiling struck at her, with a face of such malignity that I had almost thrown myself between them.—Would he never, never come?

"*You* love him? *You?* And tell that to *me*, with your shameful lips? Why don't they whip these creatures? If I could order it to be done, I would have this girl whipped to death."

A low crying on the part of Emily interrupted her. She stopped and listened to it as if it were music. "I am of a strange nature, perhaps," Rosa Dartle went on; "but I can't breathe freely in the air you breathe. I find it sickly. Therefore, I will have it cleared; I will have it purified of you. If you live here tomorrow, I'll have your story and your character proclaimed on the common stair. If, leaving here, you seek any refuge in this town in any character but your true one (which you are welcome to bear without molestation from me), the same service shall be done you, if I hear of your retreat. Being assisted by a gentleman who not long ago aspired to the favor of your hand, I am sanguine as to that. There are doorways and dust heaps for such deaths as yours—find one, and take your flight to Heaven!"

I heard a distant foot upon the stairs. It was his, thank God! It came nearer—nearer—passed Rosa Dartle as she went down—rushed into the room!

"Uncle!" A fearful cry followed the word. I saw him supporting her insensible figure in his arms. He carried her, motionless and unconscious, down the stairs.

"All night long," said Mr. Peggotty next morning to my aunt and me, "we have been together, Em'ly and me. She kneeled down at my feet, and kiender said to me, as if it was her prayers, how it all come to be.

"When my Em'ly took flight," he said, in stern wrath for the moment, "from that theer spotted snake as Mas'r Davy see, she ran along the sea beach, believing the old boat was theer and calling out to us to turn away our faces, for she was a coming by. Of a sudden—or so she thowt, you unnerstand—the day broke, and she was lying b'low a heap of stones upon the shore, and a woman was a speaking to her, that she had often talked to on the beach. She hadn't no children of her own, this woman, being a young wife; but she was a looking to have one afore long. And may my prayers go up to Heaven that 't will be a happ'ness to her and a comfort and a honor, all her life! May it love her and be dootiful to her, in her old age, helpful of her at the last, a angel to her here and hereafter!"

"Amen!" said my aunt.

"This was her as now asked what it was that had gone so much amiss. Em'ly told her, and she—took her home. She did indeed. She took her home," said Mr. Peggotty, covering his face. He was more affected by this act of kindness than by anything since the night she went away.

"It was a little cottage, you may suppose," he said presently, "but she found space for Em'ly in it—her husband was away at sea—and she kep' it secret. Em'ly was took bad with fever, but the woman nursed her till she got strong again and put her on a small trader bound for France. Em'ly made her way to England;

and she as had never seen it in her life—alone—without a penny—
young—so pretty—come to London. Here Martha found her and,
trew to her promise, saved her from worse than death. She had
knowed of her bitter knowledge wheer to watch and what to do.
How the cruel lady knowed of her being here, I can't say. Whether
that snake chanced to see 'em together, I doen't greatly ask myself.
My niece is found."

"You have quite made up your mind," said I to Mr. Peggotty,
"to emigrate, good friend?"

"Yes!" said Mr. Peggotty, with a hopeful smile. "No one can't
reproach my darling in Australia. We will begin a new life over
theer!"

Next day, at his request, I went with him to Yarmouth to
make his farewells. But I felt reluctant to be present when he first
met his sister and Ham, so I lingered behind at Omer and Joram's.
Mr. Omer surveyed me admiringly. "What a lovely work that was
of yours!" he said. "What expressions in it! I read it every word—
every word. And as to feeling sleepy! Not at all!"

I laughingly expressed my satisfaction, but I must confess
that I thought this association of ideas significant.

"I give you my word and honor, sir," said Mr. Omer, "that
when I lay that book upon the table and look at it outside, compact
in three separate and indiwidual wolumes—one, two, three—I am
as proud as Punch to think that I once had the honor of being
connected with your family. And dear me, it's a long time ago
now, ain't it? Over at Blunderstone. With a pretty little party
laid along with the other party. And you quite a small party then,
yourself."

Peggotty told me that night that Ham was as full of courage
as of sweetness, and worked harder and better than any boat-
builder in any yard in all that part. But she told me, crying, that
he was broken-hearted; and when he had spoken to me alone next
day, I believed her.

"Theer is something I could wish said or wrote to her, Mas'r
Davy," he said. I answered that I should consider it a sacred trust.

"'T ain't that I forgive her," he told me. "'T is more as I beg
of her to forgive me, for having pressed my affections upon her.
Odd times, I think that, if I hadn't had her promise fur to marry

me, she was that trustful of me that she'd have told me what was struggling in her mind and I might have saved her." We walked on before he spoke again. He was not crying when he made the pauses I shall express by lines. He was merely collecting himself to speak very plainly.

"I loved her—and I love the mem'ry of her—too deep—to be able to lead her to believe of my ownself as I'm a happy man. But if you, being so full of learning, Mas'r Davy, could think of anything to say as might bring her to believe I wasn't greatly hurt—anything as might bring her to believe as I was not tired of my life—anything as would ease her sorrowful mind—I should ask of you to say that—with my prayers for her—that was so dear."

I walked on to the old boat, which Mr. Peggotty was dismantling. I found it emptied of all its furniture, saving Emily's old locker, on which Mrs. Gummidge was seated, looking at Mr. Peggotty. "Come to bid farewell to 't, Mas'r Davy?" he said. "Bare enough, now, ain't it? Missis Gummidge has worked like a—I doen't know what Missis Gummidge ain't worked like," said Mr. Peggotty.

"Dan'l," said Mrs. Gummidge, suddenly clinging to his arm, "my dear Dan'l, the parting words I speak in this house is, I mustn't be left behind. Doen't ye think of leaving me behind, Dan'l, doen't ye! Take me 'long with you, Dan'l, with you and Em'ly! I'll be your servant, constant and trew. Doen't you leave me behind, Dan'l, that's a deary dear!"

"My good soul," said Mr. Peggotty, "you doen't know what a long voyage, and what a hard life 't is!"

"Yes, I do, Dan'l! I can guess!" cried Mrs. Gummidge. "But my parting words under this roof is, I shall go into the House and die if I'm not took. I know how 't is; I know you think that I'm lone and lorn; but, deary love, 't ain't so no more!"

Next day, when we were returning to London outside the coach, Mrs. Gummidge was on the seat behind, and Mrs. Gummidge was happy.

23

WHEN the time Mr. Micawber had appointed so mysteriously was within four and twenty hours of being come, my aunt and I consulted how we should proceed; for my aunt was very unwilling to leave Dora. Ah! How easily I carried Dora up and downstairs, now! But Dora declared that she would never forgive her bad boy if my aunt remained behind. "Tut, Blossom!" said my aunt. "You know you can't do without me!"

"Yes, I can," said Dora. "You are no use to me at all. You never run up and downstairs for me, all day long. You never sit and tell me stories about Doady, when his shoes were worn out and he was covered with dust—Oh, what a poor little mite of a fellow! You never do anything at all to please me, do you, dear?" Dora made haste to kiss my aunt and say, "Yes, you do! I'm only joking!" lest my aunt should think she really meant it. "Besides," said Dora, looking at my aunt and me, "why shouldn't you both go? I'm not very ill indeed. Am I?"

"Why what a question!" cried my aunt. So we four, my aunt, Mr. Dick, Traddles, and I, went down to Canterbury by the night mail.

Next morning we sat down to breakfast at the hotel, very anxious and impatient. When Mr. Micawber appeared, my aunt tied the strings of her bonnet and put on her shawl, as if she were ready for anything that was resolute and uncompromising. Traddles buttoned his coat with a determined air. Mr. Dick, disturbed by these formidable appearances but feeling it necessary to imitate them, pulled his hat, with both hands, as firmly over his ears as he possibly could.

"Gentlemen, and madam," said Mr. Micawber, "good morning! My dear sir," to Mr. Dick, who shook hands with him violently, "you are extremely good."

"Have you breakfasted?" said Mr. Dick. "Have a chop!"

"Not for the world, my good sir!" cried Mr. Micawber; "appetite and myself, Mr. Dixon, have long been strangers."

Mr. Dixon was so well pleased with his new name and appeared to think it so very obliging in Mr. Micawber to confer it upon him that he shook hands with him again and laughed rather childishly. "Dick," said my aunt, "attention!" Mr. Dick recovered himself with a blush.

"Now, sir," said my aunt to Mr. Micawber, as she put on her gloves, "we are ready for Mt. Vesuvius, or anything else, as soon as you please."

"Madam," returned Mr. Micawber, "I trust you will shortly witness an eruption. Mr. Traddles, I have your permission, I believe, to mention here that we have been in communication together?"

"It is undoubtedly the fact, Copperfield," said Traddles, to whom I looked in surprise. "Mr. Micawber has consulted me; and I have advised him to the best of my judgment."

"I would beg," said Mr. Micawber, "to be allowed a start of five minutes by the clock and then to receive the present company at the office of Wickfield and Heep, whose stipendiary I am." With which he included us all in a comprehensive bow and disappeared, his face extremely pale.

When the time was expired, we found Mr. Micawber at his desk. The large office ruler was stuck into his waistcoat and was not so well concealed but that a foot or more protruded from his bosom. As it appeared that I was expected to speak, I said aloud, "How do you do, Mr. Micawber? Is Mr. Wickfield at home?"

"Mr. Wickfield is unwell in bed, sir, of a rheumatic fever," he returned; "but Miss Wickfield, I have no doubt, will be happy to see old friends. Will you walk in, sir?" Flinging open the door of Mr. Wickfield's former office, he said, in a sonorous voice, "Miss Trotwood, Mr. David Copperfield, Mr. Thomas Traddles, and Mr. Dixon!"

Our visit astonished Uriah Heep, evidently; but a moment afterward he was as fawning and as humble as ever. "Well, I am sure," he said, "this is indeed an unexpected pleasure! Mr. Copperfield, I hope I see you well, and—if I may umbly express self so—friendly toward them as is ever your friends, whether or not. Things are changed in this office, Miss Trotwood, since I was an umble clerk, ain't they? But *I* am not changed, Miss Trotwood."

"Well, sir," returned my aunt, "to tell you the truth, I think you are pretty constant to the promise of your youth."

"Thank you, Miss Trotwood," said Uriah, writhing in his ungainly manner, "for your good opinion! Micawber, tell 'em to let Miss Agnes know—and mother. Mother will be quite in a state!" said Uriah, setting chairs.

I saw him watch Agnes while she greeted us; and he reminded me of an ugly and rebellious genie watching a good spirit. In the meanwhile, some slight sign passed between Mr. Micawber and Traddles; and Traddles, unobserved except by me, went out. "Don't wait, Micawber," said Uriah.

Mr. Micawber, with his hand upon the ruler in his breast, stood erect before the door, most unmistakably contemplating one of his fellow men, and that man his employer. "Micawber!" said Uriah. "Why do you wait?"

"Because I—in short, choose," replied Mr. Micawber, with a burst.

Uriah's cheeks lost color, and an unwholesome paleness over-spread them. "You are a dissipated fellow, as all the world knows," he said with an effort at a smile, "and I am afraid you'll oblige me to get rid of you. Go along! I'll talk to you presently."

"If there is a scoundrel on this earth," said Mr. Micawber, suddenly breaking out again with the utmost vehemence, "with whom I have already talked too much, that scoundrel's name is —*Heep!*"

Uriah fell back, as if he had been struck. Looking slowly round upon us with the darkest and wickedest expression that his face could wear, he said, "Oho! This is a conspiracy! You have met here by appointment! You are playing Booty with my clerk, are you, Copperfield? Now, take care. There is no love between us. You were always a puppy with a proud stomach, from your first coming here; and you envy me my rise, do you? None of your plots against me!"

"Mr. Micawber," said I, "there is a sudden change in this fellow, in more respects than the extraordinary one of his speaking the truth in one particular, which assures me that he is brought to bay. Deal with him as he deserves!"

"You are a precious set of people, ain't you?" said Uriah, break-ing out into a clammy heat, "to buy over my clerk, who is the very scum of society—as you yourself were, Copperfield, before any one had charity on you—to defame me with his lies? Miss Trot-wood, you had better stop this; or I'll stop your husband shorter than will be pleasant to you. I won't know your story professionally for nothing, old lady! Miss Wickfield, if you have any love for your father, you had better not join that gang. I'll ruin him, if you do. Now, come! I have got some of you under the harrow. Think twice, before it goes over you. Where's mother?" he said, suddenly appearing to notice, with alarm, the absence of Traddles. "Fine doings in a person's own house!"

"Mrs. Heep is here, sir," said Traddles, returning with that worthy mother of a worthy son. "I have taken the liberty of making myself known to her."

"Who are you to make yourself known?" retorted Uriah.

"I am the agent of Mr. Wickfield, sir," said Traddles, in a composed and business-like way. "And I have a power of attorney from him in my pocket."

"The old ass has drunk himself into a state of dotage," said Uriah, turning uglier than before, "and it has been got from him by fraud!"

"Something has been got from him by fraud, I know," returned Traddles quietly; "and so do you, Mr. Heep. We will refer that question to Mr. Micawber."

Mr. Micawber, whose impetuosity I had restrained thus far with the greatest difficulty, and who had repeatedly interposed with the first syllable of *scoun*-drel! without getting to the second, now burst forward, drew the ruler from his breast (apparently as a defensive weapon), produced from his pocket a foolscap document, and began to read as follows:

"'Dear Miss Trotwood and Gentlemen—'"

"Bless and save the man!" exclaimed my aunt in a low voice. "He'd write letters by the ream, if it was a capital offense!"

Mr. Micawber, without hearing her, went on.

"'In appearing before you to denounce probably the most consummate Villain that has ever existed'"—Micawber, without looking off the letter, pointed the ruler, like a ghostly truncheon, at Uriah Heep—"'I ask no consideration for myself. In an accumulation of Ignominy, Want, Despair, and Madness, I entered the office of the Firm, nominally conducted under the appellation of Wickfield and—*Heep* but in reality wielded by *Heep* alone. *Heep*, and only *Heep*, is the mainspring of that machine. *Heep*, and only *Heep*, is the Forger and the Cheat.'"

Uriah, more blue than white at these words, made a dart at

the letter as if to tear it in pieces. Mr. Micawber, with a perfect miracle of dexterity or luck, caught his advancing knuckles with the ruler and disabled his right hand. It dropped at the wrist, as if it were broken. The blow sounded as if it had fallen on wood. "The devil take you!" said Uriah, writhing in a new way.

"Approach me again, you—you—you—*Heep* of infamy," gasped Mr. Micawber, making broad-sword guards with the ruler, "and if your head is human, I'll break it. Come on, Come on!" When he was sufficiently cool, he proceeded with his letter.

"'The stipendiary emoluments in consideration of which I entered into the service of—*Heep*'"—always pausing before that word and uttering it with astonishing vigor—"'were not defined, beyond the pittance of twenty-two shillings and six per week. The rest was left contingent on the value of my professional exertions, in other words, on the baseness of my nature, the cupidity of my motives, the poverty of my family, the general moral (or rather immoral) resemblance between myself and—*Heep*. Need I say that it soon became necessary for me to solicit from—*Heep* pecuniary advances toward the support of Mrs. Micawber and our blighted but rising family? Need I say that this necessity had been foreseen by—*Heep?* That those advances were secured by I.O.Us. and other similar acknowledgments, known to the legal institutions of this country? And that I thus became enmeshed in the web he had spun for my reception? Then it was that—*Heep* began to favor me with just so much of his confidence as was necessary to the discharge of his infernal business. I found that my services were constantly called into requisition for the falsification of business and the mystification of an individual whom I will designate as Mr. W. But stimulated by the silent monitor within and by a no less touching and appealing monitor without—to whom I will briefly refer as Miss W.—I entered on a not unlaborious task of clandestine investigation, protracted now, to the best of my knowledge, information, and belief, over a period exceeding twelve calendar months.'"

He read this passage as if it were from an act of Parliament and appeared majestically refreshed by the sound of the words.

"'My charges against—*Heep*,'" he read on, glancing at him, and drawing the ruler into a convenient position under his left arm, in case of need, "'are as follows: First, when Mr. W.'s faculties and memory for business became, through causes into which it is not necessary or expedient for me to enter, weakened and confused—*Heep* designedly perplexed and complicated the whole of the official transactions. When Mr. W. was least fit to enter on business—*Heep* was always at hand to force him to enter on it. He obtained Mr. W.'s signature under such circumstances to documents of importance, representing them to be other documents of no importance. He induced Mr. W. to empower him to draw out, thus, one particular sum of trust money, amounting to twelve six fourteen, two and nine, to meet pretended business charges and deficiencies which were either already provided for or had never really existed, and has used it, ever since, to torture and constrain him.'"

"You shall prove this, you Copperfield!" said Uriah.

"Ask—*Heep*, Mr. Traddles, who lived in his house after him," said Mr. Micawber.

"The fool himself—and lives there now," said Uriah, disdainfully.

"Ask—*Heep* if he ever kept a pocketbook in that house," said Mr. Micawber.

I saw Uriah's lank hand stop, involuntarily, in the scraping of his chin.

"Or ask him," said Mr. Micawber, "if he ever burned one there. If he says yes and asks you where the ashes are, refer him to Wilkins Micawber, and he will hear of something not at all to his advantage!"

The triumphant flourish with which Mr. Micawber delivered himself of these words had a powerful effect in alarming the mother, who cried out in much agitation, "Ury, Ury! Be umble, and make terms, my dear!"

"Mother!" he retorted, "will you keep quiet?" Mr. Micawber proceeded.

"'Second. *Heep* has, on several occasions, to the best of my knowledge, information, and belief, systematically forged, to various entries, books, and documents, the signature of Mr. W., and has distinctly done so in one instance, to wit, in manner following, that is to say: The said—*Heep* deemed it expedient to have a bond ready by him, as from Mr. W., for the before-mentioned sum of twelve six fourteen, two and nine, with interest, stated therein to have been advanced by—*Heep* to save Mr. W. from dishonor, though really the sum was never advanced by him and has long been replaced. The signatures to this instrument purporting to be executed by Mr. W. and attested by Wilkins Micawber are forgeries by—*Heep.* I never attested any such document. And I have the document itself in my possession.'"

"Ury, Ury!" cried the mother, "be umble and make terms." It was singular to see how she still held to the old trick, when her son had abandoned it as useless. "Mother," he said, with an impatient bite at the handkerchief in which his hand was wrapped, "you had better take and fire a loaded gun at me."

Mr. Micawber resumed his letter. "'Third. And last. I am now in a condition to show, by—*Heep's* false books, and—*Heep's* real memoranda that the weaknesses, the faults, the very virtues, the parental affections, and the sense of honor of the unhappy Mr. W. have been for years acted on by and warped to the base purposes of—*Heep.* That his last act, completed but a few months since, was to induce Mr. W. to execute a relinquishment of his share in the partnership. That these meshes, beginning with alarming and falsified accounts of the estate of which Mr. W. is the receiver, at a period when Mr. W. had launched into imprudent and ill-judged speculations and may not have had the money for which he was morally and legally responsible in hand, perpetuated by a miscellaneous catalogue of unscrupulous chicaneries, gradually thickened until the unhappy Mr. W. could see no world beyond. Bankrupt, as he believed, alike in circumstances, in all other hope, and in honor, his sole reliance was upon the monster in the garb of man'"—Mr. Micawber was so very much struck by this happy turn of expression that he indulged himself with a second reading of it, under pretense of having lost his place—"'who, by making himself necessary to him, had achieved his destruction. All this I undertake to show. Probably much more!'"

There was a movement among us, as if Mr. Micawber had finished. He said, with exceeding gravity, "Pardon me," and proceeded, with a mixture of the lowest spirits and the most intense enjoyment, to the peroration of his letter.

"'I have now concluded. It merely remains for me to substantiate these accusations; and then, with my ill-starred family, to disappear from the landscape. That is soon done. It may be reason-

ably inferred that our baby will first expire of inanition, as being the frailest member of our circle, and that our twins will follow next in order. So be it! Let it be, in justice, merely said of me, as of a gallant naval hero, with whom I have no pretensions to cope, that what I have done, I did, in despite of mercenary and selfish objects,

"For England, Home, and Beauty."

"'Remaining always, etc., etc., WILKINS MICAWBER.'"

What was my astonishment when I beheld my aunt, who had been profoundly quiet and attentive, make a dart at Uriah Heep and seize him by the collar with both hands! "You know what *I* want?" she said. "My property! Agnes, my dear, as long as I believed it had been really made away with by your father, I wouldn't breathe a syllable of its having been placed here for investment. But now I know this fellow's answerable for it, and I'll have it!"

During the last few minutes, Mrs. Heep had been clamoring to her son to be "umble" and had been going down on her knees to all of us in succession and making the wildest promises. Her son said to me, with a ferocious look, "What do you want done?"

"I will tell you what must be done," said Traddles. "First, the deed of relinquishment must be given over to me now—here. Then, you must prepare to disgorge all that your rapacity has become possessed of and to make restoration to the last farthing."

"I won't do it!" said Uriah, with an oath.

"Copperfield," said Traddles, "will you go round to the Guild-hall and bring a couple of officers?" Here, Mrs. Heep broke out again, exclaiming that he was very humble, and it was all true, and if he didn't do what we wanted, she would. To inquire what he might have done if he had had any boldness would be like inquiring what a mongrel cur might do if it had the spirit of a tiger. "Stop!" he growled to me and wiped his hot face with his hand. "Mother, hold your noise. Well! Let 'em have that deed. Go and fetch it!"

"Good," said Traddles, when it was brought. "Now, Mr. Heep, you can retire to think." When he had gone, Mr. Micawber proffered me the satisfaction of "witnessing the reestablishment of mutual confidence between himself and Mrs. Micawber." Accordingly, my aunt and I accompanied him to his house.

Exclaiming, "Emma! my life!" Mr. Micawber rushed into Mrs. Micawber's arms. Mrs. Micawber shrieked and folded Mr. Micawber in her embrace. Miss Micawber, nursing the unconscious stranger of Mrs. Micawber's last letter to Traddles, was sensibly affected. The stranger leaped. The twins testified their joy by several inconvenient but innocent demonstrations. Master Micawber, whose disposition appeared to have been soured by early disappointment and whose aspect had become morose, yielded to his better feelings and blubbered.

When the transports were over, my aunt said musingly, "Mr. Micawber, I wonder you have never turned your thoughts to emigration."

"Capital, madam, capital," urged Mr. Micawber, gloomily.

"Capital?" cried my aunt. "But you are doing us a great service, and what could we do for you that would be half so good as to find the capital? Think of this now, both of you. Here are some people David knows, going out to Australia shortly. If you decide to go, why shouldn't you go in the same ship? You may help each other."

"There is but one question, my dear ma'am, I could wish to

ask," said Mrs. Micawber. "*Are* the circumstances of the country such that a man of Mr. Micawber's abilities would have a fair chance of rising in the social scale? I will not say, at present, might he aspire to be Governor, or anything of that sort; but would there be a reasonable opening for his talents to develop?"

"No better opening anywhere," said my aunt, "for a man who conducts himself well and is industrious."

"For a man who conducts himself well," repeated Mrs. Micawber, with her clearest business manner, "and is industrious. Precisely. It is evident to me that Australia is the legitimate sphere of action for Mr. Micawber!"

"I entertain the conviction, my dear madam," said Mr. Micawber, "that it is, under existing circumstances, the land, the only land, for myself and family, and that something of an extraordinary nature will turn up on that shore."

Shall I ever forget how, in a moment, he was the most sanguine of men, or how Mrs. Micawber presently discoursed about the habits of the kangaroo! Shall I ever recall that street of Canterbury on a market day without recalling him as he walked back with us, expressing, in the hardy roving manner he assumed, the unsettled habits of a temporary sojourner in the land, and looking at the bullocks as they came by with the eye of an Australian farmer!

24

I MUST pause yet once again. Oh, my child-wife, there is a figure in the moving crowd before my memory, quiet and still, saying in its innocent love and childish beauty, "Stop to think of me—turn to look upon the Little Blossom, as it flutters to the ground!"

I do. All else grows dim and fades away. I am again with Dora, in our cottage. I do not know how long she has been ill. It is not really long, in weeks or months; but, in my usage and experience, it is a weary, weary while. They have left off telling me to "wait a few days more." I have begun to fear, remotely, that the day may never shine when I shall see my child-wife running in the sunlight with her old friend Jip, who is grown very old.

What a strange pause in my life there seems to be—and in all life—when I sit in the quiet, shaded, orderly room, with the blue eyes of my child-wife turned toward me and her little fingers twining round my hand!

"You won't think what I am going to say, unreasonable, Doady?" she said one evening. "I want to see Agnes. Very much I want to see her."

"I will write to her, my dear."

"You are very lonely when you go downstairs, now?" Dora whispers.

"How can I be otherwise, my own love, when I see your empty chair?"

"Oh, husband! I am so glad, yet so sorry!" creeping closer to me.

It is night; and I am with her still. Agnes has arrived. Do I know, now, that my child-wife will soon leave me? They have told me so. But I hold her hand in mine, I see her love for me, alive in all its strength. I cannot shut out a pale lingering shadow of belief that she will be spared.

"I am going to speak to you, Doady. I am going to say something I have often thought of saying, lately. Doady, dear, I am afraid I was too young."

I lay my face upon the pillow by her, and she looks into my eyes and speaks very softly. Gradually, as she goes on, I feel, with a stricken heart, that she is speaking of herself as past. "I was such a silly little creature! I am afraid it would have been better, if we had only loved each other as a boy and girl and forgotten it. I have begun to think I was not fit to be a wife."

I try to stay my tears as I reply, "Oh, Dora, love, as fit as I to be a husband!"

"But as years went on, my dear boy would have wearied of his child-wife. She wouldn't have improved. It is better as it is."

"Oh, Dora, dearest, dearest, do not speak so. Every word seems a reproach!"

"No, not a syllable!" she answers, kissing me. "Oh, how my poor boy cries! Hush, hush! Now make me one promise. I want to speak to Agnes quite alone."

I promise that she shall, immediately; but I cannot leave her, for my grief.

"I said that it was better as it is!" she whispers as she holds me

in her arms. "Oh, Doady, after more years, you never could have
loved your child-wife better than you do; and, after more years,
she would so have tried and disappointed you that you might not
have been able to love her half so well! I know I was too young and
foolish. It is much better as it is!"

Agnes is downstairs, when I go into the parlor; and I
give her the message. She disappears, leaving me alone with
Jip.

I sit down by the fire, thinking with a blind remorse of every
little trifle between me and Dora, and feel the truth, that trifles
make the sum of life. How the time wears, I know not, until I am
recalled by my child-wife's old companion. He wanders to the
door and whines to go upstairs. "Not tonight, Jip! Not tonight!
Oh, Jip! It may be, never again!"

He lies down at my feet, stretches himself out as if to sleep,
and with a plaintive cry is dead.

"Oh, Agnes! Look, look, here!"

That face, so full of pity and of grief, that rain of tears, that
awful mute appeal to me, that solemn hand upraised toward
Heaven!

"Agnes?"

It is over. Darkness comes before my eyes; and, for a time, all
things are blotted out of my remembrance.

When it was first proposed that I should go abroad or how it
came to be agreed among us that I was to seek the restoration of
my peace in change and travel, I do not, even now, distinctly
know. The spirit of Agnes so pervaded all we thought and said
and did in that time of sorrow that I assume I may refer the
project to her influence.

I was to go abroad. I waited only for what Mr. Micawber
called the "final pulverization of Heep" and for the departure of
the emigrants. My aunt, Agnes, Traddles, and I held a conference
when the funeral was over.

"I am happy to say, Miss Wickfield," said Traddles, who had
just come from Canterbury, "that in your absence Mr. Wickfield
has considerably improved. Relieved of the incubus that had
fastened upon him for so long a time and of the dreadful apprehensions under which he had lived, he is hardly the same person. For

we take it to be clear that he might now wind up his business and his agency trust and exhibit no deficiency or defalcation whatever."

"Oh, thank Heaven!" cried Agnes, fervently.

"But," said Traddles, "the surplus that would be left as his means of support—and I suppose the house to be sold—would be very small, not exceeding some hundreds of pounds."

"Dear Mr. Traddles and dear Trotwood," said Agnes, "to take our future on myself will be the next great happiness that I can know. If I rent the dear old house and keep a school, I shall be useful and happy." The calm fervor of her cheerful voice made my heart too full for speech.

"Next, Miss Trotwood," said Traddles, "that property of yours."

"Well, sir," sighed my aunt. "All I have got to say about it is that, if it's gone, I can bear it and, if it's not gone, I shall be glad to get it back."

"It was originally, I think, eight thousand pounds, consols?" said Traddles.

"Right!" replied my aunt.

"I can't account for more than five," said Traddles, with perplexity.

"Thousand, do you mean?" inquired my aunt, with uncommon composure. "Or pounds?"

"Five thousand pounds," said Traddles.

"It was all there was," returned my aunt. "I sold three, myself. One, I paid for your articles, Trot, my dear; and the other two I have by me. When I lost the rest, I thought it wise to say nothing about that sum but to keep it secretly for a rainy day. I wanted to see how you would come out of the trial, Trot; and you came out nobly—persevering, self-reliant, self-denying! So did Dick. Don't speak to me, for I find my nerves a little shaken!"

Nobody would have thought so, to see her sitting upright, with her arms folded; but she had wonderful self-command.

"Then I am delighted to say," cried Traddles, beaming with joy, "that we have recovered the whole money!"

"Don't congratulate me, anybody!" exclaimed my aunt. "How so, sir?"

"Why, the fact is," returned Traddles, "Mr. Micawber had so completely hemmed the rascal in that he could not escape from us.

A most remarkable circumstance is that I really don't think he grasped this sum so much for the gratification of his avarice, which was inordinate, as in the hatred he felt for Copperfield. He said so to me, plainly."

"Ha!" said my aunt, glancing at Agnes. "And what's become of him?"

"I don't know. He left Canterbury with his mother, who had been clamoring, and beseeching, and disclosing, the whole time. They went away by one of the London night coaches, and I know no more about him. Touching those I.O.U's which Mr. Micawber gave him for the advances he had—" said Traddles, a little disconcerted.

"Well! They must be paid," said my aunt.

"Yes, but I don't know when they may be proceeded on or where they are," rejoined Traddles; "and I anticipate that, between this time and his departure, Mr. Micawber will be constantly arrested or taken in execution."

"Then he must be constantly set free again and taken out of execution," said my aunt. "What's the amount altogether?"

"Why, Mr. Micawber has entered the transactions—he calls them transactions—with great form, in a book," rejoined Traddles, smiling; "and he makes the amount a hundred and three pounds, five."

"Now what shall we give him, that sum included?" said my aunt.

Traddles and I both recommended a small sum in money and the payment of the Uriah claims as they came in. We proposed that the family should have their passage and their outfit and a hundred pounds. To this, I added the suggestion that I should give some explanation of his character and history to Mr. Peggotty and that to Mr. Peggotty should be quietly entrusted the discretion of advancing another hundred. I further proposed to interest Mr. Micawber in Mr. Peggotty and to endeavor to bring each of them to bear upon the other, for the common advantage. We all entered warmly into these views; and I may mention at once that the principals themselves did so, shortly afterward, with perfect good will and harmony.

When Agnes and Traddles had left for Canterbury, my aunt

said, "Would you ride with me a little way tomorrow, Trot? I'll tell you then what I have had on my mind lately." For a fortnight she had been in and out of London every day; but her consideration for me was so great that she would not tell me what had happened to distress her.

We drove to one of the large hospitals. Standing hard by the building was a plain hearse. "You understand it now, Trot," said my aunt. "He is gone! When he knew his state in his last illness, he asked them to send for me. He was sorry then. Very sorry. But no one can harm him now. Uriah's threat was a vain one."

We drove away, out of town, to the churchyard at Hornsey. "He was born here," said my aunt. "Six and thirty years ago, this day, my dear, I was married. God forgive us all!"

The morning post brought us the following short note:

> "Canterbury,
> Friday.

"My dear Madam, and Copperfield,
"The fair land of promise lately looming on the horizon is again envelopcd in impenetrable mists and forever withdrawn from the eyes of a drifting wretch whose Doom is sealed!

"A writ has been issued in the cause of *Heep* v. *Micawber*, and the defendant in that cause is the prey of the sheriff having legal jurisdiction in this bailiwick. Consigned to which, and to a speedy end, my course is run. Bless you, bless you! Some future traveler, visiting, from motives of curiosity, not unmingled, let us hope, with sympathy, the place of confinement allotted to debtors in this city, may, and I trust will, Ponder, as he traces on its wall, inscribed with a rusty nail,

> "The obscure initials
> "W.M.

"P.S. I reopen this to say that our common friend Mr. Thomas Traddles has paid the debt and costs, in the noble name of Miss Trotwood, and that myself and family are at the height of earthly bliss."

25

I NOW approach an event in my life, so indelible, so awful, so bound by an infinite variety of ties to all that has preceded it in these pages, that from the beginning of my narrative I have seen it growing larger and larger as I advanced, like a great tower in a plain, and throwing its forecast shadow even on the incidents of my childish days.

For years after it occurred, I dreamed of it often. I have an association between it and a stormy wind, or the lightest mention of a seashore, as strong as any of which my mind is conscious. As plainly as I behold what happened, I will try to write it down. I do not recall it but see it done, for it happens again before me.

Reflecting one evening on what had passed between Ham and myself when I was last at Yarmouth, I decided to write Emily at once. She might desire, I thought, to send some parting word by me to her unhappy lover. I therefore faithfully repeated what he had requested me to tell her, and her reply to Ham came to me next day:

"I have got your message. Oh, what can I write, to thank you for your good and blessed kindness to me! When I find what you are and what uncle is, I think what God must be and can cry to him.

"Good-by for ever. Now, my dear, my friend, good-by forever in this world. In another world, if I am forgiven, I may wake a child and come to you. All thanks and blessings. Farewell, evermore."

In the evening I started, by the mail, down the road to Yarmouth I had traversed so often.

"Don't you think that," I asked the coachman, "a very remarkable sky?"

"That's wind, sir. There'll be mischief done at sea, I expect, before long."

As the night advanced, it came on to blow harder and harder. It still increased until our horses could scarcely face the wind. We came to Ipswich—very late, having had to fight every inch of ground since we were ten miles out of London—and found a cluster of people in the market place, who had risen from their beds in the night, fearful of falling chimneys. As we struggled on, nearer and nearer to the sea from which this mighty wind was blowing dead on shore, its force became terrific. Long before we saw it, its spray was on our lips and showered salt rain upon us. When we came within sight of it, the waves on the horizon, caught at intervals above the rolling abyss, were like glimpses of another shore with towers and buildings. When at last we got into the town, the people came out to their doors, all aslant, making a wonder of the mail that had come through such a night.

Coming near the beach, I saw not only the boatmen but half the people of the town, lurking behind buildings, some now and then braving the fury of the storm to look away to sea and blown sheer out of their course in trying to get zigzag back. The tremendous sea itself, when I could find sufficient pause to look at it in the agitation of the blinding wind, the flying stones and sand, and the awful noise, confounded me. As the high watery walls came rolling in and, at their highest, tumbled into surf, they looked as if the least would engulf the town. As the receding wave swept back with a hoarse roar, it seemed to scoop out deep caves in the beach, as if its purpose were to undermine the earth.

Not finding Ham among the people whom this memorable wind—for it is still remembered down there, as the greatest ever known to blow upon that coast—had brought together, I learned that he had gone to Lowestoft, and I went back to the inn. If such a wind could rise, I think it was rising. The howl and roar, the rattling of the doors and windows, the rumbling in the chimneys, the apparent rocking of the very house that sheltered me and the prodigious tumult of the sea were more fearful than in the morning. When I finally fell asleep, I dreamed I was at the siege of some town in a roar of cannonading, until I awoke to find the storm raging, in lieu of the batteries, and someone knocking and calling at my door, "A wreck! Close by!"

Numbers of people were there before me, all running in one direction to the beach. The sea, having upon it the additional agitation of the whole night, was infinitely more terrific than when I had seen it last. Every appearance it had then presented bore the expression of being *swelled*. Then, O great Heaven, I saw it, close in upon us!

One mast was broken short off and lay over the side, entangled in a maze of sail and rigging which beat the side as if it would stave it in. As the ship turned toward us, I plainly descried her people at work with axes, especially one active figure with long curling hair, conspicuous among the rest. But a great cry, which was audible even above the wind and water, rose from the shore at this moment; the sea, sweeping over the rolling wreck, made a clean breach, and carried men, spars, casks, planks, bulwarks, heaps of such toys into the boiling surge. Four men arose with the wreck out of the deep, clinging to the rigging of the remaining mast—uppermost, the active figure with the curling hair.

There was a bell on board; and as the ship rolled and dashed, the bell rang; and its sound, the knell of those unhappy men, was borne toward us on the wind. Again we lost her, and again she rose. Two men were gone. The agony on shore increased.

The lifeboat had been bravely manned an hour ago and could do nothing; as no man would be so desperate as to attempt to wade off with a rope, there was nothing left to try; but suddenly I saw the people part, and Ham come breaking through them to the front. The determination in his face aroused me to a knowledge of his danger. I held him back with both arms and implored the men not to listen to him, not to let him stir from off that sand!

But another cry arose on shore; and, looking to the wreck, we saw the cruel sail, with blow on blow, beat off the lower of the two men and fly up in triumph round the active figure left alone upon the mast.

Against such a sight and against such determination as that of the calmly desperate man who was already accustomed to lead half the people present, I might as hopefully have entreated the wind. "Mas'r Davy," he said, cheerily grasping me by both hands, "if my time is come, 't is come. If 't ain't, I'll bide it. Lord above bless you and bless all! Mates, make me ready! I'm a going off!"

The wreck, even to my unpracticed eye, was breaking up. I saw that she was parting in the middle and that the life of the solitary man upon the mast hung by a thread. Still, he clung to it. He had a singular red cap on—not like a sailor's cap, but of a finer color—and as the few yielding planks between him and destruction rolled and bulged and his anticipative death knell rang, he was seen by all of us to wave it. I saw him do it now, and I thought I was going distracted when his action brought an old remembrance to my mind of a once dear friend.

Ham watched the sea until there was a great retiring wave, when, with a backward glance at those who held the rope which was made fast round his body, he dashed in after it and in a moment was buffeting with the water; rising with the hills, falling with the valleys, lost beneath the foam, borne in toward the shore, borne on toward the ship, striving hard and valiantly. The distance was nothing, but the power of the sea and wind made the strife deadly. At length he neared the wreck, when, a high, green, vast hillside of water moving on shoreward, from beyond the ship, he seemed to leap up into it with a mighty bound, and the ship was gone!

They drew him to my very feet—insensible—dead; he had been beaten to death by the great wave, and his generous heart was stilled for ever. As I sat beside him, a fisherman, who had known me when Emily and I were children, whispered my name. "Sir," said he, "will you come over yonder?"

The old remembrance that had been recalled to me was in his look. I asked him, terror stricken, "Has a body come ashore? Do I know it?"

He led me to the shore. And on that part of it where she and I had looked for shells, two children—on that part of it where some lighter fragments of the old boat, blown down last night, had been scattered by the wind—among the ruins of the home he had wronged—I saw him lying with his head upon his arm, as I had often seen him lie at school.

No need, O Steerforth, to have said, when we last spoke together, "Think of me at my best!" I had done that ever; and could I change now, looking on this sight! I knew that the hard duty of preparing his mother could only rest with me. Upon a mellow autumn day, about noon, I arrived at Highgate. The wind had quite gone down, and nothing moved.

Mrs. Steerforth was in his room, not in her own; the many tokens of his old sports and accomplishments, by which she was surrounded, remained there, just as he had left them. At her chair, as usual, was Rosa Dartle. From the first moment of her dark eyes resting on me, I saw she knew I was the bearer of evil tidings. The scar sprung into view that instant.

"I am sorry to observe you are in mourning, sir," said Mrs. Steerforth.

"I am unhappily a widower," said I.

"I am grieved to hear it," she returned. "I hope Time will be good to you."

"I hope Time," said I, looking at her, "will be good to all of us. Dear Mrs. Steerforth, we must all trust to that, in our heaviest misfortunes."

I tried to command my voice in gently saying his name, but it trembled. She repeated it to herself, two or three times, in a low tone. Then, addressing me, she said with enforced calmness, "My son is ill."

"Very ill."

The handsome lady—so like— oh, so like!—regarded me with a fixed look and put her hand to her forehead. Then, as she slightly turned her head toward Rosa Dartle, I said, by the motion of my lips, to Rosa, "Dead!"

"Rosa!" said Mrs. Steerforth, "come to me!"

She came, but with no sympathy or gentleness. Her eyes gleamed like fire as she confronted his mother and broke into a frightful laugh. "Now," she said, "is your pride appeased, you madwoman? *Now* has he made atonement to you—with his life! Do you hear? His life!"

Mrs. Steerforth, fallen back stiffly in her chair and making no sound but a moan, cast her eyes upon her with a wide stare.

"Ay!" cried Rosa, "look at me! Moan, and groan, and look at me! Look here!" striking the scar, "at your dead child's handi-work! Moan for your nurture of him, moan for your corruption of him, moan for your loss of him, moan for mine!" She clenched her hand and trembled through her spare worn figure, as if her passion were killing her by inches.

"I loved him better than you ever loved him!" she went on fiercely. "If I had been his wife, I could have been the slave of his caprices for a word of love a year. I could sing to him, and talk to him, and show the ardor that I felt in all he did; and I attracted him. When he was freshest and truest, he loved *me*. Yes, he did! Moan? Moan for what you made him; not for your love."

"Miss Dartle," said I, "if you can be so obdurate as not to feel for this afflicted mother, look at that figure, even as one you have never seen before, and render it some help!"

The figure looked unchangeable, motionless, rigid, staring, moaning in the same dumb way, but giving no other sign of life. Miss Dartle suddenly kneeled down before it. Taking the impassive figure in her arms, she wept over it, called it, tried every tender means to rouse the dormant senses. I went through the dreary house, darkening the windows; and all the world seemed death and silence, broken only by his mother's moaning.

One thing more I had to do, before yielding myself to the shock of these emotions. It was to conceal what had occurred from those who were going away and to dismiss them on their voyage in happy ignorance. It was not easy to whisper to Mr. Peggotty, when they were about to sail, that I had given the letter and all was well. But I did it and made them happy. Mr. Peggotty then told me that Mr. Micawber had just now been arrested again (for the last time) at the suit of Heep and that, in compliance with my request, he had paid the money.

He then took Peggotty and me, who had come to Gravesend for a last farewell, down between decks. It was such a strange scene to me, and so confined and dark, that at first I could make out hardly anything; but, by degrees, it cleared. Among the great beams, bulks, and ringbolts of the ship and heaps of miscellaneous baggage were crowded groups of people, making new friendships, taking leave of one another, talking, laughing, crying, eating and drinking; some already settled down into the possession of their few feet of space, with their little households arranged; others, despairing of a resting place, wandering disconsolate. When the time came for visitors to leave the ship, Mrs. Gummidge, assisted by some younger woman in black, was busily arranging Mr. Peggotty's goods.

"Is there any last wured, Mas'r Davy?" said he. "Is there any one forgotten thing afore we parts?"

"One thing!" said I. "Martha!"

He touched the younger woman I have mentioned, and Martha stood before me. "Heaven bless you, you good man!" cried I. "You take her with you!"

She answered for him, with a burst of tears. I could speak no more at that time, but I wrung his hand; and if ever I have loved and honored any man, I loved and honored that man in my soul.

The time was come. I embraced him, took my weeping nurse upon my arm, and hurried away. On deck, I took leave of poor Mrs. Micawber. She was looking distractedly about for her family, even then; and her last words to me were that she never would desert Mr. Micawber.

We went over the side into our boat and lay at a little distance to see the ship wafted on her course. It was then calm, radiant sunset, when I saw her for the first time, at her uncle's side. Ay, Emily, beautiful and drooping, cling to him with the utmost trust of thy bruised heart; for he has clung to thee with all the might of his great love!

Surrounded by the rosy light and standing high upon the deck, apart together, they solemnly passed away. The night had fallen on the Kentish hills when we were rowed ashore—and fallen darkly upon me.

26

I⊤ was a long and gloomy night that gathered on me, haunted by the ghosts of many hopes, of many dear remembrances, many errors, many unavailing sorrows.

I went away from England, not knowing, even then, how great the shock was that I had to bear. The knowledge came upon me, not quickly, but little by little. By imperceptible degrees, it became a hopeless consciousness of all that I had lost. I mourned for my child-wife, taken from her blooming world, so young. I mourned for him who might have won the love and admiration of thousands, as he had won mine long ago. I mourned for the broken heart that had found rest in the stormy sea and for the wandering remnants of the simple home where I had heard the night wind blowing when I was a child. Listlessness to everything but brooding sorrow was the night that fell on my undisciplined heart. Let me look up from it—as at last I did, thank Heaven!—and from its long sad, wretched dream, to dawn.

I was in Switzerland. I came, one evening, down into a valley, as the evening sun was shining on the remote heights of snow. All at once, in this serenity, great Nature spoke to me and soothed me to weep as I had not wept since Dora died. I had found a packet of letters awaiting me but a few minutes before and had it in my hand. I opened it and read the writing of Agnes.

She gave me no advice; she urged no duty on me; she only told me, in her own fervent manner, what her trust in me was. She knew (she said) how such a nature as mine would turn affliction to good. She commended me to God and in her sisterly affection cherished me always, proud of what I had done, but infinitely prouder yet of what I was reserved to do. I put the letter in my breast and thought, what had I been an hour ago! I felt that the night was passing from my mind, and there was no name for the love I bore her.

Inspired by her, I worked early and late, patiently and hard. I wrote a story with a purpose growing out of my experience, and the tidings of my growing reputation began to reach me. My third work of fiction was not half written when, in an interval of rest, I thought of returning home.

I enter now on the most secret current of my heart. I cannot say when I began to think that I might have set its earliest and brightest hopes on Agnes. I believe I may have heard some whisper of that distant thought, in the old unhappy want of something never to be realized, of which I had been sensible. I made no effort to conceal from myself, now, that I loved her; but I brought the assurance home to myself that it was now too late and that our long-subsisting relation must be undisturbed.

I could not forget that the feeling with which Agnes now regarded me had grown up in my own free choice and course. I had a sustaining sense that I must, in honor, keep away from myself the thought of turning to the dear girl in the withering of my hopes from whom I had frivolously turned when they were fresh. These were the shifting quicksands of my mind in the three years of my absence from her. Three years. And when I stood on the deck that brought me home, Agnes was very dear to me—but she was not mine. She might have been, but that was past.

They expected me home before Christmas but had no idea of my returning so soon. I had purposely misled them that I might have the pleasure of surprising them. And yet, I was perverse enough to feel a chill and disappointment in receiving no welcome and rattling, alone and silent, through the streets of London.

For some changes in the fortunes of my friends, I was pre-pared. My aunt had long been reestablished at Dover, and Traddles had chambers in Gray's Inn, whither I now made my way. In the course of my stumbling up his stairs, I fancied I heard a pleasant sound of laughter; and not the laughter of an attorney or barrister or their clerks but of two or three merry girls. When I found Traddles's door, I knocked. A considerable scuffling within ensued, but nothing else. I knocked again, and a small, sharp-looking lad, very much out of breath, presented himself. "Is Mr. Traddles within?" I said.

"Yes, sir, but he's engaged." After a moment's survey of me, however, the sharp-looking lad admitted me into a little sitting room where I came into the presence of my old friend (also out of breath) seated at a table and bending over papers.

"Good God!" cried Traddles, looking up. "It's Copperfield!"

and rushed into my arms, where I held him tight. "My beloved Copperfield, how glad I am to see you!"

"All well, my dear Traddles?"

"All well, my dear, dear Copperfield, and nothing but good news! I am married! Why, my dear boy, she's behind the window curtain! Look here!"

To my amazement, the dearest girl in the world came at that same instant, laughing and blushing, from her place of conceal-ment. I kissed her as an old acquaintance should and wished them joy with all my might of heart.

"We are all as happy as possible!" said Traddles. "Even the girls are happy—Sophy's sisters. They are staying with us. I was romping with the girls, in point of fact, when you knocked. But as that wouldn't look quite professional if they were seen by a client, they decamped. But then," said Traddles, "our domestic arrangements are, to say the truth quite unprofessional. Even Sophy's being here is unprofessional. And we have no other place of abode."

If I had beheld a thousand roses blowing in a top set of chambers, in that withered Gray's Inn, they could not have brightened it half so much as those pretty Devonshire girls. I thought of them with pleasure as I walked back to the Inn coffee house, where I found my eyes resting on a countenance associated with my earliest remembrances. Little Mr. Chillip, the doctor to whose good offices I was indebted in the very first chapter of this history, sat there reading a newspaper. "I have a kind of an impression that something in your countenance is familiar to me, sir," he said, in reply to my greeting; "but I couldn't lay my hand on your name, really."

"And yet you knew it, long before I knew it myself," I returned.

"Did I indeed, sir?" said Mr. Chillip. "Is it possible that I had the honor, sir, of officiating when—?"

On my telling him my name he was really moved. He quite shook hands with me—which was a violent proceeding for him, his usual course being to slide a tepid little fish slice, an inch or two in advance of his hip, and evince the greatest discomposure when anybody grappled with it. "We are not ignorant, sir," he said, "down in our part of the country, of your fame. I have heard of you, too, from your stepfather's sister. Very decided character there, sir?"

"The brother and sister are pursuing their old course, are they?" said I.

Mr. Chillip shook his head. "She was a charming woman, sir!" he observed in a plaintive manner.

"The present Mrs. Murdstone?"

"A charming woman indeed, sir," said Mr. Chillip; "as amiable, I am sure, as it was possible to be! Mrs. Chillip's opinion is that her spirit has been entirely broken since her marriage and that she is all but melancholy mad. They go about with her, now, more like her keepers than her husband and sister-in-law. That was Mrs. Chillip's remark to me. And the ladies," observed Mr. Chillip timorously, "are great observers."

I told Mr. Chillip that I was going down to my aunt, whom he had met on the night of my birth. The mere notion of her appeared to terrify him. He called almost immediately for a candle and went to bed, as if he were not quite safe anywhere else.

Thoroughly tired, I went to bed too, passed the next day on the Dover coach, burst safe and sound into my aunt's old parlor, and was received by her, and Mr. Dick, and dear old Peggotty, who acted as housekeeper, with open arms and tears of joy. My aunt was mightily amused by my account of my meeting with Mr. Chillip and of his holding her in such dread remembrance; and both she and Peggotty had a great deal to say about my poor mother's second husband and "that murdering woman of a sister" —on whom I think no pain or penalty would have induced my aunt to bestow any other designation.

"And when, Trot," said my aunt, "are you going over to Canterbury?"

"I shall ride over tomorrow, aunt," I said, looking thoughtfully at the fire; for I could not be so near Agnes without the revival of those regrets with which I had so long been occupied. "Oh, Trot," I seemed to hear my aunt say once more, and I understood her better now—"blind, blind, blind!" When I raised my eyes, I found that she was steadily observant of me. "Has Agnes any—" I was thinking aloud, rather than speaking.

"Well? Hey? Any what?" said my aunt, sharply.

"Any lover," said I.

"A score!" cried my aunt, with a kind of indignant pride. "She might have been married twenty times, my dear, since you have been gone!"

"No doubt," said I. "But has she any lover worthy of her?"

My aunt sat musing for a little while before she said, "I suspect she has an attachment, Trot, though I have no right to tell you even so much."

She was so true, she was so beautiful, she was so good—I owed her so much gratitude, she was so dear to me that I could find no utterance for what I felt when finally I saw her. I tried to bless her, tried to thank her, tried to tell her what an influence she had on me, but my love and joy were dumb.

At last I told her something that had been in my thoughts since Dora died. "You remember when you came down to me in our little room—pointing upward, Agnes?"

"Oh, Trotwood!" she returned, her eyes filled with tears. "So loving, so confiding, and so young! Can I ever forget?"

"As you were then, my sister, I have often thought since, you have ever been to me. Ever pointing upward, Agnes, ever leading me to something better!"

She only shook her head; through her tears I saw a sad quiet smile.

As I rode back in the lonely night, the wind going by me like a restless memory, I thought of this, and feared she was not happy. *I* was not happy; but, thus far, I had faithfully set the seal upon the past.

27

As my notoriety began to bring upon me an enormous quantity of letters, I agreed with Traddles to have my name painted up on his door; and there, at intervals, I labored through them. The girls had gone home, but Sophy was always there. "What a thoroughly good and charming wife she is," said I one day.

"My dear Copperfield," returned Traddles, "she is, without exception, the dearest girl! The way she manages this place; her domestic knowledge, economy, and order; her cheerfulness! I positively sometimes can't believe it. Then, our pleasures! Dear me, they are inexpensive, but they are quite wonderful! When we stroll into the squares and streets and see a house to let, sometimes we look up at it and say, how would *that* do, if I was made a judge? And we parcel it out—such a room for us, such rooms for the girls, and so forth. Now, you know, Copperfield, if I was Lord Chancellor, we couldn't do this!"

"You would do something pleasant and amiable, whatever you were," thought I. "And by the way," I said aloud, "I suppose you never draw any skeletons now?"

"Really," replied Traddles, laughing and reddening, "I can't wholly deny that I do. For being in one of the back rows of the King's Bench the other day, with a pen in my hand, I am afraid there's a skeleton—in a wig—on the desk." He wound up by saying, in his forgiving way, as he thought of our schoolmaster, "Old Creakle!"

"I have a letter from that old—rascal here," said I. "Among the persons who are attracted to me in my rising fame and fortune and who discover that they were always much attached to me is the self-same Creakle. He is a magistrate now and writes that he will be glad to show me the only true system of prison discipline; the only unchallengeable way of making sincere and lasting penitents—which, you must know, is by solitary confinement. If you'll read his letter, you'll find he is the tenderest of men to prisoners convicted of the whole calendar of felonies, though I can't find that his tenderness extends to any other class."

We decided to accept his offer and repaired one day to the prison, an immense and solid building, erected at vast expense. I could not help thinking what an uproar would have been made if any deluded man had proposed to spend one-half the money it had cost on the erection of an industrial school for the young or a house of refuge for the deserving old. And I found, as we went through the magnificent passages, that the most professing men were the greatest objects of interest to Mr. Creakle and his fellow magistrates, especially a certain Number Twenty-seven, who was the favorite, though Twenty-eight was also a bright particular star.

To give us an opportunity of conversing with Twenty-seven in all his purity, Mr. Creakle directed him to be invited out into

the passage; when whom should Traddles and I behold, to our amazement, but Uriah Heep!

He knew us directly and greeted us with the old writhe, which caused a general admiration in the party. I rather thought that everyone was struck by his not being proud and taking notice of us.

"Well, Twenty-seven," said Mr. Creakle, mournfully admiring him, "are you quite comfortable?"

"I am very umble, sir!" replied Uriah Heep. "I see my follies now, sir. And that makes me comfortable."

A murmur of gratification having subsided, orders were given to let out Twenty-eight. I had been so much astonished already, that I only felt a kind of resigned wonder when Mr. Littimer walked forth, reading a good book.

"Twenty-eight," said a gentleman in spectacles, who appeared to me to back him against Mr. Creakle's Twenty-seven, "what is your state of mind?"

"I thank you, sir," returned Mr. Littimer, "I see my follies now, sir. I am a good deal troubled when I think of the sins of my former companions; but I trust they may find forgiveness."

"Now, Twenty-seven," said Mr. Creakle, "is there anything we can do for you?"

"I would umbly ask, sir," returned Uriah, with a jerk of his malevolent head, "for leave to write to mother. I should wish mother to be got into my state. I never should have got into my present state if I hadn't come here. It would be better for everybody, if they got took up and was brought here."

This sentiment gave greater satisfaction than anything that had passed yet.

"I hope Mr. W. will repent, and Miss W., and all of that sinful lot," Uriah went on. "I pity all who ain't brought here!" He sneaked back into his cell amid a chorus of approbation.

It was characteristic of this repentance that I was fain to ask what these two men had done to be there at all. I addressed myself to one of the warders, who, I suspected from certain indications, knew pretty well what all this stir was worth. The answer was that Twenty-seven's last "folly" was fraud, forgery, and conspiracy. "And Twenty-eight," said my informant, looking over his shoulder as we walked along, to guard himself from being overheard in an unlawful reference to these immaculates by Creakle and the rest, "Twenty-eight got a place and robbed a young master the night before they were going abroad. I particularly recollect his case, from his being took by a dwarf."

"Not Miss Mowcher?"

"That's it! He had eluded pursuit and was going to America in such a complete disguise as you never see, when the little woman picked him out with her sharp eye in a moment—ran between his legs to upset him—and held on to him like grim death. She said in court that she'd have took him single handed (on account of what she knew concerning him) if he had been Samson."

We had now seen all there was to see. It would have been in vain to represent to such a man as the worshipful Mr. Creakle that Twenty-seven and Twenty-eight were perfectly consistent and unchanged; that the hypocritical knaves were just the subjects to make that sort of profession in such a place. We left them to their precious system and themselves.

At least once a week I rode over from my aunt's to see Agnes. When I read her what I wrote, when I moved her to smiles or tears and heard her voice so earnest on the shadowy events of that imaginative world in which I lived, I thought what a fate mine might have been, what I could have wished my wife to be.

But Christmas time being come and Agnes having reposed no new confidence in me, a doubt arose in me whether she could have a perception of the true state of my breast, which restrained her from giving me pain. I resolved to set this right. "Do you know anything more," said I to my aunt, "of that attachment of Agnes?"

She looked up in my face a little while before replying. "I think I do, Trot."

"Are you confirmed in your impression?" I inquired.

"I think I am, Trot. And what is more—I think Agnes is going to be married."

"God bless her!" said I, summoning up a determination to be cheerful.

"God bless her!" said my aunt, "and her husband too!" There was greater reason than ever to do what I had resolved. I rode to Canterbury that very day.

"Agnes," said I, "you have a secret. Let me share it."

She cast down her eyes and trembled.

"I have heard—but from other lips than yours, which seems strange—that there is someone upon whom you have bestowed the treasure of your love. Do not shut me out of what concerns your happiness so nearly!"

With an appealing, almost a reproachful, glance, she hurried across the room as if without knowing where, put her hands before her face, and burst into tears.

"Agnes! Sister! Dearest! What have I done?"

"Let me go, Trotwood, I am not well. Don't speak to me now. Don't! don't!"

Was it a selfish error that was leading me astray? Or was something opening to me that I had not dared to think of? "For Heaven's sake, Agnes, let us not mistake each other after all these years! I must speak plainly. If you have any lingering thought that I could envy the happiness you will confer, that I could not resign you to a dearer protector, of your own choosing, dismiss it, for I don't deserve it! You have not taught me quite in vain."

She was quiet now. In a little time she said in a low voice, "You are mistaken, Trotwood. If I have any secret, it is—no new one; and is—not what you suppose. I cannot reveal it or divide it." She was going away, but I detained her. New thoughts and hopes were whirling through my mind, and all the colors of my life were changing. "Dearest Agnes! If I indeed have any new-born hope that I may ever call you something more than sister, widely different from sister—"

Her tears fell fast; but they were not like those she had lately shed, and I saw my hope brighten in them. "Agnes! Ever my guide and best support! If you had been more mindful of yourself and less of me, when we grew up together, I think my heedless fancy never would have wandered from you. I went away, dear Agnes, loving you. I stayed away, loving you. I returned home, loving you!"

Still weeping, but not sadly—joyfully!—and clasped in my arms as she had never been, as I had thought she never was to be! "I am so blessed, Trotwood—my heart is so overcharged—but there is one thing I must say. Do you know, yet, what it is?"

"I am afraid to speculate. Tell me, my dear."

"I have loved you all my life!"

Oh, we were happy, we were happy! Long miles of road opened out before my mind; and, toiling on, I saw a ragged way-worn boy forsaken and neglected, who should come to call even the heart now beating against mine his own.

We were married within a fortnight. "Dearest husband!" said Agnes. "Now that I may call you by that name, I have one more thing to tell you. The night when Dora died, she made a last request to me and left me a last charge."

"And it was—"

"That only I would occupy this vacant place."

What I have purposed to record is nearly finished; but without one incident some threads in the web I have spun would have a raveled end.

I had advanced in fame and fortune, my domestic joy was perfect, I had been married ten happy years, when I was told one night that a stranger wished to see me. It was Mr. Peggotty!

"And now tell us," said I, when our first emotion was over, "everything relating to your fortunes."

"Our fortun's, Mas'r Davy," he rejoined, "is soon told. We've allus thrived. That is, in the long run. If not yesterday, why then today. If not today, why then tomorrow. And Em'ly? A slight figure," said Mr. Peggotty, looking at the fire, "kiender worn, fondly loving of her uncle, patient, liked by young and old, sowt out by all that has any trouble. That's Em'ly!" She might have married well, he told us. "'But uncle,' she says, 'that's gone forever.'" Martha was married, and even Mrs. Gummidge had had an offer!

"Now, last, not least, Mr. Micawber," said I. "He has paid off every obligation he incurred here, and therefore we may take it for granted that he is doing well. But what is the latest news of him?"

Mr. Peggotty, with a smile, handed me a little odd-looking newspaper, where I read aloud as follows:

"☞ The public dinner to our distinguished fellow colonist *Wilkins Micawber, Esq.*, Port Middlebay District Magistrate, came off yesterday in the large room of the hotel, where the beauty, fashion, and exclusiveness of Port Middlebay flocked to do honor to one so deservedly esteemed, so highly talented, and so widely popular. Doctor Mell (of Colonial Salem-House Grammar School) presided. When he proposed 'Our distinguished guest, the ornament of our town!' the cheering defied description. . . . " There was a good deal more, but I looked back to the name of Doctor Mell, pleased to have discovered, in these happier circumstances, Mr. Mell, formerly poor pinched usher to Mr. Creakle.

Before Mr. Peggotty left, he went with me to Yarmouth, to see a little tablet I had put up to the memory of Ham, and there he gathered a tuft of grass from the grave. "For Em'ly," he said, as he put it in his breast. "I promised, Mas'r Davy."

And now my written story ends. I look back, once more—for the last time—before I close these leaves.

I see myself, with Agnes at my side, journeying along the road of life. I see our children and our friends around us. What faces are the most distinct? Here is my aunt, an old woman of fourscore years and more, but upright yet. Always with her, here comes

Peggotty, my good old nurse, accustomed to do needlework at night very close to the lamp, but never sitting down to it without a bit of wax candle and a workbox with a picture of St. Paul's upon the lid. Her cheeks and arms, so hard and red in my childish days, are shriveled now; but her rough forefinger, which I once associated with a nutmeg grater, is just the same, and when I see my least child catching at it as it totters from my aunt to her I think of our old parlor at home, when I could scarcely walk. My aunt's old disappointment is set right, now. She is godmother to a real living Betsey Trotwood; and Agnes and Dora (next in order) say she spoils her.

Among my boys, this summer holiday time, I see an old man making giant kites, with a delight for which there are no words. He greets me rapturously and whispers, with many nods and winks, "Trotwood, you will be glad to hear that I shall finish the Memorial when I have nothing else to do and that your aunt's the most extraordinary woman in the world, sir!"

Working at his chambers in the Temple, with a busy aspect, and his hair more rebellious than ever by the constant friction of his lawyer's wig, I come upon my dear old Traddles. It is the talk of the town, now, that Traddles will be a judge; and Traddles's house is one of the very houses—or it easily may have been—which he and Sophy used to parcel out, in their walks. It is a large house; but Traddles and Sophy squeeze themselves into upper rooms, reserving the best bedrooms for the Beauty and the girls, three of whom, however, are married.

And now, as I close my task, these faces fade away. But one face, shining on me like a heavenly light by which I see all other objects, is above them and beyond them all. Oh Agnes, oh my soul, so may thy face be by me when I close my life indeed; so may I, when realities are melting from me like the shadows which I now dismiss, still find thee near me, pointing upward!

OLIVER TWIST

I

AMONG other public buildings in a certain town, there is one anciently common to most towns, great or small, to wit, a workhouse; and in this workhouse was born the item of mortality whose name is prefixed to this book.

For some time it remained a matter of considerable doubt whether the child would survive to bear any name at all; indeed, if Oliver had been surrounded by careful grandmothers, anxious aunts, experienced nurses, and doctors of profound wisdom, he would most indubitably have been killed in no time. There being nobody by, however, but a pauper old woman, who was rendered rather misty by an unwonted allowance of beer, and a parish surgeon, who did such matters by contract, Oliver and Nature fought out the point between them. As he finally gave proof of the free and proper action of his lungs, the pale face of a young woman was raised feebly, and a faint voice said, "Let me see the child and die."

The surgeon deposited it in her arms. She imprinted her cold lips passionately on its forehead; passed her hands over her face;

gazed wildly round; shuddered; fell back—and died. "She was a good-looking girl, too; where did she come from?" the surgeon said.

"She was brought here last night," replied the old woman. "She was found lying in the street. She had walked some distance, for her shoes were worn to pieces. But where she came from, or where she was going to, nobody knows."

The surgeon leaned over the body and raised the left hand. "The old story," he said, shaking his head; "no wedding ring, I see. Ah! Good night!"

Oliver cried lustily. If he could have known that he was an orphan, left to the tender mercies of churchwardens and overseers, perhaps he would have cried the louder.

The hungry and destitute situation of the infant orphan being duly reported by the workhouse authorities to the parish authorities, they humanely resolved that Oliver should be "farmed," in other words despatched to a branch workhouse some three miles off, where twenty or thirty other juvenile offenders against the poor laws rolled about the floor all day, without the inconvenience of too much food or clothing, under the parental superintendence of an elderly female who received the culprits for the consideration of sevenpence halfpenny per small head per week and consigned the rising parochial generation to even a shorter allowance than was originally provided for them.

It cannot be expected that this system of farming would produce any very extraordinary or luxuriant crop. Oliver Twist's ninth birthday found him a pale thin child, somewhat diminutive in stature, and decidedly small in circumference. He was keeping it in the coal cellar with a select party of two other young gentlemen, who, after participating with him in a sound thrashing, had been locked up for atrociously presuming to be hungry, when Mrs. Mann, the good lady of the house, was startled by the apparition of Mr. Bumble, the beadle, who generally presaged a visit from the parish board. He was striving to undo the garden gate.

"Goodness gracious! Is that you, Mr. Bumble, sir?" said Mrs. Mass, thrusting her head out of the window in well-affected ecstasies of joy. "(Susan, take Oliver and them two brats upstairs, and wash 'em directly.) My heart alive! Mr. Bumble, how glad I am to see you, sure-ly!"

Now, Mr. Bumble was a fat man, and a choleric; he gave the gate a tremendous shake and then bestowed upon it a kick which could have emanated from no leg but a beadle's. "Now, don't you be offended at what I'm a going to say," said Mrs. Mann, running out to let him in. "You've had a long walk, or I wouldn't mention it. Now, will you take a little drop of somethink, Mr. Bumble?"

"Not a drop. Not a drop," said Mr. Bumble, waving his hand in a placid manner.

"Now, just a leetle drop," said Mrs. Mann persuasively.

"What is it?" inquired the beadle.

"Why, it's what I'm obliged to keep a little of in the house to put into the blessed infants' Daffy, when they ain't well, Mr. Bumble," replied Mrs. Mann as she took down a bottle and glass. "It's gin. I'll not deceive you, Mr. B. It's gin."

"Do you give the children Daffy, Mrs. Mann?" inquired Bumble, following with his eyes the interesting process of mixing. "You feel as a mother, Mrs. Mann." He stirred the gin and water. "And now about business," as he swallowed half of it. "The child that was half baptized, Oliver Twist, is nine year old today. And notwithstanding the most superlative exertions on the part of the parish, we have never been able to discover who is his father or what was his mother's settlement, name, or con-dition."

"How comes he to have any name at all, then?" said Mrs. Mann, astonished.

The beadle drew himself up with great pride. "I inwented it."

"You, Mr. Bumble?"

"I, Mrs. Mann. We name our foundlings in alphabetical order. The last was a S—Swubble, I named him. This was a T—Twist, I named *him*. The next one as comes will be Unwin, and the next Vilkins. I have got names ready made to the end of the alphabet."

"Why, you're quite a literary character, sir!" said Mrs. Mann.

"Well, well," said the beadle, gratified, "perhaps I may be, Mrs. Mann." He finished the gin and water. "Oliver being now too old to remain here, the board have sent me to take him back to the house."

So Oliver was led away from the wretched home where one kind word or look had never lighted the gloom of his infant years. And yet he burst into an agony of childish grief as the gate closed after him. Wretched as were the little companions in misery he was leaving behind, they were the only friends he had known; and a sense of his loneliness in the great wide world sank into the child's heart for the first time.

Poor Oliver! The workhouse board had that very day arrived at a decision which would exercise a material influence over all his future fortunes. They had established the rule that all poor people should have the alternative (for they would compel nobody, not they) of being starved by a gradual process in the house or by a quick one out of it. With this view, they issued three meals of thin gruel a day, with an onion twice a week, and half a roll on Sundays.

The room in which the boys were fed was a large stone hall with a copper at one end, out of which the master ladled the gruel at mealtimes. Of this festive composition each boy had one porringer, and no more. The bowls never wanted washing. The boys polished them with their spoons till they shone; and when they had performed this operation, they would sit staring at the copper, with such eager eyes, as if they could have devoured the very bricks of which it was composed, employing themselves, meanwhile, in sucking their fingers most assiduously, with the view of catching up any stray splashes of gruel that might have been cast thereon. Boys have generally excellent appetites. Oliver Twist and his companions suffered the tortures of slow starvation for three months: at last they got so voracious and wild with hunger that one boy, who was tall for his age, and not used to that sort of thing, hinted darkly to his companions that unless he had another basin of gruel per diem, he was afraid he might some night happen to eat the boy who slept next him. He had a wild, hungry eye; and they implicitly believed him. A council was held; lots were cast to determine who should walk up to the master after supper that evening and ask for more; and it fell to Oliver Twist.

The evening arrived; the boys took their places. The master stationed himself at the copper; his pauper assistants ranged themselves behind him; the gruel was served out; and a long grace was said over the short commons. The gruel disappeared; the boys winked at Oliver. Child as he was, he was desperate with hunger and reckless with misery. He rose from the table and, advancing to the master, basin in hand, said, somewhat alarmed at his own temerity, "Please, sir, I want some more."

The master was a fat, healthy man; but he turned very pale.

He gazed in stupefied astonishment on the small rebel and then clung for support to the copper. The assistants were paralyzed with wonder; the boys with fear. "What!" said the master at length, in a faint voice.

"Please, sir," replied Oliver, "I want some more."

The master aimed a blow at Oliver's head with the ladle, pinioned him in his arms, and shrieked aloud for the beadle. The board were sitting in solemn conclave, when Mr. Bumble rushed into the room in great excitement and, addressing the gentleman at the top, said, "Mr. Limbkins, I beg your pardon, sir! Oliver Twist has asked for more!"

There was a general start. Horror was depicted on every countenance. "For *more!* That boy will be hung," said a gentleman in a white waistcoat. "I know that boy will be hung."

Oliver was ordered into instant confinement; and a bill was next morning pasted on the outside of the gate, offering a reward of five pounds to anybody who would take Oliver Twist off the hands of the parish. In other words, five pounds and Oliver Twist were offered to any man or woman who wanted an apprentice to any trade, business, or calling.

For a week after the commission of the impious and profane offence of asking for more, Oliver remained a prisoner in a dark and solitary room; crying bitterly all day; when the long, dismal night came on, spreading his little hands before his eyes to shut out the darkness, and crouching in a corner to sleep. As for exercise, it was nice cold weather and he was allowed to perform his ablutions under the pump in a stone yard, while Mr. Bumble prevented him catching cold by repeated applications of the cane. As for society, he was carried every other day into the hall and there sociably flogged as a public warning and example.

It chanced one morning, while Oliver's affairs were in this comfortable state, that Mr. Gamfield, chimney sweep, was deeply cogitating ways and means of paying certain arrears of rent when, passing the workhouse, his eyes encountered the bill on the gate. "Wo-o!" said Mr. Gamfield, bestowing a blow on the head of his donkey and giving its jaw a sharp wrench.

The gentleman with the white waistcoat was standing at the gate after delivering himself of some profound sentiments in the board room; and, having witnessed the little dispute between Mr. Gamfield and the donkey, he smiled joyously when that person came up to read the bill, for he saw at once that Mr. Gamfield was exactly the sort of master for Oliver Twist. Mr. Gamfield smiled, too, as he perused the document; for five pounds was just the sum he had been wishing for; and, as to the boy, Mr. Gamfield, knowing what the dietary of the workhouse was, well knew he would be a nice small pattern, just the thing for register stoves.

But the board having considered Mr. Gamfield's proposition, declared themselves against it. As Mr. Gamfield did labor under the slight imputation of having bruised three or four boys to death already, it occurred to him that the board had, perhaps, in some unaccountable freak, taken it into their heads that this extraneous circumstance ought to influence their proceedings. "So you won't let me have him, gen'lmen?" he said.

"No," replied Mr. Limbkins; "at least, as it's a nasty business, we think you ought to take something less than the premium we offered."

"What'll you give, gen'lmen?" said Mr. Gamfield, brightening. "Come! Don't be too hard on a poor man. What'll you give?"

"I should say, three pound ten was plenty," said Mr. Limbkins.

"You're desperate hard on me, gen'lmen," said Gamfield, when they remained adamant. But the bargain was made. Mr. Bumble was instructed that Oliver Twist and his indentures were to be conveyed before the magistrate for approval; and it was done that very afternoon.

"This is the boy, your worship," said Mr. Bumble.

An old gentleman reading a newspaper behind the desk raised his head. "Well," said he, "I suppose he's fond of chimney-sweeping?"

"He dotes on it, your worship," replied Bumble, giving Oliver a sly pinch to intimate that he had better not say he didn't.

"And this man that's to be his master—you, sir—you'll treat him well, and feed him, and do all that sort of thing, will you?"

"When I says I will, I means I will," replied Mr. Gamfield doggedly.

"You're a rough speaker, my friend, but you look an honest, open-hearted man," said the old gentleman, turning his spectacles in the direction of the candidate for Oliver's premium, whose villanous countenance was a regular stamped receipt for cruelty. But the magistrate was half blind and half childish, so he couldn't reasonably be expected to discern what other people did.

"I hope I am, sir," said Mr. Gamfield, with an ugly leer.

"I have no doubt you are, my friend," replied the old gentleman, fixing his spectacles more firmly on his nose, and looking about him for the inkstand.

It was the critical moment of Oliver's fate. Happening in the course of his search to look straight before him the old gentleman encountered the pale and terrified face of Oliver Twist, who, despite all the admonitory looks and pinches of Bumble, was regarding the repulsive face of his future master with horror and fear too palpable to be mistaken even by a half-blind magistrate.

"My boy!" said the old gentleman. Oliver started at the sound. He might be excused for doing so; for the words were kindly said, and strange sounds frighten one. He trembled violently and burst into tears.

"My boy!" said the old gentleman, "you look pale and alarmed. What is the matter? Stand away from him, Beadle."

Oliver fell on his knees and, clasping his hands, prayed that they would order him back to the dark room, that they would starve him—beat him—rather than send him away with that dreadful man.

"Well!" said Mr. Bumble, raising his hands and eyes with most impressive solemnity, "Well! of all the artful and designing orphans that ever I see, Oliver, you are one of the most bare-facedest."

"Hold your tongue, Beadle," said the old gentleman. "I refuse to sanction these indentures. Take the boy back to the workhouse and treat him kindly. He seems to want it."

The next morning the public were once more informed that Oliver Twist was again "To Let" and that five pounds would be paid to anybody who would take possession of him.

2

"By the bye," said Mr. Bumble, happening to meet at the gate Mr. Sowerberry, the parochial undertaker. "You don't know anybody who wants a boy, do you?" As he spoke he gave three distinct raps upon the words "five pounds" on the bill above him.

"Gadso!" said the undertaker, examining the bill, "I think I'll take the boy myself." It was at once arranged that Oliver should go to him "upon liking"—a phrase which means, in the case of a parish apprentice, that if the master find, upon a short trial, that he can get enough work out of a boy without putting too much food into him, he shall have him for a term of years, to do what he likes with.

Oliver heard the news of his destination in perfect silence. Once more attaching himself to Mr. Bumble's gold-laced cuff, he was led away. As they drew near, Mr. Bumble thought it expedient to look down and see that the boy was in good order for inspection by his new master, when he saw a tear in Oliver's eye. As he gazed sternly at him, it rolled down his cheek. It was followed by another, and another. The child made a strong effort, but it was unsuccessful. He covered his face with both hands and wept until the tears sprang out from between his chin and bony fingers.

"Well!" exclaimed Mr. Bumble, darting at his little charge a look of intense malignity. "Of *all* the ungratefullest and worst disposed boys, Oliver, you are the—"

"No, no, sir," sobbed Oliver, clinging to the hand which held the well-known cane. "No, no, sir; I will be good indeed; indeed, indeed, I will, sir! I am a very little boy, sir; and it is so—so—"

"So what?" inquired Mr. Bumble, in amazement.

"So lonely, sir! So very lonely!" cried the child. "Everybody hates me. Oh! sir, don't, don't pray be cross to me!" The child beat his hand upon his heart and looked in his companion's face with tears of real agony.

Mr. Bumble regarded Oliver with some astonishment, for a few seconds; then, once more taking his hand, walked on with him in silence.

"Oh! that's the boy, is it?" said the undertaker when they arrived. "Mrs. Sowerberry, will you have the goodness to come here a moment, my dear?"

Mrs. Sowerberry emerged, presenting the form of a short, thin, squeezed-up woman, with a vixenish countenance. "My dear," said Mr. Sowerberry deferentially, "this is the boy from the work-house." Oliver bowed.

"Dear me!" said the undertaker's wife, "he's very small."

"Why, he *is* rather small," replied Mr. Bumble. "But he'll grow—he'll grow."

"Ah! I dare say he will," replied the lady pettishly, "on our victuals. Get downstairs, little bag o' bones." With this she pushed Oliver down a steep flight of stairs into a stone cell denominated "kitchen," wherein sat a slatternly girl. "Here, Charlotte," said Mrs. Sowerberry, "give this boy some of the cold bits that were put by for Trip. I dare say the boy isn't too dainty to eat 'em—are you, boy?"

Oliver, whose eyes had glistened at the mention of meat and who was trembling with eagerness to devour it, replied in the negative; and a plateful of coarse broken victuals were set before him.

"Well," said the undertaker's wife, watching with fearful auguries the horrible avidity with which Oliver Twist tore asunder the viands that the dog had neglected, "have you done?" There being nothing eatable now within his reach, Oliver replied in the affirmative. "Then come with me," said Mrs. Sowerberry. "Your bed's under the counter. You don't mind sleeping among the coffins, I suppose?" Oliver meekly followed his new mistress; and he wished, as he crept into his narrow bed, that that were indeed his coffin.

Oliver was awakened in the morning by a loud kicking at the shop door. When he began to undo the chain, a voice cried, "Open the door, will yer?"

"I will, directly, sir," replied Oliver.

"I suppose yer the new boy, ain't yer?" said the voice through the keyhole. "How old are yer?"

"Ten, sir," replied Oliver.

"Then I'll whop yer when I get in," said the voice; "you just see if I don't, my work'us brat!" And, having made this obliging promise, the voice began to whistle.

For a second or two after he opened the door, Oliver glanced up the street, and down the street, and over the way; for nobody did he see but a big charity boy, sitting on a post in front of the house, eating bread and butter. "Yer don't know who I am, I suppose, Work'us?" said the charity boy. "I'm Mr. Noah Claypole, and you're under me. Take down the shutters, yer idle young ruffian!" With this, Mr. Claypole administered a kick to Oliver and entered the shop with a dignified air.

"Come near the fire, Noah," said Charlotte, when they went down to breakfast. "I saved a nice little bit of bacon for you. Oliver, shut that door at Mr. Noah's back and take them bits that I've put out for you over to that box. D'ye hear?"

"D'ye hear, Work'us?" said Noah Claypole. Noah was a charity boy, but not a workhouse orphan. No chance child was he, for he could trace his genealogy all the way back to his parents, who lived hard by. The shop boys in the neighborhood had long been in the habit of branding Noah, in the public streets, with the ignominious epithet of "charity"; and Noah had borne it without reply. But now that fortune had cast in his way a nameless orphan, at whom even the meanest could point with scorn, he retorted on him with interest, which affords charming food for contemplation.

Oliver had been sojourning at the undertaker's some three weeks or a month when Mr. Sowerberry said one evening, "My dear—" He was going to say more; but, Mrs. Sowerberry looking up with a peculiarly unpropitious aspect, he stopped short.

"Well," said Mrs. Sowerberry, sharply.

"Nothing, my dear, nothing," said Mr. Sowerberry.

"Ugh, you brute!" said Mrs. Sowerberry.

"Not at all, my dear," said Mr. Sowerberry, humbly. "I thought you didn't want to hear, my dear. I was only going to say—"

"Oh, don't tell me what you were going to say," interposed Mrs. Sowerberry. "I am nobody; don't consult me, pray. *I* don't want to intrude upon your secrets." As Mrs. Sowerberry said this, she gave a hysterical laugh, which threatened violent consequences.

This is a very common and much-approved matrimonial course of treatment, which is often very effective. It at once reduced Mr. Sowerberry to begging, as a special favor, to be allowed to say what Mrs. Sowerberry was most curious to hear. After a short altercation of less than three-quarters of an hour's duration, the permission was graciously conceded.

"It's only about young Twist, my dear," said Mr. Sowerberry.

"There's an expression of melancholy in his face which is very interesting. He would make a delightful mute, my love. I don't mean to attend grown-up people, but only for children's practice. You may depend on it, it would have a superb effect."

Mrs. Sowerberry, who had a good deal of taste in the undertaking way, was much struck by the novelty of this idea; but as it would have been compromising her dignity to say so under the circumstances, she merely inquired, with much sharpness, why such an obvious suggestion had not presented itself to her husband's mind before. Mr. Sowerberry rightly construed this as an acquiescence; and, the month's trial over, Oliver was formally apprenticed.

It was a nice sickly season. In commercial phrase, coffins were looking up; and many were the mournful processions which little Oliver headed, in a hat band reaching down to his knees, to the indescribable admiration and emotion of all the mothers in the town. But Noah Claypole's jealousy being aroused by the same sight, he used Oliver far worse than before. Charlotte treated him ill, because Noah did; and Mrs. Sowerberry was his decided enemy, because Mr. Sowerberry was disposed to be his friend; so, between these three on one side and a glut of funerals on the other, Oliver was not altogether comfortable.

One day, intent upon the innocent amusement of aggravating young Oliver, Noah pulled Oliver's hair; and twitched his ears; and entered upon various topics of petty annoyance, like the malicious and ill-disposed charity boy he was. But none of these taunts producing the desired effect of making Oliver cry, Noah got rather personal. "Work'us," said Noah, "how's your mother?"

"She's dead," replied Oliver; "don't you say anything about her to me!"

"What did she die of, Work'us?" said Noah.

"Of a broken heart, some of our old nurses told me," replied Oliver, more as if he were talking to himself than answering Noah. "I think I know what it must be to die of that!"

"Tol de rol lol lol, Work'us," said Noah, as a tear rolled down Oliver's cheek. "What's set you a sniveling now?"

"Not *you*," replied Oliver, hastily brushing the tear away. "Don't say anything to me about her; you'd better not!"

"Better not!" exclaimed Noah. "Well! Better not! Yer know, Work'us," speaking in a jeering tone of affected pity, "yer mother was a regular right-down bad 'un."

"What did you say?" inquired Oliver, looking up very quickly.

"A regular right-down bad 'un, Work'us," replied Noah coolly. "And it's a great deal better that she died when she did, or she'd have been transported, or hung."

Crimson with fury, Oliver started up; seized Noah by the throat; shook him, in the violence of his rage, till his teeth chattered; and, collecting his whole force into one heavy blow, felled him to the ground.

"He'll murder me!" blubbered Noah. "Charlotte! missis! Here's the new boy a murdering of me! Help! Help! Oliver's gone mad! Char-lotte!"

"Oh, you little wretch!" screamed Charlotte, rushing into the kitchen and seizing Oliver with her utmost force, which was about equal to that of a strong man in good training, "Oh, you little un-grate-ful, mur-der-ous, hor-rid villain!" Between every syllable, Charlotte gave Oliver a blow with all her might, accompanying it with a scream, for the benefit of society. Mrs. Sowerberry plunged into the kitchen and assisted to hold him with one hand, while she scratched his face with the other. In this favorable position of affairs, Noah rose from the ground and pommeled him behind. When they were all wearied out, they dragged Oliver, struggling and shouting but nothing daunted, into the dust cellar and locked him up.

"Oh! Charlotte," said Mrs. Sowerberry, "what a mercy we have not all been murdered in our beds!"

"Ah! mercy indeed, ma'am," was the reply. "Poor Noah! He was all but killed."

Noah, whose top waistcoat button might have been on a level with the crown of Oliver's head, rubbed his eyes while this commiseration was bestowed upon him and performed some affecting tears and sniffs.

"What's to be done!" exclaimed Mrs. Sowerberry. "Your master's not at home. Run to Mr. Bumble, Noah, and tell him to come here directly."

"Oh, Mr. Bumble, sir!" cried Noah, when he had run to the workhouse, "Oliver, sir, Oliver has turned wicious. He tried to murder me, sir; and then he tried to murder Charlotte; and then missis. Oh! what dreadful pain it is! Such agony, please, sir!" And here, seeing a gentleman in a white waistcoat in the yard, Noah writhed and twisted his body into an extensive variety of eel-like positions.

"By Jove!" exclaimed the gentleman in the white waistcoat, "I knew it! I felt a presentiment that that audacious young savage would come to be hung!"

"And please, sir," said Noah, "missis wants to know can Mr. Bumble spare time to step up there directly and flog him—cause master's out."

"Certainly, my boy, certainly," said the gentleman in the white waistcoat, patting Noah's head, which was about three inches higher than his own. "Don't spare him, Beadle."

"No, I will not, sir," replied the beadle. But the accounts of Oliver's ferocity, as related by Mrs. Sowerberry and Charlotte, were so startling that he judged it prudent to parley before opening the door. "Do you know this here voice, Oliver?" said Mr. Bumble through the keyhole.

"Yes," replied Oliver. "You let me out!"

"Ain't you afraid of it, sir? Ain't you a trembling while I speak, sir?"

"No!" replied Oliver boldly.

An answer so different from the one he had expected staggered Mr. Bumble not a little. "Oh, you know, Mr. Bumble, he must be mad. No boy in half his senses could venture to speak so to you," said Mrs. Sowerberry.

"It's not Madness, ma'am," replied Mr. Bumble. "It's Meat. You've overfed him, ma'am. You've raised a artificial soul and spirit in him, ma'am, unbecoming a person of his condition. He comes of a bad family, ma'am. Both the nurse and doctor said that that mother of his made her way here against difficulties and pain that would have killed any well-disposed woman, weeks before."

Mr. Sowerberry returned at this juncture, and, left no alternative by his wife's tears, gave Oliver a drubbing. Mrs. Sowerberry, after making various remarks uncomplimentary to the memory of his mother, ordered him upstairs to his dismal bed.

It was not until he was left alone that Oliver gave way to the feelings which the day's treatment may be supposed to have awakened in a mere child. He had listened to their taunts with a look of contempt; he had borne the lash without a cry. But now, when there were none to see or hear him, he wept such tears as, God send for the credit of our nature, few so young may ever have cause to pour out before him! Then, having listened intently, he gently undid the fastenings of the door. One timid look around— one moment's pause of hesitation—he had closed it behind him and was in the open street.

His way lay directly in front of the cottage where he had been brought up. He stopped and peeped into the garden. A child was weeding one of the beds. Oliver was glad to see him before he went, for he had been his little friend and playmate. "You mustn't say you saw me, Dick," he said, as the boy thrust his thin arm between the rails to greet him. "I am running away. They beat and ill-use me, Dick; and I am going to London to seek my fortune. How pale you are!"

"I heard the doctor tell them I was dying," replied the child with a faint smile. "I am very glad to see you, dear; but don't stop, don't stop! Good-by, dear! God bless you!"

The blessing was from a young child's lips, but it was the first that Oliver had ever heard invoked upon his head; and through the struggles and sufferings of his after life, he never once forgot it.

3

OLIVER had a crust of bread, a coarse shirt, two pairs of stockings, and a penny for his journey of seventy miles to London. If it had not been for a good-hearted turnpike man and a benevolent old lady his troubles would have been shortened by the very same process which had put an end to his mother's; he would most assuredly have fallen dead upon the king's highway. But the seventh morning after he left his native place found him in the little town of Barnet.

He was sitting with bleeding feet on a doorstep when a boy of about his own age, after observing him closely, walked up to him.

This was a snub-nosed, flat-browed, common-faced boy, as dirty as one could see; but he had about him all the airs and manners of a man. He was short, with bowlegs and little, sharp, ugly eyes. His hat was stuck on the top of his head so lightly that it

threatened to fall off every minute and would have done so, if the
wearer had not had a knack of every now and then giving his head
a sudden twitch, which brought it back to its old place again. He
wore a man's coat, which reached nearly to his heels. He had
turned the cuffs back, halfway up his arm, to get his hands out of
the sleeves, apparently with the ultimate view of thrusting them
into the pockets of his corduroy trousers; for there he kept them.
He was, altogether, as roistering and swaggering a young gentleman as ever stood four feet six. "Hullo, my covey! What's the
row?" he said to Oliver.

"I am very hungry and tired," replied Oliver. "I have been
walking these seven days."

"Walking for sivin days!" said the young gentleman. "Oh, I
see. Beak's orders, eh? But," he added, seeing Oliver's look of
surprise, "I suppose you don't know what a beak is, my flash
com-pan-ion?"

Oliver mildly replied that he had always heard it was a bird's
mouth.

"My eyes, how green!" exclaimed the young gentleman. "Why,
a beak's a madg'strate. But come, you want grub, and you shall
have it. I'm at low-water mark myself—only one bob and a magpie; but, *as* far *as* it goes, I'll fork out and stump."

"Going to London?" said the strange boy, when Oliver had at
length concluded his meal. "Got any lodgings?"

"No."

"Don't fret your eyelids on that score. I know a 'spectable old
gentleman as lives there, wot'll give you lodgings for nothink—that
is, if any genelman he knows interduces you. And don't he know
me? Oh, no! Not in the least! By no means!" This led to a confidential dialogue from which Oliver discovered that his friend's
name was Jack Dawkins, though among his intimate friends he was
better known as "The Artful Dodger."

When they reached London that evening, he scudded along at
a rapid pace, pushed open the door of a house near Field Lane, and
whistled. "Now, then!" cried a voice from below.

"Plummy and slam!" was the reply.

This seemed to be some watchword or signal that all was right;
for a man's face peeped out from where a balustrade of the old

kitchen staircase had been broken away. "There's two on you," said the man. "Who's t'other one?"

"A new pal," replied Jack Dawkins, pulling Oliver forward.

"Where did he come from?"

"Greenland. Is Fagin upstairs?"

"Yes, he's a sortin' the wipes. Up with you!"

The walls and ceiling of the room they now entered were perfectly black with age and dirt. In a frying pan some sausages were cooking, and standing over them was a very old shriveled Jew, whose villanous-looking face was obscured by a quantity of matted red hair. He was dressed in a greasy flannel gown and seemed to be dividing his attention between the fire and a clothes horse, over which a great number of silk handkerchiefs were hanging. Several rough beds made of old sacks were on the floor. And seated round the table were four or five boys, none older than the Dodger, smoking long clay pipes and drinking spirits with the air of middle-aged men.

"This is my friend Oliver Twist, Fagin," said Jack Dawkins.

Fagin grinned and, making a low obeisance to Oliver, took him by the hand. Upon this, the young gentlemen with the pipes came round him and shook both his hands very hard—especially the one in which he held his little bundle. "We're very glad to see you, Oliver, very," said Fagin. "Ah, you're a staring at the handkerchiefs, eh, my dear! There are a good many of 'em, ain't there? We've just looked 'em out, ready for the wash; that's all, Oliver, that's all. Ha! ha! ha!"

This was hailed by a boisterous shout from all the hopeful pupils of the merry old gentleman. Immediately after supper, Oliver felt himself gently lifted onto one of the sacks and then sank into a deep sleep.

It was late next morning when he awoke. There was no one there but the old Jew, who was whistling softly to himself as he stirred some coffee round and round. He would stop every now and then to listen when there was the least noise below; and when he had satisfied himself, he would go on whistling and stirring. Suddenly he drew forth, as it seemed to Oliver from some trap in the floor, a small box, from which he took a magnificent gold watch, sparkling with jewels.

"Aha!" he said, with a hideous grin. "Clever dogs! Clever dogs!

Staunch to the last! Never told the old parson where they were. Never peached on old Fagin. And why should they? It wouldn't have loosened the knot, or kept the drop up, a minute longer. No, no, no. Fine fellows! Fine fellows!" At least half a dozen more watches were drawn forth, besides rings, brooches, bracelets, and other jewelry.

Suddenly his bright dark eyes fell on Oliver's, fixed on his in mute curiosity. He closed the lid of the box with a crash and, laying his hand on a bread knife, started furiously up. "What's that?" said he. "Why are you awake? What have you seen? Quick!"

"I wasn't able to sleep any longer, sir," replied Oliver, meekly.

"You were not awake an hour ago?" said Fagin, scowling fiercely.

"No! No, indeed!" replied Oliver.

"Tush, tush, my dear!" said Fagin, abruptly resuming his old manner and playing with the knife a little, before he laid it down, as if he had caught it up in mere sport. "I only tried to frighten you. Ha! ha! You're a brave boy, Oliver!" He rubbed his hands with a chuckle but glanced uneasily at the box. "Did you see any of the pretty things, my dear? They—they're my little property. All I have to live upon, in my old age. The folks call me a miser, my dear. Only a miser; that's all."

When the Dodger appeared, accompanied by a very sprightly young friend, who was introduced as Charley Bates, the box had disappeared. "Well," said Fagin, glancing slyly at Oliver, "I hope you've been hard at work this morning, my dears?"

"Hard," replied the Dodger. "A couple of pocketbooks."

"Not so heavy as they might be," said Fagin, after looking at their insides carefully, "but very neat and nicely made. Ingenious workman, ain't he, Oliver?"

"Very, indeed, sir," said Oliver. At which Mr. Charles Bates laughed uproariously, much to the amazement of Oliver.

"And what have you got, my dear?" said Fagin to Charley Bates.

"Wipes," replied Master Bates, producing four handkerchiefs.

"Well," said Fagin, inspecting them closely, "they're very good ones, very. You haven't marked them well, though, Charley; so the marks shall be picked out with a needle, and we'll teach Oliver how to do it. Shall us, Oliver? Ha! ha! ha!"

When the breakfast was cleared away, the merry old gentleman and the two boys played at a very curious game, which was performed in this way. The merry old gentleman, placing a snuff box in one pocket of his trousers, a note case in the other, and a watch in his waistcoat pocket, with a guard chain round his neck, and sticking a mock diamond pin in his shirt, buttoned his coat tight round him and, putting a spectacle case and handkerchief in his pockets, trotted up and down the room with a stick, in imitation of the manner in which old gentlemen walk the streets any hour in the day. All this time, the two boys followed him closely about, getting out of his sight so nimbly, every time he turned round, that it was impossible to follow their motions. At last the Dodger trod upon his toes, accidentally, while Charley Bates stumbled up against him behind; and, in that one moment, they took from him, with the most extraordinary rapidity, snuff box, note case, watch guard, chain, shirt pin, handkerchief, spectacle case. If the old gentleman felt a hand in any one of his pockets, he cried out where it was; and then the game began all over again.

When it had been played many times, a couple of young ladies called, one of whom was named Bet and the other Nancy; and all four young people went away together, having been kindly furnished by the amiable old Jew with money to spend.

"There, my dear," said Fagin to Oliver, "that's a pleasant life, isn't it? They have gone out for the day. Is my handkerchief hanging out of my pocket?"

"Yes, sir," said Oliver.

"See if you can take it out without my feeling it, as you saw them do when we were at play this morning."

Oliver held up the bottom of the pocket with one hand, as he had seen the Dodger do, and drew the handkerchief lightly out of it with the other.

"Is it gone?" cried Fagin.

"Here it is, sir," said Oliver, showing it.

"You're a clever boy, my dear," said the playful old gentleman, patting Oliver approvingly. "I never saw a sharper lad. Here's a shilling for you. If you go on, you'll be the greatest man of the time. And now come here, and I'll show you how to take the marks out of the handkerchiefs."

For many days, Oliver remained in the Jew's room, picking the marks out of the handkerchiefs (of which a great many were brought home) and sometimes taking part in the game already described, which the two boys and Fagin played regularly every morning. At length, he began to languish for fresh air and earnestly entreated the old gentleman to allow him to go out to work with his two companions. He was rendered the more anxious to be actively employed by what he had seen of the stern morality of the old gentleman's character. Whenever the Dodger or Charley Bates came home empty-handed, he would expatiate on the misery of idle and lazy habits and would enforce the necessity of an active life by sending them supperless to bed—once, by knocking them both down a flight of stairs.

At last Oliver obtained the permission he sought. There had been no handkerchiefs to work upon for two or three days, and the dinners had been rather meager. The three boys sallied out—the Dodger with his coat sleeves tucked up, and his hat cocked, as usual; Master Bates sauntering along with his hands in his surprisingly capacious pockets; and Oliver between them, wondering what branch of manufacture he would be instructed in, first.

Suddenly the Dodger drew his companions back. "Hush!" he said. "Do you see that old cove at the book stall? He'll do."

"A prime plant," observed Master Charley Bates.

The two boys walked stealthily across the road and slunk close behind the old gentleman they had designated, while Oliver stood looking on in silent amazement.

The old gentleman was very respectable looking, with a powdered head and gold spectacles. He had taken up a book from the stall, and there he stood reading away. What was Oliver's horror and alarm to see the Dodger plunge his hand into the old gentleman's pocket and draw forth a handkerchief! To see him hand the same to Charley Bates, and finally to behold them both running round the corner at full speed.

In an instant the whole mystery of the handkerchiefs, and the watches, and the jewels, and the Jew, rushed upon the boy's mind. He stood for a moment with the blood so tingling through his veins from terror that he felt as if he were in a burning fire; then, confused and frightened, he took to his heels and, not knowing what he did, made off as fast as he could lay his feet to the ground.

In that very instant, the old gentleman turned sharp round. Missing his handkerchief and seeing the boy scudding away, he shouted, "Stop thief!" and made off after him. The Dodger and Master Bates no sooner heard the cry and saw Oliver running than they issued forth from the doorway into which they had retired and, shouting, "Stop thief!" too, joined in the pursuit.

"Stop thief! Stop thief!" There is magic in the sound. The cry is taken up by a hundred voices, and the crowd accumulates at every turning. Away they fly, splashing through the mud and rattling along the pavements; up go the windows; onward bear the mob. "Stop thief! Stop thief!" There is a passion *for hunting something* deeply implanted in the human breast. One wretched breathless child, terror in his looks, strains every nerve to make head upon his pursuers; and as they gain upon him, they hail his decreasing strength with shouts of joy. "Stop thief!" Ay, stop him for God's sake, were it only in mercy!

Stopped at last! A clever blow. "Come, get up," said a police officer, roughly.

"It wasn't me, sir. Indeed, indeed, it wasn't," said Oliver, clasping his hands.

"Don't hurt him," said the old gentleman, compassionately. "I-I would rather not press the case."

"Must go before the magistrate now, sir," replied the man who had Oliver in charge. The old gentleman looked almost as rueful as Oliver when they were ushered into the imposing presence of the renowned Mr. Fang, the magistrate. "There is something in that boy's face," he said to himself, "that touches and interests me. He looks like—Bless my soul! Where have I seen something like that look before?"

"Officer!" said Mr. Fang. "Who is this fellow?" He looked at the old gentleman with an angry scowl.

"My name, sir," said the old gentleman, speaking *like* a gentleman, "is Brownlow."

"Officer!" said Mr. Fang. "What's this fellow charged with?"

"He's not charged at all, your worship," replied the officer. "He appears against the boy, your worship."

"Appears against the boy, does he?" said Fang, surveying Mr. Brownlow contemptously. "Swear him!" With many interruptions and repeated insults, Mr. Brownlow contrived to state his case, expressing his hope that the magistrate would deal as leniently with the boy as justice would allow.

"What's your name, you hardened scoundrel?" demanded Mr. Fang of Oliver. "Officer, what's his name?"

Finding Oliver deadly pale and incapable of understanding the question, and knowing that his not replying would only infuriate the magistrate, the officer hazarded a guess. "He says his name's Tom White, your worship. I think he really is ill."

"Stuff and nonsense!" said Mr. Fang. "I know better." Oliver at this point falling to the floor in a fainting fit, "I knew he was shamming," said Fang, as if this were incontestable proof of the fact. "Let him lie there."

"How do you propose to deal with the case, sir?" inquired the clerk.

"Summarily," replied Mr. Fang. "He stands committed for three months—hard labor, of course. Clear the office."

The door was opened for this purpose, when an elderly man of decent but poor appearance rushed hastily in. "Stop! stop! don't take him away!" he cried, breathless. "I keep the book stall. The robbery was committed by another boy. I saw it done; and I saw that this boy was perfectly amazed and stupefied by it."

"Why didn't you come here before?" said Fang.

"I hadn't a soul to mind the shop," replied the man. "I could get nobody till five minutes ago; and I've run here all the way."

"The boy is discharged," said Fang. "Clear the office." In the yard lay little Oliver Twist, his face deadly white; and a cold tremble convulsed his whole frame.

"Poor boy, poor boy!" said Mr. Brownlow. "Call a coach, somebody, pray." Oliver having been carefully laid on the seat, the old gentleman got in and away they drove to a neat house near Pentonville, where a bed was prepared for Oliver; and here he was tended with a kindness and solicitude that knew no bounds.

But for many days Oliver remained insensible to all the goodness of his new friends. Weak, and thin, and pallid, he awoke at last from what seemed to have been a troubled dream, when a motherly old lady rose from an armchair close by and, smoothing back his hair from his forehead, looked so kindly and lovingly in his face that he could not help placing his little withered hand in hers and drawing it round his neck. "Save us!" said the old lady, with tears in her eyes. "What a grateful little dear it is. Pretty creetur!"

Gradually, Oliver fell into that deep tranquil sleep which ease from suffering alone imparts. In three days' time he was able to sit in an easy chair, and Mrs. Bedwin had him carried into the housekeeper's room, which belonged to her. "Are you fond of pictures, my dear?" she inquired, seeing that Oliver fixed his eyes, most intently, on a portrait which hung against the wall opposite him.

"I have seen so few, that I hardly know, ma'am," said Oliver, without taking his eyes from the canvas. "What a beautiful, mild face that lady's is! Is—is that a likeness, ma'am?"

"Yes," said the old lady, "though not of anybody that you or I know, I expect. It seems to strike your fancy, my dear."

"The eyes look so sorrowful," said Oliver; "and where I sit, they seem fixed upon me, as if they wanted to speak to me but couldn't."

Oliver looked very worn and shadowy from sickness. "Poor boy!" said Mr. Brownlow when he came in to see him. "A couple of glasses of port wine would do him some good. Wouldn't they, Tom White, eh?"

"My name is Oliver Twist, sir," replied the little invalid, with astonishment.

"Queer name!" said the old gentleman. "What made you tell the magistrate your name was White?"

"I never told him so, sir," returned Oliver in amazement. This sounded so like a falsehood that the old gentleman looked some-what sternly in Oliver's face. It was impossible to doubt him; and as he gazed, the old idea of the resemblance between his features and some familiar face came upon him. Suddenly he pointed to the portrait. "Bedwin, look there!" The eyes, the head, the mouth— every feature was the same as the boy's!

4

"Where's Oliver?" said Fagin, rising with a menacing look when the Dodger and Charley Bates returned alone from their expedition with Oliver. The young thieves eyed their preceptor with alarm and looked uneasily at each other. But they made no reply.

"Will you speak?" thundered Fagin. "Speak out, or I'll throttle you!"

"Why, the traps have got him, and that's all about it," said the Dodger, sullenly. Charley Bates at this moment raising a perfectly terrific howl, the Jew flung a pot of beer at him.

"What the blazes is in the wind now!" growled a deep voice. "Who pitched that 'ere at me? Come in, you sneaking warmint; wot are you stopping outside for, as if you was ashamed of your master! Come in!" The man who growled out these words was a stoutly built fellow of about five-and-thirty, in a black velveteen coat, very soiled drab breeches, lace-up half boots, and gray cotton stockings which enclosed a bulky pair of legs. He had a broad heavy countenance with a beard of three days' growth and two scowling eyes, one of which displayed various parti-colored symp-toms of having recently been damaged by a blow.

"Come in, d'ye hear?" growled this engaging ruffian. And a white shaggy dog, with his face scratched and torn, skulked into the room.

"What are you up to? Ill-treating the boys, you covetous, avaricious, in-sa-ti-able old fence?" said the man. "I wonder they don't murder you! *I* would."

"Hush! hush! Mr. Sikes," said Fagin, trembling. "You seem out of humor, Bill."

"Perhaps I am," replied Bill Sikes. But after swallowing two or three glasses of spirits, he condescended to hear the cause and manner of Oliver's capture. "I'm afraid," said Fagin, "that he may say something which will get us into trouble. Nancy, my dear," for that young lady had entered the room, "you go up to the office and find out what's happened to Oliver. Nobody about here knows anything of you."

Accordingly, with a clean white apron tied over her gown, and her curl papers tucked up under a straw bonnet—both articles of dress provided from the Jew's inexhaustible stock—Miss Nancy prepared to issue forth on her errand.

"Carry this in your hand, my dear," said Fagin, producing a little covered basket. "It looks more respectable."

"Give her a door key to carry in t'other hand, Fagin," said Sikes; "it looks real and genivine like."

"Oh, my brother! My poor, dear, sweet, innocent little brother!" exclaimed Nancy, bursting into tears. "Oh, do have pity, and tell me what's been done with him, gentlemen; do, gentlemen, if you please, gentlemen!" Having uttered these words in a most lamentable and heartbroken tone to the immeasurable delight of her hearers, Miss Nancy winked to the company, nodded smilingly round, and disappeared.

But the news she brought of Oliver's removal to some place at Pentonville caused instant dismay. "Nancy, my dear, I must have him found," cried Fagin. "I trust to you, my dear. I shall shut up this shop tonight. You'll know where to find me! Don't stop here a minute. Find him, find him out, that's all!"

They were happy days, those of Oliver's recovery. Everybody was so kind and gentle that after the noise and turbulence in the midst of which he had always lived, it seemed like Heaven itself.

Mr. Brownlow caused a complete new outfit of clothes to be bought for him; and as Oliver was told that he might do what he liked with the old clothes, he gave them to a servant who had been very kind to him and asked her to sell them and keep the money. He felt quite delighted that there was now no possible danger of his ever being able to wear those rags again.

"Now, Oliver," said Mr. Brownlow one evening, speaking in a serious manner, "I want you to pay great attention to what I am going to say."

"Oh, don't tell me you are going to send me away, sir, pray!" exclaimed Oliver. "Don't send me back to the wretched place I came from!"

"My dear child," said the old gentleman, moved by the warmth of Oliver's appeal, "you need not be afraid of my deserting you, unless you give me cause. I have been deceived, before, in the objects whom I have endeavored to benefit; but I feel strongly disposed to trust you, and I am more interested in you than I can well account for. Let me hear your story. Speak the truth, and you shall not be friendless while I live."

As Oliver was about to begin, a peculiarly impatient little double knock was heard at the street door; and the servant announced Mr. Grimwig, who now walked into the room, supporting himself by a thick stick. He was a stout old gentleman, lame in one leg, whose countenance was twisted into a variety of odd shapes. Holding out a small piece of orange peel, he exclaimed, in a growling voice, "Isn't it an extraordinary thing that I can't call at a man's house but I find a piece of this surgeon's friend on the staircase? I've been lamed with orange peel once, and I know orange peel will be my death at last. It will, sir; orange peel will be my death, or I'll be content to eat my own head, sir!"

This was the handsome offer with which Mr. Grimwig backed and confirmed nearly every assertion he made. "I feel strongly on this subject, sir," said the irritable old gentleman. "There's always orange peel on my pavement; and I *know* it's put there by the surgeon's boy at the corner. A young woman stumbled over a bit last night and fell against my garden railings; I saw her look toward his infernal red lamp. 'Don't go to him,' I called out of the window; 'he's an assassin! A man trap!' So he is. If he is not—" Here the irascible old gentleman gave a great knock on the ground with his stick, which was always understood, by his friends, to imply the customary offer, whenever it was not expressed in words.

"That's the boy I've heard about, is it?" said Mr. Grimwig at length, looking at Oliver. "How are you, boy?"

Mr. Brownlow, seeming to apprehend that his singular friend was about to say something disagreeable, asked Oliver to tell Mrs. Bedwin they were ready for tea. "He is a nice-looking boy, is he not?" he then said to Mr. Grimwig.

"I don't know," replied Mr. Grimwig, pettishly. "Where does he come from? Who is he? What is he? He has had a fever. What of that? Fevers are not peculiar to good people, are they? Bad people have fevers sometimes, haven't they? I knew a man who was hung in Jamaica for murdering his master. He had had a fever six times. Pooh! nonsense!" Now, the fact was, that Mr. Grimwig was strongly disposed to admit that Oliver's appearance was unusually prepossessing; but he had a strong appetite for contradiction; and, inwardly determining that no man should dictate to him whether a boy was well-looking or not, he resolved to oppose his friend. "That boy is deceiving you, my good friend," he said.

"I'll swear he is not," replied Mr. Brownlow, warmly.

"If he is not," said Mr. Grimwig, "I'll—" and down went the stick.

"We shall see," said Mr. Brownlow, checking his rising anger.

"We will," replied Mr. Grimwig, with a provoking smile; "we will."

As fate would have it, Mrs. Bedwin chanced to bring in, at this moment, a parcel of books which had just arrived. "Stop the boy!" said Mr. Brownlow. "There is something to go back."

"He has gone sir," replied Mrs. Bedwin.

"Dear me, I am sorry for that," exclaimed Mr. Brownlow; "he is a poor man, and they are not paid for. There are some books to be taken back, too."

"Send Oliver with them," said Mr. Grimwig, with an ironical smile; "he will be sure to deliver them safely, you know."

The old gentleman was just going to say that Oliver should not go out, when a most malicious cough determined him that he should. "I'll run all the way, sir," said Oliver, eagerly. Mrs. Bedwin followed him to the street door. "Bless his sweet face!" said the old lady, looking after him. "I can't bear, somehow, to let him go."

"Let me see; he'll be back in twenty minutes," said Mr. Brownlow, pulling out his watch and placing it on the table. "It will be dark by that time."

"Oh! you really expect him back, do you?" inquired Mr. Grimwig.

"Don't you?" asked Mr. Brownlow, smiling.

"No," said Mr. Grimwig, smiting the table with his fist, "I do not. The boy has a new suit of clothes on his back, a set of valuable books under his arm, and a five-pound note in his pocket. He'll join his old friends the thieves and laugh at you. If ever that boy returns here, sir, I'll eat my head."

With these words he drew his chair closer to the table; and there the two old friends sat, in silent expectation, with the watch between them. It grew so dark that the figures on the dial were scarcely discernible; but there the two old gentlemen continued to sit, in silence, with the watch between them.

Oliver was walking along on his way to the book stall, happy and content, when he was startled by a young woman screaming out very loud, "Oh, my dear brother!" And he had hardly looked up, when he was stopped by having a pair of arms thrown tight round his neck. "Come home, dear, come. Thank gracious goodness heavins, I've found him!"

"Why, it's Nancy!" exclaimed Oliver, seeing the young woman's face.

"You see he knows me!" cried Nancy, appealing to the bystanders. "Make him come home, there's good people, or he'll kill his dear mother and break my heart!"

"What the devil's this?" said a man, bursting out of a beer shop, with a white dog at his heels. "Young Oliver! Come home to your poor mother, you young dog!"

"I don't belong to them. I don't know them. Help! help!" cried Oliver, struggling in the man's powerful grasp.

"Help!" repeated the man, striking him. "I'll help you, you young rascal. Here, Bull's-eye, mind him, boy! Mind him!"

Weak with recent illness, stupefied by the blows and the suddenness of the attack, terrified by the fierce growling of the dog and the brutality of the man—what could one poor child do? Darkness had set in; it was a low neighborhood; no help was near; resistance was useless. In another moment he was dragged into a labyrinth of dark narrow courts, which terminated at length in a large open space, across which they were hurrying when a church bell struck the hour. "Eight o'clock, Bill," said Nancy. "I wonder whether *they* can hear it, poor fellows. Oh, Bill, such fine young chaps as them!"

"Yes; that's all you women think of," answered Sikes. "Fine young chaps! Well, they're as good as dead, so it don't matter." Clasping Oliver's wrist more firmly, he told him to step out again.

"Wait a minute!" said the girl. "I wouldn't hurry by, if it was you that was coming out to be hung, the next time eight o'clock struck, Bill."

"And what good would that do?" inquired the unsentimental Mr. Sikes. "Unless you could pitch over a file and twenty yards of good stout rope." The girl burst into a laugh; drew her shawl more closely round her; and they walked away. But Oliver felt her hand tremble and saw that her face had turned a deadly white.

In a filthy narrow street the dog, running forward, stopped before the door of a shop that was closed and apparently untenanted, which was opened by Mr. John Dawkins. "Won't Fagin be glad to see you? Oh, no!" said he, as they entered a low earthy-smelling room, where they were received by a shout of laughter from Master Charles Bates. "Look at his togs, Fagin! Superfine cloth, and the heavy swell cut! And his books, too! Nothing but a gentleman, Fagin!"

"Delighted to see you looking so well, my dear," said Fagin, bowing with mock humility to Oliver. "The Artful shall give you another suit, my dear, for fear you should spoil that Sunday one."

"It belongs to the old gentleman," said Oliver, wringing his hands. "Oh, pray send it back; send back the books and the money. Keep me here all my life long; but pray, pray send them back. He'll think I stole them; the old lady—all of them who were so kind to me—will think I stole them. Oh, have mercy upon me!"

"You're right, Oliver, you're right; they *will* think you have stolen 'em. Ha! ha!" chuckled Fagin, rubbing his hands; "it couldn't have happened better, if we had chosen our time. So you wanted to get away, my dear, did you?" taking up a jagged and knotted club which lay in a corner of the fireplace, "eh?" He inflicted a smart blow on Oliver's shoulders and was raising it for a second blow when Nancy, rushing forward, wrested the club from his hand.

"I won't stand by and see it done, Fagin," she cried. "You've got the boy, and what more would you have? Let him be—let him be—or I shall put that mark on some of you that will bring me to the gallows before my time."

There is something about a roused woman which few men like to provoke. Fagin cast a glance, half imploring and half cowardly, at Sikes. "What do you mean by this?" said he, seizing her. "You're a nice one to take up the humane and gen-teel side! A pretty subject for the boy to make a friend of!"

"God Almighty help me, I am!" cried the girl passionately. "And I wish I had been struck dead in the street before I lent a hand in bringing him here. He's a thief, a liar, a devil, all that's bad, from this night forth. Isn't that enough for the old wretch, without blows?"

"Come, come, Sikes," said Fagin, appealing to him in a remonstratory tone, "we must have civil words; civil words, Bill."

"Civil words!" cried the girl, whose passion was frightful to see. "Civil words, you villain! Yes, you deserve 'em from me. I thieved for you when I was a child not half as old as this!" pointing to Oliver.

Here, with many uncontrollable bursts of laughter, Master Bates produced the identical old suit of clothes which Oliver had so much congratulated himself upon leaving off at Mr. Brownlow's and the accidental display of which, to Fagin, by the man who purchased them, had been the very first clue received of his whereabouts. "Pull off the smart ones," said Charley, "and I'll give 'em to Fagin to take care of. What fun it is!" Poor Oliver unwillingly complied. Master Bates rolled up the new clothes and locked Oliver in an adjacent room.

. . . .

Mrs. Bedwin was waiting anxiously at the open door; the servant had run up the street twenty times to see if there were any traces of Oliver; and still the two old gentlemen sat, perseveringly, in the dark parlor, with the watch between them.

5

Mr. Bumble emerged at early morning from the workhouse gate and walked with portly carriage up High Street. He was in the full bloom and pride of beadlehood; his cocked hat and coat were dazzling in the morning sun; he clutched his cane with the vigorous tenacity of health and power and relaxed not in his dignified pace until he reached the farm where Mrs. Mann tended the infant paupers with parochial care.

"Drat that beadle!" said Mrs. Mann, hearing the well-known shaking at the garden gate. "If it isn't him at this time in the morning!—Lauk, Mr. Bumble, only think of its being you! Well, dear me, it *is* a pleasure, this is! And hoping you find yourself well, sir!"

"So-so, Mrs. Mann," replied the beadle. "A porochial life, ma'am, is a life of worrit, and vexation, and hardihood; but all public characters, as I may say, must suffer prosecution. Mrs. Mann, I am a going to London."

"Lauk, Mr. Bumble!" cried Mrs. Mann, starting back.

"I and two paupers, Mrs. Mann! A legal action is a coming on, about a settlement; and the board has appointed me to depose to the matter. Here is your porochial stipend for the month." He then inquired how the children were.

"Bless their little hearts!" said Mrs. Mann with emotion. "They're as well as can be, the dears! Of course, except the two that died last week. And little Dick."

"Isn't that boy no better?" inquired Mr. Bumble. "He's a ill-conditioned, wicious, bad-disposed porochial child, that. Where is he?" Having had his face put under the pump and dried upon Mrs. Mann's gown, Dick was led into the awful presence.

The child was pale and thin; his cheeks were sunken; and his eyes large and bright. The scanty parish dress hung loosely on his feeble body; and his young limbs had wasted away, like those of an old man. He stood trembling beneath the beadle's glance. "What's the matter with you, porochial Dick?" inquired Mr. Bumble, with well-timed jocularity.

"Nothing, sir," replied the child faintly.

"I should think not," said Mrs. Mann. "You want for nothing, I'm sure."

"I should like," faltered the child, "I should like if somebody would put a few words down for me on a piece of paper and keep it for me, after I am laid in the ground. I should like to leave my dear love to poor Oliver Twist and tell him," pressing his small hands together, and speaking with great fervor, "that I was glad to die when I was very young; for, perhaps, if I had lived to be a man, my little sister who is in Heaven might forget me or be unlike me, and it would be so much happier if we were both children there together."

Mr. Bumble surveyed the little speaker with indescribable astonishment and turning to his companion said, "That outdacious Oliver has demogalized them all!"

Mr. Bumble having duly arrived in London, the very first paragraph in the paper upon which his eye rested, was the following advertisement.

FIVE GUINEAS REWARD

Whereas a young boy, named Oliver Twist, absconded, or was enticed, on Thursday evening last, from his home at Pentonville and has not since been heard of, the above reward will be paid to any person who will give such information as will lead to the discovery of the said Oliver Twist or tend to throw any light upon his previous history.

Then followed the name and address of Mr. Brownlow. In five minutes Mr. Bumble was on his way to Pentonville.

He was shown into the parlor where sat Mr. Brownlow and his friend Mr. Grimwig. "Do you know where this poor boy is now?" asked Mr. Brownlow.

"No more than nobody," replied Mr. Bumble.

"Well, what *do* you know of him?" inquired the old gentleman.

"You don't happen to know any good of him, do you?" said Mr. Grimwig, caustically, after an attentive perusal of Mr. Bumble's features. Mr. Bumble, catching at the inquiry very quickly, shook his head with portentous solemnity. "You see?" said Mr. Grimwig, looking triumphantly at Mr. Brownlow.

The sum and substance of Mr. Bumble's story was: That Oliver was a foundling, born of low and vicious parents. That he had, from his birth, displayed no better qualities than treachery, ingratitude, and malice. That he had terminated his brief career in the place of his birth by making a sanguinary and cowardly attack on an unoffending lad and running away in the night time from his master's house. Mr. Brownlow paced the room sorrowfully.

At length he stopped and rang the bell. "Mrs. Bedwin," said Mr. Brownlow, when the housekeeper appeared, "that boy Oliver is an imposter."

"It can't be, sir. It cannot be," said the old lady, energetically. "He was a dear, grateful, gentle child, sir."

"Silence!" said the old gentleman, feigning an anger he was far from feeling. "Never let me hear the boy's name again. I rang to to tell you that. Never."

There were sad hearts at Mr. Brownlow's that night.

Meanwhile, having prepared Oliver's mind, by solitude and gloom, to prefer any society to the companionship of his sad thoughts, the wily Fagin had the boy in his toils. He was now placed in almost constant communication with the other two boys, who played the old game with their teacher every day, whether for their own improvement or Oliver's, Mr. Fagin best knew. He was slowly instilling into Oliver's soul the poison which he hoped would blacken it, and change its hue forever.

Emerging one night from his den, Fagin slunk through many winding and narrow ways, until he reached a house in Bethnal Green. A dog growled as he touched the handle of a room door there; and a man's voice demanded who it was. "Only me, Bill; only me, my dear," said Fagin, looking in. "Ah! Nancy."

"Now, my dear," he said, when he had seated himself, "about that crib at Chertsey; when is it to be done, Bill? Such plate, my dear, such plate!"

"Not at all," replied Sikes coldly. "At least, it can't be a put-up job as we expected. Toby Crackit has been hanging about the place for a fortnight, and he can't get one of the servants into line. The old lady has had 'em these twenty years; and if you were to give 'em five hundred pound, they wouldn't be in it."

Fagin looked blank at this information. After ruminating for some minutes he said, with a deep sigh, that if flash Toby Crackit couldn't get them over he feared the game was up. "It's a sad thing, my dear," he said, "to lose so much when we had set our hearts upon it."

"So it is," said Mr. Sikes. "Worse luck!" After a long silence,

"Fagin," said he, "is it worth fifty shiners extra if it's safely done from the outside?"

"Yes, my dear, yes," rejoined the Jew. "Is there no other help wanted?"

"None," said Sikes. "'Cept a center bit and a boy. The first we've both got; the second you must find us."

"A boy!" exclaimed Fagin. "Oh, then it's a panel, eh? Bill!" He nodded his head toward Nancy, who had been sitting silently before the fire, and intimated that he would have her told to leave the room.

"I know what he's going to say, Bill," rejoined Nancy coolly. "He needn't mind me." Swallowing a glass of brandy, she shook her head with an air of defiance and burst into sundry exclamations of "Keep the game a going!" "Never say die!" and the like, which seemed to reassure the gentlemen. "Now, Fagin, tell Bill about Oliver," she said with a laugh.

"Ha! you're a clever one, my dear; the sharpest girl I ever saw!" said the Jew. "Oliver's the boy for you, my dear. He's been in good training these last few weeks, and it's time he began to work for his bread. Once let him feel that he is one of us, once fill his mind with the idea that he has been a thief, and he's ours! Ours for his life. Oho! It couldn't have come about better!"

After some discussion, it was decided that Nancy should fetch Oliver the next evening, Fagin craftily observing that, if he evinced any disinclination to go, he would be more willing to accompany the girl who had so recently interfered in his behalf.

Oliver, left alone the next night, had fallen asleep when Nancy came "Am I to go with you?" he asked when she woke him.

"Yes. I have come from Bill," replied the girl. "You can't help yourself. I have tried hard for you, but all to no purpose. I have promised for your being silent. If you are not, you will only do harm to yourself and me, too, and perhaps be my death. See here! I have borne all this for you, already." She pointed to some livid bruises on her neck and arms. "Remember this! And don't let me suffer more for you, just now. If I could help you, I would; but I have not the power. Give me your hand. Make haste! Your hand!" A hackney cabriolet drove them rapidly to Bethnal Green.

"Now, first, do you know wot this is?" inquired Sikes when they arrived, taking up a pistol, which he loaded.

Oliver replied in the affirmative.

"Well," said the robber, grasping Oliver's wrist and putting the barrel so close to his temple that they touched, "if you speak a word when you're out o' doors with me, except when I speak to you, that loading will be in your head without notice."

So they began their journey, which ended at length near a bridge outside Chertsey, when Sikes turned suddenly down the bank. "The water!" thought Oliver, turning sick with fear. "He has brought me to this lonely place to murder me!" He was about to throw himself on the ground and make one struggle for his young life, when he saw that they stood before a solitary house. Sikes, with Oliver's hand still in his, softly raised the latch. The door yielded, and they passed in.

"Hallo!" cried a loud, hoarse voice.

"Don't make such a row," said Sikes, bolting the door. "Show a glim, Toby." They entered a low dark room with two or three broken chairs and a very old couch on which, with his legs much higher than his head, a man was reposing at full length. He was dressed in a smartly cut snuff-colored coat, with large brass buttons, an orange neckerchief, a coarse, staring, shawl-pattern waistcoat, and drab breeches. Mr. Crackit (for he it was) had no very great quantity of hair, but what he had was of a reddish dye and tortured into long corkscrew curls, through which he occasionally thrust some very dirty fingers, ornamented with large common rings.

"Bill, my boy!" said this figure, "I'm glad to see you." Having crammed their pockets with the tools of their trade, the two robbers soon issued forth with Oliver between them.

It was now half-past one, and intensely dark. After walking about a quarter of a mile beyond the town, they stopped before a detached house surrounded by a wall to the top of which Toby Crackit climbed in a twinkling. "The boy next," he said. "Hoist him up." And for the first time, Oliver, well-nigh mad with grief and terror, saw that housebreaking and robbery, if not murder, were the objects of the expedition. His limbs failed him; as the others stole cautiously toward the house, he sank to his knees.

"Get up!" murmured Sikes, trembling with rage and drawing the pistol. "Get up, or I'll strew your brains on the grass." He dragged Oliver to the back of the house, where an aperture so small

that the inmates had probably not thought it worth defending opened into a scullery. It was large enough to admit Oliver.

"Now listen, you young limb," whispered Sikes, drawing a dark lantern from his pocket and throwing the glare on Oliver's face, "I'm a going to put you through there. Take this light; go softly up the steps straight afore you, and along the hall, to the street door; unfasten it, and let us in." He put Oliver gently through the window, briefly advising him to take notice that he was within shot all the way.

In the short time he had had to collect his senses, the boy had firmly resolved that, whether he died in the attempt or not, he would make one effort to alarm the family. Filled with this idea, he advanced at once.

"Come back!" suddenly cried Sikes aloud. "Back! back!" A light appeared—a vision of two terrified men at the top of the stairs swam before Oliver's eyes—a flash—a loud noise—a crash—he staggered back into Bill's grasp and saw or heard no more.

6

BLEAK, dark, and piercing cold, it was a night for the well-housed and fed to draw around the bright fire and thank God they were at home. Mrs. Corney, the matron of the workhouse to which our readers have been already introduced as the birthplace of Oliver Twist, sat herself down before a cheerful fire in her own little room and glanced complacently at her kettle, singing on the hearth. But how slight a thing will disturb the equanimity of our frail minds! The water slightly scalding Mrs. Corney's hand as she made her tea, she was overpowered at the thought of her solitary fate, Mr. Corney having been dead five and twenty years.

"I shall never get another!" said Mrs. Corney pettishly— "like him." At that moment she was disturbed by a soft tap at the door. "Oh, come in with you!" said Mrs. Corney, sharply. "What's amiss now, eh?"

"Nothing, ma'am, nothing," replied a man's voice.

"Dear me!" exclaimed the matron, in a much sweeter tone, "is that Mr. Bumble?"

"At your service, ma'am," said Mr. Bumble. "Hard weather, ma'am. Antiporochial weather this, ma'am." Mrs. Corney bashfully inquired whether—whether he wouldn't take a cup of tea?

Mr. Bumble instantaneously drew another chair up to the table, looked at the lady, coughed, and slightly smiled.

"Sweet, Mr. Bumble?" inquired the matron, taking up the sugar basin.

"Very sweet, indeed, ma'am," replied Mr. Bumble. He fixed his eyes on Mrs. Corney as he said this; and if ever a beadle looked tender, Mr. Bumble was that beadle at that moment. "You have a cat, ma'am, I see," said Mr. Bumble, "and kittens too."

"I am so fond of them, Mr. Bumble, you can't think," replied the matron. "So fond of their home they are too, that it's quite a pleasure, I'm sure."

"Mrs. Corney, ma'am," said Mr. Bumble, slowly, "any cat, or kitten, that could live with you, ma'am, and *not* be fond of its home, must be a ass ma'am. I would drown it myself, with pleasure."

"Then you're a cruel man," said the matron vivaciously, "and a very hard-hearted man besides."

"Hard-hearted, ma'am?" said Mr. Bumble. "Hard?" He squeezed Mrs. Corney's little finger as she took his cup and, moving his chair by little and little, began to diminish the distance between himself and the matron. When the two chairs touched, Mr. Bumble stopped.

"Hard-hearted, Mrs. Corney?" said Mr. Bumble, stirring his second cup of tea. "Are *you* hard-hearted, Mrs. Corney?"

"Dear me!" exclaimed the matron, "what a very curious question from a single man."

The beadle drank his tea to the last drop, finished a piece of toast, whisked the crumbs off his knees, wiped his lips, and deliberately kissed the matron.

"Mr. Bumble!" cried that discreet lady in a whisper, for the fright was so great that she had quite lost her voice. "Mr. Bumble, I shall scream!" Mr. Bumble made no reply but, in a slow and dignified manner, put his arm round the matron's waist.

As the lady had stated her intention of screaming, of course she would have, but that the exertion was rendered unnecessary by a hasty knocking at the door. "If you please, mistress," said a withered old female pauper, putting her head in at the door, "Old Sally is a going fast."

"Well, what's that to me?" angrily demanded the matron. "I can't keep her alive, can I?"

"No, no, mistress," replied the old woman, "nobody can. But she says she has got something to tell, which you must hear. She'll never die quiet till you come, mistress." At this intelligence, the worthy Mrs. Corney muttered a variety of invectives against old women who couldn't even die without purposely annoying their betters and followed the messenger from the room with a very ill grace.

Mr. Bumble's conduct on being left to himself was rather inexplicable. He opened the closet, counted the teaspoons, weighed the sugar tongs, closely inspected a silver milk pot to ascertain that it was of the genuine metal, and, having satisfied his curiosity on these points, put on his cocked hat cornerwise, and danced with much gravity four distinct times round the table. Then, spreading himself before the fire with his back toward it, he seemed to be mentally engaged in taking an exact inventory of the furniture.

It was a bare garret room where the sick woman lay dozing. The matron, after impatiently watching by the bed for a while, said snappishly, "It's no part of my duty to see all the old women in the house die, and I won't—what's more." She was bouncing away, when a cry caused her to look round. The patient had raised herself upright and was stretching her arms toward her. "Come here! Nearer! Let me whisper in your ear," she said, clutching the matron by the arm. "In this very room—in this very bed—I once nursed a pretty young creetur that was brought into the house with her feet cut and bruised with walking. She gave birth to a boy and died. Let me think—what was the year again!"

"Never mind the year," said the impatient auditor. "What about her?"

"Ay," murmured the sick woman, relapsing into her former drowsy state, "what about her?—what about—I know!" she cried fiercely. "I robbed her, so I did! She wasn't cold—I tell you she wasn't cold, when I stole it!"

"Stole what, for God's sake?" cried the matron.

"It!" replied the woman, laying her hand over the other's mouth. "The only thing she had. It was gold, I tell you, that might have saved her life!"

"Gold!" echoed the matron. "Go on, go on—yes—what of it?"

"She charged me to keep it safe," replied the woman with a groan, "and trusted me as the only woman about her; and the child's death, perhaps, is on me besides! They would have treated him better, if they had known it all!"

"Known what?" asked the other. "Speak!"

"The boy grew so like his mother," said the woman, rambling on and not heeding the question, "that I could never forget it when I saw his face. Poor girl! poor girl! When the pains of death first came upon her, she whispered that if her baby was born alive the day might come when it would not feel so much disgraced to hear its poor young mother named."

"The boy's name?" demanded the matron.

"They *called* him Oliver," replied the woman, feebly. "The gold I stole was—"

"Yes, yes—what?" cried the other, as the woman once again rose, slowly and stiffly, and fell lifeless on the bed.

While these things were passing in the country workhouse, Mr. Fagin sat in the old den, where the Dodger, Charley Bates, and a half-witted dupe named Tom Chitling played at whist. "Hark!" cried the Dodger suddenly. "I heard the tinkler." Catching up the light, he crept softly upstairs.

After a short pause he reappeared and whispered to Fagin mysteriously. "What!" cried Fagin, "alone? Bring him down."

After casting a hurried glance round the room, the newcomer pulled off a large wrapper which had concealed the lower portion of his face and disclosed, all haggard, unwashed, and unshorn, the features of flash Toby Crackit.

"How are you, Faguey?" said this worthy. "Pop that shawl away in my castor, Dodger, so I may know where to find it when I cut; that's the time of day! First and foremost, Faguey, how's Bill?"

"What!" screamed Fagin, starting from his seat.

"Why, you don't mean to say—" began Toby, turning pale.

"Mean!" cried Fagin, stamping furiously on the ground. "Where are they? Sikes and the boy!"

"The crack failed," said Toby faintly. "They fired and hit the boy. We cut over the fields at the back, with him between us; his head hung down, and he was cold. They were close upon our heels —every man for himself, and each from the gallows! We parted company and left the youngster lying in a ditch. Alive or dead, that's all I know about him." Fagin stopped to hear no more but, uttering a loud yell, rushed from the house.

The Three Cripples, or rather The Cripples (the name by which the establishment was familiarly known to its patrons) was the public house to which he now made his way. "What can I do for you?" inquired the landlord.

"Will *he* be here tonight?" asked Fagin.

"Monks, do you mean? Certain," replied the man. "If you'll wait ten minutes, he'll be—"

"No, no," said Fagin, hastily, as though relieved by his absence. "Tell him I came here to see him and that he must come to me. Tomorrow will be time enough."

"I say," said the other, speaking in a hoarse whisper, "what a time this would be for a sell! I've got Phil Barker here so drunk that a boy might take him."

"Aha! But it's not Phil Barker's time," said Fagin. "Phil has something more to do, before we can afford to part with him; so go back to the company, my dear, and tell them to lead merry lives— *while they last*. Ha! ha! ha!" The landlord reciprocated the old man's laugh and returned to his guests.

Fagin was no sooner alone than his countenance resumed its former expression of anxiety, and he made for Bethnal Green. "Now," he muttered, as he knocked at Bill Sikes's door, "if there is any deep play here, I shall have it out of you, my girl, cunning as you are."

The girl was alone, lying with her head upon the table, and her hair straggling over it. "And where should you think Bill was now, my dear?" asked Fagin when he had recounted Toby Crackit's story.

The girl moaned out some half-intelligible reply, that she could not tell, and seemed, from the smothered noise that escaped her, to be crying.

"And the boy, too," said Fagin, straining his eyes to catch a glimpse of her face. "Poor leetle child! Left in a ditch, Nancy— only think!"

"The child," said the girl, suddenly looking up, "is better where he is than among us; and if no harm comes to Bill from it, I hope he lies dead in the ditch. I shall be glad to have him away from my eyes and to know that the worst is over. I can't bear to have him about me. The sight of him turns me against myself and all of you."

"Listen to me, you drab," said Fagin furiously. "Listen to me, who with six words can strangle Sikes as surely as if I had his bull's throat between my fingers now. When the boy's worth hundreds of pounds to me, am I to lose what chance threw me, through the whims of a drunken gang that I could whistle away the lives of! And me bound, too, to a born devil that only wants the will and has the power to—to—"

Panting for breath, the old man stammered for a word and in that instant checked the torrent of his wrath and trembled with the apprehension of having himself disclosed some hidden villainy. But, seeing Nancy in the same listless attitude, he appeared somewhat reassured and so turned his face homeward.

When he reached home, it was to find a stranger waiting for him, whom he took into an unused room. "As there are holes in the shutters and we never show lights to our neighbors, we'll set the candle on the stairs," he said, placing the candle exactly opposite the room door. They conversed for some time in whispers, when Monks—by which name Fagin had designated the strange man—said, "If you had had patience for a twelvemonth, couldn't you have got him convicted and sent safely out of the kingdom?"

"I had no hold upon him to make him worse," said Fagin, anxiously watching the contenance of his companion. "I had nothing to frighten him with. What could I do? Send him out with the Dodger and Charley? We had enough of that, at first, my dear; I trembled for us all, though if it had never happened you might never have clapped eyes upon the boy and so found that it was him you were looking for. You want him made a thief. If he is alive, I can make him one from this time; and if—if—" said Fagin, drawing nearer to the other—"it's not likely, mind—but if the worst comes to the worst and he is dead—"

"It's no fault of mine if he is!" interposed the other man, with a look of terror. "Mind that, Fagin! I had no hand in it. Anything but his death, I told you from the first. I won't shed blood; it's always found out and haunts a man besides.—Fire this infernal den! What's that yonder? I saw the shadow of a woman pass along the wainscot like a breath!"

They rushed tumultuously from the room. But the candle showed them only the empty staircase and their own white faces. They listened intently: a profound silence reigned throughout the house. "It's only your fancy," said Fagin.

7

As it would be by no means seemly in a humble author to keep so mighty a personage as a beadle waiting, with his back to the fire and the skirts of his coat gathered up under his arms, the historian whose pen traces these words hastens to pay him that respect which his position demands.

Mr. Bumble had recounted the teaspoons, reweighed the sugar tongs, made a closer inspection of the milk pot, and ascertained to a nicety the exact condition of the furniture, when he began to think that it was time for Mrs. Corney to return. As there were no sounds of her approach, it then occurred to him to allay further his curiosity by a cursory glance at the interior of Mrs. Corney's chest of drawers.

Arriving, in course of time, at the right-hand corner drawer and beholding therein a small padlocked box, which, being shaken, gave forth a pleasant sound, as of the chinking of coin, Mr. Bumble returned with a stately walk to the fireplace and, resuming his old attitude, said, with a grave and determined air, "I'll do it!"

He was placidly engaged in surveying his legs, when Mrs. Corney, hurrying into the room, threw herself into a chair and gasped for breath. "Mrs. Corney," said Mr. Bumble, stooping over the matron, "what is this, ma'am? Has anything happened, ma'am? Pray answer me; I'm on—on—" Mr. Bumble, in his alarm, could not immediately think of the word "tenterhooks," so he said "broken bottles." "Take something, ma'am," said Mr. Bumble soothingly.

"Not for the world!" replied Mrs. Corney. "I couldn't—oh! The top shelf in the right-hand corner—oh!" Uttering these words, the good lady pointed, distractedly, to the cupboard and underwent a convulsion from internal spasms. Mr. Bumble rushed to the closet and, snatching a pint green-glass bottle from the shelf, filled a teacup with its contents and held it to the lady's lips.

"I'm better now," said Mrs. Corney, falling back, after drinking half of it. Mr. Bumble raised his eyes piously to the ceiling in thankfulness and, bringing them down again to the brim of the cup, lifted it to his nose.

"Peppermint," exclaimed Mrs. Corney, in a faint voice, smiling gently on the beadle as she spoke. "Try it! There's a little—a little something else in it." Mr. Bumble tasted the medicine with a doubtful look, smacked his lips, took another taste, and put the cup down empty.

"It's very comforting," said Mrs. Corney.

"Very much so indeed, ma'am," said the beadle. As he spoke, he drew a chair beside the matron and, taking her hand, tenderly inquired what had happened to distress her.

"Nothing," replied Mrs. Corney. "I am a foolish, excitable, weak creetur."

"Not weak, ma'am," retorted Mr. Bumble, drawing his chair a little closer. "Are you a weak creetur, Mrs. Corney?"

Mrs. Corney sighed.

"Don't sigh, Mrs. Corney," said Mr. Bumble.

"I can't help it," said Mrs. Corney. And she sighed again.

"This is a very comfortable room, ma'am," said Mr. Bumble, looking round. "Another room, and this, ma'am, would be a complete thing."

"It would be too much for one," murmured the lady.

"But not for two, ma'am," rejoined Mr. Bumble, in soft accents. "Eh, Mrs. Corney?"

Mrs. Corney drooped her head, when the beadle said this; and the beadle drooped his, to get a view of Mrs. Corney's face. Mrs. Corney, with great propriety, turned her head away and released her hand to get at her pocket handkerchief but insensibly replaced it in that of Mr. Bumble.

"The board allow you coals, don't they, Mrs. Corney?" inquired the beadle, affectionately pressing her hand.

"And candles," replied Mrs. Corney, slightly returning the pressure.

"Coals, candles, and house rent free," said Mr. Bumble. "Oh, Mrs. Corney, what a Angel you are!"

The lady was not proof against this burst of feeling. She sank into Mr. Bumble's arms; and that gentleman, in his agitation, imprinted a passionate kiss upon her chaste nose.

"Such porochial perfection!" exclaimed Mr. Bumble, rapturously. "You know that Mr. Slout is worse tonight, my fascinator?"

"Yes," replied Mrs. Corney, bashfully.

"He can't live a week, the doctor says," pursued Mr. Bumble. "He is the master of this establishment; his death will cause a wacancy, that wacancy must be filled up. Oh, Mrs. Corney, what a prospect this opens! What a opportunity for a jining of hearts and housekeepings!"

Mrs. Corney sobbed.

"The little word?" said Mr. Bumble, bending over the bashful beauty. "The one little, little, little word, my blessed Corney?"

"Ye—ye—yes!" sighed out the matron.

"One more," pursued the beadle; "compose your darling feelings for only one more. When is it to come off?"

Mrs. Corney twice essayed to speak and twice failed. At length summoning up courage, she threw her arms round Mr. Bumble's neck and said it might be as soon as ever he pleased and that he was "a irresistible duck."

And now that matters here are thus amicably and satisfactorily arranged, let us set on foot a few inquiries after young Oliver Twist.

"My advice or, leastways, I should say, my *orders*, is," said the fattest man of the party of pursuers, when Sikes and Toby Crackit disappeared, "that we 'mediately go home again."

"I am agreeable to anything which is agreeable to Mr. Giles," said a shorter man, very pale in the face and very polite, as frightened men frequently are. "Whatever Mr. Giles says, it isn't our place to contradict him. No, no, I know my sitiwation!"

"You are afraid, Brittles," said Mr. Giles.

"I ain't," said Brittles.

"You are," said Giles.

"You're a falsehood, Mr. Giles," said Brittles.

"You're a lie, Brittles," said Mr. Giles.

"It's natural and proper to be afraid, under such circumstances," said the third man. "*I* am."

"So am I," said Brittles; "only there's no call to tell a man he is, so bounceably."

These frank admissions softened Mr. Giles, who at once owned that *he* was afraid, upon which, they all three faced about and ran back home.

This dialogue was held between the two men who had surprised the burglars, Mr. Giles, who acted in the double capacity of butler and steward to the old lady of the mansion, and Brittles, a lad of all work, who, having entered her service a mere child, was treated as a promising young boy still, though he was something past thirty. The third man was a traveling tinker who had been sleeping in the outhouse when the attempted robbery occurred.

They were recruiting themselves, after the fatigues and terrors of the night, with tea and sundries, in the kitchen, and Mr. Giles was recounting his exploits to the breathless interest of the cook and housemaid, when he started violently, in common with the rest of the company. The cook and housemaid screamed.

"It was a knock," said Mr. Giles, assuming perfect serenity. "Open the door, somebody."

Nobody moved.

"If Brittles would rather open the door, in the presence of witnesses," said Mr. Giles, after a short silence, "I am ready to make one."

"So am I," said the tinker. The two women, who were afraid to stay behind, brought up the rear. Brittles threw open the door; and the group, peeping timorously over each other's shoulders, beheld no more formidable object than poor little Oliver Twist, speechless and exhausted, who, having made his way to the house, mutely solicited their compassion.

Brittles, who had got behind the door to open it, no sooner saw Oliver than he uttered a loud cry. Mr. Giles, seizing the boy by one leg and one arm (fortunately not the broken limb), lugged him straight into the hall. "Here he is!" he bawled; "here's one of the thieves, ma'am! Here's a thief, miss! Wounded, miss! I shot him, miss, and Brittles held the light." In the midst of all the commotion, there was heard a sweet female voice.

"Don't be frightened, miss," said Giles; "I ain't much injured. He didn't make a very desperate resistance, miss! I was soon too many for him."

"Hush!" replied the young lady; "you frighten my aunt. Is the poor creature much hurt?" She directed that he be carried upstairs and that Brittles was to betake himself instantly to Chertsey for the doctor.

In a handsome room sat two ladies, one well advanced in years, the younger not past seventeen. Cast in so slight and exquisite a mold, so mild and gentle, so pure and beautiful, the very intelligence that shone in her deep blue eye and was stamped upon her noble head seemed scarcely of her age or of the world. They were waiting for the return of their friend Mr. Losberne, a surgeon known in the neighborhood as "the doctor," who was upstairs with the patient.

At length he returned and, in reply to an anxious inquiry, looked very mysterious. "This is a very extraordinary thing, Mrs. Maylie," he said. "Have you seen this thief?"

"No," rejoined the old lady. "Nor heard anything about him."

"Have you any objection to seeing him in my presence?"

"If it be necessary," replied the old lady, "certainly not."

"Then allow me—Miss Rose, will you permit me?"

Upon the bed, in lieu of the dogged, black-visaged ruffian they had expected to behold, there lay a mere child, worn with pain and exhaustion and sunk into a deep sleep.

"Aunt, dear aunt," said Rose, "as you love me and know that I have never felt the want of parents in your goodness and affection, but that I might have done so and might have been equally helpless and unprotected with this poor child, have pity upon him before it is too late!"

"My dear love," said the elder lady, as she folded the weeping girl to her bosom, "do you think I would harm a hair of his head? What can I do to save him, sir?"

"I think, if you give me a full and unlimited commission to bully Giles and that little boy Brittles, I can manage it," replied the doctor. Descending to the kitchen, he found that the adventures of the previous night were still under discussion.

"How is the patient to-night, sir?" asked Giles.

"So-so," returned the doctor. "I am afraid you have got yourself into a scrape there, Mr. Giles."

"I hope you don't mean to say, sir," said Mr. Giles, trembling, "that he's going to die. If I thought it, I should never be happy again. I wouldn't cut a boy off—no, not even Brittles here."

"That's not the point," said the doctor mysteriously. "Are you going to take upon yourselves to swear that that boy upstairs is the boy that was put through the little window last night? Out with it! Come! We are prepared for you!" The doctor, who was universally considered one of the best-tempered creatures on earth, made this demand in such a dreadful tone of anger that Giles and Brittles stared at each other in a state of stupefaction.

"I don't know; I really don't know," said Giles, with a rueful countenance. "I couldn't swear to him."

Mr. Brittles then involved himself and his respected superior in such a wonderful maze of fresh contradictions and impossibilities as tended to throw no particular light on anything. In short, after some more examination and a great deal more conversation, a neighboring magistrate was readily induced to take the joint bail of Mrs. Maylie and Mr. Losberne for Oliver's appearance if he should ever be called upon.

Oliver's ailings were neither slight nor few. In addition to the pain of a broken limb, his exposure to the wet and cold had brought on fever and ague, which hung about him for many weeks and reduced him sadly. But, at length, he began to get better and to be able to say how deeply he felt the goodness of the two sweet ladies and how ardently he hoped that, when he grew strong and well again, he could do something to show his gratitude. "I was thinking," he said one day, "that I am ungrateful now to the kind gentleman and the dear old nurse, who took so much care of me before. If they knew how happy I am, they would be pleased, I am sure."

"I am sure they would," rejoined Oliver's benefactress; "and Mr. Losberne has already promised that, when you are well enough, he will carry you to see them." One morning Oliver and Mr. Losberne set out, accordingly, in a carriage. When they came to Chertsey Bridge, Oliver turned pale and uttered an exclamation.

"That house, sir!" he cried. "The thieves— the house they took me to!"

"The devil it is!" cried the doctor. "Stop, coachman. Let me out!" Running down to the deserted tenement, he began kicking at the door.

"Hullo?" said a little ugly hump-backed man, opening the door. "What's the matter here?"

"Where's—confound the fellow, what's his rascally name— Sikes; that's it. Where's Sikes, you thief?" said the doctor.

The hump-backed man stared, as if in excess of amazement and indignation; then, growling forth a volley of horrid oaths, he retired into the house. The doctor followed him and looked anxiously round. But not an article of furniture, not a vestige of anything, answered the description Oliver had given him.

"Now!" said the hump-backed man, who had watched him keenly, "what do you mean by coming into my house, in this violent way? Will you take yourself off?"

"As soon as I think proper," said Mr. Losberne. "I shall find you out, some day, my friend."

"Will you?" sneered the ill-favored cripple. "If you ever want me, I'm here. I haven't lived here mad and all alone, for five and twenty years, to be scared by you."

"The boy must have made a mistake," muttered the doctor to himself. "Here! Put that in your pocket, and shut yourself up again." With these words he flung the hunchback a piece of money and returned to the carriage.

"I am an ass!" said the doctor, after a long silence. "Even if it had been the right place, and the right fellows had been there, what could I have done, single-handed? I am always involving myself in some scrape or other, by acting on impulse." Now, the fact was that the excellent doctor had never acted upon anything but impulse all through his life and had the warmest respect and esteem of all who knew him. If the truth must be told, he was a little out of temper, for a minute or two, at being disappointed in procuring corroborative evidence of Oliver's story, on the very first occasion on which he had a chance of obtaining any. He soon came round again, however; and, finding that Oliver's replies to his questions were still as straight-forward and consistent and still delivered with as much apparent sincerity and truth as they had ever been, he made up his mind to attach full credence to them, from that time forth.

"Now, my boy, which house is it?" he inquired, when they drove into the street in which Mr. Brownlow resided.

"That! That!" replied Oliver, pointing eagerly. "The white house. Oh! make haste!" The coach rolled on. It stopped. No; that was the wrong house; the next door. Oliver looked up at the windows, with tears of happy expectation. Alas! the white house was empty and there was a bill in the window. "To Let."

"Knock at the next door," cried Mr. Losberne, taking Oliver's arm in his. "What has become of Mr. Brownlow, who used to live in the adjoining house, do you know?" The servant said that Mr. Brownlow, his housekeeper, and a friend of Mr. Brownlow's had gone to the West Indies, six weeks before. Oliver clasped his hands and sank feebly backward.

"The book-stall keeper, sir?" said Oliver. "I know the way there. See him, pray, sir! Do see him!"

"My poor boy, this is disappointment enough for one day," said the doctor. "If we go to the book-stall keeper's, we shall certainly find that he is dead, or has set his house on fire, or run away. No; home again straight!"

The circumstance occasioned no alteration, however, in the

behavior of Oliver's benefactors. After another fortnight, leaving Giles in care of the house, they departed to a cottage in the country and took Oliver with them.

It was a happy time. The days were peaceful and serene; the nights brought with them neither fear nor care. Every morning Oliver went to an old gentleman who taught him to read better and to write; and every evening he would walk with Mrs. Maylie and Rose. So three months glided away.

8

ONE beautiful night, Oliver and the ladies had taken a longer walk than was customary with them. Rose had been in high spirits; but, Mrs. Maylie being fatigued, they returned home, and the young lady sat down to the piano. After running abstractedly over the keys for a few minutes, she fell into a low and very solemn air; and as she played it, they heard a sound as if she were weeping.

"What is this? In tears! My dear child, not ill?" cried Mrs. Maylie.

"No, no!" replied Rose, shuddering as though some deadly chillness were passing over her. Making an effort to recover her cheerfulness, she strove to play some livelier tune; but her fingers dropped powerless on the keys. Covering her face with her hands, she sank upon a sofa and gave vent to the tears which she was now unable to repress. "I have tried very hard and cannot help this," she said at length. "I fear I *am* ill, aunt."

She was, indeed; for when candles were brought, they saw that, in the very short time which had elapsed since their return home, she had sadly changed. An anxious night ensued. When morning came, Rose was in the first stage of a high and dangerous fever.

"This letter must be sent, with all possible expedition, to Mr. Losberne," Mrs. Maylie said to Oliver. "The people at the inn will undertake to do it. And here is another letter; but, whether to send it now or wait until I see how Rose goes on, I scarcely know."

"Is it for Chertsey, too, ma'am?" inquired Oliver, holding out his trembling hand for the letter.

"No," replied the old lady, giving it to him mechanically. Oliver glanced at it and saw that it was directed to Harry Maylie,

Esquire, at some great lord's house in the country. "I will wait until tomorrow," she decided.

Swiftly Oliver ran across the fields and down the little lanes which sometimes divided them, now almost hidden by the high corn on either side and now emerging on an open field, where the mowers and haymakers were busy at their work; nor did he stop once, until he came, in a great heat, to the market town, where he hastened to the inn. He was turning into the gateway when he accidentally stumbled against a tall man wrapped in a cloak, who was at that moment coming out of the inn door.

"Hah!" cried the man, fixing his eyes on Oliver and suddenly recoiling. "Who would have thought it! Grind him to ashes! He'd start up from a stone coffin, to come in my way!"

"I am sorry," stammered Oliver, confused by the strange man's wild look. "I hope I have not hurt you!"

"Rot you!" murmured the man, in a horrible passion, between his clenched teeth; "if I had only had the courage to say the word, I might have been free of you in a night. Curses on your head, and black death on your heart, you imp! What are you doing here?" He advanced toward Oliver, as if with the intention of aiming a blow at him, but fell violently on the ground, writhing and foaming, in a fit.

Oliver gazed, for a moment, at the struggles of the madman (for such he supposed him to be) and then darted into the house for help. But the circumstance did not dwell in his recollection long; when he reached the cottage, there was enough to drive all considerations of self from his mind. Rose Maylie had rapidly grown worse; before midnight she was delirious.

Late at night, Mr. Losberne arrived. "It is hard," said the good doctor, turning away as he spoke—"so young, so much beloved—but there is very little hope." The next day Rose fell into a deep sleep, from which she would waken, either to recovery and life or to bid them farewell and die.

Mrs. Maylie and Oliver sat, listening and afraid to speak, for hours. At last their quick ears caught the sound of an approaching footstep. They both darted to the door, as Mr. Losberne entered. "What of Rose?"

"As God is good and merciful, she will live to bless us all, for years to come."

Oliver was returning home from a long ramble, laden with flowers for the adornment of the sick chamber, when he heard the noise of a post chaise, driven at great speed. As the road was narrow, he stood leaning against a gate until it should have passed him. Suddenly a stentorian voice bellowed to the driver to stop. "Oliver, what's the news?" called the same voice. "Miss Rose! Master O-li-ver!"

"Is it you, Giles?" cried Oliver, running up to the chaise door.

"In a word!" cried a young gentleman, who occupied the other corner of the chaise. "Better or worse?"

"Better—much better!" replied Oliver, hastily.

"Thank Heaven!" exclaimed the gentleman. Oliver glanced at him with much interest and curiosity. He seemed about five and twenty years of age and was of the middle height; his countenance was frank and handsome; and his demeanor easy and prepossessing. Notwithstanding the difference between youth and age, he bore so strong a likeness to the old lady that Oliver had no great difficulty in imagining their relationship.

"Mother!" the young man said, when Mrs. Maylie met him; "why did you not write before? If Rose had—I cannot utter that word now—if this illness had terminated differently, how could I ever have known happiness again?"

"I know," said Mrs. Maylie, "that Rose deserves the best and purest love the heart of man can offer; I know that the devotion and affection of her nature require no ordinary return, but one that shall be deep and lasting. I think, my dear son, that if an enthusiastic, ardent, and ambitious man marry a wife on whose name there is a stain, which though it originate in no fault of hers may be visited by cold and sordid people upon her, he may, no matter how generous and good his nature, one day repent of the connection he formed in early life. And she may have the pain of knowing that he does so."

"Mother," said the young man, impatiently, "he would be a selfish brute. The mental agony I have suffered during the last two days wrings from me the avowal to you of a passion which, as you well know, is not one of yesterday, nor one I have lightly formed. On Rose, sweet, gentle girl! My heart is set, as firmly as ever heart of man was set on woman. Before I leave this place, Rose shall hear me."

"She shall," said Mrs. Maylie.

The melancholy which had seemed to the sad eyes of the anxious boy to hang for days past, over every object, was now dispelled by magic. The dew seemed to sparkle more brightly on the green leaves, the air to rustle among them with a sweeter music, and the sky itself to look more blue and bright. Oliver applied himself, with redoubled assiduity, to the instructions of his tutor and labored so hard that his quick progress surprised even himself. It was while he was engaged in this pursuit that he was greatly startled and distressed by a most unexpected occurrence.

The little room in which he was accustomed to sit, when busy at his books, was on the ground floor, at the back of the house. One beautiful evening Oliver sat at this window. He had been poring over his books for some time, when, the day being uncommonly sultry, he fell asleep.

There is a kind of sleep that steals upon us sometimes which, while it holds the body prisoner, does not free the mind from a sense of things about it. Oliver knew, perfectly well, that he was in his own little room, and yet he was asleep. Suddenly, the scene changed; the air became close and confined; and he thought, with a glow of terror, that he was in Fagin's house again. There sat the hideous old man, in his accustomed corner, pointing at him and whispering to another man, with his face averted, who sat beside him.

"Hush, my dear!" he thought he heard Fagin say; "it is he, sure enough. Come away."

"He!" the other man seemed to answer; "could I mistake him, think you? If a crowd of ghosts were to put themselves into his exact shape and he stood among them, there is something that would tell me how to point him out." He said this with such dreadful hatred that Oliver awoke.

Good Heaven! what was that which sent the blood tingling to his heart and deprived him of his voice and of power to move! There—there—at the window—close before him—so close, that he could have almost touched him before he started back—with his eyes peering into the room and meeting his—there stood Fagin! And beside him, white with rage or fear, or both, were the scowling features of the very man who had accosted him in the inn yard.

It was but an instant, a glance, a flash, before his eyes; and they were gone. But they had recognized him, and he them; and their look was firmly impressed upon his memory. He stood transfixed for a moment; then, leaping from the window into the garden, called loudly for help.

The search immediately instituted by Harry Maylie was all in vain. There were not even the traces of recent footsteps to be seen. "It must have been a dream, Oliver," said Harry.

"Oh, no, indeed, sir," replied Oliver, shuddering at the very recollection of the old wretch's countenance; "I saw him too plainly for that. I saw them both, as plainly as I see you now."

Giles was despatched to the different ale houses in the village, furnished with a description of the strangers; but he returned without any intelligence calculated to dispel or lessen the mystery. And, after a few days, the affair began to be forgotten.

Meanwhile, Rose was rapidly recovering. But although this happy change had a visible effect on the little circle, there was, at times, an unwonted restraint upon some there. At length, Harry Maylie begged permission to speak with Rose.

"Rose, my own dear Rose!" he said. "For years—for years—I have loved you—hoping to win my way to fame and then come proudly home and tell you it had been pursued only for you to share, thinking, in my day dreams, how I would remind you of the many silent tokens I had given of a boy's attachment and claim your hand, as in redemption of some old mute contract that had been sealed between us! That time has not arrived; but here, with no fame won and no young vision realized, I offer you the heart so long your own and stake my all upon the words with which you greet the offer."

"Your behavior has ever been kind and noble," said Rose, mastering the emotions by which she was agitated. "As you believe that I am not insensible or ungrateful, so hear my answer."

"It is, that I may endeavor to deserve you; it is, dear Rose?"

"It is," replied Rose, "that you must endeavor to forget me— not as your old and dearly attached companion, for that would wound me deeply—but as the object of your love."

There was a pause. "Your reasons, Rose," Harry said, at length.

"You have a right to know them," rejoined Rose. "You can say nothing to alter my resolution. It is a duty that I must perform. I owe it to myself that I, a friendless, portionless girl with a blight upon my name, should not give your friends reason to suspect that I had sordidly yielded to your first passion and fastened myself, a clog on all your hopes and projects. I owe it to you and yours to prevent you from opposing, in the warmth of your generous nature, this great obstacle to your progress in the world."

"One word more, Rose. Dearest Rose! one more!" cried Harry, throwing himself before her. "If I had been less—less fortunate, the world would call it—if some obscure and peaceful life had been my destiny—if I had been poor, sick, helpless—would you have turned from me then? Or has my probable advancement to riches and honor given this scruple birth? Answer me this one question!"

"Then, if your lot had been differently cast," rejoined Rose, "if you had been even a little, but not so far, above me, I should have been spared this trial."

"I ask one promise," said Harry. "Once, and only once more—say within a year, but it may be much sooner—I may speak to you again on this subject, for the last time."

"Let it be so," rejoined Rose; "it is but one pang the more, and by that time I may be enabled to bear it better."

Early next morning, casting one glance at Rose's window, Harry jumped into the carriage which Mr. Losberne had ordered to take him home. "Drive on!" he cried; "hard, fast, full gallop! Nothing short of flying will keep pace with me, today."

"Hullo!" cried the doctor, letting down the front glass in a great hurry and shouting to the postilion; "something very short of flying will keep pace with *me*. Do you hear?"

Jingling and clattering, the vehicle wound its way along the road in a cloud of dust. "He seems in high spirits and happy," Rose said to herself, gazing after the carriage until even the cloud was no longer to be seen. "I feared for a time he might be otherwise. I was mistaken. I am very, very glad." But the tears which coursed down her face seemed to tell more of sorrow than of joy.

9

MR. Bumble sat in the workhouse parlor, with his eyes moodily fixed on a paper fly cage which dangled from the ceiling; and as the heedless insects hovered round the gaudy network, Mr. Bumble would heave a deep sign, while a more gloomy shadow overspread his countenance. Mr. Bumble was meditating; it might be that the insects brought to mind some painful passage in his own past life.

Nor was Mr. Bumble's gloom the only thing calculated to show that a great change had taken place in the position of his affairs. The laced coat and the cocked hat—where were they? The mighty cocked hat was replaced by a modest one. Mr. Bumble was no longer a beadle. Strip the bishop of his apron, or the beadle of his hat and lace—what are they? Men. Mere men. Dignity, and even holiness too, sometimes, are more questions of coat and waist-coat than some people imagine.

Mr. Bumble had married Mrs. Corney and was master of the workhouse. Another beadle had come into power. "And tomorrow two months it was done!" said Mr. Bumble, with a sigh. "It seems a age. I sold myself," said Mr. Bumble, "for six teaspoons, a pair of sugar tongs, and a milk pot, with a small quantity of second-hand furniture and twenty pound in money. I went very reasonable. Cheap, dirt cheap!"

"Cheap!" cried a shrill voice in Mr. Bumble's ear; "you would have been dear at any price, and dear enough I paid for you, Lord above knows that!"

Mr. Bumble turned and encountered the face of his interesting consort, who, imperfectly comprehending the few words she had overheard of his complaint, had hazarded the foregoing remark at a venture.

"Mrs. Bumble, ma'am!" said Mr. Bumble. "Have the goodness to look at me!" ("If she stands such a eye as that," said Mr. Bumble to himself, "she can stand anything. It is a eye I never knew to fail with paupers.") On hearing the unexpected sound of a laugh, Mr. Bumble relapsed into his former state.

"Are you going to sit snoring there, all day?" inquired Mrs. Bumble.

"I am going to sit here, as long as I think proper, ma'am,"

rejoined Mr. Bumble; "and although I was *not* snoring, I shall snore, gape, sneeze, laugh, or cry, as the humor strikes me, such being my prerogative."

"*Your* prerogative!" sneered Mrs. Bumble, with ineffable contempt.

"I said the word, ma'am," said Mr. Bumble. "The prerogative of a man is to command."

"And what's the prerogative of a woman, in the name of Goodness?" cried the relict of Mr. Corney deceased.

"To obey, ma'am," thundered Mr. Bumble. "Your late unfortunate husband should have taught it you; and then, perhaps, he might have been alive now. I wish he was, poor man!"

Mrs. Bumble, seeing, at a glance, that the decisive moment had now arrived, and that a blow struck for the mastership on one side or other must necessarily be final and conclusive, dropped into a chair, and fell into a paroxysm of tears.

But tears were not the things to find their way to Mr. Bumble's soul; his heart was waterproof. He eyed his good lady with looks of great satisfaction and begged, in an encouraging manner, that she should cry her hardest, the exercise being looked upon, by the faculty, as strongly conducive to health. Putting on his hat, rather rakishly, he thrust his hands into his pockets and sauntered toward the door.

Now, Mrs. Corney, that was, had tried the tears because they were less troublesome than a manual assault; but she was quite prepared to make trial of the latter mode of proceeding. Clasping Mr. Bumble tightly round the throat with one hand, the expert lady inflicted a shower of blows (dealt with singular vigor and dexterity) upon it with the other. This done, she created a little variety by scratching his face and tearing his hair; and having, by this time, inflicted as much punishment as she deemed necessary, she defied him to talk about his prerogative again, if he dared. "Get up!" said Mrs. Bumble, in a voice of command. "And take yourself away from here."

"Certainly, my dear, certainly," rejoined Mr. Bumble, making a quicker motion toward the door. "I didn't intend to—I'm going, my dear! You are so very violent, that really I—"

At this instant, Mrs. Bumble stepped hastily forward to replace the carpet, which had been kicked up in the scuffle. Mr. Bumble immediately darted out of the room, without bestowing another thought on his unfinished sentence, leaving the late Mrs. Corney in full possession of the field.

The measure of his degradation was not yet full. After making a tour of the house, Mr. Bumble came to a room where some of the female paupers were usually employed in washing the parish linen, whence the sound of voices in conversation now proceeded.

"Hem!" said Mr. Bumble, summoning up all his native dignity. "These women at least shall continue to respect the prerogative. Hullo! Hullo there! What do you mean by this noise, you hussies?"

With these words, Mr. Bumble opened the door and walked in with a very fierce and angry manner, which was at once exchanged for a most humiliated and cowering air, as his eyes unexpectedly rested on the form of his lady wife. "What do *you* do here?" she demanded.

"I thought they were talking rather too much to be doing their work properly, my dear," replied Mr. Bumble.

"*You* thought they were talking too much?" said Mrs. Bumble. "What business is it of yours?"

"It's very true you're matron here, my dear," submitted Mr. Bumble; "but I thought you mightn't be in the way just then."

"I'll tell you what, Mr. Bumble," returned his lady. "We don't want any of your interference. You're a great deal too fond of poking your nose into things that don't concern you, making everybody in the house laugh the moment your back is turned, and making yourself look like a fool every hour in the day. Be off; come!"

Mr. Bumble, seeing with excruciating feelings, the delight of two old paupers, who were tittering together most rapturously, hesitated for an instant. Mrs. Bumble, whose patience brooked no delay, caught up a bowl of soap suds. What could Mr. Bumble do? He looked dejectedly round and slunk away; and as he reached the door, the titterings of the paupers broke into a shrill chuckle of irrepressible delight. It wanted but this.

"All in two months!" said Mr. Bumble, filled with dismal thoughts. "No more than two months ago, I was not only my own master but everybody else's, so far as the porochial workhouse was concerned, and now—!" It was too much. Mr. Bumble boxed the ears of the boy who opened the gate for him and walked distractedly to a public house.

It was deserted save for one customer, who had the air of a stranger. "I have seen you before, I think?" said he to Mr. Bumble. "You were beadle here, once, were you not?"

"I was," said Mr. Bumble, in some surprise—"porochial beadle."

"I came down to this place today," the stranger said, "to find you out; and, by one of those chances which the devil throws in the way of his friends sometimes, you walked into the very room I was sitting in. I want some information from you. I don't ask you to give it for nothing." As he spoke, he pushed a couple of sovereigns across the table. "Carry your memory back—let me see—twelve years, last winter. A boy was born in the workhouse."

"A many boys," observed Mr. Bumble, shaking his head despondingly.

"A murrain on the young devils!" cried the stranger; "I speak of one, a meek-looking, pale-faced boy, who was apprenticed down here, to a coffin maker, and who afterward ran away to London, as it was supposed."

"Why, you mean Oliver! Young Twist!" said Mr. Bumble. "There wasn't a obstinater young rascal—"

"It's not of him I want to hear," said the stranger. "It's of a woman, the hag that nursed his mother. Where is she?"

"She died last winter," rejoined Mr. Bumble.

The man seemed lost in thought. At length he breathed more freely and, observing that it was no great matter, rose to depart. But Mr. Bumble was cunning enough. He well remembered the night of old Sally's death; and although his lady had never confided to him the disclosure of which she had been the solitary witness, he had heard enough to know that it related to something that had occurred in the old woman's attendance, as workhouse nurse, upon the young mother of Oliver Twist. He informed the stranger, with an air of mystery, that one woman had been closeted with the old harridan shortly before she died and that he could produce her.

"At nine in the evening," said the stranger, writing down on a scrap of paper an obscure address by the water side, "bring her to me there."

"What name am I to ask for?" said Mr. Bumble.

"Monks!" rejoined the man, and strode hastily away.

It was a dull, close, overcast summer evening when Mr. and Mrs. Bumble directed their course toward the river. Before a large ruinous building the worthy couple paused, as the first peal of distant thunder reverberated in the air. "Come in!" Monks cried impatiently, appearing at the door. A bright flash of lightning streamed down, and a peal of thunder followed, which shook the crazy building to its center.

"Hear it!" he cried, shrinking back. "Hear it! Rolling and crashing on as if it echoed through a thousand caverns where the devils were hiding from it. I hate the sound!"

He remained silent for a few moments and then, removing his hands suddenly from his face, showed, to the unspeakable discomposure of Mr. Bumble, that it was much distorted and discolored. "These fits come over me, now and then," said Monks, observing his alarm; "and thunder sometimes brings them on. It's over.— Now," when they had seated themselves around a table upstairs, "the sooner we come to our business, the better for all."

"What's it worth to you?" asked the woman collectedly.

"It may be nothing; it may be twenty pounds," replied Monks. "Speak out, and let me know which."

"Give me five and twenty pounds in gold," said the woman, "and I'll tell you all I know. Not before."

Monks thrust his hand into a pocket and producing twenty-five sovereigns pushed them over to the woman.

"Now," he said, "gather them up; and when this cursed peal of thunder is gone, let's hear your story." The thunder, which seemed to shiver and break almost over their heads, having subsided, Monks, raising his face from the table, bent forward to listen to what the woman should say.

Having recounted the death of old Sally, the matron continued, "She clutched my gown, violently, with one hand, which was partly closed; and when I saw that she was dead and so removed the hand by force, I found it clasped a scrap of dirty paper. It was a pawnbroker's duplicate. I judge that she had pawned the trinket and had saved or scraped together money to pay the pawnbroker's interest year by year and prevent its running out so that, if anything came of it, it could still be redeemed. Noth-

ing had come of it; and, as I tell you, she died with the scrap of
paper, all worn and tattered, in her hand. The time was out in two
days; I thought something might one day come of it too and so
redeemed the pledge."

"Where is it now?" asked Monks quickly.

"*There*," replied the woman. And, as if glad to be relieved of it,
she hastily threw upon the table a small kid bag which contained a
little gold locket, in which were two locks of hair and a plain gold
wedding ring. "It has the word 'Agnes' engraved on the inside,"
said the woman. "There is a blank left for the surname; and then
follows the date, which is within a year before the child was born.
I found out that."

Monks suddenly wheeled the table aside and, pulling an iron
ring in the boarding, threw back a large trap door which opened
close at Mr. Bumble's feet and caused that gentleman to retire
several paces backward, with great precipitation. The turbid water,
swollen by the heavy rain, was rushing rapidly on below; and all
other sounds were lost in the noise of its plashing and eddying
against the green and slimy piles.

Tying the little packet to a leaden weight, Monks dropped it into the stream. It fell straight and true as a die; clove the water with a scarcely audible splash; and was gone. The three, looking into each other's faces, seemed to breathe more freely. "There!" said Monks, closing the trap door, which fell heavily back into its former position. "If the sea ever gives up its dead, as books say it will, it will keep its gold and silver to itself, and that trash among it. We have nothing more to say and may break up our pleasant party. Get away from here as fast as you can."

10

ON the following evening, Mr. William Sikes, awakening from a nap, drowsily growled forth an inquiry what time of night it was. The room in which he propounded this question was a mean and badly furnished apartment, which bespoke a state of extreme poverty, while the meager and attenuated condition of Mr. Sikes himself betrayed a recent illness.

The dog sat at the bedside. By the window, so pale and reduced with watching and privation that it was difficult to recognize her, sat Nancy. "Not long gone seven," said the girl. "How do you feel tonight, Bill?"

"As weak as water," replied Mr. Sikes, with an imprecation on his eyes and limbs. "Here; lend us a hand, and let me get off this thundering bed anyhow." Illness had not improved Mr. Sikes's temper; for as the girl raised him up and led him to a chair, he muttered various curses on her awkwardness and struck her. "Whining, are you?" said Sikes. "Come! Don't stand sniveling there. If you can't do anything better than that, cut off altogether."

"Why, you don't mean to say you'd be hard upon me tonight, Bill," said the girl, laying her hand upon his shoulder, "such a number of nights as I've been patient with you, nursing and caring for you, as if you had been a child."

"Get up and bustle about," demanded Mr. Sikes, "and don't come over me with your woman's nonsense."

At any other time, this remonstrance and the tone in which it was delivered would have had the desired effect; but the girl, being really weak and exhausted, dropped her head over the back of the chair and fainted. Mr. Sikes tried a little blasphemy and, finding that mode of treatment wholly ineffectual, called for assistance.

"What's the matter here, my dear?" said Fagin, looking in, the Artful and Charley Bates after him.

"Lend a hand to the girl, can't you?" replied Sikes impatiently. "What evil wind has blowed you here?" he asked, when their combined efforts had restored Nancy.

"No evil wind at all, my dear, for I've brought something good with me, that you'll be glad to see. Dodger, my dear, open the bundle; and give Bill the little trifles that we spent all our money on, this morning."

"Sitch a rabbit pie, Bill," exclaimed that young gentleman, disclosing to view a huge pasty; "half a pound of seven and sixpenny green, so precious strong that if you mix it with biling water it'll go nigh to blow the lid of the teapot off; a pound and a half of moist sugar; two half-quartern brans; pound of best fresh; piece of double Gloucester; and, to wind up all, some of the richest sort you ever lushed!" Mr. Dawkins poured out a wineglassful of raw spirits from the bottle he carried, which the invalid tossed down his throat without a moment's hesitation.

"Ah!" said Fagin, rubbing his hands with great satisfaction. "You'll do, Bill; you'll do now."

"Do!" exclaimed Mr. Sikes; "I might have been done for, twenty times over, afore you'd have done anything to help me. You took no more notice of me, all this mortal time, than if I was that 'ere dog. Drive him down, Charley!"

"I never see such a jolly dog as that," cried Master Bates, doing as he was desired. "Smelling the grub like a old lady a going to market! He'd make his fortun' on the stage, that dog would, and revive the drayma besides."

"Hold your din," cried Sikes. "If it hadn't been for the girl, I might have died; and I must have some blunt tonight."

"I haven't a piece of coin about me," replied the Jew.

"Then you've got lots at home," retorted Sikes. "Nancy shall go to the ken and fetch it."

The Jew then, taking leave of his affectionate friend, returned homeward, attended by Nancy. "Now," said Fagin, when they had arrived at his abode, "I'll go and get you that cash, Nancy. —Hush! who's that?"

The girl, who was sitting at the table with her arms folded, appeared in no way interested in the arrival until the murmur of a man's voice reached her ears, when she tore off her bonnet and shawl, with the rapidity of lightning, and thrust them under the table. Fagin turning round immediately afterward, she muttered a complaint of the heat. "Not a word about the money while he's here, Nance," Fagin whispered. The visitor, coming hastily into the room, was close upon the girl before he observed her. It was Monks.

"Only one of my young people," said Fagin, observing that Monks drew back on beholding a stranger. "Don't move, Nancy."

The girl drew closer to the table and, glancing at Monks with an air of careless levity, withdrew her eyes; but as he turned his toward Fagin, she stole another look, so keen and searching and full of purpose that if there had been any bystander to observe the change he could hardly have believed the two looks to have proceeded from the same person.

"Any news?" inquired Fagin.

"Great. Let me have a word with you."

The girl made no offer to leave the room, although she could see that Monks was pointing to her. The Jew, perhaps fearing she might say something aloud about the money if he endeavored to get rid of her, pointed upward and took Monks out of the room.

Before the sound of their footsteps had ceased to echo through the house, the girl had slipped off her shoes and stood at the door, listening with breathless interest. The moment the noise ceased, she glided from the room, ascended the stairs with incredible softness and silence, and was lost in the gloom above.

When she glided back, the two men were heard descending. "Why, Nance," exclaimed Fagin, when he had bade Monks good-by, "how pale you are! What have you been doing to yourself?"

"Nothing that I know of, except sitting in this close place for I don't know how long and all," replied the girl carelessly. "Come! Give me the money, that's a dear." When she got into the open street, she sat down upon a doorstep and seemed, for a few moments, wholly bewildered and unable to pursue her way.

It was fortunate for her that the possession of money occasioned Mr. Sikes so much employment next day in the way of eating and drinking that he had no time to be critical of her behavior. That she had all the abstracted and nervous manner of one who is on the eve of some bold and hazardous step would have been obvious to the lynx-eyed Fagin. As that day closed in, the girl's excitement increased; and when night came on, there was an unusual paleness in her cheek that even Sikes observed with astonishment.

"Why, burn my body!" he said; "if you haven't caught the fever, there's something more than usual in the wind, and something dangerous too. You're not a going to—. No, damme! There ain't a stauncher hearted gal going, or I'd have cut her throat three months ago. She's got the fever coming on."

Fortifying himself with this assurance, Sikes drained his glass to the bottom and then, with many grumbling oaths, called for his physic. The girl jumped up, with great alacrity; poured it quickly out, but with her back toward him; and held the vessel to his lips, while he drank off the contents. After two or three minutes, he was suddenly stricken into a deep and heavy sleep. "The laudanum has taken effect at last," murmured the girl. "I may be too late, even now." Stooping softly over the bed, she kissed the robber's lips and then hurried from the house.

Many of the shops were already closing in the back lanes and avenues through which she tracked her way, in making from Spitalfields toward the West End of London. Her headlong progress excited the curiosity of the passers-by. At length she entered a family hotel in a quiet but handsome street near Hyde Park. "Now, young woman!" said the porter, "who do you want here?"

"A lady who is stopping in this house," answered the girl. "Miss Maylie."

"You don't suppose the young lady will see such as you, do you?" said the man. But he was finally persuaded to carry her message.

"I am the person you inquired for," said Rose when she received Nancy. The kind tone, the sweet voice, the gentle manner took the girl completely by surprise, and she burst into tears.

"Oh, lady, lady!" she said. "If there was more like you, there would be fewer like me—there would—there would!"

"Sit down," said Rose, earnestly.

"Let me stand, lady," said the girl, still weeping. "Is—is—that door shut? I am about to put my life, and the lives of others, in your hands. I am the girl that dragged little Oliver back to old Fagin's, on the night he went out from the house in Pentonville."

"You!" said Rose Maylie.

"I, lady!" replied the girl. "Thank Heaven upon your knees that you had friends to care for and keep you in your childhood and that you were never in the midst of cold and hunger, and riot and drunkenness, and—and—something worse than all—as I have been from my cradle. I have stolen away from those who would surely murder me if they knew I had been here, to tell you what I have overheard. Do you know a man named Monks?"

"No," said Rose.

"He knows you," replied the girl, "and he knew you were here, for it was by hearing him tell the place that I found you out."

"I never heard the name," said Rose.

"Then he goes by some other than his own name among us," rejoined the girl, "which I more than thought before. Some time ago, and soon after Oliver was put into your house on the night of the robbery, I—suspecting this man—listened to a conversation held between him and Fagin in the dark. I found out, from what I heard, that Monks had seen Oliver accidentally with two of our boys on the day we first lost him and had known him directly to be the same child that he was watching for, though I couldn't make out why. A bargain was struck with Fagin that if Oliver was got back he should have a certain sum; and he was to have more for making him a thief, which this Monks wanted for some purpose of his own. Last night he came again. The first words I heard Monks say were these: 'So the only proofs of the boy's identity lie at the bottom of the river, and the old hag that received them from the mother is rotting in her coffin.' They laughed, and talked of his success in doing this; and Monks, talking on about the boy and getting very wild, said that though he had got the young devil's money safely now he'd rather have had it the other way, for what a game it would have been to have driven him through every jail in town and then hauled him up for some capital felony which Fagin could easily manage, after having made a good profit of him besides. 'In short, Fagin,' he says, 'you never laid such snares as I'd contrive for my brother Oliver.'"

"His brother!" exclaimed Rose.

"Those were his words," said Nancy, glancing uneasily round, as she had scarcely ceased to do since she began to speak, for a vision of Sikes haunted her perpetually. "And more. When he spoke of you and the other lady and said it seemed contrived by Heaven, or the devil, against him, that Oliver should come into your hands, he laughed and said there was some comfort in that too, for how many thousands and hundreds of thousands of pounds would you not give, if you had them, to know who your two-legged spaniel was.—But it is growing late, and I must get back quickly."

"Back! Why do you wish to return?" said Rose. "If you repeat this information to a gentleman whom I can summon in an instant from the next room, you can be consigned to some place of safety without half an hour's delay."

"I wish to go back," said the girl. "I must go back, because—how can I tell such things to an innocent lady like you?—because, among the men I have told you of, there is one, the most desperate among them all, that I can't leave—no, not even to be saved from the life I am leading now. I should be drawn back to him, I believe, if I knew that I was to die by his hand at last."

"But where can I find you again when it is necessary?" asked Rose.

"Will you promise me that you will have my secret strictly kept, and come alone, or with the only other person that knows it; and that I shall not be watched or followed?" asked the girl.

"I promise you solemnly," answered Rose.

"Every Sunday night, from eleven until the clock strikes twelve," said the girl without hesitation, "I will walk on London Bridge if I am alive."

One question occupied Rose Maylie's thoughts. What course of action should she determine upon? Mr. Losberne was with them; but Rose was too well acquainted with the excellent gentleman's impetuosity to trust him with the secret, when her representations in the girl's behalf could be seconded by no experienced person. Mrs. Maylie's first impulse would infallibly be to hold a conference with the worthy doctor. Rose had taken up the pen to write Harry Maylie, and laid it down again fifty times, when Oliver, who had been walking in the streets, with Mr. Giles for a body-guard, entered the room in breathless haste.

"To think that I should see him at last, and you should be able to know that I have told you all the truth!" he cried. "I have seen the gentleman who was so good to me—Mr. Brownlow, that we have so often talked about. I didn't speak to him—I couldn't speak to him, for he didn't see me, and I trembled so that I was not able to go up to him. But here is his address."

"Quick!" Rose said. "Tell them to fetch a hackney coach. I will take you there directly."

When they arrived Rose left Oliver in the coach, under pretense of preparing the old gentleman to receive him, and was presented to an elderly gentleman of benevolent appearance, in a bottle-green coat. At no great distance from him was seated another old gentleman, in nankeen breeches and gaiters, who did not look particularly benevolent and who was sitting with his hands clasped on the top of a thick stick and his chin propped thereupon. He was introduced as Mr. Grimwig.

"I shall surprise you very much, I have no doubt," said Rose, "but you once showed great benevolence and goodness to a very dear young friend of mine, and I am sure you will take an interest in hearing of him again."

"Indeed!" said Mr. Brownlow.

"Oliver Twist you knew him as," replied Rose.

"A bad one! I'll eat my head if he is not a bad one," growled Mr. Grimwig, without moving a muscle of his face.

"Do not heed my friend, Miss Maylie," said Mr. Brownlow; "he does not mean what he says."

"Yes, he does," growled Mr. Grimwig.

"No, he does not," said Mr. Brownlow.

"He'll eat his head, if he doesn't," growled Mr. Grimwig.

"He would deserve to have it knocked off, if he does," said Mr. Brownlow.

"And he'd uncommonly like to see any man offer to do it," responded Mr. Grimwig, knocking his stick upon the floor.

Having gone thus far, the two old gentlemen severally took snuff and afterward shook hands, according to their invariable custom. "Now, Miss Maylie," said Mr. Brownlow, "will you let me know what intelligence you have of this poor child."

Rose at once related all that had befallen Oliver since he left Mr. Brownlow's house, concluding with the information that he was waiting in a coach at the door. "At this door!" cried the old gentleman. With which he hurried out of the room, down the stairs, up the coach steps, and into the coach, without another word.

When the room door closed behind him, Mr. Grimwig rose and limped as fast as he could up and down the room at least a dozen times and then, stopping suddenly before Rose, kissed her without the slightest preface. "Hush!" he said, as the young lady rose in some alarm at this unusual proceeding. "Don't be afraid. I'm old enough to be your grandfather. You're a sweet girl. I like you. Here they are!"

Leaving Oliver to the raptures of Mrs. Bedwin, Mr. Brownlow led the way into another room and there heard from Rose a full narration of her interview with Nancy. The old gentleman readily undertook to hold solemn conference with Mr. Losberne.

Rose had by no means overrated the measure of the good doctor's wrath. Nancy's history was no sooner unfolded to him than he poured forth a shower of mingled threats and execrations.

"But reflect," said Mr. Brownlow, "whether sending these people anywhere is likely to attain the object we have in view, which is the discovery of Oliver's parentage and regaining for him the inheritance of which he seems to have been fraudulently deprived. "Before we can resolve upon any precise course of action," he went on, "it will be necessary to see the girl to ascertain from her whether she will point out this Monks on the understanding that he is to be dealt with by us and not by the law or, if she will not or cannot do that, to procure from her such an account of his haunts and description of his person as will enable us to identify him."

I I

UPON the night when Nancy, having lulled Mr. Sikes to sleep, hurried on her self-imposed mission to Rose Maylie, there advanced toward London, by the Great North Road, two persons upon whom it is expedient that this history should bestow some attention.

They were a man and woman, or perhaps they would be better described as a male and female; for the former was one of those long-limbed, knock-kneed, shambling, bony people to whom it is difficult to assign any precise age, looking as they do, when they are yet boys, like undergrown men and, when they are almost men, like overgrown boys. The woman was young but of a robust and hardy make, as she need have been to bear the weight of the heavy bundle which was strapped to her back. Her companion was not so encumbered. "Come on, can't yer? What a lazybones yer are, Charlotte," he called impatiently when they reached Highgate.

"Is it much farther?" asked the woman, resting herself against a bank. "Where do you mean to stop for the night, Noah? Near, I hope."

"No, not near," replied Mr. Claypole, for he it was. "There! Not near; so don't think it. A pretty thing it would be, wouldn't it, to go and stop at the very first public house outside the town, so that Sowerberry, if he come up after us, might poke in his old nose and have us taken back in a cart with handcuffs on."

They were soon deep in the obscurity of the intricate and dirty ways which, lying between Gray's Inn Lane and Smithfield, render that part of the town one of the lowest and worst that improvement has left in the midst of London. At length Noah stopped in front of a public house, more humble in appearance and more dirty than any he had yet seen. "What's the name of the house—t-h-r—three what?" he asked.

"Cripples," said Charlotte. They were ushered into a small back room where a single pane of glass fixed in the wall afforded a safe place of espial. Fagin, coming into the bar to inquire after some of his young pupils, applied his eye to the pane of glass, from which secret post he could see Mr. Claypole taking cold beef from the dish and porter from the pot and administering homeopathic doses of both to Charlotte, who sat patiently by, eating and drinking at his pleasure.

"Aha!" Fagin whispered, looking round to the landlord, "I like that fellow's looks. He'd be of use to us; he knows how to train the girl already. Don't make as much noise as a mouse, my dear, and let me hear 'em talk—let me hear 'em."

"So I mean to be a gentleman," said Mr. Claypole, kicking out his legs.

"But tills ain't to be emptied every day, and people to get clear off after it," said Charlotte.

"Tills be blowed!" said Mr. Claypole; "there's more things besides tills to be emptied; pockets, women's ridicules, houses, mail coaches, banks!"

"But you can't do all that, dear," said Charlotte.

"I shall look out to get into company with them as can," replied Noah. "If we could only get in with some gentlemen of this sort, it would be cheap at that twenty-pound note you've got."

Here Fagin interrupted him; and very amiable he looked, and a very low bow he made, as he seated himself at the nearest table and ordered something to drink. "A pleasant night, sir," said Fagin, putting about the liquor which the landlord reappeared with.

"Good stuff that," observed Mr. Claypole, smacking his lips.

"Dear!" said Fagin. "A man need be always emptying a till, or a pocket, or a woman's reticule, or a house, or a mail coach, or a bank, if he drinks it regularly."

Mr. Claypole no sooner heard this extract from his own remarks than he fell back in his chair and looked from the Jew to Charlotte with a countenance of ashy paleness and excessive terror.

"Don't mind me, my dear," said Fagin, drawing his chair closer. "Ha! ha! it was lucky it was only me that heard you by chance."

"I didn't take it," stammered Noah, no longer stretching out his legs like an independent gentleman, but coiling them up as well as he could under his chair; "it was all her doing."

"No matter who did it, my dear!" replied Fagin, "I'm in that way of business, myself, and I like you for it. What's more, I have got a friend that I think can gratify your darling wish and put you in the right way, where you can take whatever department of the business you think will suit you best."

"When could I see him?" asked Noah doubtfully.

"Tomorrow morning."

"Um!" said Noah. "What's the wages?"

"Live like a gentleman—board and lodging, pipes and spirits free—half of all you earn, and half of all the young woman earns," replied Mr. Fagin.

"But, yer see," observed Noah, "as she will be able to do a good deal, I should like to take something very light."

"What do you think of the old ladies?" asked Fagin. "There's a good deal of money made in snatching their bags and parcels and running round the corner."

"Don't they holler out a good deal, and scratch sometimes?" asked Noah, shaking his head. "I don't think that would answer my purpose. Ain't there any other line open?"

"Stop!" said Fagin, laying his hand on Noah's knee. "The kinchin lay."

"What's that?" demanded Mr. Claypole.

"The kinchins, my dear," said Fagin, "is the young children that's sent on errands by their mothers, with sixpences and shillings; and the lay is just to take their money away—they've always got it ready in their hands—then knock 'em into the gutter and walk off very slow, as if there were nothing else the matter but a child fallen down and hurt itself. Ha! ha! ha!"

"Ha! ha!" roared Mr. Claypole, kicking up his legs in an ecstasy. "Lord, that's the very thing! What time tomorrow shall we say?"

"Will ten do?" asked Fagin. "What name shall I tell my good friend?"

"Mr. Bolter," replied Noah, who had prepared himself for such an emergency. "Mr. Morris Bolter."

"And so it was you that was your own friend, was it?" asked Mr. Claypole, otherwise Bolter, when according to their compact, he met Fagin next day. "'Cod, I thought as much last night!"

"Every man's his own friend, my dear," replied Fagin. "He hasn't as good a one as himself anywhere. Some conjurors say that number three is the magic number, and some say seven. It's neither, my friend, neither. It's number one. And in a little community like ours, my dear, we have a general number one; that is, you can't consider yourself as number one, without considering me too as the same, and all the others. It's this mutual trust we have in each other that consoles me under heavy losses. My best hand was taken from me yesterday morning."

"You don't mean to say he died?" cried Mr. Bolter.

"No, no," replied Fagin, "not quite so bad as that. He was

charged with attempting to pick a pocket, and they found a silver snuff box on him. Ah! he was worth fifty boxes, and I'd give the price of as many to have him back. You should have known the Dodger, my dear, you should have known the Dodger."

"Well, but I shall know him, I hope; don't yer think so?" said Mr. Bolter.

"I'm doubtful about it," replied Fagin, with a sigh. And the news presently brought by Master Bates confirmed his fear that the Artful would be transported for life.

"To think of Jack Dawkins—lummy Jack—the Artful Dodger—going abroad for a common sneeze box!" cried Master Bates. "Oh, why didn't he rob some rich old gentleman of all his walables and go out *as* a gentleman, and not like a common prig, without no honor nor glory! How will he stand in the Newgate Calendar? P'raps not be there at all. Oh, my eye, my eye, wot a blow it is!"

"Never mind, Charley," said Fagin soothingly. "They'll know what a clever fellow he was; he'll show it himself, when he talks to the bigwigs, and not disgrace his old pals and teachers. We must know how he gets on today." He then persuaded Mr. Bolter that he incurred no possible risk in visiting the police office; where Noah waited, however, in some suspense, until a prisoner appeared who he felt could be no other than the object of his visit.

It was indeed Mr. Dawkins, who, shuffling into the office with the big coat sleeves tucked up as usual, preceded the jailer, with a rolling gait altogether indescribable, and, taking his place in the dock, requested in an audible voice to know what he was placed in that 'ere disgraceful sitivation for.

"Hold your tongue, will you?" said the jailer.

"I'm an Englishman, ain't I?" rejoined the Dodger. "Where are my priwileges?"

"You'll get your privileges soon enough," retorted the jailer, "and pepper with 'em."

"We'll see wot the Secretary of State for the Home Affairs has got to say to the beaks if I don't," replied Mr. Dawkins. "I shall thank the madg'strates to dispose of this here little affair, for I've got an appointment with a genelman in the City; and as I'm wery punctual in business matters, he'll go away if I'm not there to my time, and then pr'aps there won't be an action for damage. Oh no, certainly not!" At this point, the Dodger, with a show of being very

particular with a view to proceedings to be had thereafter, desired
the jailer to communicate "the names of them two files as was on
the bench," which tickled the spectators.

"Silence there!" cried the jailer.

"What is this?" inquired one of the magistrates.

"A pickpocketing case, your worship."

"Has the boy ever been here before?"

"He ought to have been, a many times," replied the jailer. "He
has been pretty well everywhere else. *I* know him well, your
worship."

"Oh! you know me, do you?" cried the Artful, making a note of
the statement. "Wery good. That's a case of deformation of character, anyway."

Here there was another laugh, and another cry of silence.

"Do you hear his worship ask if you've anything to say?"
inquired the jailer, when the evidence had been presented.

"I beg your pardon," said the Dodger, looking up with an air of
distraction. "Did you redress yourself to me, my man?"

"There! He's fully committed," interposed the clerk. "Take
him away."

"Ah!" said the Dodger to the Bench, brushing his hat with the
palm of his hand, "it's no use your looking frightened; I won't show
you no mercy, not a hap'orth of it. *You'll* pay for this, my fine
fellers. I wouldn't be you for something! Here, carry me off to
prison! Take me away!" With these words he suffered himself to be
led off by the collar, threatening, till he got into the yard, to make a
parliamentary business of it and then grinning in the officer's face,
with great glee and self-approval.

Having seen him locked up, Noah hastened back to bear to
Mr. Fagin the animating news that the Dodger was doing full
justice to his bringing up and establishing for himself a glorious
reputation.

Adept as she was in all the arts of cunning and dissimulation,
the girl Nancy could not wholly conceal the effect which the knowledge of the step she had taken wrought upon her mind. She grew
pale and thin, even within a few days. At times, she took no heed
of what was passing before her; at other times, she laughed without
merriment and was noisy without cause.

It was Sunday night, and the bell of the nearest church struck the hour. Sikes and Fagin were talking, but they paused to listen. The girl looked up too. Eleven. She put on her bonnet and was leaving the room, when Sikes spoke. "Where are you going?"

"Not far."

"I say where?" retorted Sikes. "Do you hear me?"

"I don't know where," replied the girl.

"Then I do," said Sikes, more in the spirit of obstinacy than because he had any real objection. "Nowhere. Sit down." He locked the door.

"You'll drive me on to something desperate," muttered the girl. "Bill, let me go; you don't know what you are doing. You don't, indeed. For only one hour—do—do!"

Suddenly pinioning her hands, Sikes dragged her, struggling and wrestling, to a bench, where he held her down by force. She struggled and implored by turns until twelve o'clock had struck and then, wearied and exhausted, ceased to contest the point any further. "Whew!" said the housebreaker, "wot a precious strange gal that is!"

"You may say that, Bill," replied Fagin thoughtfully. "You may say that." He asked if Nancy could light him down the dark stairs.

When they reached the passage, he laid his finger on his lip and drew close to the girl. "If you want revenge on those that treat you like a dog—like a dog! worse than his dog, for he humors him sometimes—come to me," he whispered. He had conceived the idea that Nancy, wearied of the housebreaker's brutality, had conceived an attachment for some new friend. Sikes knew too much. "With a little persuasion," thought Fagin, "what more likely than that she would consent to poison him?" If he laid a watch, discovered the object of her altered regard, and threatened to reveal the whole history to Sikes unless she entered into his designs, could he not secure her compliance? "I can," said Fagin, almost aloud.

"I want you, Bolter," said Fagin, next morning, "to do a piece of work for me, my dear, that needs great care and caution. I want you to dodge a woman."

"I can do that pretty well, I know," said Bolter. "I was a regular cunning sneak when I was at school. What am I do dodge her for?"

"To tell me where she goes, who she sees, and, if possible, what she says. I'll point her out at the proper time."

Six nights passed—six long weary nights—and, on each, Fagin intimated that it was not yet time. On the seventh, he returned home with an exultation he could not conceal. It was Sunday. "She goes abroad tonight," he said, "and on the right errand, I'm sure; for she has been alone all day, and the man she is afraid of will not be back much before daybreak. Come with me. Quick!"

In The Three Cripples, Noah was shown Nancy through the concealed pane of glass. When she left, the spy followed.

The church clocks chimed three quarters past eleven, as the two figures emerged on London Bridge. The girl had taken a few restless turns to and fro—closely watched meanwhile by her hidden observer—when the heavy bell of St. Paul's tolled for the death of another day, and a young lady, accompanied by a gray-haired gentleman, alighted from a hackney carriage. They had scarcely set foot upon the bridge when the girl made toward them.

They walked onward, looking about them with the air of persons who entertained some very slight expectation which had little chance of being realized, when they were suddenly joined by this new associate. They halted with an exclamation of surprise but suppressed it immediately, for a man in the garments of a country-man came close up at that moment.

"Not here," said Nancy hurriedly, "I am afraid to speak to you here. Come away—out of the public road—down the steps yonder!" As she uttered these words and indicated, with her hand, the direction in which she wished them to proceed, the countryman passed on and, unobserved, descended the stairs, hiding behind a pilaster; where presently he heard the sound of voices.

"This is far enough," said the gentleman. "Why did you not let me speak to you above?"

"I told you before," replied Nancy, shuddering, "that I was afraid. I have such a fear and dread upon me that I can hardly stand. I'll swear I saw 'coffin' written in every page of the book I read tonight—aye, and they carried one close to me, in the streets."

"There is nothing unusual in that," said the gentleman. "They have passed me often."

"*Real ones*," rejoined the girl. "This was not."

"You were not here last Sunday night," the gentleman said.

"I couldn't come," replied Nancy; "I was kept by him that I told the young lady of before. It's not very easy for me to leave him unless he knows why; I couldn't have seen the lady when I did, but that I gave him a drink of laudanum before I came away."

After receiving an assurance from both that any of her companions who might be implicated would go scot free, she described the public house whence she had been followed that night. When she had explained the best position from which to watch it without exciting observation, and the night and hour on which Monks was most in the habit of frequenting it, she seemed to consider for a few moments for the purpose of recalling his appearance.

"He is tall," said the girl, "and a strongly made man, but not stout; he has a lurking walk and, as he walks, constantly looks over his shoulder, first on one side, and then on the other. Don't forget that, for his eyes are sunk in his head so much deeper than any other man's that you might almost tell him by that alone. His face is dark, like his hair and eyes, and, although he can't be more than six or eight and twenty, withered and haggard. His lips are often discolored and disfigured with the marks of teeth, for he has desperate fits and sometimes even bites his hands and covers them with wounds—why did you start?" said the girl, stopping suddenly.

The gentleman replied, in a hurried manner, that he was not conscious of having done so and begged her to proceed.

"Upon his throat—so high that you can see a part of it below his neckerchief—there is—"

"A broad red mark, like a burn or scald?" cried the gentleman.

"How's this?" said the girl. "You know him!"

The young lady uttered a cry of surprise, and for a few moments they were so still that the listener could distinctly hear them breathe. "I think I do," said Mr. Brownlow at last (for it was he). "Now, you have given us most valuable assistance, young woman; what can I do to serve you?"

"Nothing, sir," rejoined the girl, weeping. "You can do nothing to help me. I am past all hope, indeed."

"You put yourself beyond its pale," said the gentleman. "Before the dawn of morning, you shall be placed in some foreign country, as entirely beyond the reach of your former associates as if you were to disappear from the earth. Quit them all, while there is time and opportunity!"

"No," replied the girl, after a short struggle. "I am chained to my old life. This fear comes over me again. I must go home."

"This purse," cried the young lady. "Take it for my sake, that you may have some resource in an hour of need and trouble."

"No!" replied the girl. "I have not done this for money. And yet—give me something that you have worn—your gloves or hand-kerchief—anything that I can keep, as having belonged to you, sweet lady. There. Bless you! God bless you. Good night, good night!" The sound of retreating footsteps were audible, and the voices ceased.

The astonished listener remained motionless for some minutes afterward and, having ascertained, with many cautious glances round him, that he was again alone, crept slowly from his hiding place. When he reached the top of the stairs, Noah Claypole darted away at his utmost speed and made for the Jew's house as fast as his legs would carry him.

12

It was nearly two hours before daybreak, that time which in the autumn of the year may be truly called the dead of night, when Fagin sat watching in his old lair, with face so distorted and pale that he looked less like a man than like some hideous phantom; moist from the grave and worried by an evil spirit. His right hand was raised to his lips; and as, absorbed in thought, he bit his long black nails, he disclosed among his toothless gums a few such fangs as should have been a dog's or rat's.

Mortification at the overthrow of his notable scheme; hatred of the girl who had dared to palter with strangers; an utter distrust of the sincerity of her refusal to yield up her companions; bitter disappointment at the loss of his revenge on Sikes; the fear of detection and ruin and death; and a fierce and deadly rage kindled by all—these were the passionate considerations which shot through the brain of Fagin, as every evil thought and blackest purpose lay working at his heart. He sat without changing his attitude until his quick ear caught a footstep in the street. "At last," he muttered, "at last!" Sikes, carrying a bundle, came into the room.

"Wot now?" he cried, as Fagin looked fixedly at him, his lips quivering violently. Fagin raised his right hand and shook his trembling forefinger in the air, but his passion was so great that the power of speech was for the moment gone.

"I've got that to tell you, Bill," said Fagin, at last, "will make you worse than me. Suppose that lad that's lying there—" pointing to Noah, asleep on the floor, "was to peach—to blow upon us all; what then?"

"What then!" replied Sikes, with a tremendous oath. "If he was left alive till I came, I'd grind his skull under the iron heel of my boot."

"What if *I* did it!" cried Fagin almost in a yell. "*I*, that know so much and could hang so many besides myself!"

"I don't know," replied Sikes, turning white at the mere suggestion. "I'd do something in the jail that 'ud get me put in irons; and if I was tried along with you, I'd fall upon you with them in the open court and beat your brains out afore the people."

"If it was Charley, or the Dodger, or Bet, or—"

"I don't care who," replied Sikes impatiently. "Whoever it was, I'd serve them the same."

Fagin looked hard at the robber; then, stooping over the bed upon the floor, he shook the sleeper to rouse him. "Bolter, Bolter! Poor lad!" he said, looking up with an expression of devilish anticipation and speaking slowly and with marked emphasis. "He's tired—tired with watching for *her* so long—watching for *her*, Bill."

When his assumed name had been repeated several times, Noah awoke. "Tell me that again—once again, just for him to hear," said the Jew, pointing to Sikes; "that about—*Nancy*," clutching Sikes by the wrist, as if to prevent his leaving the house before he had heard enough. "You followed her?"

"Yes."

"To London Bridge?"

"Yes."

"Where she met two people?"

"So she did."

"A gentleman and a lady that she had gone to of her own accord before, who asked her to give up all her pals, and Monks first, which she did—and to describe him, which she did—and to tell her what house it was that we meet at and go to, which she did —and where it could be best watched from, which she did—and what time the people went there, which she did. She did all this. And what did they say about last Sunday?" cried Fagin, half mad with fury.

"They asked her," said Noah, "why she didn't come, last Sunday, as she promised. She said she couldn't because she was kept at home by Bill, the man she told them of before."

"What more of him?" cried Fagin, tightening his grasp on Sikes, as the foam flew from his lips.

"Why, that she couldn't very easily get out of doors unless he knew where she was going to," said Noah; "and so the first time she went to see the lady, she—ha! ha! ha! it made me laugh when she said it, that it did—she gave him a drink of laudanum."

"Hell's fire!" cried Sikes, breaking fiercely from Fagin. "Let me go!" Flinging the old man from him, he rushed from the room. Without one pause or moment's consideration, his teeth so tightly compressed that the strained jaw seemed starting through his skin, the robber held on his headlong course, nor muttered a word, nor relaxed a muscle, until he reached his own door. He opened it, softly, with a key; strode lightly up the stairs; and, entering his own room, double locked the door, lifted a heavy table against it, and drew back the curtain of the bed.

The girl was lying, half dressed, upon it. He had roused her from her sleep. "It *is* you, Bill!" she said, with an expression of pleasure at his return.

"It is," was the reply. "Get up."

There was a candle burning, but the man hastily drew it from the candlestick and hurled it under the grate. Seeing the faint light of early day without, the girl rose to undraw the curtain.

"Let it be," said Sikes, thrusting his hand before her. "There's light enough for wot I've got to do."

"Bill," said the girl, in the low voice of alarm, "why do you look like that at me!"

The robber sat regarding her, for a few seconds, with dilated nostrils and heaving breast and then, grasping her by the head and throat, dragged her into the middle of the room and, looking once toward the door, placed his heavy hand upon her mouth.

"Bill, Bill!" gasped the girl, wrestling with the strength of

mortal fear, "I—I won't scream or cry—not once—hear me—speak to me—tell me what I have done!"

"You know, you she devil!" returned the robber, suppressing his breath. "You were watched tonight; every word you said was heard."

"Then spare my life for the love of Heaven, as I spared yours," rejoined the girl, clinging to him. "Bill, dear Bill, you cannot have the heart to kill me. Oh! think of all I have given up for you. You *shall* have time to think and save yourself this crime; I will not loose my hold, you cannot throw me off. Bill, Bill, for dear God's sake, for your own, for mine, stop before you spill my blood! I have been true to you, upon my guilty soul I have!"

The man struggled violently to release his arms; but those of the girl were clasped round his, and, tear her as he would, he could not tear them away.

"Bill," cried the girl, striving to lay her head upon his breast, "the gentleman and that dear lady told me tonight of a home in some foreign country where I could end my days in solitude and peace. Let me see them again and beg them, on my knees, to show the same mercy and goodness to you. It is never too late to repent, but we must have time—a little, little time!"

The housebreaker freed one arm and grasped his pistol. The certainty of immediate detection if he fired flashed across his mind even in the midst of his fury; and he beat it twice with all the force he could summon, upon the upturned face that almost touched his own.

She staggered and fell, nearly blinded with the blood that rained down from a deep gash in her forehead, but, raising herself with difficulty on her knees, drew from her bosom a white handkerchief—Rose Maylie's own—and, holding it up in her folded hands, as high toward Heaven as her feeble strength would allow, breathed one prayer for mercy to her Maker.

It was a ghastly figure to look upon. The murderer, staggering backward to the wall and shutting out the sight with his hand, seized a heavy club and struck her down.

The sun—the bright sun that brings back, not light alone, but new life, and hope, and freshness to man—burst upon the crowded city in clear and radiant glory. It lighted up the room where the murdered woman lay. He tried to shut it out, but it would stream in. If the sight had been a ghastly one in the dull morning, what was it now, in all that brilliant light!

He had not moved; he had been afraid to stir. There had been a moan and motion of the hand; and, with terror added to rage, he had struck and struck again. Once he threw a rug over it; but it was worse to fancy the eyes and imagine them moving toward him than to see them glaring upward, as if watching the reflection of the pool of gore that quivered and danced in the sunlight on the ceiling. He had plucked it off again. And there was the body—mere flesh and blood, no more—but such flesh, and so much blood!

He struck a light, kindled a fire, and thrust the club into it. There was hair upon the end, which blazed and shrunk into a light cinder and, caught by the air, whirled up the chimney. Even that frightened him, sturdy as he was; but he held the weapon till it broke and then piled it on the coals to burn away and smolder into ashes. He washed himself and rubbed his clothes; there were spots that would not be removed, but he cut the pieces out and burned them. How those stains were dispersed about the room! The very feet of the dog were bloody.

All this time he had never once turned his back upon the corpse; no, not for a moment. Such preparations completed, he moved, backward, toward the door, dragging the dog with him, lest he should soil his feet anew and carry out new evidences of the crime into the streets. He shut the door softly, locked it, took the key, and left the house.

He crossed over and glanced up at the window, to be sure that nothing was visible from the outside. There was the curtain still drawn, which she would have opened to admit the light she never saw again. It lay nearly under there. *He* knew that. God, how the sun poured down upon the very spot!

It was nine o'clock that night when the man, quite tired out, and the dog, limping and lame, crept into a small public house in Hatfield. After finishing his meal, the robber had almost dropped asleep, when a newcomer, half peddler and half mountebank, entered the bar. "And what be that stoof? Good to eat?" asked a grinning countryman, pointing to some cakes in a corner of the peddler's box.

"This," said the fellow, producing one, "this is the infallible and invaluable composition for removing all sorts of stain, rust, dirt, mildew, spick, speck, spot, or spatter, from silk, satin, linen, cambric, cloth, crepe, stuff, carpet, merino, muslin, bombazine, or woolen stuff. Wine stains, fruit stains, beer stains, water stains, paint stains, pitch stains, any stains, all come out at one rub with the infallible and invaluable composition. One penny a square! Two halfpence is all the same, and four farthings is received with joy. One penny a square! Wine stains, fruit stains, beer stains, water stains, paint stains, pitch stains, mud stains, blood stains! Here is a stain upon the hat of a gentleman in company that I'll take clean out, before he can order me a pint of ale."

"Hah!" cried Sikes, starting up. "Give that back."

"I'll take it clean out, sir," replied the man, winking to the company, "before you can come across the room to get it. Gentlemen all, observe the dark stain upon this gentleman's hat, no wider than a shilling, but thicker than a half crown. Whether it is a wine stain, fruit stain, beer stain, water stain, paint stain, pitch stain, mud stain, or blood stain—"

The man got no further, for Sikes with a hideous imprecation overthrew the table and, tearing the hat from him, burst out of the house. Getting out of the glare of the lamps of a stagecoach, he was walking past, when he recognized the mail from London and saw that it was standing at the little post office. He almost knew what was to come; but he crossed over and listened.

The guard was standing at the door, waiting for the letter bag. A man, dressed like a gamekeeper, came up at the moment. "Anything new up in town, Ben?" he asked.

"No, nothing that I knows on," replied the man. "Corn's up a little. I heerd talk of a murder, too, down Spitalfields way."

"Oh, that's quite true," said a gentleman, looking out of the window. "And a dreadful murder it was. A woman—"

"All ri—ight!" cried the guard, taking the bag. The horn sounded a few cheerful notes, and the coach was gone.

Sikes went on doggedly; but as he left the town and plunged into the solitude and darkness of the road, he felt a dread and awe creeping upon him which shook him to the core. That morning's ghastly figure seemed to be following at his heels. He could hear its garments rustling in the leaves, and every breath of wind came laden with that last low cry. If he stopped, it did the same. If he ran, it followed. At times he turned, with desperate determination, resolved to beat this phantom off, though it should look him dead; but the hair rose on his head and his blood stood still, for it had turned with him and was behind him then. He threw himself on his back upon the road. At his head it stood, silent, erect, and still—a living gravestone, with its epitaph in blood.

Let no man talk of murderers escaping justice, and hint that Providence must sleep. There were twenty score of violent deaths in one long minute of that agony of fear.

Suddenly there arose upon the night wind the noise of distant shouting, and the broad sky seemed on fire. Mingled with the ringing of an alarm bell and the crackling of flames, he could hear the cry of "Fire!" It was like new life to him. Flying from memory and himself, he plunged into the throng, now working at the pumps, and now hurrying through the smoke and flame, but never ceasing to engage himself wherever noise and men were thickest.

This mad excitement over, there returned, with tenfold force, the dreadful consciousness of his crime. He looked suspiciously about him; for the men were conversing in groups, and he feared to be the subject of their talk. He heard the firemen, who were from London, talking about the murder. "He has gone to Birmingham, they say," said one; "but they'll have him yet, for the scouts are out."

Suddenly, he took the desperate resolution of going back to London. "They'll never expect to nab me there, after this country scent," he thought. The dog, though. If any descriptions of him were out, it would not be forgotten that the dog was missing and had probably gone with him. He resolved to drown him and walked on, looking about for a pond, picking up a heavy stone and tying it to his handkerchief as he went.

The animal looked up into his master's face while these preparations were making; whether his instinct apprehended something of their purpose, or the robber's sidelong look at him was sterner than ordinary, he skulked a little farther in the rear than usual and cowered as he came more slowly along. When his master halted at the brink of a pool and looked round to call him, he stopped outright. "Do you hear me call? Come here!"

The dog wagged his tail but moved not. Sikes called again.

The dog advanced, retreated, paused an instant, turned, and scoured away at his hardest speed. The man whistled again and again. But no dog appeared, and at length he resumed his journey.

13

THE twilight was beginning to close in when Mr. Brownlow, with two sturdy men, hurried a third man into his house. This man was Monks. "If he hesitates," said Mr. Brownlow, "call for the police."

"This is pretty treatment, sir," said Monks, "from my father's oldest friend."

"It is because I was your father's oldest friend, young man," returned Mr. Brownlow; "it is because he knelt with me beside his only sister's death bed, on the morning that would—but Heaven willed otherwise—have made her my young wife; it is because even the sight of you brings with it old thoughts of him that I move to treat you gently now—yes, Edward Leeford, even now—and blush for your unworthiness who bear the name.

"You have a brother," continued Mr. Brownlow, "the whisper of whose name in your ear was, in itself, enough to make you accompany me hither."

"I have no brother,'" replied Monks. "You know I was an only child."

"I know that of the wretched marriage into which family pride forced your unhappy father when a mere boy, you were the sole and most unnatural issue. I know that at last that wretched pair wrenched the clanking bond asunder. I know that, when they had been separated for some time, your father fell among new friends, a retired naval officer whose wife had died, and his two daughters, one a beautiful creature of nineteen, the other a mere child of two or three. The end of a year found your father solemnly contracted to the elder daughter, the object of the first, true, ardent passion of a guileless girl.

"At length it was necessary that your father should immediately repair to Rome, where a relative had died, leaving his affairs in great confusion. He went; was seized with mortal illness there; was followed by your mother, who carried you with her; he died the day after her arrival, leaving no will—*no will*— so that the whole property fell to her and you."

At this part of the recital Monks held his breath and listened with a face of intense eagerness. As Mr. Brownlow paused, he changed his position with the air of one who has experienced a sudden relief.

"Before he went abroad and as he passed through London on his way," said Mr. Brownlow, slowly, fixing his eyes upon the other's face, "he came to me and left with me a portrait painted by himself of this poor girl. He was worn by anxiety and remorse almost to a shadow; talked in a wild, distracted way, of ruin and dishonor worked by himself; confided to me his intention to convert his whole property, at any loss, into money and, having settled on his wife and you a portion of his recent acquisition, to fly the country— I guessed too well he would not fly alone—and never see it more. I went," said Mr. Brownlow, after a short pause, "when all was over, to the scene of his—I will use the term the world would use— of his guilty love, resolved that that erring child should find one heart to shelter her. The family had left that part a week before, why or whither, none could tell.

"When your brother, a feeble, ragged, neglected child, was cast in my way by a stronger hand than chance and lay recovering from sickness in my house, his strong resemblance to this picture I have spoken of struck me with astonishment, though he was snared away before I knew his history."

"Brother!" said Monks, rising boldly, "You don't even know that a child was born of this maudlin pair; you don't even know that."

"I *did not*," replied Mr. Brownlow, "but within the last fortnight I have learned it all. There was a will, which your mother destroyed. It contained a reference to some child likely to be the result of this sad connection, which child was born and accidentally encountered by you, when your suspicions were first awakened by his resemblance to his father. You repaired to the place of his birth. There existed proofs of his birth and parentage, which you destroyed. Unworthy son, coward, liar—you, whose plots have brought a violent death upon the head of one worth millions such as you—you, Edward Leeford, do you still brave me?"

"No, no, no!" returned the coward, overwhelmed by these accumulated charges.

"Will you set your hand to a statement of truth and facts and repeat it before witnesses?"

"Yes, I will."

"You must do more than that," said Mr. Brownlow. "Make restitution to an innocent child. You have not forgotten the provisions of the will. Carry them into execution so far as your brother is concerned, and then go where you please."

While Monks was meditating with dark and evil looks on this proposal, Mr. Losberne entered the room. "The murderer will be taken," he cried. "His dog has been seen lurking about some old haunt, and there seems little doubt that his master either is or will be there, under cover of the darkness."

"Have you made up your mind?" asked Mr. Brownlow of Monks.

"Yes," he replied. "You—you—will be secret with me?"

"I will."

Near to that part of the Thames on which the church at Rotherhithe abuts, where the buildings on the banks are dirtiest and the vessels on the river blackest with the dust of colliers and the smoke of close-built low-roofed houses, there exists the filthiest, the strangest, the most extraordinary of the many localities that are hidden in London. In this neighborhood stands Jacob's Island, surrounded by a muddy ditch, six or eight feet deep and fifteen or twenty wide when the tide is in, known in the days of this story as Folly Ditch. In an upper room of one of the houses on Jacob's Island, there were assembled three men, Toby Crackit, Mr. Chitling, and a returned transport of fifty years whose name was Kags.

"When was Fagin took?" asked Toby Crackit.

"Just at dinner time," answered Mr. Chitling. "Charley and I made our lucky up the wash'us chimney, and Bolter got into the empty water butt, head downward; but his legs were so precious long that they stuck out at the top, and so they took him too."

"And Bet?"

"Poor Bet! She went to see the Body, to speak to who it was, and went off mad, screaming and raving and beating her head against the boards; so they put a strait weskut on her and took her to the hospital—and there she is."

"Wot's come of young Bates?" demanded Kags.

"He hung about, not to come over here afore dark, but he'll be here soon," replied Chitling. "There's nowhere else to go to now."

Suddenly a pattering noise was heard upon the stairs, and Sikes's dog bounded into the room. "What's the meaning of this?" said Toby. "He can't be coming here. I—I—hope not."

"If he was coming here, he'd have come with the dog," said Kags.

"He"—(none of them called the murderer by his old name) "he can't have made away with himself?" said Chitling.

"If he had," said Kags, "the dog 'ud want to lead us away to where he did it. No. I think he's got out of the country and left the dog behind." Suddenly was heard a hurried knocking at the door below. Crackit went to the window, then, shaking all over, drew in his head. There was no need to tell them who it was; his pale face was enough. The dog too was on the alert in an instant and ran whining to the door.

"We must let him in," he said; "there's no help for it. He *must* come in."

Crackit went down to the door and returned followed by a

man with the lower part of his face buried in a handkerchief, which he drew slowly off. Blanched face, sunken eyes, hollow cheeks, beard of three days' growth, wasted flesh, short thick breath—it was the very ghost of Sikes. When his hollow voice broke silence, the three others started.

"You that keep this house," said Sikes, turning his face to Crackit, "do you mean to sell me or to let me lie here till this hunt is over?"

"You may stop here, if you think it safe," he said. After another knock at the door, he returned with Charley.

"Toby," said the boy, falling back as he saw Sikes, "why didn't you tell me he was here? If they come after him, I'll give him up; I will." Crackit pointed with alarm to the window. There were lights gleaming below, loud voices, the tramp of hurried footsteps—endless they seemed in number—crossing the wooden bridges across Folly Ditch. Then came a loud knocking at the door, and then a hoarse murmur from such a multitude of angry voices as would have made the boldest quail.

"Help!" shrieked the boy. "He's here! Break down the door!"

Sikes flung the boy into another room. "Is the door fast?" he cried.

"Double locked and lined with sheet iron," replied Crackit.

"Damn you!" cried the desperate murderer, throwing up the sash and menacing the crowd. "I'll cheat you yet!" Of all the terrific yells that ever fell on mortal ears none could exceed the cry of the infuriated throng. Sikes staggered back and shut the faces out. "The tide was in as I came up," he said. "Give me a long rope. I may drop into the ditch and clear off that way."

The boy had never ceased to call on those without to guard the back. There were tiers and tiers of faces in every window of the houses on the opposite side of the ditch, cluster upon cluster of people clinging to every house top, as Sikes emerged on the roof. He set his foot against the stack of chimneys, fastened one end of the rope round it, and with the other made a strong running noose. At the very instant when he brought the loop over his head previous to slipping it beneath his arm pits, the murderer, looking behind him on the roof, threw his arms above his head and uttered a yell of terror. "The eyes again!" he cried in an unearthly screech.

Staggering as if struck by lightning, he lost his balance and

tumbled over the parapet. The noose was on his neck. It ran up
with his weight, tight as a bowstring. He fell for five and thirty
feet. There was a sudden jerk, a terrific convulsion of the limbs, and
there he hung.

A dog, which had lain concealed till now, ran backward and
forward on the parapet with a dismal howl and jumped for the
dead man's shoulders. Missing his aim, he fell into the ditch, and,
striking his head against a stone, dashed out his brains.

Two days later Oliver found himself, with all his friends, in the
chief inn of his native town. Mr. Losberne, Mr. Grimwig, and Mr.
Brownlow brought into the room a man whom Oliver almost
shrieked with surprise to see; for it was the same man he had met
at the market town and seen looking in with Fagin at the window
of his little room.

"This child," said Mr. Brownlow, drawing Oliver to him, "is
your half brother, the illegitimate son of your father, my dear
friend Edwin Leeford, by poor young Agnes Fleming, who died in
giving him birth."

"Yes," said Monks, scowling at the trembling boy. "Among the papers in my father's desk when he died were two, a letter to this girl Agnes and a will."

"What of the letter?" asked Mr. Brownlow.

"The letter? A sheet of paper crossed and crossed again with a penitent confession and prayers to God to help her. He had palmed a tale on the girl that some secret mystery—to be explained one day—prevented his marrying her just then; and so she had gone on, trusting patiently to him, until she trusted too far and lost what none could ever give her back."

"The will," said Mr. Brownlow, "was in the same spirit as the letter. He talked of miseries which his wife had brought upon him, of the rebellious disposition, vice, malice, and premature bad passions of you, his only son, who had been trained to hate him, and left you and your mother each an annuity of eight hundred pounds. The bulk of his property he divided into two equal portions—one for Agnes Fleming, and the other for their child, if it should be born alive and ever come of age. If it were a girl, it was to inherit the money unconditionally; but if a boy, only on the stipulation that in his minority he should never have stained his name with any public act of dishonor, meanness, cowardice, or wrong."

"My mother," said Monks, "did what a woman should have done. She burned this will. The letter never reached its destination; but that, and other proofs, she kept, in case they ever tried to lie away the blot. The girl's father, goaded by shame and dishonor, fled with his children into a remote corner of Wales; and there, after the girl had left home in secret, he died of a broken heart."

There was a short silence here, which ended when Mr. Grimwig brought in the Bumbles. "Do my hi's deceive me?" cried Mr. Bumble, with ill-feigned enthusiasm. "Or is that little Oliver? Oh O-li-ver, if you know'd how I've been a grieving for you—"

"Hold your tongue, fool," murmured Mrs. Bumble.

"Isn't natur', natur', Mrs. Bumble?" remonstrated the workhouse master. "Can't I be supposed to feel—I as brought him up porochially? I always loved that boy as if he'd been my—my—my own grandfather," said Mr. Bumble, halting for an appropriate comparison.

"Do you know that person?" Mr. Brownlow inquired, pointing to Monks. "Did you sell him a certain gold locket and ring?"

"If he has been coward enough to confess, as I see he has," replied Mrs. Bumble, "I have nothing to say. What then?"

"Nothing," replied Mr. Brownlow, "except that it remains for us to take care that neither of you is employed in a situation of trust again. You may leave the room."

"It was all Mrs. Bumble. She *would* do it," urged Mr. Bumble, first looking round to ascertain that his partner had left the room.

"That is no excuse," replied Mr. Brownlow. "You were present on the occasion of the destruction of these trinkets and, indeed, are the more guilty of the two, in the eye of the law; for the law supposes that your wife acts under your direction."

"If the law supposes that," said Mr. Bumble, squeezing his hat emphatically in both hands, "the law is a ass—a idiot. If that's the eye of the law, the law is a bachelor; and the worst I wish the law is that his eye may be opened by experience—by experience."

Laying great stress on the repetition of these two words, Mr. Bumble fixed his hat on very tight and, putting his hands in his pockets, followed his helpmate down stairs.

"Young lady," said Mr. Brownlow, turning to Rose, "give me your hand. Do not tremble. You need not fear to hear the few remaining words we have to say. The father of the unhappy Agnes had *two* daughters. What was the fate of the other?"

"The child," replied Monks, "when her father died in a strange place—without a scrap of paper that yielded the faintest clue by which his friends or relatives could be traced—the child was taken by some wretched cottagers, who reared it as their own. My mother found them, after a year of cunning search, and told them the child was illegitimate. The people believed her; and there the child dragged on a miserable existence until Mrs. Maylie saw her by chance, pitied her, and took her home."

"Not aunt," cried Oliver, throwing his arms about Rose's neck, "I'll never call her aunt—sister, my own dear sister, that something taught my heart to love so dearly from the first!"

They were a long, long time alone. A soft tap at the door at length announced that some one was without. Oliver opened it, glided away, and gave place to Harry Maylie. "Do you guess that I have come to remind you of a promise?" he said.

"The disclosure of tonight," replied Rose, "leaves me in the same position, with reference to you, as that in which I stood before."

"When I left you last," said the young man, "I left you with a firm determination to level all fancied barriers between yourself and me, resolved that, if my world could not be yours, I would make yours mine. This I have done. Such power and patronage, such relatives of influence and rank as smiled upon me then look coldly now; but there are smiling fields and waving trees in England's richest county, and by one village church—mine, Rose, my own!—there stands a rustic dwelling which you can make me prouder of than all the hopes I have renounced, measured a thousandfold. This is *my* rank and station now, and here I lay it down!"

14

FAGIN had but one more night to live. The space before the prison was cleared, and a few strong barriers had been already thrown across the road to break the pressure of the expected crowd, when Mr. Brownlow and Oliver presented an order of admission to the prisoner.

The condemned criminal was seated on his bed, rocking himself from side to side, with a countenance more like that of a snared beast than the face of a man. His mind was evidently wandering to his old life, for he continued to mutter, without appearing conscious of their presence otherwise than as a part of his vision.

"Good boy, Charley—well done—" he mumbled. "Oliver, too, ha! ha! ha! Oliver too—quite the gentleman now—quite the—take that boy away to bed!"

"Fagin," said the jailer.

"That's me!" cried the Jew, falling, instantly, into the attitude of listening he had assumed upon his trial. "An old man, my Lord; a very old, old man!"

"Steady," said the turnkey, holding him down. "Now, sir, tell him what you want. Quick, if you please, for he grows worse as the time gets on."

"You have some papers," said Mr. Brownlow advancing, "which were placed in your hands, for better security, by a man called Monks."

"It's all a lie together," replied Fagin. "I haven't one—not one."

"For the love of God," said Mr. Brownlow solemnly, "do not say that now, upon the very verge of death; but tell me where they are. You know that Sikes is dead; that Monks has confessed; that there is no hope of any further gain. Where are those papers?"

"Oliver," cried Fagin, beckoning to him. "Here, here! Let me whisper to you. The papers are in a canvas bag, in a hole a little way up the chimney in the top front room. I want to talk to you, my dear. I want to talk to you."

"Yes, yes," returned Oliver. "Let me say a prayer. Do!"

"Outside, outside," replied Fagin, pushing the boy before him toward the door and looking vacantly over his head. "Say I've gone to sleep—they'll believe *you*. You can get me out, if you take me so. Now then, now then!"

"Oh! God forgive this wretched man!" cried the boy with a burst of tears.

"That's right, that's right," said Fagin. "That'll help us on.

This first door. If I shake and tremble, as we pass the gallows, don't you mind, but hurry on. Now, now, now!"

"You had better leave him, sir," said the jailer, as some attendants entered.

"Press on, press on," cried Fagin. "Softly, but not so slow. Faster, faster!"

The men laid hands upon him and, disengaging Oliver from his grasp, held him back. He struggled with the power of desperation for an instant and then sent up cry upon cry that penetrated even those massive walls and rang in their ears until they reached the open yard.

Day was dawning when they emerged. A great multitude had already assembled; the windows were filled with people, smoking and playing cards to beguile the time; the crowd were pushing, quarreling, joking. Everything told of life and animation, but one dark cluster of objects in the center of all—the black stage, the cross beam, the rope, and all the hideous apparatus of death.

The fortunes of those who have figured in this tale are nearly closed. Before three months had passed, Rose Fleming and Harry Maylie were married in the village church which was henceforth to be the scene of the young clergyman's labors; on the same day they entered into possession of their new and happy home, where Mrs. Maylie took up her abode with them.

Mr. Brownlow adopted Oliver as his son. Removing with him and the old housekeeper to within a mile of the parsonage house, where his dear friends resided, he gratified the only remaining wish of Oliver's warm and earnest heart and thus linked together a little society whose condition approached as nearly to one of perfect happiness as can ever be known in this changing world.

Within the altar of the old village church there stands a white marble tablet, which bears but one word, "Agnes." If the spirits of the dead ever come back to earth to visit spots hallowed by the love of those whom they knew in life, I believe that the shade of Agnes sometimes hovers round that solemn nook. I believe it none the less because that nook is in a church, and she was weak and erring.

MARTIN CHUZZLEWIT

I

As no lady or gentleman with any claims to polite breeding
can possibly sympathize with the Chuzzlewit family
without being first assured of the extreme antiquity of
the race, it is a great satisfaction to know that it undoubtedly
descended in a direct line from Adam and Eve and was in the very
earliest times closely connected with the agricultural interest. If
it should ever be urged by grudging and malicious persons that a
Chuzzlewit, in any period of the family history, displayed an over-
weening amount of family pride, surely the weakness will be considered not only pardonable but laudable when the immense
superiority of the house to the rest of mankind, in respect of its
ancient origin, is taken into account.

The Chuzzlewit family having had, then, by reason of its
ancient birth, a pretty large share in the foundation and increase
of the human family, it becomes the province of this history to
submit that such of its members as shall be introduced in these

pages have still many counterparts and prototypes in the great world about us.

It was pretty late in the autumn of the year, when the declining sun, struggling through the mist which had obscured it all day, looked brightly down upon a little Wiltshire village, within an easy journey of the fair old town of Salisbury. Like a sudden flash of memory or spirit kindling up the mind of an old man, it shed a glory upon the scene, in which its departed youth and freshness seemed to live again. A moment, and its glory was no more. The sun went down; the light was all withdrawn; an evening wind uprose; and the withering leaves, no longer quiet, hurried to and fro in search of shelter from its chill pursuit.

The oddest feat they achieved was to take advantage of the sudden opening of Mr. Pecksniff's front door to dash wildly into his passage, whither the wind, following close upon them and finding the back door open, incontinently blew out the lighted candle held by Miss Pecksniff and slammed the front door against Mr. Pecksniff, who was at that moment entering, with such violence that, in the twinkling of an eye, he lay on his back at the bottom of the steps. Neither, when Miss Pecksniff inquired through the keyhole in a shrill voice, which might have belonged to a wind in its teens, "Who's there?" did he make any reply; nor, when Miss Pecksniff opened the door and peered out, did he offer any remark.

With a sharply delivered warning relative to the cage and the constable and the stocks and the gallows, Miss Pecksniff was about to close the door again, when Mr. Pecksniff (being still at the bottom of the steps) raised himself on one elbow, and sneezed.

"That voice!" cried Miss Pecksniff. "My parent!"

At this exclamation another Miss Pecksniff bounced out of the parlor; and the two Miss Pecksniffs, with many incoherent expressions, dragged Mr. Pecksniff into an upright posture.

"Pa!" they cried in concert. "Pa! Speak, pa! Do not look so wild, my dearest pa!"

"That'll do," said Mr. Pecksniff. "I'm better."

"He's come to himself!" cried the youngest Miss Pecksniff.

"He speaks again!" exclaimed the eldest. With these joyful words they kissed Mr. Pecksniff on either cheek and bore him into the house. His injuries having been comforted externally with patches of pickled brown paper, Mr. Pecksniff comforted himself internally with some stiff brandy-and-water, and the eldest Miss Pecksniff sat down to make the tea. In the meantime the youngest Miss Pecksniff took up her station on a low stool at her father's feet.

It must not be inferred from this position of humility that the youngest Miss Pecksniff was so young as to be forced to sit upon a stool by reason of the shortness of her legs. Miss Pecksniff sat upon a stool because of her simplicity and innocence, which were very great—very great. Miss Pecksniff sat upon a stool because she was all girlishness and playfulness and wildness and kittenish buoyancy. She was the most arch and at the same time the most artless creature, was the youngest Miss Pecksniff, that you can possibly imagine. It was her great charm.

Mr. Pecksniff was a moral man, a grave man, a man of noble sentiments and speech, and he had had her christened Mercy. Mercy! Oh, what a charming name for such a pure-souled being as the youngest Miss Pecksniff! Her sister's name was Charity. There was a good thing! Mercy and Charity! And Charity, with her fine strong sense and her mild yet not reproachful gravity, was so well named and did so well set off and illustrate her sister! What a pleasant sight was that, the contrast they presented! And the crowning circumstance was that both the fair creatures were so utterly unconscious of all this!

It has been remarked that Mr. Pecksniff was a moral man. So he was. Perhaps there never was a more moral man than Mr. Pecksniff, especially in his conversation and correspondence. Some people likened him to a direction post, which is always telling the way to a place and never goes there; but these were his enemies, the shadows cast by his brightness—that was all. His very throat was moral. You saw a good deal of it. You looked over a very low fence of white cravat, and there it lay, seeming to say, on the part of Mr. Pecksniff, "There is no deception, ladies and gentlemen— all is peace; a holy calm pervades me." So did his hair, just grizzled with an iron gray, which was all brushed off his forehead and stood bolt upright or slightly drooped in kindred action with his heavy eyelids. So did his person, which was sleek, though free from corpulency. So did his manner, which was soft and oily. In a word, even his plain black suit and state of widower, and dangling double eyeglass all tended to the same purpose and cried aloud, "Behold the moral Pecksniff!"

The brazen plate upon the door (which, being Mr. Pecksniff's, could not lie) bore this inscription, "Pecksniff, Architect"; though of his architectural doings nothing was clearly known, except that he had never designed or built anything, it was generally understood that his knowledge of the science was almost awful in its profundity.

Mr. Pecksniff's professional engagements, indeed, were almost if not entirely confined to the reception of pupils. His genius lay in ensnaring parents and guardians through advertisements and pocketing premiums. A young gentleman's premium being paid and the young gentleman come to Mr. Pecksniff's house, Mr. Pecksniff turned him loose in a spacious room on the two-pair front, where he improved himself, for three or five years according to his articles, in making elevations of Salisbury Cathedral from every possible point of sight and in constructing in the air a vast quantity of castles, Houses of Parliament, and other public buildings.

"Yes," said Mr. Pecksniff now, "I have again been fortunate in the attainment of my object. A new inmate will very shortly come among us."

"Is he handsome, pa?" inquired the younger daughter.

"Silly Merry!" said the eldest, Merry being fond for Mercy. "What is the premium, pa? Tell us that."

"Oh, good gracious, Cherry!" cried Miss Mercy, holding up her hands with the most winning giggle in the world, "what a mercenary girl you are! Oh, you naughty, thoughtful, prudent thing!"

"He is well looking," said Mr. Pecksniff, slowly and distinctly, "well looking enough. I do not positively expect any immediate premium with him." Notwithstanding their different natures, both Charity and Mercy concurred in opening their eyes uncommonly wide at this announcement and in looking for the moment as blank as if their thoughts had actually had a direct bearing on the main chance. "But what of that?" said Mr. Pecksniff, smiling at the fire. "There is disinterestedness in the world, I hope? Oh! let us not be forever calculating, devising, and plotting for the future." There was something in these morsels of philanthropy which reassured the sisters. They exchanged glances and brightened very much.

"What is the domestic news since yesterday?" said Mr. Pecksniff. "John Westlock is gone, I hope?"

"Indeed no," said Charity. "He slept last night at the Dragon and had Mr. Pinch to dine with him."

"Now I think," said Mr. Pecksniff, with his accustomed gentleness, though with the air of one who suffered under injury without complaint, "I think Mr. Pinch might have done better than choose for his companion one who, at the close of a long intercourse, had endeavored, as he knew, to wound my feelings. I am not quite sure that this was delicate in Mr. Pinch."

"But what can anyone expect from Mr. Pinch?" cried Charity. "Now mark my words," as a gentle rap was heard at the door, "he has come back with John Westlock for his box and is going to help him take it to the mail."

"Come in!" cried Mr. Pecksniff—not severely, only virtuously. "Come in!" An ungainly, awkward-looking man, extremely short-sighted and prematurely bald, availed himself of this permission.

"Oh! I beg your pardon, Mr. Pecksniff," he said. "Mr. Westlock, sir, hearing that you were come home—"

"Mr. Pinch, Mr. Pinch!" said Mr. Pecksniff, looking at him with an aspect of the deepest melancholy, "I did not expect this from you. I have not deserved this from you!"

"No, but do have the goodness, sir," cried Pinch, with great earnestness, "if you please. Mr. Westlock, sir, going away for good and all, wishes to leave none but friends behind him. Mr. Westlock and you, sir, have had many little differences—"

A good-looking youth, newly arrived at man's estate, stepped forward from the doorway. "Come, Mr. Pecksniff," he said, with a smile, "bear me no ill will at parting, sir."

"I bear," answered Mr. Pecksniff mildly, "no ill will to any man."

"I told you he didn't," said Pinch, in an undertone; "I knew he didn't! He always says he don't."

"Then you will shake hands, sir?" cried Westlock.

"No, John," said Mr. Pecksniff, with a calmness quite ethereal; "no, I will not shake hands, John. You cannot move me to remember any wrong you have ever done me, John."

"Wrong!" cried the other, with all the heat and impetuosity of his age. "Here's a pretty fellow! Wrong! Wrong I have done him! He'll not even remember the five hundred pounds he had with me under false pretenses, or the seventy pounds a year for board and lodging that would have been dear at seventeen! Come, Pinch, I was right, and you were wrong." He clapped his dejected companion on the shoulder and walked out.

"I'll tell you what, Pinch," he said, as they took his box between them, "you haven't half enough of the devil in you! Half enough! You haven't any! Just run over the reasons you have for being grateful to Pecksniff, will you?"

"In the first place," said Pinch, "he took me as his pupil for much less than he asked. In the second place, my poor old grandmother died happy to think that she had put me with such an excellent man. I have grown up in his house, I am in his confidence, I am his assistant, he allows me a salary; when his business improves, my prospects are to improve too."

"I believe you are one of the best fellows in the world," his companion said, "Tom Pinch. *He* didn't take less than he had asked because that less was all your poor grandmother had and more than he expected; not he, Tom! He doesn't keep you as his assistant because your wonderful faith in his pretensions is of inestimable service in all his mean disputes, because your honesty reflects honesty on him. *He* gets no credit from you, Tom, not he."

"Why, of course he don't," said Pinch, gazing at his friend with a more troubled aspect than before. "Pecksniff get credit from *me!* Well!"

But here the sound of the mail guard's horn came cheerily upon their ears, and John Westlock bade Tom an affectionate good-by. "Go your ways," said Pinch, apostrophizing the coach. "He is a fine lad and has but one fault that I know of—he don't mean it, but he is most cruelly unjust to Pecksniff."

2

FOR many years a Blue Dragon had swung and creaked complainingly before the village-ale-house door; but never in all his swinging, creaking, and flapping had there been such a stir within its dingy precincts as on the evening next after that upon which the incidents detailed in the last chapter occurred.

An old gentleman and a young lady, traveling unattended in a rusty old chariot with post horses, had turned out of the highroad and driven unexpectedly to the Blue Dragon. And here was the old gentleman, who had taken this step by reason of his sudden illness in the carriage, suffering the most horrible cramps and spasms, yet protesting and vowing, in the very midst of his pain, that he wouldn't have a doctor sent for and wouldn't take any remedies but those which the young lady administered from a small medicine chest and wouldn't, in a word, do anything but terrify the landlady out of her five wits.

So the landlady, being by this time pretty well beside herself, dispatched a messenger for Mr. Pecksniff, as a learned man who could bear a deal of responsibility and a moral man who could administer a world of comfort to a troubled mind.

The mistress of the Blue Dragon was just what a landlady should be—broad, buxom, comfortable, and good-looking. She was a widow but years ago had passed through her state of weeds and burst into flower again; and in full bloom she had continued ever since. She now sat before the fire in the sick chamber, side by side with the young lady.

The young lady's attire was extremely plain; and in her manner, even when she sat as still as she did then, there was an indefinable something which appeared to be in kindred with her scrupulously unpretending dress. She had sat at first looking anxiously toward the bed; but, seeing that the patient was at last quiet and was busy writing, she had moved away.

"The gentleman—your grandpapa—" said the landlady, "being so bent on having no assistance must terrify you very much, miss?"

"I have been very much alarmed tonight. He—he is not my grandfather."

"Father, I should have said," returned the hostess, sensible of having made an awkward mistake.

"Nor my father," said the young lady. "Nor," she added, slightly smiling, "nor my uncle. We are not related.—Did you call me, Martin?"

"Call you?" cried the old man, looking quickly up and hurriedly drawing beneath the coverlet the paper on which he had been writing. "No. Why, how you stand there, Mary, as if I had the plague! But they're all afraid of me," he added, leaning helplessly backward on his pillow—"even she! There is a curse upon me. What else have I to look for?"

"Oh, dear, no. Oh, no, I'm sure," said Mrs. Lupin, for in that name the Blue Dragon was licensed. "You forgot, for the moment, that there were none but friends here."

"Oh!" cried the old man, moaning impatiently. "Can you or anybody teach me to know who are my friends, and who my enemies?"

"At least," urged Mrs. Lupin gently, "this young lady is your friend, I am sure."

"She has no temptation to be otherwise," cried the old man, like one whose hope and confidence were utterly exhausted. "I suppose she is. Heaven knows. There—let me try to sleep." Mrs. Lupin withdrew at once; and at that moment Mr. Pecksniff at length arrived.

"Oh, dear me, sir!" she cried, "I am so very glad you have come."

"And *I* am very glad I have come," said Mr. Pecksniff, when she had acquainted him with the circumstances of her call. "I will wait upon these travelers."

"Shall I knock?" asked Mrs. Lupin.

"No," said Mr. Pecksniff; "enter, if you please."

The old gentleman was asleep. After patting the counterpane once or twice in a very solemn manner, as if by that means he gained a clear insight into the patient's disorder, Mr. Pecksniff took his seat in a large armchair and in an attitude of some thoughtfulness and much comfort waited for his waking.

Full half an hour elapsed before the old man stirred; but at length he turned himself in bed and removed the bedclothes from about his head. In course of time his eyes opened. There was nothing remarkable in these proceedings, except the influence they worked on Mr. Pecksniff, which could hardly have been surpassed by the most marvelous of natural phenomena. Gradually his hands became tightly clasped upon the elbows of the chair, his eyes dilated with surprise, his mouth opened, until, at length, when the old man rose in bed and stared at him with scarcely less emotion than he showed himself, the Pecksniff doubts were all resolved, and he exclaimed aloud,

"You *are* Martin Chuzzlewit!"

His consternation of surprise was so genuine that the old man, with all the disposition that he clearly entertained to believe it assumed, was convinced of its reality.

"I *am* Martin Chuzzlewit," he said bitterly; "and Martin Chuzzlewit wishes you had been hanged before you had come here to disturb him in his sleep."

"My good cousin—" said Mr. Pecksniff.

"There! In his very first words," cried the old man, "he asserts his relationship! I knew he would; they all do it! Ugh! What a calendar of deceit and lying and false witnessing the sound of any word of kindred opens before me!"

"Pray do not be hasty, Mr. Chuzzlewit," said Pecksniff, in a tone that was at once in the sublimest degree compassionate and dispassionate; for he had by this time recovered from his surprise and was in full possession of his virtuous self. "I came here to offer my services to a stranger. I make no offer of them to you, because I know you would distrust me if I did. And if you desire to speak to me before I go, sir, I must stipulate, in justice to myself, that you do so as to a stranger—strictly as to a stranger."

"You wish me to speak to you as to a total stranger," said the old man, "do you? You shall be gratified. Sir, I am a rich man. I have no pleasure in the possession of money. Pain and bitterness are the only goods it ever could procure for me. I hate it. The curse of my existence is that, by the golden standard which I bear about me, I am doomed to try the metal of all other men and find it false and hollow."

Mr. Pecksniff shook his head and said, "You think so."

"Oh, yes," cried the old man, "I think so! And in your telling me 'I think so' I recognize the true unworldly ring of *your* metal. I tell you, man," he added, with increasing bitterness, "that I have gone, a rich man, among people of all grades and kinds, relatives, friends, and strangers; among people in whom, when I was poor, I had confidence, and justly, for they never once deceived me then or, to me, wronged each other. But I have never found one nature, no, not one, in which, being wealthy and alone, I was not forced to detect the latent corruption that lay hid within it, waiting for such as I to bring it forth. The young girl with me is an orphan child whom, with one steady purpose, I have bred and educated. I have taken, as she knows, a solemn oath never to leave her sixpence when I die. She is bound to me in life by ties of interest and, losing by my death and having no expectation disappointed, will mourn it, perhaps—though for that I care little. This is the only kind of friend I have or will have."

Mr. Pecksniff slowly rose and, with a prefatory hem, began to speak.

"There. Go!" interposed the other. "Enough of this. I am weary of you."

"I am sorry for that, sir," rejoined Mr. Pecksniff, "because I have a duty to discharge, from which, depend upon it, I shall not shrink. No, sir, I shall not shrink. While I am forgetful of myself, I owe it to myself and to my character to tell you, without fear or favor, that it will not do for you to be unmindful of your grandson, young Martin, who has the strongest natural claim upon you. It will not do, sir. You must provide for that young man; you shall provide for him; you *will* provide for him. I believe," said Mr. Pecksniff, glancing at the pen and ink, "that in secret you have already done so. Bless you for doing so. Bless you for doing right, sir. Bless you for hating me. And good night!"

Martin lay for some time with an expression on his face of silent wonder, not unmixed with rage. At length he muttered in a whisper, "What does this mean? Can the false-hearted boy have chosen such a tool? Oh self, self, self! Every man for himself, and no creature for me!"

Universal self! Was there nothing of its shadow in these reflections, and in the history of Martin Chuzzlewit, on his own showing?

That worthy man Mr. Pecksniff, having taken leave of his cousin, haunted the Dragon at all times and seasons and, returning good for evil, evinced the deepest solicitude in the progress of the obdurate invalid. Walking into the bar of the Dragon one evening and finding no Mrs. Lupin there, he went straight upstairs, purposing, in the fervor of his affectionate zeal, to apply his ear to the keyhole and quiet his mind by assuring himself that the hard-hearted patient was getting on well. But in the dark passage he brought his head into violent contact with another head and found himself immediately collared by something which smelt like several damp umbrellas, a barrel of beer, a cask of warm brandy-and-water, and a small parlorful of stale tobacco smoke, mixed.

The gentleman who now led him downstairs was of that order of appearance which is currently termed "shabby-genteel." His fingers were a long way out of his gloves; his nether garments were so stretched and strained in a tough conflict between his braces and his straps that they appeared every moment in danger of flying asunder at the knees; his coat, in color blue and of a military cut, was buttoned and frogged up to his chin. But he wore a mustache—the regular satanic sort of thing—and he wore, besides, a vast quantity of unbrushed hair. He was very dirty and very jaunty; very bold and very mean; very swaggering and very slinking; very much like a man who might have been something better and unspeakably like a man who deserved to be something worse.

"You were eavesdropping at that door, you vagabond!" said this gentleman.

Mr. Pecksniff cast him off, as St. George might have repudiated the Dragon in that animal's last moments, and said, "Do you know, sir, that I am the friend and relative of that sick gentleman, that I am his protector, his guardian, his—"

"Not his niece's husband," interposed the stranger, "I'll be sworn; for he was there before you. And you behold in me, sir, one who has also an interest in that gentleman upstairs. My name, sir, is Tigg. Montague Tigg. I give you my brightest word of honor, sir, that I've been looking through that keyhole, with short intervals of rest, ever since nine o'clock this morning. You don't know that the Spottletoes are here, I suppose? And Mrs. Spottletoe is Chuzzlewit's own niece, isn't she?"

"Now, upon my sacred word," cried Mr. Pecksniff, looking upwards, "this is dreadful! The rapacity of these people is absolutely frightful!"

"It's not only the Spottletoes, either. Anthony Chuzzlewit and his son Jonas have got wind of it and have come down this afternoon. I saw 'em not five minutes ago."

"O Mammon, Mammon!" cried Mr. Pecksniff, smiting his forehead.

"The whole family," said Mr. Tigg, "is pouring down to this place." And, indeed, by the very next coach there came posting to the scene of action so many other affectionate members of the family that in less than four and twenty hours the scanty tavern accommodation was at a premium and Martin Chuzzlewit was in a state of siege. But he resisted bravely—refusing to receive all letters, messages, and parcels, obstinately declining to treat with anybody, and holding out no hope or promise of capitulation, being perpetually closeted with his young companion.

As no one branch of the Chuzzlewit tree had ever been known to agree with another, there was such a skirmishing as had never been known in those quiet parts before. But at length, in utter despair and hopelessness, it was agreed that there should be a general council and conference held at Mr. Pecksniff's house upon a certain day at noon.

If ever Mr. Pecksniff wore an apostolic look, he wore it on this memorable day. If ever his unruffled smile proclaimed the words "I am a messenger of peace!" that was its mission now. If ever man combined within himself all the mild qualities of the lamb, with a considerable touch of the dove and not a dash of the crocodile or the least possible suggestion of the very mildest seasoning of the serpent, that man was he. "This," said Mr. Pecksniff, looking round upon the company with folded hands, "does me good. It does my daughters good. We thank you for assembling here."

"Pecksniff," said Anthony Chuzzlewit, who had been watching the whole party with peculiar keenness from the first, "don't you be a hypocrite."

"A what, my good sir?" demanded Mr. Pecksniff.

"A hypocrite."

"Charity, my dear," said Mr. Pecksniff, "when I take my chamber candlestick tonight, remind me to be more than usually particular in praying for Mr. Anthony Chuzzlewit, who has done me an injustice." With a cheerfulness of conscience, prompting almost a sprightly demeanor, he then resumed, "We are met today to consider whether it is possible by *any* means to open the eyes of our valued relative to his present infatuation."

Before he could continue, Mr. Spottletoe burst into the chamber. "Will you venture to say," he cried to Mr. Pecksniff, "that you didn't know Mr. Chuzzlewit was going, sir, and that you don't know he's gone, sir?"

"Gone!" was the general cry.

"Gone," echoed Mr. Spottletoe. "Gone while you were sitting here. Gone. Nobody knows where he's gone. Oh, of course not! Nobody knew he was going. Oh, of course not!"

It was in vain for Mr. Pecksniff to assure his family that this new and opportune evasion was at least as great a shock and surprise to him as to anybody else. He had but one comfort, and that was the knowledge that all these his relations and friends had hated him to the very utmost extent before.

3

MR. Pinch was jogging along to Salisbury in Mr. Pecksniff's gig, one bright frosty morning, to meet the new pupil, when he saw upon the path before him a traveler on foot, who walked with a light quick step and sang as he went. He was a young fellow, of some five or six and twenty perhaps, and was dressed in a free and fly-away fashion, with a bunch of bright winter berries in the buttonhole of his velveteen coat. "Why, Mark Tapley!" said Tom Pinch, stopping. "How spruce you are!"

"It's not my fault, you know, Mr. Pinch," said Mark, with a very sudden decrease of vivacity in his whimsical face. "That's where the aggravation of it is. Any man may be in good spirits and good temper when he's well dressed. There ain't much credit in that. If I was very ragged and very jolly, then I should begin to feel I had gained a point, Mr. Pinch."

"So you were singing just now to bear up, as it were, against being well dressed, eh, Mark?" said Pinch.

"Your conversation's always equal to print, sir," rejoined Mark, with a broad grin. "That was it."

"Well," cried Pinch, "you are the strangest young man, Mark, I ever knew in my life. Get in. I more than half believed just now, seeing you so very smart, that you must be going to be married."

"Well, sir, I've thought of that too," Mark replied. "There might be some credit in being jolly with a wife, 'specially if the children had the measles and that and was very fractious indeed. I don't believe there ever was a man as could come out so strong under circumstances that would make other men miserable as I could, if I could only get a chance. But I can't get a chance. I'm a going to leave the Dragon, sir."

"Going to leave the Dragon!" cried Mr. Pinch, with great astonishment.

"Yes, sir," he rejoined. "What's the use of my stopping at the Dragon? Any man could be jolly at the Dragon. There's no credit in *that*."

"Why, what will become of Mrs. Lupin, Mark?" said Mr. Pinch. "I always supposed that Mrs. Lupin and you would make a match of it."

"Why, that would be the ruin of a man like me," returned the other. "What would be the credit of the landlord of the Dragon's being jolly? Why, he couldn't help it if he tried. I'm looking out now for something new and suitable." And when they reached the city, off he went.

Mr. Pinch was waiting in the tavern that evening when another guest came in, bringing with him such a quantity of cold air that he positively seemed at first to put the fire out. "Very hard frost tonight, sir," said he, courteously acknowledging Mr. Pinch's withdrawal from the fire. "Don't disturb yourself, I beg."

Though he said this with a vast amount of consideration for Mr. Pinch's comfort, he dragged a chair to the very center of the hearth notwithstanding and sat down in front of the fire, with a foot on each hob. He was young—one and twenty, perhaps—and handsome, with a keen, dark eye and a quickness of look and manner which made Tom sensible of a great contrast in his own bearing and caused him to feel even more shy than usual. "I have an engagement to meet a gentleman here," said the newcomer.

"So have I," said Tom. "The young gentleman I expect was to inquire for a person by the name of Pinch."

"Dear me!" cried the other, jumping up. "And I have been keeping the fire from you all this while! I had no idea you were Mr. Pinch. I am the Mr. Martin for whom you were to inquire." After drinking to each other in a glass of hot punch, they became quite confidential. "I'm a sort of relation of Pecksniff's, you know," said the young man. "My grandfather is his cousin. Chuzzlewit is my name."

"Dear me!" cried Mr. Pinch, with an involuntary start. Then,

remembering that Mr. Pecksniff had privately cautioned him to say nothing in reference to the old gentleman of the same name who had lodged at the Dragon, he proposed that they leave.

Their principal topic on the drive home was naturally Mr. Pecksniff and his family, of whom and of the great obligations they had heaped upon him Tom Pinch drew such a picture as would have inclined anyone almost to revere them, and of which Mr. Pecksniff had not the slightest foresight or he certainly (being very humble) would not have sent Tom Pinch to bring the pupil home.

"A pretty church!" said Martin, as they approached the village.

"Is it not?" cried Tom, with great pride. "There's the sweetest little organ there you ever heard. I play it for them."

"Indeed!" said Martin. "It is hardly worth the trouble, I should think. What do you get for that now?"

"Nothing," answered Tom. "That is, I get a great deal of pleasure from it. And it led to something else the other day; it led to my seeing one of the loveliest and most beautiful faces you can possibly picture to yourself, as she listened to my playing. But she is gone now; and, of all unlikely things in this wide world, it is perhaps the most improbable that I shall ever look upon her face again."

"And you never followed her when she went away?"

"Why should I distress her by doing that?" said Tom Pinch. "Is it likely that she wanted my company? She came to hear the organ, not to see me."

The new pupil was clearly very much amazed by Mr. Pinch's weakness and would probably have told him so but for their opportune arrival at Mr. Pecksniff's door. Mr. Pecksniff had clearly not expected them for hours to come—for he was surrounded by open books and was glancing from volume to volume with a pencil in his mouth and a pair of compasses in his hand. "Bless my life!" said Mr. Pecksniff, looking up and gradually exchanging his abstracted face for one of joyful recognition. "Here already! Martin, my dear boy, I am delighted to welcome you to my poor house! Nay, my dears, why blush at being detected in your every-day pursuits? We had prepared to give you the reception of a visitor, Martin, in our little room of state, but I like this better—I like this better!"

Festive preparations, however, on a rather extensive scale were already completed. There were two bottles of currant wine; a dish of sandwiches, another of apples, another of captain's biscuits, a plate of oranges cut up small and gritty with powdered sugar, and a highly geological home-made cake. The magnitude of these preparations quite took away Tom Pinch's breath; for though the new pupils were usually let down softly, particularly in the wine department, which had so many stages of declension that sometimes a young gentleman was a whole fortnight in getting to the pump, still, this was a banquet.

Perhaps to assure himself that what he saw and heard was holiday reality and not a charming dream, Mr. Pinch ate of everything; nor was he stinted in his draughts of wine, though every time he filled his glass anew Miss Charity, despite her amiable resolves, could not repress a fixed and stony glare, as if her eyes had rested on a ghost. Mr. Pecksniff also became thoughtful at those moments, not to say dejected; but as he knew the vintage,

it is very likely he may have been speculating on the probable condition of Mr. Pinch upon the morrow and discussing within himself
the best remedies for colic.

"It is not often," Mr. Pecksniff said the next morning, "that
my daughters and I desert our quiet home to pursue the giddy
round of pleasures that revolves abroad. But I have a summons to
repair to London—on professional business, my dear Martin,
strictly on professional business—and I promised my girls, long
ago, that whenever that happened again they should accompany
me.

"Let me see," he said, searching among some papers, "how
you can best employ yourself, Martin, while I am absent. Suppose
you were to give me your idea of a monument to a Lord Mayor
of London or a tomb for a sheriff or your notion of a cow house to
be erected in a nobleman's park. Do you know, now," said Mr.
Pecksniff, folding his hands and looking at his young relation with
an air of pensive interest, "that I should very much like to see
your notion of a cow house?"

But Martin by no means appeared to relish this suggestion.
"Stay," said Mr. Pecksniff. "Come! As you're ambitious and are
a very neat draftsman, you shall—ha, ha!—you shall try your
hand on these proposals for a grammar school, regulating your
plan, of course, by the printed particulars. Upon my word, now,"
said Mr. Pecksniff merrily, "I shall be very curious to see what you
make of the grammar school. Who knows but a young man of your
taste might hit upon something, impracticable and unlikely in
itself, which I could put into shape?"

Martin readily undertook this task, and Mr. Pecksniff forthwith proceeded to entrust him with the materials necessary for
its execution, dwelling meanwhile on the magical effect of a few
finishing touches from the hand of a master, which, indeed, as
some people said (and these were the old enemies again!), was
unquestionably almost miraculous, as there were cases on record
in which the masterly introduction of an additional back window
or a kitchen door or half a dozen steps or even a water spout had
made the design of a pupil Mr. Pecksniff's own work and had
brought substantial rewards into that gentleman's pocket. But
such is the magic of genius, which changes all it handles into gold!

As the coach appeared that evening, Tom Pinch, who had spent the day helping Mr. Pecksniff prepare for his journey, entreated that gentleman to undertake the delivery of a letter. "Oh!" said Mr. Pecksniff, glancing at the superscription. "For your sister, Thomas. Yes, oh, yes, it shall be delivered, Mr. Pinch." He made the promise with so much condescension and patronage that Tom felt he had asked a great deal (this had not occurred to his mind before) and thanked him earnestly. The Miss Pecksniffs, according to a custom they had, were amused beyond description at the mention of Mr. Pinch's sister. Oh, the fright! The bare idea of a Miss Pinch! Good Heavens! They drove away laughing still.

Martin Chuzzlewit, however, appeared out of spirits. "Deuce take it, I must talk openly to somebody," he cried as he and Tom sat alone before the fire. "I'll talk openly to you, Pinch.

"You must know that I have been bred up from childhood with great expectations and have always been taught to believe that I should be, one day, very rich. Now, my grandfather, who reared me, has a great many good points; but he has two very great faults. He has the most confirmed obstinacy of character you ever met with; and he is most abominably selfish. I have heard that those have been, time out of mind, the failings of our family; and I believe there's some truth in it, though I can't say of my own knowledge. All I have to do, you know, is to be very thankful that they haven't descended to me and to be very careful that I don't contract 'em."

"To be sure," said Mr. Pinch. "Very proper."

"Well, sir," resumed Martin, "I am in love with one of the most beautiful girls the sun ever shone upon. But she is wholly dependent upon the pleasure of my grandfather; and when he suspected me of loving her, he charged me with designing to corrupt the fidelity to himself (there you observe his selfishness) of a young creature whom he had trained and educated to be his only disinterested and faithful companion when he should have disposed of me in marriage to his heart's content. Upon that, I took fire immediately and told him that with his good leave I would dispose of myself in marriage; words engendered words, as they always do; and the upshot of it was that I was to renounce her or be renounced by him. Of course I was not going to yield to him or give way by so much as a thousandth part of an inch, so here

I am! I saw Pecksniff's advertisement, which I answered, having always had some natural taste, I believe, in the matters to which it referred and thinking it might suit me. It would never do, you know, for me to be plunging myself into poverty and shabbiness and love in one room up three pair of stairs and all that sort of thing."

"To say nothing of her," remarked Tom Pinch, in a low voice.

"Exactly so," rejoined Martin. "There is one odd coincidence connected with this love story, which brings it to an end. You remember what you told me about your pretty visitor in the church? That was she. After what I have just heard from Pecksniff, I have no doubt that she came and went with my grandfather."

"I knew what you were going to say!" cried Tom, looking fixedly at him and speaking very softly. "I have no power at all— I needn't tell you that—but I have an excellent will; and if I could ever be of use to you, in any way whatever, how very glad I should be!"

4

WHEN Mr. Pecksniff and the two young ladies got into the heavy coach, they found it empty, which was a great comfort, particularly as the outside was quite full and the passengers looked very frosty. For as Mr. Pecksniff justly observed—when he and his daughters had burrowed their feet deep in the straw, wrapped themselves to the chin, and pulled up both windows—it is always satisfactory to feel in keen weather that many other people are not as warm as you are.

But the tendency of mankind, when it falls asleep in coaches, is to wake up cross—to find its legs in its way and its corns an aggravation. Mr. Pecksniff, not being exempt from the common lot of humanity, found himself, at the end of a nap, so decidedly the victim of these infirmities that he had an irresistible inclination to visit them upon his daughters, which he had already begun to do in the shape of divers random kicks, when the coach stopped and the door was opened.

"Now mind," said a thin, sharp voice in the dark, "I and my son go inside because the roof is full, but you agree only to charge us outside prices. It's quite understood that we won't pay more. Is it?"

"All right, sir," replied the guard. And two people took their seats in the vehicle.

"That was lucky!" whispered the old man. "And a great stroke of policy in you, my boy, to observe it. He, he, he! We couldn't have gone outside. I should have died of the rheumatism!"

Whether it occurred to the dutiful son that he had in some degree overreached himself by contributing to the prolongation of his father's days, or not, he gave his father such a nudge in reply that that good old gentleman was taken with a cough which lasted for full five minutes and goaded Mr. Pecksniff to that pitch of irritation that he said at last, and very suddenly, "There is really no room in this coach for any gentleman with a cold in his head!"

"Mine," said the old man, after a moment's pause, "is upon my chest, Pecksniff."

"Hem! I thought," said Mr. Pecksniff, returning to his usual mildness, "that I addressed a stranger. I find that I address a relative. Mr. Anthony Chuzzlewit and his son Mr. Jonas—for they, my dear children, are our traveling companions—will excuse me for an apparently harsh remark. I may be a Hypocrite," said Mr. Pecksniff cuttingly, "but I am not a Brute."

"Pooh, pooh!" said the old man. "What signifies that word, Pecksniff? Hypocrite! Why, we are all hypocrites. The annoying quality in *you* is that you keep up appearances by a tacit understanding even before your own daughters here. Now I, when I have a business scheme in hand, tell Jonas what it is, and we discuss it openly."

Here Mr. Jonas told Mr. Pecksniff "that if it was all the same to him he would have a chat with the gals" and established himself beside them.

"Well, cousin," said Mr. Jonas "—because we *are* cousins, you know, a few times removed—so you're going to London?"

Miss Mercy replied in the affirmative, pinching her sister's arm at the same time and giggling excessively. "Merry," cried that more prudent damsel, "really I am ashamed of you. How can you go on so? You wild thing!" At which Miss Merry only laughed the more, of course.

"I saw a wildness in her eye, t'other day," said Mr. Jonas, addressing Charity. "But you're the one to sit solemn! Don't mind crowding me, I like to be crowded by gals. Come a little closer, cousin."

"No, thank you, sir," said Charity.

"There's that other one a laughing again," said Mr. Jonas. "She's a laughing at my father, I shouldn't wonder. Do you ever have the nightmare, cousin?

"Sometimes," answered Charity. "Not often."

"The other one," said Mr. Jonas, after a pause. "Does *she* ever have the nightmare?"

"I don't know," replied Charity. "You had better ask her."

"She laughs so," said Jonas; "there's no talking to her. Only hark how she's a going on now! You're the sensible one, cousin!"

"Tut, tut!" cried Charity.

After a heavy supper had been consumed by all the party, Mr. Pecksniff delivered a kind of grace after meat, in these words: "The process of digestion, as I have been informed by anatomical friends, is one of the most wonderful works of nature. I do not know how it may be with others, but it is a great satisfaction to me to know, when regaling on my humble fare, that I am putting in motion the most beautiful machinery with which we have any acquaintance. I really feel at such times as if I was doing a public service." As nothing could be added to this, nothing was said; and when the party awoke the next morning, they were in London.

Mr. Pecksniff, with one of the young ladies under each arm, dived through the streets until he knocked at the door of a very dingy edifice, on the front of which was a little oval board like a tea tray, with this inscription, "Commercial Boarding House. M. Todgers," where a small boy with a large red head and no nose to speak of let them in.

M. Todgers's Commercial Boarding House was a house of that sort which is likely to be dark at any time. There was an odd smell in the passage, as if the concentrated essence of all the dinners that had been cooked in the kitchen since the house was built lingered at the top of the kitchen stairs to that hour. In particular, there was a sensation of cabbage, as if all the greens that had ever been boiled there were evergreens and flourished in immortal strength. The parlor communicated to strangers a magnetic and instinctive consciousness of rats and mice. It had not been papered or painted, hadn't Todgers's, within the memory of man. It was very black, begrimed, and moldy.

M. Todgers was a lady, rather a bony and hard-featured lady, with a row of curls in front of her head. "Mr. Pecksniff!" cried Mrs. Todgers. "Welcome to London! My dear Miss Pecksniffs, how happy your pa has made me!"

"I know, my good madam," said Mr. Pecksniff, "that you only receive gentlemen boarders. But it occurred to me that perhaps you would give my daughters house room."

"Perhaps?" cried Mrs. Todgers, ecstatically embracing the young ladies. "Perhaps?" The truth was that, the house being full, she wanted time for consideration. "I think I can arrange it," she said at length, affection beaming in one eye and calculation shining out of the other. "Oh, you dear girls!"

By the second day of their stay in London, the Miss Pecksniffs and Mrs. Todgers were highly confidential, insomuch that the last-named lady had already communicated the particulars of three early disappointments of a tender nature. "Your pa was once a little particular in his attentions, my dears," said Mrs. Todgers; "but to be your ma was too much happiness denied me. Presiding over an establishment like this makes sad havoc with the features. The gravy alone is enough to add twenty years to one's age, I do assure you. There is no such passion in human nature as the passion for gravy among commercial gentlemen."

"Just like Mr. Pinch, Merry!" said Charity. "We have always noticed it in him, you remember?"

"Yes, my dear," giggled Merry, "but we have never given it him, you know."

"Your pa was kind enough," said Mrs. Todgers, "to invite me to take a ride with you today, and I think he mentioned that you were going to call upon Miss Pinch. Any relation to the gentleman you were speaking of just now, Miss Pecksniff?"

"For goodness' sake, Mrs. Todgers," interposed the lively Merry, "don't call him a gentleman. He's the most hideous, goggle-eyed creature in existence—quite an ogre. This is his sister, so I leave you to suppose what *she* is. I shall be obliged to laugh outright, I know I shall!" cried the charming girl.

Mrs. Todgers laughed immensely at the dear love's humor and declared she was quite afraid of her, she was so severe.

Tom Pinch's sister was governess in a family, a lofty family—perhaps the wealthiest brass and copper founder's family known to mankind. To their mansion Mr. Pecksniff, accompanied by his daughters and Mrs. Todgers, drove gallantly in a one-horse fly. They were ushered into a small room where Mr. Pinch's sister was at that moment instructing her eldest pupil—to wit, a premature little woman of thirteen years old, who had already arrived at such a pitch of whalebone and education that she had nothing girlish about her.

It is a melancholy fact, but it must be related, that Mr. Pinch's sister was not at all ugly. On the contrary, she had a very mild and prepossessing face and a pretty little figure. There was something of her brother in a gentleness of manner and in her look of timid trustfulness; but she was so far from being a fright or a dowdy or a horror or anything else predicted by the two Miss Pecksniffs that those young ladies naturally regarded her with great indignation.

"It is very kind of you," said Tom Pinch's sister, with Tom's own simplicity and Tom's own smile, "to come here, very kind indeed; though how great a kindness you have done me in gratifying my wish to see you and to thank you with my own lips, you, who make so light of benefits conferred, can scarcely think."

"Very grateful; very pleasant; very proper," murmured Mr. Pecksniff. "And how do *you* do, my very interesting child?" as his eyes wandered to the pupil. "A sweet face this, my dears." Both his daughters had been in ecstasies with the scion of a wealthy house from the first. Mrs. Todgers vowed that anything one quarter so angelic she had never seen. "She wanted but a pair of wings, a dear," said that good woman, "to be a young sirup"—meaning, possibly, young sylph or seraph.

"Missis's compliments to Miss Pinch," said a footman, suddenly appearing, "and begs to know wot my young lady is a learning of just now."

"My dears," said Mr. Pecksniff, "we are interrupting the studies. Let us go." Then he said to Miss Pinch, with more condescension and kindness than ever—for it was desirable the footman should expressly understand that they were not friends of hers, but patrons—"Good morning. Good-by. God bless you! You may depend upon my continued protection of your brother."

"Thank you," said Tom's sister heartily, "a thousand times."

"Not at all," he retorted, patting her gently on the head. "My sweet child," to the pupil, "farewell! That fairy creature," said Mr. Pecksniff, looking in his pensive mood hard at the footman, as if he meant him, "has shed a vision on my path, refulgent in its nature and not easily to be obliterated. My dears, are you ready?"

Todgers's was in a great bustle that evening, partly owing to some additional domestic preparations for the morrow, when the Miss Pecksniffs were to make their first appearance at the general table, and partly to the excitement always inseparable in that house from Saturday night, when there was always a great clinking of pattens downstairs until midnight or so, together with a frequent gleaming of mysterious lights in the area, much working at the pump, and a constant jangling of the iron handle of the pail.

The red-headed boy honored the Miss Pecksniffs with a deal of notice, seldom passing the door of Mrs. Todgers's private room, where they sat, without putting in his head and greeting them. "I say," he whispered, stopping in one of his journeys to and fro, "young ladies, there's soup tomorrow. She's a making it now. Ain't she a putting in the water? Oh! not at all!"

In the course of answering another knock, he thrust in his head again. "I say! There's fowls tomorrow. Not skinny ones. Oh, no!"

Presently he called through the keyhole, "There's fish tomorrow. Just come. Don't eat none of him!" and, with this spectral warning, vanished again.

Benjamin was supposed to be the real name of this young retainer, but he was generally known among the gentlemen as "Bailey junior," a name bestowed upon him in contradistinction to Old Bailey. When the hour for the gala Sunday dinner drew nigh, Bailey junior, testifying great excitement, appeared in a complete suit of cast-off clothes several sizes too large for him and, in particular, mounted a clean shirt of such extraordinary magnitude that one of the gentlemen (remarkable for his ready wit) called him "Collars" on the spot. At about a quarter before five, a deputation headed by Mr. Jinkins, who always took the lead in the house, besought the honor of conducting the Miss Pecksniffs upstairs, where the gentlemen were waiting to be presented.

There was considerable delay in the production of dinner, and poor Mrs. Todgers, being reproached in confidence by Jinkins, slipped in and out at least twenty times to see about it, always coming back as though she had no such thing upon her mind and hadn't been out at all. At last dinner was announced by Bailey junior in these terms, "The wittles is up!" On which notice the company immediately descended to the banquet hall.

The two Miss Pecksniffs had hardly ever felt so pleasant and so full of conversation in their lives. Mercy, in particular, was in immense request, being called on to take wine with some new admirer every minute. But at length the sun, as Mr. Jinkins says (gentlemanly creature, Jinkins—never at a loss!), is about to leave the firmament. Mrs. Todgers rises; the two Miss Pecksniffs rise; all rise. Miss Mercy Pecksniff looks downward for her scarf. Where is it? Dear me, where *can* it be? Sweet girl, she has it on, not on her fair neck, but loose upon her flowing figure. A dozen hands assist her. She is all confusion. The youngest gentleman in the company thirsts to murder Jinkins. She skips and joins her sister at the door. Her sister has her arm about the waist of Mrs. Todgers. She winds her arm around her sister. Diana, what a picture! The last things visible are a shape and a skip. "Gentlemen, let us drink the ladies!"

They go upstairs. Mr. Pecksniff takes a chair at the side of Mrs. Todgers. He also spills a cup of coffee over his legs without appearing to be aware of the circumstance. "Mr. Pecksniff!" cried Mrs. Todgers. "What a ghastly smile! Are you ill, sir?"

He pressed his hand upon her arm and answered in a solemn manner and a faint voice, "Chronic."

"Colic?" cried the frightened Mrs. Todgers.

"Chron-ic," he repeated with some difficulty. "Chron-ic. A chronic disorder. I have been its victim from childhood. It is carrying me to my grave. I am rather glad of it, upon the whole. You are like her, Mrs. Todgers. Permit me—in honor of her memory. For the sake of a voice from the tomb."

"Don't squeeze me so tight, pray, Mr. Pecksniff. If any one should see!"

"Has a voice from the grave no influence?" said Mr. Pecksniff, with dismal tenderness. "This is irreligious! My dear creature."

"Hush!" urged Mrs. Todgers. "Really, you mustn't."

"It's not me," said Mr. Pecksniff. "Don't suppose it's me; it's the voice; it's her voice." Mrs. Pecksniff, deceased, must have had an unusually thick and husky voice for a lady and, to say the truth, somewhat of a drunken voice if it had ever borne much resemblance to that in which Mr. Pecksniff spoke just then. But perhaps this was delusion on his part. "Don't be alarmed, Mrs. Todgers," said Mr. Pecksniff, falling heavily against her; "chronic—chronic! Let's have a little drop of something to drink."

"Bless my life, Miss Pecksniffs!" cried Mrs. Todgers aloud. "Your dear pa's took very poorly!" Standing on his feet, Mr. Pecksniff regarded the assembly with a look of ineffable wisdom. Gradually it gave place to a smile—a feeble, helpless, melancholy smile, bland almost to sickliness. "Do not repine, my friends," said Mr. Pecksniff tenderly. "Do not weep for me. It is chronic." And with these words, after making a futile attempt to pull off his shoes, he fell into the fireplace.

The youngest gentleman in company had him out in a second. Yes, before a hair upon his head was singed, he had him on the hearth rug. Her father! They carried him upstairs to bed and crushed the youngest gentleman at every step. But before they had gained the bottom of the staircase, a vision of Mr. Pecksniff, strangely attired, was seen to flutter on the top landing. He desired to collect their sentiments, it seemed, upon the nature of human life. "Here," cried Jinkins. "Go to bed again!"

But as often as Mr. Pecksniff was shut up in his own room, he darted out afresh. "The legs of the human subject, my friends, are a beautiful production," he said on one appearance. "Compare them with wooden legs. Do you know," said Mr. Pecksniff, leaning over the banisters, "that I should very much like to see Mrs. Todgers's notion of a wooden leg, if perfectly agreeable to herself?"

As it appeared impossible to entertain any reasonable hopes of him after this speech, Mr. Pecksniff was finally locked in his room.

5

BUT Mr. Pecksniff had come to town on business. Had he forgotten? No. Every morning, after the early breakfast, he repaired to the post office and inquired for letters. This went on for four or five days. At length, one morning, Mr. Pecksniff returned with a breathless rapidity strange to observe in him, at other times so calm, and, seeking immediate speech with his daughters, he shut himself up with them in private conference for two whole hours.

That same day an old gentleman walked toward Todgers's. Mr. Pecksniff was seated in the landlady's little room, and his visitor found him reading—by an accident; he apologized for it—an excellent theological work. There were cake and wine upon a table—by another accident, for which he also apologized. He would not venture to recommend Mr. Chuzzlewit to take the easy chair, but there it was. Old Martin sat down.

After a few moments' silence he said, "Let me thank you for coming to London so promptly, at my almost unexplained request —I need scarcely add, at my cost. It is not a caprice. It is built up on reason, proof, and cool comparison. Moreover, I am not a capricious man."

"Most assuredly not," said Mr. Pecksniff.

"How do you know?" returned the other quickly. "You are to begin to know it now; you are to test and prove it. Deserted by all in whom I have ever trusted, I fly to you for refuge. You spoke to me disinterestedly on behalf of—I needn't name him. I now confide in you to help me visit the consequences of dissimulation on the right heads. If I had known you sooner and sooner used you as you well deserve, I might have been a happier man."

Mr. Pecksniff looked up to the ceiling and clasped his hands in rapture.

"Your daughters," said Martin, after a short silence. "I could wish to see them. Are they near at hand?"

They were, very near; for they had, in fact, been listening at the door from the beginning of this conversation until now, when they precipitately retired. Having wiped the signs of weakness from his eyes and so given them time to get upstairs, Mr. Pecksniff opened the door and mildly cried in the passage, "My own darlings, where are you?"

"Here, my dear pa!" replied the distant voice of Charity.

"Come down into the back parlor, if you please, my love," said Mr. Pecksniff, "and bring your sister with you."

"Yes, my dear pa!" cried Merry; and down they came directly (being all obedient), singing as they came.

Nothing could exceed the astonishment of the two Miss Pecksniffs when they found a stranger with their dear papa. Nothing could surpass their mute amazement when he told them that Mr. Chuzzlewit and he were friends. Crying, "Thank Heaven for this!" they fell upon the old man's neck.

"You have a new inmate in your house," said Martin, then. "He must quit it. He has deceived you."

"I hope not," said Mr. Pecksniff eagerly. "I trust not. I have been extremely well disposed toward that young man."

The old man glanced at both his fair supporters, but especially at Miss Mercy. "Of course you know that he has made his matrimonial choice?" he said.

"Oh, dear!" cried Mr. Pecksniff, rubbing his hair up very stiff upon his head and staring wildly at his daughters. "Surely not without his grandfather's consent and approbation!"

"I thought he had suppressed it," said the old man. The indignation felt by Mr. Pecksniff at this terrible disclosure was only to be equaled by the kindling anger of his daughters. What! Had they taken to their hearth and home a secretly contracted serpent, a crocodile, who had made a furtive offer of his hand! Monster! How basely had they been deceived!

"I am glad you second me so warmly," said Mr. Chuzzlewit; adding presently, "You know what will be said of this new understanding between us? Some will say that I dote in my old age, that illness has shaken me, that I have lost all strength of mind and have grown childish. You can bear that?"

Mr. Pecksniff answered that it would be dreadfully hard to bear, but he thought he could, if he made a great effort.

"With the great mass of slanderers," said old Martin, "the tale, as I clearly foresee, will run thus: That to mark my contempt for the rabble whom I despised, I chose from among them the very worst, and made him do my will and pampered and enriched him at the cost of all the rest. Is your mind made up to bear this likewise?"

"My dear Mr. Chuzzlewit," cried Pecksniff, in an ecstasy, "for such a man as you have shown yourself to be this day, I hope it is no presumption to say that I, and I am sure I may add my children also, would bear anything whatever!"

"Enough," said Martin. "You can charge no consequences on me. You and your daughters may expect to see me before long; in the meantime I need not tell you that we keep our own confidence. What you will do when you get home is understood between us. My dears, good morning!"

When they were again alone, the two young ladies exhibited an unusual amount of gaiety, but at that juncture they were disturbed by the sound of voices in the next room.

"I don't care that, Mrs. Todgers!" said the young gentleman who had been the youngest gentleman in company on the day of the festival. "I don't care *that*, ma'am," said he, snapping his fingers, "for Jinkins. Don't suppose I do."

"I am quite certain you don't, sir," replied Mrs. Todgers. "You have too independent a spirit, I know, to yield to anybody."

"I have borne this long enough," said the youngest gentleman; "I left home originally because I had that within me which wouldn't be domineered over by a sister; and do you think I'm going to be put down by *him?* No."

"It is very wrong in Mr. Jinkins—I know it is perfectly inexcusable in Mr. Jinkins—if he intends it," observed Mrs. Todgers.

"If he intends it!" cried the youngest gentleman. "Don't he interrupt and contradict me on every occasion? Does he ever fail to interpose himself between me and anything or anybody that he sees I have set my mind upon? Does he make bragging remarks about his razors and insulting allusions to people who have no necessity to shave more than once a week? All I've got to say to you, Mrs. Todgers, is, a week's notice from next Saturday. If we get over the intermediate time without bloodshed, you may think yourself pretty fortunate. I don't myself expect we shall."

"Dear, dear!" cried Mrs. Todgers. "What would I have given to have prevented this! As many of the gentlemen and I have often said, you are too sensitive. That's where it is. It's your spirit."

The young gentleman coughed and was so much mollified by these and similar speeches on the part of Mrs. Todgers that in the end he withdrew his notice and went back to business.

"Goodness me, Miss Pecksniffs!" cried Mrs. Todgers, as she came into the back room. "What a trial of temper it is to keep a house like this! Of all the ridiculous young fellows that ever I had

to deal with, that is the most ridiculous and unreasonable. Mr.
Jinkins is hard upon him sometimes, but not half as hard as he
deserves."

The young ladies were greatly entertained by certain anecdotes illustrative of the youngest gentleman's character, which she
went on to tell them. But Mr. Pecksniff looked quite stern and said
in a solemn voice, "Pray, Mrs. Todgers, if I may inquire, what
does that young gentleman contribute toward the support of these
premises?"

"Why, sir, for what *he* has he pays about eighteen shillings a
week!" said Mrs. Todgers.

"Eighteen shillings a week!" repeated Mr. Pecksniff. "And
do you mean to say, ma'am—is it possible, Mrs. Todgers—that
for such a miserable consideration as eighteen shillings a week a
female of your understanding can so far demean herself as to wear
a double face, even for an instant?"

"I am forced to keep things on the square if I can, sir," faltered
Mrs. Todgers. "The profit is very small."

"The profit!" repeated Mr. Pecksniff. "The profit of dissimulation! To worship the golden calf of Baal for eighteen shillings a
week!"

"Don't in your own goodness be too hard upon me, Mr. Pecksniff," cried Mrs. Todgers, taking out her handkerchief.

"Oh, Calf, Calf!" cried Mr. Pecksniff mournfully. "Oh, Baal,
Baal! Oh, my friend Mrs. Todgers! To barter away that precious
jewel, self-esteem, and cringe to any mortal creature—for eighteen
shillings a week!"

Just, most just thy censure, upright Pecksniff! Had it been
for the sake of a place, a party, or eighteen thousand pounds, or
even eighteen hundred—but to worship the golden calf for eighteen
shillings a week! Oh, pitiful, pitiful!

The family were within two or three days of their departure
from Mrs. Todgers's, and the commercial gentlemen were to a
man despondent, when Bailey junior presented himself before
Miss Charity Pecksniff and gave her to understand that a visitor
attended to pay his respects to her. "A gentleman for me!" cried
Charity. "My dear Mercy, who *can* it be? Isn't it odd? I have a
great mind not to go to him, really. So very strange, you know."

The younger sister plainly considered that this appeal had its origin in the pride of being called upon and that it was intended as a retaliation upon her for having captured the commercial gentlemen. Therefore she replied, with great affection, that it was, no doubt, very strange indeed and that she was totally at a loss to conceive what the ridiculous person unknown could mean by it.

"Quite impossible to divine," said Charity, with some sharpness, "though you needn't be angry, my dear. I am afraid your head is turned, you silly thing."

"Do you know, my dear," said Merry, with engaging candor, "I have been afraid of that myself all along! What a relief it must be to you, my dear, to be so very comfortable in that respect, and not to be worried by those odious men! How *do* you do it, Cherry?"

This artless inquiry might have led to turbulent results, but for the strong emotions of delight evinced by Bailey, which brought to the young ladies' immediate recollection the great virtuous precept "Keep up appearances whatever you do" in which they had been educated. So Miss Charity went upstairs in state to receive her mysterious adorer.

"Ah, cousin!" he said. "Here I am, you see. You thought I was lost, I'll be bound. I say, how's the other one?"

"My sister is very well, I believe," returned the young lady. "Perhaps you would like to ask her yourself?"

"No, no, cousin," said Mr. Jonas. "Don't be in a hurry. I say! Did you think I was lost? You haven't told me. Did the other one?"

"I am sure it is impossible for me to say what my sister may or may not have thought on such a subject," cried Cherry. "She never said anything about it."

"Didn't she laugh about it?" inquired Jonas. "She's a terrible one to laugh."

"She is very lively," said Cherry.

"Liveliness is a pleasant thing—when it don't lead to spending money—ain't it?" asked Mr. Jonas. "Such liveliness as yours, I mean, you know. I called to ask you to come and take a walk, cousin, and see some of the sights, and to come to our house afterward and have a bit of something. I say—you'll bring the other one?"

Miss Charity withdrew to prepare her sister and herself for the excursion, though Miss Mercy was by no means pleased to leave the brilliant triumphs of Todgers's for the society of Mr. Jonas.

"Aha!" cried Jonas when they appeared. "You're there, are you?"

"Yes, fright," said Mercy, "here I am; and I would much rather be anywhere else, I assure you."

"Oh, you're a sharp gal!" said Mr. Jonas. "She's a regular teaser, ain't she?" He gave an arm to each cousin and proceeded to show them as many sights, in the way of bridges, churches, streets, outsides of theaters, and other free spectacles, as most people see in a twelvemonth. When they had been out for some hours and were thoroughly fatigued, he took them home with him.

The old-established firm of Anthony Chuzzlewit and Son, Manchester Warehousemen, and so forth, had its place of business in a very narrow street where every house was in the brightest summer morning very gloomy. A dim, dirty, smoky, tumble-down, rotten old house it was as anybody would desire to see, but there the firm of Anthony Chuzzlewit and Son transacted all their business and their pleasure too, such as it was; for neither the young man nor the old had any other residence or any care or thought beyond its narrow limits. The single sitting room was a chaos of boxes and old papers and had more countinghouse stools than chairs. The solitary little table for purposes of refection and social enjoyment bore as fair a proportion to the desk and other business furniture as the graces and harmless relaxations of life had ever done, in the persons of the old man and his son, to their pursuit of wealth. It was meanly laid out now for dinner; and in a chair before the fire sat old Anthony himself, who rose to greet his son and his fair cousins as they entered.

"Well, ghost!" said Mr. Jonas, dutifully addressing his parent. "Is dinner ready? Here," he said to Charity, when they sat down to table, "you sit on the right side of me, and I'll have her upon the left. Other one, will you come here?"

"You're such a fright," replied Mercy, "that I know I shall have no appetite if I sit so near you; but I suppose I must."

"Ain't she lively?" whispered Mr. Jonas to the elder sister, with his favorite elbow emphasis.

"Oh, I really don't know!" replied Miss Pecksniff tartly. "I am tired of being asked such ridiculous questions."

"What's that precious old father of mine about now?" said Mr. Jonas, seeing that his parent was traveling up and down the room. "What are you looking for?"

"I've lost my glasses, Jonas," said old Anthony.

"Sit down without your glasses, can't you?" returned his son. "And where's that sleepy-headed old Chuffey? Now, stupid. Oh! You know your name, do you?"

It would seem that he didn't, for he didn't come until the father called. As he spoke, the door of a small glass office was slowly opened, and a little blear-eyed, weazen-faced ancient man came creeping out. He looked as if he had been put away and forgotten half a century before and somebody had just found him in a closet. He looked at nothing, with eyes that saw nothing, and a face that meant nothing. "Our clerk," said Mr. Jonas, as master of ceremonies, "old Chuffey."

"Is he deaf?" inquired one of the young ladies.

"No, I don't know that he is. He ain't deaf, is he, father?"

"I never heard him say he was," replied the old man.

"Blind?" inquired the young ladies.

"N-no, I never understood that he was at all blind," said Jonas carelessly.

"What is he, then?"

"Why, I'll tell you what he is," said Mr. Jonas; "he's precious old, for one thing; and I think my father must have caught it of him. He's a strange old chap, for another, and don't understand anyone but *him!*" He pointed to his honored parent. "He's been addling his brains with bookkeeping all his life, and twenty years ago he took a fever and hasn't been quite right since. Now, Chuffey, stupid, are you ready? Ask him, father."

"Are you ready for your dinner, Chuffey?" asked the old man.

"Yes, yes," said Chuffey, lighting up into a sentient human being at the first sound of the voice, so that it was at once a curious and quite a moving sight to see him "—yes, yes. Quite ready, Mr. Chuzzlewit. Quite ready, sir. All ready, all ready, all ready." With that he stopped, smilingly, and listened for some further address; but, being spoken to no more, the light forsook his face by little and little until he was nothing again.

It was strange enough that Anthony Chuzzlewit, himself so old a man, should take pleasure in the gibings of his son at the

expense of the poor shadow at their table. But he did, unquestionably, though not so much—to do him justice—with reference to
their ancient clerk as in exultation at the sharpness of Jonas. For
the same reason, that young man's coarse allusions to himself
filled him with a stealthy glee, causing him to rub his hands and
chuckle covertly, as if he said in his sleeve, "*I* taught him. *I* trained
him. This is the heir of my bringing up. Sly, cunning, and covetous, he'll not squander my money." And the old clerk, when such
things were communicated to him, said, "He's your own son, Mr.
Chuzzlewit. Bless him for a sharp lad! Bless him, bless him!"

Miss Charity made tea by desire of Mr. Jonas and felt and
looked so like the lady of the house that she was in the prettiest
confusion imaginable—the more so from Mr. Jonas whispering a
variety of admiring expressions in her ear, while Miss Mercy
yawned over yesterday's newspaper. "Don't quarrel for your
cousin," said Anthony when they departed.

"Oh, the creature!" cried Mercy. "The idea of quarreling for
him! You may take him, Cherry my love, all to yourself."

"What! I'm a sour grape, am I, cousin?" said Jonas. Miss
Charity was more entertained by this repartee than one would
have supposed likely but in her sisterly affection took Mr. Jonas
to task for being so cruel to poor Mercy. Mercy, who really had
her share of good humor, only retorted with a laugh; and so they
walked home.

Next day, when old Anthony and his son arrived at Mrs.
Todgers's to say good-by, Anthony glanced at his son as he sat
beside Miss Charity, and then at Mr. Pecksniff. "Jonas is a shrewd
lad and careful. Look ye!" said Anthony in Mr. Pecksniff's ear.
"I think he is sweet upon your daughter. Supposing it should last,
perhaps (you having feathered your nest pretty well, and I also)
we might have an understanding."

Mr. Pecksniff, smiling gently, was about to speak, when
Anthony stopped him. "I know what you are going to say. It's
quite unnecessary. You have never thought of this for a moment;
and, in a point so nearly affecting the happiness of your dear child,
you couldn't, as a tender father, express an opinion, and so forth.
But you will excuse my taking the liberty of putting the matter
beyond a doubt and having it distinctly understood, as it is now,
that we do see it and do know it." He rose as he spoke and, giving

Mr. Pecksniff a nod of intelligence, left that good man somewhat puzzled and discomfited by such very plain dealing and not quite free from a sense of having been foiled in the exercise of his familiar weapons.

6

Mr. Pinch and Martin, little dreaming of the stormy weather that impended, made themselves very comfortable in the Pecksniffian halls and improved their friendship daily. Martin's facility, both of invention and execution, being remarkable, the grammar school proceeded with great vigor. "If I should turn out a great architect, Tom," said the new pupil one day, as he eyed his drawing with much complacency, "I'll tell you what should be one of the first things I'd build—your fortune."

"No!" said Tom Pinch, quite as much delighted as if the thing were done. "Would you though? How kind of you to say so."

"I should be married to her then, Tom, of course," said Martin.

What was that which checked Tom Pinch so suddenly, in the high flow of his gladness, bringing a remorseful feeling to his honest heart, as if he were unworthy of his friend's regard?

"In honor of old times," said Martin, "and of her having heard you play the organ in this damp little church down here—for nothing, too—we will have one in the house; and many's the summer evening she and I will sit and listen to you, Tom—be sure of that!"

It may have required a stronger effort on Tom Pinch's part to shake his friend by both hands, with nothing but serenity and grateful feeling painted on his face—it may have required a stronger effort to perform this simple act with a pure heart than to achieve many and many a deed to which the doubtful trumpet blown by Fame has lustily resounded. "That's all right," observed Martin, leaning back in his chair with a hand in each pocket and yawning drearily. "So you've heard again from Westlock, eh?"

"Yes, he has come into his property," answered Tom, smiling, "and begs that we three may have the pleasure of dining together in Salisbury." And so, when the time came, the two young men set off on foot, for the inn where John Westlock awaited them.

"Stand off a moment, Tom," cried the old pupil, laying one

hand affectionately on each of Mr. Pinch's shoulders and holding him out at arm's length. "Let me look at you! Just the same! I have ordered everything for dinner that we used to say we'd have, Tom. It's like a dream."

They were very merry and full of enjoyment the whole time, but not the least part of the festival was when they all three sat about the fire, cracking nuts, drinking wine, and talking cheer-fully. Then, when Tom Pinch deserted his warm corner to say a word to a friend, John Westlock took that opportunity of observing that he had never had even a peevish word with Tom during the whole term of their residence in Mr. Pecksniff's house.

"Yes," said Martin, "it's impossible to like Pinch better than I do or to do greater justice to his good qualities. He is the most willing fellow I ever saw."

"He's rather too willing," said John, who was quick in observa-tion. "It's quite a fault in him. You, however, who are older than the majority of Mr. Pecksniff's assistants, understand him, I have no doubt, and see how liable he is to be imposed upon."

"Certainly," said Martin, stretching out his legs. "By the bye, what's your opinion of Pecksniff? I don't like him, I tell you frankly."

"If you press me to give my opinion," returned John Westlock, "I should say that he is the most consummate scoundrel on the face of the earth. When I remember the hypocrisy, the knavery, the meannesses, the false pretenses, the lip service of that fellow, and his trading in saintly semblances for the very worst realities—! Hush! Here's Pinch. Not a word more about Pecksniff, or we shall spoil his whole enjoyment."

No slight circumstance, perhaps, could have better illustrated the difference of character between John Westlock and Martin Chuzzlewit than the manner in which each of the young men now contemplated Tom Pinch. The old pupil could not do enough to show Tom how cordially he felt toward him, whereas the new one had no impulse but to laugh at Tom's extreme absurdity, and mingled with his amusement there was something slighting and contemptuous.

"Good night!" cried Tom, when they parted from John. "And such pleasant dreams to you as should attend the sleep of the best fellow in the world!"

"Except Pecksniff," said his friend, gaily.

"Except Pecksniff," answered Tom, with great gravity, "of course."

Early the next morning, in a pouring rain, Mr. Pinch and Martin went to meet the coach by which the Pecksniffs were returning. "Dear me, Mr. Pinch! Is it possible that you are out upon this very inclement morning?" said Mr. Pecksniff.

"Yes, sir," cried Tom, advancing eagerly, "Mr. Chuzzlewit and I, sir."

"Oh!" said Mr. Pecksniff, looking not so much at Martin as at the spot on which he stood. "Oh, indeed! Do me the favor to see to the trunks, if you please, Mr. Pinch." In the same manner, and in profound silence, Mr. Pecksniff handed his daughters into the gig and, following himself and taking the reins, drove off home, where, instead of taking favorable notice of his relative and keeping Mr. Pinch in the background, he did exactly the reverse and was so lavish in his attentions to Tom that Tom was thoroughly confounded.

"Now, Mr. Pecksniff," said Martin at last, in a very quiet voice, "if you have sufficiently refreshed and recovered yourself, I shall be glad to hear what you mean by this treatment of me."

"And what," said Mr. Pecksniff, turning his eyes on Tom Pinch even more placidly and gently than before—"what have *you* been doing, Thomas, humph?"

"Mr. Pecksniff," Martin said, rapping the table twice or thrice, "do me the favor to reply, if you please."

"I lament to be obliged to say, sir," said Mr. Pecksniff, "that you have imposed upon a nature which you knew to be confiding and unsuspicious. This lowly roof, sir, must not be contaminated by the presence of one who has cruelly deceived an honorable, beloved, venerated, and venerable gentleman. I weep for your depravity, sir, I mourn over your corruption, I pity your voluntary withdrawal of yourself from the flowery paths of purity and peace —" here he struck himself upon his breast, or moral garden—"but I cannot have a leper and a serpent for an inmate. Go forth, young man! go forth!"

With what intention Martin made a stride forward at these words it is impossible to say. It is enough to know that Tom Pinch caught him in his arms and that, at the same moment, Mr. Pecksniff stepped back so hastily that he missed his footing, tumbled over a chair, and fell in a sitting posture on the ground, where he remained without an effort to get up again, with his head in a corner, perhaps considering it the safest place.

"Let me go, Pinch!" cried Martin. "Do you think a blow could make him a more abject creature than he is?" Flinging his hat upon his head, he walked from the house so rapidly that he was already clear of the village when he heard Tom Pinch calling breathlessly after him in the distance.

"Are you going now at once, in this bad weather, on foot, without your clothes, with no money?" cried Tom.

"Yes," he answered sternly, "I am."

"And where?" cried Tom. "Oh, where will you go?"

"I don't know," he said. "Yes, I do; I'll go to America!"

"No, no," cried Tom, in a kind of agony. "Don't go there. Don't be so dreadfully regardless of yourself. Don't go to America!"

"My mind is made up," he said. "I'll go to America. God bless you, Pinch!"

"Take this!" cried Tom, pressing a book upon him in great agitation. "Look at the leaf I have turned down. Good-by, good-by!"

Friendless and penniless, incensed to the last degree, deeply wounded in his pride and self-love, full of independent schemes, and perfectly destitute of any means of realizing them, Martin's most vindictive enemy might have been satisfied with the extent of his troubles. In this deplorable condition, he looked at the dingy lettering on the back of Mr. Pinch's book and, finding it to be an odd volume of the "Bachelor of Salamanca," was on the point of throwing it away when he bethought himself that Tom had referred him to a leaf and, opening it, found—well, well! not much, but Tom's all—a half sovereign.

Martin felt keenly for himself, and he felt this good deed of Tom's keenly. But after a few minutes it had the effect of raising his spirits and reminding him what a winning fellow he must be to have made such an impression on Tom. He found a curious gratification, too, in reflecting how superior he was to Tom and how much more likely to make his way in the world. Animated by these thoughts and strengthened in his design to push his fortune in another country, he resolved to get to London as a rallying point; though when he reached the metropolis, he had a pretty strong sense of being shut out, alone, upon the dreary world, without the key of it.

His first step, after he had pawned his watch, was to write a formal note to Tom Pinch (for he knew Pecksniff would see it) requesting to have his clothes forwarded to London by coach. He then began making inquiries relative to American vessels and lingering about the docks and wharves, with the faint hope of stumbling upon some engagement for the voyage, which would enable him to procure a free passage. Finding soon that no such means of employment were likely to present themselves, he drew up a short advertisement, stating what he wanted, and inserted it in the leading newspapers.

But of all the twenty or thirty answers he expected, in five weeks not one had come. His money, even the additional stock he had raised from the disposal of his spare clothes, was fast diminishing. Yet it is an illustration of a very common tendency in the mind of man that all this time he never once doubted the certainty of doing great things in the New World, if he could only get there.

The five weeks had quite run out and he was in a truly desperate plight when, most unexpectedly, a letter arrived for him. He opened it and found enclosed, without any name, address, or other inscription, or explanation of any kind whatever, a Bank of England note for twenty pounds.

To say that he was perfectly stunned with astonishment and delight, that he bewildered himself with conjectures and could make nothing of it but that there the note was, would be only to relate so many matters of course. The final upshot was that he resolved to treat himself to a comfortable but frugal meal in his own chamber in an obscure public house and, having ordered a fire to be kindled, went out to purchase it forthwith.

He had begun to eat with great appetite when there came a knock at his door. "More coals, I suppose," said Martin. "Come in!"

"It ain't a liberty, sir, though it seems so," rejoined a man's voice. "Your servant, sir. Hope you're pretty well, sir."

Martin stared at the face that was bowing in the doorway,

perfectly remembering the features and expression, but quite forgetting to whom they belonged.

"Tapley, sir," said his visitor. "Him as formerly lived at the Dragon, sir, and was forced to leave in consequence of a want of jollity, sir."

"To be sure!" cried Martin, who had met Mark Tapley with Tom Pinch. "How did you find me out?"

"Why, sir," said Mark, "I've passed you once or twice in the street if I'm not mistaken; and when I was a looking in at the beef-and-ham shop just now, along with a hungry sweep as was very much calculated to make a man jolly, sir, I see you. I made bold to foller; and as I told 'em downstairs that you expected me, I was let up."

Martin cast an angry look at him; but there was something in the fellow's merry face and in his manner, which, with all its cheerfulness, was far from being obtrusive or familiar, that quite disarmed him.

"What are you doing in London?" he asked.

"Nothing at all, sir," rejoined Mark. "I want a place to attend upon a single gentleman. Makeshifts would be preferred. Wages no object."

He said this so pointedly that Martin said, "If you mean me—"

"Yes, I do, sir," interposed Mark.

"Then you may judge, from my style of living here, of my means of keeping a man servant. Besides, I am going to America immediately."

"Well, sir," returned Mark, quite unmoved by this intelligence, "from all that ever I heard about it, I should say America is a very likely sort of place for me to be jolly in! Now, sir, here am I, without a situation, without any want of wages for a year to come—for I have saved up (I didn't mean to do it, but I couldn't help it) at the Dragon—here am I, with a liking for what's wentersome, and a liking for you, and a wish to come out strong under circumstances as would keep other men down; and will you take me, or will you leave me?"

"How can I take you?" cried Martin.

"When I say take," rejoined Mark, "I mean will you let me go along with you? For go I will, somehow or another. Now that you've said America, I see clear at once that that's the place for me to be jolly in. The only doubt I have is whether there's any credit in going with a gentleman like you, that's as certain to make his way there as a gimlet is to go through soft deal."

This was touching Martin on his weak point and having him at a great advantage. "Why, certainly, Mark," he said, "I have hopes of doing well there, or I shouldn't go. Ornamental architecture applied to domestic purposes can hardly fail to be in great request in that country; for men are constantly changing their residences there and moving further off, and it's clear they must have houses to live in.

"Come, Tapley," he added after a moment's thought, "I'll trust you with my history, such as it is." When he came to his love affair, Mark's interest was keen, for which he apologized, as one who had seen the young lady at the Blue Dragon.

"Ay! You saw her when she was not happy," said Martin. "If you had seen her in the old times, indeed—"

"Why, she certainly was a little down-hearted, sir," said Mark, "but none the worse in her looks for that. I think she seemed better, sir, after she came to London."

"Do you mean to tell me she is in London now? And you know where?"

"Yes!" cried Mark. "What! Don't you?"

"My good fellow!" exclaimed Martin, clutching him by both arms. "I have never seen her since I left my grandfather's house."

"Why, then," cried Mark, "if I ain't your nat'ral-born servant, hired by Fate, there ain't such a thing in natur' as a Blue Dragon! I went to your grandfather's hotel to see if he would engage me, but he said he couldn't make up his mind to trust nobody no more. Here, sit down, sir. Write her a letter, sir! Let it be wery pinted, sir. Be very tender, sir, if you please."

The letter being duly signed, sealed, and delivered was handed to Mark Tapley for immediate conveyance. He returned with word that the young lady would meet the gentleman at eight o'clock tomorrow morning in St. James's Park; and it was then agreed that Mark should escort her to the place of appointment.

"If you have changed at all, my love, since we parted," said Martin when they met, "it is only to be more beautiful than ever!"

"What change is there in *you*, Martin?" she replied. "For that concerns me nearest. You have paid a dear price for a poor heart, Martin; but it is at least your own, and a true one."

"Of course I feel quite certain of that," said Martin, "or I shouldn't have put myself in my present position. And don't say a poor heart, Mary, for I say a rich one. Now, I am about to break a design to you, dearest, which is undertaken for your sake. I am going abroad, to America. I am going with great prospects of doing well and of returning home very soon to claim you for my wife."

"In the meantime, dear Martin—"

"In the meantime you shall hear, constantly, of all my goings on. Living in the house of this fellow Pecksniff (of whom I fear you have heard) there is a certain poor person of the name of Pinch, who is very grateful and desirous to serve me and whom I shall ask to forward my letters to you."

"Heaven send our next meeting may come speedily and prosperously!" said Mary. "When do you go?"

"We leave for Liverpool tonight. In a month or less, we shall be there. Time will wear wings indeed! I can bear anything, so that I have swift action, Mary."

Was he thinking solely of her care for him when he took so little heed of her share in the separation—of her quiet monotonous endurance and her slow anxiety from day to day? Was there nothing jarring and discordant even in his tone of courage, with this one note "self" forever audible, however high the strain? Not in her ears. "One other question, Martin, I must ask," she said. "Have you provided money for this journey?"

"Have I?" cried Martin—it might have been in his pride; it might have been in his desire to set her mind at ease. "More than enough. A pocketful."

"Then, good-by a hundred times!" cried Mary, in a trembling voice; and when she left, Mr. Tapley followed, as in duty bound.

When he rejoined Martin again, he handed him a ring. "She sent a lot of kind words, sir, and this for a parting keepsake."

"Diamonds!" said Martin, kissing it—let us do him justice, it was for her sake, not for theirs—and putting it on his little finger. "Splendid diamonds! My grandfather is a singular character, Mark. He must have given her this, now."

Mark Tapley knew as well that she had bought it, to the end that that unconscious speaker might carry some article of sterling value with him in his necessity, as he knew that it was day and not night. Her lover's strange obtuseness promptly suggested to Mark's mind its real cause and root; and from that moment he had a clear and perfect insight into the one absorbing principle of Martin's character. Without giving vent to any articulate sound, he seemed, by a twist of his features and a motion of his lips, to release himself of this word—"Jolly!"

7

A DARK and dreary night; on, on, on, over the countless miles of angry space, roll the long, heaving billows. And onward, in gallant combat with the elements, her tall masts trembling and her timbers starting on the strain, onward comes a ship, with dim lights burning in her hull, and people there, asleep, as if no deadly element were peering in at every seam and chink.

Among these sleeping voyagers were Martin and Mark Tapley, who, rocked into a heavy drowsiness by the unaccustomed motion, were as insensible to the foul air in which they lay as to the uproar without. It was broad day when the latter awoke. "Well," said Mark, "this is the first time as ever I stood on my head all night."

"Is that you, Mark?" asked a faint voice from another berth.

"It's as much of me as is left, sir, after a fortnight of this work," Mr. Tapley replied. "How do *you* find yourself this morning, sir?"

"Very miserable," said Martin, with a peevish groan. "Ugh! This is wretched, indeed!"

"Creditable," muttered Mark, pressing one hand upon his aching head and looking round him with a rueful grin. "That's the great comfort. It *is* creditable to keep up one's spirits here. Virtue's its own reward. So's jollity." Indeed a dark, low, stifling cabin, surrounded by berths all filled to overflowing with men, women, and children, in various stages of sickness and misery, is not the liveliest place of assembly at any time; but when it is so crowded (as the steerage cabin of the *Screw* was every passage out) that mattresses and beds are heaped upon the floor, to the extinction of everything like comfort, cleanliness, and decency, it is liable to operate not only as a pretty strong barrier against amiability of temper but as a positive encourager of selfish and rough humors. Mark felt this, as he sat looking about him, and his spirits rose proportionately.

"Well, Mark," said Martin, "when will this be over?"

"Another week, they say, sir," returned Mark, "will most likely bring us into port. You'd feel all the better for it, sir, if you was to turn out."

"And be seen by the ladies and gentlemen on the after deck," returned Martin, with a scornful emphasis upon the words, "mingling with the beggarly crowd that are stowed away in this vile hole?"

"I am very sorry, sir," said Mark. "I didn't know you took it so much to heart as this comes to."

"Of course you didn't know," returned his master. "It's no trial to *you*, Mark, to make yourself comfortable and to bustle about, helping other people. It's as natural for you to do so under the circumstances as it is for me not to do so. Why, you don't suppose there is a living creature in this ship who can by possibility have half so much to undergo on board of her as *I* have?"

Soon one great sensation, however, pervaded the whole ship, and the soil of America lay close before them, so close at last that, upon a certain starlight night, they took a pilot on board, awaiting the arrival of a steamboat in which the passengers were to be conveyed ashore. When she had taken all her living freight aboard, the steamer dashed at great speed up a beautiful bay; and presently they saw some heights, and islands, and a long, flat, straggling city.

"And this," said Mr. Tapley, looking far ahead, "is the Land of Liberty, is it? Very well. I'm agreeable. Any land will do for me, after so much water!"

Some trifling excitement prevailed upon the very brink and margin of the Land of Liberty. For an alderman had been elected the day before; and, party feeling naturally running high, the friends of the disappointed candidate had found it necessary to assert the great principles of Purity of Election and Freedom of Opinion by breaking a few legs and arms. These good-humored little outbursts were not in themselves sufficiently remarkable to create any great stir, but they found fresh life and notoriety in the breath of the newsboys, who proclaimed them with shrill yells on the deck of the steamboat, which, before she touched the shore, was boarded and overrun by a legion of those young citizens.

"Here's this morning's *New York Sewer!*" cried one. "Here's this morning's *New York Stabber!* Here's the *New York Family Spy!* Here's the *New York Private Listener!* Here's the *New York Peeper!* Here's the *New York Plunderer!* Here's the *New York Keyhole Reporter!* Here's the *New York Rowdy Journal!* Here's all the New York papers! Here's full particulars of the patriotic Locofoco movement yesterday, in which the Whigs was so chawed up; and the last Alabama gouging case; and all the Political, Commercial, and Fashionable News. Here's the papers, here's the papers!"

"Here's the *Sewer!*" cried another. "Here's the *Sewer's* exposure of the Wall Street Gang, and the *Sewer's* exposure of the Washington Gang, and the *Sewer's* exclusive account of a flagrant act of dishonesty committed by the Secretary of State when he was eight years old, now communicated, at great expense, by his own nurse. Here's the *Sewer!* Here's the *Sewer!*"

"It is in such enlightened means," said a voice almost in Martin's ear, "that the bubbling passions of my country find a vent."

Martin turned involuntarily and saw, standing close at his side, a sallow gentleman, with sunken cheeks, black hair, small twinkling eyes, and a mixed expression of vulgar cunning and conceit. This gentleman wore a rather broad-brimmed hat for the greater wisdom of his appearance and had his arms folded for the greater impressiveness of his attitude. As he looked at Martin and nobody else was by, Martin inclined his head and said, "You allude to—?"

"To the Palladium of rational Liberty at home, sir, and the dread of Foreign oppression abroad," returned the gentleman. "To the Envy of the world, sir, and the leaders of Human Civilization. Let me ask you, sir," he added, "how do you like my Country?"

"I am hardly prepared to answer that question yet," said Martin, "seeing that I have not been ashore."

"You have brought, I see, sir," the gentleman said, "the usual amount of misery, and poverty, and ignorance, and crime, to be located in the bosom of the Great Republic. Well, sir, let 'em come on in shiploads from the old country! My name is Colonel Diver, sir. I am the Editor of the *New York Rowdy Journal.*"

Martin received the communication with that degree of respect which an announcement so distinguished appeared to demand; and the colonel offered, in consideration of his being an Englishman, to show him the town and to introduce him, if such were his desire, to a genteel boarding house. But before they entered on these proceedings (he said), he would beseech the honor of Martin's company at the office of the *Rowdy Journal*.

All this was so extremely kind and hospitable that Martin, instructing Mark to follow him when he had cleared the baggage, readily acquiesced. They turned up a narrow street and into other narrow streets, until at last they stopped before a house where, in a dark and dirty room, a small young gentleman of very juvenile appearance sat with a stump of a pen in his mouth and a great pair of scissors in his right hand. Martin had begun to say that he presumed this was the colonel's little boy and that it was very pleasant to see him playing at editor in all the guilelessness of childhood, when the colonel proudly interposed and said, "My War Correspondent, sir—Mr. Jefferson Brick! Let me see. When did you leave England, sir?"

"Five weeks ago," said Martin.

"Five weeks ago," repeated the colonel thoughtfully. "Now let me ask you, sir, which of Mr. Brick's articles had become at that time the most obnoxious to the British Parliament and the Court of Saint James's?"

"Upon my word," said Martin, "the truth is that I—"

"That you never heard of Jefferson Brick, sir," said the colonel. "That you never saw the *Rowdy Journal*, sir. That you never knew, sir, of its mighty influence upon the cabinets of Eu-rope. Yes?"

"That's what I was about to observe, certainly," said Martin.

"Keep cool, Jefferson," said the colonel gravely; "don't bust! O you Europeans!"

Presently they all three left the office and walked a mile or more along a handsome street which the colonel said was called Broadway and which Mr. Jefferson Brick said "whipped the universe." Turning, at length, into one of the numerous streets which branched from this main thoroughfare, they stopped before a rather mean-looking house with the name of "Pawkins" engraved on the knocker.

The colonel led the way into a room at the back of the house

upon the ground floor, light and of fair dimensions, but exquisitely uncomfortable, having nothing in it but the four cold white walls and ceiling, a mean carpet, a dreary waste of dining table reaching from end to end, and a bewildering collection of cane-bottomed chairs. In the farther region of this banqueting hall was a stove, garnished on either side with a great brass spittoon. Before it, swinging himself in a rocking chair, lounged a large gentleman with his hat on, who amused himself by spitting alternately into the spittoon on the right hand of the stove and the spittoon on the left, and then working his way back again in the same order.

"Here is a gentleman from England, Major Pawkins," the colonel said, "who has concluded to locate himself here if the amount of compensation suits him."

"I am glad to see you, sir," observed the major, shaking hands with Martin and not moving a muscle of his face. "You are pretty bright, I hope?"

"Never better," said Martin.

"You are never likely to be," returned the major. "You will see the sun shine *here*."

"I think I remember to have seen it shine at home sometimes," said Martin, smiling.

"I think not," replied the major. He said so with a stoical indifference certainly, but still in a tone of firmness which admitted of no further dispute on that point. He then referred Martin to Mrs. Pawkins for all particulars connected with the rate of board and lodging and informed him that dinner would soon be ready. This reminded him that if he were to take a bitter before dinner there was no time to lose; so he walked off to a neighboring bar room without more ado and left them to follow if they thought proper.

They were walking back very leisurely—Martin arm in arm with Mr. Jefferson Brick, and the major and the colonel side by side before them—when, as they came within a house or two of the major's residence, they heard a bell ringing violently. The instant this sound struck upon their ears the colonel and the major darted off, dashed up the steps and in at the street door (which stood ajar) like lunatics, while Mr. Jefferson Brick, detaching his arm from Martin's, made a precipitate dive in the same direction and vanished also.

"Good Heavens!" thought Martin, "the premises are on fire! It was an alarm bell!" But there was no smoke to be seen, nor was there any smell of fire. As Martin faltered on the pavement, three more gentlemen, with horror and agitation depicted in their faces, came plunging wildly round the street corner, jostled each other on the steps, struggled for an instant, and rushed into the house in a confused heap of arms and legs. Unable to bear it any longer, Martin followed. Even in his rapid progress he was run down, thrust aside, and passed by two more gentlemen, stark mad, as it appeared, with fierce excitement.

"Where is it?" cried Martin, breathlessly, to a Negro whom he encountered in the passage.

"In a eatin' room, sa. Kernel, sa, him kep a seat 'side himself, sa."

"A seat!" cried Martin.

"For a dinnar, sa."

Martin stared at him for a moment and then burst into a hearty laugh as he walked into the dining room.

It was a numerous company, eighteen or twenty perhaps. All the knives and forks were working away at a rate that was quite alarming; very few words were spoken; and everybody seemed to eat his utmost in self-defense, as if a famine were expected to set in before breakfast time tomorrow morning and it had become high time to assert the first law of nature. Spare men, with lank and rigid cheeks, came out unsatisfied from the destruction of heavy dishes and glared with watchful eyes upon the pastry. What Mrs. Pawkins felt each day at dinner time is hidden from all human knowledge. But she had one comfort—it was very soon over.

When the colonel had finished his dinner, he asked Martin what he thought of the boarders. "Pray," said Martin, "who is that sickly little girl opposite, with the tight round eyes? I don't see anybody here who looks like her mother or who seems to have charge of her."

"Do you mean the matron in blue, sir?" asked the colonel, with emphasis. "That is Mrs. Jefferson Brick, sir. Jefferson Brick is one of the most remarkable men in our country, sir!"

"Pray, Mr. Brick," said Martin, turning to him in some confusion, "who is that very short gentleman yonder, with the red nose?"

"That is Pro-fessor Mullit, sir," replied Jefferson. "He is a man of fine moral elements, sir, and not commonly endowed. He is one of the most remarkable men in our country, sir."

"There seem to be plenty of 'em," thought Martin, "at any rate."

Pursuing his inquiries, Martin found that there were no fewer than four majors present, two colonels, one general, and a captain. There seemed to be no man there without a title, for those who had not attained to military honors were either doctors, professors, or reverends, except for a middle-aged man with a dark eye and a sunburned face, who had attracted Martin's attention by having something very engaging and honest in the expression of his features, but of whom he could learn nothing from either of his neighbors. "I will not ask you," said this gentleman after dinner, with a smile, "how you like my country, for I can quite anticipate your feeling on that point."

"You have been abroad?" asked Martin.

"Oh, yes. And I do not find that we are a model of wisdom, and an example to the world, and the perfection of human reason, and a great deal more to the same purpose, which you may hear any hour in the day. But you have come here on some design of improving your fortune, I dare say, and I should grieve to put you out of heart."

The stranger's face grew infinitely longer as the domestic architecture project was developed. But he spoke in a cheerful tone and said that, although there was no such opening as Martin wished in that city, he would make it matter of immediate inquiry where one was most like to exist; and then he made Martin acquainted with his name, which was Bevan. There was a cordial candor in his manner, and an engaging confidence that it would not be abused, a manly bearing on his own part, and a simple reliance on the manly faith of a stranger, which Martin had never seen before. He linked his arm readily in that of the American gentleman, and they walked out together.

It was characteristic of Martin that all this while he had forgotten Mark Tapley as completely as if there had been no such person in existence. But, being now in the streets again, it occurred to him that Mr. Tapley might, in course of time, grow tired of waiting, so they walked to the *Rowdy Journal* office, and found Mark recumbent in the midst of a fortification of luggage, whistling "Rule Britannia" to a gray-haired black man who sat on one of the outworks (a portmanteau). "And may I ask," said Martin, glancing, but not with any displeasure, from Mark to the Negro, "who this gentleman is?"

"Why, sir," returned Mark, taking him aside and speaking confidentially in his ear, "he's a man of color, sir. I mean that he's been one of them as there's picters of in the shops—a man and a brother, you know, sir."

"A slave!" cried Martin, in a whisper.

"Ah!" said Mark, in the same tone. "Nothing else—a slave. Why, when that there man was young, he was shot in the leg, gashed in the arm, scored in his live limbs like crimped fish, beaten out of shape, had his neck galled with an iron collar, and wore iron rings upon his wrists and ankles."

"Is *this* true?" asked Martin of his friend, who stood beside them.

"I have no reason to doubt it," he answered, shaking his head. "It very often is."

"Bless you," said Mark, "I know it is, from hearing his whole story. In years and years he saved up a little money and bought his freedom, which he got pretty cheap at last, on account of his strength being nearly gone and he being ill. Then he came here. And now he's a saving up to treat himself, afore he dies, to one small purchase; it's nothing to speak of, only his own daughter— that's all!" cried Mr. Tapley, becoming excited. "Liberty for ever! Hurrah! Hail, Columbia!"

"I think," said Martin's friend, "that this young man had better return to the boarding house with us. He may get into trouble otherwise, he speaks his mind so plainly. This is not a slave state; but I am ashamed to say that the spirit of tolerance is not so common anywhere in these latitudes as the form."

The tea or the supper, or whatever else they called the evening meal, was over when they reached the major's; but at one end of the board Mrs. Jefferson Brick and two other ladies were drinking tea, out of the ordinary course, evidently, for they were bonneted and shawled and seemed to have just come home. "Have you been to meeting, Mrs. Brick?" asked Martin's friend, with something of a roguish twinkle in his eye.

"To lecture, sir."

"I beg your pardon. I forgot. What course of lectures are you attending now, ma'am?"

"The Philosophy of the Soul, on Wednesdays."

"On Mondays?"

"The Philosophy of Crime."

"On Fridays?"

"The Philosophy of Vegetables."

"You have forgotten Thursdays—the Philosophy of Government, my dear," observed one of the ladies.

"No," said Mrs. Brick; "that's Tuesdays."

"So it is!" cried the lady. "The Philosophy of Matter on Thursdays."

"You see, Mr. Chuzzlewit, our ladies are fully employed," said Bevan.

"Indeed you have reason to say so," answered Martin. "Between these very grave pursuits abroad and family duties at home, their time must be pretty well engrossed."

Martin stopped here, for he saw that the ladies regarded him with no very great favor; and when they had retired, Mr. Bevan informed him that domestic drudgery was far beneath the exalted range of these Philosophers and that the chances were a hundred to one that neither of the three could perform the easiest woman's work for herself.

"O Tom Pinch, Tom Pinch!" said Martin, when he and Mark were alone. "What would I give to be again beside you!"

"O Dragon, Dragon!" echoed Mark cheerfully. "If there warn't any water between you and me and nothing faint-hearted-like in going back, I don't know that I mightn't say the same. But there's a fortune to make, Dragon, and a beautiful young lady to make it for."

"Wisely said, Mark," cried Martin. "We must look forward. Good night!"

Leaving them to blend and mingle in their sleep the shadows of objects afar off, be it the part of this slight chronicle—a dream within a dream—as rapidly to change the scene and cross the ocean to the English shore.

8

"What a cold spring it is!" whimpered old Anthony, drawing near the evening fire. "It was a warmer season, sure, when I was young!"

"You needn't go scorching your clothes into holes, whether it was or not," observed the amiable Jonas.

"A good lad!" cried the father, breathing on his cold hands, and feebly chafing them against each other. "A prudent lad!" Suddenly Old Chuffey cried out, too, like one inspired, "He is your own son, Mr. Chuzzlewit—your own son, sir!"

"Yes, yes, Chuffey, Jonas is a chip of the old block. It's a very old block now, Chuffey," said the old man, with a strange look of discomposure.

"Precious old," assented Jonas.

"No, no, no," said Chuffey. "No, Mr. Chuzzlewit—not old at all, sir." The poor old shadow drew through his palsied arm his master's hand and held it there, with his own folded upon it, as if he would defend him. But, Anthony remaining quite still and silent, he relaxed his hold by slow degrees and lapsed into his usual niche in the corner, merely putting forth his hand at intervals and touching his old employer gently on the coat, as with the design of assuring himself that he was yet beside him.

"They've been carrying on this game," thought Jonas, in a brown study, "for the last two or three weeks. I never saw my father take so much notice of him as he has in that time. What! You're legacy hunting, are you, Mr. Chuff—eh?" When he had scowled at him to his heart's content, Jonas walked into the glass office. He opened a secret drawer in the desk. "Here's the will, Mr. Chuff," he said, unfolding a paper. "Thirty pound a year for your maintenance, old boy, and all the rest to his only son Jonas. You needn't trouble yourself to be too affectionate; you won't get anything by it.—What's that?"

It *was* startling, certainly—a face on the other side of the glass partition looking curiously at the paper in his hand. "What's the matter?" cried Jonas, falling back, as the phantom walked in. "Who is it? Why didn't you knock at the door?"

"So I did, Mr. Jonas," answered Pecksniff, "but no one heard me. I was curious," he added, in his gentle way, "to find out what part of the newspaper interested you so much; but the glass was too dim and dirty."

"How the deuce do you come to be in London again?" asked Jonas, recovering himself. "Here's father in the next room."

"And now, my good sir," said Mr. Pecksniff to Anthony when Mr. Jonas had left them, "pray tell me what I can do for you? I never in my life was so astonished as by the receipt of your letter yesterday."

"Jonas is sweet upon your daughter, Pecksniff," said the old man.

"A charming girl, sir," murmured Mr. Pecksniff, seeing that

he waited for an answer. "A dear girl, Mr. Chuzzlewit, though I say it who should not."

"You know better," cried the old man. "If your daughter was what you would have me believe, she wouldn't do for Jonas. Being what she is, I think she will. He might be deceived in a wife. She might run riot, contract debts, and waste his substance. But your daughter is not too young or heedless and comes of a good hard, griping stock. Only, don't you play too fine a game. She only holds him by a thread, and if you draw it too tight (I know his temper) it'll snap. Bind him when he's in the mood, Pecksniff; bind him." His chin sank down upon his breast, and in another minute he was quite regardless of Mr. Pecksniff's presence.

"What! My father asleep again?" Mr. Jonas cried, when he returned.

"He snores very deep," said Mr. Pecksniff.

"Snores deep!" repeated Jonas. "Yes, he'll snore for six, at any time. How's Charity?"

"Blooming, Mr. Jonas, blooming."

"And the other one—how's she?"

"Volatile trifler!" said Mr. Pecksniff, fondly musing. "She is well—she is well. Ah! were she a little less giddy than she is and had she but the sterling qualities of Cherry, my young friend!—A strange noise that, Mr. Jonas!"

"Something wrong in the clock, I suppose," said Jonas. "So the other one ain't your favorite, ain't she?"

The fond father was about to reply when the sound he had already noticed was repeated. "Upon my word, Mr. Jonas, that is a very extraordinary clock," said Pecksniff.

It would have been if it had made the noise which startled them; but another kind of timepiece was fast running down, and from that the sound proceeded. A scream from Chuffey, rendered a hundred times more loud and formidable by his silent habits, made the house ring from roof to cellar; and, looking round, they saw Anthony Chuzzlewit extended on the floor, with the old clerk upon his knees beside him. It was frightful to see how the principle of life, shut up within his withered frame, fought like a strong devil, mad to be released, and rent its ancient prison house. The fits held him so long that it was past midnight when they got him, quiet now, but quite unconscious and exhausted, into bed.

"Don't go," said Jonas, putting his ashy lips to Mr. Pecksniff's ear. "It was a mercy you were present when he was taken ill. Someone might have said it was my doing. If anything happens, Pecksniff, you must promise me to stop here till it's all over. You shall see that I do what's right."

Mr. Pecksniff was in a hackney cabriolet, for Jonas Chuzzlewit had said, "Spare no expense"; it never should be charged upon his father's son that he had grudged the money for his father's funeral. Mr. Pecksniff had been to the undertaker and was now upon his way to another officer in the train of mourning—a female functionary, a nurse and watcher and performer of nameless offices about the persons of the dead—whose name was Gamp.

This lady lodged at a bird fancier's, in a little house, and this was the more convenient; for Mrs. Gamp being, in her highest walk of art, a monthly nurse, or, as her signboard boldly had it, "Midwife," and lodging in the first-floor front, was easily assailable at night by pebbles, walking sticks, and fragments of tobacco pipe —all much more efficacious than the street-door knocker, which was so constructed as to wake the street with ease and even spread alarms of fire in Holborn without making the smallest impression on the premises to which it was addressed.

It chanced on this particular occasion that Mrs. Gamp had been up all the previous night; so when Mr. Pecksniff drove up in the hackney cab, Mrs. Gamp's curtains were drawn close, and Mrs. Gamp was fast asleep behind them. The shop was closed. Mr. Pecksniff tried the latch and shook it, causing a cracked bell inside to ring most mournfully; but no one came. He applied himself to the knocker. But at the first double knock, every window in the street became alive with female heads; and before he could repeat the performance, whole troops of married ladies (some about to trouble Mrs. Gamp themselves very shortly) came flocking round the steps, all crying out with one accord and with uncommon interest, "Knock at the winder, sir, knock at the winder. Lord bless you, don't lose no more time than you can help; knock at the winder!"

Acting upon this suggestion and borrowing the driver's whip for the purpose, Mr. Pecksniff soon made a commotion among the first-floor flowerpots and roused Mrs. Gamp, whose voice—to the great satisfaction of the matrons—was heard to say, "I'm coming."

"He's as pale as a muffin," said one lady, in allusion to Mr. Pecksniff.

"So he ought to be, if he's the feelings of a man," observed another.

A third lady (with her arms folded) said she wished he had chosen any other time for fetching Mrs. Gamp, but it always happened so with *her*.

It gave Mr. Pecksniff much uneasiness to find, from these remarks, that he was supposed to have come to Mrs. Gamp upon an errand touching, not the close of life, but the other end. Mrs. Gamp herself was under the same impression; for, throwing open the window, she cried behind the curtains as she hastily attired herself, "Is it Mrs. Perkins?"

"No!" returned Mr. Pecksniff sharply. "Nothing of the sort."

"What, Mr. Whilks!" cried Mrs. Gamp. "Don't say it's you, Mr. Whilks, and that poor creetur Mrs. Whilks with not even a pincushion ready. Don't say it's you, Mr. Whilks!"

"It isn't Mr. Whilks," said Pecksniff. "Nothing of the kind. A gentleman is dead; and, some person being wanted in the house, you have been recommended by Mr. Mould, the undertaker."

As she was by this time in a condition to appear, Mrs. Gamp, who had a face for all occasions, looked out of the window with her mourning countenance on and said she would be down directly. But the matrons took it very ill that Mr. Pecksniff's mission was of so unimportant a kind, so that when Mrs. Gamp appeared the unoffending gentleman was glad to hustle her off in the cabriolet.

Mrs. Gamp had a large bundle with her, a pair of pattens, and a species of gig umbrella—the latter article in color like a faded leaf, except where a circular patch of lively blue had been dexterously let in at the top. She was a fat old woman, this Mrs. Gamp, with a husky voice and a moist eye, which she had a remarkable power of turning up, and only showing the white of it. Having very little neck, it cost her some trouble to look over herself, if one may say so, at those to whom she talked. She wore a very rusty black gown, rather the worse for snuff, and a shawl and bonnet to correspond. In these dilapidated articles of dress she had on principle arrayed herself, time out of mind, on such occasions as the present; for this at once expressed a decent amount of veneration for the deceased and invited the next of kin to present her with a fresher suit of weeds—an appeal so frequently successful that the very fetch and ghost of Mrs. Gamp, bonnet and all, might be seen hanging up in at least a dozen of the second-hand clothes shops about Holborn. The face of Mrs. Gamp—the nose in particular—was somewhat red and swollen, and it was difficult to enjoy her society without becoming conscious of a smell of spirits.

"Ah!" repeated Mrs. Gamp—for it was always a safe sentiment in cases of mourning—"ah, dear! When Gamp was summonsed to his long home and I see him a lying in Guy's Hospital with a penny piece on each eye and his wooden leg under his left arm, I thought I should have fainted away. But I bore up."

"You have become indifferent since then, I suppose?" said Mr. Pecksniff. "Use is second nature, Mrs. Gamp."

"You may well say second nater, sir," returned that lady. "One's first ways is to find sich things a trial to the feelings, and so is one's lasting custom. If it wasn't for the nerve a little sip of liquor gives me (I never was able to do more than taste it), I never could go through with what I sometimes has to do. 'Mrs. Harris,' I says, at the very last case as ever I acted in, which it was but a young person—'Mrs. Harris,' I says, 'leave the bottle on the chimley piece; and don't ask me to take none, but let me put my lips to it when I am so dispoged and then I will do what I'm engaged to do, according to the best of my ability.' 'Mrs. Gamp,' she says in answer, 'if ever there was a sober creetur to be got at eighteenpence a day for working people and three and six for gentlefolks—night watching,'" said Mrs. Gamp, with emphasis, "'being a extra charge—you are that inwallable person.' 'Mrs. Harris,' I says to her, 'don't name the charge; for if I could afford to lay all my feller creetur's out for nothink, I would gladly do it, sich is the love I bears 'em. But what I always says to them as has the management of matters, Mrs. Harris,'"—here she kept her eye on Mr. Pecksniff—"'be they gents or be they ladies, is, Don't ask me whether I won't take none or whether I will, but leave the bottle on the chimley piece, and let me put my lips to it when I am so dispoged.'"

The conclusion of this affecting narrative brought them to the house. In the passage they encountered Mr. Mould, the undertaker, a little elderly gentleman, bald, and in a suit of black, with a notebook in his hand, a massive gold watch chain dangling from his fob, and a face in which a queer attempt at melancholy was at odds with a smirk of satisfaction, so that he looked as a man might who, in the very act of smacking his lips over choice old wine, tried to make believe it was physic.

"Well, Mrs. Gamp, and how are *you*, Mrs. Gamp?" said this gentleman, in a voice as soft as his step. "You'll be very particular here, Mrs. Gamp. This is not a common case, Mrs. Gamp. Let everything be very nice and comfortable, Mrs. Gamp, if you please. This is one of the most impressive cases, sir," he continued, addressing Mr. Pecksniff, "that I have seen in the whole course of my professional experience. There is no limitation, there is positively *no* limitation"—opening his eyes wide and standing on tiptoe—"in point of expense! Anything so filial as this—anything so honorable to human nature, so calculated to reconcile all of us to the world we live in—never yet came under my observation. Mr. Pecksniff, sir, good morning."

Mrs. Gamp and Mr. Pecksniff then ascended the staircase; and the former having been shown to the chamber in which all that remained of Anthony Chuzzlewit lay covered up, with but one loving heart, and that a halting one, to mourn it, left the latter free to enter the darkened room below and rejoin Mr. Jonas; where he was interrupted, however, by Mrs. Gamp, who, divested of her bonnet and shawl, came sidling and bridling into the room.

"I have been at a many places in my time, gentlemen," said Mrs. Gamp, "and I hope I knows what my duties is and how the same should be performed. I have seen a deal of trouble my own self, and I can feel for them as has their feelings tried; but I am not a Rooshan or a Prooshan and consequently cannot suffer spies to be set over me. Some people," said Mrs. Gamp, again entrenching herself behind her strong point, "may be Rooshans, and others may be Prooshans; they are born so and will please themselves. Them which is of other natur's thinks different."

"If I understand this good lady," said Mr. Pecksniff, turning to Jonas, "Mr. Chuffey is troublesome to her. Shall I fetch him down?"

"Do," said Jonas. "I'd go myself only—only I'd rather you went if you don't mind."

Mr. Pecksniff promptly departed, followed by Mrs. Gamp, who, seeing that he took a bottle and glass from the cupboard and carried it in his hand, was much softened. "Ah, what a wale of grief!" cried Mrs. Gamp, possessing herself of the bottle.

"Why did he die before his poor old crazy servant?" said Chuffey, before he submitted to be led away. "Oh, Chuzzlewit and Son. Your own son, Mr. Chuzzlewit; your own son, sir!"

The weight of that which was stretched out, stiff and stark, in the awful chamber above stairs so crushed and bore down Jonas that he bent beneath the load. During the whole long seven days and nights he was always oppressed and haunted by a dreadful sense of its presence in the house. Did the door move, he looked toward it with a livid face and starting eye, as if he fully believed that ghostly fingers clutched the handle. The lightest noise disturbed him; and once in the night, at the sound of a footstep overhead, he cried out that the dead man was walking, tramp, tramp, tramp, about his coffin.

At length the day arrived, and through the narrow streets and winding city ways went Anthony Chuzzlewit's funeral—Mr. Jonas glancing stealthily out of the coach window now and then to observe its effect upon the crowd; Mr. Mould, as he walked along, listening with a sober pride to the exclamations of the bystanders; the doctor whispering a story to Mr. Pecksniff; and poor old Chuffey sobbing unregarded in a corner.

"I loved him," cried the old man, sinking down upon the grave when all was done. "He was very good to me. Oh, my dear old friend and master!"

"Upon my word, my good friend," murmured the doctor, in a tone of stately reproof, "you should take example from others, my good sir. You forget that you were not connected by ties of blood with our deceased friend and that he had a very near and very dear relation, Mr. Chuffey."

"Ah, his own son!" cried the old man, clasping his hands with remarkable passion. "His own, own, only son!"

"He's not right in his head, you know," said Jonas, turning pale. "You're not to mind anything he says." His discomposure, however, was but momentary, and he soon recovered. Indeed, by the time they were returned home, he was, in every respect, himself again.

"Pecksniff," said Jonas, in the coach that was taking him down into the country for a few days' change of air and scene after his recent trials, "what do you mean to give your daughters when they marry?"

"Why, that," said Mr. Pecksniff, "would naturally depend in a great measure upon the kind of husbands they might choose, my dear young friend. To be plain with you, Mr. Jonas, if I could find two such sons-in-law as you will one day make to some deserving man, I would—forgetful of myself—bestow upon my daughters portions reaching to the very utmost limit of my means. My eldest girl I would endow with a fortune of four thousand pounds. I should sadly pinch and cramp myself to do so," was his fatherly remark; "but that would be my duty, and my conscience would reward me." For the rest of the journey, Mr. Jonas was so very buoyant—it may be said, boisterous—that Mr. Pecksniff had some difficulty in keeping pace with him.

It was a hard thing, Mr. Pecksniff said, when tea with his daughters was done and cleared away, to leave so pleasant a little party but, having some important papers to examine in his own apartment, he must beg them to excuse him for half an hour. He had not been gone five minutes when Merry, who had been sitting in the window apart from Jonas and her sister, burst into a half-smothered laugh and skipped toward the door.

"Hullo!" cried Jonas. "Don't go."

"Oh, I dare say!" rejoined Merry, looking back. "You're very anxious I should stay, fright—ain't you?"

"Yes, I am," said Jonas. "Upon my word I am. I want to speak to you." But as she left the room notwithstanding, he ran out after her and brought her back, after a short struggle in the passage, which scandalized Miss Cherry very much.

"Upon my word, Merry," urged that young lady, "I wonder at you! There are bounds even to absurdity, my dear."

"Thank you, my sweet," said Merry, pursing up her rosy lips. "Much obliged to it for its advice. Oh! do leave me alone, you monster, do!" This entreaty was wrung from her by a new proceeding on the part of Mr. Jonas, who pulled her down, all breathless as she was, into a seat beside him on the sofa, having at the same time Miss Cherry upon the other side.

"Now," said Jonas, clasping the waist of each, "I want to have some sober talk. She'll not believe what I am going to say, will she, cousin?" timidly squeezing Miss Charity.

"Really, Mr. Jonas, I don't know, until I hear what it is."

"Why, you see," said Jonas, "her way always being to make game of people, I know she'll laugh, or pretend to—I know that beforehand. But you can tell her I'm in earnest, cousin, can't you? Nobody else can tell her how hard I tried to get to know you better, in order that I might get to know her without seeming to wish it; can they? You'll bear honest witness now, won't you? Cousin Mercy, you've heard what I've been saying. She'll confirm it, every word; she must. Will you have me for your husband? Eh?"

As he released his hold of Charity, to put this question with better effect, she started up and hurried away to her own room, marking her progress as she went by such a train of passionate and incoherent sound as nothing but a slighted woman in her anger could produce.

"Let me go away. Let me go after her," said Merry, pushing him off.

"Not till you say 'Yes.' You haven't told me."

"No, I won't. You're a fright. Besides, I always thought you liked my sister best. We all thought so."

"Any trick is fair in love," said Jonas. "She may have thought I liked her best, but you didn't. You never could have thought I liked her best, when you were by."

"There's no accounting for tastes," said Merry; "at least—I didn't mean to say that. I don't know what I mean. Let me go to her."

"Say 'Yes,' and then I will."

"If I ever brought myself to say so, it should only be that I might hate and tease you all my life."

"That's as good," cried Jonas, "as saying it right out. It's a bargain, cousin. We're a pair, if ever there was one." This gallant speech was succeeded by a confused noise of kissing and slapping; and then the fair but much disheveled Merry broke away and followed in the footsteps of her sister.

Now whether Mr. Pecksniff had been listening—which in one of his character appears impossible—or divined almost by inspiration what the matter was, at the moment when the sisters came together in their own room, he appeared. "Children!" said Mr. Pecksniff, but not before he had shut the chamber door. "Girls! Daughters! What is this?"

"The wretch—the apostate—the false, mean, odious villain—has before my very face proposed to Mercy!" was his elder daughter's answer.

"Oh, fie! For shame!" said Mr. Pecksniff gravely. "Can the triumph of a sister move you to this terrible display, my child? Oh, really this is very sad! Mercy, my girl, bless you!" Uttering this apostrophe, Mr. Pecksniff walked downstairs into the parlor, where he seized his intended son-in-law by both hands. "Jonas!" cried Mr. Pecksniff. "Jonas! the dearest wish of my heart is now fulfilled!"

"Very well; I'm glad to hear it," said Jonas. "I say! as it ain't the one you're so fond of, you must come down with another thousand, Pecksniff. You must make it up five."

Mr. Pecksniff was struggling to regain his composure after this remark, when Tom Pinch, in a state of great excitement, came darting into the room. "Mr. Pinch," said Pecksniff, "this is hardly decent."

"I beg your pardon, sir," replied Tom, "for not knocking. But it's rather pressing."

"Excuse me for one moment, Mr. Jonas," said Pecksniff, taking Tom into the passage. "Now, sir, what is the reason of this rough intrusion?"

"I am very sorry, sir, I am sure," said Tom, "but the truth is I was so surprised to see them and knew you would be too that I really hadn't enough command over myself to know what I was doing. They had a posting carriage at the church porch, sir, and had stopped to hear the organ, they said. And then they said—*she* said, I mean—'I believe you live with Mr. Pecksniff, sir?' And when I said I did, they came with me across the meadows. I left 'em at the turnstile; and they'll be here, sir, in—in less than a minute's time, I should say."

"Now who," said Mr. Pecksniff, pondering, "who may these people be?"

"Bless my soul, sir!" cried Tom. "I meant to mention that at first; I thought I had. The gentleman who was ill at the Dragon, sir, last winter, and the young lady who attended him."

Tom's teeth chattered in his head, and he positively staggered with amazement, at witnessing the extraordinary effect produced on Mr. Pecksniff by these simple words. The dread of losing the old man's favor almost as soon as they were reconciled, through the mere fact of having Jonas in the house; the impossibility of dismissing Jonas; the horrible discordance prevailing in the establishment; the total hopelessness of being able to disguise or feasibly explain this state of rampant confusion—so filled the entrapped architect with dismay that, if Mr. Pecksniff could have been a Gorgon staring at Tom, Tom could not have been half so horrified.

At that moment a loud knocking was heard at the hall door.

9

THE knocking at Mr. Pecksniff's door, though loud enough, bore no resemblance whatever to the noise of an American railway train at full speed. It may be well to begin the present chapter with this frank admission, for Mr. Pecksniff's house is now more than a thousand leagues away, and again this happy chronicle has Liberty and Moral Sensibility for its high companions. Martin and Mark Tapley are seated side by side in the train.

"And so, Mark," said Martin, "you are glad we have left New York far behind us, are you? Were you not 'jolly' there?"

"On the contrary, sir," returned Mark. "The jolliest week as ever I spent in my life was that there week at Pawkins's."

"What do you think of our prospects?" inquired Martin, with an air that plainly said he had avoided the question for some time.

"Uncommon bright, sir," returned Mark. "Impossible for a place to have a better name, sir, than the Walley of Eden."

"And that's a fact," said a voice so close in his ear that it tickled him. "That's dreadful true."

Mark looked round and found that a gentleman, on the seat behind, had thrust his head between himself and Martin and sat with his chin resting on the back rail of their little bench, entertaining himself with their conversation. "Well," the stranger said, "how's the unnat'ral old parent by this time?"

"You mean the old country?" Martin said.

"Ah!" was the reply. "How's she? Progressing back'ard, I expect, as usual? Well, how's Queen Victoria?"

"In good health, I believe," said Martin.

"Queen Victoria won't shake in her royal shoes at all in her luxurious lo-cation in the Tower of London when she reads the next double-extra *Watertoast Gazette*," the stranger observed.

Several other gentlemen had left their seats and gathered round during the foregoing dialogue. They were highly delighted with this speech. One very lank gentleman, in a loose, limp, white cravat, a long white waistcoat, and a black great coat, who seemed to be in authority among them, felt called upon to acknowledge it.

"Hem! Mr. La Fayette Kettle," he said, taking off his hat. "In the name of this company, sir, and in the name of our common country, I thank you."

"General Choke," said Mr. La Fayette Kettle, "you warm my heart."

"I think," said Martin, addressing himself to the general, "that I have the pleasure of being the bearer of a letter of introduction to you, sir. From Mr. Bevan."

The general took the letter and read it attentively. "Well," he said, "and you think of settling in Eden?"

"Subject to your opinion and the agent's advice," replied Martin. "I am told there is nothing to be done in the old towns."

"I can introduce you to the agent, sir," said the general. "I know him. In fact, I am a member of the Eden Land Corporation myself."

This was serious news to Martin, for his friend had laid great stress upon the general's having no connection, as he thought, with any land company and therefore being likely to give him disinterested advice. The general explained that he had joined the corporation only a few weeks ago and that no communication had passed between himself and Mr. Bevan since.

"We have very little to venture," said Martin anxiously "—only a few pounds—but it is our all. Now, do you think that, for an architect, this would be a speculation with any hope or chance in it?"

"Would I," said the general gravely, "with my principles, invest capital in this speculation if I didn't think it full of hopes and chances for my brother man? What are the Great United States for, sir, if not for the regeneration of man? But it is nat'ral in you to make such an enquerry; for you come from England, and you do not know my country."

They came to their journey's end late in the evening. Close to the railway was an immense white edifice, like an ugly hospital, on which was painted "National Hotel." There was a wooden gallery or veranda in front, in which it was rather startling to behold a great many pairs of boots and shoes and the smoke of a great many cigars. But within the house and without, wherever half a dozen people were collected together, there, in their looks, dress, morals, manners, habits, intellect, and conversation, were Mr. Jefferson Brick, Colonel Diver, Major Pawkins, General

Choke, and Mr. La Fayette Kettle, over, and over, and over again. They did the same things; said the same things; judged all subjects by, and reduced all subjects to, the same standard.

"Now, Mark, my good fellow," said Martin that night, "we must hold a solemn council, for our fate is decided tomorrow morning. You are determined to invest these savings of yours in the common stock, are you?"

"If I hadn't been determined to make that wenture, sir," answered Mr. Tapley, "I shouldn't have come."

"Now, Mark," said Martin in his old way, "your share will be very much larger than mine, even after the sale of *her* ring. But I have thought of a means of making this up to you and very materially elevating your prospects in life. You shall be a partner in the business. I will put in, as my additional capital, my professional knowledge and ability; and half the annual profits, as long as it is carried on, shall be yours."

Poor Martin! Forever building castles in the air. Forever, in his very selfishness, forgetful of all but his own teeming hopes and sanguine plans. Swelling, at that instant, with the consciousness of patronizing and most munificently rewarding Mark!

"I'll stand by you, sir, to the best of my ability, and to the last," Mark rejoined, much more sadly than his custom was. "That's all."

"We quite understand each other, my good fellow," said Martin, rising in self-approval and condescension. "We are no longer master and servant, but friends and partners: Chuzzlewit and Tapley."

"Lord love you, sir," cried Mark, "don't have my name in it. I must be 'Co.,' I must."

Next morning they went with the general to the office of the Eden Settlement. "Heyday!" cried Martin, as his eye rested on a great plan which occupied one whole side of the office. "What's that?"

"That's Eden," said the agent, whose name was Scadder, picking his teeth with a sort of young bayonet that flew out of his knife when he touched a spring.

"Why, I had no idea it was a city." A flourishing city, too! An architectural city! There were banks, churches, cathedrals, market places, factories, hotels, stores, mansions, wharves; an exchange, a theater; public buildings of all kinds, down to the office of the *Eden Stinger*, a daily journal—all faithfully depicted in the view before them. "I am afraid," said Martin, "that there's nothing left for me to do."

"Well, it ain't all built," replied the agent. "Not quite."

"I suppose," said Martin, feigning to look more narrowly at the plan but showing by his tremulous voice how much depended, in his mind, upon the answer, "I suppose there are—several architects there?"

"There ain't a single one," said Mr. Scadder.

"Mark," whispered Martin, pulling him by the sleeve, "do you hear that?—But whose work is all this before us, then?" he asked aloud.

"The soil being very fruitful, public buildings grows spontaneous, perhaps," said Mark.

"I entreat, Mark," Martin said with some irritation, "that you will not obtrude remarks of that nature."

"The Co.'s a putting his foot in it already," thought Mark. "He must be a sleeping partner—fast asleep and snoring, Co. must, *I* see."

The agent said nothing, but he set his back against the plan and thrust his toothpick into the desk some twenty times, looking at Mark all the while as if he were stabbing him in effigy.

"You haven't said whose work it is," Martin ventured to observe, at length, in a tone of mild propitiation.

"Well, never mind whose work it is or isn't," said Scadder sulkily. "P'raps he cleared off, handsome, with a heap of dollars; p'raps he wasn't worth a cent. P'raps he was a loafing rowdy; p'raps a ring-tailed roarer. Now!"

"I hope you're satisfied with the success of your joke, Mark," said Martin.

But here the general interposed and asked the agent to give his friends the particulars of that little lot of fifty acres with the house upon it, which, having belonged to the company formerly, had lately lapsed again into their hands.

"You air a deal too open handed, gen'ral," was the answer. "It is a lot as should be rose in price. It is." He grumblingly opened his books notwithstanding.

"Now, where upon the plan may this place be?" Martin inquired. The agent reflected for a short time, as if, having been put upon his mettle, he was resolved to be particular to the very minutest hair's breadth of a shade. At length, he made a dart at the drawing and pierced the very center of the main wharf through and through.

"There!" he said, leaving his knife quivering in the wall. "That's where it is!"

Martin glanced with sparkling eyes upon his Co., and his Co. saw that the thing was done.

As soon as it was generally known in the National Hotel that the young Englishman, Mr. Chuzzlewit, had purchased a "location" in the Valley of Eden and intended to betake himself to that earthly Paradise by the next steamboat, he became a popular character. Captain Kedgick, the landlord, kindly came upstairs to see how he was getting on. "Well, sir," he said, "you're quite a public man, I calc'late. Our citizens, sir, intend to pay their respects to you. You will have to hold a sort of le-vee, sir, while you're here."

"Powers above!" cried Martin. "I couldn't do that, my good fellow!"

"You wouldn't be unpop'lar, *I* know," said the captain, paring his nails. "Our citizens ain't long of riling up, I tell you; and our *Gazette* could flay you like a wildcat."

"But will you," said Martin, "at least tell me this? What do they want to see me for? What have I done? And how do they happen to have such a sudden interest in me?"

Captain Kedgick passed one hand all down his face, beginning at the forehead and ending at the chin; looked at Martin; then at Mark; then at Martin; winked; and walked out.

"Upon my life, now!" said Martin. "Mark, what do you say to this?"

"Why, sir," returned his partner, "my opinion is that we must have got to the *most* remarkable man in the country at last. So I hope there's an end to the breed, sir."

Punctually at two o'clock, Captain Kedgick returned to hand Martin to the room of state; and he had no sooner got him safe there than he bawled down the staircase, to his fellow citizens below, that Mr. Chuzzlewit "was receiving." Up they came with a rush. One after another, one after another, up they came—all shaking hands with Martin. If they spoke to him, which was not often, they invariably asked the same questions, in the same tone—with no more remorse, or delicacy, or consideration, than if he had been a figure of stone, purchased, and paid for, and set up there for their delight. Martin might have done something desperate if the gong had not, at last, sounded for supper.

In the meantime Mark was busy getting on board the steamboat such provisions, tools, and other necessaries as they had been forewarned it would be wise to take. Dispirited and weary to the last degree, but a greater lion than ever, Martin walked down to the wharf through a concourse of people and went on board. But Mark was bent on solving the riddle of this lionship and so, not without the risk of being left behind, ran back to the hotel. "I want to ask you a question," he said to Captain Kedgick. "What have they been making so much of him for, now? Come!"

The captain looked at him as if he were half inclined to unburden his mind of a capital joke. "You air a going?" he said.

"Going?" cried Mark. "Ain't every moment precious?"

"Our people like ex-citement," said the captain, whispering. "He ain't like emigrants in gin'ral; and he excited 'em along of this"—he winked and burst into a smothered laugh—"along of this. Scadder is a smart man, and—and—nobody as goes to Eden ever comes back a-live!"

"Mark! Mark!" cried Martin.

"Here am I, sir!" shouted Mark. "Never was half so jolly, sir," as he leapt aboard. The sparks from the wood fire streamed upward from the two chimneys, as if the vessel were a great firework just lighted; and they roared away upon the dark water.

At first they parted with some of their passengers once or twice a day and took in others to replace them. But by degrees the towns upon their route became more thinly scattered, and for many hours together they would see no other habitations than the huts of the woodcutters, where the vessel stopped for fuel. Sky, wood, and water all the livelong day, and heat that blistered everything it touched. On they toiled through great solitudes where the trees upon the banks grew thick and close—on, until return appeared impossible, and restoration to their home a miserable dream.

"Mark," Martin said one day, "are there really none but ourselves on board this boat who are bound for Eden?"

"None at all, sir. Most of 'em, as you know, have stopped short, and the few that are left are going further on. What matters that? More room there for us, sir."

"Oh, to be sure!" said Martin. "But I was thinking how—how odd that people should have arranged to try their fortune at such wretched holes as we have passed, when there is such a very different kind of place near at hand!" He spoke in a tone so very different from his usual confidence and with such an obvious dread of Mark's reply that the good-natured fellow was full of pity.

"Why, you know, sir," said Mark, gently, "we must guard against being too sanguine."

At last they stopped—at Eden too. The waters of the Deluge might have left it but a week before, so choked with slime and matted growth was the hideous swamp which bore that name. There were a few log houses visible among the dark trees, the best a cow shed or a rude stable. But for the wharves, the market place, the public buildings! "Here comes an Edener," said Mark as a figure appeared. "Keep a good heart, sir."

The man advanced toward them through the thickening gloom very slowly, leaning on a stick. As he drew nearer, they observed that he was pale and worn and that his anxious eyes were deeply sunken in his head. "You couldn't recommend us someone as would lend a hand to help carry our things up to the—to the town, could you, sir?" said Mark.

"My eldest son would do it if he could," replied the man; "but today he has his chill upon him and is lying wrapped up in the blankets. My youngest died last week. You must look for such folk here," knocking his stick upon the ground, "or yonder in the bush, toward the north. We've buried most of 'em. The rest have gone away." He conducted them to their miserable cabin, rudely constructed of the trunks of trees, the door of which had either fallen down or been carried away long ago, and which was consequently open to the wild landscape and the dark night.

Many a man who would have stood within a home dismantled, strong in his passion and design of vengeance, has had the firmness of his nature conquered by the razing of an air-built castle. When the log hut received them, Martin lay down upon the ground and wept aloud. "Lord love you, sir!" cried Mr. Tapley, in great terror. "Don't do that! Don't do that, sir! Anything but that!"

"I ask your forgiveness a thousand times, my dear fellow," said Martin. "I couldn't have helped it if death had been the penalty." And by the next morning he was very pale and languid; he spoke of pains and weakness in his limbs and complained that his sight was dim. "Do the best you can for yourself," he said to Mark. "You'll soon have only yourself to consider. And then God speed you home, and forgive me for bringing you here!"

"Wait half a minute," said Mark cheerily, "till I run up to one of our neighbors and ask what's best to be took and borrow a little of it to give you; and tomorrow you'll find yourself as strong as ever again. I won't be gone a minute. Don't give in, while I'm away, whatever you do!"

"Now, Mr. Tapley," he said to himself, "things is looking about as bad as they *can* look, young man. You'll not have such another opportunity for showing your jolly disposition, my fine fellow, as long as you live. And therefore, Tapley, now's your time to come out strong—or Never!"

10

"Hullo, Pecksniff!" cried Mr. Jonas, from the parlor. "Isn't somebody a going to open that precious old door of yours?"

"Immediately, Mr. Jonas, immediately. Thomas Pinch"—he couldn't make up his mind, in his great agitation, whether to call Tom his dear friend or a villain, so he shook his fist at him pro tem—"go up to my daughters' room and tell them who is here. Say, Silence, silence! Do you hear me, sir?"

"Directly, sir!" cried Tom, departing, in a state of much amazement, on his errand.

"You'll—ha, ha, ha!—you'll excuse me, Mr. Jonas, if I close this door a moment, will you?" said Pecksniff. "This may be a professional call." Then, gently warbling a rustic stave, he put on his garden hat, seized a spade, and opened the street door.

Seeing a gentleman and lady before him, he started back; but recognition came upon him the next moment, and he cried, "Mr. Chuzzlewit! Can I believe my eyes! Pray, my dear sir, walk in. You find me in my garden dress. You will excuse it, I know. It is an ancient pursuit, gardening—" He had by this time got them into the best parlor. "My daughters," said Mr. Pecksniff, "will be overjoyed. Mr. Pinch," raising his voice for the edification of Tom upon the stairs, "was about, I dare say, to tell me of your coming, when I begged him first to knock at my daughters' chamber and inquire after Charity, my dear child, who is not so well as I could wish."

"Pecksniff," the old man said, after a pause, "I was much shocked on hearing of my brother's death. We had been strangers for many years, but we were playfellows once, and it would have been better for us both if we had died then."

Finding him in this gentle mood, Mr. Pecksniff began to see another way out of his difficulties besides the casting overboard of Jonas. "That any man, my dear sir, could possibly be the happier for not knowing you," he returned, "you will excuse my doubting. But Mr. Anthony, in the evening of his life, was happy in the affection of his excellent son—a pattern, my dear sir, a pattern to all sons."

"His son a pattern!" cried old Martin. "A greedy expectant, who measured every day and hour the lessening distance between his father and the grave and cursed his tardy progress on that dismal road!"

"No!" cried Mr. Pecksniff boldly. "Not at all, sir! That bereaved young man is now in this house, sir, seeking in change of scene the peace of mind he has lost. Shall I be backward in doing justice to that young man, when even undertakers and coffin makers have been moved by the conduct he has exhibited?"

The old man gazed at him for a moment with a look of wonder, before he said, "Here now—in this house! Let me see him."

"I will break this happiness to him," said Mr. Pecksniff, as he left the room. But, however well he had taught Jonas the lesson of dutiful behavior to his uncle in the quarter of an hour that elapsed before he returned, that young man's bearing was anything but manly or engaging. Perhaps, indeed, so singular a mixture of defiance and obsequiousness, of fear and hardihood, of dogged sullenness and an attempt at cringing and propitiation never was expressed in any one human figure as in that of Jonas. And not even Mr. Pecksniff's guileless merriment could set such a party at their ease.

The unspeakable jealousy and hatred which that night's explanation had sown in Charity's breast was not to be so easily kept down. The beauteous Merry, too, with all the glory of her conquest fresh upon her, so probed and lanced the rankling disappointment of her sister by her capricious airs and thousand little trials of Mr. Jonas's obedience that she almost goaded her into a fit of madness. The constraint imposed upon the family by the presence among them for the first time of Mary Graham (for by that name old Martin Chuzzlewit had introduced his companion) did not at all improve this state of things, gentle and quiet though her manner was. Perhaps Mr. Pecksniff had never in his life felt such relief as when old Martin announced that it was time to go, and asked Mr. Pinch to light them to the Dragon.

"And so, Mr. Pinch," said Martin on the way, "you are very comfortably situated here, are you?"

Tom answered, with even more than his usual enthusiasm, that he was under obligations to Mr. Pecksniff which the devotion of a lifetime would but imperfectly repay. The old man had felt kindly toward Tom at first but was now disgusted by what in his suspicious nature he considered a shameless and fulsome puff of his employer. "You're like the rest," he thought. "You had nearly imposed upon me, but you are too zealous a toadeater, Mr. Pinch."

As Tom approached the first stile on his way home, a man slipped past him and took his seat upon it. It was Jonas. "Good gracious me!" cried Tom. "You followed us, then?"

"What's that to you?" said Jonas. "Go to the devil!"

"You are not very civil, I think," remarked Tom.

"Civil enough for *you*," retorted Jonas. "Who are you?"

"One who has as good a right to common consideration as another," said Tom mildly.

"You're a liar," said Jonas. "Pauper 'prentices haven't a right to anything. Ecod, we manage 'em a little better in the City!"

"Never mind what you do in the City," said Tom. "What have you got to say to me?"

"Just this, Mr. Pinch," retorted Jonas. "I advise you to keep your own counsel, and to avoid tittle tattle, and not to cut in where you're not wanted. Ecod, I should like to know what goes on between you and a vagabond member of my family."

"I know no vagabond member of your family," cried Tom stoutly. "Your uncle's namesake, if you mean him, is no vagabond. Any comparison between you and him"—Tom snapped his fingers at him, for he was rising fast in wrath—"is immeasurably to your disadvantage."

"Oh, indeed!" sneered Jonas. "And what do you think of his deary, his beggarly leavings, eh, Mr. Pinch?" He flourished his stick over Tom's head; but in a moment it was spinning harmlessly in the air, and Jonas himself lay sprawling in the ditch. In the momentary struggle for the stick, Tom had brought it into violent contact with his opponent's forehead, and the blood welled out profusely from a deep cut on the temple.

"I didn't know the road," Jonas said, when they reached home. "The night's very dark; and just as I came up with Mr. Pinch, I ran against a tree. It's only skin deep."

"Cold water, Merry, my child!" cried Mr. Pecksniff. "Brown paper! Scissors! A piece of old linen! Charity, my dear, make a bandage. Bless me, Mr. Jonas!"

Miss Charity, though called upon to lend her aid, sat upright in one corner, with a smile upon her face, and didn't move a finger or say a word. But when Mr. Jonas's head was bound up and he had gone to bed and everybody else had retired, she spoke to Tom. "Mr. Pinch," she whispered, "dear Mr. Pinch! Tell me the truth! You did that? There was some quarrel between you, and you struck him? I am sure of it!"

It was the first time she had ever spoken kindly to Tom in all the many years they had passed together. He was stupefied with amazement. "Ye-yes. We had a struggle for the path," said Tom. "But I didn't mean to hurt him so much."

"Not so much!" she repeated, clenching her hand and stamping her foot, to Tom's great wonder. "Don't say that. It was brave of you. I honor you for it. Dear Mr. Pinch, I am your friend from tonight."

Tom went to bed, full of uncomfortable thoughts. That any train of circumstances should have led to the commission of an assault and battery by Thomas Pinch upon any man calling himself the friend of Seth Pecksniff was a matter of such deep and painful cogitation that he could not close his eyes. But he fell asleep at last and dreamed—new source of waking uneasiness—that he had betrayed his trust and run away with Mary Graham.

One day the lively Merry, sitting under a shady tree in the churchyard whither she had retired after fatiguing herself by the imposition of sundry trials on the temper of Mr. Jonas, was not a little surprised to see old Martin take his seat upon the turf beside her and open a conversation thus: "When are you to be married?"

"Oh! dear Mr. Chuzzlewit, my goodness me! I'm sure I don't know. Not yet awhile, I hope."

"You hope?" said the old man. It was very gravely said, but she took it for banter and giggled excessively. "Come," said the old man, with unusual kindness, "you are young, good-looking, and I think good-natured! Do you love the young man you are to marry?"

"Why, my dear Mr. Chuzzlewit, I'm sure I tell him a hundred times a day that I hate him. You must have heard me tell him that."

"Often," said Martin. When he spoke again, it was in a tone of severity. "Look about you," he said, pointing to the graves, "and remember that, from your bridal hour to the day which sees you brought as low as these and laid in such a bed, there will be no appeal against him. Think, and speak, and act, for once, like an accountable creature. Is any control put upon your inclinations? Are you forced into this match?"

"No," said Merry, shrugging her shoulders. "If anyone had tried to make me have him, I wouldn't have had him at all."

"Have you any wish—or is there anything within your breast that whispers you may form the wish, if you have time to think— to be released from this engagement?"

Again Miss Merry pouted, and looked down, and plucked the grass, and shrugged her shoulders. No, she didn't know that she had; she was pretty sure she hadn't—quite sure, she might say. She "didn't mind it."

"Has it ever occurred to you," said Martin, "that your married life may perhaps be miserable, full of bitterness, and most unhappy?"

"My dear Mr. Chuzzlewit, what shocking words! Of course, I shall quarrel with him. I should quarrel with any husband. But as to being miserable, and bitter, and all those dreadful things, you know, why, I couldn't be absolutely that unless he always had the best of it, and I mean to have the best of it myself."

"Let it go on," said Martin rising. "Let it go on! I sought to know your mind, my dear, and you have shown it me. I wish you joy—joy!" he repeated, looking full upon her and pointing to the wicket gate where Jonas entered at the moment. And then, without waiting for his nephew, he passed out at another gate and went away.

Mr. Jonas sat down upon the grass and sulkily inquired, "What's my uncle been a talking about?"

"About you," rejoined Merry. "He says you're not half good enough for me.—Griffin! What are you doing, Griffin?"

"Only giving you a squeeze," said the discomfited Jonas. "There's no harm in that, I suppose?"

"But there is a great deal of harm in it if I don't consider it agreeable," returned his cousin. Mr. Jonas withdrew his arm and for a moment looked at her more like a murderer than a lover. But he cleared his brow by degrees and broke silence with "I say, Mel! When is it to be? I can't afford to go on dawdling about here half my life. What do you say to next week, now?"

"To next week! If you had said next quarter, I should have wondered at your impudence."

"But I didn't say next quarter," retorted Jonas; "I said next week."

"Then, Griffin," cried Miss Merry, pushing him off and rising, "I say no! Not next week. It shan't be till I choose, and I may not choose it to be for months. There! If it's next month, that shall be the very earliest. And if you don't do everything I order you to do, it shall never be at all. So don't follow me. There, Griffin!" And with that she skipped away among the trees.

"Ecod, my lady," said Jonas, looking after her and biting a piece of straw almost to powder, "you'll catch it for this when you *are* married! It's all very well now—it keeps one on somehow, and you know it—but I'll pay you off scot and lot by and by. Take your own way as long as it's in your power, my lady!"

I I

Mr. Mould was enjoying the sweets of domestic repose one day when a knock was heard at the room door and a servant announced that Mrs. Gamp wished to speak to him. "Tell Mrs. Gamp to come upstairs," said Mould.—"Now, Mrs. Gamp, what's *your* news?"

The lady in question was by this time in the doorway, curtsying to Mrs. Mould. At the same moment a peculiar fragrance was borne upon the breeze, as if a passing fairy had hiccuped and had previously been to a wine vaults.

Mrs. Gamp made no response to Mr. Mould but curtsied to Mrs. Mould again and held up her hands and eyes, as in a devout thanksgiving that she looked so well. "There are some happy creeturs," Mrs. Gamp observed, "as time runs back'ards with, and you are one, Mrs. Mould. Only t'other day, I says to Mrs. Harris—when she says to me, 'Years and our trials, Mrs. Gamp, sets marks upon us all,'—'Say not the words, Mrs. Harris, if you and me is to be continual friends, for sech is not the case. Mrs. Mould,' I says, 'is one of them that goes agen the obserwation straight; and never, Mrs. Harris, whilst I've a drop of breath to draw, will I set by, and not stand up, don't think it.' 'I ast your pardon, ma'am,' says Mrs. Harris, 'and I humbly grant your grace; for if ever a woman lived as would see her feller creeturs into fits to serve her friends, well do I know that woman's name is Sairey Gamp.'"

At this point she was fain to stop for breath; and advantage may be taken of the circumstance to state that a fearful mystery surrounded this lady of the name of Harris, whom no one in the circle of Mrs. Gamp's acquaintance had ever seen, neither did any human being know her place of residence, though Mrs. Gamp appeared on her own showing to be in constant communication with her. There were conflicting rumours on the subject; but the prevalent opinion was that she was a phantom of Mrs. Gamp's brain—as Messrs. Doe and Roe are fictions of the law—created for the express purpose of holding visionary dialogues with her on all manner of subjects and invariably winding up with a compliment to the excellence of her nature.

"And what's your news, Mrs. Gamp?" asked Mould again. "How's Mr. Chuffey?"

"Mr. Chuffey, sir," she replied, "is jest as usual; he ain't no better, and he ain't no worse. I take it very kind in the gentleman to have wrote up to you and said, 'Let Mrs. Gamp take care of him till I come home'; but ev'rythink he does is kind. There ain't a many like him. If there was, we shouldn't want no churches."

"What do you want to speak to me about, Mrs. Gamp?" said Mould, coming to the point.

"Jest this, sir," Mrs. Gamp returned, "with thanks to you for asking. There *is* a gent, sir, at the Bull in Holborn, as has been took ill there and is bad abed. They have a day nurse as was recommended from Bartholomew's; and well I knows her, Mr. Mould, her name being Mrs. Prig, the best of creeturs. But she is otherways engaged at night, and they are in wants of night watching."

"Night watching, eh?" said Mould, rubbing his chin.

"From eight o'clock till eight, sir. I will not deceive you," Mrs. Gamp rejoined.

"And then go back, eh?" said Mould.

"Quite free then, sir, to attend to Mr. Chuffey. His ways bein' quiet, and his hours early, he'd be abed, sir, nearly all the time."

"Well, Mrs. Gamp," observed Mould, "I don't see any particular objection to your earning an honest penny under such circumstances. I should keep it quiet, I think, Mrs. Gamp."

"The very words was on my lips, sir," Mrs. Gamp rejoined. "Supposing that the gent should die, I hope I might take the liberty of saying as I know'd someone in the undertaking line, and yet give no offense to you, sir?"

"Certainly, Mrs. Gamp," said Mould, with much condescension. "But don't obtrude it—don't obtrude it. Easy, easy! My dear, you may as well give Mrs. Gamp a card or two, if you please."

Mrs. Gamp took her departure and, arriving shortly after at the house of Anthony Chuzzlewit and Son, lay down to rest. Remaining there until seven o'clock in the evening and then persuading poor old Chuffey to betake himself to bed, she sallied forth upon her new engagement. As she turned into the yard of the Bull, she stopped, for the landlord was on the threshold talking earnestly with a young gentleman. The first words that struck upon Mrs. Gamp's ear obviously bore reference to the patient; and, it being expedient that all good attendants should know as much as possible about the case on which their skill is brought to bear, Mrs. Gamp listened as a matter of duty.

"Poor fellow!" said the gentleman. "I am sorry to hear he is no better. The worst of it is that I have no idea what friends or relations he has, or where they live, except that it certainly is not in London. We were schoolfellows together; but since that time I have only met him twice. The letter bearing my name and address which you found upon his table and which led to your applying to me is in answer, you will observe, to one he wrote from his house the very day he was taken ill, making an appointment with him at his own request. He has very little luggage, you say?"

"Nothing but a portmanteau," said the landlord.

"A few pounds in his purse, though?" inquired the gentleman, who was no other than our old friend John Westlock. "Then you have enough to go upon for the present; and I will readily undertake to pay the doctor and the nurses."

"Ah!" cried Mrs. Gamp. "A rayal gentleman!" She groaned her admiration so audibly that they turned round, and Mrs. Gamp introduced herself. "The night nurse," she observed, "well beknown to Mrs. Prig, the day nurse and the best of creeturs. It ain't the fust time by a many score that Mrs. Prig and me has nussed together, turn and turn about, one off, one on." She then betook herself to the sick chamber, where she found Mrs. Prig bonneted and shawled and all impatience to be gone.

Mrs. Prig was of the Gamp build, but not so fat; and her voice was deeper and more like a man's. She had also a beard. "I began to think you warn't a coming!" Mrs. Prig observed, in some displeasure.

"It shall be made good tomorrow night," said Mrs. Gamp, "*honorable*. Anythin' to tell afore you goes, my dear?"

"The pickled salmon," Mrs. Prig replied, "is quite delicious. I can partick'ler recommend it. Don't have nothink to say to the cold meat, for it tastes of the stable. The drinks is all good. The physic and them things is on the drawers and mankleshelf," said Mrs. Prig, cursorily. "He took his last slime draught at seven. The easy chair ain't soft enough. You'll want his piller." Mrs. Gamp thanked her for these hints and entered on her occupation of the sick chamber.

When she had exhausted the prospect, she strolled up to the bedside to take a look at the patient. A young man—dark, and not ill-looking—with long black hair. His eyes were partly open, and he never ceased to roll his head from side to side upon the pillow. Mrs. Gamp solaced herself with a pinch of snuff and stood looking at him with her head inclined a little sideways, as a connoisseur might gaze upon a doubtful work of art. Stooping down, she pinned his wandering arms against his sides. "Ah!" said Mrs. Gamp, walking away from the bed, "he'd make a lovely corpse."

She now filled a small kettle, as a preliminary to refreshing herself with a cup of tea in the course of the night; laid what she called "a little bit of fire," for the same philanthropic purpose; and also set forth a small tea board, that nothing might be wanting

for her comfortable enjoyment. These preparations occupied so long that when they were brought to a conclusion it was high time to think about supper; so she rang the bell and ordered it.

"I think, young woman," said Mrs. Gamp to the assistant chambermaid, in a tone expressive of weakness, "that I could pick a little bit of pickled salmon, with a nice little sprig of fennel, and a sprinkling of white pepper. I takes new bread, my dear, with jest a little pat of fresh butter, and a mossel of cheese. In case there should be such a thing as a cowcumber in the 'ouse, will you be so kind as bring it, for I'm rather partial to 'em, and they does a world of good in a sick room. If they draws the Brighton Tipper here, I takes *that* ale at night, my love, it being considered wakeful by the doctors. And whatever you do, young woman, don't bring more than a shilling's worth of gin-and-water warm when I rings the bell a second time, for that is always my allowance, and I never takes a drop beyond!"

"Ah!" sighed Mrs. Gamp, as she meditated over the warm

shilling's worth, "what a blessed thing it is to make sick people happy in their beds, and never mind oneself as long as one can do a service. I don't believe a finer cowcumber was ever grow'd. I'm sure I never see one!" She moralized in the same vein until her glass was empty and then administered the patient's medicine by the simple process of clutching his windpipe to make him gasp and immediately pouring it down his throat. "I almost forgot the piller, I declare!" said Mrs. Gamp, drawing it away. "There! Now he's comfortable as he can be, I'm sure! I must try to make myself as much so as I can."

Having formed the best couch that the circumstances admitted of, she took out of her bundle a yellow nightcap of prodigious size, in shape resembling a cabbage, which article of dress she fixed and tied on with the utmost care, previously divesting herself of a row of bald old curls that could scarcely be called false, they were so very innocent of anything approaching to deception. These arrangements made, she lighted the rush light, coiled herself up on her couch, and went to sleep.

Still, without a moment's interval, the burning head tossed to and fro. Still, from time to time, fatigue, impatience, suffering, and surprise found utterance upon that rack, and plainly too, though never once in words. At length, in the solemn hour of midnight, he began to talk, waiting awfully for answers sometimes, as though invisible companions were about his bed, and so replying to their speech and questioning again.

Mrs. Gamp awoke. "Come! Hold your tongue!" she cried, in sharp reproof. "Don't make none of that noise here."

There was no alteration in the face or in the incessant motion of the head, but he talked on wildly. "That makes five hundred and twenty-one men, all dressed alike and with the same distortion on their faces, that have passed in at the window and out at the door," he cried anxiously. "Look there! Five hundred and twenty-two—twenty-three—twenty-four. Do you see them?"

"Ah! *I* see 'em," said Mrs. Gamp. "You'll take your next draught when I've made the kettle bile."

"Five hundred and twenty-eight, five hundred and twenty-nine, five hundred and thirty—look here! What's that upon the arm of every man?"

"Spiders, p'raps," said Mrs. Gamp.

"Crape! Black crape! Good God! why do they wear it outside?"

The fire she had lit beginning by this time to impart a grateful warmth, Mrs. Gamp fell into a heavy doze. She was awakened by the room ringing with a name she knew—"Chuzzlewit!" The sound was so distinct and real and so full of agonized entreaty that Mrs. Gamp jumped up in terror. But the patient now was silent.

She brewed her tea, made some buttered toast, and sat down at the tea board, with her face to the fire—when once again, in a tone more terrible than that which had vibrated in her slumbering ear, these words were shrieked out: "Chuzzlewit! Jonas! No!"

It was bright morning the next time Mrs. Gamp looked out of window, and the sun was rising cheerfully. Mrs. Prig relieved punctually, having passed a good night at her other patient's. The doctor came at the same time. "What sort of a night, nurse?"

"Restless, sir," said Mrs. Gamp.

"Talk much?"

"Middling, sir," said Mrs. Gamp.

"Well," said the doctor, "we must keep him quiet; keep the room cool; give him his draughts regularly; and see that he's carefully looked to. That's all!"

"And as long as Mrs. Prig and me waits upon him, sir, no fear of that," said Mrs. Gamp.

"I suppose," observed Mrs. Prig, when they had curtsied the doctor out, "there's nothin' new?"

"Nothin' at all, my dear," said Mrs. Gamp. "He's rather wearin' in his talk from making up a lot of names; elseways you needn't mind him."

"Oh, I shan't mind him," Mrs. Prig returned. "I have somethin' else to think of."

"I pays my debts tonight, you know, my dear, and comes afore my time," said Mrs. Gamp. "But, Betsey Prig"—speaking with great feeling, and laying her hand upon her arm—"try the cowcumbers, God bless you!"

The bird fancier who had the honor of entertaining Mrs. Gamp as his first-floor lodger was named Paul Sweedlepipe, commonly called Poll; for, with the exception of the staircase and his lodger's private apartment, his house was one great bird's nest. He had closed the door of his shop one evening and was hastening down the street when he ran against a young gentleman in a livery, who halted on the pavement and went round and round in circles, for the better exhibition of his figure. "Beau-ti-ful!" cried Poll. "A grass-green frock coat, bound with gold! And a cockade in your hat!"

"*I* should hope so," replied Bailey junior. "Blow the cockade though, for, except that it don't turn round, it's like the wentilator that used to be in the kitchin winder at Todgers's. I've got the right sort of governor now. Wot are you up to, old feller?" asked Mr. Bailey.

"Why, I am going to fetch my lodger home," said Poll, explaining that she was a nurse who had been acting as a kind of housekeeper to a gentleman for some weeks past. "He's newly married, and he brings his young wife home tonight. So I'm going to fetch my lodger away—Mr. Chuzzlewit's, close behind the post office—and carry her box for her."

"Jonas Chuzzlewit's?" said Bailey.

"Ah!" returned Poll. "Do you know him?"

"Oh, no!" cried Mr. Bailey. "Not at all. And I don't know her! Not neither! Why, they first kept company through me, almost. But her sister was the best. *She* was the merry one. I often used to have a bit of fun with her, in the hold times." He was good enough to bear the bird fancier company to Mr. Chuzzlewit's, where he was introduced to Mrs. Gamp.

"He knows Mrs. Chuzzlewit," said Poll.

"There's nothin' he don't know; that's my opinion," observed Mrs. Gamp, who was much astonished by Mr. Bailey's affable manners and great ease. "All the wickedness of the world is Print to him."

Mr. Bailey received this as a compliment and said, adjusting his cravat, "Reether so."

"As you know Mrs. Chuzzlewit, you knows, p'raps, what her chris'en name is?" Mrs. Gamp observed.

"Charity," said Bailey.

"That it ain't!" cried Mrs. Gamp. "It begins with a M."

"Whew!" cried Mr. Bailey, slapping his left leg. "Then he's been and married the merry one!" As these words were spoken, the sound of wheels announced the arrival of the newly married couple. Mrs. Gamp took up the candle and hurried away to welcome the young mistress of the house.

"Wishing you 'appiness and joy with all my 'art," said Mrs. Gamp, dropping a curtsy as they entered the hall; "and you too, sir. Your lady looks a little tired with the journey, Mr. Chuzzlewit—a pretty dear!—But you don't," added Mrs. Gamp, internally—"you don't look much like a merry one, I must say!" It was true; she did not. "Ain't there," said Mrs. Gamp, with a look of great sweetness and rummaging all the time in her pocket, "ain't there nothing I can do for you, my little bird?"

"No," said Merry, almost crying. "You had better go away, please."

With a leer of mingled sweetness and slyness—with one eye on the future, one on the bride, and an arch expression in her face, partly spiritual, partly spirituous, and wholly professional and peculiar to her art—Mrs. Gamp rummaged in her pocket again and took from it a printed card, whereon was an inscription copied from her signboard.

"Would you be so good, my darling dovey of a dear young married lady," Mrs. Gamp observed, in a low voice, "as put that somewheres where you can keep it in your mind? I'm well beknown to many ladies, and it's my card. Livin' quite handy, I will make so bold as call in now and then and make inquiry how your health and spirits is, my precious chick!" And with innumerable leers, winks, coughs, nods, smiles, and curtsies, all leading to the establishment of a mysterious and confidential understanding between herself and the bride, Mrs. Gamp, invoking a blessing upon the house, leered, winked, coughed, nodded, smiled, and curtsied herself out of the room.

As the door closed heavily behind her, Mrs. Jonas sat down in a chair and felt a strange chill creep upon her while she looked about the room. "It ain't good enough for you, I suppose?" said Jonas, watching her looks.

"Why, it *is* dull," said Merry, trying to be more herself.

"It'll be duller before you're done with it," retorted Jonas, "if you give me any of your airs. You're a nice article, to turn sulky on first coming home! Ecod, you used to have life enough when you could plague me with it."

As she roused herself, the old man Chuffey laid his hand softly

on her arm. "You are not married?" he said eagerly. "Not married?"

"Yes; a month ago. Good Heaven! What is the matter?"

He answered nothing was the matter and turned from her. But in her fear and wonder, turning also, she saw him raise his trembling hands above his head and heard him say, "Oh! woe, woe, woe upon this wicked house!"

It was her welcome—*home*.

12

MR. Bailey junior drove slowly up and down Pall Mall about the hour of noon, in waiting for his "governor," who presently appeared, a world of jet-black shining hair upon his head, upon his cheeks, upon his chin, upon his upper lip. His clothes, symmetrically made, were of the newest fashion and the costliest kind;

precious chains and jewels sparkled on his breast; his fingers, clogged with brilliant rings, were as unwieldy as summer flies but newly rescued from a honey pot; and yet, though changed his name and changed his outward surface, it was Tigg. Though no longer Montague Tigg, but Tigg Montague, still it was Tigg —the same satanic, gallant, military Tigg. The brass was burnished, lacquered, newly stamped; yet it was the true Tigg metal notwithstanding.

Beside him sat a smiling gentleman, of less pretensions and of business looks, whom he addressed as David. "The secretary's salary, David," said Mr. Montague, "is eight hundred pounds per annum. Is that enough?"

David smiled and nodded and coughed behind a little locked portfolio which he carried, with an air that proclaimed him to be the secretary in question. "It was a capital thought, wasn't it— the Anglo-Bengalee?" he tittered.

"The Anglo-Bengalee Disinterested Loan and Life Insurance Company is rather a capital concern, I hope, David," said Montague.

"Capital indeed," cried Mr. David Crimple, with another laugh "—in one sense! What will be the paid-up capital, according to the next prospectus?"

"A figure of two, and as many noughts after it as the printer can get into the same line," replied his friend. "Ha, ha!"

The Anglo-Bengalee Disinterested Loan and Life Insurance Company had started into existence one morning, not an Infant Institution, but a Grown-up Company running along at a great pace, with main offices in a new street in the City. As the cabriolet now drove up to the door, a magnificent porter appeared bareheaded on the pavement, crying aloud, "Room for the chairman, room for the chairman, if you please!" much to the admiration of the bystanders, who, it is needless to say, had their attention directed to the Anglo-Bengalee Company thenceforth by that means. Mr. Tigg leaped gracefully out and ascended the stairs, still preceded by the porter, who cried as he went, "By your leave there—by your leave! The Chairman of the Board, Gentle—*men!*" In like manner, he ushered the chairman through the public office, where some humble clients were transacting business, into an awful chamber, labeled "Board Room," the door of which sanctuary immediately closed and screened the great capitalist from vulgar eyes.

"Bullamy!" said Mr. Tigg.

"Sir," replied the porter.

"Let the Medical Officer know, with my compliments, that I wish to see him." The medical officer (he was the same medical officer who had followed poor old Anthony Chuzzlewit to the grave and who had attended Mrs. Gamp's patient at the Bull) promptly appeared.

In certain quarters of the City and its neighborhood Mr. John Jobling was a very popular character. He had a portentously sagacious chin and a pompous voice. Perhaps he could shake his head, rub his hands, or warm himself before a fire better than any man alive; and he had a peculiar way of smacking his lips and saying "Ah!" at intervals while patients detailed their symptoms which inspired great confidence. He was for many reasons exactly the sort of person whom the Anglo-Bengalee Company wanted for a medical officer.

"Commission to you, doctor, on four new policies and a loan this morning, eh?" said Crimple. "Well done!"

"No, no; nonsense," said the doctor. "I don't recommend anybody here. I only say what I know." The words were on his lips when Bullamy entered with a card for the medical officer. "Shall I introduce him?" asked Jobling.

"I shall be eternally delighted," answered Tigg, kissing his hand and smiling sweetly.

The doctor disappeared into the outer office and immediately returned with Jonas Chuzzlewit. "Mr. Montague," said Jobling. "Allow me. My friend Mr. Chuzzlewit. My dear friend—our Chairman. You two gentlemen have business to discuss, I know, so I will leave you."

Now there is a simplicity of cunning no less than a simplicity of innocence, and in all matters involving a faith in knavery Mr. Jonas was the most credulous of men. If Mr. Tigg had preferred any claim to high and honorable dealing, Jonas would have suspected him though he had been a very model of probity; but since he now gave utterance to Jonas's own thoughts of everything and everybody, Jonas began to feel that he was one to be talked to freely. "The truth is—" he said.

"Don't say the truth," interposed Tigg, with a grin; "it's so like humbug."

Greatly charmed by this, Jonas began again, "The long and the short of it is that I didn't consider myself very well used by one or two of the old companies in some negotiations I have had with 'em. They started objections they had no right to start and put questions they had no right to put and carried things much too high for my taste. Now I've been and got married, and I'm thinking of insuring her life. Because offense has been given me in other quarters, I wouldn't mind patronizing this company. But I want to know what sort of security there is for the company's going on."

"The paid-up capital, my dear sir—" said Tigg.

"Oh! I understand all about paid-up capitals, you know," said Jonas.

"You do?" cried Tigg, stopping short. Moving nearer to Jonas, he said in his ear, "I know you do; I know you do. Look at me! You've seen me before?"

"Why, I thought I remembered your face when I first came in," said Jonas, gazing at it; "but I couldn't call to mind where I had seen it."

"Was it in Pecksniff's parlor?" said Tigg.

"In Pecksniff's parlor!" echoed Jonas, "You don't mean—"

"Yes," cried Tigg. "Do you find me at all changed since that time?" Jonas looked hard at his waistcoat and jewels and said, "Rather, ecod!"

"Why don't you"—Tigg whispered this and nudged him in the side with his elbow—"why don't you *take* premiums, instead of paying 'em? That's what a man like you should do. Join us! Do you see that crowded street? *I* can tell you how many people will come in here merely because they find this office here, knowing no more about it than they do of the Pyramids. Ha, ha! I can tell you how many of them will buy annuities, effect insurances, bring us their money in a hundred shapes and ways, force it upon us, trust us as if we were the Mint, yet know no more about us than you do of that crossing sweeper at the corner—not so much. Ha, ha!"

Jonas gradually broke into a smile.

"Yah!" said Montague, giving him a pleasant thrust in the breast. "You're too deep for us, you dog, or I wouldn't have told you. Dine with me tomorrow, in Pall Mall!"

"I will," said Jonas.

Mr. Montague, being left alone, pondered for some moments and then said, raising his voice, "Is Nadgett in the office there?"

"Here he is, sir." And there promptly entered, shutting the board-room door after him as carefully as if he were about to plot a murder, the man who made the Anglo-Bengalee inquiries. It was no virtue or merit in Nadgett that he transacted all his business secretly and in the closest confidence, for he was born to be a secret. "Mr. Nadgett," said Montague, copying Jonas Chuzzlewit's address upon a piece of paper, "any information about this name I shall be glad to have *myself*."

It was with a faltering hand and yet with an imbecile attempt at a swagger that Mr. Jonas, vastly impressed, knocked at his new friend's door in Pall Mall when the appointed hour arrived. The room in which he was received was a spacious and elegant apartment, furnished with extreme magnificence. The dinner was as good as money (or credit, no matter which) could produce. Everything was elegantly served. The plate was gorgeous. Mr. Jonas was in the midst of a calculation of the value of this item alone, when his host disturbed him.

"I thought it best not to have a party," said Tigg.

"Why, what do you call this?" retorted Jonas. "You don't mean to say you do this every day, do you?"

"My dear fellow," said Montague, shrugging his shoulders, "every day of my life, when I dine at home. This is my common style. It was of no use having anything uncommon for you. You'd have seen through it. But I hope you'll often dine with me?"

"Ah!" said Jonas. "I don't mind. On the contrary." It was especially in his way and character to drink copiously at his entertainer's expense, and it ended in the slumber of Mr. Jonas upon one of the sofas.

As he could not be made to understand where he was, Mr. Bailey received orders to call a hackney coach and take him home, where the merry one herself opened the door—but sadly, strangely altered! So careworn and dejected, so faltering and full of fear, so fallen, humbled, broken, that to have seen her quiet in her coffin would have been a less surprise.

"Don't be frightened," said Bailey. "There ain't nothing the matter. I've brought home Mr. Chuzzlewit." The ill-favored brute, with dress awry and sodden face and rumpled hair, sat blinking and drooping and rolling his idiotic eyes about until, becoming conscious by degrees, he recognized his wife and shook his fist at her.

"Ah!" cried Mr. Bailey, squaring his arms with a sudden emotion. "What, you're wicious, are you? Would you, though? You'd better not!"

"Pray, go away!" said Merry. "Bailey, my good boy, go home. Jonas!" she said, timidly laying her hand upon his shoulder and bending her head down over him. "Jonas!"

"Look at her!" cried Jonas, pushing her. "Look here! Look at her! You're a pretty clog to be tied to a man for life, you mewling, white-faced cat!"

With affected gaiety she gave Bailey a piece of money and again implored him to be gone. Her entreaty was so earnest that the boy had not the heart to stay there. But he stopped at the bottom of the stairs and listened.

"Hark ye!" cried Jonas, stamping his foot upon the ground. "You made me bear your pretty humors once, and ecod I'll make you bear mine now. I always promised myself I would. I married you that I might. I'll know who's master and who's slave!"

It might have softened him—indeed it might—to hear her turn a little fragment of a song he used to say he liked, trying, with a heart so full, to win him back.

"Oho!" he said. "You're deaf, are you? You don't hear me, eh? So much the better for you. I hate you." She went up to him and spoke lovingly, saying that she would defer to him in everything and would consult his wishes and obey them and they might be very happy if he would be gentle with her. He answered with an imprecation and—not with a blow? Yes. Stern truth against the base-souled villain—with a blow.

No angry cries, no loud reproaches. Even her weeping and her sobs were stifled by her clinging round him. She only said, repeating it in agony of heart, how could he, could he, could he! And lost utterance in tears.

Having provided for his younger daughter that choicest of blessings, a tender and indulgent husband, Mr. Pecksniff renewed his youth and, spreading the plumage of his own bright conscience, felt himself equal to all kinds of flights.

But, however much inclined the good man was to be jocose and playful, the gentle Cherry, stung by a sense of slight and injury, was in flat rebellion. "I must beg you, pa," she announced one day, "to provide me with a home. Place me at Mrs. Todgers's, or somewhere, on an independent footing; I will not live here. I am not quite a fool, and I am not blind. All I have got to say is I won't submit to it."

It is possible that Miss Pecksniff saw in Mrs. Todgers's a vision of enthusiastic men pining to fall, in adoration, at her feet. It is possible that Mr. Pecksniff, in his new-born juvenility, saw in the suggestion an easy means of relieving himself from an irksome charge; it was soon arranged between them that Cherry's not being well should form the excuse for her departure, to Mr. Chuzzlewit and Mary, who had come to live with them.

Old Martin Chuzzlewit had gradually undergone an important change; his character seemed to have softened down into a dull indifference for almost everyone but Mr. Pecksniff. But when Mr. Pecksniff pondered on the train of circumstances which had delivered the old gentleman into his hands for the confusion of evil doers and the triumph of a righteous nature, he always felt that Mary Graham was his stumbling block. Let the old man say what he would, Mr. Pecksniff knew he had a strong affection for her. That her unprotected state was no light burden on the old man's mind, he also knew, for Mr. Chuzzlewit had plainly told him so. "Then," said Mr. Pecksniff to himself, "what if, making sure of his approval first—he is nearly imbecile, poor gentleman—I married her!"

As to consulting the wishes of her heart in such a case, it formed no part of Mr. Pecksniff's moral code; for he knew what a good man he was and what a blessing he must be to anybody. Coming upon her as she walked alone that day, he joined her. "Take my arm, sweet girl," said Mr. Pecksniff.

Mary declined it and walked so very fast that he remonstrated. "You were loitering when I came upon you," Mr. Pecksniff said. "Why be so cruel as to hurry now? You would not shun me, would you?"

"Yes, I would," she answered, turning her glowing cheek

indignantly upon him. "You know I would. Release me, Mr. Pecksniff. Your touch is disagreeable to me."

His touch! What? That chaste patriarchal touch which Mrs. Todgers—surely a discreet lady—had endured, not only without complaint, but with apparent satisfaction! "Mary," said Mr. Pecksniff, in his tenderest tones——indeed, they were so very tender that he almost squeaked—"my soul! I love you!"

A fantastic thing, that maiden affection! She made believe to shudder. "If you force me by your superior strength," said Mary, "to be the subject of your insolence, you cannot constrain the expression of my thoughts. I hold you in the deepest abhorrence. I know your real nature and despise it. By what arts or unhappy chances you have gained your influence over Mr. Chuzzlewit, I do not know, but he shall know of this, trust me, sir."

Mr. Pecksniff raised his heavy eyelids languidly and let them fall again. "Come, come," said that good gentleman, "I am not angry, my love. Neither are you; and I will tell you why. There are two Martin Chuzzlewits, my dear; and your carrying your anger to one might have a serious effect—who knows?—upon the other. You wouldn't wish to hurt him, would you? I'd have compassion on Martin junior, do you know?" said Mr. Pecksniff, with a persuasive smile. "Yes. He don't deserve it, but I would."

She wept so bitterly now and was so much distressed that he thought it prudent to unclasp her waist and let her go.

One sultry afternoon, about a week after Miss Charity's departure for London, Mr. Pecksniff, being out walking by himself, took it into his head to stray into the church, where Tom was practicing. He entered very softly, glided into the red-curtained pew of state, and fell asleep. After a while he began to have at intervals the dreamy impression of voices and, awakening to an indolent curiosity upon the subject, opened his eyes and peeped through the curtains. Tom Pinch and Mary.

"No," Tom was saying. "No letters have ever reached me, except that one from New York. But I should like to know (if you will tell me) why you have been so very silent about Martin."

"Because I have been afraid," said Mary, "of injuring you with your employer." The gentleman in question dived.

"With Pecksniff!" rejoined Tom, with cheerful confidence. "Oh dear, he'd never think of us! He is not a spy."

"Mr. Pinch," said Mary, "you mistake him."

"No, no!" cried Tom. "*You* mistake him. But," he added, with a rapid change in his tone, "what is the matter? Don't cry. Pray tell me what it is."

"I wouldn't have told you, Mr. Pinch," said Mary, "if I could have helped it; but your delusion is so absorbing, and it is so necessary that we should be upon our guard. That person whom you think the best of men is the worst—the falsest, craftiest, meanest, cruelest, most sordid, most shameless. What is he—O

Mr. Pinch, what *is* he—who, thinking he could compass his designs the better if I were his wife, assails me with the coward's argument that, if I marry him, Martin, on whom I have brought so much misfortune, shall be restored to something of his former hopes and, if I do not, shall be plunged in deeper ruin?"

"I say," cried Tom, in great excitement, "he is a scoundrel and a villain!" When Mary had left him, the full agitation and misery of the disclosure came rushing upon Tom indeed. "O Pecksniff, Pecksniff," he cried aloud, "there is nothing I would not have given to have had you deserve my old opinion of you—nothing!" Then, locking the door, he left the church.

Mr. Pecksniff got out into the churchyard through a window and walked straight home. He was not angry, he was not vindictive, he was not cross, he was not moody, but he was grieved—he was sorely grieved. As he sat down by the side of Mr. Chuzzlewit, two tears stole down his meritorious cheeks. "My good, my worthy friend, I am deceived. Ah!" cried Mr. Pecksniff, in an agony, "deceived, Mr. Chuzzlewit, by Thomas Pinch. And, worst of all, on a subject nearly concerning *you*." After a close conference with his friend, he sent for Mr. Pinch.

Tom came—constrained and altered in his manner, downcast and dejected, visibly confused, not liking to look Pecksniff in the face. The honest man bestowed a glance on Mr. Chuzzlewit, as who should say, "You see!" and addressed himself to Tom in these terms. "Mr. Pinch, I will not dismiss you without a word of explanation. Therefore I will say to you what I have already said to Mr. Chuzzlewit. From fragments of a conversation which I overheard in the church just now, Mr. Pinch, between yourself and Miss Graham, I ascertained that you, forgetful of all ties of duty and of honor, sir, regardless of the sacred laws of hospitality to which you were pledged as an inmate of this house, have presumed to address Miss Graham with unreturned professions of attachment and proposals of love. Do you deny it, sir?"

"No, sir," replied Tom. "I do not." He saw that Mr. Pecksniff had devised this fiction as the readiest means of getting rid of him at once, and that a denial and an explanation might incense the old man more than ever against Martin and against Mary.

"We part, Mr. Pinch, at once, and are strangers from this time. I will not say," cried Mr. Pecksniff, shedding tears, "what a blow this is. It may be a comfort to you to know that I shall endeavor not to think the worse of my fellow creatures in general for what has passed between us. Farewell!"

Tom went upstairs for his things. At any other time he would have parted from his room with a pang, thinking of all he had learned there, of the many hours he had passed there, for the love of his very dreams. But there was no Pecksniff; there never had been a Pecksniff; and the unreality of Pecksniff extended itself even to the chamber to which he now said farewell.

"And how, my sweet Miss Pecksniff," said Mrs. Todgers when they met, "how is your princely pa?"

Miss Pecksniff signified (in confidence) that he contemplated the introduction of a princely ma and repeated the sentiment that she wasn't blind and wasn't quite a fool and wouldn't bear it.

Mrs. Todgers was more shocked by the intelligence than anyone could have expected. She was quite bitter. She protested, with tears in her eyes, that she loved Miss Pecksniff like a sister and felt her injuries as if they were her own.

"Your real darling sister I have not seen more than once since her marriage," said Mrs. Todgers; "and then I thought her looking poorly. But the misery we have had from that match, here among ourselves, in this house, my dear Miss Pecksniff, nobody would believe. You recollect our youngest gentleman, my dear? When the marriage took place, I thought he had taken leave of his senses, I did indeed. The clinching way in which he bit his bread and butter, the manner in which he taunted Mr. Jinkins—all combined to form a picture never to be forgotten. And now he is the meekest of men. You can almost bring the tears into his eyes by looking at him."

Towards this most unhappy Mr. Moddle, Miss Pecksniff conducted herself at first with distant haughtiness, being in no humor to be entertained with dirges in honor of her married sister. But Mr. Moddle having confided to Mrs. Todgers that "when she talks and when she smiles, I think I am looking on *Her* who is Another's," Miss Pecksniff began to speculate on the probability of its being her mission to become ultimately Mrs. Moddle. Besides, besides, he had been regarded as devoted to Merry. And he was better looking, better spoken, better tempered, better mannered than Jonas.

"You give Mr. Moddle a little encouragement, Miss Pecksniff," said Mrs. Todgers, "and he'll speak fast enough, depend upon it." Accordingly, Moddle was goaded on to ask whether Miss Pecksniff could be contented with a blighted heart; and it appearing that she could be, the dismal troth was plighted.

13

From Mr. Moddle to Eden is an easy and natural transition. Mr. Moddle, living in the atmosphere of Miss Pecksniff's love, dwelt (if he had but known it) in a terrestrial Paradise. The thriving city of Eden was also a terrestrial Paradise, upon the showing of its proprietors. Mark Tapley went up to the nearest cabin and knocked. "Neighbor," said he "—for I *am* a neighbor, though you don't know me—I've come a begging. I wish you'd come and give me your opinion of my partner."

They found Martin in the house, lying wrapped up in his blanket on the ground. He was, to all appearance, very ill indeed and shook and shivered horribly. Their neighbor pronounced his disease an aggravated kind of fever, accompanied with ague, which was very common in those parts and which he predicted would be worse tomorrow and for many more tomorrows.

With all his various duties of attendance upon Martin (who became the more exacting in his claims the worse he grew), Mark worked out of doors early and late, though, within himself, he looked on their condition as beyond all hope. "There's one good thing in this place, sir," he said to Martin, "as disposes me to be jolly— and that is, that it's a reg'lar little United States in itself. There's two or three American settlers left; and they coolly comes over one, even here, sir, as if it was the wholesomest and loveliest spot in the world. Here's one now—Hannibal Chollop."

"If this ain't Mr. Chuzzlewit, ain't it!" exclaimed the visitor. "How do *you* git along, sir?"

Martin shook his head and drew the blanket over it involuntarily; for he felt that Hannibal was going to spit.

"You need not regard me, sir," observed Mr. Chollop complacently; "I am fever proof and likewise agur."

"Mine was a more selfish motive," said Martin, looking out again. "I was afraid you were going to—"

"I can calc'late my distance, sir," returned Mr. Chollop, "to an inch." With a proof of which happy faculty he immediately favored him. "How do you like our country, sir?" he inquired.

"Not at all," was the invalid's reply.

"I am not surprised to hear you say so. It re-quires An elevation and A preparation of the intellect. You don't feel yourself at home in Eden, either?" Chollop asked Mark.

"No," said Mark. "I don't."

"You miss the imposts of your country. You miss the house dues?"

"And the houses—rather!" said Mark.

"No window dues here, sir," observed Chollop.

"And no windows to put 'em on," said Mark.

Many weeks elapsed before Martin was strong enough to move about. He was yet in a feeble and weak condition when the misfortune he had dreaded fell upon them. Mark was taken ill. "Floored for the present, sir," Mark said one morning, sinking back upon his bed "—but jolly!" And whenever Martin gave him drink or medicine or tended him in any way, the patient Mr. Tapley brightened up and cried, "I'm jolly, sir; I'm jolly!"

Now, when Martin began to think of this and to look at Mark as he lay there, never reproaching him by so much as an expression of regret, never murmuring, always trying to be manful and stanch, he began to think, how was it that this man, who had had so few advantages, was so much better than he who had had so many? It was natural for him to reflect—he had months to do it in—upon his own escape and Mark's extremity. This led him to consider which of them could be the better spared, and why. Then the curtain slowly rose a very little way, and Self, Self, Self was shown below. He made a solemn resolution that he would not resist the conviction that selfishness was in his breast and must be rooted out.

As soon as Mark was well enough to talk without fatigue, Martin consulted him upon a project he had in his mind and which a few months back he would have carried into execution without troubling anybody's head but his own. "The only hope left us," he said "is to quit this settlement for ever and get back to

England. Shall I ask Mr. Bevan for money enough to enable us by the cheapest means to reach New York, explaining that I will endeavor to repay him, even through my grandfather, immediately on our arrival in England?"

"Why, to be sure," said Mark, "he can only say no, and he may say yes. If you don't mind trying him, sir—"

"Mind!" exclaimed Martin. "I am to blame for coming here, and I would do anything to get away. If I had taken your opinion sooner, Mark, we never should have been here."

Mr. Tapley was very much surprised at this admission. "I don't know what to make of him," he thought. "I'll try him again. —Ah, sir! Dear me! You've ventured a good deal for a young lady's love!"

"I tell you what, I'm not so sure of that, Mark," was the reply. "She has sacrificed her peace of mind; she has endangered her interests very much; she can't run away from those who are jealous of her and opposed to her, as I have done. I begin to think she has more to bear than ever I have had!"

"I'm regularly defrauded," thought Mr. Tapley, with a happy face. "It's a swindle. There'll be no credit in being jolly with *him!*"

The time wore on, and at last came the answer to the letter Martin had written to Mr. Bevan, and in it a little roll of dollar notes. When the first stage of excitement was passed, each of them believed that he would surely die before the boat returned for them. But at sunrise, on an autumn day, they stood upon her deck and looked their last on Eden.

In New York again, they had the satisfaction of being received by their good friend with his own warmth and heartiness. "I am truly sorry and ashamed," said Martin, "to have begged of you. But look at us, see what we are, and judge to what we are reduced!"

"So far from claiming to have done you any service," returned Mr. Bevan, "I reproach myself with having been, un-wittingly, the original cause of your misfortunes. I no more supposed that you would do anything but be dispossessed of your idea that fortunes were so easily made here than I thought of going to Eden myself."

"The fact is, I closed with the thing in a mad and sanguine

manner," said Martin, "and the less said about it the better for me. But how shall I ever thank you for your kindness?"

"If you ever become a rich man or a powerful one," returned his friend, "you shall try to make your government more careful of its subjects when they roam abroad to live. Tell it what you know of emigration in your own case and impress upon it how much suffering may be prevented with a little pains!"

Cheerily, lads, cheerily! Anchor weighed. Ship in full sail. Her sturdy bowsprit pointing true to England. America a cloud upon the sea behind them. "If I was a painter and was called upon to paint the American Eagle," observed Mark, "I should want to draw it like a Bat, for its short-sightedness; like a Bantam, for its bragging; like a Magpie, for its honesty; like a Peacock, for its vanity; like an Ostrich, for its putting its head in the mud and thinking nobody sees it—"

"And like a Phoenix, for its power of springing from the ashes of its faults and vices and soaring up anew into the sky!" said Martin. "Well, Mark, let us hope so."

In health and fortune, prospect and resource, the two travelers came back to England poorer men than they had gone away. But it was home! Being set ashore with very little money in their pockets, they sought out a cheap tavern, where they regaled upon a smoking steak and certain flowing mugs of beer, then drew back the glowing curtain from the window and gazed blissfully into the street. Suddenly their gaze was arrested by a figure which slowly, very slowly and reflectively, passed the window at that moment.

Mr. Pecksniff—placid, calm, but proud! The landlord, too, looked after him with great respect, almost with veneration. "That, gentlemen," he observed, "is the great Mr. Pecksniff! The celebrated architect, gentlemen, who has come down here to help to lay the first stone of a new and splendid public building, for which he carried off the first premium."

Learning that the ceremony would take place at any minute, Mark and Martin hurried off to it. And when Mr. Pecksniff unrolled his plans and people gathered round to admire them, Martin was looking straight over the shoulder of the unconscious architect. He returned to Mark, boiling with rage. "This is *my* building!" he cried. "My grammar school. I invented it; I did it all. He has only put four windows in it, the villain, and spoiled it. Yet compare that fellow's situation today with ours!"

"Lord bless you, sir!" cried Mark. "What's the use? In the meantime, we have a deal to do and far to go. So sharp's the word, and Jolly!"

"You are the best master in the world, Mark," said Martin; "and I will not be a bad scholar if I can help it, I am resolved! So come! Best foot foremost, old fellow!"

It was on the morning of this very day that Mr. Nadgett had suddenly appeared before Mr. Montague's house in Pall Mall— he always made his appearance as if he had that moment come up a trap—when the clocks were striking nine. He rang the bell in a covert, underhanded way, as though it were a treasonable act, and was immediately received by the chairman. "Well, Mr. Nadgett, any news?"

"I think we have some news at last, sir. I am disposed to think it's a good case. We'll begin at the beginning and take that one first, if you please, sir," handing him a document.

The chairman had not read half a dozen lines when his face was full of grave and serious attention. "Number Two," said Mr. Nadgett, handing him another. Mr. Montague went on with Number Two and afterward with Numbers Three and Four and Five, and so on.

"You are a wonderful man, Mr. Nadgett!" he said at last, drawing a long breath. "There is a deeper impression of Somebody's Hoof here than I had expected.—I think I heard a double knock. Will you put your head out of window and tell me whether there is anybody at the door?"

Mr. Nadgett looked out and observed, "Mr. Jonas Chuzzlewit!"

"I thought so," Tigg retorted. "Remain here, Mr. Nadgett, if you please. Don't you leave us alone together. Mind you don't now!"

"Hullo!" said Jonas, when he came in. "Who's that? Oh, old what's-his-name, looking (as usual) as if he wanted to skulk up the chimney. He's afraid of me, I think."

"It's my belief," said Tigg, "that you are Poison to him. Nadgett, give me that towel!" He had as little occasion for a towel as Jonas had for a start. But Nadgett brought it quickly and, having lingered for a moment, fell back upon his old post by the fire. "You see, my dear fellow," resumed Tigg, "you are too—what's the matter with your lips? They're white!"

"I took some vinegar just now," muttered Jonas, rubbing them upon his handkerchief. "I want to have a word with you. I am not satisfied with the state of affairs."

"Not satisfied!" cried Tigg. "The money comes in well."

"The money comes in well enough," retorted Jonas, "but it don't come out well enough. I haven't sufficient power; it's all in your hands. If you should take it into your honorable head to go abroad with the bank, I don't see much to prevent you."

"I am unfortunate to find you in this humor," said Tigg, with a remarkable kind of smile; "for I was going to propose to you—for your own advantage, solely for your own advantage—that you should venture a little more with us. And to suggest that surely you have friends who would answer our purpose admirably and whom we should be delighted to receive."

"How kind of you! You'd be delighted to receive 'em, would you?" said Jonas, bantering.

"It will be very much to your advantage," answered Montague, looking steadily upon him. "It will be very much to your advantage, I assure you. Shall I tell you how?"

"I think you had better," said Jonas. "Strange things have been done in the insurance way before now."

"Chuzzlewit!" replied Montague. "We strangely happen, sometimes, to come into the knowledge of very strange events." He beckoned to Jonas to bring his chair nearer and whispered in his ear.

From red to white, from white to red again, from red to yellow, then to a cold, dull, awful, sweat-bedabbled blue—in that short whisper all these changes fell upon the face of Jonas Chuzzlewit; and when at last he laid his hand upon the whisperer's mouth, appalled, lest any syllable of what he said should reach the ears of the third person present, it was as bloodless and as heavy as the hand of Death.

"You'll not object," his companion said, "to venture further with us, Chuzzlewit, my friend?"

His pale lips faintly stammered out a no.

"Well said! That's like yourself. Do you know, I was thinking yesterday that your father-in-law would join us, if the thing were well presented to him. Shall I leave Mr. Pecksniff to you?"

"I'll try. I'll do my best."

"A thousand thanks," replied the other, clapping him upon the shoulder. "Shall we walk downstairs? Mr. Nadgett, follow us, if you please."

14

YOHO, past donkey chaises drawn aside into the ditch and empty carts with rampant horses, held by struggling carters close to the five-barred gate, until the coach had passed the narrow turning in the road. Yoho, down the pebbly dip, and through the merry water splash, and up at a canter to the level road again. Yoho! Yoho! Tom Pinch is on his way to London.

See the bright moon! High up before we know it—making the earth reflect the objects on its breast like water. Clouds too! And a mist upon the hollow! Not a dull fog that hides it, but a light, airy, gauze-like mist, which gives a new charm to the beauties it is spread before. Now Day comes leaping up. Yoho! Two stages, and the country roads are almost changed to a continuous street. Yoho! Down countless turnings, and through countless mazy ways, until an old inn yard is gained, and Tom Pinch, getting down, quite stunned and giddy, is in London!

Arriving before the great bell handle of the brass-and-copper founder's mansion, Tom gave it a gentle pull. The porter appeared.

"Pray, does Miss Pinch live here?" said Tom.

"Miss Pinch is governess here," replied the porter, ringing the house bell.

"Hullo, there!" called a footman from the doorstep. "This way, young man!"

"Oh!" said Tom, hurrying toward him. "Pray, is Miss Pinch at home?"

"She's *in*," replied the footman, as much as to say, "But if you think she has anything to do with the proprietorship of this place, you had better abandon that idea." He condescended to show Tom into a parlor. "Hany neem?"

"Say her brother, if you please," said Tom.

"Mother?" drawled the footman.

"Brother," repeated Tom, slightly raising his voice. "Dear me!" he thought, "this is very disrespectful and uncivil behavior. I hope these are new servants here and that Ruth is very differently treated." His cogitations were interrupted by the sound of voices in the adjoining room. They seemed to be engaged in high dispute or in indignant reprimand of some offender. He was wondering what domestic quarrel might have caused these sounds, when the door opened and his sister ran into his arms.

"Why, bless my soul!" said Tom, looking at her with great pride when they had tenderly embraced each other. "You are so womanly; you are so—positively, you know, you are so handsome! But what's the matter? You have been crying. What is it, dear? I'm not with Mr. Pecksniff now. I am going to try and settle myself in London; and if you are not happy here, you shall not remain."

"We will talk about it, Tom," said Ruth, giving him another kiss to pacify him. "I am afraid I cannot stay here."

"Cannot!" replied Tom. "Why, then you shall not, my love. Heyday! You are not an object of charity! Upon my word!" Tom was stopped in these exclamations by the footman, who brought a message from his master, importing that he wished to speak with him before he went.

They entered the adjoining room, where they found a middle-aged gentleman, with a pompous voice and manner, a middle-aged lady, and that eldest pupil of Miss Pinch whom Mrs. Todgers, on a previous occasion, had called a sirup and who was now weeping and sobbing spitefully. "My brother, sir," said Ruth Pinch, timidly presenting Tom.

"Oh!" cried the gentleman. "You really are Miss Pinch's brother? I am sorry to inform you that we are not at all satisfied with your sister. What are my feelings as a father when, after my desire (repeatedly expressed to Miss Pinch) that my daughter should be choice in her expressions, genteel in her deportment, as becomes her station in life, and politely distant to her inferiors in society, I find her, only this very morning, addressing Miss Pinch herself as a beggar! But for my knowing Miss Pinch to be an unprotected young person, I would have severed the connection between us at that moment and from that time."

"Bless my soul, sir," cried Tom, unable to contain himself any longer, "don't allow such considerations to influence you, pray! She is not unprotected; she is ready to depart this instant. Ruth, my dear, get your bonnet!"

"Oh, a pretty family!" cried the lady. "Oh, he's her brother! There's no doubt about that!"

"As little doubt, madam," said Tom, "as that the young lady yonder is the child of your teaching, and not my sister's. Ruth, my dear, get your bonnet on!"

"You speak with extreme impertinence, young man," observed the gentleman.

"I speak without passion, but with extreme indignation and contempt for such a course of treatment and for all who practice it," said Tom. "I will stand in your garden until my sister is ready."

It was not until they had walked some short distance that Tom was quite restored to himself by his sister's saying, in her pleasant little voice, "Where are we going, Tom?"

"Dear me!" said Tom, stopping. "I don't know. We must have some lodgings." So they walked off arm in arm; and at length, in a singular little old-fashioned house, they discovered two small bedrooms and a triangular parlor, which promised to suit them well enough. Then Tom walked out again to narrate all these marvelous occurrences to his friend John Westlock.

He was about to inquire the way to Furnival's Inn, where John lived, when a well-known voice behind him cried, "Mr. Pinch!" It was Charity. "I hope you have run away," said Miss Pecksniff. "Won't you walk in?"

"You live here, then?" said Tom.

"Yes," returned Miss Pecksniff, pointing with her parasol to Todgers's; "I reside with this lady *at present*." Simpering very much when Tom asked her if she knew the way to Furnival's Inn, she at length found courage to reply, "A gentleman who is a friend of mine, or at least who is not exactly a friend so much as a sort of acquaintance—oh, upon my word, I hardly know what I say, Mr. Pinch; you mustn't suppose there is any engagement between us, or at least, if there is, that it is at all a settled thing as yet—is going to Furnival's Inn immediately, I believe, and I am sure he would be very glad to accompany you. You had better walk in. You will very likely find my sister Merry here," she said, preceding him into the house. "Augustus, my child, where are you?" With these words she screamed her way out of the parlor, calling on Augustus Moddle to appear, and left Tom Pinch alone with her sister.

If she had always been his kindest friend, if she had lightened every moment of those many years and had ever spared and never wounded him, his honest heart could not have swelled before her with a deeper pity or a purer freedom from all base remembrance than it did then.

"If you should talk with old Mr. Chuzzlewit at any time," Mercy said, when she had greeted him, "will you promise me to tell him that you saw me here and that I said I bore in mind the time we talked together in the churchyard? Many times since then, when I have wished I had been carried there before that day, I have recalled his words. Tell him," said Mercy, "that I sent the message, not for myself, but that he might be more forbearing and more patient and more trustful to some other person, in some other time of need. Tell him that, if he could know how my heart trembled in the balance that day and what a very little would have turned the scale, his own would bleed with pity for me." Touched to the quick, Tom took her hand and said, or meant to say, some words of consolation.

When she had gone, Miss Pecksniff entered with her friend.

"Mr. Thomas Pinch," said Charity, performing the ceremony of introduction with evident pride, "Mr. Moddle. My sister has gone?"

"She's greatly altered since she's been Anoth—since she's been married," observed Moddle.

"My dear Augustus," said Miss Pecksniff, in a low voice, "I verily believe you have said that fifty thousand times in my hearing. What a Prose you are!" This was succeeded by some trifling love passages, which appeared to originate with, if not to be wholly carried on by, Miss Pecksniff. At any rate, Mr. Moddle was much slower in his responses than is customary with young lovers and exhibited a lowness of spirits which was quite oppressive.

He did not improve at all when Tom and he were in the streets but sighed so dismally that it was dreadful to hear him. As a means of cheering him up, Tom told him that he wished him joy. "Joy!" cried Moddle. "Ha, ha!" Tom inferred from this and other expressions of the same nature that he was jealous. Therefore, he allowed him to take his own course, which was such a gloomy one that Tom felt a load removed from his mind when they parted company at the gate of Furnival's Inn, where John Westlock received him with all his old friendship and kindness.

Pleasant little Ruth! Cheerful, tidy, bustling, quiet little Ruth! No doll's house ever yielded greater delight to its young mistress than little Ruth derived from her glorious dominion over the triangular parlor and the two small bedrooms. She was busily engaged in the manufacture of a beefsteak pudding the next day, when suddenly she started and turned very red. Following her eyes, Tom saw John Westlock in the room.

"I beg your pardon," said John "—your sister's pardon especially—but I met your landlord at the street door, who requested me to enter here." He held out his hand to Miss Pinch, who couldn't take it by reason of the flour and paste upon her own, and this had the best effect in the world; for neither of them could help laughing, and so they both found themselves on easy terms immediately.

"How is it, Tom, that you never told me you had friends in London?" John asked presently. "This morning a grave, business-like, sedate-looking stranger came to see me and amazed me by saying, 'I believe you are acquainted, sir, with Mr. Thomas Pinch?' I told him I was. Did I know where you were at present residing? Yes. He had casually heard, in a roundabout way, that you had left your situation with Mr. Pecksniff. Did you want another? Yes, you did. 'Then,' said he, 'I think I can accommodate him.' Of course I begged him," pursued John Westlock, glancing at Tom's sister, who was not less eager in her interest than Tom himself, "to proceed, and said that I would undertake to see you immediately. He went on to tell me that a friend of his was in want of a kind of secretary and librarian and that although the salary was small, being only a hundred pounds a year, there the post was."

"Good gracious me!" cried Tom. "A hundred pounds a year! My dear John! Ruth, my love! A hundred pounds a year!"

"But the strangest part of the story," resumed John Westlock, "is that he doesn't know Tom and isn't at liberty to enter into any explanations!"

Tom observed that this was the most unaccountable circumstance he had ever heard of in his life.

"Unaccountable?" his friend repeated. "I declare I half suspected him to be a supernatural visitor until he handed me this card."

"Mr. Fips," said Tom, reading it aloud, "Austin Friars."

"Tom," said Ruth, after a little hesitation, "perhaps Mr. Westlock, in his friendship for you, knows more of this than he chooses to tell."

"No, indeed!" cried John eargerly. "It is not so, I assure you. I wish it were."

Tom, being in a great flutter, wished to start for Austin Friars instantly; and there, in a very dark passage, they found a little blear-eyed glass door with "Mr. Fips" painted on it. "Walk in," said Mr. Fips. He looked at Tom Pinch curiously and asked if Mr. Pinch thought the offer worth his while.

"I think it a piece of great good fortune, sir," said Tom. "I am exceedingly obliged to the gentleman with whom I am to engage and whose confidence I shall endeavor to deserve."

"My friend is not at this present moment," said Mr. Fips, "in town; but with reference to your duties I can set you going, and with reference to your salary I can pay it—weekly. The place is in the Temple."

Thither they accordingly repaired, to an apartment covered thick with dust, where piles of books were scattered on the floor. "Before anything else can be done, we must have them put in order, catalogued, and ranged upon the bookshelves, Mr. Pinch. That will do to begin with, I think, sir," said Mr. Fips.

"An occupation full of interest for me, I assure you," Tom said. "It will occupy me, perhaps, until Mr.—I forgot that you had not mentioned the gentleman's name."

"Oh!" cried Mr. Fips, pulling on his glove, "didn't I? No, by the bye, I don't think I did. Ah! I dare say he'll be here soon. You won't forget to shut the door?" And Mr. Fips walked coolly out.

"Why, he's gone!" cried Tom.

"And what's more, Tom," said John Westlock, "he is evidently not coming back again; so here you are, installed."

There was a ghostly air about these uninhabited chambers in

the Temple, and attending every circumstance of Tom's employment there, which had a strange charm in it. Though the books
were never so interesting, and never so full of novelty to Tom, they
could not so enchain him, in those mysterious chambers, as to
render him unconscious for a moment of one recurring, never-
failing source of speculation. This employer—would he come today, and what would he be like?

But now a circumstance occurred which helped to divert
Tom's thoughts from even this mystery. The way it came about was
this. Having always been an early riser, it was his habit to take a
long walk before going to the Temple; and he became a great
frequenter of the market places, bridges, quays, and especially
the steamboat wharves. In most of these morning excursions, Ruth
accompanied him; and as their landlord was generally up and
away at his business (whatever that might be, no one seemed to
know) at a very early hour, the habits of the people of the house
in which they lodged corresponded with their own.

On one particular occasion, Tom, with Ruth upon his arm,
stood looking down from the wharf at the steamboats, as nearly
regardless as it was in the nature of flesh and blood to be of an
elderly lady behind him, who had brought a large umbrella with
her, when she gave him such a poke with it that he could not
refrain from turning round.

The owner of the umbrella was struggling on tiptoe, with a
countenance expressive of violent animosity, to look down upon
the steamboats. She had been grievously knocked about; so,
instead of pursuing the altercation, Tom civilly inquired what
boat she wanted to go on board of.

"I suppose," returned Mrs. Gamp (for it was no other than that
experienced practitioner), "as nobody but yourself can want to
look at a steam package without wanting to go a boarding of it,
can they? Booby!"

"What boat did you want?" asked Ruth.

"The Ankworks package," Mrs. Gamp replied. "I will not
deceive you, my sweet; why should I?"

"That is the Antwerp packet in the middle," said Ruth.

Mrs. Gamp leaned her chin upon the cool iron and groaned.
"I wouldn't," said Mrs. Gamp, "I wouldn't be a man and have

such a think upon my mind—! There is a dear young creetur a comin' down this mornin' to that very package, which is no more fit to trust herself to sea than nothin' is! Them Confugion steamers has done more to throw us out of our reg'lar work and bring ewents on at times when nobody counted on 'em (especially them screeching railroad ones) than all the other frights that ever was took. I have heerd of one young man, a guard upon a railway only three year opened—well does Mrs. Harris know him, which, indeed, he is her own relation by her sister's marriage with a master sawyer—as is godfather at this present time to six and twenty blessed little strangers, equally unexpected, and all on 'em named after the Ingeins as was the cause.—There she identically goes! Poor sweet young creetur, there she goes, like a lamb to the sacrifige. If there's any illness when that wessel gets to sea," said Mrs. Gamp prophetically, "it's murder, and I'm the witness for the persecution."

"Do you mean the lady who is with that man wrapped up from head to foot in a large cloak, so that his face is almost hidden?" asked Ruth. "He seems to be hasty with her."

At this moment a hand upon his sleeve caused Tom to look round and find his landlord, to his great surprise. "I beg your pardon, Mr. Pinch," he said in his ear. "Do you see a gentleman muffled up from head to foot down yonder? Will you do me a kindness, sir, a great kindness? Will you put that letter in his hand?"

To hesitate in the performance of a good-natured office was not in Tom's way. He ran down the steps with all the expedition he could make. But as he advanced to give the letter, what was his astonishment to find in the object of his search the man with whom he had had the conflict in the field—poor Mercy's husband, Jonas!

"I was asked to give you this letter," said Tom.

Jonas took the letter and opened it. The contents were evidently very brief, but they struck upon him like a stone from a sling. He reeled back as he read. When a hoarse voice inquired if there was anyone to go ashore, "Yes," cried Jonas, "I—I am coming. Give me time. Where's that woman? Come back here!" He dragged, rather than led her forth, pale and frightened; and he turned, even in the madness of his hurry, and scowling darkly back at Tom shook his clenched hand at him.

Suddenly a gentleman of foreign appearance, with a black moustache and whiskers, saluted Jonas Chuzzlewit by name. "Chuzzlewit, my good fellow," said Mr. Montague, raising his hat in compliment to Mrs. Chuzzlewit, "I ask your pardon twenty thousand times. I am most unwilling to interfere between you and a domestic trip of this nature, but the bee hive, my dear friend, the bee hive—"

"Your great discovery," Jonas countered, sullenly, "is it known to anybody else?"

"No!" said Montague, without the smallest hesitation. "What would it be worth, do you think, unless I had the keeping of it?"

Now, for the first time, Jonas looked at him. After a pause, he put out his hand, and said, with a laugh, "Come! Make things easy to me, and I'm yours. Come with me to Pecksniff. We must make a dash—go down in state, and carry documents. As I can't take your lodgings or your dinners down, I must take you. Will you come tonight?"

"I will," said Montague, "if that's your opinion." And they shook hands upon it.

They got into a handsome cabriolet, which was waiting for them, and drove away. Merry too was gone now; and Tom and his sister were left to walk away and wonder.

15

IT was one of those hot, silent nights when people sit at windows listening for the thunder which they know will shortly break. It was very dark; and now, a very few large drops of rain began to fall, and thunder rumbled in the distance. Jonas sat in a corner of the carriage, with a bottle resting on his knee and gripped as tightly in his hand as if he would have ground its neck to powder if he could. Louder and louder the deep thunder rolled, as through the myriad halls of some vast temple in the sky; fiercer and brighter became the lightning; more and more heavily the rain poured down.

The lightning, being very crooked and very dazzling, may have presented or assisted a curious optical illusion, which suddenly rose before the startled eyes of Montague in the carriage and as rapidly disappeared. He thought he saw Jonas with his hand lifted and the bottle clenched in it like a hammer, making as if he would aim a blow at his head. At the same time he observed (or so he believed) an expression in his face which might have rendered a wolf a less terrible companion.

He uttered an involuntary exclamation. But it could hardly have been as he supposed, for he now saw that his companion sat reclining in his corner as before. "I wish we had never started on this journey. This is not," said Montague, speaking in a voice that betrayed his agitation, "this is not a night to travel in."

Arrived at Salisbury, they went to the inn. After examining his chamber and looking under the bed and in the cupboards, Montague double locked the door by which he had entered and retired to rest. There was another door in the room, but it was locked on the outer side, and with what place it communicated he knew not.

His fears or evil conscience reproduced this door in all his dreams. He dreamed that a dreadful secret was connected with it—a secret which he knew and yet did not know; for although he was heavily responsible for it and a party to it, he was harassed even in his vision by a distracting uncertainty in reference to its import. Incoherently entwined with this dream was another which represented it as the hiding place of an enemy, a shadow, a phantom and made it the business of his life to keep the terrible creature closed up and prevent it from forcing its way in upon him. With this view, Nadgett and he and a strange man with a bloody smear upon his head worked with iron plates and nails to make the door secure. But his greatest terror was when the man with the bloody smear demanded of him if he knew the creature's name and said that he would whisper it. Looking at the speaker's lips, he saw that they formed the letter "J"; and, crying out aloud that the secret was discovered, he awoke.

Awoke to find Jonas standing at his bedside watching him and that very door wide open! As their eyes met, Jonas retreated a few paces, and Montague sprang out of bed. "What are you doing here?" he stammered.

"My room is on the other side of that door," said Jonas. "I thought it led into a passage and was coming out to order breakfast. There's—there's no bell in my room." When he had retired, whistling, Montague dragged a table against the door and sat

down to collect himself, as if his dreams still had some influence upon his mind.

"An evil journey," he repeated several times; "an evil journey. But I'll travel home alone. I'll have no more of this!"

On the night of the storm, Mrs. Lupin, hostess of the Blue Dragon, sat by herself in her little bar. Her solitary condition or the bad weather, or both united, made Mrs. Lupin thoughtful, not to say sorrowful. "Dear me! Ah, dear, dear me!" she was saying, when a traveler came in, wrapped up to the eyes in a rough blue sailor's coat, who said, rather gruffly, "Pint of the best old beer here."

"There's a fire in the kitchen," said Mrs. Lupin, "and very good company there. Hadn't you better go and dry yourself?"

"No, thankee," said the man. In the act of lifting the tankard, he added, "You've got a sort of relation of mine here, ma'am, a young man of the name of Tapley."

This was touching Mrs. Lupin on a tender point. She turned to trim the candle on the chimney piece and said, with her back toward the traveler, "Nobody should be made more welcome at the Dragon, master, than any one who brought me news of Mark. But it's many and many a long day since he left here and England. And whether he's alive or dead, poor fellow, Heaven above us only knows!" She shook her head, and her voice trembled.

"Where did he go, ma'am?" asked the traveler, in a gentler voice.

"He went," said Mrs. Lupin, with increased distress, "to America. How could he! Why didn't he go to some of those countries where the savages eat each other fairly, and give an equal chance to every one?" Quite subdued, Mrs. Lupin sobbed and was retiring to a chair to give her grief free vent, when the traveler caught her in his arms, and she uttered a glad cry of recognition.

"Yes, I will!" cried Mark. "Another—one more—twenty more! You didn't know me in that coat? I thought you would have known me anywheres! Ten more! Lord bless you, what a treat it is to see you! One more! Well, I never was so jolly. Just a few more, on account of there not being any credit in it!"

When Mr. Tapley stopped in these calculations in simple addition, he did it, not because he was at all tired of the exercise, but because he was out of breath. The pause reminded him of other duties. "Mr. Martin Chuzzlewit's outside," he said. "I'll bring him in now to hear all the news."

"Little did I ever think," said Mrs. Lupin, adjusting her cap and laughing heartily, when Martin had hugged her, "that any of Mr. Pecksniff's young gentlemen would ever make so free as you, Mr. Martin! Still less that I should ever have the changes to relate that I shall have to tell you of!"

"And now," said Mark, when she had related, as the common talk of the neighborhood, what entire possession Mr. Pecksniff had obtained over old Mr. Chuzzlewit, "what will you do, sir? If you started wrong with your grandfather (which, you'll excuse my taking the liberty of saying, appears to have been the case), up with you, sir, and tell him so, and make an appeal to his affections."

"You are right, Mark," said Martin. "Right or wrong, it shall be done." Accordingly, Martin knocked at Mr. Pecksniff's door next morning and, without a word of notice or announcement, stood in the presence of his grandfather. Mr. Pecksniff also was in the room; and Mary. In the swift instant of their mutual recognition, Martin saw the old man hide his face in his hands.

It smote him to the heart. He hurriedly advanced to seize the old man's hand in his, when Mr. Pecksniff interposed himself between them.

"No, young man!" said Mr. Pecksniff, striking himself upon the breast and stretching out his other arm toward his guest, as if it were a wing to shelter him. "No, sir; none of that. Strike here, sir, here! Launch your arrows at Me, sir, if you'll have the goodness, not at Him!"

"Grandfather," cried Martin, "hear me! I implore you, let me speak!"

"Would you, sir? Would you?" said Mr. Pecksniff, dodging about, so as to keep himself always between them.

"Pecksniff," said the old man, in a feeble voice, "calm yourself. Be quiet." He looked steadily at his grandson. "And that," he said, "is he. Say what you wish to say, but come no nearer."

"Grandfather!" said Martin, with great earnestness, "from a painful journey, from a hard life, from a sickbed, from privation and distress, from gloom and disappointment, from almost hopelessness and despair, I have come back to you. Upon that subject," glancing at Mary, "which first occasioned a division between us, my mind and heart are incapable of change. But that I might have trusted to your love, if I had thrown myself manfully upon it; that I might have won you over with ease, if I had been more yielding and more considerate; that I should have best remembered myself in forgetting myself and recollecting you—reflection, solitude, and misery have taught me. Do not for one fault, however thankless, quite reject me!"

As he ceased, the gray head of the old man dropped again, and he concealed his face behind his outspread fingers. "My dear sir," cried Mr. Pecksniff, bending over him, "you must not give way to this. Rouse yourself. Think," said Mr. Pecksniff, "think of Me, my friend. Shall I give expression to your thoughts?"

"Yes," said old Martin, leaning back in his chair and looking at him, half in vacancy and half in admiration, as if he were fascinated by the man. "Speak for me, Pecksniff. Thank you. You are true to me. Thank you!"

"Young man," said Mr. Pecksniff, "blush if you can; begone without a blush if you can't."

Martin looked as steadily at his grandfather as if there had been a dead silence all this time. The old man looked no less steadily at Mr. Pecksniff. "You have nothing more to say?" he inquired, laying his hand with unusual earnestness on Mr. Pecksniff's sleeve. "I will oppose nothing that you ask of me."

The tears rose in abundance to Mr. Pecksniff's eyes, but he said, with great emotion, that he had no other observation whatever to make.

For a few moments the old man sat looking at him, with that blank and motionless expression which is not uncommon in the faces of those whose faculties are on the wane, in age. Then he walked toward the door on Mr. Pecksniff's arm. "You have heard him. Go away," he said to Martin. "Go!"

Mr. Pecksniff murmured certain cheering expressions of sympathy and encouragement as they retired; and Martin caught the innocent cause of all in his embrace and pressed her to his heart. A parting word that he would write from London, whither they would go at once, and Mark and he stood on the outside of the Pecksniffian halls.

Coming in sight of the Dragon, they saw a traveling carriage at the door, in which Mrs. Lupin showed them a portmanteau with the name of "Chuzzlewit" upon it. "Miss Pecksniff's husband that was," she explained.

"Upon my word! Miss Pecksniff's husband travels gaily!" observed Martin.

He was at that moment being clasped in the paternal arms of Mr. Pecksniff. "Jonas! My child! She is well? There is nothing the matter?"

"What, you're at it again, are you?" replied his son-in-law. "Even with me? Get away with you, will you?"

"Tell me she is well then," said Mr. Pecksniff. "You have come to stay?"

"No. I've got a friend with me," said Jonas.

"Bring your friend!" cried Mr. Pecksniff, in a gush of hospitality. "Bring any number of your friends!"

"This ain't the sort of man to be brought," said Jonas contemptuously. "I think I see myself 'bringing' him to your house for a treat! Thankee all the same; but he's a little too near the top o' the tree for that, Pecksniff. I'll tell you what you may do if you like, though; you may come and dine with us at the Dragon. We were forced to come down to Salisbury last night on some business, and I got him to bring me over here this morning in his carriage."

"Some young nobleman who has been borrowing money of you at good interest, eh?" said Mr. Pecksniff, shaking his forefinger facetiously. "I shall be delighted to know the gay sprig."

"Borrowing!" echoed Jonas. "Borrowing! When you're a twentieth part as rich as he is, you may shut up shop! Why, since I was lucky enough to get a share in the insurance office that he's president of, I've made—never mind what I've made." Inch by inch, and bit by bit, Jonas rather allowed the dazzling prospects of the Anglo-Bengalee establishment to escape him than paraded them before his greedy listener.

"Really, my dear Jonas," cried Mr. Pecksniff, with much warmth, "a gentleman like this should receive some attention." As Jonas made no attempt to conciliate him but, on the contrary, was more boorish and rude to him than usual, Mr. Pecksniff, so far from suspecting his real design, laid himself out to be attacked to advantage. At dinner time he presented himself in such a state of suavity, benevolence, cheerfulness, politeness, and cordiality as even he had perhaps never attained before.

They were as frank and merry as three honest men could be. "Money cannot be turned and turned again quickly enough in the ordinary course, Mr. Pecksniff," Mr. Montague cried frankly. "There is nothing like building our fortunes on the weaknesses of mankind. *We* do it!" And as often as he repeated this sentiment, just as often Mr. Pecksniff repeated, "Oh, fie! Oh, fie, for shame! I am sure you don't. How *can* you, you know?" laying a greater stress each time on those last words.

Books, papers, statements, tables, calculations of various kinds were soon spread out before him; and as they were all framed with one object, it is not surprising that they should all have tended to one end, which was that Mr. Pecksniff agreed to become the last partner and proprietor in the Anglo-Bengalee and made an appointment to dine with Mr. Montague at Salisbury on the next day but one, then and there to complete the negotiation.

"You mean to wait at Salisbury over the day after tomorrow, do you, then?" said Jonas, when Mr. Pecksniff had departed.

"You heard our appointment," returned Montague. "If you wish to go home, I can manage Mr. Pecksniff."—"This brings about," he thought with relief, "what I wanted. I shall travel home alone."

16

THERE was a little plot between Tom and his sister that Tom should always come out of the Temple by one way, and that was past the fountain; and if Ruth had come to meet him, there he would see her. Now, either she was a little too soon, on the afternoon of which this history treats, or Tom was a little too late—no Tom was there. Well! But was anybody else there that she blushed so deeply, after looking round, and tripped off down the steps with such unusual expedition? Why, the fact is that Mr. Westlock was passing at that moment. (Merrily the tiny fountain played, and merrily the dimples sparkled on its sunny face.) John Westlock hurried after her. Oh, foolish, panting, timid little heart, why did she feign to be unconscious of his coming? Why wish herself so far away, yet be so flutteringly happy there?

"What an extraordinary meeting!" said Tom, when he, in turn, appeared. "I should never have dreamed of seeing you two together here."

"Quite accidental," John was heard to murmur. "But I have a proposition to make. It is that you and your sister—if she will so far honor a poor bachelor's dwelling—give me a great pleasure and come and dine with me." John was very pathetic on the subject of his dreary life and the deplorable makeshifts it involved. It was a wretched life, he said—a miserable life.

"Well," said Tom, when they had dined sumptuously together, "I don't know where you can go, John, to be more comfortable— that's all I can say. What do *you* say, Ruth?" Ruth trifled with the cherries on her plate and said that she thought Mr. Westlock ought to be quite happy and that she had no doubt he was. Ah, foolish, panting, frightened little heart, how timidly she said it! "But you are forgetting what you had to tell, Tom—what occurred this morning," she added in the same breath.

On Tom's relating what had passed upon the wharf (with which the reader is already acquainted), his friend took a great interest in the narrative. "It is quite clear to me," he said, "that whatever the business is there is little good in it; and it is so desirable for you to disentangle yourself from any appearance of willful connection with it that I would counsel you to see Mr. Jonas Chuzzlewit and wash your hands of it by a plain statement of the facts. I have a misgiving that there is something dark at work here, Tom. I will tell you why, at another time—when I have made an inquiry or two myself." All this sounded very mysterious to Tom Pinch. But he resolved to follow his friend's advice.

He and Ruth were, accordingly, passing through a street in the City the next day, when Tom pointed to two persons who were looking at the window of a large furniture warehouse. "Hush!" Tom whispered. "Miss Pecksniff and the young gentleman to whom she is going to be married."

"Why does he look as if he was going to be buried, Tom?" inquired his little sister.

Miss Pecksniff, indeed, had quite the air of having taken the unhappy Moddle captive and brought him up to the contemplation of the furniture like a lamb to the altar. But when she became conscious of the observation of Tom Pinch and his sister, she glanced about her, as if for some convenient means of sinking into the earth.

"Upon my word, I—there never was such a—the indelicacy of meeting any gentleman under such circumstances! Mr. Augustus Moddle, Miss Pinch!" Miss Pecksniff was quite gracious to Miss Pinch in this triumphant introduction—exceedingly gracious— and offered to accompany them to her sister's house.

"Of course, my love," she said, linking her arm in Ruth's, "it would be useless for me to disguise, after what you have seen, that I am about to be united to Mr. Moddle. I am curious to know whether you have observed that he is of a rather melancholy turn?"

Ruth acknowledged that he had impressed her at first sight as looking "rather low."

"No, really?" said Miss Pecksniff. "Well, that is quite remarkable! Everybody says the same. My dear, I shouldn't wish it to be known, but I don't mind mentioning it to you, having known your brother for so many years—I refused Augustus three times;

and he has never recovered the effect of that cruelty. Let me be a warning to you. If you ever feel toward a person as I really felt toward him at the very time when I was driving him to distraction, let that feeling find expression, if that person throws himself at your feet as Augustus Moddle did at mine."

Arrived at Mrs. Jonas Chuzzlewit's, she led the way into the house. "Merry, my darling!" said the fair Miss Pecksniff, opening the door of the usual sitting room. "Here are Mr. Pinch and his sister come to see you! How do you do, Mrs. Gamp? And how do you do, Mr. Chuffey, though it's of no use asking you the question, I am well aware. Augustus, my sweet pet, bring me a chair."

It is to be hoped, for the general cheerfulness of mankind, that such a doleful little pet was never seen as Mr. Moddle looked when he complied. But the ecstasies of Mrs. Gamp were sufficient to have furnished forth a score of young lovers, and they were chiefly awakened by the sight of Tom Pinch and his sister. "To think as I should see that smilin'est and sweetest face which me and another friend of mine, which her name, I'll not deceive you, Mrs. Chuzzlewit, is Harris, took notige of among the packages down London Bridge, in this promiscuous place, is a surprige in-deed!" With these words, the worthy woman, who appeared to have dropped in as a delicate little attention (her patient at the Bull having recovered), crossed to Mr. Chuffey. "Rouge yourself, and look up!" she said.

"I know I'm in the way," cried the old man, "but I've nowhere else to go to. Where is she?" Merry went to him. "Ah!" he said, patting her on the cheek. "Here she is! She's never hard on poor old Chuffey."

As she took her seat upon a low chair by the old man's side, Merry looked up once at Tom, as if to say, "You see how misery has changed me. I can feel for a dependent *now*." Suddenly the old man cried out, "Who's dead upstairs?"

"No one," said Merry. "We're all here."

"All here!" cried the old man. "All here! Where is he then— my old master, Mr. Chuzzlewit, who had the only son? There's someone dead or dying, and I want to know who it is. Foul play!" he whispered.

"Why, highty-tighty, sir!" cried Mrs. Gamp. "Is these your manners?" She took him by the collar of his coat and gave him some dozen or two of hearty shakes backward and forward in his chair, that exercise being considered by the disciples of the Prig school of nursing (who are very numerous among professional ladies) as exceedingly conducive to repose and highly beneficial to the performance of the nervous functions. Its effect in this instance was to render the patient so giddy that he could say nothing more, which Mrs. Gamp regarded as the triumph of her art.

"There!" she said, loosening the old man's cravat, in consequence of his being rather black in the face after this scientific treatment. "Now, I hope you're easy in your mind. If you should turn at all faint, we can soon revive you, sir, I promige you. Bite a person's thumbs, or turn their fingers the wrong way," said Mrs. Gamp, smiling with the consciousness of at once imparting pleasure and instruction to her auditors, "and they comes to wonderful, Lord bless you!"

As this excellent woman had been formally entrusted with the care of Mr. Chuffey on a previous occasion, neither Tom Pinch nor anybody else had the resolution to interfere; but Tom now rose to go. "I will write to your husband," he said to Merry, "and explain to him, as I would have done if I had met him here, that if he has sustained any inconvenience through my means it is not my fault—a postman not being more innocent of the news he brings than I was when I handed him that letter on the boat."

"I thank you," said Merry. "It may do some good." At that moment a key was heard in the lock. It was Jonas, Merry said timidly.

The instant he presented himself, Jonas grasped a chair as if he would have felled Tom to the ground with it. "You have no cause to be violent, sir," said Tom. "I wish you to understand that I am no party to the contents of the letter I gave you; that I had it from—"

If Nadgett's name could have passed his lips, if Jonas could have learned what unsuspected spy there was upon him—he would have been saved from the commission of a guilty deed, then drawing on toward its black accomplishment. But the fatality was of his own working; the pit was of his own digging; the gloom that gathered round him was the shadow of his own life. Merry ran between them, crying to Tom for the love of Heaven to leave the house.

"Listen to me," said Jonas, when he had gone. "If you don't obey exactly what I order, you'll repent it. I have been traveling day and night and am tired. Put my supper in the little off room below, and have the truckle bed made. I shall sleep there tonight and maybe tomorrow; if I can sleep all day tomorrow, so much the better. Keep the house quiet, and don't call me. Mind! Don't call me."

He was brooding in his chair when Mrs. Gamp came in to tell him the little room was ready. "How is he now, sir?" she said, going up to Mr. Chuffey. "The creetur's head's so hot, you might 'eat a flat iron at it. And no wonder, I am sure, considerin' the things he said!"

"Said!" cried Jonas. "What did he say?"

Turning up her eyes, Mrs. Gamp replied in a faint voice, "The awfullest things, Mr. Chuzzlewit, as ever I heerd! Who's lyin' dead upstairs, and where was Mr. Chuzzlewit as had the only son—"

"Why, the old fool's mad!" cried Jonas, much disturbed.

"That's my opinion, sir," said Mrs. Gamp, "and I will not deceive you. I believe as Mr. Chuffey, sir, rekwires attention."

"Could you—could you take care of such an idiot now?" asked Jonas.

"Me and a friend of mine, one off, one on, could do it," replied the nurse. "Me and Betsey Prig, sir, would undertake Mr. Chuffey reasonable and give every satigefaction."

Leaving Mrs. Gamp in the act of producing some of the more remarkable opinions of the celebrated Mrs. Harris, Jonas descended to the little room and locked it. It was now growing dark. As the gloom of evening, deepening into night, came on, another dark shade emerging from within him seemed to overspread his face and slowly change it—slowly, slowly; darker and darker—until it was black within him and without.

The room was on the ground floor and had a door opening into an alley which had an outlet in a neighboring street. He put the key in the lock and turned it. The door resisted, then came stiffly open. He looked out, passed out, locked it after him. All was clear and quiet as he fled away. . . .

At sunset the next day two men, riding in a gig, came out of Salisbury by a road not much frequented. It was the day on which Mr. Pecksniff had agreed to dine with Montague. He was now going home, and his host was riding with him for a short distance, meaning to return by a pleasant track through some fields. Jonas knew their plans. He had hung about the inn yard while they were at dinner.

When his new partner had disappeared, Montague sat down on a stile with looks so altered that he might have grown ten years older in the meantime. The effort of sustaining his difficult part before his late companion had fatigued him, perhaps; or it may be (as it *has* been) that a shadowy veil was dropping round him, closing out all thoughts but the presentiment and vague fore-knowledge of impending doom. He rose up shivering from his seat and hastily resumed his walk, then checked himself, undecided whether to pursue the footpath, which was lonely and retired, or to go back by the road. He took the footpath.

As evening fell upon the wood, he entered it. Moving here and there a bramble which stretched across his path, he slowly disappeared. At intervals a narrow opening showed him passing on; then he was seen no more. Never more beheld by mortal eye—one man excepted. That man, parting the leaves and branches on the other side near where the path emerged again, came leaping out soon afterward. What had he left within the wood that he sprang out of it as if it were a hell?

The body of a murdered man. In one thick, solitary spot, it lay among last year's leaves just as it had fallen headlong down. . . .

The passageway near his house was empty when the murderer's face looked into it. He stole to his door on tiptoe, as if he dreaded to disturb his own imaginary rest. He went in and went to bed.

The morning advanced. There were footsteps in the house. He tried to call out more than once, but his mouth was dry. At last he cried, "Who's there?"

It was his wife.

"Did—did no one knock at my door yesterday?" he faltered. "Something disturbed me; but unless you had knocked the door down, you would have got no notice."

"No one," she replied. "Mr. Nadgett wanted to see you, but I told him you had requested not to be disturbed. As I was opening my window I saw him passing through the street this morning very early; but he hasn't been again."

In his secret dread of meeting the household for the first time, after what he had done, Jonas lingered at the door on slight pretexts, that they might see him without looking on his face. But whatsoever guard he kept upon himself, he could not help listening, and showing that he listened. For he knew it must come; and his present punishment, and torture, and distraction were—to listen for its coming. Hush!

17

TOM PINCH and Ruth were sitting at breakfast that morning when a knock at the door ushered in two unexpected visitors. "Good gracious me!" cried Tom. "What a surprise this is! My sister, Martin. Mr. Chuzzlewit, my love. Mark Tapley from the Dragon, my dear. Sit down, sit down. How *are* you? Lord bless me!" When he had somewhat recovered from his excitement, he asked what Martin's prospects were.

"No longer to make your fortune, Tom," said Martin, "but to try to live. If you will give me the benefit of your advice, I may succeed better."

"Why, of course," cried Tom. "But you shall have better advice than mine. You shall consult John Westlock. We'll go there immediately."

John Westlock was at home but, strange to say, was rather embarrassed to see them and, when Tom was about to go into the room where he was breakfasting, said he had a stranger there. "But the matter on which I am engaged," he added to Martin, "relates to a member of your family and is of a serious nature." Tom accordingly left them together, and John related all the circumstances connected with his having presided over the illness and slow recovery of the patient at the Bull, whom he then introduced to Martin as Mr. Lewsome. "The short statement that I wish you to hear from his own lips, Mr. Chuzzlewit," John pursued, "he made to me for the first time yesterday and repeated to me this morning."

Mr. Lewsome said in a low, weak, hollow voice, "What relation was Mr. Anthony Chuzzlewit, who—"

"Who died—to me?" said Martin. "He was my grandfather's brother."

"I fear he was made away with—murdered!"

"My God!" said Martin. "By whom?"

Lewsome looked up in his face and, casting down his eyes again, replied, "I fear, by me. Not by my act, but by my means. I was bred a surgeon. Jonas Chuzzlewit is the principal in this deed."

"What do you mean?" demanded Martin sternly. "Do you know he is the son of the old man of whom you have spoken?"

"I have reason to know it, for I have often heard him wish his old father dead. He was in the habit of doing so at a place of meeting we had—three or four of us—to drink and game. He generally won. Whether or no, he lent money at interest to those who lost; and in this way came to be the master of us. One night when I was alone with him he said that he wanted me to get him some of two sorts of drug, one that was instantaneous in effect, one that was slow and not suspicious in appearance. He said 'drugs' and never used any other word. Neither did I. I asked him what he wanted the drugs for. He said for no harm; to physic cats; what did it matter to me? He would forgive me a small debt and pay me five pounds. On his saying I was a fool to think he should ever use them for any harm, I gave him the drugs. We have never met since. I only know that the poor old father died soon afterward, just as he would have died from this cause, and that I have undergone, and suffer now, intolerable misery."

Martin was so amazed, so shocked and confounded by what he had heard that it was some time before he could reduce it to any order in his mind. When John Westlock acquainted him with Tom's account of the strange behavior of old Chuffey, they concluded that to arrive at a knowledge of that old man's mind would be to take an important stride forward. And since Mr. Chuffey was influenced by Mrs. Gamp, it was decided that Mrs. Gamp should be approached without delay.

Mrs. Gamp's apartment was swept and garnished for the reception of a visitor, Mrs. Prig. The chimney piece was ornamented with a small almanac, marked here and there with the date at which some lady was expected to fall due. It was also embellished with three profiles—one, in colors, of Mrs. Gamp herself in early life; one, in bronze, of a lady in feathers, supposed to be Mrs. Harris, as she appeared when dressed for a ball; and one, in black, of Mr. Gamp, deceased. The last was full length, in order that the likeness might be rendered more forcible by the introduction of the wooden leg.

A pair of bellows, a pair of pattens, a toasting fork, a kettle, a pap boat, a spoon for the administration of medicine to the refractory, and, lastly, Mrs. Gamp's umbrella, which, as something of great price and rarity, was displayed with particular ostentation, completed the decorations of the chimney piece and adjacent wall. Toward these objects Mrs. Gamp raised her eyes in satisfaction when she had concluded her arrangements.

"There's the bell a ringing now," she said, hurrying to the stair head and looking over. "Betsey Prig, my—why, it's that there disappintin' Sweedlepipes, I do believe."

"Yes, it's me," said the bird fancier. "You recollect young Bailey? His master can't be found. It's in the papers. The other manager of their office—Crimple, David Crimple—has gone off with the money and is advertised for, with a reward. Mr. Montague is advertised for too. Their office is a smash—a swindle altogether."

"Don't you hear nothink of Mr. Chuzzlewit in all this?" asked Mrs. Gamp.

"No," said Poll, "nothing to speak of. His name wasn't printed as one of the board, though some people say it was just going to be."

At this juncture the little bell rang, and the deep voice of Mrs. Prig struck into the conversation. "Oh, you're a talkin' about it, are you!" observed that lady. "Well, I hope you've got it over, for I ain't interested in it myself."

"My precious Betsey," said Mrs. Gamp, "how late you are!"

The worthy Mrs. Prig replied with some asperity that "if perwerse people went off dead, it warn't no fault of her'n." Her first words, after glancing at the pickled salmon on the table, were, "I know'd she wouldn't have a cowcumber!"

Mrs. Gamp changed color. "Lord bless you, Betsey Prig, your words is true!"

Mrs. Prig, looking steadfastly at her friend, put her hand in her pocket and, with an air of surly triumph, drew forth a green vegetable of an expansive nature, a handful of mustard and cress, three bunches of radishes, an onion rather larger than a turnip, and a short prong or antler of celery, recommending that these productions of nature should be sliced up for immediate consumption in plenty of vinegar. "And don't go a dropping none of your snuff in it," said Mrs. Prig. "In gruel, barley water, mutton broth, and that, it don't signify. It stimilates a patient. But I don't relish it myself."

"Why, Betsey Prig!" cried Mrs. Gamp. "How *can* you talk so!"

"Why, ain't your patients, wotever their diseases is, always a sneezin' their wery heads off along of your snuff?" said Mrs. Prig.

"And wot if they are?" said Mrs. Gamp.

"Nothing if they are," said Mrs. Prig. "But don't deny it, Sairah."

"Who deniges of it, Betsey?" Mrs. Gamp inquired. "*Who* deniges of it?"

It was the nearest possible approach to a very decided difference of opinion between these ladies; but Mrs. Prig's impatience for the meal being greater than her impatience of contradiction, the matter was dropped. For a quarrel can be taken up any time, but a limited quantity of salmon cannot.

The temper of both parties was improved for the time being by the enjoyment of the table. "Betsey," said Mrs. Gamp, filling her own glass and passing the teapot, which contained the spirits, "I will now propose a toast. My frequent pardner, Betsey Prig!"

"Which, altering the name to Sairah Gamp, I drink," said Mrs. Prig, "with love and tenderness." From this moment, symptoms of inflammation began to lurk in the nose of each lady, and perhaps in the temper also. "Now, Sairah," said Mrs. Prig, "joining business with pleasure, wot is this case in which you wants me?" Mrs. Gamp hesitating, Betsey added, "*Is* it Mrs. Harris?"

"No, Betsey Prig, it ain't," was Mrs. Gamp's reply.

"Well," said Mrs. Prig, with a short laugh, "I'm glad of that, at any rate."

"Why should you be glad of that, Betsey?" Mrs. Gamp retorted warmly. "She is unbeknown to you except by hearsay; why should you be glad?"

"Well, it ain't her, it seems," said Mrs. Prig coldly; "who is it then?"

"You have heard me mention, Betsey," Mrs. Gamp replied, "a person as I took care on at the time as you and me was pardners off and on at the Bull?"

"Old Snuffey," Mrs. Prig observed.

Sarah Gamp looked at her with an eye of fire, for she saw in this mistake of Mrs. Prig another willful and malignant stab at that same custom of hers, an ungenerous allusion to which had first disturbed their harmony that evening. And she saw it still more clearly when, politely but firmly correcting Betsey by the distinct enunciation of the word "Chuffey," Mrs. Prig received the correction with a diabolical laugh, her arms folded and one eye shut up in an offensive manner.

Mrs. Gamp, observing this, felt it the more necessary that Mrs. Prig should know her place. She therefore assumed an air of greater patronage and importance. "Mr. Chuffey's friends, Betsey," said Mrs. Gamp, "has made propojals for his bein' took care on and has said to me, 'Mrs. Gamp, *will* you undertake it, at your own price, day and night, and by your own self?' 'No,' I says, 'I will not. There is,' I says, 'but one creetur in the world as I would undertake on sech terms, and her name is Harris. But,' I says, 'I am acquainted with a friend, whose name is Betsey Prig, that I can recommend, and will assist me. Betsey,' I says, 'is always to be trusted, under me, and will be guided as I could desire.'"

Here Mrs. Prig, without any abatement of her offensive manner, counterfeited abstraction of mind and stretched out her hand to the teapot. It was more than Mrs. Gamp could bear. She stopped the hand of Mrs. Prig with her own and said, with great feeling, "No, Betsey! Drink fair, wotever you do!"

Mrs. Prig, thus baffled, threw herself back in her chair and, closing the same eye more emphatically, suffered her head to roll slowly from side to side, while she surveyed her friend with a contemptuous smile.

Mrs. Gamp resumed, "Mrs. Harris, Betsey—"

"Bother Mrs. Harris!" said Betsey Prig. "I don't believe there's no sech a person!" After the utterance of which, she leaned forward and snapped her fingers once, twice, thrice—each time nearer to the face of Mrs. Gamp—and then rose to put on her bonnet, as one who felt that there was now a gulf between them which nothing could ever bridge across.

"What!" said Mrs. Gamp, gasping for breath. "You bage creetur, have I know'd Mrs. Harris five and thirty year, to be told at last that there ain't no sech a person livin'! Go along with you."

"I'm a goin', ma'am, ain't I?" said Mrs. Prig, stopping as she said it.

"You had better, ma'am," said Mrs. Gamp.

"Do you know who you're talking to, ma'am?" inquired her visitor.

"Aperiently," said Mrs. Gamp, surveying her with scorn from head to foot, "to Betsey Prig. Aperiently so."

"And you was a goin' to take me under you!" cried Mrs. Prig, surveying Mrs. Gamp from head to foot in her turn. "You was, was you? Oh, how kind! Why, deuce take your imperence," said Mrs. Prig, with a rapid change from banter to ferocity, "what do you mean?"

"Go along with you!" said Mrs. Gamp. "I blush for you."

"Why, bless my life!" exclaimed Mr. Sweedlepipe, as Mrs. Prig angrily withdrew, "what's amiss? The noise you ladies have been making, Mrs. Gamp! Why, these two gentlemen have been standing on the stairs nearly all the time, trying to make you hear!"

"Oh, Mr. Sweedlepipes, which Mr. Westlock also, if my eyes do not deceive, and a friend not havin' the pleasure of bein' beknown, wot I have took from Betsey Prig this blessed night no mortal creetur knows! The words she spoke of Mrs. Harris, lambs could not forgive. No, Betsey," said Mrs. Gamp, in a violent burst of feeling, "nor worms forget!"

John Westlock sat down on one side of Mrs. Gamp. Martin supported her on the other. "To think," said Mrs. Gamp, "as she should ever have helped to nuss that friend of your'n and been so near of hearing things that—Oh, Betsey Prig, what wickedness you've showed this night; but never shall you darken Sairey's doors agen, you twining serpiant!"

"You were always so kind to her, too!" said John consolingly. "I hope you have time to find another assistant, Mrs. Gamp?"

"Which short it is, indeed," cried Mrs. Gamp. "Tomorrow

evenin', sir, I waits upon his friends. Mr. Chuzzlewit apinted it from nine to ten."

"From nine to ten," said John, with a significant glance at Martin; "and then Mr. Chuffey retires into safe keeping, does he?"

"He needs to be kep' safe, I do assure you," Mrs. Gamp replied, with a mysterious air. "Other people besides me has had a happy deliverance from Betsey Prig. The torters she inflicts is frightful!" Closing her eyes as she made this remark, in the acuteness of her commiseration for Betsey's patients, she forgot to open them again.

"Rely upon it," whispered John to Martin, "you shall question old Chuffey though you go as Mrs. Harris herself."

The night had now come when the old clerk was to be delivered over to his keepers. In the midst of his guilty distractions Jonas had not forgotten it. "He shall be gagged if he speaks," said Jonas, looking at him, for they sat alone together.

Hush! Still listening! To every sound. He had listened ever since, and it had not come yet. The exposure of the insurance office, the flight of Crimple with the plunder, his immense losses and peril of being still called to account as a partner in the broken firm—all these things rose in his mind at one time and always, but he could not contemplate them. He thought of the one dread question only, when they would find the body.

Suddenly the old clerk cried out, "Give her up! Tell me what you have done with her. Quick! I have made no promises on that score. Where is she?"

"How can I give you up what I haven't got, idiot?" said Jonas. "She is out."

"If she has come to any harm," cried Chuffey, "mind! I-I-I can speak."

"You can speak, can you?" thought Jonas. "So, so, we'll stop your speaking." A hand upon the door. "What's that?"

"A pleasant evenin'," said the voice of Mrs. Gamp, "though warm. How does Mr. Chuffey find hisself tonight, sir?" Mrs. Gamp kept particularly close to the door in saying this and curtsied more than usual. She did not appear to be quite so much at her ease as she generally was.

"Get him to his room," said Jonas; "then come down again."

"Poor sweet dear!" cried Mrs. Gamp, with uncommon tenderness. "He's all of a tremble. Come with Sairey!—Mr. Chuffey is a lyin' down," she said, returning.

"Where is the other woman?" said Jonas hoarsely. "You told me her name."

"I mentioned Betsey Prig," said Mrs. Gamp.

"She is to be trusted, is she?"

"That she ain't," said Mrs. Gamp; "nor have I brought her, Mr. Chuzzlewit. I've brought another, which engages to give every satigefaction."

"What is her name?" asked Jonas.

Mrs. Gamp looked at him in an odd way before she answered. "Her name," said Mrs. Gamp, "is Harris."

"Well," said Jonas, "you and she have arranged to take care of him, have you? Let me see her."

"The t'other person, sir?" said Mrs. Gamp. She took two or three backward steps toward the door and stopped there. "It is your wishes, Mr. Chuzzlewit," she said, in a sort of quavering croak, "to see the t'other person, is it?"

But the ghastly change in Jonas told her that the other person was already seen. Before she could look round toward the door, she was put aside by old Martin's hand, and Chuffey and John Westlock entered with him.

"Let no one leave the house," said Martin."—Come in there!"

An irrepressible exclamation burst from the lips of Jonas as Lewsome entered the door.

"Oh, brother!" cried old Martin, clasping his hands and lifting up his eyes. "Oh, brother, brother! Were we strangers half our lives that you might breed a wretch like this and I make life a desert by withering every flower that grew about me?—For the love of your old friend," he said to Chuffey, "speak out, good fellow!"

"I have been silent for his love!" cried the old man. "He made me promise it upon his dying bed. I never would have spoken, but for your finding out so much. He bought the stuff," stretching out his hand toward Jonas, "and mixed it—look at him!—with some sweetmeat in a jar. But his courage failed him, or his heart was touched—my God! I hope it was his heart! He was his only son!—and he did not put it in the usual place, where my old master would have taken it twenty times a day. When my master found it, he told me that his own son had it in his mind to poison him. 'He shall not weary for my death, Chuff'—that was what he said next," pursued the old clerk, as he wiped his eyes. "'He shall have it now. He shall marry where he has a fancy, Chuff, although it doesn't please me; and you and I will go away and live upon a little. I have sown, and I must reap.' But his mind, like mine, went a little wrong through grief, and then his heart broke."

Jonas could look at his company now, and vauntingly too. "Well," he said, after a pause, "do you see the door?"

"Do *you* see the door?" returned John Westlock. "Look at it!"

He looked, and his gaze was nailed there. Fatal, ill-omened, blighted threshold, cursed by his father's footsteps in his dying hour, cursed by his young wife's sorrowing tread, cursed by the daily shadow of the old clerk's figure, cursed by the crossing of his murderer's feet—what men were standing in the doorway?

Nadgett foremost. "Murder," said Nadgett, looking round on the astonished group. "Let no one interfere!"

Martin was the first to speak. "What terrible history is this?"

"Ask *him*," said Nadgett. "He knows more of it than I do, though I know much. I never watched a man so close as I have watched him."

The game was up; the race was at an end; the rope was woven for his neck. But, left alone with an officer for a moment, Jonas made one last effort.

"Put your hand in my pocket. Here! One hundred pound for only five minutes in the next room!" He whispered something in the officer's ear.

The officer took the purse. "Are you guilty?" he asked.

"Yes!" said Jonas and closed the door.

It was not easy, when the five minutes were up, to open the door. The officer started back as his eyes met those of Jonas, standing in an angle of the wall and staring at him. His neckerchief was off; his face was ashy pale.

"You're too soon," said Jonas, with an abject whimper. "I've not had time. I have not been able to do it. I—five minutes more—two minutes more—only one!" He whined, and cried, and cursed, and submitted, in the same breath, and had no power to stand. But they got him away and into the coach, where he soon fell moaning down among the straw and lay there.

Happening to pass a fruiterer's on their way, one of the officers remarked how faint the peaches smelled. The other assented at the moment but presently stooped down in quick alarm and looked at the prisoner. "Stop the coach! He has poisoned himself! The smell comes from this bottle!"

They dragged him out into the dark street; but jury, judge, and hangman could have done no more and could do nothing now. Dead, dead, dead!

18

"No Mr. Fips's friend today, I suppose," thought Tom, as he ascended the stairs in the Temple. Not yet, at any rate; but it looked a different place, it was so orderly and neat. Tom had labored away at the catalogue he was making for an hour or more, when he heard a footstep in the entry below. "Ah!" said he, looking toward the door. "Time was when that would have set me wondering and expecting. But I have left off now."

The footstep came on, up the stairs. The door stood open. As the tread advanced, Tom looked impatiently and eagerly toward it. When a figure came upon the landing and, arriving in the doorway, stopped and gazed at him, he rose up from his chair and half believed he saw a spirit. Old Martin Chuzzlewit! The same whom he had left at Mr. Pecksniff's weak and sinking!

The same? No, not the same; for this man, though old, was strong. One glance at the resolute face, the watchful eye, the vigorous hand upon the staff, the triumphant purpose in the figure, and such a light broke in on Tom as blinded him.

"You have expected me," said Martin, "a long time?"

"I was told that my employer would arrive soon," said Tom, "but—"

"I know. You were ignorant who he was. I intended to have been with you much sooner. I thought I could know no more, and no worse, of him than I did on that day when I saw you last. But I was wrong. I have lived in his house, Pinch, and had him fawning on me, days, and weeks, and months. You know it. I have suffered him to treat me like his tool and instrument. You know it. I have seen him offer love to Mary. You know it; who better—who better, my true heart! I have had his base soul bare before me, day by day, and have not betrayed myself once. I never could have undergone such torture but for looking forward to this time. The time now drawing on," said the old man hurriedly, his eyes and whole face brightening as he spoke, "will make amends for all."

Mark Tapley arrived, having delivered Mr. Chuzzlewit's summons to the Temple, and waited at the door. A knock. Mr. Westlock and Miss Pinch. The old man went to meet them, took her hands in his, and kissed her on the cheek. As this looked promising, Mr. Tapley smiled benignantly.

Young Martin entered. The old man, scarcely looking at him, pointed to a distant seat. This was less encouraging, and Mr. Tapley's spirits fell.

He was quickly summoned to the door by another knock. He did not start, or cry, or tumble down at sight of Miss Graham and Mrs. Lupin, but he drew a very long breath, which seemed to say that nothing could surprise him any more.

The last appointed footstep sounded now upon the stairs. They all knew it. It was Mr. Pecksniff's; and Mr. Pecksniff was in a hurry too, for he came bounding up with such uncommon expedition that he stumbled twice or thrice. "Where is my venerable friend?" he cried upon the upper landing and then with open arms came darting in.

Old Martin merely looked at him; but Mr. Pecksniff started back as if he had received the charge of an electric battery. He then looked round on the assembled group and shook his head reproachfully—for such a man severely, quite severely. "Oh, vermin!" said Mr. Pecksniff. "Oh, bloodsuckers! Horde of unnatural plunderers and robbers! Leave him! Leave him, I say! Begone! And you, my tender sir," in a tone of gentle remonstrance, "how could you ever leave me, though even for this short period!"

He advanced with outstretched arms to take the old man's hand. But he had not seen how the hand clasped and clutched the stick within its grasp. As he got within its reach, old Martin, with his burning indignation crowded into one vehement burst, rose up and struck him down upon the ground.

"Hear me, rascal!" said Mr. Chuzzlewit. "I have summoned you here to witness your own work—come hither, my dear Martin —look here, here, here!" At every repetition he pressed his grand-

son closer to his breast. "The passion I felt, Martin, when I dared not do this, when I could only send you an anonymous gift," he said, "was in the blow I struck just now. How could we ever part?—Mary, my love, come here." Drawing her hand through Martin's arm, he said to Mr. Pecksniff, "Listen, hypocrite! When I lay ill in Mrs. Lupin's house and your meek spirit pleaded for my grandson, you had already caught him, had you? Counting on the restoration of the love you knew I bore him, you designed him for one of your daughters, did you?"

"I am not angry," observed Mr. Pecksniff. "I am hurt, Mr. Chuzzlewit—wounded in my feelings—but I am not angry, my good sir."

Mr. Chuzzlewit resumed. "Once resolved to try this rascal, I was resolute to pursue the trial to the end; but while I was bent on fathoming the depth of his duplicity, I made a sacred compact with myself that I would give him credit on the other side for any latent spark of goodness, honor, forbearance—any virtue—that might glimmer in him. From first to last there has been no such thing. Not once."

"I beg your pardon, sir," said Mr. Tapley, stepping forward, "but you was mentionin' just now a lady of the name of Lupin, sir. It seems almost a pity to change such a name into Tapley, don't it, sir?"

"That depends upon the lady. What is *her* opinion?"

"Why, sir," said Mr. Tapley, retiring, with a bow, toward the buxom hostess, "her opinion is as the name ain't a change for the better but the individual may be; and therefore, if nobody ain't acquainted with no jest cause or impediment, et cetrer, the Blue Dragon will be con-werted into the Jolly Tapley. A sign of my own inwention, sir. Wery new, conwivial, and expressive."

The whole of these proceedings were so agreeable to Mr. Pecksniff that he stood with his eyes fixed upon the floor and his hands clasping one another alternately as if a host of penal sentences were being passed upon him. "I have been struck this day," said Mr. Pecksniff, "with a walking stick (which I have every reason to believe has knobs upon it), on that delicate and exquisite portion of the human anatomy, the brain. Several blows have been inflicted, sir, without a walking stick, upon that tenderer portion of my frame, my heart. But if you ever contemplete the silent tomb, sir, think of me. If you should wish to have anything inscribed upon your silent tomb, sir, let it be that I, the humble individual who has now the honor of reproaching you, forgave you. May you find a consolation in it when you want it, sir! Good morning!"

With this sublime address Mr. Pecksniff departed; and Mrs. Gamp was seen in the doorway, out of breath from coming up so many stairs, and panting fearfully, but dropping curtsies as she stated her business. "Which, Mr. Chuzzlewit," she said, "is well beknown to Mrs. Harris as has one sweet infant (though she *do* not wish it known) in her own family by the mother's side, kep' in spirits in a bottle. And Mrs. Harris, Mr. Chuzzlewit, has knowed me many year and can give you information that the lady which is widdered can't do better and may do worse than let me wait upon her, which I hope to do. Permittin' the sweet faces as I see afore me."

"Oh!" said Mr. Chuzzlewit, "is that your business?—Was this good person paid for the trouble we gave her?"

"I paid her, sir," returned Mark Tapley "—liberal."

"Then here we will close our acquaintance, Mrs. Gamp," retorted Mr. Chuzzlewitt, "with a word or two of good advice—such as hinting at the expediency of a little less liquor and a little more humanity, and a little less regard for yourself and a little more regard for your patients, and perhaps a trifle of additional honesty."

Mrs. Gamp clasped her hands, turned up her eyes until they were quite invisible, threw back her bonnet for the admission of fresh air to her heated brow, and in the act of saying faintly, "Less liquor!—Sairey Gamp!—Bottle on the chimley piece, and let me put my lips to it when I am so dispoged!" fell into a walking swoon, in which pitiable state she was conducted forth.

The old man looked about him with a smile, until his eyes rested on Tom Pinch's sister, when he smiled the more. "I must see your lodgings, Tom," he said. "But suppose you go on first, my dear," to Ruth. "Mr. Westlock, I dare say, will escort you, while Martin and Mary stay together here."

Brilliantly the Temple fountain sparkled in the sun, and laughingly its liquid music played as little Ruth and her companion came toward it. What a good old place it was, John said, with quite an earnest affection for it. The more they talked, the more afraid this fluttering little Ruth became of any pause. When they reached their destination, she sat down on the little sofa and untied her bonnet strings. He sat down by her side, and very near her—very, very near her. Oh rapid, swelling, bursting little heart, you knew that it would come to this and hoped it would. Why beat so wildly, heart?

"Dear Ruth! Sweet Ruth! If I had loved you less, I could have told you that I loved you long ago. I have loved you from the first. There never was a creature in the world more truly loved than you, dear Ruth, by me!"

She clasped her little hands before her face. The gushing tears of joy, and pride, and hope, and innocent affection would not be restrained. Fresh from her full young heart they came to answer him.

They soon began to talk of Tom. "I am never to leave him, *am* I, dear?" she said. "I could never leave Tom. I am sure you know that."

"Do you think I would ask you?" he returned, with a—well,

never mind with what. And just then they heard him knocking at the door.

When Ruth saw his dear old face come in, her heart was so touched that she ran into his arms and laid her head down on his breast and sobbed out, "Bless me, Tom! My dearest brother!"

Tom looked up in surprise and saw John Westlock holding out his hand. "Dear Tom," said his friend, "we are brothers."

"I am glad you chose today," said Mr. Chuzzlewit to John when he had been told the news. "I thought you would. I must play the part of a father here, Tom, also. There are not many fathers who marry two such daughters on the same day; but we will overlook the improbability for the gratification of an old man's fancy."

Todgers's was in high feather, and mighty preparations for a late breakfast were astir in its commercial bowers. The blissful morning had arrived when Miss Pecksniff was to be united in holy matrimony to Augustus. The wedding guests had not yet assembled when a carriage stopped at the door, and Mrs. Todgers conducted Mr. Chuzzlewit into the little back chamber, where, sadly different from when it had first been her lodging, sat poor Merry, old Chuffey beside her.

"I judged you hastily," Mr. Chuzzlewit said to her in a low voice. "I fear I judged you cruelly. Let me know that I have your forgiveness. Your late husband's estate," he went on, "will be seized upon by law; for it is not exempt, as I learn, from the claims of those who have suffered by the fraud in which he was engaged. Your father's property was all, or nearly all, embarked in the same transaction. There is no home *there*."

"I couldn't return to him," she said.

"I know it," Mr. Chuzzlewit resumed. "Come with me. Your sister is careless of you, I know. She hurries on and publishes her marriage in a spirit which (to say no more of it) is barely decent, is unsisterly, and bad. Leave the house before her guests arrive, and come with me!"

Mrs. Todgers added her persuasions. Even poor old Chuffey (of course included in the project) added his. She hurriedly attired herself, and they departed.

And now the wedding party began to assemble. Mr. Jinkins, the only boarder invited, was on the ground first. Mrs. Todgers soon joined him, followed by Mr. and Mrs. Spottletoe. Mr. Spottletoe honored Jinkins with an encouraging bow. "Give you joy," he said, under the impression that Jinkins was the happy man.

Mr. Jinkins explained. He was merely doing the honors for his friend Moddle, who had ceased to reside in the house and had not yet arrived.

"Not arrived, sir!" exclaimed Spottletoe, in a great heat. "Upon my soul, he begins well!"

The door was thrown open at this juncture, and Miss Pecksniff entered, tottering. "You do not know Augustus," said Miss Pecksniff tearfully. "Wait till you see Augustus, and I am sure he will conciliate your affections."

"The question arises," said Spottletoe, folding his arms, "how long we are to wait."

As time went on, the bride became seriously alarmed—good Heavens, what could have happened! Dear Augustus!—when Jinkins, having met the postman at the door, came back with a letter, which he put into her hand.

Miss Pecksniff opened it, glanced at it, uttered a piercing shriek, and fainted away. They picked it up and read this communication.

"Off Gravesend,

"Clipper Schooner 'Cupid,'

"Wednesday night

"Ever injured Miss Pecksniff,

"Ere this reaches you, the undersigned will be on the way to Van Diemen's Land. Send not in pursuit. I never will be taken alive!

"I love another. She is Another's. O Miss Pecksniff, why didn't you leave me alone? Was it not cruel, *cruel?* But I will not reproach you, for I have wronged you. May the Furniture make some amends!

"Farewell! Be the proud bride of a ducal coronet, and forget me! Long may it be before you know the anguish with which I now subscribe myself—amid the tempestuous howlings of the—sailors,

"Unalterably, never yours,

"Augustus."

What sounds are these that fall so grandly on the ear? What darkening room is this? And that mild figure seated at an organ, who is he? Ah, Tom, dear Tom, old friend!

Thy life is tranquil, calm, and happy, Tom. In the soft strain which ever and again comes stealing back upon the ear, the memory of thine old love may find a voice perhaps; but it is a pleasant, softened, whispering memory and does not pain or grieve thee, God be thanked!

Touch the notes lightly, Tom, but never will thine hand fall half so lightly on that instrument as on the head of thine old tyrant, brought down very low. For a drunken, begging, squalid letter-writing man, called Pecksniff (with a shrewish daughter), haunts thee, Tom; and when he makes appeals to thee for cash, reminds thee that he built thy fortunes better than his own; and when he spends it, entertains the ale-house company with tales of thine ingratitude. All known to thee, and yet all borne with, Tom!

And coming from a garden, Tom, bestrewn with flowers by children's hands, thy sister, little Ruth, as light of foot and heart as in old days, sits down beside thee. From the Present, and the Past, with which she is so tenderly entwined in all thy thoughts, thy strain soars onward to the Future. As it resounds within thee and without, the noble music, rolling round ye both, shuts out the grosser prospect of an earthly parting and uplifts ye both to Heaven!

I

THE first ray of light which illumines the gloom and converts into a dazzling brilliancy that obscurity in which the earlier history of the immortal Pickwick would appear to be involved is derived from the following entry in the Transactions of the Pickwick Club:

"May 12, 1827, Joseph Smiggers, Esq., P.V.P.M.P.C.,* presiding. The following resolutions unanimously agreed to:

"That this Association has heard read, with feelings of unmingled satisfaction and unqualified approval, the paper communicated by Samuel Pickwick, Esq., G.C.M.P.C.,† entitled

* Perpetual Vice-President, Member Pickwick Club
† General Chairman, Member Pickwick Club.

'Speculations on the Source of the Hampstead Ponds, with Some Observations on the Theory of Tittlebats'; and that this Association does hereby return its warmest thanks to the said Samuel Pickwick, Esq., G.C.M.P.C., for the same.

"That this Association cannot but entertain a lively sense of the inestimable benefits which must inevitably result from carrying the speculations of that learned man into a wider field.

"That the Corresponding Society of the Pickwick Club is therefore hereby constituted; and that Samuel Pickwick, Esq., G.C.M.P.C., Tracy Tupman, Esq., M.P.C., Augustus Snodgrass, Esq., M.P.C., and Nathaniel Winkle, Esq., M.P.C., are hereby nominated and appointed members of the same; and that they be requested to forward, from time to time, authenticated accounts of their journeys and investigations to the Pickwick Club, stationed in London."

A casual observer, adds the secretary, might possibly have remarked nothing extraordinary in the bald head and circular spectacles, which were intently turned toward his (the secretary's) face, during the reading of the above resolutions: to those who knew that the gigantic brain of Pickwick was working beneath that forehead and that the beaming eyes of Pickwick were twinkling behind those glasses, the sight was indeed an interesting one. On his right hand sat Mr. Tracy Tupman—the too susceptible Tupman, who to the wisdom and experience of maturer years superadded the enthusiasm and ardor of a boy, in the most pardonable of human weaknesses, love. Time and feeding had expanded that once romantic form; but the soul of Tupman had known no change—admiration of the fair sex was still its ruling passion. On the left of his great leader sat the poetic Snodgrass, and near him again the sporting Winkle, the former poetically enveloped in a mysterious blue coat with a canine-skin collar, and the latter communicating additional luster to a new green shooting coat, plaid neckerchief, and closely fitted drabs.

We have no official statement of the facts which the reader will find recorded in the following pages, but they have been carefully collated from letters and other manuscript authorities, so unquestionably genuine as to justify their narration in a connected form.

That punctual servant of all work, the sun, had just risen on the morning of the thirteenth of May, one thousand eight hundred and twenty-seven, when Mr. Samuel Pickwick burst like another sun from his slumbers, threw open his chamber window, and looked out upon the world beneath. In another hour he was in a cab.

"How old is that horse, my friend?" inquired Mr. Pickwick of the driver.

"Forty-two," replied the man, eyeing him askant.

"What!" ejaculated Mr. Pickwick, laying his hand upon his notebook. "And how long do you keep him out at a time?"

"Two or three veeks," replied the man.

"Weeks!" said Mr. Pickwick in astonishment—and out came the notebook again. The entry was scarcely completed when they reached the Golden Cross. Mr. Tupman, Mr. Snodgrass, and Mr. Winkle, who had been anxiously waiting the arrival of their illustrious leader, crowded to welcome him.

"Here's your fare," said Mr. Pickwick, holding out a shilling to the driver.

What was his astonishment when the man flung the money on the pavement and requested in figurative terms to be allowed the pleasure of fighting him (Mr. Pickwick) for the amount! "Come on!" he said, sparring away like clockwork. "Come on— all four on you."

"What's the row, Sam?" inquired a gentleman in the crowd.

"Row!" replied the cabman. "What did he take my number for?"

"I didn't take it," said Mr. Pickwick, indignantly.

"Would anybody believe," continued the cab driver, "as an informer 'ud go about in a man's cab, not only takin' down his number, but ev'ry word he says into the bargain?" (A light flashed upon Mr. Pickwick—it was the notebook.) "Come on," cried the cabman, who had been sparring the whole time.

As the intelligence of the Pickwickians being informers was spread among the crowd, there is no saying what acts of personal aggression they might have committed had not the affray been unexpectedly terminated by the interposition of a rather tall thin young man, in a green coat, to whom Mr. Pickwick managed to explain the real state of the case.

"Come along, then," said he, lugging Mr. Pickwick after him to the waiting room and talking the whole way. "Here, No. 924, take your fare, and take yourself off—respectable gentleman—know him well—none of your nonsense—this way, sir—where's your friends?—all a mistake, I see—never mind—damned rascals. Here, waiter! Glasses round—brandy-and-water, hot and strong, and sweet, and plenty." And the stranger, without stopping to take a breath, swallowed at a draught full half a pint. His face was thin and haggard; but an indescribable air of jaunty impudence and perfect self-possession pervaded the whole man.

Mr. Pickwick was returning in chosen terms his warmest thanks for his assistance, when the "Commodore" coach was announced and all five travelers climbed aboard. "Any luggage, sir?" inquired the coachman.

"Who—I? Brown paper parcel here, that's all—other luggage gone by water—packing cases, nailed up—big as houses—heavy, heavy, damned heavy," replied the stranger, as he forced into his pocket as much as he could of the brown paper parcel, which presented most suspicious indications of containing one shirt and a handkerchief.

"Heads, heads—take care of your heads!" cried the loquacious stranger, as they came out under the low archway. "Terrible place —dangerous work—other day—five children—mother—tall lady, eating sandwiches—forgot the arch—crash—knock—children look round—mother's head off—sandwich in her hand—no mouth to put it in—shocking, shocking!"

"I am ruminating," said Mr. Pickwick, "on the strange mutability of human affairs."

"Ah! I see.—Philosopher, sir?"

"An observer of human nature, sir," said Mr. Pickwick.

"Ah, so am I. Most people are when they've little to do and less to get. Poet, sir?"

"My friend Mr. Snodgrass has a strong poetic turn," said Mr. Pickwick.

"So have I," said the stranger. "Epic poem—ten thousand lines—revolution of July—composed it on the spot—Mars by day, Apollo by night—bang the fieldpiece, twang the lyre.—Sportsman, sir?" abruptly turning to Mr. Winkle.

"A little, sir," replied that gentleman.

"Fine pursuit, sir—fine pursuit.—Dogs, sir?"

"Not just now," said Mr. Winkle.

"Ah! You should keep dogs—fine animals—sagacious creatures—dog of my own once—pointer—surprising instinct—out shooting one day—entering enclosure—whistled—dog stopped—whistled again—Ponto, Ponto—wouldn't move—dog transfixed—staring at a board—looked up, saw an inscription—'Gamekeeper has orders to shoot all dogs found in this enclosure'—wouldn't pass it—wonderful dog—valuable dog that—very."

"Singular circumstance that," said Mr. Pickwick. "Will you allow me to make a note of it?"

"Certainly, sir, certainly—hundred more anecdotes of the same animal.—Fine girl, sir" (to Mr. Tracy Tupman, who had been bestowing sundry anti-Pickwickian glances on a young lady by the roadside). "English girls not so fine as Spanish—noble creatures—jet hair—black eyes—lovely forms—sweet creatures—beautiful."

"You have been in Spain, sir?" inquired Mr. Tupman.

"Lived there—ages."

"Many conquests, sir?" said Mr. Tracy Tupman.

"Conquests! Thousands. Don Bolaro Fizzgig—grandee—only daughter—Donna Christina—splendid creature—loved me to distraction—jealous father—high-souled daughter—handsome Englishman—Donna Christina in despair—prussic acid—stomach pump in my portmanteau—operation performed—old Bolaro in ecstasies—consent to our union—romantic story—very."

"Is the lady in England now, sir?" inquired Mr. Tupman, on whom the description of her charms had produced a powerful impression.

"Dead, sir—dead," said the stranger, applying to his right eye the brief remnant of a very old cambric handkerchief. "Never recovered the stomach pump—undermined constitution—fell a victim."

"And her father?" inquired the poetic Snodgrass.

"Remorse and misery," replied the stranger. "Sudden disappearance—talk of the whole city—search made everywhere—without success—public fountain in the great square suddenly ceased playing—water drawn off—father-in-law discovered sticking headfirst in the main pipe, with a full confession in his right boot—took him out, and the fountain played away again, as well as ever."

"Will you allow me to note that little romance down, sir?" said Mr. Snodgrass, deeply affected.

"Certainly, sir, certainly—fifty more if you like to hear 'em— strange life mine—rather curious history—not extraordinary, but singular."

In this strain did the stranger proceed, until they reached Rochester bridge, by which time the notebooks, both of Mr. Pickwick and Mr. Snodgrass, were completely filled with selections from his adventures.

2

THE whole population of Rochester and the adjoining towns rose from their beds at an early hour of the following morning, in a state of the utmost bustle and excitement. A grand review was to take place upon the Lines. The maneuvers of half a dozen regiments were to be inspected by the eagle eye of the commander in chief; temporary fortifications had been erected, the citadel was to be attacked and taken, and a mine was to be sprung.

Mr. Pickwick was an enthusiastic admirer of the army. Nothing could have been more delightful to him—nothing could have harmonized so well with the feeling of his companions—as this sight. Accordingly they were soon walking in the direction of the scene of action, where they stationed themselves in the front rank of the crowd and patiently awaited the commencement of the proceedings.

At length the military bands struck up all together; column after column poured onto the plain; the horses stood upon two legs each, cantered backward, and whisked their tails about in all directions; and nothing was to be seen on either side, as far as the eye could reach, but a long perspective of red coats and white trousers, fixed and motionless.

Mr. Pickwick had been so fully occupied in falling about and disentangling himself, miraculously, from between the legs of horses that he had not enjoyed sufficient leisure to observe the scene before him, until it assumed the appearance we have just described. When he was at last enabled to stand firmly on his legs, his gratification and delight were unbounded. "We are in a capital situation now," said he, looking round him. The crowd had gradually dispersed in their immediate vicinity, and they were nearly alone.

"Capital!" echoed both Mr. Snodgrass and Mr. Winkle.—Mr. Tupman had unaccountably disappeared.

"What are they doing now?" inquired Mr. Pickwick, adjusting his spectacles.

"I—I—rather think," said Mr. Winkle, changing color, "I rather think they're going to fire."

"Nonsense," said Mr. Pickwick, hastily.

"I—I—really think they are," urged Mr. Snodgrass, somewhat alarmed.

"Impossible," replied Mr. Pickwick. He had hardly uttered the word, when the whole half-dozen regiments leveled their muskets as if they had but one common object, and that object the Pickwickians, and burst forth with the most awful and tremendous discharge that ever shook the earth to its center, or an elderly gentleman off his.

"We had better throw ourselves on our faces, hadn't we?" said Mr. Snodgrass.

"No, no—it's over now," said Mr. Pickwick. His lip might quiver, and his cheek might blanch, but no expression of fear or concern escaped the lips of that immortal man.

Mr. Pickwick was right: the firing ceased. But he had scarcely time to congratulate himself on the accuracy of his opinion when a quick movement was visible in the line. The hoarse shout of the word of command ran along it; and before either of the party could form a guess at the meaning of this new maneuver, the whole of the half-dozen regiments, with fixed bayonets, charged at double-quick time down upon the very spot on which Mr. Pickwick and his friends were stationed.

Man is but mortal, and there is a point beyond which human courage cannot extend. Mr. Pickwick gazed through his spectacles for an instant on the advancing mass and then fairly turned his back and trotted away, at as quick a rate as his legs would convey him; so quickly indeed, that he did not perceive the awkwardness of his situation, to the full extent, until too late.

The opposite troops were drawn up to repel the mimic attack

of the sham besiegers of the citadel; and the consequence was that
Mr. Pickwick and his two companions found themselves suddenly
enclosed between two lines of great length, the one advancing at a
rapid pace and the other firmly waiting the collision in hostile
array.

"Hoi!" shouted the officers of the advancing line.

"Get out of the way!" cried the officers of the stationary one.

"Where are we to go to?" screamed the agitated Pickwickians.

"Hoi—hoi—hoi!" was the only reply. There was a moment of
intense bewilderment, a heavy tramp of footsteps, a violent con-
cussion, a smothered laugh; the half-dozen regiments were half a
thousand yards off, and the soles of Mr. Pickwick's boots were
elevated in air.

Mr. Snodgrass and Mr. Winkle had each performed a com-
pulsory somersault with remarkable agility, when the eyes of the
latter beheld his venerated leader at some distance off, running after
his own hat, which was gamboling playfully away in perspective.

There are very few moments in a man's existence when he
experiences so much ludicrous distress or meets with so little
charitable commiseration as when he is in pursuit of his own hat.
A vast deal of coolness and a peculiar degree of judgment are
requisite in catching a hat. There was a fine gentle wind, and Mr.
Pickwick's hat might have rolled far beyond his reach, had it not
providentially been blown with some violence against the wheel
of a carriage. Mr. Pickwick, perceiving his advantage, darted
briskly forward and had secured his property, when he heard his
own name eagerly pronounced by Mr. Tupman's voice. Looking
upward, he beheld a sight which filled him with pleasure and
surprise.

In an open barouche stood a stout old gentleman, two young
ladies in scarves and feathers, a young gentleman apparently
enamored of one of the young ladies, a lady of doubtful age,
probably the aunt of the aforesaid, and Mr. Tupman. On the box
sat a fat and red-faced boy, in a state of somnolency. "Come along,
sir. Pray, come up," said the stout gentleman. "Joe!—Damn that
boy, he's gone to sleep again.—Joe, let down the steps." The fat
boy rolled slowly off the box, let down the steps, and held the
carriage door invitingly open. Mr. Snodgrass and Mr. Winkle
came up at the moment.

"Room for you all, gentlemen," said the stout man. "Very glad to see you. Know you very well, gentlemen, though you mayn't remember me. I spent some ev'nin's at your club last winter—picked up my friend Mr. Tupman here this morning. —My daughters, gentlemen—my gals these are; and that's my sister, Miss Rachel Wardle. This is my friend Mr. Trundle." So the stout gentleman put on his spectacles, and Mr. Pickwick pulled out his glass, and everybody looked over somebody else's shoulder at the evolutions of the military.

The young Miss Wardles were so frightened that Mr. Trundle was actually obliged to hold one of them up in the carriage, while Mr. Snodgrass supported the other; and Mr. Wardle's sister suffered under such a dreadful state of nervous alarm, that Mr. Tupman found it indispensably necessary to put his arm round her waist, to keep her up at all. Everybody was excited, except the fat boy, and he slept as soundly as if the roaring of cannon were his ordinary lullaby.

"Joe, Joe!" said the stout gentleman, when the citadel was taken. "Damn that boy, he's gone to sleep again. Be good enough to pinch him, sir—in the leg, if you please; nothing else wakes him —thank you. Undo the hamper, Joe." The fat boy proceeded to unpack the hamper, with more expedition than could have been expected from his previous inactivity, and the work of destruction of the food commenced.

"How dear Emily is flirting with the stranger gentleman," whispered the spinster aunt, with true spinster-aunt-like envy, to her brother Mr. Wardle.

"Oh! I don't know," said the jolly old gentleman; "all very natural, I dare say—nothing unusual."

"Young girls have *such* spirits," said Miss Wardle to Mr. Tupman, with an air of gentle commiseration. "Do you think my dear nieces pretty?"

"I should, if their aunt wasn't here," replied the ready Pickwickian.

"Oh, you naughty man—but really, if their complexions were a *little* better, don't you think they would be nice-looking girls— by candle light?"

"Yes; I think they would," said Mr. Tupman, with an air of indifference.

"What a sarcastic smile," said the admiring Rachel. "I declare, I'm quite afraid of you."

"I'm sure aunt's talking about us," whispered Miss Emily Wardle to her sister Isabella. "I'm quite certain—she looks so malicious."

"Damn that boy," said Mr. Wardle, "he's gone to sleep again."

"Very extraordinary boy, that," said Mr. Pickwick; "does he always sleep in this way?"

"Sleep!" said the old gentleman. "He's always asleep. Goes on errands fast asleep, and snores as he waits at table. I'm proud of that boy—wouldn't part with him on any account—he's a natural curiosity! Here, Joe—Joe—take these things away, and open another bottle—d'ye hear?"

The fat boy rose, opened his eyes, swallowed the huge piece of pie he had been in the act of masticating when he last fell asleep, and slowly obeyed his master's orders—gloating languidly over the remains of the feast, as he removed the plates and deposited them in the hamper.

"Now mind," said the old gentleman, as he shook hands with Mr. Pickwick at the conclusion of a conversation which had been carried on at intervals, "we shall see you all tomorrow at Manor Farm, Dingley Dell." The carriage rattled off. As the Pickwickians turned round to take a last glimpse of it, the setting sun cast a rich glow on the faces of their entertainers and fell upon the form of the fat boy. His head was sunk upon his bosom: and he slumbered again.

3

"Now, about Manor Farm," said Mr. Pickwick, the next morning. "How shall we go?"

"We had better consult the waiter, perhaps," said Mr. Tupman.

"Fifteen miles, gentlemen—cross road. Very nice four-wheeled chaise, sir—seat for two behind—one in front for the gentleman that drives—oh! beg your pardon, sir—that'll only hold three.

Perhaps one of the gentlemen would like to ride, sir?" suggested the waiter, looking toward Mr. Winkle.

"The very thing," said Mr. Pickwick. "Winkle, will you go on horseback?"

Mr. Winkle did entertain considerable misgivings, in the very lowest recesses of his own heart, relative to his equestrian skill; but as he would not have them even suspected on any account, he at once replied with great hardihood, "Certainly. I should enjoy it of all things."

Mr. Winkle had rushed upon his fate; there was no resource.

It was a curious little green box drawn by an immense brown horse that drove up at eleven. A hostler stood near, holding by the bridle another immense horse—apparently a near relative of the animal in the chaise—ready saddled for Mr. Winkle. "Bless my soul!" said Mr. Pickwick. "Who's to drive?"

"Oh, you, of course," said Mr. Tupman.

"Of course," said Mr. Snodgrass.

"I!" exclaimed Mr. Pickwick.

"Not the slightest fear, sir," interposed the hostler. "Warrant him quiet, sir; a hinfant in arms might drive him." Mr. Pickwick ascended to his perch.

"Wo—o!" cried Mr. Pickwick, as the tall quadruped evinced a decided inclination to back into the coffee-room window.

"Wo—o!" echoed Mr. Tupman and Mr. Snodgrass, from behind.

"Only his playfulness, gen'lm'n," said the head hostler encouragingly; "jist kitch hold on him, Villiam." The deputy hostler restrained the animal's impetuosity, and the principal ran to assist Mr. Winkle in mounting.

"T'other side, sir, if you please."

"Blowed if the gen'lm'n worn't a gettin' up on the wrong side," whispered a grinning postboy to the inexpressibly gratified waiter.

Mr. Winkle, thus instructed, climbed into his saddle, with about as much difficulty as he would have experienced in getting up the side of a first-rate man-of-war.

"All right?" inquired Mr. Pickwick, with an inward presentiment that it was all wrong.

"All right," replied Mr. Winkle faintly.

"Let 'em go," cried the hostler. "Hold him in, sir," and away went the chaise, and the saddle horse, with Mr. Pickwick on the box of the one and Mr. Winkle on the back of the other, to the delight and gratification of the whole inn yard.

"What makes him go sideways?" said Mr. Snodgrass to Mr. Winkle.

"I can't imagine," replied Mr. Winkle. His horse was drifting up the street in the most mysterious manner—side first, with his head toward one side of the way and his tail toward the other.

Suddenly there was a shout from Mr. Pickwick. "I have dropped my whip!"

"Winkle," said Snodgrass, as the equestrian came trotting up on the tall horse, with his hat over his ears, and shaking all over, "pick up the whip, there's a good fellow." Mr. Winkle pulled at the bridle of the tall horse till he was black in the face and, having at length succeeded in stopping him, dismounted, handed the whip to Mr. Pickwick, and prepared to remount. He had no sooner touched the reins than the horse slipped them over his head and darted backward to their full length.

"Poor fellow," said Mr. Winkle, soothingly, "poor fellow—good old horse." The "poor fellow" was proof against flattery: the more Mr. Winkle tried to get nearer him, the more he sidled away; and, notwithstanding all kinds of coaxing and wheedling, there were Mr. Winkle and the horse going round and round each other for ten minutes, at the end of which time each was at precisely the same distance from the other as when they first commenced. "What am I to do?" shouted Mr. Winkle, after the dodging had been prolonged for a considerable time. "Do come and hold him."

Mr. Pickwick was the very personation of kindness and humanity: he threw the reins on the horse's back and, having descended from his seat, carefully stepped back to the assistance of his distressed companion.

The horse no sooner beheld Mr. Pickwick advancing toward him with the chaise whip in his hand than he exchanged the rotary motion for a retrograde movement of so very determined a character that it at once drew Mr. Winkle, who was still at the end of the bridle, at a rather quicker rate than fast walking in the direction from which they had just come. Mr. Pickwick ran to his assistance; but the faster Mr. Pickwick ran forward, the faster the horse ran backward. There was a great scraping of feet and kicking up of the dust; and at last Mr. Winkle, his arms nearly pulled out of their sockets, fairly let go his hold. The horse paused, stared, shook his head, turned round, and quietly trotted home to Rochester, leaving Mr. Winkle and Mr. Pickwick gazing on each other with countenances of blank dismay. A rattling noise at a little distance attracted their attention. "Bless my soul!" exclaimed the agonized Mr. Pickwick. "There's the other horse running away!"

The heat was a short one. Mr. Tupman threw himself into the hedge, Mr. Snodgrass followed his example, the horse dashed the four-wheeled chaise against a wooden bridge, and the party walked slowly forward, leading the horse among them, and abandoning the chaise to its fate.

An hour's walking brought them to a little roadside public house. "Hullo there!" called Mr. Pickwick to the proprietress. "Can we put this horse up here, my good woman?"

"No," replied the woman, after a little consideration, "I'm afeer'd on it. It got us in trouble last time."

"I—I—really believe," whispered Mr. Winkle, "that she thinks we have come by this horse in some dishonest manner."

"It's like a dream," ejaculated Mr. Pickwick, "a hideous dream. The idea of a man's walking about, all day, with a dreadful horse that he can't get rid of!" The depressed Pickwickians turned moodily away, with the tall quadruped, for which they all felt the most unmitigated disgust, following slowly at their heels.

It was late in the afternoon when the four friends and their four-footed companion turned into the lane leading to Manor Farm, their pleasure materially damped as they reflected on the singularity of their appearance and the absurdity of their situation. Torn clothes, lacerated faces, dusty shoes, exhausted looks, and, above all, the horse. Oh, how Mr. Pickwick cursed that horse: he had eyed the noble animal from time to time with looks expressive of hatred and revenge; more than once he had calculated the probable amount of the expense he would incur by cutting his throat; and now the temptation to destroy him or to cast him loose upon the world rushed upon his mind with tenfold force. He was roused from a meditation on these dire imaginings by the sudden appearance of Mr. Wardle and the fat boy.

"Why, where *have* you been?" said the hospitable old gentleman. "Welcome to Manor Farm."

"Hullo!" was the sound that roused Mr. Pickwick next morning from his contemplation of the beauties of the countryside. "Your friend and I," said his host, "are going out rook shooting before breakfast. He's a very good shot, ain't he?"

"I've heard him say he's a capital one," replied Mr. Pickwick; "but I never saw him aim at anything."

"Come along," shouted the old gentleman, addressing Mr. Winkle, who now came up with the other Pickwickians; "a keen hand like you ought to have been up long ago, even to such poor work as this."

Mr. Winkle responded with a forced smile and took up his gun with an expression of countenance which might have been keenness but looked remarkably like misery.

"Shall I begin?" said Mr. Wardle.

"If you please," said Mr. Winkle, glad of any respite.

"Stand aside, then. Now for it." Half a dozen young rooks in violent conversation flew out, the old gentleman fired, down fell a bird.

"Now, Mr. Winkle," said the host, reloading his gun. "Fire away."

Mr. Winkle advanced and leveled his gun. Mr. Pickwick and his friends cowered involuntarily to escape damage from the heavy fall of rooks, which they felt quite certain would be occasioned by the devastating barrel of their friend. There was a solemn pause— a flapping of wings—a faint click. "Missed fire," said Mr. Winkle, who was very pale—probably from disappointment.

"Odd," said the old gentleman, taking the gun. "Why, I don't see anything of the cap."

"Bless my soul," said Mr. Winkle. "I declare I forgot the cap!"

The slight omission was rectified. Mr. Pickwick crouched again. Mr. Winkle stepped forward with an air of determination and resolution; and Mr. Tupman looked out from behind a tree. Mr. Winkle fired. There was a scream as of an individual—not a rook—in corporeal anguish. Mr. Tupman had saved the lives of innumerable unoffending birds by receiving a portion of the charge in his left arm.

To describe the confusion that ensued would be impossible. To tell how Mr. Pickwick in the first transports of his emotion called Mr. Winkle "Wretch"; how Mr. Tupman lay prostrate on the ground; how Mr. Winkle knelt horror stricken beside him; how Mr. Tupman called distractedly upon some feminine Christian name and then fell back;—all this would be as difficult to describe in detail as it would be to depict the gradual recovering of the unfortunate individual, the binding up of his arm with pocket handkerchiefs, and the conveying him back by slow degrees supported by the arms of his anxious friends.

"Why, what *is* the matter with the little old gentleman?" said Isabella Wardle, as they approached. The spinster aunt heeded not the remark; she thought it applied to Mr. Pickwick. In her eyes Tracy Tupman was a youth; she viewed his years through a diminishing glass.

"Don't be frightened," called out the host. "Mr. Tupman has met with a little accident; that's all." The spinster aunt uttered a piercing scream, burst into a hysteric laugh, and fell backward in the arms of her nieces. "Throw some cold water over her," said the old gentleman.

"No, no," murmured the spinster aunt; "I am better now. Is he wounded?—Is he dead?"

"Calm yourself," said Mr. Tupman, affected almost to tears by this expression of sympathy with his sufferings. "Dear, dear madam, calm yourself."

"It is his voice!" exclaimed the spinster aunt. "Then you are not dead! Oh, say you are not dead!"

Mr. Tracy Tupman gently pressed her hand to his lips and sank upon the sofa, where a surgeon pronounced his wound a slight one.

"Are you a cricketer?" inquired Mr. Wardle presently of the marksman.

At any other time, Mr. Winkle would have replied in the affirmative. He felt the delicacy of his situation and modestly replied, "No."

"I subscribe to the club here," said the host. "The grand match with Muggleton is played today. Of course," to Mr. Pickwick, "you would like to see it."

"I, sir," replied Mr. Pickwick, "am delighted to view any

sports which may be safely indulged in, and in which the impotent effects of unskillful people do not endanger human life." Mr. Pickwick paused and looked steadily on Mr. Winkle, who quailed beneath his leader's searching glance.

"Capital game—smart sport—fine exercise—very" were the words which fell upon Mr. Pickwick's ear as he entered the tent at the cricket field; and the first object that met his eyes was his green-coated friend of the Rochester coach, holding forth to a select circle of the All-Muggleton team. The stranger recognized his friends immediately and, darting forward, seized Mr. Pickwick by the hand, talking all the while as if the whole of the arrangements were under his especial patronage and direction. "This way—this way—capital fun—lots of beer—hogsheads; rounds of beef—bullocks; mustard—cart loads; glad to see you—very."

"Mr. Wardle—a friend of mine," said Mr. Pickwick.

"Friend of yours!—My dear sir, how are you?—Friend of *my* friend's—give me your hand, sir"—and the stranger grasped Mr. Wardle's hand with fervor.

"Well—and how came you here?" said Mr. Pickwick.

"Stopping at the Crown," said the stranger, "—Crown at Muggleton—met a party—flannel jackets—white trousers—anchovy sandwiches—deviled kidneys—splendid fellows—glorious." Throughout the play he was eating, drinking, and talking, without cessation. "Capital game—well played—some strokes admirable," he concluded, as both sides crowded into the tent after the game.

Two of the principal members of the Dingley Dell club approached Mr. Pickwick and said, "We are about to partake of a plain dinner at the Blue Lion, sir; we hope you and your friends will join us."

"Of course," said Mr. Wardle, "among our friends we include Mr.—" and he looked toward the stranger.

"Jingle," said that versatile gentleman, taking the hint at once. "Jingle—Alfred Jingle, Esq., of No Hall, Nowhere."

"I shall be very happy, I am sure," said Mr. Pickwick.

"So shall I," said Mr. Alfred Jingle.

4

It was evening of the same day. The cricketers had not yet returned; Isabella and Emily had strolled out with Mr. Trundle; Mr. Wardle's deaf old mother had fallen asleep in her chair; the snoring of the fat boy penetrated from the distant kitchen. And there sat the spinster aunt and Mr. Tupman in a garden bower.

"Miss Wardle," said Mr. Tupman, "you are an angel."

"Mr. Tupman!" exclaimed Rachel, blushing. "Men are such deceivers."

"They are, they are," ejaculated Mr. Tupman, "but not all men. There lives at least one being who can never change—one being who would be content to devote his whole existence to your happiness." And ere the lady was aware of his intention, Mr. Tupman had sunk upon his knees at her feet.

"Mr. Tupman, rise," said Rachel.

"Never!" was the valorous reply. "Oh, Rachel! Say you love me."

"Mr. Tupman," said the spinster aunt, with averted head, "I can hardly speak the words; but—but—you are not wholly indifferent to me." There is no telling how many kisses Mr. Tupman might have bestowed on her, if the lady had not suddenly given a very unaffected start and exclaimed in an affrighted tone, "Mr. Tupman, we are observed! We are discovered!"

Mr. Tupman looked round. There was the fat boy, perfectly motionless, with his large circular eyes staring into the arbor, but without the slightest expression on his face. Mr. Tupman took the arm of the spinster aunt and walked toward the house; the fat boy followed behind. "He must have been fast asleep," whispered Mr. Tupman. But Mr. Tupman was wrong.

Eleven—twelve—one o'clock struck, and the gentlemen had still not arrived. Could they have been waylaid and robbed? Hark! There they were: Mr. Pickwick, with his hands in his pockets and his hat cocked completely over his left eye, shaking his head from side to side, and producing a constant succession of the blandest and most benevolent smiles without being moved thereunto by any discernible cause or pretense whatsoever; old

Mr. Wardle, with a highly inflamed countenance, grasping the hand of a strange gentleman, muttering protestations of eternal friendship!

"Is anything the matter?" inquired the three ladies.

"Nothing the matter," replied Mr. Pickwick. "We—we're—all right. I say, Wardle, we're all right, ain't we?"

"I should think so," replied the jolly host.—"My dears, here's my friend, Mr. Jingle—Mr. Pickwick's friend, Mr. Jingle, come 'pon—little visit."

"What a nice man!" whispered the spinster aunt to Mr. Tupman; and his mind was troubled. Nor was the succeeding half hour's conversation of a nature to calm his perturbed spirit. The new visitor was very talkative, and the number of his anecdotes was only to be exceeded by the extent of his politeness. Mr. Tupman felt that as Jingle's popularity increased he (Tupman) retired further into the shade. His laughter was forced—his merriment feigned. But worse was to follow the next day.

It was old Mrs. Wardle's habit on fine summer mornings to repair to the arbor in which Mr. Tupman had already signalized himself. She was not a little surprised on this particular morning to see the fat boy look carefully round him and then return toward her with great stealth.

The old lady was timorous—most old ladies are—and her first impression was that the bloated lad was about to do her some grievous bodily harm. Her terror was in no degree diminished by his coming close up to her and shouting in her ear in an agitated tone—"Missus!"

Now it so happened that Mr. Jingle was walking in the garden close to the arbor at this moment. He too heard the shout of "Missus" and stopped to hear more.

"Well, Joe," said the trembling old lady. "I'm sure I have been a good mistress to you, Joe. What can you want to do now?"

"I wants to make your flesh creep," replied the boy. "What do you think I see in this very arbor last night?"

"Bless us! What?" exclaimed the old lady.

"The strange gentleman—him as had his arm hurt—a kissin' and huggin'—"

"Who, Joe? None of the servants, I hope."

"Worser than that," roared the fat boy. "Miss Rachel."

"My da'ter!" Fragments of angry sentences reached the ears of Mr. Jingle.

It was a remarkable coincidence perhaps, but it was nevertheless a fact, that Mr. Jingle within five minutes after his arrival at Manor Farm on the preceding night had inwardly resolved to lay siege to the heart of the spinster aunt, without delay. He immediately sought her out. "Miss Wardle," said Mr. Jingle, with affected earnestness, "forgive intrusion—short acquaintance—no time for ceremony—all discovered. Treacherous dog, Joe—told the old lady—old lady furious—wild—raving—arbor—Tupman—came to warn you—tender my services—prevent the hubbub."

"Oh, Mr. Jingle, what *can* I say!" exclaimed the spinster aunt.

"Say he dreamed it," replied Mr. Jingle, coolly. "Blackguard boy—lovely woman—fat boy horsewhipped—you believed—end of the matter—all comfortable." That insinuating gentleman then sighed deeply, fixed his eyes on her face for a couple of minutes, started melodramatically, and suddenly withdrew them. "Ha!" exclaimed Mr. Jingle. "Your love bestowed upon a man who— but no; he is my friend; I will not expose his vices. Miss Wardle— farewell!"

"Mr. Jingle," said the aunt, "I entreat—I implore you, if there is any dreadful mystery connected with Mr. Tupman, reveal it."

"Can I," said Mr. Jingle, fixing his eyes on the aunt's face— "can I see—lovely creature—sacrificed at the shrine—heartless avarice! Tupman only wants your money. More than that, loves another. Short girl—black eyes—niece Emily."

Now, if there were one individual in the whole world of whom the spinster aunt entertained a mortal and deeply rooted jealousy, it was this identical niece. Biting her thin lips, she said, "It can't be. I won't believe it."

"Watch 'em," said Jingle.

"I will," said the aunt.

"He'll pay her every possible attention."

"Let him."

"And he'll cut you."

"Cut *me!*" screamed the spinster aunt. "*He* cut *me—will* he!" And she trembled with rage and disappointment.

"You'll not have him afterward?"

"Never."

"You'll take somebody else?"

"Yes."

"You shall." Mr. Jingle fell on his knees, remained thereupon for five minutes thereafter, and rose the accepted lover of the spinster aunt—conditionally upon Mr. Tupman's perjury being made clear and manifest.

The burden of proof lay with Mr. Alfred Jingle; and he produced his evidence that very day at dinner. The spinster aunt could hardly believe her eyes. Mr. Tracy Tupman was established at Emily's side, ogling, whispering, and smiling, in opposition to Mr. Snodgrass. Not a word, not a look, not a glance, did he bestow upon his heart's pride of the evening before.

"Damn that boy!" thought old Mr. Wardle to himself—he had heard the story from his mother. "He *must* have been asleep. It's all imagination."

"Traitor!" thought the spinster aunt. "Dear Mr. Jingle was not deceiving me. Ugh! How I hate the wretch!"

The following conversation may serve to explain to our readers this apparently unaccountable alteration of deportment on the part of Mr. Tupman.

"How did I do it?" he inquired secretly of Mr. Jingle.

"Splendid—capital—couldn't act better myself."

"Does Rachel still wish it?"

"Of course—she don't like it—but must be done."

"Oh, my friend!" said poor Mr. Tupman. "Receive my warmest thanks for your disinterested kindness. Can I ever repay you?"

"Don't talk of it," replied Mr. Jingle. He stopped short, as if suddenly recollecting something, and said, "By the bye—can't spare ten pounds, can you? —very particular purpose—pay you in three days."

"I dare say I can," replied Mr. Tupman, in the fullness of his heart. "Three days, you say?"

"Only three days—all over then—no more difficulties."

Mr. Tupman counted the money into his companion's hand.

"Where's Rachel?" said Mr. Wardle at supper. "And Jingle?"

Suddenly one of the servants burst into the room. "They ha'
gone, Mas'r! Gone right clean off, sir!" (At this juncture Mr.
Tupman was observed to lay down his knife and fork and to turn
very pale.)

"Who's gone?" said Mr. Wardle, fiercely.

"Mus'r Jingle and Miss Rachel, in a po'chay, from Blue Lion,
Muggleton. I was there; but I couldn't stop 'em; so I run off to
tell you."

"I paid his expenses!" said Mr. Tupman, jumping up franti-
cally. "He's got ten pounds of mine! Stop him! He's swindled me!
I won't stand it!"

"Put the horse in the gig!" cried the host. "I'll get a chaise at
the Lion and follow 'em instantly."

"I'll go with you," said Mr. Pickwick.

They jumped into the gig. "How much are they ahead?" shouted Wardle, as they drove up to the door of the Blue Lion.

"Not above three-quarters of an hour," was everybody's reply.

"Chaise and four directly!" And away they went, fast and furiously.

5

THERE are in London, in the Borough especially, several old inns, once the headquarters of celebrated coaches. It was in the yard of one of these inns—the White Hart—that a man was busily employed in brushing the dirt off a pair of boots, early on the morning succeeding the events narrated in the last chapter. A bright red handkerchief was wound in a very loose and unstudied style round his neck, and an old white hat was carelessly thrown on one side of his head.

A loud ringing of one of the bells belonging to a double tier of bedroom galleries was followed by the appearance of a smart chambermaid, who called over the balustrades, "Sam! Number twenty-two wants his boots."

"Ask number twenty-two, wether he'll have 'em now or wait till he gets 'em," was the reply of the man with the white hat.

There was another loud ring, and the bustling old landlady appeared. "Here, clean them shoes for number seventeen directly, and take 'em to private sitting room, number five," she cried, flinging down a pair of lady's shoes.

"She came in early this morning," said the chambermaid, "with a gentleman; and it's him as wants his boots, and you'd better do 'em, that's all."

"Vy didn't you say so before?" said Sam, with great indignation. "Private room! And a lady too! If he's anything of a gen'lm'n, he's vorth a shillin' a day." Stimulated by this inspiring reflection, Mr. Samuel brushed away with such hearty good will that in a few minutes he stepped into the presence of a lady and gentleman seated at breakfast.

"Boots," said the gentleman, "do you know Doctors' Commons?"

"Yes, sir. Paul's Churchyard, sir; two porters in the middle as touts for licenses."

"What do they do?" inquired the gentleman.

"Do! *You*, sir! That ain't the wo'st on it, neither. They puts things into old gen'lm'n's heads as they never dreamed of. My father, sir, wos a coachman. A widower he wos, and fat enough for anything. His missus dies and leaves him four hundred pound. Down he goes to the Commons, to see the lawyer—up comes the touter, touches his hat—'License, sir, marriage license?'—'Dash my veskit,' says my father, 'I never thought o' that.—No,' says he, 'damme, I'm too old, b'sides I'm a many sizes too large,' says he. 'Not a bit on it, sir,' says the touter. 'This way, sir—this way!' And sure enough my father walks arter him, like a tame monkey behind a horgan. 'What's your name, sir,' says the lawyer. 'Tony Weller,' says my father. 'And what's the lady's name?' My father was struck all of a heap. 'Blessed if I know,' says he. 'Can't I put that in arterward' 'Impossible!' says the lawyer. 'Wery well,' says my father, after he'd thought a moment, 'put down Mrs. Clarke.' 'What Clarke?' says the lawyer, dipping his pen in the ink. 'Susan Clarke, Markis o'Granby, Dorking,' says my father. 'She'll have me, if I ask, I dessay—I never said nothing to her, but she'll have me, I know.' The license was made out, and she *did* have him, and what's more she's got him now.—Beg your pardon, sir," said Sam and left the room.

"Half past nine—just time for the license—off at once," said the gentleman, whom we need hardly introduce as Mr. Jingle. Skipping playfully up to the spinster aunt, he imprinted a chaste kiss upon her lips.

"Dear man!" said the spinster as the door closed after him.

"Rum old girl," said Mr. Jingle, as he walked down the passage.

He was yet on his way back to the White Hart, when two plump gentlemen and one thin one entered the inn yard. "My friend," said the thin gentleman, going up to Mr. Samuel Weller, "this is a curious old house of yours."

"If you'd sent word you was a coming, we'd ha' had it repaired," replied the imperturbable Sam.

The little man seemed rather baffled by this remark, and one of the plump gentlemen, who in addition to a benevolent countenance, possessed a pair of spectacles and a pair of black gaiters, interfered. "The fact of the matter is," said he, "that my friend here (pointing to the other plump gentleman) will give you half a guinea, if you'll answer one or two—"

"Now, my dear sir," said the little man, "if you place a matter in the hands of a professional man, you must in no way interfere in the progress of the business—really Mr. Pickwick, my dear sir, really."

"You want me to except of half a guinea," broke in Sam Weller. "Wery well, I'm agreeable. I can't say no fairer than that, can I, sir?" Mr. Pickwick smiled. "Then the next question is, what the devil do you want with me, as the man said w'en he see the ghost?"

"We want to know," said the little man, solemnly, "who you've got in this house, at present?"

"Who there is in the house!" said Sam, in whose mind the inmates were always represented by that particular article of their costume which came under his immediate superintendence. "There's a wooden leg in number six; there's a pair of Hessians in thirteen; there's two pair of halves in the commercial; there's these here painted tops in the snuggery inside the bar; and five more tops in the coffee room."

"Nothing more?" said the little man.

"Stop a bit," replied Sam, suddenly recollecting. "Yes; there's a pair of Wellingtons a good deal worn, and a pair o' lady's shoes, in number five."

"What sort of shoes?" hastily inquired Wardle.

"Country make," replied Sam. "Muggleton."

"It *is* them," exclaimed Wardle. "By Heavens, we've found them. Show us the room." Sam led the way; old Wardle opened the door; and they walked into the room just as Mr. Jingle produced the license to the spinster aunt. "You—you are a nice rascal, aren't you?" exclaimed Wardle, breathless with passion.

"My dear sir, my dear sir," said the little man, who was Mr. Wardle's lawyer Mr. Perker, "pray consider—pray. Defamation of character—action for damages."

"And you, Rachel," continued Mr. Wardle, "at a time of life when you ought to know better, what do *you* mean by running away with a vagabond. Get on your bonnet."

"Do nothing of the kind," said Jingle. "Leave the room, sir—

no business here—lady's free to act as she pleases—more than one and twenty.—Boots, get me an officer."

"Stay, stay," said little Mr. Perker. "Consider, sir, consider."

"I'll *not* consider," replied Jingle. "She's her own mistress—see who dares to take her away—unless she wishes it."

"I *won't* be taken away," shrieked the spinster aunt. "I *don't* wish it."

"My dear sir," said the little man, in a low tone, taking Mr. Wardle and Mr. Pickwick apart, "we're in a very awkward situation. We must be content to suffer some pecuniary loss."

"I'll suffer any, rather than submit to this disgrace and let her, fool as she is, be made miserable for life," said Wardle.

"I rather think it can be done," said the bustling little man. "Mr. Jingle, will you step with us into the next room for a moment? —Now, sir, the fact is that, beyond a few hundreds, the lady has little or nothing till the death of her mother—fine old lady, my dear sir; only one member of her family hasn't lived to eighty-five, and *he* was beheaded by one of the Henrys. The old lady is not seventy-three, my dear sir. Don't you think that fifty pounds and liberty would be better than Miss Wardle and expectation?"

"Won't do—not half enough!" said Mr. Jingle, rising.

"Well, my dear sir, just tell me what *will* do."

"Expensive affair," said Mr. Jingle. "Money out of pocket, twelve pounds—compensation, a hundred—breach of honor—and loss of the lady—"

"Yes, my dear sir, yes," said the little man, with a knowing look, "never mind the last two items. That's a hundred and twelve —say a hundred."

"And twenty," said Mr. Jingle. The check was written by the little gentleman and pocketed by Mr. Jingle.

"Now, leave this house instantly!" said Wardle, starting up.

"Off directly," said the unabashed Jingle. "Bye-bye, Pickwick. Here," tossing the license at his feet, "get the name altered—take home the lady—do for Tuppy."

Slowly and sadly did the two friends and the deserted lady return to Muggleton. Mr. Tupman having already departed, the other Pickwickians followed him immediately to London.

Mr. Pickwick's apartments in Goswell Street, although on a

limited scale, were of a very neat and comfortable description. His landlady, Mrs. Bardell—the relict of a deceased custom-house officer—was a comely woman of agreeable appearance, with a natural genius for cooking. The only other inmates of the house were a large man and a small boy, the first a lodger, the second a production of Mrs. Bardell's. Cleanliness and quiet reigned throughout the house; and in it Mr. Pickwick's will was law.

"Mrs. Bardell," said Mr. Pickwick, the morning after his return home, "your little boy is a very long time gone."

"Why, it's a good long way to the Borough, sir," remonstrated Mrs. Bardell.

"Ah," said Mr. Pickwick, "very true; so it is.—Mrs. Bardell," said Mr. Pickwick, at the expiration of a few minutes, as she dusted his apartment, "do you think it a much greater expense to keep two people, than to keep one?"

"La, Mr. Pickwick," said Mrs. Bardell, coloring up to the very border of her cap, as she fancied she observed a species of matrimonial twinkle in the eyes of her lodger, "that depends a good deal upon the person, and whether it's a saving and careful person, sir."

"That's very true," said Mr. Pickwick, "but the person I have in my eye (here he looked very hard at Mrs. Bardell) I think possesses these qualities and has, moreover, a considerable knowledge of the world and a great deal of sharpness, Mrs. Bardell, which may be of material use to me."

"La, Mr. Pickwick," said Mrs. Bardell, the crimson rising again.

"You'll think it very strange now," said the amiable Mr. Pickwick, "that I never consulted you about this matter, and never mentioned it, till I sent your little boy out this morning— eh?"

Mrs. Bardell could only reply by a look. She had long worshiped Mr. Pickwick at a distance, but here she was, all at once, raised to a pinnacle to which her wildest and most extravagant hopes had never dared to aspire.

"Well," said Mr. Pickwick, "what do you think?"

"Oh, Mr. Pickwick," said Mrs. Bardell, trembling with agitation, "it is so kind of you, Mr. Pickwick, to have so much consideration for my loneliness."

"Ah, to be sure," said Mr. Pickwick; "I never thought of that. When I am in town, you'll always have somebody to sit with you. So you will."

"Oh, you dear—" said Mrs. Bardell. Mr. Pickwick started. "Oh you kind, good, playful dear," said Mrs. Bardell; and, without more ado, she rose from her chair and flung her arms round Mr. Pickwick's neck, with a cataract of tears and a chorus of sobs.

"Bless my soul," cried the astonished Mr. Pickwick. "Mrs. Bardell, my good woman—dear me, what a situation—pray consider—I hear somebody coming up the stairs. Don't, don't, there's a good creature, don't." But entreaty and remonstrance were alike unavailing, for Mrs. Bardell had fainted in Mr. Pickwick's arms; and before he could gain time to deposit her on a chair,

Master Bardell entered the room, ushering in Mr. Tupman, Mr. Winkle, and Mr. Snodgrass.

Mr. Pickwick was struck motionless and speechless. Master Bardell at first stood at the door astounded and uncertain. But, by degrees, the impression that his mother must have suffered some personal damage pervaded his partially developed mind; and, considering Mr. Pickwick as the aggressor, he set up an appalling and semi-earthly kind of howling and commenced assailing that immortal gentleman about the back and legs.

"Take this little villain away," said the agonized Mr. Pickwick; "he's mad. Now, lead this woman downstairs." And downstairs she was led.

"I cannot conceive," said Mr. Pickwick, "what has been the matter with that woman. I had merely announced to her my intention of keeping a manservant, when she fell into the extraordinary paroxysm in which you found her. Very extraordinary thing."

"Very," said his three friends.

"Placed me in such an extremely awkward situation," he continued.

"Very," was the reply of his followers, as they coughed slightly and looked dubiously at each other. "There is a man in the passage now," said Mr. Tupman.

"It's the man I spoke to you about," said Mr. Pickwick. "I sent for him to the Borough this morning." And Mr. Samuel Weller presented himself. "Now with regard to the matter on which I sent for you," said Mr. Pickwick.

"That's the p'int, sir," interposed Sam; "out vith it, as the father said to the child, w'en he swallowed a farden."

A sunbeam of placid benevolence played on Mr. Pickwick's features as he said, "I have half made up my mind to engage you."

"Wages?" inquired Sam.

"Twelve pounds a year," replied Mr. Pickwick.

"Clothes?"

"Two suits."

"Work?"

"To attend upon me and travel about with me and these gentlemen here."

"Take the bill down," said Sam, emphatically. "I'm let to a

single gentleman, and the terms is agreed upon.—I wonder," he added, when he found himself furnished with a gray coat with the P.C. button, a black hat with a cockade to it, a pink striped waist-coat, and tight breeches and gaiters, "I wonder whether I'm meant to be a footman, or a groom, or a gamekeeper, or a seeds-man. I looks like a sort of compo of every one on 'em. Never mind; there's change of air, plenty to see, and little to do; and all this suits my complaint uncommon; so long life to the Pickvicks, says I!"

6

THE next journey undertaken by the Pickwick Club was to Eatans-will, where they had been for some days established when Mr. Pickwick's faithful valet put into his hand a card, on which was engraved the following inscription:

MRS. LEO HUNTER
The Den, Eatanswill

"Person's a waitin'," said Sam, epigrammatically. "He wants you particklar."

On Mr. Pickwick's entrance, a grave man started up and said, with an air of profound respect, "Allow me, sir, the honor of grasping your hand. The noise of your fame has reached the ears of Mrs. Leo Hunter. My wife, sir—Mrs. Leo Hunter—is proud to number among her acquaintance all those who have rendered themselves celebrated by their works and talents. Tomorrow morn-ing we give a public breakfast—a *fête champêtre*—to a great number of those who have rendered themselves celebrated by their works and talents. Permit Mrs. Leo Hunter, sir, to have the gratification of seeing you at the Den."

"With great pleasure," replied Mr. Pickwick.

"You have a gentleman in your train, who has produced some beautiful little poems, I think, sir," said the grave man.

"My friend Mr. Snodgrass has a great taste for poetry," replied Mr. Pickwick.

"So has Mrs. Leo Hunter, sir. She dotes on poetry, sir. She adores it; I may say that her whole soul and mind are wound up and entwined with it. She has produced some delightful pieces, herself, sir. You may have met with her 'Ode to an Expiring Frog,'

> Can I view thee panting, lying
> On thy stomach, without sighing;
> Can I unmoved see thee dying
> On a log,
> Expiring frog!"

"Beautiful!" said Mr. Pickwick.

"All point, sir," said Mr. Leo Hunter, "but you shall hear Mrs. Leo Hunter repeat it. *She* can do justice to it, sir. She will repeat it, in character, sir, tomorrow morning."

"In character!"

"As Minerva. But I forgot—it's a fancy-dress breakfast."

"Dear me," said Mr. Pickwick, glancing at his own figure, "I can't possibly—"

"Can't, sir, can't!" exclaimed Mr. Leo Hunter. "Soloman Lucas, in the High Street, has thousands of fancy dresses. But I may venture to promise an exception in your case, sir. We will expect you and your distinguished friends."

Intelligence of the fancy ball had already reached Mr. Pickwick's distinguished friends. "I shall go as a bandit," announced Mr. Tupman.

"What!" said Mr. Pickwick, with a sudden start. "You don't mean to say, Mr. Tupman, that it is your intention to put yourself into a green velvet jacket, with a two-inch tail?"

"Such *is* my intention, sir," replied Mr. Tupman warmly. "And why not, sir?"

"Because, sir," said Mr. Pickwick, considerably excited, "because you are too old, sir. And if any further ground of objection be wanting, you are too fat, sir."

"Sir," said Mr. Tupman, his face suffused with a crimson glow, "this is an insult."

"Sir," replied Mr. Pickwick in the same tone, "it is not half the insult to you that your appearance in my presence in a green velvet jacket, with a two-inch tail, would be to me."

"Sir," said Mr. Tupman, "you're a fellow."

"Sir," said Mr. Pickwick, "you're another!"

Mr. Tupman advanced a step or two and glared at Mr.

Pickwick. "My attachment to your person, sir," said he, speaking in a voice tremulous with emotion, and tucking up his wristbands meanwhile, "is great—very great—but upon that person I must take summary vengeance."

"Come on, sir!" replied Mr. Pickwick. Stimulated by the exciting nature of the dialogue, the heroic man actually threw himself into a paralytic attitude, confidently supposed by the two bystanders to have been intended as a posture of defense.

"For shame, gentlemen, for shame," exclaimed Mr. Snodgrass, suddenly recovering the power of speech and rushing between the two.

Mr. Pickwick's countenance gradually resumed its usual benign expression. "I have been hasty," said he; "Tupman, your hand. You will wear the green velvet jacket? To oblige me?" It was settled.

Never was such a blaze of beauty and fashion and literature as appeared next day at Mrs. Leo Hunter's! There were hosts of local geniuses and, more than these, there were half a dozen lions from London—authors, real authors, who had written whole books and printed them afterward. Above all, there was Mrs. Leo Hunter in the character of Minerva.

"Mr. Pickwick," said Mrs. Leo Hunter, "I must make you promise not to stir from my side the whole day. There are hundreds of people here that I must positively introduce you to.—Count, Count," she screamed to a well-whiskered individual in a foreign uniform, who was passing by. "I want to introduce two very clever people to each other. Mr. Pickwick, I have great pleasure in introducing you to Count Smorltork." She added in a hurried whisper to Mr. Pickwick, "The famous foreigner—gathering materials for his great work on England—hem!—Count Smorltork, Mr. Pickwick."

"What you say, Mrs. Hunt?" inquired the count, drawing forth a set of tablets, "Pig Vig or Big Vig—what you call—lawyer—eh? I see—that is it. Big Vig."

"No, No, Count," said the lady, "Pick-wick."

"Ah, ah, I see," replied the count. "Peek, Christian name—Weeks, surname—good, ver' good. Peek Weeks. How you do, Weeks?"

"Quite well, I thank you," replied Mr. Pickwick, with all his usual affability. "Have you been long in England?"

"Long—ver' long time—fortnight—more."

"Do you stay here long?"

"One week."

"You will have enough to do," said Mr. Pickwick, smiling, "to gather all the materials you want, in that time."

"Eh, they are gathered," said the count, tapping his forehead.

"Count," said Mrs. Leo Hunter, "this is Mr. Snodgrass, a poet."

"Stop," exclaimed the count, bringing out the tablets once more. "Head, po'try—chapter, literary friends—name, Snowgrass —ver' good. Introduced to Snowgrass by Mrs. Hunt, which wrote other sweet poem—what is that name?—'Fog'—'Perspiring Fog'— ver' good—ver' good indeed." And the count put up his tablets, thoroughly satisfied that he had made most valuable additions to his stock of information.

Mrs. Leo Hunter's usual course of proceeding was to issue cards for a hundred and breakfast for fifty, or in other words to feed only the very particular lions and let the smaller animals take care of themselves. She had gathered the Pickwickians about her this morning when Mr. Leo Hunter suddenly called out, "My dear, here's Mr. Charles Fitz-Marshall."

"Pray make room," said Mrs. Leo Hunter, "to let Mr. Fitz-Marshall pass."

"Coming, my dear ma'am," cried a voice, "as quick as I can —crowds of people—full room—hard work—very." Mr. Pickwick's knife and fork fell from his hand. "Ah!" cried the voice, as its owner pushed his way among the last five and twenty Turks, officers, cavaliers, and Charles the Seconds that remained between him and the table, "regular mangle—not a crease in my coat, after all this squeezing—might have 'got up my linen'—ha! ha!"

A young man dressed as a naval officer had had barely time to take Mrs. Leo Hunter's proffered hand when his eyes encountered the indignant orbs of Mr. Pickwick. "Hullo!" said Jingle. "Quite forgot—no directions to postilion—back in a minute," and he disappeared among the crowd.

"Will you allow me to ask you, ma'am," said the excited Mr.

Pickwick, rising from his seat, "who that young man is, and where he resides?"

"He is a gentleman of fortune, Mr. Pickwick," said Mrs. Leo Hunter, "who resides at the Angel at Bury St. Edmunds, not many miles from here.—But dear me, Mr. Pickwick, you are not going to leave us?"

Long before Mrs. Leo Hunter had finished speaking, Mr. Pickwick had plunged through the throng. In another hour he and Sam Weller were on their way to Bury St. Edmunds. "He deceived a worthy man once, and we were the innocent cause," said Mr. Pickwick. "He shall not do it again, if I can help it.— Do not mention my name, Sam," he cautioned, when they reached the Angel, "but ascertain that he is in the house."

Sam returned with the information that Mr. Charles Fitz-Marshall was spending the evening at some private house in the neighborhood and had taken his servant with him. "If I can get a talk with this here servant in the mornin', he'll tell me all his master's concerns," said Mr. Weller.

Accordingly, the next morning, he introduced himself to a young fellow in mulberry-colored livery who was sitting on a bench in the yard, reading what appeared to be a hymn book. "I should like to know you," said Mr. Weller, going up to him. "I like your appearance, old feller."

"Well, that is very strange," said the mulberry man, with great simplicity of manner. "I like yours so much that I wanted to speak to you, from the very first moment I saw you."

"Wery sing'ler," said Sam, inwardly congratulating himself upon the softness of the stranger. "What's your name, my patriarch?"

"Job Trotter. What's yours?"

Sam bore in mind his master's caution and replied, "My name's Walker. Will you take a drop o' somethin', Mr. Trotter? And what sort of a place have you got?"

"Bad," said Job, "very bad. My master's going to run away with an immense rich heiress, from boarding school."

"What a dragon!" said Sam, refilling his companion's glass. "It's some boarding school in this town, I suppose, ain't it?"

"No, no," said Mr. Trotter, "that is a secret—a great secret."

"Well, don't you think, old feller," remonstrated Mr. Weller, "that if you let your master take in this here young lady, you're a precious rascal?"

"I know that," said Job Trotter, turning upon his companion a countenance of deep contrition. "But who'd believe me?"

"Come this way," said Sam, suddenly jumping up, "my mas'r's the man you want." And, after a slight resistance on the part of Job Trotter, Sam presented him to Mr. Pickwick.

"I am very sorry to betray my master, sir," said Job Trotter, applying to his eyes a pink checked pocket handkerchief. "I know it is my duty, sir, but it is a hard trial."

"You are a very good fellow," said Mr. Pickwick, much affected; "an honest fellow."

"Come, come," interposed Sam, who had witnessed Mr. Trotter's tears with considerable impatience, "blow this here water-cart bis'ness. Now, where is this boarding school?"

"It is a large, old, red-brick house, just outside the town," replied Job Trotter.

"And when," said Mr. Pickwick, "is this elopement to take place?"

"Tonight, sir," replied Job.

"Instant measures must be taken," said Mr. Pickwick. "I will see the lady who keeps the establishment immediately."

"I beg your pardon, sir," said Job, "but that course of proceeding will never do. Nothing but taking him in the very fact of eloping will convince the old lady, sir. My master and I, being in the confidence of the servants, will be secreted in the kitchen. I have been thinking that if you were waiting in the back garden, alone, and I was to let you in at exactly half past eleven, you would be just in time to assist me in frustrating the designs of this bad man, by whom I have been unfortunately ensnared." Here Mr. Trotter sighed deeply.

"I don't like the plan," said Mr. Pickwick; "but as I see no other and as the happiness of this young lady's whole life is at stake, I adopt it. I shall be sure to be there."

7

THE day wore on, evening came, and a little before ten o'clock Sam Weller reported that Mr. Jingle and Job had gone out together, that their luggage was packed up, and that they had ordered a chaise. The plot was evidently in execution, as Mr. Trotter had foretold.

Half past ten arrived, and it was time for Mr. Pickwick to issue forth on his delicate errand. Scaling the wall of the boarding school, he crouched into an angle and awaited the appointed time. When half past eleven rang, he tapped on the door.

Now the door opened outward; and as it opened wider and wider, Mr. Pickwick receded behind it, more and more. What was his astonishment when he just peeped out, by way of caution, to see that the person who had opened it was—not Job Trotter, but a servant girl! Mr. Pickwick drew in his head again swiftly. "It must have been the cat, Sarah," said the girl, addressing herself to someone in the house; and she refastened the door.

"This is very curious," thought Mr. Pickwick. "They are sitting up beyond their usual hour, I suppose." Suddenly a vivid flash of lightning was followed by a loud peal of thunder. Mr. Pickwick was perfectly aware that a tree is a very dangerous neighbor in a thunderstorm. If he remained where he was, he might fall the victim of an accident; if he showed himself in the garden, he might be consigned to a constable. He would try the signal again. No reply; very odd. Another knock. He listened again. There was a low whispering inside, and then a voice cried, "Who's there?"

"That's not Job," thought Mr. Pickwick, hastily drawing himself straight up against the wall again. "It's a woman." What was his discomfiture, when he heard the chain and bolts withdrawn and saw the door slowly opening, wider and wider! He retreated into the corner, step by step.

"Who's there?" screamed a numerous chorus of treble voices, consisting of the spinster lady of the establishment, three teachers, five female servants, and thirty boarders, all half dressed and in a forest of curl papers. Suddenly an inquisitive boarder, who had been peeping between the hinges, set up a fearful screaming of four young-lady-power. "Oh, the man—the man—behind the door!"

Never was such a screaming, and fainting, and struggling, beheld. In the midst of the tumult Mr. Pickwick emerged from his concealment and presented himself among them. "Ladies— dear ladies," said Mr. Pickwick. "You may bind me hand and leg, only let me speak to the lady of the house." He stepped into a closet of his own accord; and, the lady having been brought to, the conference began.

"What did you do in my garden, Man?" said the lady in a faint voice.

"I came to warn you that one of your young ladies was going to elope tonight," replied Mr. Pickwick, from the interior of the closet, "with your friend Mr. Charles Fitz-Marshall."

"*My* friend! I don't know any such person."

"Well, Mr. Jingle, then."

"I never heard the name in my life."

"Then I have been deceived and deluded," said Mr. Pickwick. "Send to the Angel for Mr. Pickwick's manservant, I implore you, ma'am."

When, after an hour, Mr. Pickwick was rescued, he seemed bewildered and amazed. Only after Sam had got him safely to bed did he speak. "Sam," said he then, looking out from under the bedclothes, "Jingle suspected my design and set that fellow on you, with this story, I suppose?"

"Just that, sir," replied Mr. Weller. "Reg'lar do, sir; artful dodge. And whenever I catches hold o' that there melan-cholly chap, if I don't bring some real water into his eyes, for once in a way, my name ain't Weller."

The process of being washed in the night air and rough dried in a closet is as dangerous as it is peculiar. Mr. Pickwick was laid up with an attack of rheumatism. His friends, having been sent for, were surprised to find also at the Angel Mr. Wardle and Trundle, who had come down for the shooting.

"How are you?" said the old man, grasping their hands. "I have just been telling Pickwick that we must have you all down at Christmas. We're going to have a wedding—a real wedding this time. Trundle and Bella." While they were talking, Sam entered with a letter.

"Mercy on us!" cried Mr. Pickwick, when he had read it. "What's this? It must be a jest; it—it—can't be true."

Mr. Tupman, with a trembling voice, read the letter, of which the following is a copy:

Freeman's Court, Cornhill, Aug.
28, 1830
Bardell against *Pickwick*

Sir,
   Having been instructed by Mrs. Martha Bardell to commence an action
against you for a breach of promise of marriage, for which the plaintiff
lays her damages at fifteen hundred pounds, we beg to inform you that a
writ has been issued against you in this suit in the Court of Common Pleas
and request to know, by return of post, the name of your attorney in
London, who will accept service thereof.

We are, sir,
Your obedient servants,
Dodson and Fogg

Mr. Samuel Pickwick

"It's a conspiracy," said Mr. Pickwick. "Who ever saw me with
her? Not even my friends here—"

"Except on one occasion," said Mr. Tupman.

   Mr. Pickwick changed color. "Gracious powers!" he ejaculated, as the recollection of the scene in question struck forcibly
upon him. "What a dreadful instance of the force of circumstances!
I'll have it explained, though. I'll see this Dodson and Fogg! I'll
go to London tomorrow."

"Not tomorrow," said Wardle; "you're too lame. And next
day is the first of September, and you're pledged to ride out with
us to Sir Geoffrey Manning's grounds, for lunch, if you don't
take the field."

"Where did you tell the boy to meet us with the snack, Martin?"
inquired Wardle of the tall gamekeeper, when the sportsmen had
gathered.

"Side of One-tree Hill, at twelve o'clock, sir."

"That's not Sir Geoffrey's land, is it?"

"No, sir, but it's close by it. It's Captain Boldwig's land."

"Will you join us at twelve, then, Pickwick?" said old Wardle.

"I should very much like to go with you," said Mr. Pickwick,
wistfully.

"There's a barrow t'other side the hedge," said the gamekeeper's boy. "If the gentleman's lame, the gentleman's servant
could wheel it along the paths."

"The wery thing," said Mr. Weller, who ardently longed to

see the sport. Mr. Pickwick was placed in the barrow, and off the party set.

"Stop, Sam," said Mr. Pickwick, when they had got half across the first field. "I won't suffer this barrow to be moved another step unless Winkle carries that gun of his in a different manner."

"How *am* I to carry it?" said the wretched Winkle.

"Carry it with the muzzle to the ground," replied Mr. Pickwick.

"It's so unsportsman-like," reasoned Winkle.

"I don't care whether it's unsportsman-like or not," replied Mr. Pickwick; "I am not going to be shot in a wheelbarrow, for the sake of appearances, to please anybody."

"Well, well—I don't mind," said poor Winkle, turning his gun stock uppermost; "—there." And on they went.

The dogs suddenly came to a dead stop, and the party, advancing stealthily a single pace, stopped too.

"What's the matter with the dogs' legs?" whispered Mr. Winkle. "How queer they're standing."

"Hush, can't you?" replied Wardle, softly. "Don't you see they're making a point? Now then." There was a sharp whirring noise that made Mr. Winkle start back as if he had been shot himself. Bang, bang went a couple of guns.

"Where are they?" said Mr. Winkle, in a state of the highest excitement, turning round and round in all directions. "Where are they? Tell me when to fire. Where are they—where are they?"

"Where are they?" said Wardle, taking up a brace of birds which the dogs had deposited at his feet. "Why, here they are."

On they crept; and very quietly they would have advanced if Mr. Winkle, in the performance of some very intricate evolutions with his gun, had not accidentally fired, at the most critical moment, over the boy's head, exactly in the very spot where the tall gamekeeper's brain would have been, had he been there instead.

"Why, what on earth did you do that for?" said old Wardle, as the birds flew unharmed away.

"I never saw such a gun in my life," replied poor Mr. Winkle, looking at the lock, as if that would do any good. "It goes off of its own accord. It *will* do it."

"Will do it!" echoed Wardle, with something of irritation in his manner. "I wish it would kill something of its own accord."

"It'll do that afore long, sir," observed the tall gamekeeper, in a low, prophetic voice.

"What do you mean by that observation, sir?" inquired Mr. Winkle, angrily.

"Never mind, sir, never mind," replied the long gamekeeper; "I've no family myself, sir; and this here boy's mother will get something handsome from Sir Geoffrey, if he's killed on his land. Load again, sir, load again."

"Take away his gun," cried Mr. Pickwick from the barrow, horror stricken at the long man's dark insinuations. "Take away his gun, somebody."

We are bound, on the authority of Mr. Pickwick, to state that Mr. Tupman's mode of proceeding evinced far more of prudence and deliberation than that adopted by Mr. Winkle. With the quickness and penetration of a man of genius, he had at once observed that the two great points to be attained were, first, to discharge his piece without injury to himself and, secondly, to do so without danger to the bystanders; obviously, the best thing to do, after surmounting the difficulty of firing at all, was to shut his eyes firmly and fire into the air.

On one occasion, after performing this feat, Mr. Tupman, on opening his eyes, beheld a plump partridge in the act of falling wounded to the ground. "Tupman," said Mr. Wardle, grasping him warmly by the hand, "I noticed you as you raised your piece to take aim; and the best shot in existence could not have done it more beautifully." It was in vain for Mr. Tupman to protest. From that time forth, his reputation was established.

Lunch arrived. "Weal pie," said Mr. Weller, soliloquizing, as he arranged the eatables on the grass. "Wery good thing is weal pie, when you know the lady as made it and is quite sure it ain't kittens; and arter all though, where's the odds, when they're so like weal that the wery piemen themselves don't know the difference?"

"Don't they, Sam?" said Mr. Pickwick.

"Not they, sir," replied Mr. Weller, touching his hat. "It's the seasonin' as does it."

"Well, that certainly is most capital cold punch," said Mr. Pickwick, as Mr. Wardle served him with a glass. "I'll take another. Cool; very cool. Tupman, my dear friend, a glass of punch?"

The constant succession of glasses produced considerable effect upon Mr. Pickwick. After rising, finally, to his legs to address the company in an eloquent speech, he fell into the barrow and fast asleep, in which state it was decided to leave him, while the others went on.

But he was not suffered to remain in peace. He had not been asleep half an hour when little Captain Boldwig, the owner of the property, followed by two gardeners, came striding along as fast as his size and importance would let him. "Remind me to have a board done about trespassers, and spring guns, and all that sort of thing, to keep the common people out," he said. "D'ye hear?" Suddenly his eyes encountered the wheelbarrow and Mr. Pickwick. "Who are you, you rascal?" said the captain, prodding Mr. Pickwick. "What's your name?"

"Cold punch," murmured Mr. Pickwick, as he sank to sleep again.

"That's his impudence, that's his confounded impudence," said Captain Boldwig. "He's drunk. Wheel him away, Wilkins, wheel him directly to the pound."

If the most intense gratification of three-fourths of the population was excited by seeing Mr. Pickwick wheeled into the pound, how many hundredfold was their joy increased when, after a few indistinct cries of "Sam," he sat up in the barrow and gazed with indescribable astonishment on the faces before him. "Let me out," cried Mr. Pickwick. "Where are my friends?"

"You ain't got no friends. Hurrah!" Then there came a turnip, then a potato, and then an egg; and how long this scene might have lasted, no one can tell, had not a carriage, which was driving swiftly by, suddenly pulled up, from whence there descended old Wardle and Sam Weller.

8

ON the Friday succeeding these events, Mr. Pickwick presented himself at the office of Messrs. Dodson and Fogg in London. Leaving Sam Weller below, he stepped upstairs. "I came, gentlemen," said Mr. Pickwick, gazing placidly on the two partners, "to express the surprise with which I received your letter and to inquire what grounds of action you can have against me."

"I do not hesitate to say, sir," said Dodson, "that our grounds of action, sir, are strong and not to be shaken."

"I am to understand, then," said Mr. Pickwick, "that it really is your intention to proceed with this action?"

"That you certainly may," replied Dodson.

"Very well, gentlemen, very well," said Mr. Pickwick, rising in person and wrath at the same time; "you shall hear from my solicitor, gentlemen. And before I go, gentlemen, permit me to say, that of all the disgraceful and rascally proceedings—"

"Stay, sir, stay," interposed Dodson, with great politeness. "Mr. Jackson! Mr. Wicks!"

"Sir," said two clerks, appearing at the bottom of the stairs.

"I mercly want you to hear what this gentleman says," replied Dodson. "Pray, go on, sir—disgraceful and rascally proceedings, I think you said?"

"I did," said Mr. Pickwick. "I repeat it, sir."

"You hear that, Mr. Wicks?" said Dodson.

"You won't forget these expressions, Mr. Jackson?" said Fogg. —"Perhaps you would like to call us swindlers, sir."

"I do," said Mr. Pickwick. "You *are* swindlers."

"Go on, sir," said Fogg; "you had better call us thieves, sir; or perhaps you would like to assault one of us. Pray do it, sir."

As Fogg put himself very temptingly within the reach of Mr. Pickwick's clenched fist, there is little doubt that that gentleman would have complied with his earnest entreaty, but for the inter-position of Sam. "You just come avay," said Mr. Weller. "Battle-dore and shuttlecock's a wery good game, ven you ain't the shuttlecock and two lawyers the battledores."

"Well, well, Sam," said Mr. Pickwick, when they were on the street, "you had better go to Goswell Street to collect my things and pay the rent. As I have been rather ruffled, I should like a glass of brandy-and-water first."

They entered a tavern which was apparently under the especial patronage of stage coachmen, among the number a stout, red-faced, elderly man, smoking with great vehemence, who took particular notice of them. Having blown a thick cloud of smoke from his pipe, a hoarse voice, like some strange effort of ventrilo-quism, emerged at last from beneath the capacious shawls which muffled his throat and chest, and he slowly uttered these sounds: "W'y, Sammy!"

"Why, I wouldn't ha' bclieved it!" said Mr. Weller with astonished eyes. "It's the old 'un!—My father, sir.—How are you, my ancient? And how's stepmother?"

"W'y, I'll tell you what, Sammy," said Mr. Weller senior, with much solemnity; "there never was a nicer woman as a widder, than that 'ere second wentur o' mine—a sweet creetur she was, Sammy; all I can say on her now is that, as she was such an un-common pleasant widder, it's a great pity she ever changed her con-dition. Take example by your father, my boy, and be wery careful o' widders all your life, specially if they've kept a public house.—Beg your pardon, sir," addressing Mr. Pickwick; "I hope you hain't got a widder, sir."

"Not I," replied Mr. Pickwick, laughing. "Won't you take anything?"

"You're wery good, sir," replied Mr. Weller; "perhaps a small glass o'brandy."

"Take care," said Sam, "or you'll have a touch of your old complaint, the gout."

"I've found a sov'rin cure for that, Sammy," said Mr. Weller.

"A sovereign cure for the gout," said Mr. Pickwick, hastily producing his notebook. "What is it?"

"The gout, sir," replied Mr. Weller, "the gout is a complaint as arises from too much ease and comfort. If ever you're attacked with the gout, sir, jist you marry a widder as has got a good loud woice, with a decent notion of usin' it, and you'll never have the gout agin. It's a capital prescription, sir."

"What do you think of what your father says, Sam?" inquired Mr. Pickwick, with a smile.

"Think, sir!" replied Mr. Weller. "Why, I think he's the wictim o'connubiality, as Blue Beard's domestic chaplain said, with a tear of pity, ven he buried him."

"Beg your pardon, sir," said Mr. Weller senior when Mr. Pickwick's relation to his son was made known to him. "I hope you've no fault to find with Sammy, sir?"

"None whatever," said Mr. Pickwick.

"Wery glad to hear it, sir," replied the old man; "I took a good deal o' pains with his eddication, sir; let him run in the streets when he was wery young and shift for hisself. It's the only way to make a boy sharp, sir."

"Not a wery sure one," said Mr. Weller; "I got reg'larly done the other day." And he proceeded to relate how he had fallen a ready dupe to the stratagems of Job Trotter.

Mr. Weller senior listened to the tale with the most profound attention and at its termination said, "Worn't one o' these chaps slim and tall, with long hair, and the gift of the gab wery gallopin'? And t'other's a black-haired chap in mulberry livery? Then I know where they are. They're at Ipswich, safe enough, them two. I drove 'em down there myself."

"I'll follow him," said Mr. Pickwick, with an emphatic blow on the table.

"I shall work down to Ipswich the day arter tomorrow, sir," said Mr. Weller the elder, "from the Bull in Whitechapel; and if you really mean to go, you'd better go with me."

"How's stepmother this mornin'?" asked Mr. Weller the younger, when he met his parent at the Bull.

"Queer, Sammy, queer," replied the elder Mr. Weller, with impressive gravity. "She's been gettin' rayther in the Methodistical order lately, Sammy; and she is uncommon pious, to be sure. She's too good a creetur for me, Sammy. I feel I don't deserve her."

"Ah," said Mr. Samuel, "that's wery self-denyin' o' you."

"Wery," replied his parent, with a sigh. "She's got hold o' some inwention for grown-up people being born again, Sammy; the new birth, I think they calls it. I should wery much like to see your stepmother born again. Wouldn't I put her out to nurse! What do you think them women does t'other day, Sammy? Goes and gets up a grand tea drinkin' for a feller they calls their shepherd, a lanky chap with a red nose and a white neckcloth. Such goin's on, Sammy! 'The kiss of peace,' says the shepherd; and then he kissed the women all round. Such a precious loud hymn, while the tea was a brewing; such a grace, such eatin' and drinkin'! I wish you could ha' seen that red-nosed shepherd walkin' into the ham and muffins.—Hullo! here's the governor." And the coach being ready, away they went to Ipswich.

In the main street of Ipswich there stands an inn called the Great White Horse, which is famous for its enormous size. After a long and leisurely dinner, Mr. Pickwick was conducted through a multitude of tortuous windings to a tolerably large double-bedded room with a fire. "Nobody sleeps in the other bed, of course," he said.

"Oh, no, sir." The chambermaid retired. And Mr. Pickwick suddenly recollected that he had left his watch downstairs. As it was pretty late and he was unwilling to ring his bell, he walked quietly down again.

The more stairs Mr. Pickwick went down, the more stairs

there seemed to be to descend. Passage after passage did he explore; room after room did he peep into. But at length he opened the door of the identical room in which he had spent the evening, seized his watch in triumph, and proceeded to retrace his steps to his bedchamber.

If his progress downward had been attended with difficulties and uncertainty, his journey back was infinitely more perplexing. A dozen times did he softly turn the handle of some door which resembled his own, when a gruff cry from within of "Who the devil's that?" caused him to steal away. He was reduced to the verge of despair, when an open door attracted his attention. He peeped in. Right at last! There were the two beds, whose situation he perfectly remembered, and the fire still burning.

Having carefully drawn the curtains of his bed on the outside, Mr. Pickwick took off his coat, waistcoat, and neckcloth and, slowly drawing on his tasseled nightcap, had secured it firmly on his head, when he was suddenly stopped by a most unexpected interruption; to wit, the entrance into the room of some person with a candle, who, after locking the door, advanced to the dressing table and set down the light upon it.

The only way in which Mr. Pickwick could catch a glimpse of his mysterious visitor with the least danger of being seen himself was by peeping out from between the curtains of his bed. He mustered up courage and looked out—then almost fainted with horrow and dismay. Standing before the dressing glass was a middle-aged lady, in yellow curl papers, busily engaged in brushing what ladies call their "back hair."

"I never met with anything so awful as this," thought poor Mr. Pickwick, the cold perspiration starting in drops upon his nightcap. "By the self-possession of that lady it is clear to me that I must have come into the wrong room. If I call out, she'll alarm the house; but if I remain here, the consequences will be still more frightful." He shrank behind the curtains, and called out very loudly, "Ha—hum!"

"Gracious Heaven!" said the middle-aged lady. "What's that?"

"It's—it's—only a gentleman, ma'am," said Mr. Pickwick from behind the curtains.

"A gentleman!" said the lady with a terrific scream. Her garments rustled as she rushed toward the door.

"Ma'am," said Mr. Pickwick, thrusting out his head, in the extremity of his desperation, "ma'am!"

Now, although Mr. Pickwick was not actuated by any definite object in putting out his head, it was instantaneously productive of a good effect. "Wretch," said the lady, stopping and covering her eyes with her hands, "what do you want?"

"Nothing, ma'am; nothing, whatever, ma'am," said Mr. Pickwick earnestly; "I am almost ready to sink, ma'am, beneath the confusion of addressing a lady in my nightcap, but I can't get it off, ma'am." Here Mr. Pickwick gave it a tremendous tug, in proof of the statement. "It is evident to me, ma'am, now, that I have mistaken this bedroom for my own."

"If this improbable story be really true, sir," said the lady, sobbing violently, "you will leave it instantly." She pointed to the door.

One excellent quality of Mr. Pickwick's character was beautifully displayed at this moment, under the most trying circumstances. Although he had hastily put on his hat over his nightcap, although he carried his coat and waistcoat over his arm, nothing could subdue his native politeness. "I trust, ma'am," said he, bowing very low, "that my unblemished character and the devoted respect I entertain for your sex will plead as some slight excuse for this—" But before Mr. Pickwick could conclude the sentence, the lady had thrust him into the passage and locked and bolted the door behind him.

His position in the open passage was by no means enviable; but, to his great joy, his faithful attendant, who had sat up late, presently appeared and led the way to his long-sought apartment.

"I'm wery sorry, Sammy," said the elder Mr. Weller next morning, "to hear as you let yourself be gammoned by that 'ere mulberry man. I always thought, up to now, that the names of Veller and gammon could never come into contract, Sammy, never."

"Always exceptin' the case of a widder, of course," said Sam.

"Widders, Sammy," replied Mr. Weller, slightly changing color—"widders are 'ceptions to ev'ry rule. I *have* heerd how many

ord'nary women one widder's equal to, in p'int o' comin' over you.
I think it's five and twenty, but I don't rightly know vether it ain't
more. Besides, that's a wery different thing. You know what the
counsel said, Sammy, as defended the gen'l'm'n as beat his wife
with the poker, venever he got jolly. 'And arter all, my lord,' says
he, 'it's a amiable weakness.' So I says respectin' widders, Sammy,
and so you'll say, ven you gets as old as me. If ever you gets up'ard
o' fifty, Sammy, and feels disposed to go a marryin' anybody—no
matter who—jist you shut yourself up in your own room, if you've
got one, and p'ison yourself off hand. Hangin's wulgar, so don't
you have nothin' to say to that. P'ison yourself, Samivel, my boy,
p'ison yourself, and you'll be glad on it arterward." With these
affecting words, Mr. Weller looked steadfastly on his son and
departed for London.

In the contemplative mood which the words had awakened,
Mr. Samuel Weller was walking abroad in Ipswich, when he was
transfixed by a sudden appearance: the green gate of a garden
at the bottom of a yard opened, and a man emerged therefrom,
who no sooner caught sight of Mr. Weller than he faltered and
stopped. Then, advancing, he contorted his face into the most
fearful and astonishing grimaces that ever were beheld.

He was obliged to pass very near Sam, however, and the
scrutinizing glance of that gentleman enabled him to detect,
under all these appalling twists of feature, something too like the
small eyes of Mr. Job Trotter to be easily mistaken. "Hullo, you
sir!" shouted Sam, fiercely. "It won't do, Job Trotter. Bring them
'ere eyes o' yourn back into their proper places, or I'll knock 'em
out of your head. D'ye hear?"

As Mr. Weller appeared fully disposed to act up to the spirit
of this address, Mr. Trotter gradually allowed his face to resume
its natural expression and then, giving a start of joy, exclaimed,
"What do I see? Mr. Walker! Oh, Mr. Walker, if you had but
known how I have looked forward to this meeting!" And Mr.
Trotter burst into a regular inundation of tears.

"Wot's the matter vith the man," said Sam, indignantly.
"Chelsea water works is nothin' to you. What are you melting vith
now? The consciousness o' willainy? I shall perhaps be asking
arter you, at the other side of that green gate, my man."

The green gate belonged to the residence of George Nupkins, Esq., the principal magistrate of Ipswich.

"I beg the magistrate's pardon," said Mr. Pickwick, appearing before Mr. Nupkins. "Is my servant right in suspecting that a certain Captain Fitz-Marshall is in the habit of visiting here? Because, if he be, I know that person to be an unprincipled adventurer—a dishonorable character—a man who preys upon society and makes easily deceived people his dupes, sir."

"Dear me," said Mr. Nupkins, turning very red. "Captain Fitz-Marshall?"

"Don't call him a cap'en," said Sam, "nor Fitz-Marshall neither; he ain't neither one nor t'other. He's a strolling actor, and his name's Jingle."

As the narrative proceeded, all the warm blood in the body of Mr. Nupkins tingled up into the very tips of his ears. He had picked up the captain at a neighboring race course. Charmed with his long list of aristocratic acquaintance, his extensive travel, and his fashionable demeanor, Mrs. Nupkins and Miss Nupkins had exhibited Captain Fitz-Marshall and quoted Captain Fitz-Marshall and hurled Captain Fitz-Marshall at the devoted heads of their select circle of acquaintance until their bosom friends Mrs. Porkenham and the Miss Porkenhams were ready to burst with jealousy.

"Confront me with him," said Mr. Pickwick; "that is all I ask."

"Why," said Mr. Nupkins, "that might be very easily done, for he will be here tonight, and then there would be no occasion to make the matter public, just—just—for the young man's own sake, you know." So Mr. Pickwick and his friends were introduced to the ladies and soon afterward to their dinner; and Mr. Weller was consigned to the care of Mr. Muzzle, the footman.

"Mary," said Mr. Muzzle to the pretty servant girl in the kitchen, "this is Mr. Weller; a gentleman as master has sent down, to be made as comfortable as possible."

"And your master has just sent me to the right place," said Mr. Weller, with a glance of admiration at Mary. "If I wos master o' this here house, I should alvays find the materials for comfort vere Mary wos."

"Lor,' Mr. Weller," said Mary, blushing.

"Mr. Weller, let me introduce you to cook," said Mr. Muzzle.

"How are you, ma'am," said Mr. Weller. "Wery glad to see you, indeed, and hope our acquaintance may be a long 'un, as the gen'l'm'n said to the fi' pun' note."

Mr. Weller's easy manners and conversational powers had such irresistible influence with his new friends that, before the dinner was half over, they were on a footing of perfect intimacy and in possession of a full account of the delinquency of Job Trotter.

In the midst of all this jollity and conviviality, the kitchen door opened, and in walked Mr. Trotter himself. "Here he is!" said Sam, rising with great glee and laying his hand on the mulberry collar. "Only think' o' my master havin' the pleasure o' meeting yourn, upstairs, and me havin' the joy o' meetin' you down here." At this moment, the bell rang. "That's for you, Job Trotter," said Sam; and before Mr. Trotter could offer remonstrance or reply, Sam seized one arm and Mr. Muzzle the other, and they conveyed him upstairs and into the parlor.

It was an impressive tableau. Alfred Jingle, Esq., alias Captain Fitz-Marshall, was standing near the door with his hat in his hand and a smile on his face, wholly unmoved by his very unpleasant situation. Confronting him, stood Mr. Pickwick, who had evidently been inculcating some high moral lesson; for his left hand was beneath his coat tail, and his right extended in air, as was his wont when delivering himself of an impressive address.

"What prevents me," said Mr. Nupkins, with magisterial dignity, "from detaining these men as rogues and impostors? What prevents me?"

"Pride, old fellow, pride," replied Jingle, quite at his ease. "Wouldn't do—no go.—Look stupid—very! Now, Job—trot!" With these words, Mr. Jingle stuck on his hat and strode out of the room. Job Trotter, with a bow of mock solemnity to Mr. Pickwick and a wink to Mr. Weller, followed the footsteps of his hopeful master.

"Sam," said Mr. Pickwick, as Mr. Weller was following, "stay here."

Mr. Weller seemed uncertain. "Mayn't I polish that 'ere Job off, sir?"

"Certainly not," replied Mr. Pickwick.

For the first time since his engagement, Mr. Weller lookcd,

for a moment, discontented and unhappy. But his countenance immediately cleared up, for the wily Mr. Muzzle contrived with great dexterity to overturn both Mr. Jingle and his attendant down the flight of steps.

"Get your hat, Sam," said Mr. Pickwick.

"It's below stairs, sir," said Sam, and he ran after it. Now there was nobody in the kitchen but the pretty housemaid; and as Sam's hat was mislaid, he had to look for it; and the pretty housemaid helped him. They got in an awkward corner—they were necessarily so very close together; and Sam kissed her.

"You don't mean to say you did that on purpose," she said, blushing.

"No, I didn't then," said Sam; "but I will now." So he kissed her again.

"Sam," called Mr. Pickwick. "How long you have been!"

"There was something behind the door, sir," replied Sam, "which prevented our getting it open." And this was the first passage of Mr. Weller's first love.

9

As brisk as bees, if not altogether as light as fairies, did the four Pickwickians assemble on the morning of the twenty-second day of December. Christmas was close at hand, in all his bluff and hearty honesty; it was the season of hospitality, merriment, and open-heartedness; the old year was preparing, like an ancient philosopher, to call his friends around him and amidst the sound of feasting and revelry to pass gently and calmly away. How many old recollections and how many dormant sympathies does Christmas time awaken! Happy, happy Christmas, that can win us back to the delusions of our childish days; that can recall to the old man the pleasures of his youth; that can transport the sailor and the traveler, thousands of miles away, back to his own fireside and his quiet home!

But we are keeping Mr. Pickwick and his friends waiting in the cold on the outside of the Muggleton coach. The coachman mounts to the box, Mr. Weller jumps up behind, the Pickwickians pull their coats round their legs and their shawls over their noses, the coachman shouts out a cheery "All right," and away they go, the lively notes of the guard's key bugle vibrating in the clear cold air. And when they arrived at Manor Farm, what was the warmth and cordiality of their reception!

First, there was Wardle himself, looking, if possible, more jolly than ever; then there were Bella and her faithful Trundle; and, lastly, there were Emily and some eight or ten young ladies, who had all come down to the wedding, which was to take place next day. A happy party they were, that night. Long after the ladies had retired did the hot elder wine go round, and round, and round again; and pleasant were the dreams that followed. It is a remarkable fact that those of Mr. Snodgrass bore constant reference to Emily Wardle; and that the principal figure in Mr. Winkle's visions was a young lady with black eyes and an arch smile, whose name was Arabella Allen.

Mr. Pickwick was awakened, early in the morning, by a hum of voices and a pattering of feet, as the female servants and female visitors ran constantly to and fro. The occasion being an important one, he dressed himself with peculiar care and descended to the breakfast room, where he found Mr. Trundle in high feather and spirits, but a little nervous withal. The hearty old host was trying to look very cheerful and unconcerned but failing signally in the attempt. All the girls were in tears and white muslin. So let us briefly say that the wedding ceremony was performed in the parish church of Dingley Dell, that the old church bell rang as gaily as it could, and that then the company returned to breakfast.

"Vere does the mince pies go, young boa constructer?" said Mr. Weller to the fat boy, as he assisted in laying out some of the articles of consumption. "Come, wake up, young dropsy!"

The fat boy pointed to the destination of the pies.

"Wery good," said Sam. "Now we look compact and comfortable, as the father said ven he cut his little boy's head off, to cure him o' squintin'."

"Wardle," said Mr. Pickwick, almost as soon as they were seated, "a glass of wine, in honor of this happy occasion!"

"I shall be delighted, my boy," said Mr. Wardle. "Joe—damn that boy, he's gone to sleep."

"No, I ain't, sir," replied the fat boy, starting up from a remote corner, where, like the patron saint of fat boys—the immortal Horner—he had been devouring a Christmas pie.

"Ladies and gentlemen," said Mr. Pickwick, rising to his feet.

"Hear, hear! Hear, hear! Hear, hear!" cried Mr. Weller, in the excitement of his feelings.

"Call in all the servants," cried old Wardle. "Give them a glass of wine each, to drink the toast in. Now, Pickwick."

"My dear friends," resumed Mr. Pickwick, "I am going to propose the health of the bride and bridegroom—God bless 'em [cheers and tears]. My young friend Trundle I believe to be a very excellent and manly fellow; and his wife I know to be a very amiable and lovely girl, well qualified to transfer to another sphere of action the happiness which for twenty years she has diffused around her, in her father's house. [Here, the fat boy burst forth into stentorian blubberings and was led forth by Mr. Weller.] I wish," added Mr. Pickwick, "I was young enough to be her sister's husband [cheers], but, failing that, I am happy to be old enough to be her father; for, being so, I shall not be suspected of any latent designs when I say that I admire, esteem, and love them both [cheers and sobs]. The bride's father, our good friend there, is a noble person, and I am proud to know him [great uproar]. That his daughter may enjoy all the happiness even he can desire and that he may derive from the contemplation of her felicity all the gratification of heart and peace of mind which he so well deserves is, I am persuaded, our united wish. So, let us drink their healths, and wish them prolonged life, and every blessing!"

The dinner was as hearty an affair as the breakfast and was quite as noisy, without the tears. Then came the tea and coffee, and then the ball.

The best sitting room at Manor Farm was a good, long, dark-paneled room with a high chimney piece and a capacious chimney. At the upper end of the room, seated in a shady bower of holly and evergreens, were the two best fiddlers and the only harp in all Muggleton. In all sorts of recesses and on all kinds of brackets stood massive old silver candlesticks with four branches each. The carpet was up, the candles burned bright, the fire blazed and crackled on the hearth, and merry voices and light-hearted laughter rang through the room.

"We are all ready, I believe," said Mr. Pickwick, who was stationed with old Mrs. Wardle at the top of the dance and had already made four false starts, in his excessive anxiety to commence.

"Then begin at once," said Wardle. "Now!"

Up struck the two fiddles and the one harp, and off went Mr. Pickwick into hands across—down the middle—poussette everywhere—loud stamp on the ground—ready for the next couple—off again—all the figure over once more—never was such going! Long before he was weary of dancing, the newly married couple had retired from the scene. There was a glorious supper downstairs, notwithstanding; and next evening they all repaired to the large kitchen, according to annual custom on Christmas Eve.

From the center of the ceiling of this kitchen, old Wardle suspended, with his own hands, a huge branch of mistletoe, and

this same branch of mistletoe instantaneously gave rise to a scene of general and delightful struggling and confusion, the younger ladies screaming and running into corners until some of the less adventurous gentlemen were on the point of desisting, when they all at once found it useless to resist any longer and submitted to be kissed with a good grace, the plainer portions of the young-lady visitors, in their excessive confusion, running right under the mistletoe, as soon as it was hung up, without knowing it!

It was a pleasant thing to see Mr. Pickwick, blinded with a silk handkerchief, going through all the mysteries of blindman's buff. When they were tired, they sat down by the huge fire of blazing logs to a substantial supper and a mighty bowl of wassail, in which the hot apples were hissing and bubbling with a rich look and a jolly sound that were irresistible.

"This," said Mr. Pickwick, looking round him, "this is, indeed, comfort."

"Our invariable custom," replied Mr. Wardle. "Everybody sits down with us on Christmas Eve, as you see them now—servants and all—and here we wait, until the clock strikes twelve, to usher Christmas in and beguile the time with forfeits, songs, and stories. Trundle, my boy, rake up the fire. Fill up all round!"

When Mr. Pickwick descended to breakfast on Christmas Day, he found there Miss Allen's brother, Mr. Benjamin Allen, and his friend Mr. Bob Sawyer. "What say you," said Wardle, "to an hour on the ice?"

"Capital!" said Mr. Benjamin Allen.

"Prime!" ejaculated Mr. Bob Sawyer.

"You skate, of course, Winkle?" said Wardle.

"Ye-yes; oh, yes," replied Mr. Winkle. "I—I—am *rather* out of practice."

"Oh, *do* skate, Mr. Winkle," said Arabella. "I like to see it so much."

"Oh, it is *so* graceful," said another young lady.

A third young lady said it was elegant, and a fourth expressed her opinion that it was "swan-like."

"I should be very happy, I'm sure," said Mr. Winkle, reddening; "but I have no skates."

This objection was at once overruled. The fat boy announced that there were half a dozen pair downstairs, whereat Mr. Winkle expressed exquisite delight and looked exquisitely uncomfortable.

Old Wardle led the way to a pretty large sheet of ice; Mr. Bob Sawyer adjusted his skates with a dexterity which to Mr. Winkle was perfectly marvelous and described circles with his left leg and cut figures of eight, while old Wardle and Benjamin Allen performed other mystic evolutions.

All this time, Mr. Winkle, with his face and hands blue with the cold, had been forcing a gimlet into the soles of his feet, and putting his skates on with the points behind, and getting the straps into a very complicated and entangled state, with the assistance of Mr. Snodgrass, who knew rather less about skates than a Hindu. At length, however, with the assistance of Mr. Weller, the unfortunate skates were firmly screwed and buckled on, and Mr. Winkle was raised to his feet.

"Now, then, sir," said Sam, in an encouraging tone, "off vith you, and show 'em how to do it."

"Stop, Sam, stop!" said Mr. Winkle, trembling violently and clutching hold of Sam's arms with the grasp of a drowning man. "How slippery it is, Sam!"

"Not an uncommon thing upon ice, sir," replied Mr. Weller, endeavoring to disengage himself. "Now, sir, start off!"

"Stop an instant, Sam," gasped Mr. Winkle, clinging most affectionately to Mr. Weller. "I find I've got a couple of coats at home that I don't want, Sam. You may have them, Sam."

"Thank'ee sir," replied Mr. Weller.

"Never mind touching your hat, Sam," said Mr. Winkle, hastily. "You needn't take your hand away to do that. I meant to have given you five shillings this morning for a Christmas box, Sam. I'll give it to you this afternoon, Sam. Just hold me at first, will you?"

Mr. Winkle, stooping forward with his body half doubled up, was being assisted over the ice by Mr. Weller, in a very singular and un-swan-like manner, when Mr. Pickwick most innocently shouted from the opposite bank, "Sam! I want you."

With a violent effort, Mr. Weller disengaged himself from the grasp of the agonized Pickwickian and, in so doing, administered a considerable impetus to the unhappy Mr. Winkle. With an accuracy which no degree of dexterity or practice could have ensured, that unfortunate gentleman bore swiftly down at the very moment when Mr. Bob Sawyer was performing a flourish of unparalleled beauty. Mr. Winkle struck wildly against him, and with a loud crash they both fell heavily down. Mr. Pickwick ran to the spot. Bob Sawyer had risen to his feet, but Mr. Winkle was far too wise to do anything of the kind, in skates. He was seated on the ice, making spasmodic efforts to smile; but anguish was depicted on every lineament of his countenance.

Mr. Pickwick was excited and indignant. He beckoned to Mr. Weller and said in a stern voice, "Take his skates off." Then, fixing a searching gaze on his friend, he uttered in a low, but distinct and emphatic, tone these remarkable words: "You're a humbug, sir."

Meanwhile Mr. Weller and the fat boy, having by their joint endeavors cut out a slide, were exercising themselves thereupon, in a very masterly and brilliant manner. It was a good long slide, and there was something in the motion which Mr. Pickwick, who was very cold with standing still, could not help envying. "Try it," said Wardle.

Mr. Pickwick paused, considered, pulled off his gloves and put them in his hat, took two or three short runs, balked himself as often, and at last took another run, and went slowly and gravely down the slide, with his feet about a yard and a quarter apart, amidst the gratified shouts of all the spectators.

"Keep the pot a bilin', sir!" said Sam; and down went Wardle, and then Mr. Pickwick, and then Sam, and then Mr. Winkle, and then Mr. Bob Sawyer, and then the fat boy, and then Mr. Snodgrass, following closely upon each other's heels and running after each other with as much eagerness as if all their future prospects in life depended on their expedition.

The sport was at its height, the sliding was at the quickest, the laughter was at the loudest, when a sharp smart crack was heard. A large mass of ice disappeared; the water bubbled up over it; Mr. Pickwick's hat, gloves, and handkerchief were floating on the surface; and this was all of Mr. Pickwick that anybody could see.

Dismay and anguish were depicted on every countenance. Mr. Tupman, by way of rendering the promptest assistance and at the same time conveying to any persons who might be within hearing the clearest possible notion of the catastrophe, ran off across country at his utmost speed, screaming "Fire!" with all his might.

It was at this moment, when old Wardle and Sam Weller were approaching the hole with cautious steps, that a face, head, and shoulders emerged from beneath the water and disclosed the features and spectacles of Mr. Pickwick. After a vast quantity of splashing and cracking and struggling, he was at length fairly extricated from his unpleasant position, wrapped in shawls, and started off home under the guidance of Mr. Weller, who paused not an instant until Mr. Pickwick was snug in bed, when he lighted a blazing fire in the room and took up his dinner. A bowl of punch was carried up afterward, a grand carouse was held in honor of Mr. Pickwick's safety, and the jovial party broke up next morning.

IO

INFORMED on his return to London that his case would come up on the fourteenth of February, Mr. Pickwick at once consulted his attorney, Mr. Perker. "What course do we pursue?" he inquired of that gentleman.

"We have only one to adopt, my dear sir," replied Perker. "I have retained Sergeant Snubbin. Cross-examine the witnesses; trust to Snubbin's eloquence; throw dust in the eyes of the judge; throw ourselves on the jury."

"And suppose the verdict is against me?" said Mr. Pickwick. Mr. Perker shrugged his shoulders. "You mean that in that case I must pay the damages?"

Perker said, "I am afraid so."

"Then I beg to announce to you my unalterable determination to pay no damages whatever," said Mr. Pickwick, most emphatically. "None, Perker. Not a pound, not a penny, of my money, shall find its way into the pockets of Dodson and Fogg. That is my deliberate and irrevocable determination." Mr. Pickwick gave a heavy blow on the table before him, in confirmation of the irrevocability of his intention.

The thirteenth of February arrived. Mr. Weller, having obtained leave of absence from Mr. Pickwick, who in his then state of excitement and worry was by no means displeased at being left alone, set forth to meet his parent at the Blue Boar, whither Mr. Weller senior had summoned him.

As he was sauntering along, he paused before a small stationer's window; and his eyes no sooner rested on certain pictures which were exposed for sale therein than he exclaimed with energy, "If it hadn't been for this, I should ha' forgot all about it, till it was too late!"

The particular picture on which Sam Weller's eyes were fixed was a highly colored representation of a couple of human hearts skewered together with an arrow, cooking before a cheerful fire. He at once stepped into the stationer's shop and requested to be served with a sheet of the best gilt-edged letter paper and a hard-

nibbed pen which could be warranted not to splutter. Arrived at the Blue Boar, he had unconsciously been a full hour and a half writing words in small text, smearing out wrong letters with his little finger, and putting in new ones which required going over very often to render them visible through the old blots, when he was roused by the entrance of his parent.

"Vell, Sammy," said the father. "Wot's that you're a doing of?"

"I've done now," said Sam with slight embarrassment; "I've been a writin'."

"So I see," replied Mr. Weller. "Not to any young 'ooman, I hope, Sammy?"

"Why, it's no use a sayin' it ain't," replied Sam. "It's a walentine."

"Samivel, Samivel," said Mr. Weller, in reproachful accents, "I didn't think you'd ha' done it. To see you married, Sammy—to see you a dilluded wictim, and thinkin' in your innocence that it's all wery capital—it's a dreadful trial to a father's feelin's."

"Nonsense," said Sam. "I ain't a goin' to get married. I'll read you the letter." He dipped his pen into the ink to be ready for any corrections and began with a very theatrical air, "'Lovely—'"

"Stop," said Mr. Weller, ringing the bell. "A double glass o' the inwariable, my dear.—'Tain't in poetry, is it?"

"No, no," replied Sam.

"Wery glad to hear it," said Mr. Weller. "Poetry's unnat'ral. Begin agin, Sammy."

"'Lovely creetur i feel myself a dammed—'"

"That ain't proper," said Mr. Weller, taking his pipe from his mouth.

"No; it ain't 'dammed,'" observed Sam, holding the letter up to the light; "it's 'shamed'—there's a blot there—'I feel myself ashamed and completely cir—' I forget what this here word is."

"Circumwented, p'raps," suggested Mr. Weller.

"No, it ain't that," said Sam; "'circumscribed'—that's it."

"That ain't as good a word as 'circumwented,' Sammy," said Mr. Weller, gravely.

"Think not?" said Sam.

"Nothin' like it," replied his father.

"But don't you think it means more?" inquired Sam.

"Vell, p'raps it is a more tenderer word," said Mr. Weller, after a few moments' reflection. "Go on, Sammy."

"'Feel myself ashamed and completely circumscribed in a dressin' of you, for you *are* a nice gal and nothin but it.'"

"That's a wery pretty sentiment," said the elder Mr. Weller. "Wot I like in that 'ere style of writin' is that there ain't no callin' names in it—no Wenuses, nor nothin' o' that kind. Wot's the good o'callin' a young 'ooman a Wenus or a angel, Sammy?—Drive on."

"'Afore I see you, I thought all women was alike.'"

"So they are," observed the elder Mr. Weller, parenthetically.

"'But now,'" continued Sam, "'now I find what a reg'lar soft-headed, ink-red'lous turnip I must ha' been; for there ain't nobody like you, though *I* like you better than nothin' at all.' I thought it best to make that rayther strong," said Sam, looking up.

Mr. Weller nodded approvingly, and Sam resumed. " 'Except of me Mary my dear as your walentine and think over what I've said. My dear Mary I will now conclude.' That's all," said Sam.

"That's rather a sudden pull up, ain't it, Sammy?" inquired Mr. Weller.

"Not a bit on it," said Sam; "she'll vish there wos more, and that's the great art o' letter writin'."

"Well," said Mr. Weller, "there's somethin' in that; and I wish your stepmother 'ud only conduct her conwersation on the same gen-teel principle. Ain't you a goin' to sign it?"

"That's the difficulty," said Sam; "I don't know what *to* sign it."

"Sign it 'Veller,' " said the oldest surviving proprietor of that name.

"Won't do," said Sam. "Never sign a walentine with your own name."

"Sign it 'Pickvick,' then," said Mr. Weller; "it's a wery good name, and a easy one to spell."

"The wery thing," said Sam. "I *could* end with a werse." So he signed it

> Your love-sick
> Pickwick.

This important business having been transacted, Mr. Weller the elder proceeded to open that on which he had summoned his son. "This here red-nosed shepherd, Sammy," said he, "this here Stiggins that calls hisself a wessel wisits your stepmother vith a kindness and constancy as I never see equaled; and the way he empties the pineapple rum, Samivel—"

"What do you let him show his red nose in the Markis o'Granby at all for?" said Sam reproachfully.

Mr. Weller the elder fixed on his son an earnest look and replied, " 'Cause I'm a married man, Samivel, 'cause I'm a married man. W'en you're a married man, Samivel, you'll understand a good many things as you don't understand now, but vether it's worth while goin' through so much to learn so little, as the charity boy said ven he got to the end of the alphabet, is a matter o' taste.

I rayther think it isn't. Now, these here shepherds, my boy, are a goin' tonight to the monthly meetin' o' the Brick Lane Branch o' the United Grand Junction Ebenezer Temperance Association. Your stepmother *wos* a goin', Sammy, but she's got the rheumatics and can't; and I, Sammy—I've got the two tickets as wos sent her. You and I'll go, punctiwal to the time. But her shepherd won't, Sammy; her shepherd won't." Here Mr. Weller was seized with a paroxysm of chuckles.

"What are you a laughin' at, corpilence?" said Sam.

"Hush! Sammy," said Mr. Weller, speaking in a whisper. "Two friends o' mine has got the shepherd safe in tow; and ven he does come to the Ebenezer Junction, he'll be as far gone in rum as ever he wos at the Markis o' Granby, Dorkin', and that's not sayin' a little neither." With this, Mr. Weller once more laughed immoderately, and father and son took their way to Brick Lane.

Previous to the commencement of business there, the ladies of the association sat upon forms and drank tea to a most alarming extent. "Why, this here old lady next me is a drowndin' herself in tea," Mr. Weller whispered to Sam. "If this here lasts much longer, I shall feel it my duty, as a human bein', to rise and address the cheer. There's a young 'ooman on the next form but two as has drunk nine breakfast cups and a half; and she's a swellin' wisibly before my wery eyes."

There is little doubt that Mr. Weller would have carried his benevolent intention into immediate execution if the president of the United Grand Junction Ebenezer Temperance Association, Mr. Anthony Humm, had not now moved that the assembly regale itself with a temperance song. "My friends," said Mr. Humm, at its conclusion, "a delegate from the Dorking branch of our society, Brother Stiggins, attends below. Let him come forth."

"He's a comin', Sammy," whispered Mr. Weller, purple in the countenance with suppressed laughter.

The reverend Mr. Stiggins no sooner entered than there was a great clapping of hands, and stamping of feet, and flourishing of handkerchiefs, to all of which manifestations of delight Brother Stiggins returned no other acknowledgment than staring, with a wild eye and a fixed smile, at the extreme top of the wick of the candle on the table, swaying his body to and fro, meanwhile, in a very unsteady and uncertain manner.

"Are you unwell, Brother Stiggins?" whispered Mr. Anthony Humm.

"I am all right, sir," replied Mr. Stiggins, in a tone in which ferocity was blended with an extreme thickness of utterance; "I am all right, sir."

"Oh, very well," rejoined Mr. Anthony Humm, retreating a few paces. "Will you address the meeting, Brother?"

"No, sir," rejoined Mr. Stiggins. "No, sir. I will not, sir."

The meeting looked at each other with raised eyelids, and a murmur of astonishment ran through the room.

"It's my opinion, sir," said Mr. Stiggins, unbuttoning his coat and speaking very loudly, "it's my opinion, sir, that this meeting is drunk, sir. *You* are drunk, sir!" With this, Mr. Stiggins, entertaining a praiseworthy desire to promote the sobriety of the meeting and to exclude therefrom all improper characters, hit Brother Humm on the summit of the nose.

Upon this, the women set up a loud and dismal screaming and, rushing in small parties before their favorite brothers, flung their arms around them to preserve them from danger. The greater part of the lights were quickly put out; and nothing but noise and confusion resounded on all sides.

"Now, Sammy," said Mr. Weller, taking off his great coat with much deliberation, "just you step out, and fetch in a watchman; I shall ockipy myself in havin' a small settlement with that 'ere Stiggins till he comes."

II

THE judge had no sooner taken his seat, on the eventful morning of the fourteenth of February, than the officer on the floor of the court called out "Silence!" in a commanding tone, upon which another officer in the gallery cried "Silence!" in an angry manner, whereupon three or four more ushers shouted "Silence!" in a voice of indignant remonstrance. This being done, a gentleman in black proceeded to call over the names of the jury; and, after a great deal of bawling, it was discovered that only ten special jurymen were present. Upon this, Mr. Sergeant Buzfuz, who was counsel for the plaintiff, prayed a tales; the gentleman in black then proceeded to press into the special jury two of the common jurymen; and a green-grocer and a chemist were caught directly.

"Answer to your names, gentlemen, that you may be sworn," said the gentleman in black. "Richard Upwitch."

"Here," said the green-grocer.

"Thomas Groffin."

"Here," said the chemist.

"Take the book, gentlemen. You shall well and truly try—"

"I beg this court's pardon," said the chemist, "but I hope this court will excuse my attendance."

"On what grounds, sir?" said Mr. Justice Stareleigh.

"I have no assistant, my lord," said the chemist.

"I can't help that, sir," replied Mr. Justice Stareleigh. "You should hire one."

"I can't afford it, my lord," rejoined the chemist.

"Then you ought to be able to afford it, sir," said the judge, reddening. "Swear the gentleman."

"Very well, my lord," replied the chemist, in a resigned manner. "Then there'll be murder before this trial's over; that's all. Swear me, if you please, sir." And sworn the chemist was, before the judge could find words to utter.

"I merely wanted to observe, my lord," said the chemist, taking his seat with great deliberation, "that I've left nobody but an errand boy in my shop. He is a very nice boy, my lord, but he is not acquainted with drugs; and I know that the prevailing impression on his mind is that Epsom salts means oxalic acid; and sirup of senna, laudanum. That's all, my lord." With this, the tall chemist composed himself into a comfortable attitude and, assuming a pleasant expression of countenance, appeared to have prepared himself for the worst.

Mr. Pickwick was regarding the chemist with feelings of the deepest horror, when a slight sensation was perceptible in the body of the court; and immediately afterward Mrs. Bardell, supported by her friend Mrs. Cluppins, was led in and placed, in a drooping state, at the other end of the seat on which Mr. Pickwick sat. An extra-sized umbrella was then handed in by Mr. Dodson and a pair of pattens by Mr. Fogg, each of whom had prepared a most sympathizing and melancholy face for the occasion. Mrs. Sanders, another friend, then appeared, leading in Master Bardell, who was placed in a commanding position in which he could not fail to awaken the full commiseration of both judge and jury.

"Bardell and Pickwick," cried the gentleman in black, calling on the case, which stood first on the list.

Sergeant Buzfuz then rose and, having whispered to Dodson and conferred briefly with Fogg, pulled his gown over his shoulders, settled his wig, and addressed the jury.

He began by saying, that never, in the whole course of his professional experience—never, from the very first moment of his applying himself to the study and practice of the law—had he approached a case with feelings of such deep emotion or with such a heavy sense of the responsibility imposed upon him—a responsibility, he would say, which he could never have supported were he not buoyed up and sustained by a conviction so strong that it amounted to positive certainty that the cause of truth and justice, or, in other words, the cause of his much-injured and most oppressed client, must prevail with the high-minded and intelligent dozen of men whom he now saw in that box before him.

"The plaintiff, gentlemen," continued Sergeant Buzfuz, in a soft and melancholy voice, "the plaintiff is a widow; yes, gentlemen, a widow. The late Mr. Bardell, after enjoying for many years the esteem and confidence of his sovereign, as one of the guardians of his royal revenues, glided almost imperceptibly from the world, to seek elsewhere for that repose and peace which a custom house can never afford."

At this pathetic description of the decease of Mr. Bardell, who had been knocked on the head with a quart pot in a public-house cellar, the learned sergeant's voice faltered, and he proceeded with emotion.

"Some time before his death, he had stamped his likeness upon a little boy. With this little boy, the only pledge of her departed exciseman, Mrs. Bardell shrank from the world and courted the retirement and tranquillity of Goswell Street; and here she placed in her front parlor window a written placard, bearing this inscription, 'Apartments furnished for a single gentleman. Inquire within.'

"Did it remain there long? No. The serpent was on the watch, the train was laid, the mine was preparing, the sapper and miner was at work. Before the bill had been in the parlor window three days—three days, gentlemen—a Being, erect upon two legs and bearing all the outward semblance of a man, and not of a monster, knocked at the door of Mrs. Bardell's house. This man was Pickwick—Pickwick, the defendant."

Here Mr. Pickwick, who had been writhing in silence, gave a violent start; and Sergeant Buzfuz, having partially recovered from the state of moral elevation into which he had lashed himself, resumed. "I shall show you, gentlemen, that for two years Pickwick continued to reside constantly, and without interruption or intermission, at Mrs. Bardell's house. I shall prove to you, gentlemen, that, about a year ago, Pickwick suddenly began to absent himself from home, as if with the intention of gradually breaking off from my client. But I shall show you also that his resolution was not at that time sufficiently strong or that his better feelings conquered, if better feelings he has, by proving to you that, on one occasion, when he returned from the country he distinctly and in terms offered her marriage; and I am in a situation to prove to you, on the testimony of three of his own friends—most unwilling witnesses, gentlemen—that on that morning he was discovered by them holding the plaintiff in his arms and soothing her agitation by his caresses and endearments."

A visible impression was produced upon the auditors by this part of the learned sergeant's address. Drawing forth two very small scraps of paper, he proceeded. "And now, gentlemen, but one word more. Two letters have passed between these parties, letters which bespeak the character of the man. They are not open, fervent, eloquent epistles, breathing nothing but the language of affectionate attachment. They are covert, sly, underhanded communications, but fortunately far more conclusive than if couched in the most glowing language and the most poetic imagery. Let me read the first. 'Garraway's, twelve o'clock. Dear Mrs. B.: Chops and tomato sauce. Yours, Pickwick.' Gentlemen, what does this mean? Chops and tomato sauce! Yours, Pickwick! Chops! Gracious Heavens! And tomato sauce! Gentlemen, is the happiness of a sensitive and confiding female to be trifled away by such shallow artifices as these? The next has no date whatever, which is in itself suspicious. 'Dear Mrs. B.: I shall not be at home till tomorrow. Slow coach.' And then follows this remarkable expression. 'Don't trouble yourself about the warming pan.' The warming pan! Why, gentlemen, who *does* trouble himself about a warming pan? Why is Mrs. Bardell so earnestly entreated not to agitate herself about this warming pan, unless (as is no doubt the case) it is a mere cover for hidden fire, artfully contrived by Pickwick with a view to his contemplated desertion.

"My client's hopes and prospects are ruined. All is gloom and silence in the house; even the voice of the child is hushed. But Pickwick, gentlemen, Pickwick, the ruthless destroyer of this domestic oasis in the desert of Goswell Street—Pickwick, who comes before you today with his heartless tomato sauce and warming pans—Pickwick still rears his head with unblushing effrontery and gazes without a sigh on the ruin he has made. Damages, gentlemen— heavy damages—is the only punishment with which you can visit him, the only recompense you can award to my client. And for those damages she now appeals to an enlightened, a high-minded, a right-feeling, a conscientious, a dispassionate, a sympathizing, a contemplative jury of her civilized countrymen." With this beautiful peroration, Mr. Sergeant Buzfuz sat down, and Mr. Justice Stareleigh woke up.

"Call Elizabeth Cluppins," said Sergeant Buzfuz, rising a minute afterward, with renewed vigor.

The nearest usher called for Elizabeth Tuppins; another one, at a little distance off, demanded Elizabeth Jupkins; and a third rushed in a breathless state into King Street and screamed for Elizabeth Muffins till he was hoarse.

Meanwhile Mrs. Cluppins, with the combined assistance of Mrs. Bardell, Mrs. Sanders, Mr. Dodson, and Mr. Fogg, was hoisted into the witness box.

"Do you recollect, Mrs. Cluppins," said Sergeant Buzfuz, after a few unimportant questions, "being in Mrs. Bardell's back one pair of stairs, on one particular morning in July last, when she was dusting Pickwick's apartment?"

"Yes, my lord and jury, I do," replied Mrs. Cluppins.

"What were you doing in the back room, ma'am?" inquired the judge.

"My lord and jury," said Mrs. Cluppins, with interesting agitation, "I will not deceive you."

"You had better not, ma'am," said the little judge.

"I was there," resumed Mrs. Cluppins, "unbeknown to Mrs.

Bardell; I had been out with a little basket, gentlemen, to buy three pound of red kidney pertaties, which was three pound tuppence ha'penny, when I see Mrs. Bardell's street door on the jar."

"On the what?" exclaimed the little judge.

"Partly open, my lord," said Sergeant Snubbin.

"She *said* on the jar," said the little judge, with a cunning look.

"It's all the same, my lord," said Sergeant Snubbin. The little judge looked doubtful and said he'd make a note of it. Mrs. Cluppins then resumed. "I walked in, gentlemen, just to say good mornin', and went, in a permiscuous manner, upstairs and into the back room. Gentlemen, there was the sound of voices in the front room, and—"

"And you listened, I believe, Mrs. Cluppins?" said Sergeant Buzfuz.

"Beggin' your pardon, sir," replied Mrs. Cluppins, in a majestic manner, "I would scorn the haction. The voices was very loud, sir, and forced themselves upon my ear."

"Well, Mrs. Cluppins, you were not listening, but you heard the voices. Was one of those voices Pickwick's?"

"Yes, it were, sir." And Mrs. Cluppins, after distinctly stating that Mr. Pickwick addressed himself to Mrs. Bardell, repeated the conversation with which our readers are already acquainted.

The jury looked suspicious, and Mr. Sergeant Buzfuz smiled and sat down. They looked positively awful when Sergeant Snubbin intimated that he should not cross-examine the witness.

"Nathaniel Winkle!" said Mr. Skimpin, junior counsel with Sergeant Buzfuz.

"Here!" replied a feeble voice. Mr. Winkle entered the witness box and, having been duly sworn, was examined by Mr. Skimpin, who, being a promising young man of two or three and forty, was of course anxious to confuse a witness, who was notoriously predisposed in favor of the other side, as much as he could.

"Now, sir," said Mr. Skimpin, "have the goodness to let his lordship and the jury know what your name is, will you?"

"Winkle," replied the witness.

"What's your Christian name, sir?" angrily inquired the little judge.

"Nathaniel, sir."

"Daniel—any other name?"

"Nathaniel, sir—my lord, I mean."

"Nathaniel Daniel, or Daniel Nathaniel?"

"No, my lord, only Nathaniel; not Daniel at all."

"What did you tell me it was Daniel for, then, sir?" inquired the judge.

"I didn't, my lord," replied Mr. Winkle.

"You did, sir," replied the judge, with a severe frown. "How could I have got Daniel on my notes, unless you told me so, sir?"

This argument was, of course, unanswerable.

"Mr. Winkle has rather a short memory, my lord," interposed Mr. Skimpin, with a significant glance at the jury. "We shall find means to refresh it before we have quite done with him, I dare say."

"You had better be careful, sir," said the little judge, with a sinister look at the witness.

Poor Mr. Winkle bowed and endeavored to feign an easiness of manner, which, in his then state of confusion, gave him rather the air of a disconcerted pickpocket.

"Now, Mr. Winkle," said Mr. Skimpin, "attend to me, if you please, sir; and let me recommend you, for your own sake, to bear in mind his lordship's injunction to be careful. I believe you are a particular friend of Pickwick, the defendant, are you not?"

"I have known Mr. Pickwick now, as well as I recollect at this moment, nearly—"

"Pray, Mr. Winkle, do not evade the question. Are you, or are you not, a particular friend of the defendant's?"

"I was just about to say that—"

"Will you, or will you not, answer my question, sir?"

"If you don't answer the question, you'll be committed, sir," interposed the little judge, looking over his notebook.

"Come, sir," said Mr. Skimpin, "yes or no, if you please."

"Yes, I am," replied Mr. Winkle.

"Yes, you are. And why couldn't you say that at once, sir?" The witness having been by these means reduced to the requisite ebb of nervous perplexity, the examination was continued as follows: "Pray, Mr. Winkle, do you remember calling on the defendant Pickwick at these apartments in the plaintiff's house in

Goswell Street, on one particular morning, in the month of July last?"

"Yes, I do."

"Were you accompanied on that occasion by a friend of the name of Tupman and another of the name of Snodgrass?"

"Yes, I was."

"Now, sir, tell the gentlemen of the jury what you saw on this particular morning. Come, out with it, sir; we must have it, sooner or later."

"The defendant, Mr. Pickwick, was holding the plaintiff in his arms, with his hands clasping her waist," replied Mr. Winkle with natural hesitation, "and the plaintiff appeared to have fainted away."

"Did you hear the defendant say anything?"

"I heard him call Mrs. Bardell a good creature, and I heard him ask her to compose herself, for what a situation it was, if anybody should come, or words to that effect."

"Now, Mr. Winkle, I have only one more question to ask you, and I beg you to bear in mind his lordship's caution. Will you undertake to swear that Pickwick, the defendant, did not say on the occasion in question, 'My dear Mrs. Bardell, you're a good creature; compose yourself to this situation, for to this situation you must come,' or words to *that* effect?"

"I—I didn't understand him so, certainly," said Mr. Winkle.

"But you will not swear that Pickwick did not make use of the expressions I have quoted? Do I understand that?"

"No, I will not," replied Mr. Winkle; and down sat Mr. Skimpin with a triumphant countenance.

Mr. Pickwick's case had not gone off in so particularly happy a manner, up to this point, that it could very well afford to have any additional suspicion cast upon it. But as it could afford to be placed in a rather better light, if possible, Mr. Phunky, Sergeant Snubbin's junior, rose for the purpose of getting something important out of Mr. Winkle in cross-examination. Whether he did get anything important out of him, will immediately appear.

"You have told my learned friend," said Mr. Phunky, "that you have known Mr. Pickwick a long time. Had you ever any reason to suppose or believe that he was about to be married?"

"Oh, no; certainly not," replied Mr. Winkle with so much

eagerness that Mr. Phunky ought to have got him out of the box with all possible dispatch.

"I will even go further than this, Mr. Winkle," continued Mr. Phunky in a most smooth and complacent manner. "Has Mr. Pickwick's behavior, when females have been in the case, always been that of a man who, having attained a pretty advanced period of life, treats them only as a father might his daughters?"

"Not the least doubt of it," replied Mr. Winkle, in the fullness of his heart. "That is—yes—oh, yes—certainly."

"You have never known anything in his behavior toward Mrs. Bardell or any other female in the least degree suspicious?" said Mr. Phunky, preparing to sit down; for Sergeant Snubbin was winking at him.

"N—n—no," replied Mr. Winkle, "except on one trifling occasion, which, I have no doubt, might be easily explained." The moment the words fell from Mr. Winkle's lips, Sergeant Snubbin rather hastily told him he might leave the box, when Sergeant Buzfuz stopped him.

"Stay, Mr. Winkle, stay!" said Sergeant Buzfuz. "Will your lordship have the goodness to ask him what this one instance of suspicious behavior toward females was?"

"You hear what the learned counsel says, sir," observed the judge, turning to the miserable and agonized Mr. Winkle. "Describe the occasion to which you refer."

"My lord," said Mr. Winkle, trembling with anxiety, "I—I'd rather not."

"Perhaps so," said the little judge; "but you must."

Amid the profound silence of the whole court, Mr. Winkle faltered out that the trifling circumstance of suspicion was Mr. Pickwick's being found in a lady's sleeping apartment at midnight.

"You may leave the box, sir," said Sergeant Snubbin. Mr. Winkle *did* leave the box and rushed with delirious haste to the George and Vulture, where he was discovered some hours after, by the waiter, groaning in a hollow and dismal manner, with his head buried beneath the sofa cushions.

Tracy Tupman and Augustus Snodgrass were severally called into the box; both corroborated the testimony of their unhappy friend; and each was driven to the verge of desperation by excessive badgering.

Susanna Sanders was then called and examined by Sergeant Buzfuz and cross-examined by Sergeant Snubbin. Had always said and believed that Mrs. Bardell's being engaged to Pickwick was the current topic of conversation in the neighborhood, after the fainting in July; thought Mrs. Bardell fainted because Pickwick asked her to name the day; knew that she (witness) fainted away stone dead when Mr. Sanders asked *her* to name the day, and believed that everybody as called herself a lady would do the same, under similar circumstances.

During the period of her keeping company with Mr. Sanders, had received love letters, like other ladies. In the course of their correspondence Mr. Sanders had often called her a "duck," but

never "chops," nor yet "tomato sauce." He was particularly fond
of ducks. Perhaps if he had been as fond of chops and tomato sauce,
he might have called her that, as a term of affection.

Sergeant Buzfuz now rose with more importance than he had
yet exhibited, if that were possible, and vociferated, "Call Samuel
Weller."

It was quite unnecessary to call Samuel Weller; for Samuel
Weller stepped briskly into the box the instant his name was pronounced and, placing his hat on the floor and his arms on the rail,
took a bird's-eye view of the bar and a comprehensive survey of
the bench, with a remarkably cheerful and lively aspect.

"What's your name, sir?" inquired the judge.

"Sam Weller, my lord," replied that gentleman.

"Do you spell it with a 'V' or a 'W'?" inquired the judge.

"That depends upon the taste and fancy of the speller, my
lord," replied Sam; "I never had occasion to spell it more than
once or twice in my life, but I spells it with a 'V.'"

Here a voice in the gallery exclaimed aloud, "Quite right too,
Samivel, quite right. Put it down a we, my lord, put it down a
we."

"Who is that, who dares to address the court?" said the little
judge.—"Do you know who that was, sir?" turning to the witness.

"I rayther suspect it was my father, my lord," replied Sam.

"Do you see him here now?" said the judge.

"No, I don't, my lord," replied Sam, staring right up into the
lantern in the roof of the court.

"If you could have pointed him out, I would have committed
him instantly," said the judge. Sam bowed his acknowledgments.

"Now, Mr. Weller," said Sergeant Buzfuz.

"Now, sir," replied Sam.

"I believe you are in the service of Mr. Pickwick, the defendant in this case. Speak up, if you please, Mr. Weller."

"I mean to speak up, sir," replied Sam; "I am in the service o'
that 'ere gen'l'm'n, and a wery good service it is."

"Do you recollect anything particular happening on the morning when you were first engaged by the defendant—eh, Mr.
Weller?" said Sergeant Buzfuz.

"Yes, I do, sir," replied Sam.

"Have the goodness to tell the jury what it was."

"I had a reg'lar new fit out o' clothes that mornin', gen'l'm'n, of the jury," said Sam, "and that was a wery partickler and uncommon circumstance vith me in those days."

Hereupon there was a general laugh; and the little judge, looking with an angry countenance over his desk, said, "You had better be careful, sir."

"So Mr. Pickwick said at the time, my lord," replied Sam; "and I was wery careful o' that 'ere suit o' clothes; wery careful indeed, my lord."

The judge looked sternly at Sam for full two minutes, but Sam's features were so perfectly calm and serene that the judge said nothing and motioned Sergeant Buzfuz to proceed.

"Do you mean to tell me, Mr. Weller," said Sergeant Buzfuz, "that you saw nothing of this fainting on the part of the plaintiff in the arms of the defendant, which you have heard described by the witnesses?"

"Certainly not," replied Sam. "I was in the passage."

"Now, attend, Mr. Weller," said Sergeant Buzfuz. "You were in the passage and yet saw nothing of what was going forward. Have you a pair of eyes, Mr. Weller?"

"Yes, I have a pair of eyes," replied Sam, "and that's just it. If they wos a pair o' patent double-million magnifyin' gas microscopes of hextra power, p'raps I might be able to see through a flight o' stairs and a deal door; but bein' only eyes, you see, my wision's limited."

At this answer, which was delivered without the slightest appearance of irritation, the spectators tittered, the little judge smiled, and Sergeant Buzfuz looked particularly foolish. After a short consultation with Dodson and Fogg, the learned sergeant again turned toward Sam. "Now, Mr. Weller," said he, "when you went up to Mrs. Bardell's house one night when Mrs. Cluppins and Mrs. Sanders were with her, I suppose you went to have a little talk about this trial?" looking knowingly at the jury.

"I went up to pay the rent; but we *did* get a talkin' about the trial," replied Sam.

"Oh, you did get a talking about the trial," said Sergeant Buzfuz, brightening. "Will you have the goodness to tell us what passed, Mr. Weller?"

"Vith all the pleasure in life, sir," replied Sam. "Arter a few unimportant obserwations from the two wirtuous females as has been examined here today, the ladies gets into a wery great state o' admiration at the honorable conduct of Mr. Dodson and Fogg— them two gen'l'men as is settin' near you now. They said what a wery gen'rous thing it was o' them to have taken up the case on spec, and to charge nothing at all for costs, unless they got 'em out of Mr. Pickwick."

At this unexpected reply, the spectators tittered again, and Dodson and Fogg, turning very red, leaned over to Sergeant Buz-fuz and in a hurried manner whispered something in his ear. "You are quite right," said Sergeant Buzfuz aloud, with affected composure. "I will not trouble the court by asking this witness any more questions. Stand down, sir."

"Would any other gen'l'm'n like to ask me anythin'?" inquired Sam, taking up his hat and looking round most deliberately.

"Not I, Mr. Weller, thank you," said Sergeant Snubbin, laughing.

"You may go down, sir," said Sergeant Buzfuz, waving his hand impatiently. Sam went down accordingly, after doing Messrs. Dodson and Fogg's case as much harm as he conveniently could and saying just as little respecting Mr. Pickwick as might be, which was precisely the object he had had in view all along.

Sergeant Snubbin then addressed the jury on behalf of the defendant; and Mr. Justice Stareleigh summed up. The jury retired to their private room and, after an anxious quarter of an hour, came back. "Gentlemen," said the individual in black, "are you all agreed upon your verdict?"

"We are," replied the foreman.

"Do you find for the plaintiff, gentlemen, or for the defendant?"

"For the plaintiff."

"With what damages, gentlemen?"

"Seven hundred and fifty pounds."

Mr. Pickwick took off his spectacles, carefully wiped the glasses, folded them into their case, and put them in his pocket; then, having drawn on his gloves with great nicety, he mechanically followed Mr. Perker out of court, where he encountered Messrs. Dodson and Fogg, rubbing their hands with every token of outward satisfaction.

"Well, gentlemen," said Mr. Pickwick, "you imagine you'll get your costs?"

Fogg said they thought it rather probable. Dodson smiled and said they'd try.

"You may try, and try, and try again, Messrs. Dodson and Fogg," said Mr. Pickwick vehemently, "but not one farthing of costs or damages do you ever get from me, if I spend the rest of my existence in a debtor's prison."

12

MR. Pickwick was fast asleep in his bed at the George and Vulture one morning some months later, when the noise made by an early visitor entering his room awoke him. "Shaving water, Sam," said Mr. Pickwick, from within the curtains.

"Shave you directly, Mr. Pickwick," said the visitor. "I've got an execution against you, at the suit of Bardell. Here's the warrant —Common Pleas. Here's my card. I suppose you'll come over to my house?" There Mr. Perker promptly arrived.

"Aha, my dear sir," said the little man, "nailed at last, eh? Come, come, I'm not sorry for it either, because now you'll see the absurdity of this conduct."

"Perker," said Mr. Pickwick, "let me hear no more of this, I beg. I see no advantage in staying here, so I shall go to prison tonight." The usual forms having been gone through, the body of Samuel Pickwick was soon afterward confided to the custody of the tipstaff, to be by him taken to the warden of the Fleet Prison and there detained until the amount of the damages and costs in the action of Bardell against Pickwick was fully paid and satisfied.

"And that," said Mr. Pickwick, laughing, "will be a very long time. Perker, my dear friend, good-by." And so Mr. Pickwick found himself, for the first time in his life, within the walls of a ʼdebtor's prison.

Looking down a dark and filthy staircase, which appeared to lead to a range of damp and gloomy stone vaults, beneath the ground, "Those, I suppose," said Mr. Pickwick, "are the little cellars where the prisoners keep their small quantities of coals. Unpleasant places to have to go down to, but very convenient, I dare say."

"Yes, I shouldn't wonder if they was convenient," replied the gentleman who was guiding him, "seeing that a few people live there, pretty snug."

"My friend," said Mr. Pickwick, "you don't really mean to say that human beings live down in those wretched dungeons?"

"Live down there! Yes, and die down there, too, wery often!" replied the gentleman, whose name was Roker.

There is no disguising the fact that Mr. Pickwick felt very low spirited and uncomfortable. There was a perpetual slamming and banging of doors as the people went in and out; and the noise of their voices and footsteps echoed and re-echoed through the passages constantly. A young woman, with a child in her arms, who seemed scarcely able to crawl from emaciation and misery, was walking up and down the passage in conversation with her husband, who had no other place to see her in. Mr. Pickwick's heart was really too full to bear it, and he asked to be shown to his room.

"The room where you're a going to sleep tonight is the warden's room," said Mr. Roker, disclosing an apartment of an appearance by no means inviting, containing eight or nine iron bedsteads. Requesting Mr. Weller to seek a bed in some adjacent public house and to return early in the morning with his master's wardrobe from the George and Vulture, Mr. Pickwick went to bed and to sleep.

"Bravo! Heel over toe—cut and shuffle—pay away at it, Zephyr! Hooray!" These expressions, delivered in a most boisterous tone and accompanied with loud peals of laughter, roused Mr. Pickwick, who started up, and remained for some minutes fixed in mute astonishment at the scene before him.

On the floor of the warden's room, a man with a broad-skirted green coat was performing the most popular steps of a hornpipe. Another man, evidently very drunk, was sitting up between the sheets, warbling a comic song; while a third, seated on one of the bedsteads, was applauding both performers with the air of a profound connoisseur and encouraging them by such ebullitions of feeling as had already roused Mr. Pickwick from his sleep.

This figure was the first to perceive that Mr. Pickwick was

looking on, upon which he winked to the Zephyr and entreated him, with mock gravity, not to wake the gentleman. "Why, bless the gentleman's honest heart and soul!" said the Zephyr, turning round and affecting the extremity of surprise. "The gentleman *is* awake. Hem, Shakespeare! How do you do, sir? How is the dear old lady at home, sir? Will you have the kindness to put my compliments into the first little parcel you're sending that way, sir? Allow me to have the felicity of hanging up your nightcap, sir." With this, the speaker snatched that article from Mr. Pickwick's head and fixed it on that of the drunken man.

Taking a man's nightcap from his brow by violent means and adjusting it on the head of an unknown gentleman of dirty exterior is unquestionably one of those witticisms which come under the denomination of practical jokes. Mr. Pickwick, without the slightest intimation of his purpose, sprang vigorously out of bed, struck the Zephyr a smart blow, and then, recapturing his nightcap, boldly placed himself in an attitude of defense.

"Now," said Mr. Pickwick, gasping no less from excitement than from the expenditure of so much energy, "come on—both of you—both of you!" With this liberal invitation the worthy gentleman communicated a revolving motion to his clenched fists, by way of appalling his antagonists with a display of science.

It might have been Mr. Pickwick's very unexpected gallantry, or it might have been the complicated manner in which he had got himself out of bed and fallen all in a mass upon the hornpipe man, that touched his adversaries. Touched they were; for, instead of then and there making an attempt to commit manslaughter, as Mr. Pickwick implicitly believed they would have done, they paused, stared, and finally laughed outright. "Well, you're a trump, and I like you for it," said the Zephyr. "Now jump into bed again, or you'll catch the rheumatics. No malice, I hope?" And Mr. Pickwick once again dropped off to sleep.

When he opened his eyes next morning, the first object upon which they rested was Samuel Weller, seated upon a small black portmanteau. "I shall get up," said Mr. Pickwick; "give me some clean things."

After breakfasting in a small closet attached to the coffee room, which bore the imposing title of the Snuggery, and after dispatching Mr. Weller on some necessary errands, Mr. Pickwick

repaired to the Lodge, where he learned from Mr. Roker that money was, in the Fleet, just what money was out of it; that it would instantly procure him almost anything he desired; and that, if he signified his wish to have a room to himself, he might take possession of one, furnished and fitted to boot, in half an hour's time.

"Are there any people here who are able to go outside and run on errands?" he asked Mr. Roker, when he was satisfactorily installed.

"Yes," said Roker. "There's an unfortunate devil, who has got a friend on the poor side, that's glad to do anything of that sort."

"The poor side, you say?" said Mr. Pickwick. "I should like to see it. I'll go to him myself."

The poor side of a debtor's prison is, as its name imports, that in which the most miserable and abject class of debtors are confined. A prisoner having declared upon the poor side pays no rent and becomes entitled to a share of some small quantities of food, to provide which a few charitable persons have, from time to time, left trifling legacies in their wills. Mr. Pickwick had no sooner cast his eyes on the figure of a man in the room he had been directed to, than he stood perfectly fixed with astonishment.

Yes, in tattered garments and without a coat, his features changed with suffering and pinched with famine, there sat Mr. Alfred Jingle. The noise of someone stumbling hastily into the room roused Mr. Pickwick; and in the newcomer, through his rags and dirt, he recognized the familiar features of Mr. Job Trotter.

"Mr. Pickwick!" exclaimed Job aloud.

"Eh?" said Jingle, starting from his seat. "Mr.—! So it is—queer place—strange thing—serves me right—very."

Mr. Pickwick was affected. Looking Jingle full, but not unkindly, in the face, he saw that his eyes were moist with tears.

"Good fellow," said Jingle, pressing his hand and turning his head away. "Ungrateful dog—boyish to cry—can't help it—bad fever—weak—ill—hungry. Deserved it all—but suffered much—very." Wholly unable to keep up appearances any longer, the dejected stroller sobbed like a child.

"Here, Job," said Mr. Pickwick, trying to look stern, with four large tears running down his waistcoat. "Take that, sir."

Take what? In the ordinary acceptation of such language, it should have been a blow, for Mr. Pickwick had been duped, deceived, and wronged by the destitute outcast who was now wholly in his power. Must we tell the truth? It was something from Mr. Pickwick's waistcoat pocket, which chinked as it was given into Job's hand.

Sam had returned when Mr. Pickwick reached his own room. "Listen to what I am going to say, Sam," said Mr. Pickwick. "I have felt from the first that this is not the place to bring a young man to."

"Nor an old 'un neither, sir," observed Mr. Weller.

"You're quite right, Sam," said Mr. Pickwick; "but old men may come here, through their own heedlessness and unsuspicion, and young men may be brought here by the selfishness of those they serve. It is better for those young men that they should not remain here. Do you understand me, Sam?"

"Vy, no, sir, I do *not*," replied Mr. Weller, doggedly.

"Sam," said Mr. Pickwick, "for a time, you must leave me. Your wages I shall continue to pay. Any one of my three friends will be happy to take you, were it only out of respect to me. And if I ever do leave this place, Sam," added Mr. Pickwick, with assumed cheerfulness, "I pledge you my word that you shall return to me instantly."

"Now I'll tell you wot it is, sir," said Mr. Weller, in a grave and solemn voice, "this here sort o' thing won't do at all, so don't let's hear no more about it."

"I am serious and resolved, Sam," said Mr. Pickwick.

"You air, air you, sir?" inquired Mr. Weller, firmly. "Wery good, sir. Then so am I." Thus speaking, Mr. Weller fixed his hat on his head with great precision and abruptly left the room.

"I went all the way down to the Markis o' Granby, arter you, last night," said Mr. Weller, when he came on his father next day.

"How was the Marchioness o' Granby lookin'?" inquired Mr. Weller senior.

"Wery queer," said Sam. "I think she's a injurin' herself gradivally vith too much o' that 'ere pineapple rum and other strong medicines o' the same natur'."

"You don't mean that, Sammy?" said the senior, earnestly. There was an expression on his countenance, not of dismay or apprehension, but partaking more of the sweet and gentle character of hope.

"Vell, now," said Sam, "about my affair." And he related the last memorable conversation he had had with Mr. Pickwick.

"Stop there by himself, poor creetur!" exclaimed the elder Mr. Weller, "without nobody to take his part! Vy, they'll eat him up alive, Sammy!"

"Well," said Sam, "don't you see any vay o' takin' care on him?"

"No, I don't, Sammy," said Mr. Weller, with a reflective visage.

"Well, then I'll tell you wot it is," said Sam; "I'll trouble you for the loan of five and twenty pound. P'raps you may ask for it, five minits arterward; p'raps I may say I von't pay and cut up rough. You von't think o' arrestin' your own son for the money and sendin' him off to the Fleet, will you, you unnat'ral wagabone?" At this, the father and son exchanged a complete code of telegraphic nods and gestures, after which the elder Mr. Weller sat himself down on a stone step and laughed till he was purple.

"The have-his-carcase," said Sam, "next to the perpetual motion, is vun of the blessedest things as wos ever made. I'll patronize the inwention and go in, that vay." Which he accordingly did. And having thus been formally delivered into the warden's custody, he knocked at his master's door.

"Ah, Sam, my good lad!" said Mr. Pickwick, "I had no intention of hurting your feelings yesterday, my faithful fellow. Let me explain my meaning."

"Won't presently do, sir? The fact is," said Sam, with a desperate effort, "p'raps I'd better see arter my bed afore I do anythin' else. I was arrested, this here wery arternoon, for debt."

"You arrested for debt!" exclaimed Mr. Pickwick, sinking into a chair.

"Yes, for debt, sir," replied Sam. "And the man as puts me in 'ull never let me out, till you go yourself. Now the murder's out, and damme, there's an end on it!" With these words Sam Weller dashed his hat upon the ground, in a most unusual state of excitement, and then, folding his arms, looked firmly and fixedly in his master's face.

Mr. Pickwick felt a great deal too much touched by the warmth of Sam's attachment to be able to exhibit any manifestation of anger or displeasure at the precipitate course he had adopted. The only point on which he persevered in demanding any explanation was the name of Sam's detaining creditor, but this Mr. Weller as perseveringly withheld.

"It ain't o' no use, sir," said Sam, again and again. "He's a malicious, bad-disposed, vorldly minded, spiteful, windictive creetur, with a hard heart as there ain't no soft'nin'."

13

A few mornings after his incarceration, Mr. Samuel Weller was asked by his master to go for a walk round the prison. "I see a prisoner we know coming this way, Sam," said Mr. Pickwick, smiling. "He is an old friend of yours."

As Mr. Pickwick spoke, Jingle walked up. He looked less miserable than before, being clad in a half-worn suit of clothes, which, with Mr. Pickwick's assistance, had been released from the pawnbroker's. He was very pale and thin, however, and crept slowly up, leaning on a stick.

Following close at his heels came Mr. Job Trotter, in the catalogue of whose vices want of faith and attachment to his companion could at all events find no place. He was still ragged and squalid, but his face was not quite so hollow as on his first meeting with Mr. Pickwick, a few days before. As he took off his hat to our benevolent old friend, he murmured some broken expressions of gratitude and muttered something about having been saved from starving.

"Well, well," said Mr. Pickwick, impatiently interrupting him, "you can follow with Sam. I want to speak to you, Mr. Jingle."

During the whole of this time, the countenance of Mr. Samuel Weller had exhibited an expression of the most overwhelming and absorbing astonishment. "Things has altered with me, sir," said Job.

"I should think they had," exclaimed Mr. Weller, surveying his companion's rags with undisguised wonder. "This is rayther a change for the worse, Mr. Trotter, as the gen'l'm'n said, w'en he got two doubtful shillin's and sixpenn'orth o'pocket pieces for a good half crown. Wot have you been a doin' to yourself?"

"Nothing," replied Job; "and eating and drinking almost as little."

Sam took one comprehensive glance at Mr. Trotter's thin face and wretched apparel and then, seizing him by the arm, commenced dragging him away with great violence.

"Where are you going, Mr. Weller?" said Job, vainly struggling in the powerful grasp of his old enemy.

"Come on," said Sam; "come on!" He deigned no further explanation until they reached the tap and then called for a pot of porter, which was speedily produced.

"Now," said Sam, "drink that up, ev'ry drop on it, and then turn the pot upside down, to let me see as you've took the med'cine. —Now," when this was done, "wot do you say to some wittles?"

"Thanks to your worthy governor, sir," said Mr. Trotter, "we have half a leg of mutton, baked, at a quarter before three, with the potatoes under it to save boiling."

"Wot! Has *he* been a purwidin' for you?" asked Sam, emphatically.

"He has, sir," replied Job. "More than that, Mr. Weller; my master being very ill, he got us a room—we were in a kennel before —and paid for it, sir, and come to look at us, at night, when nobody should know. Mr. Weller," said Job, with real tears in his eyes, for once, "I could serve that gentleman till I fell down dead at his feet."

"I say!" said Sam. "I'll trouble you, my friend! None o' that! No man serves him but me. And now we're upon it, I'll let you into another secret besides that. I never heerd, mind you, nor read of in story books, nor see in picters, any angel in tights and gaiters, but mark my vords, Job Trotter, he's a reg'lar thoroughbred angel for all that; and let me see the man as wenturs to tell me he knows a better vun."

Mr. Pickwick, having by now been all over the prison, had seen enough. "Henceforth," he announced, "I will be a prisoner in my own room." And he steadfastly adhered to this determination. For three long months he remained shut up, all day, only stealing out at night to breathe the air when the greater part of his fellow prisoners were in bed or carousing in their rooms. His health was beginning to suffer from the closeness of the confinement, but neither the often-repeated entreaties of Perker and his friends, nor the still more frequently repeated warnings and admonitions of Mr. Samuel Weller, could induce him to alter one jot of his inflexible resolution.

Mrs. Bardell was enjoying herself in company with Mrs. Cluppins, Mrs. Sanders, and Master Bardell, at the Spaniard Tea Gardens, Hampstead, when the sound of approaching wheels was heard, and the ladies, looking up, saw a hackney coach stop at the garden gate. "Well, if it ain't Mr. Jackson, the young man from Dodson and Fogg's!" cried Mrs. Bardell. "Why, gracious! Surely Mr. Pickwick can't have paid the damages. Has anything taken place, Mr. Jackson?"

"Nothing whatever, ma'am," replied Mr. Jackson. "Our people want you down in the city directly, Mrs. Bardell."

There was a certain degree of pride and importance about being wanted by one's lawyers in such a monstrous hurry that was by no means displeasing to Mrs. Bardell. The party got into the coach.

"Sad thing about these costs of our people's, ain't it?" said Jackson, when Mrs. Cluppins and Mrs. Sanders had fallen asleep. "Your bill of costs, I mean."

"I'm very sorry they can't get them," replied Mrs. Bardell. "But if you law gentlemen do these things on speculation, why you must get a loss now and then, you know."

"You gave them a *cognovit* for the amount of your costs, after the trial, I'm told?" said Jackson.

"Yes. Just as a matter of form," replied Mrs. Bardell.

"Certainly," replied Jackson, dryly. "Quite a matter of form. Quite."

On they drove, and Mrs. Bardell also fell asleep. She was awakened, after some time, by the stopping of the coach. "Have the goodness to step out," said Jackson.

Mrs. Bardell, not yet thoroughly awake, complied. The others followed. It was a curious place—a large wall, with a gate in the middle, and a gas light burning inside. "Here we are, at last," said Jackson, when they were safely inside. "This is the Fleet, ma'am. Wish you good night, Mrs. Bardell. Good night, Tommy!" As Jackson hurried away, Mrs. Bardell screamed violently; Tommy roared; Mrs. Cluppins shrank within herself; and Mrs. Sanders made off without more ado.

Early next morning Mr. Perker appeared, having been sent for by Sam when he heard of Dodson and Fogg's latest maneuver. "What papers are those?" inquired Mr. Pickwick, as the little man deposited on his table a small bundle of documents tied with red tape.

"The papers in Bardell and Pickwick," replied Perker.

"I would rather that the subject should be never mentioned between us, Perker," interposed Mr. Pickwick, hastily.

"Pooh, pooh, my dear sir," said the little man. "It must be

mentioned. The first question I have to ask is, whether Mrs. Bardell is to remain here?"

"How can you ask me?" said Mr. Pickwick. "It rests with Dodson and Fogg; you know that, very well."

"I know nothing of the kind," retorted Perker, firmly. "It rests solely, wholly, and entirely with you. Nobody but you can rescue her from this den of wretchedness, and you can only do that by paying the costs of this suit. By paying the costs, you can obtain a full release and discharge from the damages; and further—this I know is a far greater object of consideration with you, my dear sir—a voluntary statement, under her hand, in the form of a letter to me, that this business was, from the very first, fomented and encouraged and brought about by these men Dodson and Fogg and that she entreats me to intercede with you and implore your pardon."

Before Mr. Pickwick could reply, there was a low murmuring of voices outside, and there rushed tumultuously into the room Mr. Nathaniel Winkle, leading by the hand—

"Miss Arabella Allen!" exclaimed Mr. Pickwick, rising from his chair.

"No," replied Mr. Winkle, dropping on his knees, "Mrs. Winkle. Pardon, my dear friend, pardon!"

Mr. Pickwick could scarcely believe the evidence of his senses and perhaps would not have done so, but for the corroborative testimony afforded by the smiling countenance of Perker and the bodily presence, in the background, of Sam and Mary, the identical pretty housemaid whom he had first met at Ipswich.

"Oh, Mr. Pickwick!" said Arabella, "can you forgive my imprudence?"

Mr. Pickwick returned no verbal response to this appeal; but he took off his spectacles in great haste and, seizing both the young lady's hands in his, kissed her a great number of times, perhaps a greater number than was absolutely necessary. "Why, my dear girl," said Mr. Pickwick, "how has all this come about? How long have you been married?"

Arabella looked bashfully at her lord and master, who replied, "Only three days."

"Only three days, eh?" said Mr. Pickwick. "What have you been doing these three months?"

"Why, the fact is," replied Mr. Winkle, "that I could not persuade Bella to run away, for a long time, from her aunt's in Ipswich. And when I had persuaded her, it was a long time more, before we could find an opportunity. Mary had to give a month's warning, too, before she could leave her place next door, and we couldn't possibly have done it without her assistance."

"Upon my word," exclaimed Mr. Pickwick, "you seem to have been very systematic in your proceedings. And is your brother acquainted with all this, my dear?"

"Oh, no, no," replied Arabella, changing color. "Dear Mr. Pickwick, he must only know it from you—from your lips alone."

"Ah, to be sure," said Perker gravely. "You must take this matter in hand for them, my dear sir."

"You forget, my love," said Mr. Pickwick, gently, "that I am a prisoner."

"No, indeed I do not, my dear sir," replied Arabella. "I never have forgotten it. But I hoped that what no consideration for yourself would induce you to do, a regard to our happiness might. If my brother hears of this, first, from you, I feel certain we shall be reconciled."

At last, Mr. Pickwick, fairly argued and remonstrated out of all his resolution, caught Arabella in his arms and said he could never find it in his heart to stand in the way of young people's happiness and they might do with him as they pleased.

Mr. Weller's first act, on hearing this concession, was to despatch Job Trotter for the formal discharge which his prudent parent had had the foresight to have ready for him; his next proceeding was to invest his whole stock of ready money in the purchase of five and twenty gallons of mild porter, which he himself dispensed to everybody who would partake of it; this done, he hurrahed in divers parts of the building until he lost his voice and then quietly relapsed into his usual collected and philosophical condition.

At three o'clock that afternoon, Mr. Pickwick took a last look at his room and made his way, as well as he could, through the throng of debtors who pressed eagerly forward to shake him by the hand, until he reached the Lodge steps. He turned here, to look about him, and his eye lightened as he did so. In all the crowd of wan, emaciated faces, he saw not one which was not the happier for his sympathy and charity. "God bless you, my friends!" he said and hurried from the prison.

14

"Dear me, Mr. Weller," said Mary, meeting Sam at the George and Vulture, where the Winkles were also staying.

"Dear *me* I vish it vos, my dear," replied Sam. "Wot a sweet-lookin' creetur you are, Mary!"

"Lor', Mr. Weller, what nonsense you do talk!" said Mary. "Oh! *don't*, Mr. Weller."

"Don't what, my dear?" said Sam.

"Why, that," replied the pretty housemaid. "There's a letter waiting here for you."

Sam refreshed himself with a kiss and read as follows:

> Markis Gran
> By dorken
> Wensdy

My dear Sammle,

I am wery sorry to have the pleasure of bein a Bear of ill news your step Mother cort cold consekens of imprudently settin too long on the damp grass in the rain a hearing of a shepherd who warnt able to leave off till late at night owen to his havin vound hisself up vith brandy-and-water and not being able to stop hisself till he got a little sober which took a many hours to do she died at twenty minutes afore six o'clock yesterday evenin your father says that if you will come and see me Sammy he vill take it a wery great favor for I am wery lonely Samivel n b he *vill* have it spelt that vay vich I say ain't right and as there is such a many things to settle he is sure your guvnor wont object of course he will not Sammy for I knows him better so he sends his dooty in which I join and am Samivel infernally yours

> Tony Veller.

"Wot a incomprehensible letter," said Sam; "who's to know wot it means vith all this he-ing and I-ing! It ain't my father's writin', 'cept this here signater in print letters; that's his."

"Perhaps he got somebody to write it for him, and signed it himself afterward," said the pretty housemaid.

"You're right, Mary, my dear," said Sam. "That's just the wery sort o' thing he'd do.—And so the poor creetur's dead! I'm sorry for it. She warn't a bad-disposed 'ooman, if them shepherds had let her alone. I'm wery sorry for it."

The blinds of the Marquis of Granby were pulled down and the shutters partly closed when Sam arrived there. The widower was seated at a small round table in the little room behind the bar, smoking a pipe, with his eyes intently fixed upon the fire. "Sammy," said Mr. Weller, "I wos a thinkin' that upon the whole I wos wery sorry she wos gone."

"Vell, and so you ought to be," replied Sam.

Mr. Weller nodded his acquiescence. "Those wos wery sensible observations as she made, Sammy," said he, "arter she was took ill. 'Veller,' she says, 'I'm afeared I've not done by you quite wot I ought to have done; you're a wery kind-hearted man, and I might ha' made your home more comfortabler. I begin to see now,' she says, 'ven it's too late, that if a married 'ooman vishes to be religious she should begin vith dischargin' her dooties at home and makin' them as is about her cheerful and happy.'"

"Vell," said Sam, venturing to offer a little homely consolation, after the lapse of three or four minutes, consumed by the old gentleman in slowly shaking his head from side to side and solemnly smoking, "vell, guvnor, ve must all come to it, one day or another."

"So we must, Sammy," said Mr. Weller the elder.

"There's a Providence in it all," said Sam.

"O' course there is," replied his father with a nod of grave approval. "Wot 'ud become of the undertakers vithout it, Sammy?"

While the old gentleman was lost in the immense field of conjecture opened by this reflection, a very buxom-looking cook, dressed in mourning, who had been bustling about in the bar, glided into the room. "Have a cup of tea, there's a good soul," said she, coaxingly.

"I von't," replied Mr. Weller, in a somewhat boisterous manner. "I'll see you—" Mr. Weller hastily checked himself and added in a low tone, "furder fust."

"I really never saw a man so cross," said the buxom female. "As I was telling him yesterday, Mr. Samuel, he *will* feel lonely, he can't expect but what he should, sir, but he should keep up a good heart, because, dear me, there's no situation in life so bad, Mr. Samuel, that it can't be mended. Which is what a very worthy person said to me when my husband died." Here the speaker looked affectionately at the elder Mr. Weller.

"As I don't rekvire any o' your conversation just now, mum,

vill you have the goodness to re-tire?" inquired Mr. Weller in a grave and steady voice. Falling back in his chair in a violent perspiration, when she had gone, he said, "Sammy, if I wos to stop here alone vun veek—only vun week, my boy—that 'ere 'ooman 'ud marry me by force and wiolence afore it was over. The breath wos scarcely out o' your poor stepmother's body, ven vun old 'ooman sends me a pot o' jam, and another a pot o' jelly, and another brews a blessed large jug o' camomile tea, vich she brings in vith her own hands." Mr. Weller paused with an aspect of intense disgust and, looking round, added in a whisper, "They wos all widders, Sammy, all on 'em."

"Somebody's a tappin' at the door," said Sam, after a long silence.

"Let 'em tap," replied his father, with dignity.

Sam acted upon the direction. There was another tap, and another, and then a long row of taps, upon which Sam inquired why the tapper was not admitted.

"Hush," whispered Mr. Weller, with apprehensive looks, "don't take no notice on 'em, Sammy, it's vun o' the widders, p'raps." No notice being taken of the taps, the unseen visitor ventured to open the door and peep in. It was no female head, but the red face of Mr. Stiggins. Mr. Weller's pipe fell from his hands.

The reverend gentleman gradually opened the door by almost imperceptible degrees, until the aperture was just wide enough to admit the passage of his lank body, when he glided into the room and closed it after him with great care and gentleness. Turning toward Sam and raising his hands and eyes in token of the unspeakable sorrow with which he regarded the calamity that had befallen the family, "Oh, my young friend," said Mr. Stiggins, "here's a sorrowful affliction! For the man of wrath, too! It makes a vessel's heart bleed!"

Mr. Weller was overheard by his son to murmur something relative to making a vessel's nose bleed; but Mr. Stiggins heard him not.

"Do you know, young man," whispered Mr. Stiggins, drawing his chair closer to Sam, "whether she has left Emmanuel anything?"

"Who's he?" inquired Sam.

"The chapel," replied Mr. Stiggins; "our chapel; our fold, Mr. Samuel."

"She hasn't left the fold nothin', nor the shepherd nothin', nor the animals nothin'," said Sam decisively; "nor the dogs neither."

"Perhaps," said Mr. Stiggins, hesitatingly, "perhaps she recommended me to the care of the man of wrath, Mr. Samuel?"

"I think that's wery likely," rejoined Sam.

"Ah! He's changed, I dare say," exclaimed Stiggins, brightening up. "We might live very comfortably together now. I could take good care of his property."

Mr. Weller the elder gave vent to an extraordinary sound, which, being neither a groan, nor a grunt, nor a gasp, nor a growl, seemed to partake in some degree of the character of all four. Mr. Stiggins, encouraged by this sound, which he understood to betoken remorse or repentance, walked softly across the room to a well-remembered shelf, took down a tumbler, walked softly into the bar, and, presently returning with the tumbler half full of pineapple rum, advanced to the kettle, mixed his grog, sipped it, sat down, and, taking a long and hearty pull, stopped for breath.

Suddenly the elder Mr. Weller darted upon him, and, snatching the tumbler from his hand, threw the remainder of the rum and water in his face. Then, seizing the reverend gentleman firmly by the collar, he fell to kicking him most furiously. "Sammy," said Mr. Weller, "put my hat on tight for me."

Sam dutifully adjusted the hat, and the old gentleman, resuming his kicking with greater agility than before, tumbled with Mr. Stiggins through the bar, and through the passage, out at the front door, and so into the street. It was a beautiful and exhilarating sight to see the red-nosed man writhing in Mr. Weller's grasp and his whole frame quivering with anguish as kick followed kick in rapid succession; it was a still more exciting spectacle to behold Mr. Weller, after a powerful struggle, immersing Mr. Stiggins' head in a horse trough full of water and holding it there until he was half suffocated.

"There!" said Mr. Weller, throwing all his energy into one most complicated kick, as he at length permitted Mr. Stiggins to withdraw his head from the trough, "send any vun o' them lazy shepherds here and I'll pound him to a jelly first and drownd him

artervard! Sammy, help me in, and fill me a small glass of brandy. I'm out o' breath, my boy."

Mr. Pickwick was engaged in settling his account with Mr. Perker when Jingle and Job Trotter entered the office but, seeing Mr. Pickwick, stopped short in some confusion. "Well," said Perker, "don't you know that gentleman?"

"Good reason to," replied Mr. Jingle, stepping forward. "Mr. Pickwick—deepest obligations—life preserver—made a man of me—you shall never repent it, sir."

"I am happy to hear you say so," said Mr. Pickwick.

"With regard to such an outfit as was indispensable for Jingle to take to the West Indies," said Perker, "I have taken upon myself to make an arrangement for the deduction of a small sum from his quarterly salary, which, being made only for one year, and regularly remitted, will provide for that expense. I entirely disapprove of your doing anything for him, my dear sir, which is not dependent on his own exertions and good conduct."

"Certainly," interposed Jingle, with great firmness. "Clear head—man of the world—quite right—perfectly."

"By compounding with his creditor, releasing his clothes from the pawnbroker's, relieving him in prison, and paying for his passage," continued Perker, "you have already lost upward of fifty pounds."

"Not lost," said Jingle, hastily. "Pay it all—stick to business—cash up—every farthing. Yellow fever, perhaps—can't help that—if not—"

"He means to say," said Job, "that if he is not carried off by the fever, he will pay the money back again. If he lives, he will, Mr. Pickwick. I will see it done. I know he will, sir," said Job, with energy. "I could undertake to swear it."

"A worthy couple!" said Perker, as the door closed behind them.

"I hope they may become so," replied Mr. Pickwick.

At this moment the clerk, Mr. Lowten, came in with a great air of mystery. "Who wants me?" inquired Mr. Perker.

"Why, sir," replied Lowten, "it's Dodson; and Fogg is with him."

"Bless my life!" said Mr. Perker, "it's very awkward. What will you do, my dear sir?"

Mr. Pickwick replied that he would remain where he was, the more especially as Messrs. Dodson and Fogg ought to be ashamed to look him in the face, instead of his being ashamed to see them.

"Very well, my dear sir, very well," replied Perker. "I can only say that if you expect either Dodson or Fogg to exhibit any symptom of shame or confusion at having to look you, or anybody else, in the face, you are the most sanguine man in your expectations that *I* ever met with. Show them in, Mr. Lowten."

There was a great comparing of papers, and turning over of leaves, by Fogg and Perker, after which Dodson said in an affable manner to Mr. Pickwick, "I don't think you are looking quite so stout as when I had the pleasure of seeing you last, Mr. Pickwick."

"Possibly not, sir," replied Mr. Pickwick, who had been flashing forth looks of fierce indignation, without producing the smallest effect on either of the sharp practitioners; "I believe I am not, sir. I have been persecuted and annoyed by Scoundrels of late, sir."

Perker coughed violently and asked Mr. Pickwick whether he wouldn't like to look at the morning paper? To which inquiry Mr. Pickwick returned a most decided negative.

"I am very happy," said Fogg, softened by the check for costs, which he was pocketing, "to have had the pleasure of making Mr. Pickwick's acquaintance. I hope you don't think quite so ill of us, Mr. Pickwick, as when we first had the pleasure of seeing you."

"Lowten!" cried Perker at this moment. "Open the door."

"Wait one instant," said Mr. Pickwick. "—Perker, I *will* speak. —Do you know," turning to the partners, "that I have been the victim of your plots and conspiracies? Do you know that I am the man whom you have been imprisoning and robbing? Do you know that you were the attorneys for the plaintiff, in Bardell and Pickwick?"

"Yes, sir, we do know it," replied Dodson.

"Of course we know it, sir," rejoined Fogg, slapping his pocket —perhaps by accident.

"You are," continued Mr. Pickwick, "a well-matched pair of mean, rascally, pettifogging robbers."

"Well," interposed Perker, "is that all?"

"It is all summed up in that," rejoined Mr. Pickwick; "they are mean, rascally, pettifogging robbers."

"There!" said Perker in a most conciliatory tone. "My dear sirs, he has said all he has to say. Now pray go. Lowten, *is* that door open?"

"If there's a law in England, sir," said Dodson, looking toward Mr. Pickwick, as he put on his hat, "you shall smart for this."

"You are a couple of mean—"

"Remember, sir, you pay dearly for this," said Fogg.

"—Rascally, pettifogging robbers!" continued Mr. Pickwick, taking not the least notice of the threats that were addressed to him.

"Robbers!" cried Mr. Pickwick, running to the stairhead, as the two attorneys descended.

"Robbers!" shouted Mr. Pickwick, breaking from Lowten and Perker and thrusting his head out of the staircase window.

When Mr. Pickwick drew in his head again, his countenance was smiling and placid; and, walking quietly back into the office, he declared that he had now removed a great weight from his mind and that he felt perfectly comfortable and happy.

15

Mr. Pickwick was sitting alone in his room at the George and Vulture, musing over many things, when Sam Weller entered, followed by his father. "I wanted to have a little bit o' conwersation with you, sir," said Mr. Weller, "if you could spare me five minits or so, sir."

"Certainly," replied Mr. Pickwick.

Here, old Mr. Weller was seized with a violent fit of coughing, which being terminated he nodded his head and winked and made several supplicatory and threatening gestures to his son, all of which Sam Weller steadily abstained from seeing. "I never see sich a aggerawatin' boy as you are, Samivel," said Mr. Weller at last, looking indignantly at his son, "never in all my born days."

"What is he doing, Mr. Weller?" inquired Mr. Pickwick.

"He von't begin, sir," rejoined Mr. Weller. "It ain't filial conduct, Samivel," wiping his forehead; "wery far from it."

"You said you'd speak," replied Sam; "how should I know you wos done up at the wery beginnin'? The fact is, sir, the guvnor's been a drawin' his money: five hundred and thirty pound, it is, sir, reduced counsels. To vich sum, he has added for the house and bisness—"

"Lease, good vill, stock, and fixters," interposed Mr. Weller.

"—As much as makes it," continued Sam, "altogether, eleven hundred and eighty pound."

"Indeed!" said Mr. Pickwick. "I am delighted to hear it. I congratulate you, Mr. Weller, on having done so well."

"This here money," said Sam, with a little hesitation, "he's anxious to put someveres, vere he knows it'll be safe, for vich reasons, he's draw'd it out today and come here vith me to say, leastvays to offer, or in other words to—"

"—To say this here," said the elder Mr. Weller, impatiently, "that it ain't o' no use to me. I'm a goin' to vork a coach reg'lar and ha'nt got novers to keep it in. If you'll take care on it for me, sir, I shall be wery much obliged to you. P'raps," said Mr. Weller, walking up to Mr. Pickwick and whispering in his ear, "p'raps it'll go a little vay toward the expenses o' that 'ere conwiction. All I say is, just you keep it till I ask you for it again." With these words, Mr. Weller placed the pocketbook in Mr. Pickwick's hands, caught up his hat, and ran out of the room with a celerity scarcely to be expected from so corpulent a subject.

"Stop him, Sam!" exclaimed Mr. Pickwick, earnestly. "Overtake him; bring him back instantly! Mr. Weller—my good friend," taking the old man by the hand, "your honest confidence overpowers me, but I assure you, I have more money than I can ever need. I must beg you to take this back, Mr. Weller."

"Wery well," said Mr. Weller with a discontented look. "Mark my vords, Sammy, I'll do somethin' desperate vith this here property; somethin' desperate!"

Mr. Weller seemed so deeply mortified by Mr. Pickwick's refusal that that gentleman, after a short reflection, said, "Well, well, Mr. Weller, I will keep the money. I can do more good with it, perhaps, than you can. Now sit down again. I want to ask your advice. Wait outside a few minutes, Sam, will you?"

Mr. Weller looked uncommonly wise and very much amazed when Mr. Pickwick opened the discourse by saying, "You are not an advocate for matrimony, I think, Mr. Weller?"

Mr. Weller shook his head. He was wholly unable to speak; vague thoughts of some wicked widow having been successful in her designs on Mr. Pickwick choked his utterance.

"Did you happen to see a young girl downstairs when you came in just now with your son?" inquired Mr. Pickwick.

"Yes. I see a young gal," replied Mr. Weller, shortly.

"What did you think of her, now? Candidly, Mr. Weller, what did you think of her?"

"I thought she wos wery plump and vell made," said Mr. Weller, with a critical air.

"That young person," said Mr. Pickwick, "is attached to your son."

"To Samivel Veller!" exclaimed the parent.

"Yes," said Pickwick.

"It's nat'ral," said Mr. Weller, after some consideration, "nat'ral, but rayther alarmin'. Sammy must be careful that he ain't led avay, in a innocent moment, to say anythink as may lead to a conwiction for breach. You're never safe vith 'em, Mr. Pickwick, ven they vunce has designs on you."

"You give me no great encouragement to conclude what I have to say," observed Mr. Pickwick, "but I had better do so at once. This young person is not only attached to your son, Mr. Weller, but your son is attached to her."

"Vell," said Mr. Weller, "this here's a pretty sort o' thing to come to a father's ears, this is!" But as Mr. Pickwick laid great stress on the fact that Mary was not a widow, he gradually became more tractable, and Mr. Pickwick joyfully called Sam back into the room.

"Sam," said Mr. Pickwick, clearing his throat, "I am not so blind as not to have seen that you entertain something more than a friendly feeling toward Mrs. Winkle's maid. I have had a little conversation with your father; and, finding that he is of my opinion—"

"The lady not bein' a widder," interposed Mr. Weller, in explanation.

"The lady not being a widow," said Mr. Pickwick, smiling, "I wish to free you from the restraint which your present position imposes upon you and to mark my sense of your fidelity and many excellent qualities by enabling you to marry this girl at once and to earn an independent livelihood for yourself and family. I shall be proud, Sam," said Mr. Pickwick, whose voice had faltered a little hitherto but now resumed its customary tone, "proud and happy to make your future prospects in life my grateful and peculiar care."

There was a profound silence for a short time, and then Sam said, in a low husky sort of voice, but firmly withal, "I'm wery much obliged to you for your goodness, sir, as is only like yourself; but it can't be done. Vages or no vages, notice or no notice, board or no board, lodgin' or no lodgin', Sam Veller, as you took from the old inn in the Borough, sticks by you, come what come may; and let ev'rythin' and ev'rybody do their wery fiercest, nothin' shall ever perwent it!"

For a whole week after this, Mr. Pickwick and Sam Weller were from home all day long, only returning just in time for dinner, and then wearing an air of mystery and importance quite foreign to their natures. But at last Mr. Pickwick made an announcement, at a dinner given him by his friends. "All the changes that have taken place among us," he said, "I mean the marriage that *has* taken place and the marriage of Snodgrass and Emily Wardle that *will* take place, with the changes they involve, rendered it necessary for me to think, soberly and at once, upon my future plans. I determined on retiring to some quiet pretty neighborhood in the vicinity of London; I saw a house which exactly suited my fancy; I have taken it and furnished it. Sam accompanies me there; and when he and Mary are married, she will act as housekeeper.

"I have communicated," Mr. Pickwick continued, "with the club, acquainting them with my intention. During our long absence, it had suffered much from internal dissensions; and the withdrawal of my name, coupled with this and other circumstances, has occasioned its dissolution. The Pickwick Club exists no longer. I shall never regret," said Mr. Pickwick in a low voice, "having devoted the greater part of two years to mixing with different varieties and shades of human character—frivolous as my pursuit of novelty may have appeared to many. If I have done but little good, I trust I have done less harm, and that none of my adventures will be other than a source of amusing and pleasant recollection to me in the decline of life. God bless you all!"

With these words, Mr. Pickwick filled and drained a bumper with a trembling hand, and his eyes moistened as his friends rose with one accord and pledged him from their hearts. Let us leave our old friend in one of those moments of unmixed happiness, of which, if we seek them, there are ever some, to cheer our transitory existence here.

It is the fate of all authors or chroniclers to create imaginary friends, and lose them in the course of art. Nor is this the full extent of their misfortunes, for they are required to furnish an account of them besides.

Mr. Pickwick continued to reside in his new house, employing his leisure hours in arranging the memoranda which he afterward presented to the secretary of the once famous club or in hearing Sam Weller read aloud, with such remarks as suggested themselves to his mind, which never failed to afford Mr. Pickwick great amusement. He was much troubled at first by the numerous applications made to him by Mr. Snodgrass, Mr. Winkle, and Mr. Trundle, to act as godfather to their offspring; but he has become used to it now and officiates as a matter of course. Mr. Tupman, when his friends married and Mr. Pickwick settled, took lodgings at Richmond, where he has ever since resided; he has never proposed again. Mr. Pickwick is somewhat infirm now; but he retains all his former juvenility of spirit and may still be frequently seen, enjoying a walk about the pleasant neighborhood on a fine day. He is known by all the poor people about, who never fail to take their hats off, as he passes, with great respect. The children idolize him, and so indeed does the whole neighborhood. Every year, he repairs to a large family merrymaking at Mr. Wardle's; on this, as on all other occasions, he is invariably attended by the faithful Sam, between whom and his master there exists a steady and reciprocal attachment which nothing but death will terminate.